Creation
Gore Vidal

"AMBITIOUS . . . LEARNED . . .
IT ENTERTAINS
by giving a bystander's view of great events
and men."
Paul Theroux
The New York Times Book Review

"A RICH, COLORFUL AND FULFILLING
TAPESTRY . . .
One of the finest books of this decade, even
with almost nine years ahead of us."
Ed Hutshing
The San Diego Union

Creation
Gore Vidal

A Novel

BALLANTINE BOOKS • NEW YORK

Library of Congress Catalog Card Number: 79-5528

ISBN 0-345-34020-5

This edition published by arrangement with Random House, Inc.

Manufactured in the United States of America

First Ballantine Books Edition: February 1982
Ninth Printing: August 1987

Map by Raphael Palacios

Author's Note

To the people of the fifth century B.C., India was a Persian province on the Indus River, while Ch'in was only one of a number of warring principalities in what is now China. For clarity's sake, I've used the word India to describe not only the Gangetic plain but also those regions that currently enjoy the names Pakistan and Bangladesh. Since China would be a real misnomer at this period, I've used the archaic word Cathay to describe those states between the Yangtze and Yellow rivers. Whenever possible, I have chosen the contemporary word in English for such entities as the Mediterranean and Confucius; on the other hand, I prefer to call unhappy Afghanistan—and equally unhappy Iran—by their ancient names, Bactria and Persia.

For measuring distances I've used homely nonmetric miles. As for dates, the narrator is usually careful to relate events to the time when he began to dictate his answer to Herodotus (not yet known as "the father of history")—the evening of what we would call December 20, 445 B.C.

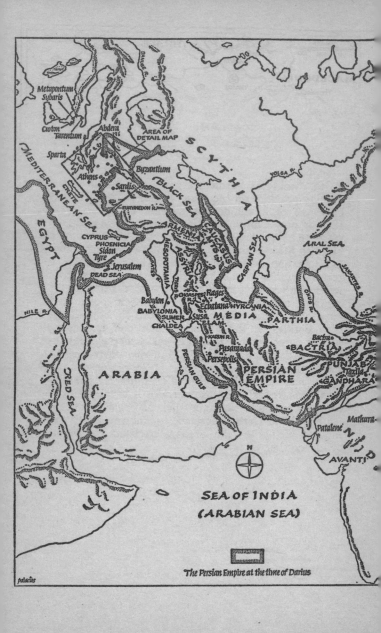

The Persian Empire at the time of Darius

BOOK ONE

Herodotus
Gives a Reading
at the Odeon in Athens

1

I AM BLIND. BUT I AM NOT DEAF. Because of the incompleteness of my misfortune, I was obliged yesterday to listen for nearly six hours to a self-styled historian whose account of what the Athenians like to call "the Persian Wars" was nonsense of a sort that were I less old and more privileged, I would have risen in my seat at the Odeon and scandalized all Athens by answering him.

But then, I know the origin of the *Greek* wars. He does not. How could he? How could any Greek? I spent most of my life at the court of Persia and even now, in my seventy-fifth year, I still serve the Great King as I did his father—my beloved friend Xerxes—and his father before him, a hero known even to the Greeks as Darius the Great.

When the painful reading finally ended—our "historian" has a thin monotonous voice made even less charming by a harsh Dorian accent—my eighteen-year-old nephew Democritus wanted to know if I would like to stay behind and speak to the traducer of Persia.

"You should," he said. "Because everyone is staring at you. They know you must be very angry." Democritus is studying philosophy here at Athens. This means that he delights in quarrels. Write that down, Democritus. After all, it is at your request that I am dictating this account of how and why the Greek wars began. I shall spare no one —including you. Where was I? the Odeon.

I smiled the poignant smile of the blind, as some unobservant poet characterized the expression of those of us who cannot see. Not that I ever paid much attention to blind men when I could see. On the other hand, I never expected to live long enough to be old, much less go blind, as I did three years ago when the white clouds that had been settling upon the retinas of my eyes became, suddenly, opaque.

2

The last thing that I ever saw was my own blurred face in a polished-silver mirror. This was at Susa, in the Great King's palace. At first I thought that the room was filling up with smoke. But it was summertime, and there was no fire. For an instant I saw myself in the mirror; then saw myself no longer; saw nothing else, ever again.

In Egypt the doctors perform an operation that is supposed to send the clouds scurrying. But I am too old to go to Egypt. Besides, I have seen quite enough. Have I not looked upon the holy fire, which is the face of Ahura Mazdah, the Wise Lord? I have also seen Persia and India and farthest Cathay. No other man alive has traveled in as many lands as I.

I am digressing. This is a habit of old men. My grandfather in *his* seventy-fifth year used to talk for hours without ever linking one subject to another. He was absolutely incoherent. But then, he was Zoroaster, the prophet of Truth; and just as the One God that he served is obliged to entertain, simultaneously, every aspect of all creation, so did His prophet Zoroaster. The result was inspiring if you could ever make sense of what he was saying.

Democritus wants me to record what happened as we were leaving the Odeon. Very well. It is your fingers that will grow tired. My voice never deserts me, nor does my memory . . . Thus far.

There was deafening applause when Herodotus of Halicarnassus finished his description of the Persian "defeat" at Salamis thirty-four years ago. By the way, the acoustics of the Odeon are dreadful. Apparently, I am not alone in finding the new music hall inadequate. Even the tone-deaf Athenians know that something is wrong with their precious Odeon, recently thrown together in record time by order of Pericles, who paid for it with money that had been collected from all the Greek cities for their common defense. The building itself is a copy in stone of the tent of the Great King Xerxes which somehow fell into Greek hands during the confusions of Persia's last campaign in Greece. They affect to despise us; then they imitate us.

As Democritus led me to the vestibule of the music hall, I heard on every side the phrase "The Persian ambassador!" The throaty syllables struck my ears like those potsherds on which Athenians periodically write the names of anyone who had happened to offend or bore them. The man who gets the most votes in this election—

3

or rejection—is exiled from the city for a period of ten years. He is lucky.

I give a few of the remarks that I heard en route to the door.

"I'll bet he didn't like what he heard."

"He's a brother of Xerxes, isn't he?"

"No, he's a Magian."

"What's that?"

"A Persian priest. They eat snakes and dogs."

"And commit incest with their sisters and mothers and daughters."

"What about their brothers and fathers and sons?"

"You are insatiable, Glaucon."

"Magians are always blind. They have to be. Is that his grandson?"

"No. His lover."

"I don't think so. Persians are different from us."

"Yes. They lose battles. We don't."

"How would you know? You weren't even born when we sent Xerxes running home to Asia."

"That boy is very good-looking."

"He's Greek. He has to be. No barbarian could look like that."

"He's from Abdera. The grandson of Megacreon."

"A medizer! Scum of the earth."

"Rich scum. Megacreon owns half the silver mines in Thrace."

Of my two remaining and relatively unimpaired senses —touch and smell—I cannot report much of the first, other than the wiry arm of Democritus, which I clutched in my right hand, but as for the second! In summer Athenians do not bathe often. In winter—and we are now in the week that contains the shortest day of the year—they bathe not at all, while their diet appears to consist entirely of onions and preserved fish—preserved from the time of Homer.

I was jostled, breathed upon, insulted. I am of course aware that my position as the Great King's ambassador at Athens is not only a perilous one but highly ambiguous. It is perilous because at any moment these volatile people are apt to hold one of their assemblies in which every male citizen may speak his mind and, worst of all, vote. After listening to one of the city's many corrupt or demented demagogues, the citizens are quite capable of breaking a sacred treaty, which is what they did fourteen

4

years ago when they sent out an expedition to conquer the Persian province of Egypt. They were roundly defeated. This adventure was doubly shameful because, sixteen years ago, an Athenian embassy had gone up to Susa with instructions to make a permanent peace with Persia. The chief ambassador was Callias, the richest man in Athens. In due course, a treaty was drafted. Athens acknowledged the Great King's sovereignty over the Greek cities of Asia Minor. In turn, the Great King agreed to keep the Persian fleet out of the Aegean Sea, and so on. The treaty was very long. In fact, I have often thought that during the composition of the Persian text, I permanently damaged my eyes. Certainly, the white clouds began to thicken during those months of negotiation when I was obliged to read every word of what the clerks had written.

After the Egyptian debacle, another embassy went up to Susa. The Great King was superb. He ignored the fact that the Athenians had broken the original treaty by invading his province of Egypt. Instead, he spoke warmly of his friendship for Sparta. The Athenians were terrified. Quite rightly, they fear Sparta. In a matter of days it was agreed that the treaty, which neither side could ever acknowledge, was once more in force, and as a proof of the Great King's faith in his Athenian slaves—so he calls them—he would send to Athens the friend closest to the bosom of his late father Xerxes, Cyrus Spitama, myself.

I cannot say that I was entirely pleased. I never thought that the last years of my life would be spent in this cold and windy city amongst a people as cold and windy as the place itself. On the other hand, and what I say is for your ears alone, Democritus—in fact, this commentary is largely for your benefit, to be used in any way you like once I am dead . . . a matter of days, I should think, considering the fever that now burns me up and the fits of coughing that must make this dictation as tiring for you as it is for me . . . I have lost my train of thought.

On the other hand . . . Yes. Since the murder of my beloved friend Xerxes and the accession of his son Artaxerxes, my position at Susa has been less than comfortable. Although the Great King is kind to me, I am too much associated with the previous reign to be entirely trusted by the new people at court. What little influence that I still exert derives from an accident of birth. I am the last living grandson in the male line of Zoroaster, the prophet of the One God, Ahura Mazdah—in Greek, the Wise Lord. Since the Great King Darius converted to Zoroastrianism a half-century ago, the royal family has always treated our family with reverence, which makes me feel something of an impostor. After all, one cannot choose one's grandfather.

At the door of the Odeon, I was stopped by Thucydides, a somber middle-aged man who has led the conservative party at Athens since the death of his famous father-in-law Cimon three years ago. As a result, he is the only serious rival to Pericles, the leader of the democratic party.

Political designations hereabouts are imprecise. The leaders of both factions are aristocrats. But certain nobles —like the late Cimon—favor the wealthy landowning class, while others—like Pericles—play to the city mob whose notorious assembly he has strengthened, continuing the work of *his* political mentor Ephialtes, a radical leader who was mysteriously murdered a dozen years ago. Naturally, the conservatives were blamed for the murder. If responsible, they should be congratulated. No mob can govern a city, much less an empire.

Certainly, if my father had been Greek and my mother Persian—instead of the other way around, I would have been a member of the conservative party, even though that party can never resist using the idea of Persia to frighten the people. Despite Cimon's love of Sparta and hatred of us, I would like to have known him. Everyone here says that his sister Elpinice resembles him in character. She is a marvelous woman, and a loyal friend to me.

Democritus reminds me, courteously, that I am again off the subject. I remind *him* that after listening all those hours to Herodotus, I can no longer move with any logic from one point to the next. He writes the way a grasshopper hops. I imitate him.

Thucydides spoke to me in the vestibule of the Odeon. "I suppose that a copy of what we've just heard will be sent on to Susa."

"Why not?" I was both bland and dull, the perfect ambassador. "The Great King enjoys wondrous tales. He has a taste for the fabulous."

Apparently I was insufficiently dull. I could sense the displeasure of Thucydides and the group of conservatives

6

who were in attendance. Party leaders in Athens seldom walk out alone for fear of murder. Democritus tells me that whenever one sees a large group of noisy men at whose center looms either a helmeted onion or a scarlet moon, the first is bound to be Pericles, the second Thucydides. Between onion and autumnal moon the city is irritably divided.

Today was the day of the scarlet moon. For some reason the helmeted onion had not attended the reading in the Odeon. Could it be that Pericles is ashamed of the acoustics in *his* building? But I forget. Shame is not an emotion known to the Athenians.

Currently Pericles and his cabal of artists and builders are constructing a temple to Athena on the Acropolis, a grandiose replacement for the shabby temple that the Persian army burned to the ground thirty-four years ago, a fact that Herodotus tends not to dwell on.

"Do you mean, Ambassador, that the account we have just heard is untrue?" Thucydides was insolent. I daresay he was drunk. Although we Persians are accused of heavy drinking because of our ritual use of haoma, I have never seen a Persian as drunk as certain Athenians and, to be fair, no Athenian could ever be as drunk as a Spartan. My old friend King Demaratus of Sparta used to say that the Spartans never took wine without water until the northern nomads sent Sparta an embassy shortly after Darius laid waste their native Scythia. According to Demaratus, the Scythians taught the Spartans to drink wine without water. I don't believe this story.

"What we have heard, my dear young man, is only a version of events that took place before you were born and, I suspect, before the birth of the historian."

"There are still many of us left who remember well the day the Persians came to Marathon." An old voice sounded at my elbow. Democritus did not recognize its owner. But one hears that sort of old voice often enough. All over Greece, strangers of a certain age will greet one another with the question, "And where were you and what did you do when Xerxes came to Marathon?" Then they exchange lies.

"Yes," I said. "There are those who still remember the ancient days. I am, alas, one. In fact, the Great King Xerxes and I are exactly the same age. If he were alive today, he would be seventy-five years old. When he came to the throne, he was thirty-four—the prime of life. Yet

7

your historian has just finished telling us that Xerxes was a rash *boy* when he succeeded Darius."

"A small detail," Thucydides began.

"But typical of a work that will give as much delight at Susa as that play of Aeschylus called *The Persians*, which I myself translated for the Great King, who found delightful the author's Attic wit." None of this was true, of course; Xerxes would have gone into a rage had he ever known to what extent he and his mother had been travestied for the amusement of the Athenian mob.

I have made it a policy never to show distress when insulted by barbarians. Fortunately, I am spared their worst insults. These they save for one another. It is a lucky thing for the rest of the world that Greeks dislike one another far more than they do us outlanders.

A perfect example: When the once applauded dramatist Aeschylus lost a prize to the currently applauded Sophocles, he was so enraged that he left Athens for Sicily, where he came to a most satisfying end. An eagle, looking for a hard surface on which to break up the turtle that he held in his claws, mistook the bald head of the author of *The Persians* for a rock and let slip the turtle, with fatal accuracy.

Thucydides was about to continue what looked to be the beginning of a most ugly scene, when young Democritus suddenly propelled me forward with the cry, "Way for the ambassador of the Great King!" And way was made.

Fortunately, my litter was waiting just outside the portico.

I have had the good luck to be able to rent a house built before we burned down Athens. It is somewhat more comfortable if less pretentious than the houses currently being built by wealthy Athenians. There is nothing like having your native city burned to the ground to inspire ambitious architects. Sardis is now far more splendid after the great fire than ever it was in the time of Croesus. Although I never saw the old Athens—and cannot of course see the new Athens—I am told that private houses are still built of mud brick, that the streets are seldom straight and never wide, that the new public buildings are splendid if makeshift—like the Odeon.

At present, most of the building is taking place on the Acropolis, a lion-colored lump of rock, Democritus' poetic phrase, that overhangs not only most of the city but this

8

house. As a result, in winter—right now—we get less than an hour of sun a day.

But the rock has its charms. Democritus and I often stroll there. I touch ruined walls. Listen to the clatter of the masons. Ponder that splendid family of tyrants who used to live on the Acropolis before they were driven out of the city, as everyone truly noble is driven out sooner or later. I knew the last tyrant, the gentle Hippias. He was often at the court of Susa when I was young.

Today the principal feature of the Acropolis is the houses or temples that contain the images of the gods which the people pretend to worship. I say pretend because it is my view that despite the basic conservatism of the Athenian people when it comes to maintaining the *forms* of old things, the essential spirit of these people is atheistic—or as a Greek cousin of mine pointed out not long ago, with dangerous pride, man is the measure of all things. I think that in their hearts the Athenians truly believe this to be true. As a result, paradoxically, they are uncommonly superstitious and strictly punish those who are thought to have committed impiety.

2

DEMOCRITUS WAS NOT PREPARED FOR some of the things that I said last night at dinner. Not only has he now asked me for a true account of the Greek wars but, more important, he wants me to record my memories of India and Cathay, and of the wise men that I met at the east—and at the east of the east. He has offered to write down everything that I remember. My guests at dinner were equally urgent. But I suspect that they were simply polite.

We are seated now in the courtyard of the house. It is the hour when we get the sun. The day is cool but not cold and I can feel the sun's warmth on my face. I am comfortable, because I am dressed in the Persian fashion. All parts of the body are covered except the face. Even the hands in repose are covered by sleeves. Naturally, I wear trousers—an article of clothing that always disturbs the Greeks.

Our notions of modesty greatly amuse the Greeks, who

are never so happy as when they are watching naked youths play games. Blindness spares me the sight not only of Athens' romping youths but of those lecherous men who watch them. Yet the Athenians are modest when it comes to their women. Women here are swathed from head to toe like Persian ladies—but without color, ornament, style.

I dictate in Greek because I have always spoken Ionian Greek with ease. My mother, Lais, is a Greek from Abdera. She is a daughter of Megacreon, the great-grandfather of Democritus. Since Megacreon owned rich silver mines and you are descended from him in the male line, you are far richer than I. Yes, write that down. You are a part of this narrative, young and insignificant as you are. After all, you have stirred my memory.

Last night I gave dinner to the torchbearer Callias and to the sophist Anaxagoras. Democritus spends many hours a day with Anaxagoras, being talked at. This is known as education. In my time and country, education meant memorizing sacred texts, studying mathematics, practicing music, and archery . . .

"To ride, to draw the bow, to tell the truth." That is Persian education in a proverbial phrase. Democritus reminds me that Greek education is much the same—except for telling the truth. He knows by heart the Ionian Homer, another blind man. This may be true but in recent years traditional methods of education have been abandoned— Democritus says supplemented—by a new class of men who call themselves sophists. In theory, a sophist is supposed to be skilled in one or another of the arts. In practice, many local sophists have no single subject or competence. They are simply sly with words and it is hard to determine what, specifically, they mean to teach, since they question all things, except money. They see to it that they are well paid by the young men of the town.

Anaxagoras is the best of a bad lot. He speaks simply. He writes good Ionian Greek. Democritus read me his book *Physics*. Although I did not understand a lot of it, I marvel at the man's audacity. He has attempted to explain all things through a close observation of the visible world. I can follow him when he describes the visible but when it comes to the invisible, he loses me. He believes that *there is no nothing*. He believes that all space is filled with something, even if we cannot see it—the wind,

10

for instance. He is most interesting (and atheistic!) about birth and death.

"The Greeks," he has written, "have a wrong conception of becoming and perishing. Nothing comes to be or perishes, but there is mixture and separation of things that exist. Thus they ought properly to speak of generation as mixture, and extinction as separation." This is acceptable. But what are these "things"? What makes them come together and go apart? How and when and why were they created? By whom? For me, there is only one subject worth pondering—creation.

In answer, Anaxagoras has come up with the word mind. "Originally, from the infinitely small to the infinitely large, all things were at rest. Then mind set them in order." Then those things (*what* are they? *where* are they? *why* are they?) started to rotate.

One of the largest things is a hot stone that we call the sun. When Anaxagoras was very young, he predicted that sooner or later a piece of the sun would break off and fall to earth. Twenty years ago, he was proved right. The whole world saw a fragment of the sun fall in a fiery arc through the sky, landing near Aegospotami in Thrace. When the fiery fragment cooled, it proved to be nothing more than a chunk of brown rock. Overnight Anaxagoras was famous. Today his book is read everywhere. You can buy a secondhand copy in the Agora for a drachma.

Pericles invited Anaxagoras to Athens and gave him a small pension, which currently supports the sophist and his family. Needless to say, conservatives hate him almost as much as they do Pericles. Whenever they wish to embarrass Pericles politically, they accuse his friend Anaxagoras of blasphemy and impiety and all the usual nonsense . . . no, not nonsense for Anaxagoras is as much an atheist as all the other Greeks, but unlike the rest he is not a hypocrite. He is a serious man. He thinks hard about the nature of the universe, and without a knowledge of the Wise Lord you must think very hard indeed for otherwise nothing will ever make sense.

Anaxagoras is about fifty years old. He is an Ionian Greek from a town called Clazomenae. He is small and fat, or so I am told by Democritus. He comes from a wealthy family. When his father died, he refused to administer the ancestral estate or hold political office. He was interested only in observing the natural world. Finally he turned over all his property to distant relatives and left

11

home. When asked whether or not his native land concerned him at all, Anaxagoras said, "Oh, yes, my native land very much concerns me." And he pointed to the sky. I forgive him this characteristic Greek gesture. They do like to show off.

During the first table, as we dined on fresh rather than preserved fish, Anaxagoras was curious to know my reaction to the tales of Herodotus. I tried several times to answer him, but old Callias did most of the talking. I must indulge Callias because our invisible peace treaty is by no means popular with the Athenians. In fact, there is always a danger that our agreement will one day be renounced and I shall be obliged to move on, assuming that my ambassadorial status is recognized and I am not put to death. The Greeks do not honor ambassadors. Meanwhile, as co-author of the treaty, Callias is my protector.

Callias described yet again the battle of Marathon. I am very tired of the Greek version of this incident. Needless to say, Callias fought with the bravery of Hercules. "Not that I was obliged to. I mean, I'm hereditary torchbearer. I serve the mysteries of Demeter, the Great Goddess. At Eleusis. But you know all about that, don't you?"

"Indeed I do, Callias. We have that in common. Remember? I am also hereditary . . . torchbearer."

"*You* are?" Callias has not much memory for recent information. "Oh, yes. Of course. *Fire*-worship. Yes, very interesting, all that. You must let us watch one of your ceremonies. I'm told it's quite a sight. Particularly the part where the Arch-Magian eats the fire. That's you, isn't it?"

"Yes." I no longer bother to explain to Greeks the difference between Zoroastrians and Magians. "But we don't *eat* the fire. We tend it. The fire is the messenger between us and the Wise Lord. The fire also reminds us of the day of judgment when each of us must pass through a sea of molten metal—rather like the real sun, if Anaxagoras' theory is true."

"But then what happens?" Although Callias is an hereditary priest, he is most superstitious. I find this odd. Hereditary priests usually tend to atheism. They know too much.

I answered him, traditionally: "If you have served the Truth and rejected the Lie, you will not feel the boiling metal. You will—"

"I see." Callias' mind, such as it is, flits about like a threatened bird. "We have something like that, too. Anyway, I want to watch you eat fire one of these days. Naturally, I can't return the favor. Our mysteries are very deep, you know. I can't tell you a thing about them. Except that you'll be reborn once you've got through the whole lot. *If* you get through them. And when you're dead, you'll be able to avoid—" Callias stopped; the bird settled upon a bow. "Anyway, I fought at Marathon, even though I was obliged to wear these priestly robes that I must always wear, as you can see. Well, no, you can't see them, of course. But priest or not, I killed my share of Persians that day—"

"—and found your gold in a ditch." Anaxagoras finds Callias as exasperating as I do. Unlike me, he does not have to endure him.

"That story has been much distorted in the telling." Callias was suddenly precise. "I happened to take a prisoner who thought I was some sort of general or king because I wear this fillet around my head, which you can't see. Since he spoke only Persian and I spoke only Greek, there was no way to sort the matter out. I couldn't tell him that I was of no importance at all, outside of being torch-bearer. Also, since I was only seventeen or eighteen, he should have figured out that I wasn't important. But he didn't. He showed me a riverbank—*not a ditch*—where he had hidden this chest of gold. Naturally, I took it. Spoils of war."

"And what happened to the owner?" Like everyone in Athens, Anaxagoras knew that Callias had promptly killed the Persian. Then, thanks to that chest of gold, Callias was able to invest in wine and oil and shipping. Today he is the richest man in Athens. He is deeply envied. But then, at Athens everyone is envied for something—even if it be nothing more than the absence of any enviable quality.

"I set him free. Naturally." Callias lied easily. Behind his back he is known as rich-ditch Callias. "The gold was by way of ransom. Normal sort of thing in battle. Happens every day between Greeks and Persians—or used to. That's all over now, thanks to us, Cyrus Spitama. The whole world owes me and you eternal gratitude."

"I will be quite happy with a year or two of gratitude."

Between the removal of the first tables and the arrival of the second tables, Elpinice joined us. She is the only Athenian lady who dines with men whenever she chooses. She is privileged because she is wife to the rich Callias and sister to the splendid Cimon—sister and true widow, too.

Before she married Callias, she and her brother lived together as man and wife, scandalizing the Athenians. It is a sign of the essential crudity of the Greeks that they do not yet understand that a great family is made even greater when brother marries sister. After all, each is a half of the same entity. Combine the two in marriage and each is doubly formidable.

It is also said that Elpinice, not Cimon, actually ruled the conservative party. At the moment, she has great influence with her nephew Thucydides. She is admired and feared. She is good company. Tall as a man, Elpinice is handsome in a ravaged way—my informant is Democritus, who at the age of eighteen regards anyone with so much as a single gray hair as an unlawful fugitive from the tomb. She speaks with that soft Ionian accent which I like as much as I dislike the hard Dorian accent. But I learned my Greek from an Ionian mother.

"I am a scandal. I know it. I can't help it. I dine with men. Unattended. Unashamed. Like a Milesian companion—except I'm not musical." Hereabouts, the elegant prostitutes are called companions.

Although women have few rights in any Greek city, there are barbarous anomalies. The first time that I attended the games in one of the Ionian Greek cities of Asia Minor, I was startled to note that although the unmarried girls were encouraged to attend the games and examine potential husbands in the nude, the married ladies were forbidden to watch, on the no doubt sensible ground that any alternative to a lawful husband must not be viewed. In conservative Athens, wives and maidens are seldom allowed to leave their quarters, much less attend games. Except for Elpinice.

I could hear the great lady as she settled herself—like a man—on a couch instead of sitting modestly in a chair or on a stool, the way Greek ladies are supposed to do on those rare occasions when they dine with men. But Elpinice ignores custom. She does as she pleases and no one dares complain . . . to her face. As sister of Cimon, wife of Callias, aunt of Thucydides, she is the greatest lady in Athens. She is often tactless, and seldom bothers to disguise the contempt she has for Callias, who admires her inordinately.

I can never decide whether or not Callias is stupid. I daresay it takes a kind of cleverness to make money with or without a treasure found in a ditch. But his shrewdness

14

in business matters is undone by his silliness in all other aspects of life. When his cousin the noble, the honest, the selfless (for an Athenian) statesman Aristides was living in poverty, Callias was much criticized for not helping him and his family.

When Callias realized that he was getting a reputation for meanness, he begged Aristides to tell the assembly how often he had refused to take money from Callias. The noble Aristides told the assembly exactly what Callias wanted him to say. Callias thanked him, and gave him no money. As a result Callias is now regarded not only as a miser but as a perfect hypocrite. Aristides is known as the just. I am not sure why. There are great blanks in my knowledge of this city and its political history.

Last night one blank was promptly filled by Elpinice. "*She* has had a son. Early this morning. *He* is delighted." *She* and *he* pronounced with a certain emphasis always mean the companion Aspasia and her lover, General Pericles.

The conservative Callias was much amused. "Then the boy will have to be sold into slavery. That's the law."

"That is not the law," said Anaxagoras. "The boy is freeborn because his parents are freeborn."

"Not according to that new law Pericles got the assembly to vote for. The law's very clear. If your mother is foreign. Or your father is foreign. I mean Athenian . . ." Callias was muddled.

Anaxagoras set him right. "To be a citizen of Athens, both parents must be Athenian. Since Aspasia is a Milesian by birth, her son by Pericles can never be a citizen or hold office. But he is not a slave, any more than his mother is—or the rest of us foreigners."

"You're right. Callias is wrong." Elpinice is brisk and to the point. She reminds me of Xerxes' mother, the old Queen Atossa. "Even so, I take some pleasure in the fact that it was Pericles who forced that law through the assembly. Now his own law will forever exclude his own son from citizenship."

"But Pericles has other sons. By his *lawful* wife." Callias still resents deeply, or so he maintains, the fact that many years ago the wife of his eldest son left her husband in order to marry Pericles, thus making two families wretched instead of one.

"Bad laws are made to entrap those who make them," said Elpinice, as if quoting some familiar proverb.

15

"Did Solon say that?" I asked. Solon is a legendary wise man, often quoted by Athenians.

"No," said Elpinice. "I said it. I like to quote myself. I am not modest. Now, who will be the king of our dinner party?"

As soon as the second tables are taken away, it is the Athenian custom for the company to elect a leader who will then decide, first, how much water should be mixed with the wine—too little obviously means a frivolous evening—and, second, to choose the topic of conversation. The king then guides, more or less, the discussion.

We elected Elpinice queen. She ordered three parts water to one of wine. A serious discussion was intended. And there was indeed a very serious discussion about the nature of the universe. I say very serious because there is a local law—what a place for laws!—which forbids not only the practice of astronomy but any sort of speculation as to the nature of the sky and the stars, the sun and the moon, creation.

The old religion maintains that the two largest celestial shapes are deities called, respectively, Apollo and Diana. Whenever Anaxagoras suggests that the sun and moon are simply great fiery stones rotating in the heavens, he runs a very real risk of being denounced for impiety. Needless to say, the liveliest of the Athenians speculate on these matters all the time. But there is the constant danger that some enemy will bring a charge of impiety against you in the assembly, and if you happen to be unpopular that week, you can be condemned to death. Athenians never cease to astonish me.

But before we got to dangerous matters, I was quizzed by Elpinice about Herodotus' performance at the Odeon. I was careful not to defend the Great King Xerxes' policy toward the Greeks—how could I? But I did mention with what horror I had heard Herodotus slander our queen mother. Amestris does not in the least resemble the bloodthirsty virago that Herodotus saw fit to invent for his audience. When he said that she had recently buried alive some Persian youths, the audience shuddered with delight. But the true story is quite different. After Xerxes was murdered, certain families went into rebellion. When order was restored, the sons of those families were executed in the normal manner. Magian ritual requires the exposure of the dead to the elements. As a good Zoroastrian, Amestris defied the Magians and ordered the dead youths buried. This was a calculated political gesture, demonstrating once again the victory of Zoroaster over the devil-worshipers.

I told them of Amestris' perfect loyalty to her husband the Great King. Of her heroic behavior at the time of his murder. Of the hard intelligence which she demonstrated in securing for her second son the throne.

Elpinice was delighted. "I should have been a Persian lady. Obviously I am wasted in Athens."

Callias was shocked. "You are far too free as it is. I'm also certain that not even in Persia is a lady allowed to lie on a couch, swilling wine with men and talking blasphemy. You'd be locked up in a harem."

"No, I'd be leading armies like what's-her-name from Halicarnassus. Artemisia? You must," Elpinice said to me, "prepare an answer to Herodotus."

"And tell us all about your travels," said Callias. "About all those eastern places you've seen. The trade routes . . . That would be really useful. I mean, just *how* does one get to India or Cathay?"

"But more important than trade routes are the notions about creation that you've encountered." Anaxagoras' dislike of trade and politics sets him apart from other Greeks. "And you must put into writing the message of your grandfather Zoroaster. I have heard of Zoroaster all my life, but no one has even made clear to me who he was or what he actually believed to be the nature of the universe."

I leave to Democritus the recordinig of the serious discussion that followed. I note that Callias was predictable; he believes in all the gods, he says. How else was he able to win three times the chariot race at Olympia? But then, he is torchbearer of the mysteries of Demeter at Eleusis.

Elpinice was skeptical. She likes evidence. That means a well-made argument. For Greeks, the only evidence that matters is words. They are masters of making the fantastic sound plausible.

As always, Anaxagoras was modest; he speaks as one "who is simply curious." Although that stone which fell from the sky proved his theory about the nature of the sun, he is more than ever modest, since "there is so much else to know."

Democritus asked him about those famous *things* of his; the things that are everywhere all the time and cannot to be seen.

17

"Nothing," Anaxagoras said, after his third cup of Elpinice's highly deluted wine, "is either generated or destroyed. It is simply mixed and separated from existing things."

"But surely," I said, "nothing is no thing and so has no existance at all."

"The word nothing will not do? Then let us try everything. Think of everything as an infinite number of small seeds that contain everything that there is. Therefore, everything is in everything else."

"This is a lot harder to believe than the passion of holy Demeter after her daughter went down into Hades," said Callias, "taking the spring and the summer with her, an *observable* fact." Callias then muttered a prayer, as befitted a high priest of the Eleusinian mysteries.

"I made no comparison, Callias." Anaxagoras is always tactful. "But you will admit that a bowl of lentils has no hair in it."

"At least we hope not," said Elpinice.

"Or fingernail parings? Or bits of bone?"

"I agree with my wife. I mean, I hope that none of these things gets mixed in with the lentils."

"Good. So do I. We also agree that no matter how closely you observe a lentil bean, it does not contain anything but bean. That is, there are no human hairs in it or bones or blood or skin."

"Certainly not. Personally, I don't like beans of any kind."

"That's because Callias is really a Pythagorean," said Elpinice. Pythagoras forbade members of his sect to eat beans because they contain transmigrating human souls. This is an Indian notion that somehow got taken up by Pythagoras.

"No, because I am really a victim of flatulence." Callias thought this amusing.

Anaxagoras made his point. "On a diet of nothing but lentils and invisible water, a man will grow hair, nails, bone, sinew, blood. Therefore, all the constituents of a human body are somehow present in the bean."

Democritus will record for himself but not for me the rest of our dinner party, which was pleasant and instructive.

Callias and Elpinice left first. Then Anaxagoras came over to my couch and said, "I may not be able to visit you for some time. I know you will understand."

18

"Medism?" This is what Athenians call those Greeks who favor the Persians and their brother-race the Medes.

"Yes."

I was more exasperated than alarmed. "These people are not sane on that subject. If the Great King didn't want peace, I wouldn't be ambassador at Athens. I would be military governor." This was unwise—the wine's effect.

"Pericles is popular. I am his friend. I also come from a city that was once subject to the Great King. So, sooner or later, I shall be charged with medism. For Pericles' sake, I hope it is later." As a very young man Anaxagoras fought at Marathon on *our* side. Neither of us has ever alluded to this episode in his life. Unlike me, he has no interest at all in politics. Therefore, he is bound to be used by the conservatives as a means of striking at General Pericles.

"Let us hope that you are never charged," I said. "If they find you guilty, they'll put you to death."

Anaxagoras gave a soft sigh which might have been a laugh. "The descent into Hades," he said, "is the same no matter where or when you start."

I then asked the grimmest of Greek questions, first phrased by the insufficiently hard-headed author of *The Persians*, " 'Is it not better for a man never to have been born?' "

"Certainly not." The response was brisk. "Just to be able to study the sky is reason enough to be alive."

"Unfortunately, I can't see the sky."

"Then listen to music." Anaxagoras is always to the point. "Anyway, Pericles is convinced that the Spartans are behind the rebellion of Euboea. So this season Sparta is the enemy, not Persia." Anaxagoras lowered his voice to a whisper. "When I told the general that I was coming here to dinner, he asked me to apologize to you. He has wanted to receive you for some time. But he is always watched."

"So much for Athenian freedom."

"There are worse cities, Cyrus Spitama."

As Anaxagoras was taking his leave I asked, "Where was all this infinitesimal matter *before* it was set in motion by mind?"

"Everywhere."

"No real answer."

"Perhaps no real question."

I laughed. "You remind me of a wise man that I met

19

in the east. When I asked him how this world began, he made a nonsensical answer. When I told him that his answer made no sense, he said, 'Impossible questions require impossible answers.' "

"A wise man," said Anaxagoras, without conviction.

"But *why* was it that mind set creation in motion?"

"Because that is the nature of mind."

"Is this demonstrable?"

"It has been demonstrated that the sun is a rock which rotates so quickly that it has caught fire. Well, the sun must have been at rest at some point or it would have burned out by now, the way its fragment did when it fell to earth."

"Then why won't you agree with me that the mind which set all these seeds in motion was that of the Wise Lord, whose prophet was Zoroaster?"

"You must tell me more about the Wise Lord, and what he said to your grandfather. Perhaps the Wise Lord *is* mind. Who knows? I don't. You must instruct me."

I find Anaxagoras agreeable. He does not push himself forward like most sophists. I think of my kinsman Protagoras. Young men pay him to teach them something called morality. He is the wealthiest sophist in the Greek world, according to the other sophists—who should know.

Many years ago I met Protagoras in Abdera. He came one day to my grandfather's house to deliver wood. He was young, charming, quick-witted. Later, somehow, he became educated. I don't think that my grandfather helped him, though he was a very rich man. Protagoras has not been in Athens for several years. He is said to be teaching in Corinth, a city filled with wealthy, idle, impious youths, according to the Athenians. Democritus admires our kinsman and has offered to read me one of his many books. I have declined this pleasure. On the other hand, I should not mind meeting him again. Protagoras is another favorite of Pericles'.

Except for one brief public meeting with General Pericles at government house, I have not come within half a city of him. But then, as Anaxagoras said last night, Pericles is always watched. Although he is, in effect, the ruler of Athens, he can still be charged in the assembly with medism or atheism—or even the murder of his political mentor Ephialtes.

Democritus finds the great man dull. On the other hand, the boy admires Aspasia. Lately, he has had the

20

run of her house, where a half-dozen charming girls from Miletus are permanently in residence.

Since Democritus is taking dictation, I cannot give my views on the ideal behavior of a young man in society. He assures me that Aspasia is still good-looking despite her advanced age—she is about twenty-five—and recent motherhood. She is also fearless, which is a good thing, since there is much to fear in this turbulent city; particularly, for a metic—the local word for foreigner—who happens to be the mistress of a man hated by the old aristocracy and their numerous hangers-on. She also surrounds herself with brilliant men who do not believe in the gods.

Currently, a mad soothsayer is threatening to charge Aspasia with impiety. If he does, she could be in real danger. But according to Democritus, she laughs at the mention of the soothsayer's name. Pours the wine. Instructs the musicians. Listens to the talkers. Attends to Pericles; and to their new son.

3

AT THE BEGINNING THERE WAS FIRE. All creation seemed to be aflame. We had drunk the sacred haoma and the world looked to be as ethereal and as luminous as the fire itself that blazed upon the altar.

This was in Bactra. I was seven years old. I stood next to my grandfather Zoroaster. In one hand I held the ritual bundle of sticks and watched . . .

Just as I was beginning to see again that terrible day, there was a banging at the door. Since the servant is never in the house, Democritus unlatched the door and admitted the sophist Archelaus and one of his pupils, a young mason.

"He's been arrested!" Archelaus has the loudest voice of any Greek that I've ever met, which means the loudest voice in the world.

"Anaxagoras," said the young mason. "He's been arrested for impiety."

"And for medism!" thundered Archelaus. "You must do something."

"But"—I was mild—"since I am *the* Mede at Athens, I don't think anything that I might say is apt to impress the assembly. Quite the contrary."

But Archelaus thinks otherwise. He wants me to go before the authorities and say that since the treaty of peace, the Great King has no designs on the Greek world. More to the point, since there is now, demonstrably, a perfect peace between Persia and Athens, Anaxagoras cannot be guilty of medism. I found this argument moderately ingenious, like Archelaus himself.

"Unfortunately," I said, "it is a condition of the treaty that the terms not be discussed in public."

"Pericles can discuss it." The sound reverberated in the courtyard.

"He can," I said. "But he won't. The matter is too delicate. Besides, even if the treaty were discussable, the Athenians are still capable of finding Anaxagoras guilty of medism, or of anything else that strikes their fancy."

"Quite true," said the pupil. The young mason is called Socrates. Uncommonly ugly, according to Democritus, he is uncommonly intelligent. Last summer, as a favor to Democritus, I hired him to repair the front wall of the house. He made such a botch of it that we now have a dozen new chinks through which the icy wind can whistle. As a result, I have been obliged to abandon the front room entirely. Socrates has offered to re-do the wall but I fear that if he so much as touches the house with his trowel, the whole mud edifice will fall down about our ears. As an artisan, he is most disconcerting. In the midst of plastering a wall he is apt, suddenly, to freeze and stare straight ahead for minutes at a time, listening to some sort of private spirit. When I asked Socrates what sort of things the spirit told him, he simply laughed and said, "My daimon likes to ask me questions."

This struck me as a highly unsatisfactory sort of spirit. But, I dare say, the lively Socrates is as highly unsatisfactory a sophist as he is a mason.

Archelaus agreed with me that since the conservatives don't dare to attack Pericles personally, they must satisfy themselves with an indictment of his friend Anaxagoras. But I disagreed with Archelaus when he said that I should tell the assembly that the charge of medism is false.

"Why should they listen to me?" I asked. "Besides, the main charge is bound to be impiety—of which he's guilty. As are you, Archelaus. As am I, in the eyes of the mob and those who've accused him. Who did bring the charge?"

"Lysicles, the sheep dealer." The name broke upon my ears like some huge wave. Lysicles is a vulgar, hustling sort of man who is bent on making his fortune by serving Thucydides and the conservative interest.

"Then it's quite clear," I said. "Thucydides will attack Anaxagoras—and his friend Pericles in the assembly. Pericles will defend Anaxagoras—and his own administration."

"And you . . . ?"

"Will do nothing." I was firm. "My own position here is fragile, to say the least. The moment that the conservatives decide that it is time for another war with Persia, I shall be put to death—if time does not anticipate your politicians." I made myself cough pathetically; then could not stop coughing. I am indeed ill.

"What," asked Socrates abruptly, "happens when you die?" I gasped for air: it seemed an eternity before the air filled up my chest. "For one thing," I said, "I shall have left Athens."

"But do you think that you yourself will continue in another fashion?" The young man seemed genuinely interested in what I thought or, rather, what Zoroastrians think.

"We believe that all souls were created at the beginning by the Wise Lord. In due course, these souls are born once, and once only. On the other hand, in the east, they believe that a soul is born and dies and is born again, thousands and thousands of times, in different forms."

"Pythagoras held the same view," said Socrates. "When Archelaus and I were in Samos, we met one of Pythagoras' oldest disciples. He said that Pythagoras got this doctrine from the Egyptians."

"No." I was firm. I can't think why. I don't really know anything about Pythagoras. "He got it from those who live beyond the Indus River, where I have traveled . . ."

Archelaus was impatient. "This is most fascinating, Ambassador. But the fact remains that our friend has been arrested."

"The fact also remains," said Socrates coolly, "that men die, and what happens or does not happen to the mind that inhabits their flesh is of considerable interest."

"What shall we do?" Archelaus seemed close to stormy tears. In his youth, he had been a student of Anaxagoras'.

23

"I'm hardly the person to ask," I said. "Go to General Pericles."

"We did. He's not at his house. He's not at government house. He's not at Aspasia's house. He's vanished."

Eventually I got rid of Archelaus. Meanwhile Anaxagoras is in prison, and at the next meeting of the assembly he will be prosecuted by Thucydides. I assume that he will be defended by Pericles.

I say assume because early this morning the Spartan army crossed the border into Attica. General Pericles has taken the field, and the war that everyone has been anticipating for so long has at last begun.

I am fairly certain that Athens will be defeated. Democritus is upset. I tell him that it makes no difference at all who wins. The world goes on. In any case, between Athens and Sparta, there is not much choice. Each is Greek.

I shall finish explaining to you, Democritus, what I was not able to tell your friend who asked me what happens after death. Once free of the body, the soul returns to the Wise Lord. But, first, the soul must cross the bridge of the redeemer. Those who have followed in life the Truth will go to the house of good mind, and happiness. Those who have followed the Lie—that is, the way of the Wise Lord's twin brother Ahriman, who is evil—will go the house of the Lie, and there suffer every sort of torment. Eventually, when the Wise Lord overwhelms evil, all souls will be as one.

Democritus wants to know why the Wise Lord created Ahriman in the first place. This is a good question, which my grandfather answered once and for all.

At the moment of creation, the Wise Lord said of his twin, "Neither our thoughts, nor our deeds, nor our consciences, nor our souls agree."

Democritus says that this is not a proper answer. I say it is. You say that it is merely a statement about oppositions. I say that it is deeper than that. You say that the Wise Lord does not explain *why* he created his evil brother. Because each was created simultaneously. By whom? You are very annoying in your Greek way. Let me explain.

At the moment of creation there was only infinite time. But then the Wise Lord decided to devise a trap for Ahriman. He proceeded to create time of the long dominion within infinite time. The human race is now encased in

24

time of the long dominion rather like a fly in a piece of amber. At the end of time of the long dominion, the Wise Lord will defeat his twin, and all darkness will be burned away by light.

Democritus wants to know why the Wise Lord has gone to so much trouble. Why did he consent to the creation of evil? Because, Democritus, he had no choice. *Whose* choice was it? you ask. I have devoted my life to trying to answer that question, a question which I have put to Gosala, the Buddha, Confucius, and many other wise men to the east and to the east of the east.

So make yourself comfortable, Democritus. I have a long memory, and I shall indulge it. As we wait in this drafty house for the Spartan army to come—not a moment too soon as far as I'm concerned—I shall begin at the beginning and tell you what I know of the creation of this world, and of all other worlds too. I shall also explain why evil is—and is not.

BOOK TWO

In the Days
of Darius
the Great King

1

AT THE BEGINNING THERE WAS FIRE. All creation seemed to be aflame. We had drunk the sacred haoma and the world looked to be as ethereal and as luminous and as holy as the fire itself that blazed upon the altar.

This was in Bactra. I was seven years old. I stood next to my grandfather Zoroaster. In one hand, I held the ritual bundle of sticks and watched closely as Zoroaster lit the fire on the altar. As the sun set and the fire flared upon the altar, the Magians began to chant one of those hymns that Zoroaster had received directly from Ahura Mazdah the Wise Lord. In my grandfather's thirtieth year, he had begged the Wise Lord to show him how a man could practice righteousness in order to achieve a pure existence, now and forever. It was then that the miracle happened.

The Wise Lord appeared to Zoroaster. The Wise Lord told Zoroaster exactly what must be done in order that he —and all mankind—might be purified *before* the end of time of the long dominion. As the Wise Lord lit with fire the way of Truth that we must follow if we do not succumb to the Lie, so Zoroaster and those who follow the true religion light the sacred fire in a sunless place.

I can still see the light from the fire altar as it illuminated the row of golden jars that held the sacred haoma. I can still hear the Magians as they chanted the hymn in celebration of the Wise Lord. I can still remember the point at which they had got in the hymn when, suddenly, death came to us out of the north.

We were chanting the verses that describe world's end "when all men will become of one voice and give praise with a loud voice to the Wise Lord and at this time he will have brought his creation to its consummation, and there will be no further work he need do."

Since the haoma had done its work, I was not entirely in or out of my body. As a result, I am not exactly cer-

28

tain what happened. I can still recall the characteristic tremor of my grandfather's hands when, for the last time, he raised to his lips the jar of haoma. To me he was awe-inspiring. But who was not awed by Zoroaster? I thought him immensely tall. But then, I was a child. Later I learned that Zoroaster was of middle height, and inclined to stoutness.

I remember that in the light from the fire the curls of his long white beard seemed to be spun from gold. I remember that in the light from the fire his blood looked like molten gold. Yes, I remember, most vividly, the murder of Zoroaster at the fire altar.

How did this happen?

The province of Bactria is on the northeastern border of the empire. The provincial capital Bactra is a midway point not only between Persia and India but also between the northern marauding tribes and those ancient civilizations that look upon the southern seas.

Although there had been rumors for some weeks that the northern tribes were on the move, no preparations had been made to defend Bactra. I suppose that the people felt safe because our satrap—or governor—was Hystaspes, father of the Great King Darius. The Bactrians thought that no tribe would dare attack the city of Darius' father. They were wrong. While Hystaspes and most of his army were on the road to Susa, the Turanians swept through the city. What they did not loot, they burned.

At the fire altar we knew nothing until the Turanians were suddenly and silently among us. They are enormous men, with blond hair, red faces, pale eyes. When the entranced Magians finally saw them, they screamed. When the Magians tried to flee, they were butchered. As the haoma jars were smashed the golden haoma mingled with the darker gold of blood.

Democritus wants to know what haoma is. I haven't the slightest notion. Only the Magians are allowed to mix haoma, and I am not a Magian—that is, hereditary priest. All I know is that the basis for this sacred, inspiring, mystical potion is a plant that grows in the Persian highlands and resembles, I am told, what you people call rhubarb.

Over the years all sorts of stories have been invented about Zoroaster's death. Since he was so firmly opposed to the old devas, or devil-gods, worshipers of these dark spirits give credit to this devil or that for having killed the prophet of the Wise Lord. This is nonsense. Those blond animals from the north were simply looting and burning a rich city. They had no idea who Zoroaster was.

I did not move from the position to which I had been assigned at the beginning of the ritual. I continued to clutch the bundle of twigs. I suppose that I was still in the haoma trance.

As for Zoroaster, he ignored the killers. He continued with the ritual, never ceasing to stare at the flame on the altar. Although I did not stir from my place, I'm afraid that I no longer looked into the fire, as required by ritual.

I stared with wonder at the slaughter all about me. I was not afraid, again due to the haoma. In fact, I found unexpectedly beautiful the way that nearby houses turned to yellow fire. Meanwhile Zoroaster continued to feed the sacred flame on the altar. As he did, the white bearded lips posed for the last time the famous questions:

"This I ask thee, O Lord, answer me truly:
Who among those to whom I speak is righteous
    and who is wicked?
Which of the two? Am I evil myself, or is he the
    evil one who would wickedly keep me far from
    thy salvation?
How should I *not* think him the wicked one?"

Zoroaster dropped to his knees.

For nearly seventy years I have told the story of what happened next so often that there are times when I think that I am like a child in school, simply repeating endlessly by rote a half-understood text.

But other times, in dreams, I do see that fire again, smell the smoke, observe the Turanian warrior's fat arm hold high the ax which suddenly falls hard on the neck of Zoroaster. As the golden blood foams and sprays, the old man's lips continue to move in prayer and the barbarian looks at him in stupid wonder. Then Zoroaster raises his voice, and I hear every word that he says. Usually Zoroaster put ritual questions to the Wise Lord. But now the Wise Lord himself speaks with the tongue of his dying prophet: "Because Zoroaster Spitama has renounced the glories of eternal life until the end of infinite time, as I shall give this same blessing to all who follow Truth."

The Turanian's ax struck again. As Zoroaster fell forward upon the altar, he deliberately gathered to his breast what remained of the Wise Lord's son, the embers of the fire.

I would have been butchered too, had not a Magian carried me to safety. Fortunately for me, he had arrived too late to drink haoma, and so, thanks to his clear head, I was saved. We spent the night together in the smoking ruins of the central market.

Shortly before dawn the barbarians left, taking with them what plunder they could. Everything else was burned except for the town's citadel, where my mother and several members of our family had taken refuge.

I remember very little of the next few days. Our satrap Hystaspes hurried back to the city. On the way he captured a number of Turanians. My mother tells me that I was asked to look at the prisoners to see if I could identify the murderer of Zoroaster. I was not able to. In any case, I remember none of this with any clarity. At the time, I was still in a half-world between waking and dreaming, the haoma state. I do remember watching the Turanian captives as they were impaled on sharpened stakes outside the ruins of the city gate.

A few weeks later Hystaspes personally brought my mother and me up to the imperial court at Susa, where my mother and I were not exactly welcome. In fact, if it had not been for Hystaspes, I very much doubt if I would still be alive, enjoying every moment of a glorious old age in this jewel of a city that I never for one moment contemplated visiting, much less living in.

Democritus thinks that Athens is marvelous. But you have not seen the civilized world. I hope that one day you will travel, and transcend your Greekness. Democritus has been with me three months. I try to educate him. He tries to educate me. But he agrees that when I'm dead —very soon, I should think—he must go to the east. Meanwhile, he is altogether too Greek, too Athenian. Write that down.

I liked old Hystaspes. Even when I was a child he treated me as if I were an adult. He also treated me as if I were in some way a holy man—at the age of seven! True, I was the last person to hear Zoroaster's final words, which were the first words ever spoken through a man's lips by the Wise Lord himself. As a result, to this day, I am regarded as not quite earthly by those Magians who follow the way of Truth as opposed to that of the Lie. On the other hand, I am not, in any true sense, the

31

heir of Zoroaster despite a number of well-meaning—also ill-meaning—attempts to install me as the chief of the order.

Democritus reminds me that I have still not explained what a Magian is. Certainly, Herodotus got it all wrong during that interminable recitation at the Odeon.

The Magians are the hereditary priests of the Medes and the Persians, just as the Brahmans are the hereditary priests of India. Except for the Greeks, every Aryan tribe has a priestly caste. Although the Greeks retain the Aryan pantheon of gods and rituals, they have lost the hereditary priests. I don't know how this happened but, for once, the Greeks are wiser or luckier than we.

Persian custom requires that *all* religious ceremonies be conducted by Magians. This makes for enormous tension. Although most Magians are not Zoroastrians, they are obliged by custom to assist in our sacred rites. My grandfather did his best to convert the whole lot of them from devil-worship to mono-theism. But his best has proved so far to be not good enough. Perhaps every tenth Magian follows the Truth; the rest celebrate, exuberantly, the Lie.

My father was Zoroaster's third and youngest son. As a cavalry commander, he fought beside the Great King Darius during the Scythian campaign. In a skirmish near the Danube River, my father was wounded. He came home to Bactra; and died. I was too young to remember him. I am told that he was dark—very much a Spitama, with the onyx-bright eyes and magical voice of the prophet, or so my mother, Lais, tells me. She is Greek . . .

Democritus is surprised that I use the present tense. So am I. But there it is. Lais is now living on the island of Thasos, just opposite the coastal city of Abdera, where she was born to an Ionian Greek family.

Lais' father was a loyal subject of the Great King—the disgusting word medizer had not yet been coined largely because all the Greek cities of Asia Minor and most of those along the Hellespont and the Thracian coast happily paid tribute to the Great King. The troubles came later, thanks to the Athenians.

Democritus wants to know how old Lais is, and how she happened to marry my father. To start with the last question first, they met shortly after Darius came to the throne. This was a time of turmoil. There were rebellions in Babylon, Persia, Armenia. Darius needed money, soldiers, alliances. To that end, he sent my father as ambassador to the brilliant court of Polycrates, the tyrant of Samos.

For many years Polycrates had been an ally of the Egyptian pharaoh against Persia. But when he saw that Egypt was no longer able to withstand our armies, he took—or pretended to take—our side.

My father's task was to get money and ships from Polycrates. The negotiations were long and unpleasant. Whenever there was a rumor that Darius had lost a battle, my father would be ordered to leave Samos. Then just as he was about to set sail, a messenger would come from the palace. Please return. The tyrant has just consulted the oracle and . . . In other words, Darius had not lost but won a battle.

During this arduous negotiation my father was much helped by Megacreon of Abdera, the owner of numerous silver mines in Thrace. Megacreon was a good friend to Persia, and a wise councilor to the slippery Polycrates. He was also father of the eleven-year-old Lais. When my father asked to marry her, Megacreon was most agreeable. Darius was not. He disapproved of mixed marriages even though he himself had made several, for political reasons.

Finally Darius consented to the marriage on condition that my father promptly take at least one Persian wife. As it turned out, my father never did marry a Persian lady or anyone else. The month that I was born, my father died. Lais was then thirteen . . . which now makes her about eighty-eight. That answers your first question.

Lais lives contentedly on Thasos in a house that faces Abdera. This means that the north wind constantly blows her way. But she never feels the cold. She is like a Scythian. She even looks like one. She has—or had—fair hair; and her blue eyes are like mine. Or the way mine were before the blue turned to white.

For once I have been diverted in my narrative not by a new thought but by you, Democritus.

Where was I? Midway between Bactra and Susa. Between an old life and a new life.

It is night. I remember this scene vividly. I have just entered the tent of Hystaspes, satrap of Bactria and Parthia. At the time I looked on Hystaspes as being as ancient as my grandfather, yet he must not have been more than fifty-five. Hystaspes was a short, broad vigorous man with

33

a useless left arm; in his youth, the muscles had been cut to the bone in battle.

Hystaspes was seated on a traveling chest. Torches flared on either side of him. As I started to fall onto my belly before him, he reached down with his good arm and set me on a stool.

"What do you want to be?" He spoke to children—or at least to me—in the same straightforward way that he spoke to everyone else, including his son the Great King.

"A soldier, I think." I had given the matter no real thought. I did know that I wanted never to be a priest. A priest, mind you, not a Magian. Although all Magians are born priests, not all priests are Magians. Certainly, we Spitamas are not Magians. I should also make the point that from childhood on, religious ceremonies have bored me, and the constant memorizing of sacred texts used to make my head ache. In fact, there were times when I felt that my head was like a jar being filled to overflowing with my grandfather's hymns. The Cathayans, by the way, believe that the soul or mind of a man is located not in the head but in the stomach. Doubtless this explains why they fret so much about the preparation and the serving of food. It may also explain why their memories are so much better than ours. Information is stored not in the finite head but in the expandable stomach.

"A soldier? Well, why not? You'll be put to school in the palace with the other boys your age. And if you show promise at archery, and so on . . ." Hystaspes' voice trailed off. He used very easily to lose his train of thought. I was accustomed to his unfinished speeches, long silences.

As I waited for him to continue, I stared idly into the flame of one of the torches. Hystaspes took this as a sort of omen. "See? You can't keep your eyes from the son of the Wise Lord. That's natural."

I quickly looked away. Even at the age of seven, I could see what was coming next. And it came. "You are the grandson of the greatest man ever to walk the earth. Don't you want to follow him?"

"Yes. I'd like to. I try to." I knew how to play the boy-priest; and did. "But I would also like to serve the Great King."

"There is no higher task for anyone on earth—except for you. You are different. You were there. In the temple. *You* heard the voice of the Wise Lord." Although

34

my good fortune—if that is the phrase—in being present at the murder of Zoroaster has made me of permanent interest to all who follow the Truth and renounce the Lie, I sometimes think that my life might have been a good deal less complicated had I been born an ordinary Persian noble, unmarked by deity. Certainly, I have always felt an impostor whenever one of our Magians kisses my hand and asks me to tell, yet again, what it was that the Wise Lord said. I am a believer, of course. But I am not a zealot. Also, I was never satisfied by Zoroaster's explanation—or nonexplanation—of how the Wise Lord was created. What existed *before* the Wise Lord? I have traveled the whole earth in search of an answer to that all-important question. Democritus wants to know if I found it. Wait.

I suppose that my share of Lais' Ionian blood has made me more skeptical in religious matters than is usual for a Persian, much less a member of the holy family of Spitama. Yet of all Ionians, those from Abdera are the least inclined to skepticism. In fact, there is an old saying that it is not humanly possible to be stupider than an Abderan. Apparently Thracian air has had a dulling effect on the wits of those Grecian colonists from whom Democritus and I descend.

Democritus reminds me that the most brilliant of the Greek sophists is an Abderan—and our cousin. Abdera can also claim the greatest living painter, Polygnotus, who painted the long porch in the market-place, or Agora, here. I shall never see it.

Hystaspes told me yet again of his veneration for my grandfather. As he talked he kneaded his useless arm. "I was the one who saved him from the Magians. Well, no. That's not strictly true. The Wise Lord saved Zoroaster. I was simply the instrument used." Hystaspes was now launched on a story that he never tired of and that I never listened to. "The Great King Cyrus had just made me satrap of Bactria. I was young. I believed everything that the Magians had taught me. I worshiped all the devas, particularly Anahita and Mithras. I often drank haoma for pleasure and not for holiness, and I never once gave the right portions of the sacrifice to the Wise Lord because I did not know who he was. Then Zoroaster came to Bactra.

"He had been driven out of his native Rages. He had traveled east, from city to city. But whenever he preached the Truth, the Magians would force him to move on. Finally he came to Bactra. The Magians begged me to expel him. But I was curious. I made them argue with Zoroaster in my presence. For seven days he spoke. One by one, he confounded their arguments. He exposed their gods as devils, as agents of the Lie. He proved that there is only one creator, the Wise Lord. But with this one creator, there is also Ahriman, the spirit of evil. He is the Lie that Truth must ever contend with . . ."

Looking back, I realize that in temperament Hystaspes was a born Magian, or priest. *He* should have been Zoroaster's grandson or son. But then, spiritually, he was. When Hystaspes accepted my grandfather's teachings, he commanded the Magians of Bactria to do so, too. Officially they have complied. Privately, to this day, most of them continue, as they always have, to worship devils.

Zoroaster's appearance on the scene was like the earthquake that recently leveled Sparta. He told the Magians that the gods they prayed to were really devils. He also found their conduct of the various rituals—particularly, the ones of sacrifice—not only impious but scandalous. He accused them of conducting orgies in the name of religion. For instance, the Magians used to hack up a *living* ox while guzzling sacred haoma. They then kept for themselves to eat those parts of the ox that belong, rightfully, to the Wise Lord. Needless to say, the Magians bitterly resented Zoroaster. But thanks to Hystaspes, the Bactrian Magians were obliged to revise many of their rituals.

As I recollect that scene in the tent with Hystaspes, I begin to understand what hopes as well as fears that he had for me at the court of his son the Great King.

A few years earlier, with much fanfare, Darius had accepted the Wise Lord and his prophet Zoroaster. When my grandfather was murdered, Hystaspes decided to send me to Darius, as a permanent and visible reminder of Zoroaster. I would be educated as if I were a member of one of the six noble families that had helped Darius to ascend the throne.

"You will find many enemies at Susa." Hystaspes spoke to me as if I were a thoughtful statesman and not a child. "Most of the Magians are devil-worshipers. Particularly the ones from ancient Media. They follow the Lie. They are also very powerful at court. My son is much too tolerant in his dealings with them."

Hystaspes' willingness to criticize his son Darius always shocked the old-fashioned Persian nobility. But neither he nor Darius had been brought up at court. In fact, to tell the truth, the main line of the imperial family—the Achaemenids—ended when the sons of Cyrus the Great were murdered. As a distant relative of the Achaemenids, young Darius seized the throne with the aid of The Six—and of the Wise Lord. He then invited Zoroaster to attend him at Susa. But my grandfather would not leave Bactra. If he had, he might have had a longer life and I would not have lived in such peril for so many years.

Hystaspes arranged and rearranged the useless arm. "My son swears to me that he follows the Truth. As he is a Persian, he cannot lie." Now that I have become a historian or counterhistorian, I must note that for us Persians there is nothing worse than the telling of a lie while for the Greeks there is no pleasure more exquisite. I believe that this is because Greeks must live by selling things to one another and, of course, all merchants are dishonest. Since the Persian nobility are forbidden by custom either to buy or to sell, they may not lie.

Hystaspes was never happy with his son's lack of religious zeal. "I know that Darius must govern more than a thousand cities, each with different gods. When he restored our fire temples, your grandfather was pleased. But when he restored the temple of Bel-Marduk at Babylon, your grandfather was horrified. So was I. But since my son rules all the lands, he believes that he must accept all religions, no matter how abominable."

Hystaspes passed his good hand very slowly through the flame of the torch beside him, an old Magian trick. "The Great King's court is split into many factions. Be on your guard. Serve only the Great King—and the Wise Lord. Each of the principal wives has her supporters. Avoid them. Avoid the Greeks at court. Many are tyrants, driven out by the new democracies. They are forever trying to get my son to go to war against other Greeks. They are bad men, and very persuasive. Since your mother is Greek . . ." Hystaspes left that sentence unfinished, too. He disliked my mother because she was not Persian, and he would have disliked her son had not the hybrid child been chosen to hear the words of the Wise Lord himself. This must have mystified Hystaspes. A half-Greek boy had been chosen to hear the voice of

37

the Wise Lord. Plainly the ways of divinity are not easily understood. This is a point that everyone agrees on.

"You will have the run of the harem until you are old enough for school. Be alert. Study the wives. Three of the wives are important. The eldest wife is a daughter of Gobryas. Darius married her when he was sixteen. They have three sons. The eldest is Artobazanes. He is now a grown man. He is expected to succeed Darius. But the Great King is under the spell of Atossa, the second wife, who is queen because she is the daughter of Cyrus the Great. Since she bore Darius three sons after he became Great King, she claims that the eldest of the three sons is the only legitimate heir. Also, as Cyrus' grandson, the boy is truly royal. He is called Xerxes." Thus did I hear for the first time the name of the man who was to be my lifelong—as long as his life, that is—friend.

Hystaspes gazed at me gravely. I fought off sleep; did my best to look alert. "Atossa is the one that you must please," said Hystaspes, having just warned me to avoid *all* the wives and factions. "But do not make enemies of the other wives or of their eunuchs. You must be sly as the serpent. For the sake of the Wise Lord, you must survive. It won't be easy. The harem is an unholy place. Astrologers, witches, devil-worshipers, every kind of wickedness is popular among the women. And the worst of the lot is Atossa. She believes that she ought to have been born a man so that she could have been Great King like her father, Cyrus. But since she's not a man, she tries to compensate through magic. She has a private chapel where she prays to the devil-goddess Anahita. Between Atossa on the one hand and the Magians on the other, your life won't be easy. The Magians will try to convert you to the Lie. But never give way. Never forget that you are the agent on earth of the Wise Lord, that you have been sent by him to pursue at Susa the way of Truth, to continue the work of Zoroaster, the holiest man that ever lived."

This was all somewhat overwhelming for a sleepy child who wanted to grow up to be a soldier because soldiers did not have to spend as much time in school as Magians and priests—or sophists.

2

IN FREEZING WEATHER WE WENT UP TO
Susa. Wrapped in wool, I rode beside my mother atop a
camel, the one form of transportation that I have never
learned to like. The camel is a disagreeable creature
whose motion can make one every bit as sick as the toss-
ing of a ship. As we approached the city, my mother kept
muttering Greek spells to herself.

Incidentally, Lais is a witch. She admitted this to me
some years after our arrival at court. "A Thracian witch.
We are the most powerful on earth." At first I thought
that she was joking. But she was not. "After all," she
used to say, "if I hadn't been a witch, we'd never have
survived at Susa." She may have a point there. Yet all the
time that she was secretly indulging herself in Thracian
mysteries, she was piously advancing her son as the true
heir to the unique prophet of the Wise Lord who had
been, of course, the sworn enemy of all those devils that
she secretly worshiped. Lais is a clever woman.

It was dawn when we came to the Karun River. In
slow single file the caravan crossed a wooden bridge,
whose planks sagged and groaned. Beneath us the water
of the river was solid ice while just ahead of us was Susa,
sparkling in the sun. I had no idea that a city could be so
large. All of Bactra could have fitted into one of the mar-
ketplaces. It is true that most Susan houses are ramshackle affairs, built of mud brick or—most oddly— built
below ground in narrow earth trenches covered with
layers of palm fronds to keep out the melting summer
heat, the petrifying winter cold. But it is also true that
the palace Darius had recently completed was by far the
most splendid building in the world. On its high platform
the palace dominates the city in much the same way that
Susa is dominated by the snow-striped peaks of the Zagros
Mountains.

Susa lies between two rivers in a fertile plain ringed on
all sides by mountains. For as long as anyone can re-

39

member, the city was the capital of Anshan, a territory subject first to the Elamites, then to the Medes. The south-west corner of Anshan contains the Persian highlands, whose clan leader was Cyrus the Achaemenid, hereditary lord of Anshan. When Cyrus finally broke out of Anshan, he conquered Media and Lydia and Babylon. His son Cambyses conquered Egypt. As a result, the whole world from the Nile to the Indus River is now Persian, thanks to Cyrus and Cambyses; thanks to Darius and to his son Xerxes and to *his* son, my current master, Artaxerxes. Incidentally, from the accession of Cyrus to the present day, only one hundred and seven years have passed, and for most of this marvelous century I have been alive, and at the court of Persia.

In summer, Susa is so hot that lizards and snakes have been found cooked in the streets at midday. But by then the court has moved two hundred miles north to Ecbatana, where the Median kings had built for themselves the largest and perhaps least comfortable palace in the world; made entirely of wood, this building occupies more than one square mile in a high cool valley. During Susa's cold months the Great King used to remove the court two hundred and twenty-five miles to the east, to that most ancient and voluptuous of cities, Babylon. But, later, Xerxes preferred Persepolis to Babylon. So the court now winters in the original homeland of the Persians. Old courtiers—like me—very much miss languorous Babylon.

At the gate to Susa we were met by a king's eye. At any moment there are at least twenty king's eyes, one for each of the twenty provinces, or satrapies. This official is a sort of general inspector and surrogate for the Great King. It was the task of this particular king's eye to look after members of the royal family. Reverently he greeted Hystaspes. He then provided us with a military escort, a necessity at Susa, since the streets so twist and turn that a stranger is soon lost—sometimes forever, if he is not attended by guards.

I was delighted by the vast, dusty marketplace. As far as the eye could see there were tents and pavilions, while bright banners marked the start or terminus of this or that caravan. There were merchants from every part of the earth. There were also jugglers, acrobats, soothsayers. Snakes writhed to the music of pipes. Veiled and unveiled women danced. Magicians cast spells, pulled teeth, restored virility. Astonishing colors, sounds, smells . . .

The new palace of Darius is approached by a wide straight avenue, lined with huge winged bulls. The palace's façade is covered with glazed brick on which bas-reliefs depict Darius' victories from one end of the world to the other. These delicately colored life-size illustrations are modeled in the brick itself, and I have yet to see anything as splendid in a Greek city. Although the figures tend to resemble one another—each is shown in profile, according to the old Assyrian style—one can still identify the features of the various Great Kings as well as those of certain of their close companions.

On the palace's west wall, near the corner, opposite a monument to some long-dead Median king, there is a portrait of my father at the court of Polycrates in Samos. My father is shown holding a cylindrical message, marked with the seal of Darius. He is facing Polycrates. Just back of the tyrant's chair is the famous physician Democedes. Lais thinks the resemblance to my father poor. But then, she dislikes the strict conventions of our traditional art. As a child, she used to watch Polygnotus at work in his studio at Abdera. She likes the realistic Greek style. I don't.

The palace at Susa is built around three courtyards on an east-west axis. Before the main gate the king's eye turned us over to the commander of the palace guard, who escorted us into the first courtyard. To one's right is a portico of tall wooden columns on stone bases. Beneath the portico a row of royal guardsmen—known as the immortals—saluted us.

We passed through high corridors into the second courtyard. This one is even more impressive than the first. Young as I was, I was relieved to see the sun symbol of the Wise Lord guarded by sphinxes.

Finally we entered the so-called private court, where Hystaspes was greeted by the palace chamberlain and by the principal clerks of the chancellery who do the actual work of governing the empire. All chamberlains and most clerks are eunuchs. While the old chamberlain—Bagopates, I think it was—greeted Hystaspes, a number of aged Magians extended bowls of smoking incense toward us. As they chanted their incomprehensible prayers they stared at me closely. They knew who I was. They were not friendly.

When the ceremonies were ended, Hystaspes kissed me on the lips. "As long as I live, I shall be your protector,

41

Cyrus, son of Pohuraspes, son of Zoroaster." Hystaspes then turned to the chamberlain, who cringed dutifully. "I commend this youth to you." I tried not to weep when Hystaspes left.

A minor functionary escorted my mother and me to our quarters in the harem, which is a small city within the large city of the palace. He showed us into a small empty room that looked onto a chicken yard.

"Your quarters, Lady." The eunuch smirked.

"I had expected a house." Lais was furious.

"In due course, Lady. Meanwhile Queen Atossa hopes that you and the child will be happy here. Whatever you want, you need only command."

This was my first acquaintance with the style of a court. One is promised everything; then given nothing. No matter how often Lais commanded, pleaded, begged, we were kept confined to that small room which looked onto a dusty courtyard containing a dry fountain and a dozen chickens that belonged to one of Queen Atossa's ladies-in-waiting. Although the noise of the chickens annoyed my mother, I quite liked them. For one thing, I had no other company. Democritus tells me that chickens are now being imported to Athens. They are called—what else?—Persian fowl!

Despite Hystaspes' official protection, Lais and I were kept prisoner for almost a year. We were never received by the Great King, whose various arrivals and departures were accompanied by a tumultuous sound of drums and tambourines that caused the chickens to run about the yard most comically—that caused my mother's face to set most tragically. Worse, when summer came we did not follow the court to Ecbatana. I have never been so hot.

We saw none of the wives except for Artystone, full sister to Queen Atossa—and so a daughter of Cyrus the Great. Apparently she was curious about us. One afternoon she appeared in our courtyard. I must say that she proved to be every bit as beautiful as people had said she was. This came as a surprise to Lais, who has always taken the view that whatever a famous personage is noted for tends to be the one thing that he notoriously lacks. For a witch, everything is illusion. Perhaps they are right. I do think that it was something of an illusion that Artystone was the only woman whom Darius had ever loved. Actually, he loved nothing on earth except earth itself; that is, he loved his dominion over all the lands.

42

Xerxes was the opposite. He loved too many people; and so lost dominion over earth, over all the lands.

Artystone was accompanied by two handsome Greek eunuchs not much older than I. They had been sold to the harem by an infamous merchant of Samos who trafficked in abducted Greek youths. Since Greeks are the most reluctant to be castrated, they are the most sought-after eunuchs. The Samian became very rich.

Actually, the most agreeable and *useful* eunuchs are Babylonian. Each year five hundred Babylonian youths joyously undergo castration in order to serve in the harems of the Great King and his nobles. By and large, these boys are uncommonly intelligent; they are also uncommonly ambitious. After all, if one has not been born a noble, eunuchhood is the only way to rise at court. It is no secret that to this day the true source of power at the Persian court is found not upon the throne but in the harem where ambitious women and sly eunuchs plot. Today, not only are the eunuchs the attendants and guardians of the wives and concubines, they are also councilors to the Great King, ministers of state and even, sometimes, generals and satraps.

Artystone wore a mantle of gold thread; carried an ivory wand. She had a high natural color, and looked always to be sulking.

Since Lais was Greek and I was half-Greek, Artystone commanded the boys to talk to us in Greek.

Lais cut her short. "We need no translator, Lady. My son is grandson of the true prophet."

"Yes, I know." Artystone pointed her ivory wand at me. "Can you eat fire?"

I was too shocked to answer.

Lais has a bad temper. "Fire is the son of the Wise Lord, Lady. It is not safe to make jokes about divinity."

"Oh?" The pale-gray eyes opened very wide. She resembled her father, Cyrus the Great, who was a remarkably handsome man. I know. I have seen his wax-covered body at holy Pasargada. "Well, Bactria is so far away."

"Bactria is the home of the Great King's father, Lady."

"It is not his home. He is simply satrap there. He is an Achaemenid, from holy Pasargada."

Wearing a faded woollen robe and surrounded by chickens, Lais faced up not only to the daughter of Cyrus but to the best-loved wife of Darius. Lais has always been fearless. Witchcraft?

"It was from Bactria that Darius came to regain the empire of your father," said Lais. "And it was in Bactria that Zoroaster first spoke with the voice of the Wise Lord, in whose name your husband the Great King rules over all the lands. Lady, beware that you do not bring down upon yourself the wrath of the One God."

In answer, Artystone raised her right arm; the golden sleeve hid her face—an odd, protective gesture. Then she was gone.

Lais turned to me, eyes bright with anger. "Never forget who you are. Never renounce the Truth and follow the Lie. Never forget that we are stronger than all the devil-worshipers."

I was deeply impressed. Particularly when I knew even then that Lais had not the slightest interest in religion of any kind. I do not count Thessalian witchcraft as religion. But Lais is a very shrewd and practical woman. In Bactra she had forced herself to learn a thousand hymns and rituals in order to convince Zoroaster that she was a follower of the Truth. Then she instilled in me the knowledge that I was not like others, that I had been especially chosen by the Wise Lord to bear constant witness to the Truth.

In youth, I never doubted Lais. But now as my life draws to a close, I have no idea whether or not I have fulfilled the mission set me by the Wise Lord, assuming that there was ever a mission. I must also confess that in the seventy years which have passed since the death of Zoroaster, I have looked upon so many faces of deity in so many parts of this huge world that I know for certain nothing.

Yes, Democritus, I know that I told you I would explain creation. And I shall—to the extent that it is knowable. As for the existence of evil, that is more easily answered. In fact, I am surprised that you have not guessed the genesis of the Lie, which defines—that's a hint—the Truth.

44

3

SHORTLY AFTER ARTYSTONE'S APPEAR-
ance, all of the chickens in our courtyard were massacred.
I missed their company. My mother did not.

It was early autumn when we received a visit from a
minor chancellery official. He had come from the office of
the chamberlain, where it had been decided that I was to
attend the palace school. Apparently, there had been no
place for me the previous spring when the court was in
residence. But now he himself would escort me to class.

Lais pressed our mysterious advantage. She demanded
new quarters. That was not possible, he said. There were
no instructions. She asked for an audience with Queen
Atossa. The eunuch tried not to laugh at the outrageous-
ness of the request.

So while poor Lais continued to live as a prisoner, I at
least attended school. I was delighted.

The palace school is divided into two parts. The first
section contains the members of the imperial family—at
that time some thirty princes, ranging in age from seven
to twenty—as well as various sons of The Six.

In the second section are the sons of the minor nobility
and the young guests of the Great King, as the hostages
are called. When Lais learned that I was not in the first
section, she was furious. Actually, she had no idea how
lucky we both were not to be dead.

I enjoyed the school which was held in a large room
that looked out upon a walled-in park where each day
we were taught archery and riding.

Our teachers were all Magians of the old school; they
hated Zoroaster and feared his influence. As a result, I
was ignored as much by the teachers as by the Persian
students. My only companions were the guests of the
Great King because, in a sense, I was a guest too. I was
also half-Greek.

I soon made friends with a boy my age named Milo
whose father, Thessalus, was stepbrother to Hippias, the

reigning tyrant of Athens. Although Hippias had continued the golden age of his father, the great Pisistratus, the Athenians had become bored with him and his family. But then, whenever the Athenians have too much of a good thing, they promptly seek something bad. This quest is not apt to be either arduous or unrewarded.

Also, in my class were the sons of Histiaeus, the tyrant of Miletus. Histiaeus himself had also been detained as a guest simply because he had become too rich and powerful. Yet Histiaeus had proven his loyalty—and practicality—at the time of Darius' invasion of Scythia.

In order to transport the Persian army into Scythia, Darius built a bridge of boats across the Hellespont. When Darius was turned back at the Danube—where my father was wounded—many of the Ionian Greeks wanted to burn the bridge and leave Darius to be hacked to pieces by the Scythians. With Darius dead or captured, the Ionian Greek cities would then declare themselves independent of Persia.

But Histiaeus opposed the plan. "Darius is our Great King," he told his fellow tyrants. "We have sworn fealty to him." Privately he warned them that without Darius' support, the Ionian nobility would ally itself with the rabble and overthrow the tyrants in much the same way that a similar alliance at Athens was in the process of expelling the last of the Pisistratids. The tyrants followed Histiaeus' advice, and the bridge was left intact.

Darius returned home safely. In gratitude he gave Histiaeus some silver mines in Thrace. Suddenly, between the lordship of the city of Miletus and the rich Thracian holdings, Histiaeus was no longer just another city tyrant—he was a powerful king. Ever cautious, Darius invited Histiaeus and two of his sons up to Susa, where they became guests. A subtle, restless man, Histiaeus was not cut out to be a guest . . . I mention all this in order to explain those wars which Herodotus refers to as Persian.

In school I spent most of my time with the Greek hostages. Although the Magians forbade us to speak Greek, we spoke nothing else whenever we were out of earshot of our teachers.

One cold winter day Milo and I were sitting on the frozen ground, watching our classmates throw the javelin. Dressed in the Persian manner—thick trousers and three sets of drawers—we did not feel the cold. I still dress properly, and often advise the Greeks to do the same. But you cannot convince any Greek that several layers of light cloth will make you not only warm in winter but cool in summer. When Greeks are not nude, they are wrapped in sweat-soaked wool.

From his father Milo had inherited a taste—as opposed to talent—for intrigue. He enjoyed explaining to me the divisions at court. "Everyone wants Artobazanes to succeed if Darius dies, because he's the eldest son. Artobazanes is also the grandson of Gobryas, who still thinks that *he* should have been Great King instead of Darius. But the other five nobles picked Darius."

"They had to. Darius is the Achaemenid. He's the nephew of Cyrus the Great."

Milo gave me a pitying look. Yes, even boys at Susa went in for such looks. At a court, even boys want to be thought to know secrets that others do not know.

"Darius," said Milo, "is no more related to Cyrus than you are or I am. Of course, all Persian nobles are related. So he's probably got some Achaemenid blood in him, just as I have through my Persian mother and you have through your father. Except *you* don't, because the Spitamas aren't really noble. In fact, they're not even Persian, are they?"

"Our family is greater than any noble family. We are holy." I became the prophet's grandson. "We have been chosen by the Wise Lord, who spoke to me—"

"Can you really eat fire?"

"Yes," I said. "And breathe it, too, when I'm divinely inspired or very angry. Anyway, if Darius isn't related to Cyrus, how did he get to be Great King?"

"Because he personally killed the Magian chancellor who was pretending that he was Cyrus' son and fooling everybody."

"But maybe the Magian really was the son of Cyrus." Even at an early age I had a sense of how the world is managed.

Milo's face suddenly looked very Greek—Dorian Greek. The blue eyes became round; the rosy lips slipped ajar. "How could they tell such a lie?"

"People do." It was my turn to be worldly. "*I* can't lie, because I am the grandson of Zoroaster." I was sublimely superior, and annoying. "But others can lie, and do."

"Are you calling the Great King a liar?"

I saw the danger, and stepped neatly around it. "No. That's why I was so surprised just now to hear *you* call him a liar. After all, *he* says that he is the Achaemenid and related to Cyrus, while you're the one who says that he isn't."

Milo was thoroughly confused, and alarmed. "To tell a lie is not possible for any Persian noble, like my mother's father. Or for an Athenian tyrant like me . . ."

"You mean a tyrant like your uncle *was*."

"He still is. Athens is still our city. Because Athens was nothing before my grandfather Pisistratus became tyrant and everyone knows it, no matter what the demagogues in the assembly say. Anyway, the Great King is the Achaemenid, if he says so. He can't lie. All I meant was that we are all Achaemenids. Related to them, that is. Particularly Gobryas and his family and Otanes and his family and—"

"I guess I misunderstood you." I let him escape. At Susa one must become a skilled courtier even before the first beard's grown. The world of a court is a supremely dangerous place: one misstep—and death, or worse.

I had already heard a good deal about the way that Darius had overthrown the false son of Cyrus. But since no one had ever dared say aloud in my presence that Darius was not related to Cyrus, I had learned something of importance from the dull Milo.

The fact that Darius was as much a usurper as the Magian he replaced explained a good deal about the factions at court. I could now see why Darius' father-in-law Gobryas had wanted to be Great King. He was Darius' senior. He was one of The Six, and as noble as Darius. But Darius had outwitted him. Gobryas accepted Darius as Great King on condition that the succession go to his grandson Artobazanes. But Darius promptly took as second wife Cyrus' daughter Atossa. Two years later, on the same day of the same year as myself, their son Xerxes was born. If Darius' relationship to the Achaemenids was tenuous, there was no doubt about the ancestry of his son Xerxes. *He* was the grandson of Cyrus the Great; he was the Achaemenid.

At Xerxes' birth, the court split between the factions of Queen Atossa and that of Gobryas' daughter. The Six tended to support Gobryas, while the other nobles supported Atossa . . . as did the Magians. My mother maintains that Darius deliberately encouraged everyone to connive against everyone else on the sensible ground that they would be too busy with one another ever to plot

48

against him. This is somewhat simple, and whatever Darius was, he was not simple. Even so, it is a fact that Darius appeared to encourage first one faction; then the other.

Susa was also the scene of another significant struggle. Since the Magians who worshiped the devas were in the majority, they did their best to make suffer the handful of Magians who followed Zoroaster. Those who followed the Lie had the help of Queen Atossa. Those who followed the Truth ought to have had the support of the Great King. But Darius was evasive. He spoke lovingly of my grandfather; then gave money to the Jews to rebuild their temple at Jerusalem, to the Babylonians to repair the temple of Bel-Marduk, and so on.

Although I was too young to play an active part in this religious war, my presence at court was deeply offensive to the deva-worshipers. Because Queen Atossa was close to them, Lais and I had been confined to that dismal harem chicken yard—from which we were saved by Hystaspes. Apparently he wrote his son to ask about my progress in the palace school. As a result of that letter I was assigned to the second section. As a result of that letter Lais and I were saved from what is called the fever, a mysterious disease that invariably kills those with powerful enemies at court.

One bright spring morning my life was again changed, entirely by accident if one rules out fate—the only deity you Greeks appear to take seriously.

I was in class, sitting cross-legged at the back of the room. I always tried to appear invisible; and usually succeeded. A Magian instructor was boring us with a religious text. I forget what it was. Probably one of those endless hymns to the fertility of Anahita, whom the Greeks call Aphrodite. It was well known at court that Queen Atossa was a devotee of Anahita, and Magians always please the great.

At a signal from the teacher, the class began to chant the praises of Anahita. All but me. Whenever called upon to sing the praises of this deva or that, I would remain silent and the Magian teachers would affect not to notice me. But this morning was different from all other mornings.

Suddenly the Magian stopped his wailing and moaning. The class fell silent. The old man looked straight at me. Was this by accident, or through fate? I shall never know.

49

I do know that I took his gaze to be a challenge. I stood up. I was ready for . . . I don't know what. Battle, I suppose.

"You did not join us in the hymn, Cyrus Spitama."

"No, Magian. I did not."

Astonished heads turned toward me. Milo's mouth fell open and stayed open. My manner was supremely disrespectful.

"Why not?"

I struck an attitude that I had seen my grandfather assume a thousand times before the fire altar at Bactra. One leg is carefully placed in front of the other while the arms are held straight forward, palms turned upward.

"Magian!" I imitated as best I could the voice of Zoroaster. " 'I sacrifice only to the undying, shining, swift-horsed sun. For when the sun rises up, then the earth, made by the Wise Lord, becomes clean. The running waters become clean. The waters of the wells become clean. The waters of the sea become clean. The standing waters become clean. All the holy creatures become clean.' "

The Magian made a gesture to ward off evil while my fellow students stared at me, appalled and frightened. Even the dullest realized that I was calling the swift-horsed sun down from the sky to be my witness.

" 'Should not the sun rise up,' " I began the last part of the invocation, " 'then the devas will destroy all things in the material world. But he who offers up a sacrifice to the undying, shining, swift-horsed sun, he will withstand darkness, and the devas, and that death which creeps in unseen . . .' "

The Magian was muttering spells to counter me.

But I could not have stopped if I had wanted to. In a loud voice I launched the Truth against the Lie. " 'As you stand for Ahriman and all that is evil, I cry out to the sun that you be destroyed, first, in time of the long dominion . . .' "

I never got to the end of my anathema.

With a scream the Magian fled, and the others followed.

I remember standing for a long time alone in the classroom, trembling like a new leaf in an equinoctal wind.

I have no idea how I got back to the courtyard with its ghosts of chickens.

I do know that word of what I had said and done echoed from one end of the palace at Susa to the other and, shortly before nightfall, I was commanded to wait upon Queen Atossa.

4

IT IS SAID OF THE PALACE AT SUSA THAT no one knows where all the corridors lead. I believe this. It is also said that there are exactly ten thousand rooms, which I very much doubt. I daresay that if Herodotus were told this story, he would report that there are twenty thousand rooms.

I recall being led through what seemed to me to be at least a mile of narrow, musty, ill-lit corridors whose floors are stained an ominous dark red. Yet we never once left the women's quarters, soon to be denied me: at about the age of seven, Persian boys are removed from the harem and turned over to the male members of the family. Since Lais was my only relative at Susa, I was allowed to live in the harem until the fairly advanced age of nine. Not that Lais and I could be said to have actually lived in the harem. Except for servants, we saw no court ladies in our squalid annex.

Two uncommonly tall and thin Babylonian eunuchs received me at the door to the private apartments of Queen Atossa. One of them told me that before the queen's entrance, I was to lie face down on an elaborate Indian carpet. As the queen entered the room I was to wriggle toward her and kiss her right foot. Unless told to rise, I was to remain face down until dismissed. Then I would wriggle backwards across the rug to the door. At no point was I ever to look directly at her. This is the way a suppliant is expected to approach the Great King or his surrogate. Members of royal or noble families are expected to bow low to the sovereign while kissing the right hand, as a sign of submission. If the Great King is so minded, he will allow a favored personage to kiss his cheek.

Protocol was particularly strict at the court of Darius, as it tends to be whenever a monarch is not born to the throne. Although the court of Darius' son Xerxes was far more glittering than that of his father, protocol was much less intrusive. As the son and grandson of Great Kings,

Xerxes did not need to remind the world of his greatness. Yet I have often thought that had he been as ill at ease with sovereignty as his father, he might have survived as long. But when it comes to fate, as the Athenians like to remind us in those tragedies that they are forever mounting so expensively at the theater, one cannot win. At the height of a bald man's fame, an eagle is bound to drop a turtle on his head.

Lais says that at the age of eight I was unique, the true heir to Zoroaster, and so on. Although she is naturally prejudiced, others seem to agree that I was unusually bold and self-assured. If I gave this impression, I must have been a skillful actor, for I was in a state of terror most of the time—and never more so than I was on that chilly evening when I lay face down on the red-and-black rug in the queen's apartment, my heart racing, as I awaited her entrance.

The room was small, the only furniture was an ivory chair with a silver footstool, and a small statue of the goddess Anahita. In front of the statue, a brazier contained burning incense. As I breathed the heavy scented air I shuddered uncontrollably. I knew where I was: I was in the hands of a deva-worshiper.

Silently a carved cedar door opposite me opened. With a rustling sound Queen Atossa entered the room and sat in the ivory chair. I crawled toward her, my nose pushed this way and that by the rough folds of the rug. Finally I saw two gold slippers set side by side on the footstool. In my panic I kissed the left slipper. But the Queen did not appear to notice my mistake.

"Stand up." Atossa's voice was almost as deep as that of a man. She also spoke the elegant old Persian of the original court of Anshan, an accent seldom heard nowadays at Susa or anywhere else for that matter. Listening to Atossa—so the old courtiers used to say—one heard again the voice of the dead Cyrus.

Although I was careful not to look at the queen directly, I did look at her out of the corner of my eye. She was a startling sight. No larger than I, she was like a fragile doll on whose neck had been set, most incongruously, the large head of Cyrus, the curve to whose Achaemenid nose so resembled that of a rooster I had got to know in our courtyard that I almost expected to see nostrils like slits set atop the bridge.

Atossa's hair or wig was dyed red; and the large gray-red eyes were surrounded not by normal white but by a red as fiery as her hair. Although she had some incurable disease of the eyes, she never went blind, lucky woman. Thick white enamel covered her face in order to hide—everyone said—a man's beard. She had tiny hands; each finger was heavy with rings.

"You were named for my father the Great King." The style of the old court made it impossible for a member of the imperial family ever to ask a question. For those unused to court life, conversation could be most confusing since direct questions always sounded like statements while answers tended to sound like questions.

"I was named for the Great King." I then recited all of Atossa's titles, the optional as well as the obligatory ones. Lais had instructed me with great care.

"I knew your father," said the queen when I had finished. "I did not know your grandfather."

"He was the prophet of the Wise Lord, who is the only creator."

Two sets of eyes shifted briefly to the smiling statue of Anahita. Like a blue snake, the incense rose in coils between Atossa and me. My eyes watered.

"So you said in the schoolroom. You frightened your teacher. Now tell me the truth, boy. Did you put a curse on him?" This was a true question, very much in the style of the modern court.

"No, Great Queen. I have not the power—that I know of," I added. I was not about to let slip any possible weapon. "I merely serve the Wise Lord, and his son the fire." Was I really so wise, so prodigious at eight years old? No. But I had been well coached by Lais, who had made up her mind not only to survive but to prevail at Susa.

"My father the Great King Cyrus worshiped the sun. Therefore, he worshiped fire. But he also worshiped the other high gods. He restored the temple of Bel-Marduk at Babylon. He built temples to Indra and Mithra. He himself was much loved by the goddess Anahita." Atossa inclined her head to the bronze statue. The idol's neck was garlanded with fresh summer flowers. I took this to be some sort of sinister miracle. I did not know that at Susa flowers are grown indoors all winter long, a luxury invented by the Medes.

Atossa questioned me about my grandfather. I told her as much as I could about his revelations. I also described

53

his death. She was particularly impressed to learn that I myself had heard the voice of the Wise Lord.

Although Atossa and her Magians were followers of the Lie, they were obliged to recognize that the Wise Lord was a singularly powerful god if only because the Great King himself had proclaimed from one end of the world to the other that his crown and his victories had come to him as a gift from the Wise Lord. Since Atossa could hardly oppose her husband, Darius, she approached the entire subject with understandable caution.

"Zoroaster is venerated here." Atossa spoke without much conviction. "And of course you and your mother are . . ." In search of the right phrase, Atossa frowned. Then she uttered an elegant old Persian phrase which does not translate at all to Greek but means something like "most dear to us in a cousinly way."

I bowed very low, wondering what I was supposed to say next. Lais had not prepared me for so much civility.

But Atossa did not expect an answer. For a long moment the queen stared at me with those curious blue-red eyes. "I have decided to move you to better quarters. You must tell your mother how surprised I was to learn that you had been living in the old palace. That was a mistake. Those who made it have been punished. You may also tell her that before the court moves to Ecbatana, I shall receive her. It has also been decided that you will attend the first section of the palace school. You will be taught with the royal princes."

I must have shown my delight, for the queen seemed less delighted.

Years later, when Atossa and I were friends, she told me that the actual decision to improve things for my mother and me came not from her but from Darius himself. Apparently one of Lais' messages had got through to Hystaspes. Furious, he had complained to his son, who had then commanded Atossa to treat us with all due honor.

"But," said Atossa, twenty years later, bestowing on me her most charming black-toothed smile, "I had no intention of obeying the Great King. Quite the contrary. I was going to put you and your mother to death. You see, I was entirely under the influence of those wicked Magians. Hard to believe, isn't it? How they poisoned our minds against the Wise Lord and Zoroaster and the Truth! Why, I was actually a follower of the Lie!"

54

"And still are!" In private, I was always bold with Atossa, which amused her.

"Never!" Atossa nearly smiled. "Actually, what saved you was that scene you made in the schoolroom. Until then hardly anyone had heard of you or your mother. But when the word started to spread that Zoroaster's grandson was in the palace, launching curses at the Magians. . . . Well, there was no way you could be ignored, or killed.

"I mean, if you and your mother had been discovered at the bottom of a well, strangled—which is what I had in mind, the fever takes too long—Darius' other wives would have blamed me and then he would have been irritated. So I was obliged to change course. Just as Lais was trying to save her own life and yours, I was trying to make my eldest son the heir to Darius. If I had fallen into disgrace, the Persian empire would have gone not to my son but to Artobazanes, who has not a drop of royal blood, any more than Darius did."

"Or Cyrus the Great," I added. The old Atossa could be played with up to a point.

"Cyrus was hereditary chief of all the highland clans." Atossa was serene. "He was born the Achaemenid. He was born lord of Anshan. As for the rest of the world . . . Well, he conquered that in the normal way, and if his son Cambyses had not . . . died, there would have been no Darius. But that is past. Today Xerxes is Great King, and all things have turned out for the best."

Atossa spoke too soon, of course. All things turn out ill, in the end. But that is the ill nature of things, to end.

Lais and I moved into the new palace. Unknown to us, we had been lodged originally in a part of the kitchen of the old palace. Although I now attended the first section of the palace school, I did not meet my exact contemporary Xerxes until that summer, after the court moved to Ecbatana.

The first section of the palace school proved to be no different from the second except that there were no Greek boys to talk to. I missed them. I was not treated badly by the young Persian nobles, but I was hardly made to feel at home. Of course, to be precise, I was not at home. For one thing, I was not a noble. For another, my peculiar status as grandson of Zoroaster made both teachers and pupils uneasy.

Because of the anathema that I had hurled at the old

55

Magian, I was thought to have supernatural powers and though, for a time, I denied that I was in any way different from the others, I soon realized that the secret of power—or in this case magic—resides not in its exercise but in its aura. If my schoolmates wanted to think of me as a magic-worker, then I would let them. I also found it useful to *see*, suddenly, the Wise Lord. Whenever I did, the Magian teachers shuddered and I would not be called upon to recite what I did not want to recite. All in all, none of this playacting did me any harm. If one is not supported at court by a powerful family, it is best then to be a protégé of the Wise Lord.

Queen Atossa kept her promise. Before the court removed to Ecbatana, she had received Lais. The fact that Lais did not annoy her with disquisitions on the Truth versus the Lie pleased her no end. Lais has always had the gift of knowing what it is that people most want to hear. She can charm anyone. Although she would ascribe this to witchcraft, I suspect that she is simply more intelligent than most people—the ultimate magic.

Since the queen was a devotee of witchcraft, Lais obliged her with every sort of potion and spell and Thracian nonsense—not to mention subtle philters and poisons. Nevertheless, despite the queen's patronage, Lais' position at court was based on the fact that she was the mother of the grandson of Zoroaster, the scourge of every sort of deva—not to mention magic. This meant that whenever I found the queen and Lais staring into a smoking cauldron and muttering spells, I would accept Lais' explanation that they were simply experimenting with some exotic medicine. Early on, I realized that what is *not* said at court can never turn, as if by—yes, magic, into a sharp knife in the dark or a draught of some slow poison.

5

THE COURT LEFT SUSA IN FOUR CONtingents. Since the harem's progress is always the slowest, the women and eunuchs depart first. Needless to say, Lais traveled by litter in the train of Queen Atossa. Lais was now an important lady of the court. The treasury and the furniture of the Great King come immediately after the harem. Next to depart are the clerks of the chancellery with their endless files. Finally the officers of state, the law-bearers, the nobles and the Great King take to the road on horseback or in war chariots. Thanks to Milo, I traveled with the nobles, in a war chariot drawn by four horses.

Shortly after I was assigned to the first section of the palace school, Thessalus insisted that his son Milo be promoted to the same class on the ground that the nephew of the tyrant of Athens was the equal of any Persian noble or priest. So Milo joined our classes and I had someone to talk Greek to. When it came time for us to leave for Ecbatana, Thessalus insisted that I travel with him and Milo.

We left Susa at sunrise. Both rivers were overflowing with swift white water from the snow that had begun to melt in the Zagros Mountains. Yet in a month's time, those swift rivers would be muddy rivulets. I have never known any place in the world to be as hot as Susa in the summertime, and I have lived in India; or as cold as Susa in the wintertime, and I have crossed the high Himalayas.

Thessalus himself drove the four-horse chariot. He had won the chariot race at the Olympic games, and he was every bit as overwhelming on the subject as Callias. There is something about those quadrennial games at Olympia that maddens even the most intelligent of the Greeks. I think that if Thessalus had had to choose between being tyrant of Athens and winning a victor's crown at the thirty-ninth Olympiad, he would have preferred the tangle of olive twigs.

For the slow-moving litters and wagons of the harem, the trip from Susa to Ecbatana takes at least a dozen days. For two small boys and a champion charioteer, the trip takes four days. Incidentally, this was my first encounter with the superb road system that Darius was creating. Out of Susa, Darius' highways go to the north, to the southwest, to the east. Every ten or fifteen miles, there is a post house, as well as an inn and stables. Small villages tend to grow up around the post houses.

At our first stop I could see through the white and pink blossoms of a thousand fruit trees in bloom, the wooden huts of a new settlement. Above Susa, the land is unusually fertile.

Due to Thessalus' rank, the innkeeper assigned us a small room with a low ceiling and an earth floor. Lesser

57

notables slept in the stables and cattle sheds or on the ground beneath the stars.

Although men of high rank usually travel with their own tents and furniture and retinue of slaves, Thessalus wanted us to travel "the way real soldiers do. Because that's what you're both going to be."

"Not Cyrus," said Milo. "He's going to be a priest. He's always praying, and thinking up curses." Although Milo could not have had much memory of the city of his birth, his style was very much the mocking Athenian one. I daresay it's in the bones.

Thessalus looked at me with some interest. "Are you a born Magian?"

"No, I'm not. I'm a Persian . . ."

"He's not a Persian. He's a Mede." Milo was tactless. It has never been considered good taste at court to mention the fact that the prophet sent by the Wise Lord to convert the Persians was not a Persian but a Mede from Rages. Despite the pretensions of various members of our family, Zoroaster had no Persian blood. On the other hand, I don't think that we are Medes, either. I have a suspicion that we derive from some truly ancient stock—Assyrian or Chaldean or even Babylonian. Except for me, the Spitamas are much too dark, too intense-looking, too exotic to be Medes. I, of course, am not typical of the family. Because of Lais, I am fair; and look to be Greek.

Thessalus lit charcoal in a brazier. He then made us soldiers' bread out of broken grain mixed with water. The result looked and no doubt tasted like sun-dried cow's dung.

"You have a great heritage," said Thessalus. He was a handsome man. Early in life he had married a Persian lady from Miletus. Although the Athenians of those days were not as opposed to mixed marriages as they are now, everyone at Athens thought that if a member of their reigning dynasty were to marry a Persian lady she should be, at the very least, a member of our imperial house.

I am told that Thessalus loved his wife in a most un-Athenian way. Certainly, he was an unusually passionate man. So fierce, if brief, had been the love between him and the future tyrannicide Harmodius that Athenian history was changed.

I don't think that anyone now alive understands exactly what happened. Elpinice, who is usually knowledgeable in such matters, thinks that both Thessalus and his step-

58

brother Hipparchus were enamored of Harmodius, a beautiful young athlete from Tanagra. Naturally, Harmodius was flattered to be loved by the two brothers of the tyrant of Athens. Harmodius was also something of a flirt. Officially, he was the boy-lover of another Tanagran, a cavalry at Athens, everyone quarreled with everyone matters at Athens, everyone quarreled with everyone else. Aristogeiton was furious at the tyrant's brothers, while Thessalus was angry at *his* brother for trying to take the boy away from him. While the boy himself . . . The whole thing is a perfect tangle, and of interest only to an Athenian. On the other hand, the outcome of this mess changed history.

Hipparchus insulted Harmodius' virginal sister at a public ceremony. He is supposed to have said that he hoped that she was less of a wanton than her brother. In a rage Harmodius went to his old lover Aristogeiton, and together they vowed to avenge this insult. At the Great Pan-Athenaic Festival, not only did Harmodius and Aristogeiton murder Hipparchus, they tried but failed to kill the tyrant Hippias. Although they themselves were promptly put to death, the tyranny was shaken and Hippias' position became so difficult that he felt obliged to send Thessalus up to Susa to make an alliance with Darius. But things had gone too far at Athens. Because of a lovers' quarrel, the house of Pisistratus fell, and statues of the lovers were put up in the Agora. Incidentally, when Xerxes conquered Athens, he brought the statues home to Susa where, upon my advice, they were placed beneath a monument to the family of Pisistratus. To this day the young killers can be seen, looking up at those good tyrants whom their jealousy and folly drove from a city that will never again know anything like the long and glorious peace so honorably maintained by the Pisistratids. The whole business is very strange. Only in Athens does one find sexual passion mixed up with politics.

Democritus reminds me that at the Persian court, favorite wives or concubines of the Great King are often influential. This is true. But whenever our queens exert power, it is not due so much to their sexual charms as to the fact that they govern the three houses of the harem and that the queen consort receives a large income *separate* from the Great King's. Finally, the queen consort is able to deal directly with those eunuchs who control the chancellery. Although I have never known a man as susceptible to beautiful women as Xerxes, I cannot think of a single instance in which his private lust affected public policy. Well, there was one such incident—but that was at the end of his life. If I live long enough, I will tell you about it.

As we ate soldiers' bread, I did my best to convince Thessalus that I, too, wanted to be a proper soldier.

"It is the best life," said Thessalus. "Necessary, too. The world is dangerous if you cannot fight. Or lead an army." He pushed at the coals in the brazier. "Or *raise* an army." He looked sad.

We all knew that Thessalus had failed to persuade Darius to come to the aid of Hippias. In those days, Darius paid little attention to the Greek world. Although he controlled the Greek cities of Asia Minor and exercised a degree of suzerainty over a number of islands like Samos, the Great King was never much interested in the western world, particularly after his defeat on the Danube.

Although Darius was fascinated by the east, he was never able, except for one expedition to the Indus River, to turn his full attention to the east and to the east of the east. Like Cyrus before him, Darius was constantly distracted by those fair-skinned northern horsemen who are forever pressing on our borders. But then, they are we. A thousand years ago the original Aryans swept down from the north and enslaved what we still refer to as the black-haired people, the original inhabitants of Assyria and Babylonia. Now, as Medes and Persians, the tribesmen are civilized and our clan leader is the Great King. Meanwhile, our cousins from the steppes look at us covetously; and await their turn.

Wistfully Thessalus spoke of Athens and, young as I was, I knew that he was speaking with a purpose. Queen Atossa was my mother's friend. Words said to me would be repeated to the queen. "Hippias is a good friend of Persia. Hippias' enemies at Athens are Persia's enemies and Sparta's friends." Thessalus' frowning face was rosy in the brazier's light. "Hippias needs the Great King's help."

Outside the inn someone shouted, "Way for the Great King's post!" There was a jangling sound as the messenger changed horses. Even in those days, royal messengers could travel the fifteen hundred miles from Susa to Sardis in less than a week. Darius always said that it was not his armies but his roads that sustained the empire.

60

"One day Sparta will make an alliance with my brother's enemies at Athens. When that happens, they will attack Persia."

Even to a child, this sounded ludicrous. Persia was a whole world. Although I had no notion just what Sparta was, I did know that it was Greek and small and weak and far away. I also knew that Persians invariably defeated Greeks. That was a natural law.

"My brother Hippias is all that stands between Persia and Sparta." I don't think that Thessalus was of very great intelligence. Since he was dead before I was full-grown, I never got to know him as one man does another. On the other hand, I had many dealings with his brother Hippias during the tyrant's long exile in Persia. Hippias was not only impressive but learned.

"Why is Sparta so dangerous?" I asked.

"They live for war. They are not like other people. Sparta is a barracks, not a city. They want to conquer all of Greece. They envy Athens. They hated our father, Pisistratus, because he was loved by all of the people and by all of the gods. In fact, the goddess Athena herself led my father up to the Acropolis, and in front of all the citizens she gave him and his heirs power over her city." I have no idea whether or not Thessalus believed this story. Certainly no modern Athenian does. Did they in those days? I doubt it.

The truth of the matter is that Pisistratus and his friends persuaded a tall girl named Phya to dress up as Athena. I have met her grandson, who delights in telling how his grandmother then escorted Pisistratus along the sacred way to Athena's temple on the Acropolis. Since a majority of the people supported Pisistratus anyway, they pretended that Phya was really Athena. The others kept silent—out of fear.

In due course Pisistratus was driven from Athens. He went to Thrace, where he owned silver mines. For a time he was associated with my grandfather Megacreon. As soon as Pisistratus had amassed a brand-new fortune, he paid off the leaders of the aristocratic party of Lycurgus. Then he bought off the commercial party of Megacles. Since he himself commanded the party of the ordinary people of the city, he was now able to return as tyrant of Athens, where he died, old and happy. He was succeeded by his sons Hippias and Hipparchus.

There are two theories—two? there are a thousand!—

as to the motives of Hipparchus' murderers. Some think that they were politically inspired. Others think that they were simply a pair of lovers gone berserk. I suspect the latter. So does Elpinice. As she pointed out only recently, neither of the two young men was connected with the celebrated family that was the focal point for those aristocrats who opposed the tyranny. I mean, of course, the descendants of the accursed . . . literally, accursed Alcmeon, who put to death a number of men who had taken refuge in a temple. In consequence, Alcmeon was cursed with the sort of curse that goes from father to son for generations. Incidentally, Pericles is an Alcmeonid, on his mother's side. Poor man! Although I don't believe in the various Greek gods, I tend to believe in the power of curses. In any case, from a base at Delphi, Alcmeon's grandson Cleisthenes led the opposition to the popular Hippias.

"Cleisthenes is a dangerous man." Thessalus was somber. "He is also ungrateful, like all the Alcmeonids. When Hippias succeeded our father, he made Cleisthenes a magistrate. Now Cleisthenes has gone to Sparta, trying to get them to invade Athens. He knows that only a foreign army could ever drive us out. No Athenian would. We are popular. The Alcmeonids are not."

Thessalus' account proved to be true, if not disinterested. A year or so after this conversation, Cleisthenes arrived at Athens with the Spartan army, and Hippias was overthrown. Hippias then swore allegiance to the Great King, and settled himself and his family at Sigeum, a modern town near the ruins of Troy.

Hippias was close to Apollo's priests at Delphi. He also helped preside over those mysteries at Eleusis where Callias bears his hereditary torch. He is said to have known more about oracles than any Greek. He could also predict the future. Once, in my green and insolent youth, I asked the tyrant if he had foreseen his own downfall.

"Yes," he said.

I waited for details. He offered none.

Whenever there is a political or moral mystery, the Athenians like to quote their wise man Solon. I shall do the same. Solon correctly blamed not Pisistratus but the Athenians for the rise of the tyrant. He said . . . what?

Democritus has now found me Solon's actual words: "You yourselves have made these men great by giving them support, and that is why you have fallen into evil

62

slavery. Each of you walks with the step of a fox, but taken all together your mind is vain. For you look to the tongue and the words of a crafty man, and you do not see the deed which is being done."

This seems to me to be as good an analysis of the Athenian character as we are ever apt to get—and from an Athenian! There is only one false note. No one had fallen into evil slavery. The tyrants were popular, and had it not been for the Spartan army, Cleisthenes would never have overthrown Hippias. Later, in order to consolidate his rule, Cleisthenes was obliged to make all sorts of political concessions to the mob that had once supported the tyrants. The result? The famous Athenian democracy. At this time, Cleisthenes' only political rival was Isagoras, the leader of the aristocratic party.

Now, half a century later, nothing has changed except that instead of Cleisthenes, there is Pericles; instead of Isagoras, Thucydides. As for the heirs of Pisistratus, they are contented landowners near the Hellespont. All except my friend Milo. He died at Marathon, fighting for his family—and for the Great King.

That evening on the road from Susa to Ecbatana, I became a fervent partisan of the Pisistratids. Naturally, I do not mention my enthusiasm to present-day Athenians, who have been taught for half a century to hate the family that their grandparents loved.

Once, most delicately, I brought up the subject with Elpinice. She was surprisingly sympathetic. "They gave us the best rule we've ever had. But Athenians prefer chaos to order. We also hate our great men. Look what the people did to my brother Cimon."

I pity Pericles. Since everyone agrees that he is a great man, he is bound to end badly. Elpinice thinks that he will be ostracized in a year or two.

Where was I? Ecbatana.

Even now, in my head, where most of my memories are without pictures of any kind—in some mysterious way, the blindness seems to have extended to much of my memory—I can still *see* the astonishingly beautiful approach to Ecbatana.

One travels upcountry through a dark forest. Then, just as it seems that the city has been misplaced or one is lost, there it is, like a vision of a fortress-city, ringed by seven concentric walls, each of a different color. At the city's exact center, a golden wall surrounds the hill on which the palace stands.

Because the highlands of Media are thickly forested, the palace is made entirely of cypress and cedar wood. As a result, the rooms smell oppressively of old wood, and fires are constantly breaking out. On the other hand, the facade of the palace is covered with squares of green copper, like armor plating. Some people think that this was done by the Medes in order to prevent enemies from firing the palace. I suspect that it was done simply for ornament. Certainly, the effect is singularly beautiful when the sun makes the pale green of the copper glow against the dark-green conifer trees that cover the mountains behind the city.

The afternoon that we entered Ecbatana, we were able to enjoy its legendary beauties for nine hours—the length of time that it took to get all of us through the seven gates. For turmoil and confusion, there is nothing to compare with the Persian court arriving at a capital city.

During those long hours before the gates of Ecbatana, I learned from Thessalus a number of Greek phrases that have since given me much pleasure in the saying.

6

IN MY TIME, SCHOOL LIFE WAS STRENUOUS. We were up before dawn. We were taught to use every kind of weapon. We were even taught farming and husbandry as well as mathematics and music. We learned to read and even to write, if necessary. We were taught how to build not only bridges and fortresses but palaces, too. We were given only one meager meal a day.

By the time a Persian noble is twenty, there is very little that he cannot do for himself if he has to. Originally, this educational system was much simpler: a youth was taught to ride, to draw the bow, to tell the truth; and that was that. But by the time of Cyrus, it was plain that the Persian nobility would have to know a great deal about nonmilitary matters, too. Finally, by the time of Darius, we were being deliberately educated for the sole purpose of administering the better part of the world.

But there was one aspect of governance that was kept

secret from us—the harem. Although many of our instructors were eunuchs, none of us was ever told anything about the inner workings of the harem, that mysterious world forever closed to all Persian males except the Great King—and me. I have often thought that my relatively long sojourn in the harem was enormously helpful to my later career.

When I finally moved into the quarters of the royal princes, I had spent nearly three years in the harem. Ordinarily, a young noble is removed from his mother at least three years before puberty and sent to the palace school. I was an exception. As a result, I got to know not only the wives of Darius but the harem eunuchs who work closely with their counterparts in the first and second rooms of the chancellery.

Democritus wants to know what these rooms are. The first room is always located at the back of the first courtyard of whatever palace the Great King happens to be occupying. At long tables a hundred clerks receive the Great King's correspondence as well as all petitions. After these documents are sorted out, the clerks of the second room then decide what should be shown the Great King or, more likely, which letter or petition should be given to this or that councilor of state or law-bearer. The second room exerts enormous power. Needless to say, it is in the hands of eunuchs.

In later life, Xerxes used to tease me by saying that I had all the subtlety and craft of a harem eunuch. I teased *him* by saying that if he had stayed longer in the harem, he might have learned statecraft from his mother. He would laugh; and agree. Later, there was nothing to laugh about.

I should note here that until the reign of Darius, married women of the ruling class could mingle with men, and it was not uncommon for a rich widow, say, to, to manage her own estates just as if she were a man. In Cyrus' time, women were not sequestered except, of course, during menstruation. But Darius had different notions from Cyrus. He kept the royal ladies entirely from public view. Naturally, the nobles imitated him, and their wives were also sequestered. Today it is not possible for a Persian lady to see and talk to any man except her husband. Once married, she can never again look upon her father or her brothers—or even her sons, once they have left the harem.

I am not sure why Darius was so intent on removing

65

the royal ladies from public life. I know that he feared them politically. Even so, I don't know why he thought that they would be less dangerous if confined to the harem. Actually, their power increased once they were removed from public gaze. In perfect secrecy they used the eunuchs, and the eunuchs used them. During the reign of Xerxes, many of the great offices of state were controlled by eunuchs in close partnership with one or another of the royal wives. This was not always a good thing. To say the least.

But even in the strict era of Darius, there were exceptions to his rules. Queen Atossa received whomever she pleased: man, woman, child or eunuch. Curiously enough, there was never any scandal about her—in my day. Years before, it was whispered that she had had an affair with Democedes, the physician who removed her breast. I rather doubt this. I knew Democedes, and he was far too clever and too nervous a man to get himself involved with a royal lady.

In her youth, Atossa preferred eunuchs to men. Most ladies do. After all, if a eunuch is sexually mature at the time of his castration, he is still capable of a normal erection. Handsome eunuchs are much fought over by the ladies of the harem. Wisely, our Great Kings choose to ignore these goings-on: women are sequestered not so much for their moral good as to make certain that their children will be legitimate. Whatever a lady may do with her eunuch or with another lady is of no concern to her master, if he be wise.

Another exception to the harem's rules was Lais. Because she was my only relative at court, she and I saw each other regularly in her apartments, which were always just outside the precinct of the harem. A lusty woman, Lais did not feel obliged to avail herself of eunuchs or women. She was pregnant at least twice that I know of. Each time, she arranged for an abortion, which is a capital crime in Persia. But Lais has the courage of a lion. Although anyone could have denounced her, no one did. She would attribute this to the fact that she had, literally, enchanted the court. Perhaps she had. Certainly, she enthralled the tyrant Histiaeus, with whom she had a long affair.

It is curious that I have no memory of my first meeting with the most important figure in my life, Xerxes. He could never remember that meeting either. But then, why should he? Xerxes was a royal prince who was already spoken of as Darius' heir, while I was neither noble nor priest, an anomaly at court. No one knew my rank, or what to do with me. Nevertheless, I had two powerful protectors—Hystaspes and Atossa.

Obviously, Xerxes and I met that summer at Ecbatana. Obviously, we must have seen each other at the first state reception that I ever attended: the wedding between Darius and one of his nieces, an occasion forever vivid to me because that was when I saw, at last, the Great King Darius.

For weeks the harem was in an uproar. The ladies spoke of nothing else but the marriage. Some approved the match between Darius and his niece—an eleven-year-old granddaughter of Hystaspes; some thought that the Great King should have married outside the imperial family this time. Endless and, to me, boring discussions filled the three houses of the harem.

Democritus wants to know what the three houses are. I thought everyone knew that the harem is divided into three sections. The so-called third house is occupied by the queen or the queen mother. If there is a queen mother, she will outrank the queen consort. The next house is for the women the Great King has already known. The first house contains the virgins, new acquisitions still being trained in music, dance, conversation.

On the day of the wedding there was a military display in front of the palace. To my disgust, while the rest of my schoolmates were at the palace gate attending the Great King, I was obliged to watch maneuvers from the roof of the harem.

Crushed in a mob of ladies and eunuchs, I watched with fascination the intricate drill of the ten thousand immortals, as the Great King's personal guard are known. In the bright sun their armor looked like the silver scales of fresh-caught fish. When they threw their spears in perfect unison, the sun itself was eclipsed by a cloud of wood and iron.

Unfortunately, from where I stood, cheek pressed against a splintery wood column, I could not see the Great King, who was directly below me, beneath a canopy of gold. But I did have a good view of the bride. She was seated on a stool between the chairs of her mother and Queen Atossa. A nice-looking child, she was plainly scared out of her wits by what was happening. From time to time during the military display, either her mother or Atossa would whisper something to her. Whatever they told her did no good. She looked more and more alarmed.

Later that day the wedding of Darius and his little niece took place in private. Afterwards there was a reception in the main hall of the palace, which I attended with my schoolmates. Under Darius, court ceremonial became so intricate that something almost always went wrong. In Cathay, when any aspect of a ceremony is botched, the whole thing must begin again from the beginning. Had we been obliged to observe this rule at the Persian court, we would never have had time to govern the world.

I ascribe a certain tendency to confusion at the Persian court to the large amounts of wine that Persians drink on ceremonial occasions. This goes back to the days when they were a wild mountain clan, given to endless drinking bouts. Note that I say they and not we. The Spitamas are Medes, if not something older; and, of course, Zoroaster hated drunkenness. That is one of the reasons why the Magians so hated him. Magians guzzle not only wine but sacred haoma.

I can still recall the awe that I felt when I first saw the lion throne on its dais. Made for King Croesus of Lydia, the back of the throne is a life-size lion, golden face turned to look over the left shoulder, emerald eyes aglitter, ivory teeth bared. A canopy of hammered gold is suspended over the throne by a long chain, while to the left and the right of the dais, elaborate silver braziers contain burning sandalwood.

At Ecbatana, the walls of the apadana—or hall of columns—are hung with tapestries depicting events in the life of Cambyses. Although the conquest of Egypt is shown in considerable detail, the Great King Cambyses' mysterious death is tactfully omitted.

I stood with my schoolmates to the right of the throne. The royal princes were closest to the throne. Next to the princes were the sons of The Six—and next to them were the boy guests of the Great King. I had been placed at the dividing line between the guests and the nobles, between Milo and Mardonius, the youngest son of Gobryas by the Great King's sister.

At the left of the throne stood the six nobles who had made it possible for Darius to become Great King. Although one of the original Six had been recently put to death for treason, his eldest son was permitted to represent a permanently ennobled and honored family.

As the world knows, when Cambyses was in Egypt, a Magian named Gaumata pretended to be Mardos, brother of Cambyses. When Cambyses died on his way home from Egypt, Gaumata seized the throne. But young Darius, with the aid of The Six, killed the pseudo-Mardos, married Atossa, the widow of both Gaumata and Cambyses, and became Great King. This is what all the world knows.

Of The Six, I was particularly interested in Gobryas, a tall, slightly stooped man whose hair and beard had been dyed blood-red. Lais told me later that the hairdresser had made the fatal error of using the wrong dyes—fatal for the hairdresser, that is. He was put to death. Largely because of that somewhat ludicrous first impression, I could never take Gobryas as seriously as everyone else did in those days.

I have often wondered what Gobryas thought of Darius. I suspect that he hated him. Certainly, he envied him. After all, Gobryas had as much or as little right to the throne as Darius. But it was Darius who became Great King, and that was that. Now Gobryas wanted his grandson Artobazanes to be Darius' heir, and the court had divided on that issue. The Six inclined to Artobazanes; Atossa and the family of Cyrus wanted Xerxes. As always, Darius himself was cryptic. The succession had not been decided.

There was a sudden clatter of drums and cymbals. The carved cedar doors opposite the throne were flung open and Darius stood in the doorway. He wore the cidaris, a high round felt hat that only the Great King and the crown prince may wear. At the base of the cidaris, Darius wore the blue-and-white fillet of sovereignty that had belonged to Cyrus and before him to the ten successive kings of Media.

I got no more than a quick glimpse of the Great King as I prostrated myself on the floor. Although the royal princes and high nobles remained standing, each bowed low to the Great King and kissed his own right hand. Needless to say, like everyone else, I kept furtive eyes on the Great King, even though it is a serious offense to look upon him without his permission.

Darius was then thirty-eight years old. Although not tall, he was beautifully proportioned, and his sinewy legs

69

were shown to advantage by the tight scarlet trousers that he wore beneath a purple Median robe on which had been embroidered, in gold, a falcon about to strike. As he approached the throne, I noticed that his saffron-dyed leather shoes were buttoned with lumps of amber.

In Darius' right hand, he carried a slender golden rod, emblem of his power to guide the state. In the left hand, he held a golden lotus with two buds, the universal symbol of immortality.

The Great King's undyed beard was long and naturally curly, and glistened like the sleek fur of the red fox, while the face was beautifully painted. The dark lines drawn about the eyelids made brilliant the sky-blue eyes. The legendary Cyrus was reported to have been the handsomest man in Persia. If Darius was not the most beautiful of the Persians, he was certainly a dazzling sight as he moved between the twenty-two columns of the apadana—rather like a lion, stalking.

Darius was followed by his turbaned cupbearer and by the court chamberlain, who carries the Great King's personal napkin and fly whisk. He was also accompanied by Hystaspes, and by the father of the child that he had just married, and by his eldest son, Artobazanes, a sturdy young man of twenty whose natural beard was almost as red as his grandfather Gobryas' disastrously dyed beard. Artobazanes was already a commander on the northern frontier.

As Darius approached the throne he playfully flicked Gobryas with the golden scepter; then he made a gesture for the older man to embrace him. This was a sign of special favor. With eyes cast down and arms folded so that each hand would be hidden in the opposite sleeve, Gobryas kissed Darius. Incidentally, no one may show his hands to the Great King unless in obeisance or in some normal business that has nothing to do with the court. The reason for this is obvious. Since no one may enter the presence of the Great King bearing arms, courtiers and supplicants are searched before they attend him. Then, to be doubly safe, they are obliged to hide their hands from him. This ancient Median custom was adopted, like so many others, by Cyrus.

At the foot of the lion throne, Darius clapped his hands. Everyone stood up straight, ready for the styling of the sovereign. As often as I have heard this ancient ceremony, I never cease to be thrilled by it—not that I am apt ever to hear it again.

As first of The Six, Gobryas was first to hail the Great King. "The Achaemenid!" Gobryas' harsh voice sounded almost hostile; doubtless an inadvertent reflection of his true feelings.

Next was Hystaspes. "By the grace of the Wise Lord," he shouted, "Great King!" This was meant as a challenge to the Magians who follow the Lie, a majority of the Magians in the hall that day. Although I could not see the Magians from where I was standing, I was told later that when they heard the Wise Lord's name, they made secret signs to one another.

One by one, from different parts of the room, the brothers of Darius proclaimed his titles. By four wives, Hystaspes had twenty sons who were all living at this time and, presumably, they were all present in Ecbatana that day. Fortunately, Darius had a great many titles. After the naming of each title there was a rattling of drums, a striking of cymbals.

Darius' eldest brother declaimed, "King of Persia!" The next brother: "King of Media!" The next brother: "King of Babel!"—a title discarded by Xerxes when he was obliged to dissolve forever that ancient kingdom. Then, from the opposite end of the room: "Pharaoh of Egypt!," followed by Darius' Egyptian name. Like Cambyses before him, Darius pretended that he was the earthly incarnation of the Egyptian god Ra, and so the legitimate god-king of Egypt. I am afraid that Darius proved to be every bit as opportunistic in religious matters as Cyrus. But Cyrus had never acknowledged that he had got the world as a gift from the Wise Lord while Darius had publicly declared that if it had not been for the Wise Lord, he would never have been Great King. Then Darius proceeded to tell the Egyptians that his ancestor Ra was a greater god than the Wise Lord! I am happy to say that I was able to persuade Xerxes not to style himself pharaoh. As a result, Egypt is now a satrapy like any other, and gone forever are those devilish god-kings of the Nile valley.

One by one, Darius' titles were shouted—and in triumph! Why not? Between Cyrus and Darius most of the world was Persian and our Great King is known to everyone not only as one king of many but as king of this great earth far and wide.

To everyone's surprise it was Darius' eldest son, Artobazanes, who stepped forward and proclaimed, in a low voice, that unique title, "King of kings."

The fact that Artobazanes had been chosen to declaim —no matter how softly—the ultimate title was taken as a sign of singular favor, and the cause of Queen Atossa promptly received a setback.

I looked at Gobryas. Grimly, through fire-red whiskers, he was smiling.

Then the Great King sat in the lion throne.

7

LAIS BEGAN HER AFFAIR WITH HISTIAEUS shortly after we settled into the palace at Ecbatana. Histiaeus was a swarthy man who never ceased to frown. I cannot say that I ever liked him. He was a most unhappy man who spread gloom about him in a most aggressive way. Admittedly, he had every reason to be unhappy. At the height of his glory as tyrant of Miletus, he was ordered to come up to Susa as a guest of the Great King. That is to say, he was made a prisoner. Meanwhile the wealthy city of Miletus was governed by his son-in-law Aristagoras.

Whenever Lais received a man, she was always attended by two eunuchs. Since Lais' pair of eunuchs were not only very old but remarkably ugly, she was confident that her obvious discretion in the choice of eunuchs made her peculiar widowhood entirely respectable in the eyes of the harem ladies. Actually, Lais need not have worried about her reputation. From the beginning she was regarded by the court as entirely alien, and the usual laws of the harem were never applied to her. After Atossa, she was the freest lady at court, and no one minded what she did since she was in no way related to the Great King. Lais was also careful never to antagonize any of the wives. Finally, as mother of Zoroaster's grandson, she occupied a sort of religious place at court, a situation she was not above exploiting. She enjoyed wearing mysterious costumes that were neither Greek nor Persian. In public she affected an other-worldly air; in private, she let it be known that, for a price, she would cast horoscopes, make love philters, administer slow-acting poisons. She was very popular.

At Ecbatana, Histiaeus' head was shaved because he was in mourning for Sybaris, a city closely connected to Miletus; earlier that year Sybaris had been entirely destroyed by the army of Croton.

Scowling, Histiaeus would sit in a wooden chair opposite the folding stool on which Lais perched in the tiny courtyard of her apartment while the decrepit eunuchs dozed in the sun. Occasionally I was allowed to join Histiaeus and Lais; my presence was supposed to lend an air of respectability to their goings-on—not that I was often with Lais. I spent most of that first summer at Ecbatana with the royal princes, being trained as a soldier.

"You are lucky to be at school here." Histiaeus always made an effort to talk to me. "Later in life there'll be no post that you won't be able to fill."

"He already has a post. He is to be head of the Zoroastrian order, and archpriest of all Persia." In those days Lais was dedicated to securing for me this high, unwanted, not to mention entirely imaginary office. There is no Zoroastrian archpriest of all Persia. We comprise not a priesthood but an order.

"In case he decides not to, he can be a satrap, a councilor of state, anything." Histiaeus had the Ionian Greek's contempt for all religion. "But no matter what you do in life," he said gravely, "never forget your mother's language."

Since we always spoke Greek with Histiaeus, this seemed a needless injunction. "I speak Greek to Milo," I said helpfully. "We're not supposed to, but we do."

"Milo, son of Thessalus?"

I nodded. "He is my best friend."

"Well, I have done what I could for that family." Histiaeus looked more than ever grim. "I've told the Great King that he should send a fleet to Athens *before* the old landowners call in the Spartan army, which they will. Certainly it's better to help Hippias while he's still tyrant rather than later when it will be too late. Persia must act now, but unfortunately—" Histiaeus stopped. He could not, directly, criticize the Great King. "I've even offered to go myself, as admiral. But . . ." There was a long pause. We listened to the soft snoring of the eu-

73

nuchs. Lais and I knew what everyone else knew: Darius did not trust Histiaeus out of his sight.

We were joined by Democedes, who always said that he was teaching Lais medicine. I now suspect that she was teaching him magic, if the two are not the same. When the tyrant of Samos was put to death by the Persian satrap at Sardis, his physician Democedes was enslaved. Later, when Darius came to Sardis, he fell from his horse and tore the muscles of the right foot. Despite a lifetime in the field, the Great King was not a good horseman.

Egyptian physicians were summoned. As a result of their elaborate ministrations and melodious chants, Darius' right foot was entirely crippled. He was furious.

Someone then recalled that the celebrated physician Democedes was a slave at Sardis, working in a warehouse. Now, Democedes was a bold as well as a crafty man. He knew that if Darius discovered that he was a master of medicine, he would never be able to buy his freedom and go home to Croton in Sicily. When sent for, he denied any knowledge of medicine. "That was not I," he declared. "That was another Democedes."

Darius ordered branding irons and pincers. Boldness promptly gave way to craft, and Democedes took on the case. He put Darius to sleep for two days. During this time he massaged the foot; practiced his art. On the third day Darius was cured, and Democedes' worst fears were realized. He was appointed physician to the entire imperial family. He was even allowed the unique privilege of being able to attend the ladies in the harem at any time of day or night, without the presence of eunuchs.

It was Democedes who saved the life of Queen Atossa. When a large painful growth on one of her breasts began to spread, Democedes neatly removed the breast. To everyone's amazement, Atossa recovered. The chagrin of the Egyptian physicians was equalled only by that of the Great King's other wives.

Although not happy about the loss of a breast, Atossa realized that had she followed the usual Egyptian cure (a paste of mare's milk, serpent's venom and ground ivory which, when applied to the diseased part, kills the patient more swiftly than any sword), she would have died. The fact that she was now able to live to a great old age changed not only my life—a small matter—but that of the world, a great matter. Had Atossa died then, her son

74

Xerxes would not have succeeded his father. It is no secret that the elevation of Xerxes to the throne was entirely his mother's work.

One curious thing. After the removal of the breast, Atossa began to grow hairs on her face. Although she removed them daily with Egyptian depilatories, the hairs kept growing back. Finally she took to enameling her face with white lead to disguise the raw redness from the depilatories. The result looked very odd indeed. My mother always said that after the mutilation, Atossa was more man than woman.

Shortly after Democedes saved Atossa's life, he arranged to be sent to Italy on the Great King's business. At Tarentum he skipped ship; and hurried home to his native city of Croton where he married the daughter of Milo, the Greek world's most famous wrestler and—yes, another winner at the Olympic games. This same Milo was also the general who commanded the army that destroyed Sybaris.

But Democedes was soon bored by life in his native Croton. After all, most of his life had been spent at glittering courts. He had served Pisistratus at Athens, Polycrates in Samos, and the Great King himself at Susa. He was used to palace life. He could not bear provincial life. Meekly Democedes asked Darius if he might return to Susa, with his bride. The Great King was pleased to forgive him, and Democedes returned to Persia, where he was honored by everyone except his old friend Atossa. She could not bear Democedes' wife, which was odd. Since the girl was never able to speak more than a few words of Persian, she could not have unduly bored the queen. Lais thinks that Atossa was jealous. If this was the case, then the rumor that she had had an affair with the physician who removed her breast must be true.

After Democedes had bowed low to the former tyrant of Miletus, the two men kissed on the lips, as Persian men do when they greet a friend who is also an equal. A friend of inferior rank is offered only a cheek to be kissed. Strictly speaking, Histiaeus should have offered a cheek —as tyrant of Miletus he outranked Democedes. But fellow Greeks who are guests of the Great King tend to ignore differences in rank.

Democedes was also an eager partisan of Hippias. "I have known Hippias since he was a boy. He was always most unusual. He is both profound and just. That's a rare combination—for a tyrant." Democedes smiled a toothless smile. "In our day, only Athens and Miletus are happy with their tyrants."

"*Were* happy." Histiaeus was like a dark cloud full of rain. "Have you talked to the Great King about Hippias?"

"I try. But Greece does not interest him. He keeps talking about India, and about those countries to the east of the east."

"India is a world away from Persia." Histiaeus mixed water with the wine that Lais had poured him. "But Athens is just across the sea from Miletus."

Democedes nodded. "And Italy is just across the sea from Greece. As everyone knows, I was sent to Croton to prepare the way for the Great King. But he never came —and I came home." This was nonsense. But Democedes could hardly admit that he had actually fled the service of the Great King. Officially, his defection was always described as a highly secret diplomatic mission for the second room of the chancellery.

"The Great King has no ambitions in the west." Democedes coughed at length into a piece of cloth. I have seldom known a good physician who was not himself constantly ill.

"Except for Samos," said Histiaeus. Briefly the frown disappeared as he raised his eyebrows. "*That* was a Greek island to the west."

"A difficult man, Polycrates." Democedes studied the cloth for signs of blood. I looked, too. Everyone did. But there was no blood—a mild disappointment for all but Democedes. "I got on with him. Of course, most people found him—"

"Treacherous, vain, foolish," said Lais.

"I always forget you were at the court of Samos, too." Democedes smiled. He had three bottom teeth set in pale gums, and no top teeth. Before he ate he would insert a piece of wood so carved that it clove to the roof of his mouth. He was then able to chew, rather slowly, all but the toughest meat or hardest bread. Now that I am old, I think quite a lot about teeth—and what their absence means. "Yes, yes. I remember you as a child with your father. From Thrace, wasn't he? Yes, of course. The rich Megacreon. Silver mines. Yes, yes."

"I met my husband at Polycrates' court," said Lais, looking sad. "That was the only good thing I remember from those days. I hated Samos. Polycrates, too. He was nothing but a pirate. He actually told my father that when he gave back to his friends the cargoes that he'd stolen, they were more pleased than if he had never taken them in the first place."

"He was a pirate," Democedes agreed. "But he was also a most splendid figure. I can remember when the court at Samos was even more dazzling than that of Pisistratus. Remember Anacreon? The poet? Before your time, I suppose. He lived in darkest Thrace before he came to Samos."

"Anacreon lived," said Lais, most firmly, "in Abdera. *Greek* Abdera."

The two men laughed. Democedes bowed to Lais. "He lived in light-filled Thrace until he came to Samos. Then he moved on to Athens. He was a favorite of poor Hipparchus. That was a sad story, wasn't it? Anyway, you must credit Polycrates with one thing: he always looked to the west. He was a true sea lord."

"Yes," said Histiaeus, again raising his eyebrows, "a sea lord who wanted to be lord of *all* the isles."

Democedes turned to the former tyrant. "Perhaps you should speak to the Great King of islands. After all, Darius was happy to acquire Samos. He was even happier to gain possession of the Samian fleet. Well, once you have at your disposal a splendid fleet—" Democedes stopped, looked at Histiaeus.

"When I was still at Miletus"—Histiaeus spoke almost dreamily—"I could very easily have conquered Naxos."

Democedes nodded. "A beautiful island. Fertile soil. Vigorous people."

The two men exchanged looks.

Thus the Greek wars began.

As a child, listening to adults, I did not recognize the significance of this cryptic exchange. Years later I realized how, almost idly, these two meddling Greeks began what proved to be a successful conspiracy to embroil the Great King in the affairs of Greece.

But this is hindsight. At the time I was more interested when Democedes spoke of the wonder-worker Pythagoras. "I knew him in Samos," said the old physician. "He was still a jeweler then—like his father, who was private jeweler to Polycrates until they fell out. Sooner or later, you always fell out with Polycrates. Anyway, Pythagoras was—is—I saw him again when I was

77

at Croton—an unusual man. With curious notions. He believes in the transmigration of souls . . ."

Although Persian children are not supposed to ask questions of adults, I was always given a certain license. "What," I asked, "is the transmigration of souls?"

"How like his grandfather!" exclaimed Lais, at this perfectly unremarkable question. Lais was forever alluding to my alleged resemblance to Zoroaster.

"It means that at death one's soul goes into another body," said Democedes. "No one knows where this idea comes from . . ."

"From Thrace," said Histiaeus. "Every crazy witch notion starts in Thrace."

"I," said Lais firmly, "am Thracian."

"Then, Lady, you know exactly what I mean." Histiaeus nearly smiled.

"I know that we are the land closest to heaven and to hell," said Lais, in her special witch voice. "So Orpheus sang when he went below the earth."

We let this pass. Democedes continued, "I don't know how the idea came to Pythagoras. I do know that he spent a year or two in the temples of Egypt. He might have picked up the notion there. I don't know. I do know that Egyptian rituals are most impressive if you are susceptible. Luckily, I'm not. He was. I also seem to remember that Polycrates had given him a letter to his friend the pharaoh. That was old Amasis. So Pythagoras must have been shown all sorts of secret rituals that people don't usually see or hear. But then Cambyses attacked Egypt and Amasis died and poor Pythagoras was taken captive, and even though he kept insisting that he was a friend of the tyrant Polycrates, the Persians sold him to a jeweler in Babylon. Luckily, the jeweler was indulgent. He let Pythagoras study with Magians—"

"Not a good thing," said Lais firmly.

"Wise men take whatever they can find, even in the most unlikely places." Democedes had a practical turn of mind. "Anyway, Pythagoras was a different man when he finally bought his freedom from the jeweler and came back to Samos. For one thing, he stayed with me, and not at court. He told me that he had learned to read and write Egyptian hieroglyphs. He had also learned Persian. He had new theories about the nature and the ordering of what he called the universe."

Yes, it was Pythagoras who first coined the word that

78

is now used a thousand times a day here at Athens by sophists who have no idea just what subtleties the word's inventor had in mind.

As I understand Pythagoras—and who does in his complex entirety?—he thought that the single unit was the basis of all things. From the single unit derives number. From numbers, points. From points, lines of connection. From lines, planes and, hence, solids. From solids, the four elements—fire, water, earth, air. These elements commingle and form the universe, which is constantly alive and shifting—a sphere containing at its center a smaller sphere, the earth.

Pythagoras believed that of all solids the sphere is the most beautiful and that of all plane figures the most holy is the circle—since all points connect and there is no beginning or end. Personally, I could never follow his mathematical theorems. Democritus says that *he* understands them. I am very pleased that you do.

Democedes also described how Polycrates quarreled with Pythagoras, and sent his bowmen to arrest the wise man. "Fortunately, I was able to persuade Polycrates' chief engineer to hide him in that tunnel they were building next to the city. Then, one dark night, we got Pythagoras aboard a ship for Italy. I gave him a letter to my old friend, now my father-in-law, Milo of Croton . . ."

"The destroyer of Sybaris." Histiaeus's scowl had returned. This Milo was a true destroyer. After he defeated the Sybarite armies, he diverted the course of a river in such a way that the entire city vanished beneath the water.

"What can I say?" Democedes was polite. "I have known Milo since he was a boy. In fact, I'm old enough to be his grandfather. When he won his first wrestling match at the Olympic games . . ."

Democritus thinks that the destruction of Sybaris took place several years later. I don't. But then, I must note that when I reconstruct a conversation of sixty years ago, I am bound to mix together various meetings.

Over a period of years I heard a good deal about Pythagoras from Democedes. This means that what I report is always accurate in the sense that I repeat exactly what I was told. Chronology is something else again. I do not keep annals. All I know for certain is that during my first summer at Ecbatana I heard the name Pythagoras. Of even greater importance, on that same day I listened to Histiaeus and Democedes discuss the sea lord Polycrates. Because of certain glances exchanged and silences charged with meaning, I later came to realize that it was at this meeting that the two men joined forces in order to embroil Darius in the Greek world. It was their policy to tempt the Great King with the one title that he lacked, sea lord. They also did their best to persuade him to support the tyrant Hippias—through war, if necessary. Naturally, eventually, war was necessary thanks, largely, to the idle conniving of two Greeks at Ecbatana on a summer day.

"Your wife tells me that Pythagoras has built himself a school in Croton." Lais quite liked Democedes' wife, since she posed no threat. "People come from all over the world to study with him."

"It's not a school in the proper sense. It's more . . . Well, he and a number of other holy men have a house where they live in accordance with what Pythagoras calls the proper life."

"They don't eat beans." Histiaeus allowed himself a laugh. To this day, the surest way to make an Athenian audience laugh is to mention Pythagoras' injunction against eating beans. The Athenians think this taboo wondrously funny, particularly when the Athenian comic actor's accompaniment to a bean joke is a series of loud farts.

"He believes that beans contain the souls of men. After all, they do resemble human foetuses." Democedes was always the man of science, and there was no notion about creation that he did not at least consider seriously. "Pythagoras also refuses to eat flesh for fear that he might, inadvertently, be eating an ancestor or a friend whose soul happens to have passed into that particular animal."

"How long," I asked, "does Pythagoras think that souls keep passing from creature to creature?"

The two Greeks looked at me with real curiosity. I had asked a crucial question. For an instant I was no longer a child but the heir to Zoroaster.

"I don't know, Cyrus Spitama." Democedes said my name with due reverence.

"To the end of time of the long dominion? Or before?" I was genuinely fascinated by what was, for me, a dazzling new conception of death and rebirth and . . . what? "Certainly, nothing can be born *after* the end of infinite time."

80

"I cannot speak in terms of Zoroaster's view . . . I mean, of his *truth*." Democedes was not about to question the religion of the Great King. "I can only say that, according to Pythagoras, it should be the aim of each man's life to free the spark of deity that resides in him so that it can rejoin the entire universe, which he sees as a kind of shifting, living aether . . . a perfect and harmonious whole."

" 'I am a child of earth and of starry heaven,' " announced Lais. I listened impatiently while she sang a very long and very mysterious song about creation, as viewed by the witches of Thrace.

When she had finished, Democedes resumed. "To break out of the constant cycle of death and rebirth is the aim of Pythagoras' teaching. He thinks that this can be done by self-denial, by ritual, by purification through diet, by the study of music, mathematics. Whether true or not as a doctrine, thanks to him and his school, Croton now controls most of southern Italy."

"That's not the reason," said Histiaeus. "You'd better thank your father-in-law, Milo. He is a great soldier." For a Greek, Histiaeus was remarkably uninterested in philosophy—the word that Pythagoras invented to describe a true love of wisdom.

It was also Pythagoras, with the aid of Democedes—or so Democedes told me—who established that the human brain is the center of all our thinking. I have not seen the proofs of this theory, nor would I understand them if I did. But I believe this to be true. I used to argue the matter with the Cathayans, who think that the stomach is the mind's center, since the stomach is more sentient than any other part of the body due to its windy gurgling. Democritus tells me that I have said this before. You must bear with me. Besides, repetition is the secret of the learning process.

"I attribute the success of Croton to the virtue of its inhabitants." Democedes coughed into his cloth. "They believe that their teacher is a god, and I think that perhaps he is."

"Does *he* think that he is?" Histiaeus was to the point.

Democedes shook his head. "I think that Pythagoras believes that all things are interrelated, that we all partake of the one cosmos, that each of us shares in the entire divinity. But we cannot re-join the whole until we have got free of the flesh, which is our tomb."

"Why?" asked Lais.

"To transcend the pain of this world, the sense of incompleteness . . ."

"Orpheus went down into hell," said Lais, as if she were making a relevant response; perhaps she was. I have never known very much about the cult of Orpheus. A Thracian, he went down into hell to reclaim his dead wife. He came back, but she did not—the dead tend not to. Later he was torn to pieces—for impiety, I should think.

The cult of Orpheus has always been popular in the back country, particularly in witch-haunted Thrace. Lately the cult has started to spread throughout the Greek world. From what little I know of Orphism, I should think that it is nothing more than a coarse variation on the beautiful and truly ancient legend of the hero Gilgamesh. He also went down into hell in order to bring back his dead lover Enkidu. No, Democritus, Gilgamesh was not a Greek but he was very much a hero, and like most heroes he wanted too much. There was nothing that he could not defeat save nothing itself, death. The hero wanted to live forever. But not even the glorious Gilgamesh could reverse the natural order. When he accepted this ultimate truth, he was at peace . . . and died.

I learned the Gilgamesh story at Babylon. Once upon a time Gilgamesh was a world cult figure. Today he is largely forgotten, except at Babylon. Time of the long dominion is very long indeed. The trouble with the Greeks is that they have no idea how old this earth is. They seem not to realize that everything has already happened that will ever happen, save the end. In India, they think that the end *has* happened, over and over again, as cycles of creation burn out—and rekindle.

Democritus now sees fit to instruct me in Orphism. Apparently they, too, believe in the transmigration of souls, a process that ends only when, through ritual and so on, the spirit is purified. I defer to Democritus. You are Thracian-born, after all. You have also convinced me that Lais, for all her familiarity with the dark arts, never understood the cult of Orpheus.

"I am not sure that Pythagoras claims to have visited Hades, but he did tell me a strange story." Democedes looked faintly troubled, as if he did not much like what he was about to tell us. "Shortly after he came back from Babylon, we were walking on that new mole which Polycrates had just built in the harbor. Suddenly Pythagoras stopped. He stared down at me. He's much taller than I. 'I can remember,' he said. 'I can remember everything.' I had no idea what he was talking about. 'Everything about what?' I asked.

" 'My previous lives,' he said. He was most compelling. He told me that in an early incarnation he had been the son of the god Hermes by a human being. Now, Hermes was so fond of this boy that he told him that he would give him anything that he asked for except immortality. Only the gods are immortal. So the boy asked for the next best thing. 'Let me remember at each new incarnation who and what I was in my previous lives.' Hermes agreed.

" 'And,' said Pythagoras, 'I can remember what it was like to be a bird, a warrior, a fox, an Argive at Troy. All these things I was, and am, and will be until I am reunited with the whole.' "

I was deeply impressed by what Democedes told me, and I have often regretted that I never knew Pythagoras. When he was driven out of Croton by a rival faction, he took refuge in a temple at Metapontum where he slowly starved himself to death. Since I was about twenty years old at the time, I could have gone to see him. They say that he received visitors until the end. At least, I *assume* that it was the end. If not, he may be walking the streets of Athens today, his mind filled with all the memories of a thousand earlier selves.

Democritus tells me that there is a Pythagorean school at Thebes, presided over until recently by a Crotonian named Lysis. Democritus is much struck by something that Lysis is supposed to have said: "Men must die because they cannot join the beginning to the end."

Yes, that is indeed wise. A man's life can be drawn as a straight and descending line. But when the soul or the fragment of the divine fire in each of us rejoins the original source of life, then the perfect form has been achieved, and what was a straight line is now a circle and the beginning has joined the end.

I should say here that as a child I was in no way a prodigy. I certainly don't want to give the impression that I was a prophet or a wonder-worker or philosopher at an early age or, indeed, at any age. It was my fate to have been born a Spitama and, all in all, I cannot pretend that I ever found my place in the world anything but enjoyable despite the constant enmity of the Magians who follow the Lie, an enmity more than compensated for by the kindness shown me by the three Great Kings—Darius, Xerxes, Artaxerxes.

Although my mind has never been much inclined to religion or magic, I do have a speculative nature. I also feel obliged to examine other religions or systems of thought in order to see how much they vary from the way of Truth that I was ordained at birth to follow.

In the course of a long life I have been startled to find in other religions elements that I always took to be special revelations from the Wise Lord to Zoroaster. But now I realize that the Wise Lord is able to speak in all the languages of the world, and in all the languages of the world his words are seldom understood or acted upon. But they do not vary. Because they are true.

8

DURING CHILDHOOD I LED TWO LIVES: a religious life at home with Lais and the Magians who followed Zoroaster, and life at school. I was happier at school, in the company of my exact contemporaries Xerxes and his cousin Mardonius, the son of Gobryas. Except for Milo, all my classmates were Persians. For some reason, the sons of Histiaeus were never taken into the first section. I cannot think that this exclusion pleased that ambitious man.

Although our military training was hard, I enjoyed it if only because no Magians were involved. We were taught by the best of the immortals. That is, by the best soldiers in the world.

The morning that I first became aware of Xerxes is more vivid to me than this morning. But then I was young. I could see. Saw what? Sun like a plate of gold set against a blue-white sky. Forests of dark-green cedars. High mountains capped with snow. Yellow fields at whose corners brown deer grazed. Childhood is all color. Age . . . ? The absence of color—for me, sight too.

We began our day's march before sunrise. We walked in twos; each carried a spear. For some reason I was paired with Xerxes. He paid no attention to me. Needless to say, I examined him closely. As a child of the harem, I knew that if Atossa's faction prevailed over that of Gobryas, he would be Great King one day.

Xerxes was a tall boy whose pale-gray eyes shone beneath dark brows that grew together in a straight line. Young as he was, whorls of dark-gold down grew on his ruddy cheeks. Sexually, he was precocious.

If Xerxes was at all conscious of his destiny, he did not betray it. In manner, he was neither more nor less than one of the Great King's many sons. He had a charming smile. Unlike most men, he kept all his teeth to the end.

I did not speak to him; nor he to me.

At noon we were given the order to stop beside a forest spring. We were allowed to drink water but not to eat. For some reason, instead of stretching out on the moss with the others, I wandered off into the forest.

Green laurel suddenly parts. I see the snout; the curved yellow tusks. I freeze, spear in hand, unable to move as the huge bristling body breaks through the hedge of laurel.

The boar gets wind of me; backs away. No doubt, the beast is as alarmed as I. But then, in an odd circling movement, the boar wheels about and charges.

I am thrown high into the air. Before I reach earth again, I realize that all the wind has left my chest.

I thought that I was dead until I found that although I could no longer breathe, I could at least hear—and heard an almost human cry from the boar as Xerxes dug his spear deep into the animal's neck. I drew my first uneven breath as the bleeding boar staggered into the laurel, where it stumbled, fell, died.

Everyone hurried forward to congratulate Xerxes. No one paid the slightest attention to me. Fortunately, I had not been hurt. In fact, no one noticed me except Xerxes.

"I hope you're all right." He looked down at me and smiled.

I looked up at him and said, "You saved my life."

"I know." He was matter-of-fact.

Since there was so much that we might have said at that point, neither of us said another word or ever mentioned the episode again.

Over the years I have had occasion to notice that when a man saves the life of another man, he often has a proprietary sense about the one saved. In no other way can I explain why it was that Xerxes chose me to be his particular friend. Shortly after our forest adventure, at his insistence, I moved into the princes' quarters.

I continued to visit Lais but I no longer lived with her. She was delighted that I was close to Xerxes, or so she said. Years later she told me that our friendship had worried her. "In those days everyone thought that Artobazanes would succeed Darius. If he had, Xerxes would have been put to death, with all his friends."

If I was aware of any danger at that time, I have no sense of it now. Xerxes was a beguiling companion. Everything came easily to him. He was an expert horseman; he was proficient with every sort of weapon. Although he was not much interested in the lessons that the Magians gave us, he could read with some ease. I don't think that he could write.

Each year, with the seasons, we followed the Great King from Susa to Ecbatana to Babylon and then back to Susa. Xerxes and I preferred Babylon to the other capitals. But what young man does not?

As students, our lives were entirely controlled by army officers, Magians and eunuchs. Also, the court was the court no matter in what city it was held, and so was the palace school. We had no more freedom than those slaves who worked my grandfather's silver mines. Yet in Babylon we were aware that a truly marvelous life existed beyond the strict confines of Darius' court. Wistfully, Xerxes and Mardonius and I used to wonder what it would be like to visit the city when the court was *not* in Babylon. In our nineteenth year, we got our wish.

Mardonius was a quick-witted youth whom Darius appeared to like very much. I say appeared because one never knew what Darius really felt about anyone. He was a consummate manipulator of men, and brutally charming. The Great King was also the most inscrutable of men, and no one ever knew precisely where he stood with him until, sometimes, too late. Certainly Darius was influenced by the fact that Mardonius' father was Gobryas, a difficult man at best and a potential rival. As a result, Darius was most indulgent of both father and son.

At the Great King's birthday, in the presence of members and close connections of the royal family, he anoints his head according to ritual and grants the wishes of those close to him. That year at Susa, it was Xerxes who held the silver ewer filled with rosewater, and it was Mardonius who dried with a silk cloth Darius' beard and hair.

"What may I grant you, Mardonius?" The Great King was in a good mood despite his dislike of all anniversaries, and the death that each one presages.

"The governorship of Babylon for the third month of the new year, Great King."

Although protocol requires that the Great King never show surprise, Xerxes told me that his father was plainly astonished. "Babylon? Why Babylon? And why the governorship for only a month?"

But Mardonius did not answer; he simply crouched at Darius' feet—the ceremonial position that means: I am your slave, do as you like with me.

Darius stared hard at Mardonius. Then he looked about the crowded hall. Although no one may look directly at him, Xerxes did. When Darius caught his son's eye, Xerxes smiled.

"I have never known anyone so modest." Darius affected bewilderment. "Of course, many fortunes have been made in less than a month. But surely not in Babylon. When it comes to money, the black-haired people are much cleverer than us Persians."

"I shall go with him, Great King, if you grant me that, as my wish," said Xerxes. "I will keep Mardonius virtuous."

"But who will look to *your* virtue?" Darius was grave.

"Cyrus Spitama, if you grant *his* wish, which he has asked me to make for him." Xerxes had been well rehearsed by Mardonius. "He will see to our religious training."

"Cyrus Spitama has sworn to convert the high priest of Bel-Marduk to the way of Truth." Mardonius was pious.

"I am the victim of a plot," said Darius. "But I must do as kings do on this day. Mardonius, son of Gobryas, you are entrusted with the administering of my city of Babylon for the third month of the new year. Xerxes and Cyrus Spitama will attend you. But why the third month?" Darius knew, of course, exactly what we had in mind.

"The high gardens by the Euphrates will be in bloom, Great King," said Mardonius. "It is a lovely time of year."

"Made more lovely by the fact that in the third month the Great King will be many miles away at Susa." Darius laughed, a plebeian habit he retained to the end of his days. I never found it offensive, rather the contrary.

9

BABYLON IS MORE OVERWHELMING than beautiful. Everything is made of the same dull brick, baked from Euphrates mud. But the temples and palaces are of Egyptian proportions and, of course, in those days the city walls were so wide that—as the inhabitants never ceased to remind you—a four-horse chariot could make a full turn on the parapets. Not that I ever saw a chariot of any kind on the walls, or anything else for that matter. There were no guards. Such was the totality of the Great King's peace in those days.

There is something curiously haunting about a city that has existed for more than three thousand years. Although Babylon has often been wrecked in wars, the inhabitants —known simply as the black-haired people—always rebuild their city exactly the way it was before, or so they tell us. The city is at the center of a huge square that is almost evenly divided by the swift, dark Euphrates River. Originally Babylon was well protected by an outer wall, an inner wall and a deep moat. But the second time that Darius was obliged to subdue the city, he razed part of the outer wall. Years later, after Xerxes had put down a rebellion in the city, he destroyed practically all of the walls and filled in the moat. I now think it unlikely that the Babylonians will ever again give us trouble. By nature, the black-haired people are indolent and sensual and obedient. For centuries they have been governed by a highly corrupt and complex priesthood. From time to time the priests of one temple will arouse the people against the priests of another temple and there is violence, like a summer storm—and like a summer storm it is soon over. But these periodic confusions are a nuisance to administrators.

Although I am glad that I was not born a Babylonian, I must say that no place on earth so perfectly caters for the taste of young men, particularly young men brought up in the austere Persian manner.

At sundown we passed through the gate of Ishtar,

named for a goddess not unlike Anahita or Aphrodite except that she is a man as well as a woman. In either guise, Ishtar is sexually insatiable and her worship sets the tone for the whole city. The Ishtar gate is really two gates—one to the city's outer wall, one to the inner wall. The enormous gates are covered with tiles that have been glazed blue and yellow and black, and depict all sorts of strange and terrible beasts, including dragons. The effect is more alarming than beautiful. Of the city's nine gates —each named for a god—that of Ishtar is the most important for it leads straight into the heart of the left bank of Babylon where the temples and palaces and treasuries are.

Just inside the first gate, Mardonius was greeted by the city's actual governor and his retinue. For obvious reasons, the identity of Xerxes and myself was kept a secret. We were simply the companions of the third month's governor.

After the ritual offering of bread and water, we were escorted along the processional way. This impressive avenue is paved with well-fitted slabs of limestone. On either side of the processional way, the walls of the buildings are covered with enameled tiles depicting lions.

To the left of the processional way is a temple to some devil-god; to the right is the so-called new palace, built by King Nebuchadnezzar in fifteen days, according to the local people. The last of Babylon's hero-kings, Nebuchadnezzar drove the Egyptians out of Asia; he also conquered Tyre and Jerusalem. Unfortunately, like so many Babylonians, he was religion-mad. I daresay he had no choice: the priests of Bel-Marduk control the city, and no king of Babylon is really king until he dresses up as a priest and takes, literally, the hands of Bel, which means he must grasp the hands of the golden statue of Bel-Marduk at the great temple. Cyrus, Cambyses, Darius and Xerxes each took the hands of Bel.

Most of Nebuchadnezzar's last days were engaged in religious ceremonies during which he often pretended that he was the sacrificial goat. On one occasion he got down on all fours and ate grass in the high gardens. But unlike the usual goat, he was never actually sacrificed. Some fifty years before our visit in Babylon, he died, raving mad. I have never met a Babylonian who did not enjoy talking about him. He was their last true king. Incidentally, he was of ancient Chaldean stock as is I am as certain as one can be without any proof at all—the family of Spitama.

Thirty years after Nebuchadnezzar's death, Cyrus was welcomed to Babylon by the antipriest party, an association of international merchants and moneychangers who had deposed the last king, a dim figure named Nabonidus. Because this very odd sovereign was interested only in archaeology, he was usually to be found not at Babylon but out in the desert, digging up the lost cities of Sumeria. Because of the king's total absorption in things past, the priests assumed charge of things present. They governed the state, and let it go to ruin or, properly speaking, to glory, since it went to Cyrus.

We were assigned splendid apartments in the new palace. Directly beneath our quarters was the stone bridge that connects the left and right banks of the city. Each night the wooden sections of the bridge are taken up so that thieves may not cross from one side to the other.

Under the river, Nebuchadnezzar constructed a tunnel. This remarkable work of engineering is about twenty feet wide, and almost as high. Because of constant seepage from the Euphrates, the floor and walls are alarmingly muddy and the air is foul not only from the oxen who draw the carts but from the smoking pitch torches that each traveler is encouraged to rent as he enters. I was short of breath by the time we got to the other side, and Xerxes said that he felt as if he had been buried alive. Nevertheless, the tunnel has been in use for half a century without incident.

Our apartments were at the top of the new palace, some four stories above the city. From a central loggia we had a fine view of what the Babylonians call a ziggurat, or high place. This particular ziggurat is known as the House of the Foundation of Heaven and Earth. It is the world's largest building, dwarfing even the greatest of Egypt's pyramids—or so the Babylonians like to tell you. I have never been to Egypt.

Seven enormous cubes of brick have been set one atop the other. The largest cube is the base; the smallest the peak. A staircase goes around the whole pyramidal shape. Since each level is sacred to a different divinity, each is colored accordingly. Even by moonlight we could make out the ghostly shining blues and reds and greens of the various sun and moon and star gods.

Close to the ziggurat is the temple of Bel-Marduk, a

complex of huge mud-colored buildings and dusty court-yards. The temple is of no particular external beauty save for the tall bronze doors to the room of the god. In fact, there is only one remarkable thing about the temple: it is supposed to be in no way different from what it was three thousand years ago. The true god or spirit of this city is immutability. Nothing is ever allowed to change.

It is a pity that so few Athenians ever visit Babylon. They might be able to learn humility at the thought of time's long duration, and of the shortness of our own petty days—not to mention works. In the presence of so much history, it is no wonder that the black-haired people live so entirely for pleasure in the here and now. All in all, Babylon is a place well calculated to depress the ambitious. Certainly none of our Great Kings ever really liked holding court there. It was Xerxes, finally, who discontinued what had been an annual practice since Cyrus.

The governor of the city had prepared a banquet for us in the gardens on top of the new palace. These celebrated gardens were created for Nebuchadnezzar. First, the engineers built a series of colonnades strong enough to support earth six feet deep. Then, trees and flowers were planted to make happy a queen homesick for—of all places!—Ecbatana. Finally, mechanical pumps were installed. Day and night, ceaselessly, buckets of water from the Euphrates nourish the high gardens. As a result, even in the heat of high summer, the gardens are always green and cool. I must say that to sit in a grove of pine trees on top of a palace surrounded by palm trees is a pleasure like no other.

For the first time in our lives, we were free men, and I remember that evening as one of the most magical that I ever spent. We reclined on couches beneath what looked to be by moonlight solid silver wisteria. To this day, I can never smell wisteria without recalling Babylon—and youth. No, Democritus, the sight or feel of silver does *not* stimulate memory. I am not a merchant or a banker.

The city's governor wore a gold turban and carried a staff of ivory. Although he knew who Xerxes was, he managed to contain that terror which the Great King and his sons so often inspire. A most solicitous host, he produced for us a dozen girls, well trained in the arts of Ishtar.

"The satrap Zopyrus is at his house upriver, young lords," said the governor. "He has been ill for some months. Otherwise he would have greeted you himself."

"Send him our compliments." Mardonius played with gusto the role of governor, while Xerxes and I pretended to fawn on him in the best court tradition. Later we agreed that it was a lucky thing that we had not been received by the satrap, since he would be obliged to kiss the Great King's companions, and Zopyrus, of course, had no lips—or nose or ears.

When Darius laid siege to Babylon the second time, the city had withstood him for nearly two years. Zopyrus was a son of one of The Six, and an officer in the Persian army. Finally Zopyrus asked the Great King how much the possession of Babylon meant to him. A somewhat simple question, I would have thought, after nineteen months of siege. When Darius acknowledged that the city was all-important to him, Zopyrus said that he would make the Great King a present of Babylon.

Zopyrus called in a butcher and ordered him to cut away his ears, lips and nose. Then Zopyrus defected to the Babylonians. Pointing to his ruined head, he said, "Look what the Great King has done to me!" He was believed. In that condition, how could he not be?

Eventually Zopyrus was taken into the high counsels of the priests who governed the city. When food was in short supply, he advised them to kill most of the women in order to leave sufficient food for the soldiers. Fifty thousand women were killed. Then, one night, when the Babylonians were celebrating one of their religious ceremonies, Zopyrus opened the Nannar Gate and Babylon was conquered yet again.

Darius' justice was swift. Three thousand men were crucified outside the walls. A number of gates and a part of the outer wall were torn down. In order to repopulate the city, Darius imported thousands of women from various parts of the world. At the time of our visit the foreign ladies had already done their work, and most of the city's population was under sixteen-years of age.

As custom required, Darius took once more the hands of Bel and became—once more—legitimate king of Babel, as the nation was known. He then made Zopyrus satrap for life. Curiously enough, I met his grandson only a few days ago in the Agora. He is a merchant, he told me, and "no longer a Persian." I said that he would always be the grandson of the man Darius called the greatest Persian since Cyrus. Well, we are not responsible for

92

our descendants. Ironically, this grandson is called Zopyrus; he is the son of Megabyzus, until recently Persia's finest general.

"Where is the treasure of Queen Nitocris?" Mardonius was in a playful mood.

"I swear to you that it is not in her tomb, Lord." The governor's manner was so serious that we could not help laughing.

"As the Great King discovered." Xerxes drank cup after cup of beer. He could drink more than any man I have ever known, and show it less. I should note also that at nineteen, he was remarkably beautiful, and that evening, by moonlight, the pale eyes resembled moonstones and the new beard was like Scythian fox fur.

"How," I asked, "was it possible for a woman to be the ruler of this country?"

"Because, Lord, certain of our queens used to pretend that they were men, in the Egyptian fashion. And of course, the goddess Ishtar is a man as well as a woman."

"We shall want to see her temple," said Xerxes.

"Perhaps the famous treasure is hidden there," said Mardonius. Looking back, I now realize how well Darius had understood the youthful Mardonius. The joke that Darius had made about the possible acquisition of a fortune in a month's time was seriously intended. The Great King knew even then what it took me years to learn—that my friend Mardonius was a most avaricious man.

Xerxes wanted to look at the queen's tomb, which is above one of the city's gates. On the inner wall of the gate is carved the sentence: "Should any future ruler of my land be in need of money, let him open my tomb."

Since Darius always needed money, he had ordered the queen's tomb opened. Except for the queen's body, preserved in honey, there was nothing in the sepulcher except a stone tablet on which she had written: "Had you been less greedy and importunate, you would not have turned graverobber." Darius personally threw the queen's body into the Euphrates. This was not a tactful thing to do; but he was very angry.

The governor assured us that the treasure of Nitocris was simply legend. On the other hand, though he did not mention the fact, what looked to be most of the gold in the world was on view in the temple of Bel-Marduk.

Years later Xerxes removed all the golden objects from the temple, including the statue of Bel-Marduk. He then melted everything down in order to make darics—gold coins—to pay for the Greek wars. Predictably, modern-day Babylonians like to say that Xerxes' later troubles were due entirely to this sacrilege, which is nonsense. As it was, Cyrus and Darius and the young Xerxes made far too many concessions to the numerous local gods of the empire. Although our Great Kings shrewdly allow the people to worship local deities, they themselves ought never to acknowledge any god other than the Wise Lord. Half-Truth is equal to whole Lie, said Zoroaster.

Zopyrus proved to be the perfect host. He remained in his house upriver, and we never saw him. Disguised as ordinary Medes, we were free to explore the city. Needless to say, the guards were never far from Xerxes; Queen Atossa had seen to that. In fact, she had even gone to Darius and begged him to keep Xerxes home. But since a promise made by the Great King cannot be unmade, Atossa insisted that she at least be allowed to select Xerxes' guards. She also made me swear to keep an eye on Mardonius. She thought him capable of killing Xerxes, and nothing that I could say would convince her to the contrary. "The boy's father is Gobryas. The boy's nephew is Artobazanes. That's enough. This is a plot. The moment my son is alone in Babylon . . ." But for once, Atossa was wrong. Mardonius was devoted to Xerxes. More to the point, he disliked his father and felt nothing for his nephew Artobazanes.

Like every visitor to Babylon, we went straight to the temple of Ishtar, where the women prostitute themselves. According to an ancient law of the land, each Babylonian woman is required to go, once in a lifetime, to the temple of Ishtar and wait in the courtyard until a man offers her silver to make love to him. The first to offer her the money gets her. In other temples to the goddess, young men and boys act as prostitutes, and the man who goes with a temple catamite is thought to have earned himself the special blessing of the goddess. Luckily for the Babylonian male, he is *not* required once in a lifetime to be a temple prostitute. Only the ladies are so honored.

Wide-eyed, the three of us stood at the edge of the outer courtyard. Perhaps a thousand women of every size, shape, age, class were seated on the ground in the hot sun. There were no awnings. The portico at the far end of the courtyard is reserved for the languid temple eunuchs, who see to it that the visitors do not stray from the lines which have been drawn on the ground. Each man is obliged to keep to a given line. Otherwise the confusion would be too great. Between the lines, the women sit.

Strangely enough, Babylonian men seldom visit the temple. I suppose that they are used to it. Also, they must experience a certain embarrassment at the sight of their wives or sisters or daughters serving the goddess. Fortunately, a sufficient number of strangers come from every part of the world to help the ladies achieve Ishtar's blessing.

In single file Xerxes, Mardonius and I followed a line that led through a flock of seated women. We had been warned that those who appeared to be enjoying themselves are actual prostitutes, pretending to serve Ishtar yet again. Attractive as they sometimes are, these women are to be avoided. To be preferred are the women who look rather soulful and grave, as if they have somehow detached themselves from those bodies that they are offering up to deity.

Since most of the men who come to the sacred precinct are singularly unattractive, I can see what a joy it must be for an ill-made baker, say, to get for one piece of silver the beautiful daughter of some distinguished lord. As it was, even for a handsome trio of Persian princes—I inflate my rank—the situation was highly pleasurable. Also, because we were young, we got many appealing glances.

According to custom, you make your choice by dropping silver into a woman's lap. She then rises, takes your arm and leads you into the temple, where hundreds of wooden partitions have been set up to create a series of doorless cells. If you can find an empty cell, you couple on the floor. Although spectators are not encouraged by the eunuchs, good-looking women or men often attract a considerable audience—briefly. The circumstances are such that precipitous speed tends to be the rule in Ishtar's service. For one thing, to disguise the all-pervading odor of sexuality, so much incense is burned in braziers that not only is the stifling air an opaque blue but if one stays too long in celebration of the goddess, one is apt to turn blue oneself.

While most of the foreign men stripped to the skin, we decorous Persian youths removed nothing, which particularly amused the Greeks. In no time at all, we made holy three girls of what we took to be fairly high rank. They seemed to be pleased with us. But when Mardonius asked his girl if she would see him again, she told him quite seriously that if she did, she would be forever damned by Ishtar. Besides, she was married. She then thanked him politely for what he had done.

The girl that I chose appeared to be highly embarrassed by the whole thing. She told me that she was only recently married. Originally, she had wanted to serve Ishtar while she was still a virgin but her mother had advised against it. Apparently, too many Babylonian virgins have had unfortunate experiences at the hands of rough strangers. So she had waited until now. All in all, she said, she was glad. We straightened our clothes after the brief sexual act that had so much amused a pair of blond northern men who kept saying, in bad Greek, "But how can they do anything with all those clothes on?" We ignored them.

"The terrible thing," she said, as we made our way to the courtyard, "is getting some sort of illness. There is really no way of knowing who you're going to get. My mother did tell me that if a really filthy-looking man came near, I was to make awful faces and drool like an idiot. On the other hand, if I saw someone who looked clean, I was to smile. I'm certainly glad that I did."

I was flattered, as she intended. As we stood in the courtyard, clearing our lungs of all the scented smoke that we had inhaled, she told me that "the really ugly women have to come here day after day and, sometimes, month after month, waiting for a man to buy them. I've even heard stories of families that were forced to pay a stranger to take the woman. That's wrong, of course. Quite unholy, too. But not as unholy in the eyes of the goddess as not doing it at all."

We parted amiably. The experience was thoroughly enjoyable until, a week later, I realized that she had given me lice. I shaved off my pubic hair, something that I have done ever since.

The area around the temple of Ishtar is given over to houses of prostitution of a secular rather than religious sort. Usually these establishments are to be found above wine or beer shops. They are almost all owned by women; in fact, the low-class women of Babylon are freer than any women in the world. They can own property. They do much of the buying and selling in the markets. I have even seen them working alongside men in the brick kilns or removing silt from the canals.

After we left the temple of Ishtar, we were taken in

hand by an aide to the satrap Zopyrus. He acted as our guide while, at a discreet distance, Xerxes' guards kept us in view.

In Babylon the main avenues run parallel to one another. Smaller streets intersect them at right angles. I have seen similar cities in India and Cathay, but nowhere else. The effect is quite splendid, particularly when one stands in the shadow of the ziggurat and looks down the long straight busy avenue to its terminus, a low iron gate that marks the river's bank.

One broad highway was lined with every sort of diseased person. As we came into view, they shouted out their symptoms. According to our guide, "Babylonians don't trust physicians. So the sick people come here. Whenever they see someone who looks knowledgeable, they tell him their particular illness. If he knows of a cure, he'll discuss it with them."

As we watched, quite a number of passers-by did indeed stop to talk to the sick, and tell them which herb or root might prove to be effective.

"Democedes would be shocked," said Xerxes. "He thinks of medicine as an art."

"Witchcraft, more likely." Mardonius made the sign to ward off evil.

At the foot of the broad staircase that leads to the top of the House of the Foundation of Heaven and Earth, we were met by the high priest of Bel-Marduk. A bad-tempered old man, he was not in the least impressed by Persian princes. Great Kings come and go; the priesthood of Bel-Marduk is eternal.

"In the name of the lord Bel-Marduk, approach." The old man extended his hands toward us. As Mardonius started to take the hands, they were promptly withdrawn. Our guide never did explain to us what we were expected to do. I don't think that he knew. The high priest made us an incomprehensible speech in the ancient language of the Babylonians. Then, abruptly, at the first level of the ziggurat, the old man left us.

There are one thousand steps to the top of the House of the Foundation of Heaven and Earth. At the halfway point we stopped, sweating like horses. Below us was the city, precisely squared by the high walls and divided in two by the dull river that enters the city between fortified banks. Like a desert mirage, the green cloud of the high gardens floats above the dusty dun colored brick of the city.

Our guide explained to us the intricate system of canals that not only irrigate what is the richest earth in the Persian empire but also makes for easy transportation. Water that goes where you want it to go is the cheapest form of travel, even if you travel in a circular Babylonian boat. Incidentally, no Babylonian has ever been able to explain to me why their boats are not only round in shape but remarkably inefficient.

Breathing hard, we continued to the top of the ziggurat, where two sentries stood guard at the door to a small temple of bright yellow brick.

"What's that?" asked Mardonius.

"A shrine to Bel-Marduk." The guide seemed reluctant to tell us more.

In my capacity as religious authority, I asked to know what was inside. "After all"—I was disingenuous—"if there is any sort of image to the god, we must do it proper honor." Zoroaster would have been horrified to hear his grandson speak so respectfully of a deva. On the other hand, he would have approved of my perfect insincerity. He always said that we live in a world not of our own making.

"There is no image of any kind. You have already seen the only true image of Bel-Marduk." That morning our guide had taken us to the great temple, where he had shown us a huge solid-gold statue of a man standing next to a massive gold table on which, as prescribed, we placed flowers. The right hand of the statue was smoother and brighter than the rest because that is the hand which each king of Babylon has been obliged to hold in his own two hands for no one knows how many centuries. In a low voice I had said a prayer to the Wise Lord, requesting him to strike down the idol. Twenty years later, my prayer was answered.

The guide's evasions about the shrine atop the ziggurat aroused our curiosity to such an extent that Xerxes finally said, "We shall go in."

Since there is no quarreling with the Great King's heir, our guide spoke to the guards. Grimly, they opened the door to the shrine and we entered a windowless room that was pleasantly cool after our long climb. A single hanging lamp revealed the room's only contents, a large bed.

"Who sleeps here?" asked Xerxes.

"The god Bel-Marduk." The guide looked unhappy.

98

"Have you ever seen him?" I asked.

"No. Of course not."

"But do the priests see him?" These questions always interest me.

"I don't know."

"Then how," asked Mardonius, "do you know that the god actually sleeps on that bed?"

"We are told."

"By whom?" Xeres gave the man the full gray Achaemenid stare. The effect is most unnerving.

"The women, Lord," whispered the guide. "At sundown, each evening, a different woman is brought here. She is chosen by Ishtar, the wife of Bel-Marduk. At midnight the god comes to the woman in this room, and possesses her."

"What does he look like?" I was truly curious.

"The women cannot say. They dare not say. They are forever silent. That is the law."

"A very good law," said Xerxes.

When we returned to the new palace, Mardonius ordered the governor of the city to present to us the two priests who tended the shrine at the top of the House of the Foundation of Heaven and Earth.

When the priests arrived, Xerxes asked, "Who really appears to the woman in the shrine?"

"Bel-Marduk himself, Lord." The priests answered in unison.

When they had given Mardonius the same answer three times, he sent for a bowstring of the sort that strangles in an instant. When the question was posed a fourth time, we learned that each night of the week Bel-Marduk is impersonated by a different priest.

"Exactly what I thought." Xerxes was pleased. "Tonight," he said graciously, "I shall relieve one of your priests of his task. Tonight I shall be Bel-Marduk."

"But you are not a priest." The guardians of the ziggurat were horrified.

"But I can pretend to be Bel-Marduk just as easily as any priest can. It's all a matter of costume, isn't it?"

"But the priest *is* Bel-Marduk. He becomes the god. The god enters him."

"As he in turn enters the girl? Yes. I get the point. A circuit of absolute holiness is created." Xerxes was always very good at this sort of thing. "Rest assured that the god will enter me, too. After all—and I tell you this in confidence, by way of reassurance—my father has taken the hands of Bel-Marduk."

"Even so, this is sacrilege, Lord Prince."

"Even so, this is my will."

Xerxes then told them that Mardonius and I would also join him at the shrine. Although the priests were horrified, there was nothing that they could do. Wriggling on their bellies, they begged us at least to appear as gods. Xerxes would be dressed as Bel-Marduk, the lord of all the gods, while Mardonius would be got up to resemble the sun god Shamash and I would be dressed as the moon god Nannar—a deva worshiped at Ur. The priests then implored us not to speak to the woman—no doubt on the grounds that Bel-Marduk never speaks Persian to his Babylonian brides.

This is as good a place as any to note that the Babylonians worship sixty-five thousand gods. Since only the high priest knows all sixty-five thousand names, he is obliged to spend a good deal of time teaching their names to his heir apparent.

Shortly before midnight we climbed to the top of the ziggurat. Our costumes were waiting for us, and the sentries helped us dress. They must have been specially chosen for the sacrilege because they were most good-humored, unlike the sullen guardians of the day.

I wore on my head the silver disk of the full moon. I carried in my hand a silver staff mounted by a crescent moon. Mardonius was crowned with the sun's gold disk. Xerxes wore chains of gold; he also carried a short golden ax, necessary equipment for the ruler of sixty-five thousand unruly gods.

When we were ready, the guards opened the door to the shrine and we stepped inside. On the bed lay a girl even younger than we. She was extremely pretty, with obsidian black hair and dead-white skin, very much in the Babylonian style. She was naked except for a linen sheet of the sort that corpses are wrapped in. After one wild look at the three resplendent high gods of Babylonia she showed the whites of her eyes—and fainted.

In low voices, we discussed what to do next. Mardonius thought that the girl might revive if Xerxes joined her on the bed. Xerxes agreed to honor her with his body. I was delegated to pull back the linen sheet, which I did. The girl was not only beautifully formed but she had managed to faint in the most enticing of poses.

100

Eagerly, Xerxes got onto the bed.

Mardonius was mischievous. "Babylonians make love without their clothes."

"Not their gods." Xerxes was embarrassed.

"Especially their gods. After all, you are the first man. She is the first woman. You haven't invented clothes yet."

As I have noted before, not only do Persian men never undress in front of one another, they are never seen entirely naked by their wives or concubines—unlike the Greeks, who are modestly clothed in front of their women, except at the games, and shamelessly nude with one another. But this was a singular moment. After all, never again were we to play at gods in Babylon, where nude flesh is omnipresent, even atop the House of the Foundation of Heaven and Earth. We were, also, young. Xerxes removed his clothes. I was struck by the extraordinary beauty of his body. Obviously he took after the perfectly proportioned Cyrus rather than the somewhat short-legged, long-torsoed Darius.

Without self-consciousness, Xerxes mounted the now entirely conscious girl. As Mardonius and I watched the two figures in the lamp's glow, they did indeed seem to be the first man and first woman on earth. I must confess that there *is* something very odd about Babylon and its ancient ways.

When Xerxes was finished, he dried himself with the linen sheet, and we helped him to dress. Then, impressively, Xerxes raised the ax of Bel-Marduk. But before he could speak, the girl smiled and said in perfect Persian, "Farewell, Xerxes, son of Darius the Achaemenid."

Xerxes almost dropped the ax. The quick-witted Mardonius said, in the Babylonian tongue, "This is Bel-Marduk, girl. And I am the sun god Shamash. And there stands the moon god . . ."

"I know who all of you are." She was astonishingly self-possessed for thirteen years of age. "I'm Persian, too. Or half-Persian. I've seen you at Susa, Lord Prince. You too, Mardonius. And Cyrus Spitama."

"Did the priests tell you who we were?" Xerxes was grim.

The girl sat up in bed. "No," she said. She was quite unawed. "My mother is a priestess of Ishtar, and this is her year to select the girls for the shrine. Today she told me that it was now my turn to be taken by Bel-Marduk, and so I was. It was simply a coincidence."

101

We later learned that the girl's mother was a Babylonian and her father was a Persian. They lived part of the year at Susa and part of the year at Babylon where the father was connected with the banking house of Egibi and sons, a high recommendation in the eyes of the money-mad Mardonius. The girl's mother was a niece of the last Babylonian king, Nabonidus, which was of interest to Xerxes. She was intelligent and unsuperstitious, which delighted me.

Nineteen years later, Xerxes married her. She is of course the redoubtable Roxanna. "Whom we take as wife," Xerxes declared at Persepolis, "to show our love for our loyal kingdom of Babel and for the house of Nebuchadnezzar."

Actually, Xerxes married her because the affair that had begun so bizarrely on top of the ziggurat continued in a most satisfactory, if clandestine way, until Darius' death. Once married, Xerxes ceased to make love to her. But they were always on good terms. In fact, of Xerxes' many wives, Roxanna was easily the most charming. Certainly, she was the best actress.

"I knew perfectly well what was going to happen even before you three came into the shrine," Roxanna told me years later at Susa. "When the high priest warned my mother that the impious Persian prince was planning to impersonate Bel-Marduk, she was horrified. She was a very devout woman, and quite stupid. Luckily, I overheard them. So when the priests left, I told her that I was willing to make the supreme sacrifice. I would go to the shrine. She said, Never! When I insisted, she struck me. I then told her that if she did not let me go, I would tell everyone about Xerxes' impiety. I would also tell everyone how the priests imitate Bel-Marduk. She let me go, and that is how I was ravished by Xerxes and became the queen of Persia."

This was an exaggeration. She was not queen. In fact, among the wives, Roxanna ranked seventh. But Xerxes always delighted in her company, as did those of us who were admitted to her presence in the harem. She carried on Atossa's tradition of receiving whom she pleased, but always in the presence of eunuchs and only after menopause.

To everyone's surprise, Queen Amestris did not hate Roxanna. Women are incalculable.

BOOK THREE

The
Greek Wars
Begin

1

DURING THE YEARS THAT XERXES, Mardonius and I were growing up, we became more and more—rather than less and less—attached to each other. Great Kings and their heirs do not make friends as easily as they make enemies. Consequently, those friends made in youth are friends for life if the prince be not mad and the friend covetous.

As the years passed, Hystaspes was more often at court than in Bactria. He was always a good influence on Darius. In fact, had he lived a few years longer, I am sure that he would have neutralized the Greek faction at court, sparing us those tedious and expensive wars.

In my twentieth year Hystaspes made me commander of his personal military staff at Susa. Since he had no military forces outside his satrapy, this position was entirely honorary. Hystaspes wanted me near him so that I could help him follow the way of Truth as opposed to that of the Lie. I felt an impostor. I was not religious. In all matters that concerned the Zoroastrian order, I deferred to my uncle who was now settled in a Susan palace where, regularly, he would light the secret fire for Darius himself. Now that my uncle is dead, I can say that he had the soul of a merchant. But he was the eldest son of Zoroaster, and that was all that mattered.

Despite Hystaspes' constant pressure upon me to develop my spiritual and prophetic gifts, my life had been so entirely shaped by the Great King's court that I could think of nothing but soldiering and intrigue, of travel to far-off places.

In the twenty-first year of Darius' reign, at about the time of the winter solstice, Hystaspes summoned me to his quarters in the palace at Susa.

"We are going hunting," he said.

"Is this the season, Lord?"

"Each season has its game." The old man looked somber. I asked no more questions.

104

Although Hystaspes was well into his seventies and invariably ailing—the two conditions are the same—he refused to be carried in a litter even on the coldest winter days. As we drove out of Susa he stood very straight beside his charioteer. The slow-falling snowflakes that adhered to the long white beard made him glitter in the white winter light. I rode horseback. Except for me, Hystaspes had no escort of any kind. This was unusual. When I commented on the fact, he said, "The fewer people that know, the better." Then he gave the order to his driver. "We take the road for Pasargada."

But we did not go to Pasargada. Shortly before midday we came to a hunting lodge, set in a heavily wooded valley. This lodge had been built by the last Median king and then rebuilt by Cyrus. Darius liked to think that when he was at the lodge, no one knew where he was. But, of course, the harem always knew exactly where the Great King was at any given minute of any day, and with whom. Every day except this day.

In absolute secrecy, the Great King had arrived at the lodge the previous night. It was plain that he had given the household no warning. The main hall was chilly. The charcoal braziers had just been lit. The rugs on which the Great King walks—his feet must never touch the earth or a plain floor—had been scattered about so hastily that I took it on myself to straighten them.

On a dais was the Persian throne: a high golden chair with a footstool. In front of the dais, six stools had been set in a row. This was unusual. At court, only the Great King sits. But I had heard of certain secret councils where important figures do sit in the Great King's presence. Needless to say, I was much excited at the thought of seeing the Great King in his secret and truest role, the warrior chieftain of the highland clan that had conquered the world.

We were greeted by Hystaspes' son Artaphrenes, the satrap of Lydia. Although this powerful figure kept royal state at Sardis, the capital of the wealthy and ancient kingdom of Lydia which Cyrus had taken from Croesus, he was a mere servant here, slave to his younger brother the Great King. As Artaphrenes embraced his father, the old man asked, "Is *he* here?"

At court we can tell by the way the word "he" is said whether or not it means the Great King. This "he" was plainly someone else.

"Yes, Lord Father. He's with the other Greeks."

Even then, I knew that secret meetings with Greeks meant trouble.

"You know what I think." Old Hystaspes fondled his useless arm.

"I know, Lord Father. But we must listen to them. Things are changing in the west."

"When do they not?" Hystaspes was sour.

I think that Artaphrenes had hoped to have his father to himself for a moment, but before I could excuse myself we were interrupted by the chamberlain, who bowed low to the two satraps and said, "Will your lordships receive the guests of the Great King?"

Hystaspes nodded, and the least important guest entered first. This was my old friend the physician Democedes. He always acted as translator whenever Darius received important Greeks. Next came Thessalus of Athens. Then Histiaeus, who needed no translator; he was as fluent in the Persian language as he was resourceful at Persian intrigue.

The last Greek to enter the room was a lean, gray-haired man. He moved slowly, gravely, hieratically. He had that sublime ease with others that one finds only in those who have been born to rule. Xerxes had this quality. Darius did not.

The chamberlain announced: "Hippias, son of Pisistratus, tyrant of Athens, by the people's will." Slowly Hystaspes crossed the room to the tyrant and embraced him. In an instant Democedes was beside them, rapidly translating back and forth the ceremonial phrases. Hystaspes always treated Hippias with true respect. Hippias was the only Greek sovereign that the old man could bear.

At the lodge, the comings and goings of the Great King are always silent. There are no drums, cymbals, flutes. And so, before we knew it, Darius was in his chair, with Xerxes standing to his right and the commanding general Datis to his left.

Although Darius was only in his fifties, he was beginning to show signs of age. He often complained of chest pains. He had trouble breathing. Since Democedes said nothing to anyone about his patient, no one ever knew the exact state of Darius' health. Nevertheless, to be on the safe side—as well as observing an ancient Median custom—Darius had already ordered a tomb to be built

106

for himself near Persepolis, some twenty miles west of holy Pasargada.

That day Darius was swathed in heavy winter clothes. Except for the blue-and-white fillet, there was no mark of royalty. He fiddled constantly with the dagger at his belt. He could never be entirely still—another sign that unlike Xerxes or Hippias, he had not been born a sovereign.

"I have already welcomed the tyrant of Athens," he said. "As the rest of you are always close to me, you need no welcome in my house." Darius was impatient of ceremony when the work to be done was not the ceremony itself.

"Now I begin. This is a council of war. Sit." Darius' face was flushed, as if he had a fever. He was prone to fevers in cold weather.

Everyone sat except Xerxes, Datis and me.

"Hippias has just come from Sparta." This was a shock to us all, as Darius intended. Had it not been for the help of the Spartan army, the landowners and merchants would never have been able to drive out the popular Hippias.

Darius pulled the silver curved dagger half out of its scarlet sheath. I can still see the bright blade in that part of my memory where things are visible.

"Speak, Tyrant of Athens."

Considering the fact that the tyrant was obliged to pause every minute or two so that Democedes could translate what he had just said, Hippias was not only impressive but eloquent.

"Great King, I am grateful for all that you have done for the house of Pisistratus. You have allowed us to retain our family's land at Sigeum. You have been the best of overlords. And if heaven obliges us to be the guests of any earthly power, we are happy to be yours."

As Hippias spoke, Histiaeus gazed at Darius with all the intensity of one of those Indian snakes that first immobilize with a glassy stare some frightened rabbit; then strike. But Darius was no frightened rabbit. Despite a decade at court, Histiaeus never understood the Great King. If he had, he would have known that Darius' face told you nothing, ever. In council, the Great King resembled a stone monument to himself.

"But, Great King, we now wish to go home to the city from which, seven years ago, we were exiled by a handful of Athenian aristocrats who had been able to enlist the

107

aid of the Spartan army. Happily, the alliance between our enemies and Sparta is now broken. When King Cleomenes consulted the oracle on the Acropolis at Athens, he was told that it had been a grievous mistake for Sparta to join the enemies of our family."

The Greeks put great faith in their confusing and, sometimes, corrupt oracles. It is possible that the Spartan king was really persuaded by an oracle that had always favored the family of Pisistratus. But I think it more likely that he found uncongenial the landowner faction at Athens, led at that time by one of the accursed Alcmeonids, a man called Cleisthenes, whose enthusiasm for democracy was not apt to delight a highly conventional Spartan king. In any case, Cleomenes called for a congress of representatives of all the Greek states. The congress met at Sparta. Cleomenes made the case against Cleisthenes. Incidentally, I have been told that Cleomenes would have settled for the aristocrat Isagoras as tyrant—for anyone, in fact, but Cleisthenes.

Hippias made an eloquent case for himself at Sparta. But the other Greeks were not persuaded, and refused to form a league against Athens on the sensible ground that since they themselves feared the Spartan army, they did not want a pro-Spartan government at Athens. It was as simple as that. But Greeks are seldom direct. The representative from Corinth was particularly subtle. In front of Hippias he denounced *all* tyrants, good and bad. Outvoted, the Spartans were obliged to swear that they would not revolutionize Athens.

"At that point, Great King, I told the congress that as a lifelong student of oracles, I felt it my duty to warn the Corinthians that, in due course, their city will be crushed by that very same faction at Athens which they now support."

Hippias' prophecy came to pass. But then, anyone who knows the mercurial Greek character can assume that, sooner or later, two neighboring cities will fall out and that the stronger will crush the weaker and if not divert a river over the remains, as Croton did to Sybaris, so darken the reputation of the defeated city that the truth of the war will never be known. Quite spontaneously, Greeks follow the Lie. It is their nature.

"Great King, should you support the restoration of our house, you will be aided by Sparta. They will forswear their oath. They will follow King Cleomenes. And the usurpers—who are *your* enemies too—will be driven from the city that their unholiness has polluted."

Hippias stopped. Darius nodded. Hippias sat down. Darius motioned to Datis. The commanding general was well prepared. He spoke rapidly, and as he spoke, Democedes made for Hippias a swift translation of Datris' Median-accented Persian.

"Tyrant," said Datis, "under Spartan law there are always two kings. They are of equal rank. One of Sparta's kings favors your restoration. The other does not. Before a military campaign, the kings draw lots to see which one will lead the army. What would happen if the Spartan command in a war against Athens were to be given not to your ally King Cleomenes but to your enemy King Demaratus?"

Hippias' answer had been equally well prepared. "There are, General, as you say, two kings in Sparta. One supports me. The other does not. The one who does not support me will soon cease to be king. The oracle at Delphi has said so."

Hippias looked at the floor while this was translated. Darius maintained his stonelike expression. Like the rest of us, he was not much impressed by Greek oracles. He had bought more than a few in his time.

Hippias became practical. "Demaratus will be deposed as king of Sparta because he is illegitimate. Cleomenes himself has told me that he has the proof."

When Darius heard the translation, he smiled for the first time. "I shall be interested," he said mildly, "to learn how legitimacy is proved or disproved thirty years after conception."

Democedes' translation was somewhat less blunt than Darius' joke. But, curiously enough, Hippias turned out to be absolutely right. Demaratus *was* proved to be illegitimate, and deposed. He then came straight up to Susa, where he served most loyally the Great King—and Lais. Not long after, Cleomenes died raving mad. Unable to stop biting himself, he bled to death. Demaratus always delighted in describing his rival's peculiar end.

Darius clapped his hands, and the cupbearer brought him a silver flagon containing boiled water from the river that flows past Susa. No matter where the Great King is, he drinks water from the Choaspes River which he never offers to anyone else. He also drinks only Helbon wine, eats only Assos wheat, and uses salt only from the Am-mon oasis in Egypt. I don't know how these customs started. They are probably an inheritance from the Median kings, whom the Achaemenids imitate in so many things.

As Darius drank, I noticed that Democedes was studying his patient carefully: constant thirst is a sign of skin fevers. Darius always drank large quantities of water, and he was often feverish. Yet he was a hearty man, and able to withstand all sorts of hardship in the field. Nevertheless, at any court anywhere on earth, there is always one constant, yet never-voiced question: How much longer will the monarch live? That winter day in the hunting lodge on the road to Pasargada, Darius had thirteen more years of life, and we need not have been particularly attentive to the quantities of water that he drank.

Darius dried his beard with the back of one thick, square, much-scarred hand. "Tyrant of Athens," he began. Then he stopped. Democedes started to translate. Then he stopped too. Darius had spoken Greek.

Darius looked up at the cedar beams that held up the ill-chinked ceiling. Cold winds whistled through the lodge. Although highland Persian nobles are not supposed to notice extremes of weather, everyone in that hall was shivering with cold except the much-swathed Darius.

The Great King began to improvise—something that I had never heard him do, since I had never attended him except on those ceremonial occasions when questions and responses are as ritualized as my grandfather's sacred antiphonies.

"The north comes first," he said. "That is where the danger is. That is where my ancestor Cyrus died, fighting the tribes. That is why I went to the Danube River. That is why I went to the Volga River. That is why I slaughtered every Scythian that I could find. But not even the Great King can find them all. They are still there. The hordes are always waiting. Waiting to move south. One day they will. If it is in my time, I shall slaughter them once again, but—" Darius stopped; his eyes were half shut, as if he were surveying a field of battle. Perhaps he was reliving his defeat—at this date one may use the precise word—in the Scythian forests. If Histiaeus had not kept the Ionian Greeks from burning the bridge between Europe and Asia, the Persian army would have perished. Darius never ceased to be grateful to Histiaeus. He also never ceased to distrust him. That is why he

110

thought that if Histiaeus was the Great King's guest, he would be less dangerous than at home in Miletus. This proved to be a mistake.

I could see that Histiaeus was eager to remind us all of his crucial role in the Scythian war, but he dared not speak until given leave—unlike the Great King's brother Artaphrenes, who had the right to speak whenever he chose in council.

I found all of this, by the way, most illuminating. For one thing, I realized that although I had been brought up at court, I knew nothing about the way in which Persia was actually governed. When Xerxes spoke to me of his father, he said only conventional things. Hystaspes sometimes grumbled about his son; but said nothing more.

It was not until the meeting at the lodge that I began to understand just who and what Darius was, and even in his old age—I am now old enough to have been his father that day!—I was able to glimpse something of the fiery ingenious youth who overthrew the so-called Magian usurper and made himself master of the world while retaining the loyalty of the six nobles who had helped him to the throne.

Darius motioned for the cupbearer to withdraw. Then he turned to Artaphrenes. The brothers looked not at all alike. Artaphrenes was a somewhat coarser version of their father Hystaspes.

"Great King and brother." Artaphrenes bowed his head. Darius blinked; no more. When the chiefs of the Persian clans are together, it is often what is *not* said in words that is the true substance of the meeting. Years later Xerxes told me that Darius had a wide range of gestures with which he communicated his will. Unfortunately I was never in attendance on him long enough to learn the all-important code.

Artaphrenes began: "I believe that Hippias is our friend, as was his father, whom we allowed the lordship at Sigeum. I believe that it is in our interest to see restored at Athens the house of Pisistratus."

Thessalus' face showed delight. But Hippias' face was as impassive as that of Darius. He was a wary man, accustomed to disappointment.

Artaphrenes provided the disappointment when he suddenly shifted the subject. "Two weeks ago, at Sardis, I received Aristagoras of Miletus."

111

Histiaeus sat up very straight. The small dark eyes studied every gesture of the satrap.

"As the Great King knows"—the phrase which is used at court to prepare the Great King for something that he either does not know or has forgotten or does not want to know—"Aristagoras is the nephew as well as the son-in-law of our loyal friend and ally who honors us with his presence here today." Artaphrenes indicated Histiaeus with a gesture of the right hand. "The tyrant of Miletus who prefers, as who does not, the company of the Great King to his native land."

I think that Darius smiled at this point. Unfortunately, the beard was too thick about the lips for me to be certain.

"Aristagoras acts at Miletus in the name of his father-in-law," said the satrap. "He claims to be as loyal to us as to the tyrant himself. I believe him. After all, the Great King has never failed to support the tyrants of those Greek cities that belong to him." Artaphrenes stopped. He turned to Darius. A look—some sort of code?—was exchanged.

Darius said, "Aristagoras is dear to us." He smiled at Histiaeus. "For he is dear to you, our friend."

Histiaeus took this glance to mean that he could speak. He rose. "Great King, my nephew is a natural warrior. He is a naval commander of proven worth."

The history of the world might have been changed if at that point someone had asked where and when and how Aristagoras had shown any competence as a military leader.

I now know that Histiaeus and Artaphrenes were in league together. But at the time I was simply a green boy with only the haziest notion of where Miletus and Sardis and Athens were, much less *what* they were. I knew that it was Persian policy to support Greek tyrants. I also knew that our favorite tyrants were constantly being driven into exile by the rising class of merchants in combination with the nobility—if one can use that word to describe any Greek class. Hereabouts, the possession of two horses and a farm with one olive tree makes for a noble.

"Aristagoras believes that the island of Naxos is vulnerable," said the satrap. "If the Great King will provide him with a fleet, he swears that he will add Naxos to our empire."

Suddenly I remembered that day in Ecbatana, years before, when Democedes and Histiaeus had spoken of Naxos and, inexperienced though I was, I was quick to make the connection.

"Once we hold Naxos, we will control that chain of islands called the Cyclades. Once we control these islands, the Great King will be sea lord as well as lord of all the lands."

"I am sea lord," said Darius. "I hold Samos. The sea is mine."

Artaphrenes made a cringing gesture. "I spoke of *islands*, Great King. You are all-powerful, of course. But you will need islands if you are to approach, step by step, the mainland of Greece in order that our friends may rule once again in Athens." Neatly, Artaphrenes had connected Aristagoras' ambition to conquer Naxos with the restoration of the house of Pisistratus, the ostensible reason for the high council.

There was a long silence. Thoughtfully Darius arranged and then rearranged his heavy woollen outer robe. Finally he spoke. "Trade is bad in our Greek cities. The shipyards are idle. Tax revenues have fallen off." Darius stared at the arrangement of spears on the wall opposite him. "When Sybaris fell, Miletus lost the Italian market. That is a serious matter. Where will Miletus sell all that wool the Italians used to buy?" Darius looked at Histiaeus.

The tyrant said, "There is no comparable market anywhere else. That is why I shaved my head when Sybaris was drowned."

I was amazed that Darius knew anything at all about something so prosaic as the Milesian wool trade. I was later to discover that Darius spent most of his days fretting about caravan routes, world markets, trade. I had made the common mistake of thinking that the Great King was the same in private as he was in public—hieratic, gorgeous, immaterial. The opposite was the case.

In fact, as we sat in that cold room of the hunting lodge, Darius had already grasped a point overlooked by all his councilors. While they wanted to make him sea lord, he wanted to revive the lagging industries of the Ionian Greek cities of Asia Minor. Darius always preferred gold to glory—no doubt on the excellent ground that the first can always buy the second. "How many

113

ships," he asked, "would be needed for the conquest of Naxos?"

"Aristagoras thinks that he can take Naxos with a hundred battleships under sail." Artaphrenes spoke precisely. He was never at a loss for words. He always appeared to know the right answer to every question. He was also perfectly incompetent, as later events proved.

"With two hundred ships," said Darius, "he can make himself sea lord. In *my* name, of course." Darius' smile was plainly visible now; and altogether charming.

"I swear that he will serve you as loyally as I have—and do, Great King." Histiaeus spoke the absolute truth as, again, later events proved.

"I am certain of that." Darius then commanded: "One hundred new triremes are to be built in the shipyards of our Ionian cities. They are to be ready at the spring equinox. They will then proceed to Miletus, where they will be joined by one hundred ships from our Samian fleet. Our brother the satrap of Lydia will see to the execution of this plan."

"You will be obeyed in all things, Great King." Artaphrenes made the ceremonial response. He was careful not to show how delighted he was. On the other hand, Histiaeus was plainly aglow with pleasure. Only the Athenians looked glum: it is a long way from Naxos to Athens.

"We shall place the fleet under the command of our most loyal admiral . . ."

Histiaeus's heavy face was now ajar with a broad smile.

". . . and cousin Megabetes." Darius could not resist watching Histiaeus' lips snap shut.

"Second in command will be Aristagoras." As Darius stood up, we all bowed low. "Such is the Great King's will," said Darius and, as is the custom, we repeated in unison, "Such is the Great King's will."

The Greek wars were now under way.

Hystaspes and I stayed for two days at the hunting lodge. Each day Darius entertained us with a formidable feast. Although the Great King himself dined alone or with Xerxes, he would join us later for wine drinking. Since all highlanders pride themselves on the amounts of wine they can consume, I was not surprised to note that as each drinking-party progressed, less and less water from the Choaspes River was mixed with the Great King's Helbon wine. But like all his clan, Darius had a strong

114

head. No matter how much he drank, he was never foolish. But he did tend to fall asleep abruptly. The moment that he did, his cupbearer and his charioteer would carry him off to bed. The highlanders outdrank the low-land Greeks. Except for Hippias, who simply looked more and more sad as he realized that for the moment, his mission had failed.

I remember very little else about that famous council. I do recall that Xerxes was looking forward to taking part in the campaign against Naxos, but that there was some question whether or not he would be allowed to go.

"I am the heir," he told me as we rode together on a cold, bright winter morning. "It's all been decided. But no one's supposed to know—just yet."

"Everyone knows in the harem," I said. "They talk of nothing else." This was true.

"Even so, it's still just a rumor until the Great King actually speaks, and he won't speak until he leaves to go to war." Under Persian law, the Great King must name his heir before he goes to war; otherwise, should he be killed, there could be chaos of the sort that followed upon Cambyses' unexpected death.

As we raced our horses, the cold winter air clearing our brains of the previous day's drinking, I had no way of knowing that we were living through the high noon of the Persian empire. Ironically, in the vigor of my youth and at the apex of Persia's golden age, I suffered from constant headaches and heaviness of the stomach, the result of those interminable banquets and drinking parties. A few years later I simply announced that, as the prophet's grandson, I could only drink on ritual occasions. This wise decision made it possible for me to live as long as I have. Since long life is a curse, I now realize that I should have drunk more Helbon wine.

2

In the summer of the next year, Mardonius and I left Babylon for Sardis. We traveled with four companies of cavalry and eight companies of foot soldiers. As we left by the Ishtar Gate the ladies of the

115

harem waved to us from the roof of the new palace; but then, so did the eunuchs.

We junior officers were much in awe of the dozen or so —to us, depressingly old—men who had fought with Darius from one end of the world to the other. I even met a senior officer who had actually known my father; unfortunately, he could not remember anything of interest to tell me about him. Darius' brother Artanes commanded our small army. A dim figure, he later became a leper and was forced to live alone in the wilderness. It is said that lepers have great spiritual powers. Happily, I've not been close enough to one to find out.

I have never enjoyed myself more than I did during the weeks that it took us to travel from Babylon to Sardis. Mardonius was an enchanting companion. Since both of us missed the company of Xerxes, much of the affection that each felt for the absent friend was transferred to the other.

Every night we would pitch our tents beside one of the post houses that are set at thirteen-mile intervals along the fifteen-hundred mile highway from Susa to Sardis. Then we would go carousing. I even developed a taste for palm wine, a potent drink much favored in Babylonia.

I remember one particular evening when Mardonius and I and several girls who traveled with the baggage train decided to see how much palm wine we could drink. We were sitting on the parapet of the so-called Median wall, an ancient structure that was crumbling into the dust from which its bricks and asphalt had been shaped. I can still see the golden full moon above me as I rolled along the parapet. I can still see the equally golden sun blazing in my eyes as I lay in a sand dune at the base of the high wall. During the night I had fallen off the wall; soft sand had saved my life. Mardonius was amused. I was ill for days from the palm wine.

We kept the Euphrates to our right as we moved up-country to the sea. I was impressed, as never before, by the extent and diversity of our empire. We rode from the hot and heavily irrigated countryside of Babylonia through the desert land of Mesopotamia to the forested high country of Phrygia and Caria. Every few miles the landscape changed. The people, too. The low-land river people are small, dark, quick; they have large heads. In the mountains the people are tall, pale, slow, with small heads. In the Greek coastal cities, there are extraordinary racial

116

mixtures. Although Ionian and Dorian Greeks predominate, they have intermarried with blond Thracians, dark Phoenicians, papyrus-pale Egyptians. Physically, human variety is quite as startling as is the sameness of human character.

For obvious reasons we did not turn off the king's highway at Miletus. Instead, we left the road at Halicarnassus, the southern-most of the Great King's Greek cities. The inhabitants of Halicarnassus are Dorian Greek, and traditionally loyal to Persia.

We were received graciously by King Lydagmis, who quartered us in his sea palace, a damp gray stone barracks of a building that dominates the coast. Mardonius and I shared a room with a view of the high green island of Cos in the distance. I was always at the window. For the first time in my life I beheld the sea. I must have mariner's blood in my veins—from Lais' Ionian ancestry?—because I could not stop staring at those agitated purple waters. Driven by autumn winds, thick waves struck the base of the sea palace with such a roar that I could not sleep at night, while in the intervals between the striking of the waves, I could hear—if I strained my ears, and I did—sea foam frothing and whispering beneath my window.

Mardonius thought my fascination with the sea absurd. "Just wait till you set sail! You're bound to be sick. Magians always are." From boyhood, Mardonius liked to refer to me as the Magian. Since he was a good-natured youth, I never resented too much the epithet.

In those days I knew Mardonius so well that in a sense I did not really know him at all. I never examined his character, the way that one does with new acquaintances or with those important personages one is privileged to observe at a distance.

Since Mardonius was to become world-famous, I suppose I ought to try to recall what he was like when we were young and—most important—what he was like when we were in Halicarnassus and I began to realize that he was not just another young nobleman whose only distinction was his family's rank and his position as table companion to Xerxes.

I had always known that Mardonius was swift to take advantage of whatever situation he found himself in. He was also deeply secretive about his actions, not to mention motives. One seldom had the slightest notion just what he was up to. He never willingly revealed himself. But at Halicarnassus I discovered a good deal about the sort of man he was. Had I been more attentive, I might even have begun to understand him. Had I understood him . . . Well, there is no point in speculating on what might have been.

What was, was this.

Twenty of us were entertained that night by King Lydagmis. An insignificant-looking man in his fifties, Lydagmis lay upon a couch at the far end of the room; to his right was the Great King's brother Artanes; to his left was Mardonius, the second highest-ranking Persian in the room. The rest of us were arranged in a semicircle before the three principals. Slaves brought us each a three-legged table loaded with every sort of fish. That evening I ate my first oyster, and saw but did not dare to eat a squid, seethed in its own ink.

The banquet hall was a long room in the somewhat bleak and always—to my eye—unfinished Dorian style. Molding rushes were strewn about the floor from which sea water never ceased to ooze. It is no wonder that the rulers of Halicarnassus are prone to those diseases that stiffen the joints.

Just behind Lydagmis was a chair on which sat the king's daughter, Artemisia. She was a slender blond-haired girl. Since her husband was constantly ill, she would dine with her father as if she were his son or son-in-law. She was said to have a brother, who was mad. As a result, under Dorian law, she was herself the king's actual heiress. Like the others, I could not keep my eyes off her. For one thing, it was the first time that I had ever dined in the presence of a lady other than Lais. My fellow Persians were equally intrigued.

Although Artemisia did not speak unless addressed first by her father, she listened very carefully to what was said and comported herself modestly. I was too far away to hear a word that she said. But I did learn how to eat a sea urchin from observing the delicate way she plucked the flesh with her fingers from the center of the bristling shell. Even today I cannot eat a sea urchin without thinking of Artemisia. Although, to be precise, I no longer eat sea urchins. They are too dangerous for the blind. Perhaps that explains why I have not thought of Artemisia for so many years.

There was a good deal of wine drinking in the Dorian

manner, which is like the Thracian. A horn filled with wine makes the rounds. One drinks deeply from it before passing it along to one's neighbor. The last drops in the horn are always sprinkled on the person nearest the last drinker. This messy gesture is thought to bring good luck.

When I went to bed, Mardonius was not in the room. At dawn when I awakened, he was beside me in the bed, sleeping soundly. I waked him and proposed that we visit the port.

I do not think that there is any part of the world quite so beautiful as the coast of Asia Minor. The land is craggy and full of odd inlets. The hills are heavily wooded, while the coastal plains are fertile and well watered. In the distance, sharp blue mountains look as if they had been erected as special fire temples for the worship of the Wise Lord; yet in those days the Wise Lord was unknown in that beautiful if spiritually deprived part of the world.

The port was filled with every sort of ship, and the air smelled of that pitch mariners use to caulk hulls and decks. As the fishing boats docked, the men would throw on to the shore nets filled with writhing shining fish, and the merchants on the quay would start to haggle. The noise was deafening but cheerful. I like seaports.

Just before noon or at the time of the full market—a Greek phrase that I first heard in Halicarnassus—a tall mariner came toward us from the mole. Gravely, he saluted Mardonius, who introduced me to Scylax. Mardonius took it for granted that I knew the name, but I am ashamed to say that I had not heard of the man who was even then the finest navigator in the world. A Greek from nearby Caria, Scylax was often sent on expeditions by Darius. It was he who charted the southern ocean of India as well as the westernmost parts of the Mediterranean. It was he who persuaded Darius to build the canal between the Mediterranean and the Arabian Sea. When Xerxes became Great King, he wanted Scylax to circumnavigate all Africa. Unfortunately, the Carian was too old by then to make the voyage.

"Is there to be a war?" asked Mardonius.

"You should know, Lord." Scylax squinted down at Mardonius. Like so many mariners, his eyes were always half shut as if he had stared once too often at the sun. Although the skin of his face was Nubian-black from weather, the neck was white as sea foam.

"But *you* are Greek." Mardonius' manner was always wry with those he chose to regard, no matter how temporarily, as equals. "What is Aristagoras doing?"

"He's not been here. He's in the north, they say. I doubt if he'll come this far south. We're Dorian, you know. We have our own king. There are no tyrants here."

"How large a fleet does he have?"

Scylax smiled. "No matter how many ships Aristagoras has, he will manage to sink them all."

"He is not sea lord?"

"No, he is not sea lord. But"—and Scylax frowned— "if Histiaeus were at Miletus, *he* would be sea lord."

"You really think him able?" Like the rest of the young courtiers of our generation, Mardonius took for granted that those men at court who were older than we must of necessity be inferior to us in every way. Youth tends to this sort of vain foolishness.

"I know him well. So does the Great King. Darius is right to keep him nearby. Histiaeus could be a dangerous man."

"I shall remember that."

Scylax excused himself, and Mardonius and I walked up the steep and narrow streets that lead from the crowded fish-smelling port to the sea palace of Lydagmis.

We talked of the coming war. Since we had no information of any kind, we were not unlike the schoolboys that we had so recently been and, as schoolboys will, we discussed what great deeds we would one day do when we were grown. Happily, the future was—and always is—a perfect mystery.

At the sea palace, Mardonius turned to me and said, "There is someone who wants to talk to you. Someone who cares deeply about the Wise Lord." Although Mardonius never dared make fun openly of the religion of the Achaemenids, he had Atossa's gift for delicate offensiveness whenever the subject came up.

"I am a follower of the Truth." I was severe, as I always am when others expect me to reflect the Wise Lord's wisdom.

To my astonishment, we were led by two old women to the apartments of Artemisia. In those days, eunuchs were unknown at Dorian courts. As we entered the small room Artemisia rose to greet us. Close to, I saw that she was not altogether plain. She motioned for the old women to withdraw.

"You must sit," said Artemisia. "I give you my husband's greetings. He wanted to receive both of you. But he is not well. He is in the next room." Artemisia pointed to a carved wooden door crudely set in an undressed stone wall. The only arts that the Dorians know are warfare and thievery.

Artemisia then proceeded to ask me some perfunctory questions about the Wise Lord. It was not until I had given my dozenth perfunctory answer that I realized that Mardonius had slept with Artemisia the night before. Now he was using me so that he could make a respectable visit in daylight on the plausible ground that nothing could be more natural than for a king's daughter to discuss religion with the prophet's grandson.

Annoyed, I ceased to answer the girl's questions. She hardly noticed. She kept staring at Mardonius as if she wanted to devour him then and there the way that she had so deftly managed to ingest a series of prickly sea urchins the previous evening.

When Mardonius saw that I was not going to be helpful, *he* talked religion to her, and she listened solemnly. But eventually Mardonius ran out of religious texts. He knew as little of the Wise Lord as I did of his beloved Mithra.

Finally, the three of us just sat there. While the lovers stared at each other I pretended to be lost in a vision of the world at the end of time of the long dominion. I do this very well. Better, even, than my cousin the current heir of Zoroaster, who always looks as if he were about to try to sell you a camel's pack of rugs.

King Lydagmis entered, without fanfare—to say the least: he positively crept into the room. Startled, we leapt to our feet. If he knew that Artemisia and Mardonius had made love on the floor of that very room the previous night, he betrayed nothing. Instead, he treated us with all the gravity befitting a host who knows how to receive the Great King's table companions—or companion. Mardonius dined with Darius. I never did. Later, of course, I was to be Xerxes' table companion until the end of his life. This was a great honor, since I was neither royal nor one of The Six.

"Cyrus Spitama is the grandson of Zoroaster," said Artemisia. She was not in any way embarrassed by the situation. Plainly, Mardonius was not the first to enjoy her.

"I know. I know." King Lydagmis was benign. "I was told that you had received these two fine young princes. Obviously they have so charmed you that you've forgotten you were to ride with me in the park."

Artemisia was suddenly apologetic. "I *had* forgotten. I am sorry. Can they come too?"

"Of course. If they like."

"Come where?" asked Mardonius.

"We're hunting deer," said Artemisia. "Join us."

So that curious day ended with Mardonius and me hunting invisible deer with Lydagmis and Artemisia. The girl rather showily rode ahead of us, cloak streaming in the wind, javelin at the ready.

"She's like the goddess Artemis, isn't she?" Lydagmis was proud of his Amazonian daughter.

"More beautiful, more swift," said Mardonius, not looking at me.

Since Artemis is a chief devil, I made a sign to ward off evil; and succeeded all too well. Artemisia was promptly swept from her horse by a low branch. As I was nearest the lady, I heard her curse like a Dorian cavalryman. But when Mardonius came within earshot she began, softly, to weep. Tenderly Mardonius helped her to remount her horse.

On the inland road from Halicarnassus to Sardis we discussed Artemisia at some length. Mardonius admitted that he had seduced her. "Or the other way around," he added. "She's very strong-willed. Are all Dorian ladies like that?"

"I don't know any. Lais is Ionian."

Side by side, we proceeded through a heavily wooded gorge. During the night there had been a light frost in the mountains and the hooves of our horses made a cracking sound as frozen twigs, leaves, plants splintered beneath their weight. In double file, before us, and behind us, the cavalry made its way through steep cold woods.

Mardonius and I always traveled at dead center, just behind our commander Artanes. In case of battle, Artanes would lead the attack from the center, as the front column always becomes the left wing and the rear column becomes the right. Naturally, I speak of open country. In that high mountain ravine, anyone who attacked us would have killed us all. But our minds were not on danger—of the military kind.

Abruptly Mardonius said, "I want to marry her."

"The lady is married." I thought this worth mentioning.

"He'll die soon, her husband. She thinks it's only a matter of weeks, months."

"Does she plan to . . . hurry things?"

Mardonius nodded; he was entirely serious. "The moment that I am able to tell her I can marry her, she will be a widow. She promised me that, on the floor."

"Such a wife would make me nervous."

Mardonius laughed. "Once she marries me she enters the harem and never comes out again. No wife of mine will ever receive a man the way she received me. Or hunt deer."

"Why do you want her?"

Mardonius turned and bestowed upon me the full handsomeness of his smiling, square-jawed face. "Because I want Halicarnassus, Cos, Nisyros and Calymna. When Artemisia's father dies, she will be queen of those places in her own right. That's Dorian law. Her mother was also a Dorian, from Crete. Artemisia can lay claim to Crete, too, she told me. And she will, *if* her husband is strong enough."

"That would make you sea lord."

"That would make me sea lord." Mardonius turned away. The smile was gone.

"The Great King would never allow such a marriage." I was to the point. "Look at Histiaeus. As soon as he got those silver mines in Thrace, he was summoned up to Susa."

"But he is Greek. I am Persian. I am the nephew of Darius. I am the son of Gobryas."

"Yes. And because you are who you are, such a marriage is impossible."

Mardonius said nothing. He knew of course that I was right, and he never dared mention the subject to Darius. But some years later, when Artemisia was sole queen, he asked Xerxes for permission to marry her. Xerxes had been much amused; he had even teased Mardonius. "Highlanders," he had said from the throne, "must never mix their blood with that of an inferior race."

Irreverent as Mardonius could often be, Xerxes knew that Mardonius dared not remind him of all the Achaemenid blood that Xerxes himself had so blithely—and often so illegally—intermingled with that of foreign women. Curiously enough, the offspring of Xerxes' foreign wives all turned out badly. But to be fair, they were not given much chance to show their quality. Most of them were put to death in the next reign.

3

WE ARRIVED AT SARDIS IN EARLY AUTUMN.

I had heard all my life about this fabulous city, created or re-created by Croesus, the richest man on earth, whose defeat by Cyrus is the subject of a thousand ballads, plays, legends—even Milesian stories of lechery and excess.

I cannot remember now what I had expected to see. Buildings of solid gold, I suppose. Instead, I found an entirely undistinguished city of perhaps fifty thousand people, all crowded together in mud-and-thatch houses. Since the streets were simply haphazard lanes, it was even easier to get lost in Sardis than it is in the equally unlovely Susa or Athens.

After Mardonius and I had helped establish our troops in a camp to the south of the city, we rode together into Sardis, where we promptly lost our way. To make matters worse, the people speak neither Persian nor Greek, while no one on earth speaks Lydian except the Lydians.

We rode for what seemed hours, this way and that. Overhanging balconies and upper stories were a constant danger . . . particularly when disguised by laundry. We both found the people uncommonly handsome. The men plait their hair in long braids, and pride themselves on the pallor of their soft skin. No man of rank ever ventures out into the sun. Yet the Lydian cavalry is the best in the world, and a mainstay of the Persian army.

Finally we dismounted and led our horses along the river that runs not only through the center of the town but also through the center of the great marketplace. When in doubt, follow a river, as Cyrus the Great is said to have said.

The marketplace at Sardis was even larger than the one at Susa. Surrounded by a brick wall, ten thousand tents and bazaars offer everything there is on earth to buy. As we wandered about, mouths agape like a pair of

124

Carian peasants, no one paid the slightest attention to us. Persian officers are hardly a novelty at Sardis.

Traders from every corner of the world offered their wares. From Athens there were amphorae and kraters. From the satrapy of India, cotton cloth and rubies. From the Persian highlands, rugs. Beside the muddy river there was a row of palm trees to which a hundred ill-natured camels were tethered. Some were being relieved of their exotic burdens while others were being loaded with such Lydian goods as red figs, twelve-stringed harps, gold . . . Yes, Sardis is indeed a city of gold because the muddy river is full of gold dust and it was the father of Croesus who first began to pan the gold and turn it into jewelry; he also minted the first gold coins.

In the hills back of Sardis there are mines of the world's rarest metal, silver. I used to own a silver Lydian coin that was thought to be more than a century old. If it was, then it was minted by Croesus' grandfather, and so coinage, as we know it, did indeed originate in Lydia, as the Lydians claim. My Lydian silver piece was embossed with a lion, worn almost smooth. I was robbed of it in Cathay.

"They are so rich!" exclaimed Mardonius. He looked capable of sacking the market place single-handed.

"That's because they waste no money on their houses." I was still disappointed by the ugliness of the fabled city.

"Pleasure comes first, I suppose." Mardonius then hailed a Median merchant, who consented to act as our guide. As we made our slow way across the marketplace, I was quite groggy from so many bright colors and pungent odors, from the tiring babble of a hundred languages.

Just past the market wall is a small park with shade trees. At the far end of the park is the old palace of Croesus, a two-story building of mud brick and timber. Here lives the Persian satrap for Lydia.

As we followed a chamberlain down a dusty corridor to Croesus' throne room, Mardonius shook his head. "If I'd been the richest man in the world, I would certainly have done better than this."

Artaphrenes was seated in a chair next to the throne, which is always kept empty unless the Great King is in the room. I was surprised to see that the throne was an exact replica in ugly electrum of the Great King's lion throne.

Although Artaphrenes was holding an audience with u

125

group of Lydians, he rose when he saw Mardonius and kissed him on the mouth. I kissed the satrap on the cheek.

"Welcome to Sardis." Artaphrenes reminded me more than ever of his father, Hystaspes. "You will be quartered with us here." Artaphrenes then presented the Lydians to us. One very old man proved to be Ardes, the son of Croesus. In due course, I came to know well this fascinating link with the past.

The next few days we met often with Artaphrenes—and the Greeks. It seemed as if every Greek adventurer on earth had found his way to Sardis. Needless to say, every last one of them was for hire; and Artaphrenes had hired them because they are not only excellent soldiers and sailors but every bit as intelligent as they are treacherous.

Democritus is too polite to disagree with me. But I have seen a side to Greeks that Greeks normally do not present to one another. I have seen them at the Persian court. I have listened to them beg the Great King to attack their native cities because no Greek can endure the success of another Greek. Had it not been for the Greeks in Persia during those years, the Greek wars would not have taken place and Xerxes would have extended our empire to include all of India as far as the Himalayas and perhaps beyond. But the category of what might have been is already too crowded.

Hippias was at the first council meeting I attended in Sardis. He was accompanied by Thessalus and my old school friend Milo.

Hippias recalled our meeting at the lodge the previous winter. "I have since read deeply in the works of your grandfather."

"I am pleased that you follow the Truth, Tyrant." I was polite. I did not mention that in those days very little of my grandfather's teachings had been written down. Now, of course, a thousand oxhides have been covered with prayers and hymns and dialogues, all attributed to Zoroaster.

At the very first council that I attended at Sardis, Hippias proposed an all-out Persian attack on Miletus. The old tyrant spoke with his usual gravity. "We know that Aristagoras is still at Cyprus with his fleet. We know that the demagogues at Athens have sent him twenty ships. By now those ships cannot be too far from Cyprus. Before the two fleets join, we must regain Miletus."

126

"The city is well defended." Artaphrenes was always slow to commit himself to any strategy. No doubt on the ground that it is the essence of statecraft to know when to do nothing at all.

"Miletus," said Hippias, "began its history as a colony of Athens, and even to this day there are many Milesians who look to my family with affection."

This was nonsense. If Miletus was ever a colony of Athens, it was long before the Pisistratids. In any case, there were few tyrant-lovers at Miletus, as Aristagoras discovered when he made his bid for independence. The upper classes of the city refused to revolt against Persia unless Aristagoras allowed them to have an Athenian-style democracy. So the adventurer was obliged to give them what they wanted. As we were soon to discover, the age of the tyrants had been artificially prolonged by the Great King's policy toward his Greek cities. Apparently the ruling classes could not bear either the tyrants or their allies the common people. So all the Greek cities are now democracies in name but oligarchies in fact. Democritus thinks that the present governance of Athens is more complicated than that. I don't.

Mardonius seconded Hippias' proposal. He saw a chance to distinguish himself militarily. "This will be the making of me," he said one night when we had drunk too much sweet Lydian wine. "If they let me lead the attack on Miletus, we'll be home next summer."

Mardonius was right when he said that the war would be the making of him. But we did not go home the next summer. The war with the Ionian rebels lasted six years.

After a week of argument in council, Artaphrenes agreed to commit half the Persian army and half the Lydian cavalry to an attack on Miletus. Mardonius was appointed second in command to Artobazanes, the eldest son of Darius, and rival to Xerxes. I was to remain on the satrap's staff at Sardis.

The first bad news arrived during a ceremony at the temple of Cybele. I thought it fitting. After all, I had no business taking part in the rites of a devil-cult but Artaphrenes had insisted that his entire staff join him at the temple. "We must humor the Lydians. Like us, they are slaves to the Great King. Like us, they are loyal."

I watched with distaste as the priestesses danced with the eunuchs. It was not always easy to tell which was priestess and which was eunuch, since each was dressed

127

as a woman. Actually, the eunuchs were usually better dressed than the priestesses. I have never understood the veneration that so many benighted races have for Anahita or Cybele or Artemis or whatever name the voracious mother-goddess happens to bear.

At Sardis, on the day of the goddess, those young men who wish to serve her slash off their genitals and run through the streets, holding in one hand their severed parts. Less ambitious devotees of the goddess think it good luck to be splashed with the blood of a new eunuch. This is not difficult. There is a lot of blood. Finally, exhausted, the self-made eunuch throws his severed genitals through the open doorway of a house, whose owner is then obliged to take in the creature and nurse him back to health.

I have seen this ceremony a number of times in Babylon as well as at Sardis. Since the young men appear to be quite mad, I think that they must first drink haoma or else take some mind-deranging substance like that honey from Colchis which induces hallucinations. Otherwise, I cannot imagine anyone in his right mind serving any devil in such a fashion.

At Sardis that day, I saw one poor wretch throw his genitals at an open door. Unfortunately, he missed. He then proceeded, slowly, to bleed to death in the roadway, since it is considered blasphemous to come to the aid of a would-be priest of Cybele who has failed to find, as it were, a proper home for his sexuality.

The ceremony to Cybele was endless. The incense was so thick that the image of the tall goddess which stands— stood—in a Grecian-style portico was almost obscured. She was depicted between a lion and a pair of writhing snakes.

Old Ardes stood next to the high priestess, doing whatever it was that the last member of the Lydian royal house was expected to do on such a high occasion. The Sardians were properly ecstatic, while Artaphrenes and Hippias did their best not to look bored. But Milo yawned. "I hate all this," he said to me, in his simple, boyish way.

"So do I." I was perfectly sincere.

"They're even worse than those Magians back in school."

"You mean, worse than the Magians who follow the Lie." I was properly reverent.

128

Milo giggled. "If you're still a fire-worshiper, what are you doing dressed up as a soldier?"

Before I could think of some chilling response, a cavalryman clattered into view; he dismounted and tethered his horse within the temple precinct, committing sacrilege. Artaphrenes glared as the man approached him with a message. Artaphrenes' glare was even more intense when he had read the message. The Ionian fleet had made a rendezvous with the Athenian fleet and the two navies were now at anchor off Ephesus. Worse, from Miletus in the south to Byzantium in the north, all of the Ionian Greek cities were in open rebellion against the Great King.

A week later Artaphrenes gave a banquet at Croesus' palace. I cannot remember why. I do remember that it was not until midnight that one of the guests noticed that there was fire in the city. Since Sardis was so ill made, no one thought anything of it. Every day houses burn down; every day they are rebuilt. The emblem of Sardis should be not the lion but the phoenix.

While Hippias was reminding us yet again of the affection that all Greeks felt for his family, a series of messages arrived. Greek forces had disembarked at Ephesus. They were marching upon Sardis. They were at the city's gates. They were within the city. They had fired the city.

Not only was Artaphrenes stunned but he showed it, a clear sign that he was not fit to conduct what was developing into a major war. On the other hand, who would have believed that a band of reckless Ionian and Athenian Greeks would have had the temerity to march deep into Persian territory and set fire to the capital of Lydia?

Artaphrenes ordered the call to arms. Since the destroying flames made day of night, we were able to see one another clearly as we hurried to the park where the troops were assembling. To a man, they were ready for battle. But where was the enemy? Meanwhile, the sky was bright with red-gold flames, and what had been a cool night was now as sweltering as a Susan summer.

Finally one of Artaphrenes' aides appeared. We were to withdraw, he said, "in good order" to the acropolis. Unfortunately, the order came too late. Every road out of the city was blocked by flames. So we did the only thing that we could do: we hurried to the marketplace. If worst came to worst, we could swim in the river until the fire had burned itself out. Needless to say, the same thought had occurred to everyone in Sardis. By the time we arrived in the market enclosure, it was already crowded with townspeople as well as with Persian and Lydian troops.

I suppose the last day of creation will be something like the burning of Sardis. Deafening noise of people screaming, animals howling, buildings crashing one upon another as the fire leapt this way and that in obedience to a fickle wind.

But the wind that destroyed Sardis saved our lives. Had it not blown with some steadiness, we would have suffocated from the flames. As it was, there was sufficient heavy air for us to breathe. Also, the high wall that ringed the marketplace acted as a firebreak. Nothing inside the market caught fire except the row of palm trees that edged the deep fire-reflecting river.

I prayed to the Wise Lord, and shuddered at the thought of the molten metal at creation's end. I have never felt so entirely helpless.

"We could make a raft," Milo said. "We could float downstream."

"That's where your Athenians are. When we float past them, they'll kill us, one by one."

"Well, we could use logs. We could duck under them —like those people."

A great many Sardians were splashing about in the water, holding on to bits of wood or air-filled bladders.

"We'd have to get rid of our armor." I preferred drowning to burning, but at that moment I was willing to wait as long as possible before making a terminal choice.

Milo shook his head. "I can't disarm." As a professional soldier and heir of tyrants, he must die in battle. Only there was no battle save the one against two of the four elements.

Suddenly the Lydian cavalry charged across the marketplace. The mane of one horse was aflame: so were the long braids of its rider. As if by common consent, both horse and rider plunged into the river.

Luckily, Artaphrenes' chief of staff appeared on the scene. I forget his name, which is ungrateful of me because he saved our lives. I do remember that he was a large man and that he carried a short whip, which he used freely on everyone, military and civilian.

"Fall in! Take your positions. Cavalry to the left, by the wall. Infantry, by companies, along the riverbank. Keep clear of the burning trees. All civilians to the other side!"

To my amazement, we were once again a disciplined army. I remember thinking: Now we'll be burned alive in perfect formation. But the fire stayed outside the market wall. On the other hand, the Greeks did not. With a noisy paean, they came running into the marketplace. When they saw the Persian army and the Lydian cavalry drawn up for battle, they stopped in their tracks.

As the citizens of Sardis ran for cover, the Persian commander gave the command to attack. Without a sound, the Greeks vanished the way they had come. Although the cavalry tried to follow them through the city's fiery winding lanes, the Greeks were too quick for them, and the fire too fierce.

By noon the next day, two thirds of Sardis was ashes —ashes that smoldered for weeks. But the city that had been built so haphazardly in the first place was rebuilt with astonishing speed and in six months Sardis was its somewhat improved old self again, except for the temple of Cybele, which was left in ruins. This turned out to be a good thing for us. Although Lydians tend to be pro-Greek, they were in such a fury at the sacrilege shown to Cybele that the Lydian cavalry annihilated half the Greek forces on the road to Ephesus.

Nevertheless, the overall Greek strategy had been successful. They had challenged the Great King in the heart of his empire. They had burned the capital of Lydia. They had forced Artobazanes to lift the siege of Miletus in order to defend Lydia. Meanwhile, at sea, the combined fleets of Aristagoras and the Athenians proved to be invulnerable and, for a time, invincible.

Later that winter the Ionian cities were joined in their rebellion by the island of Cyprus, and Persia was now at war with a formidable new entity known as the Ionian Commonwealth.

4

I STAYED AT SARDIS FOR TWO YEARS. I did my work as a staff officer. I was sent on a number of expeditions upcountry. At one point we tried and failed to take back the northern city of Byzantium. I was at Sardis when I learned of Hystaspes' death. He had died while supervising the construction of Darius' tomb. I mourned him. He was the best of men.

At Sardis, I helped Mardonius celebrate, first, his victory in Cyprus, which he had regained for Persia; then, his marriage to Artazostra, the Great King's daughter. According to Lais, she was a pretty girl but stone-deaf from birth. Mardonius was to have four sons by her.

Shortly before I returned to Susa, Histiaeus went into rebellion against the Great King, and Lais decided that it was time to visit her family in Abdera. She always knew when to vanish, when to reappear. By then Lais had trouble remembering his name.

When I came home to Susa, I was surprised—I was still innocent in those days—to find that hardly anyone wanted to hear about the Ionian revolt. Although the burning of Sardis had been a shock, the court was confident that the Greeks would soon be punished. Meanwhile, everyone was far more intrigued by the latest pretender to the throne of Babylon. I have never known a time when there was not a pretender to that ancient throne. Even to this day, from time to time, some wild man will appear out of the Babylonian countryside and announce that he is the true heir to Nebuchadnezzar. This is always embarrassing for what is left of the old royal family, and annoying for the Great King. Despite their native indolence, Babylonians are subject to fits of violence, particularly the countryfolk when they drink too much palm wine.

"I'm being sent to put down the rebellion," said Xerxes. We were in the exercise ground where so much of our childhood had been spent. Nearby the next generation of Persian nobility was practicing archery. I remember thinking how old we both were now, and how relieved I was to be free of those Magian teachers.

"Have they much support?"

"No. The king's eye says it shouldn't take me more than a few days . . ." Xerxes frowned. I had never seen him so distracted. I soon found out the reason. "Mardonius has won a real victory, hasn't he?"

"Cyprus is ours again." I had not spent a life at court for nothing. I knew how to address a jealous prince. "But Mardonius was hardly alone. The invasion plan was Artaphrenes'. And then the admiral in charge . . ."

"Mardonius has got the credit. That's all that matters. And here I sit, doing nothing."

"You've married. That's something." Xerxes had recently married Amestris, the daughter of Otanes.

"That's nothing."

"Your father-in-law is the richest man in the world. That's something."

Ordinarily, Xerxes would have been amused. But he was not now. He was genuinely upset. "All of you are real soldiers."

"Some less than others," I said, wanting to make him laugh. But he did not hear me.

"I'm practically a eunuch," he said, "a harem fixture."

"You go to Babylon."

"Only because it's safe."

"You are the Great King's heir."

"No," said Xerxes, "I am not the heir."

I was too stunned to do more than gape.

"There has been a change," he said.

"Artobazanes?"

Xerxes nodded. "He's doing well in Caria. Or so they say. My father talks of him constantly."

"That is no sign."

"The Great King has said from the lion throne that the succession will not be determined until Athens has been destroyed."

"But suppose he dies first?"

"The Great King is all-powerful. He will die at a time of his own choosing." Only with me did Xerxes ever betray any bitterness toward his father. But then, in some ways, I was closer to him than any of his brothers. After all, I was not royal. I was no threat.

"What does Queen Atossa say?"

"What does she *not* say!" Xerxes managed a smile. "You've never seen such a parade of Magians and priests and witches as she has got, all marching through her apartments."

"Does Darius . . . march through her quarters?"

"No." The answer was short, but hardly conclusive. Since Atossa controlled much of the administration of the empire through the eunuchs of the harem, she was often able to influence Darius at a discreet distance.

"I shall go to her," I said.

"I'll be gone by the time you've talked to her. I shall be conquering Babylon." Xerxes tried but failed to joke. Suddenly he said, "Cyrus made *his* son king of Babel before he died."

I made no comment. I did not dare.

As we practiced with the javelin I told Xerxes about the siege of Miletus and the burning of Sardis. But he was more interested in Mardonius' affair with Artemisia.

"I envy him," said Xerxes—with sadness, not envy.

5

LAIS HAD NUMEROUS COMPLAINTS about Abdera, her sea journey, recent events at court. She had grown rather fat. "Thracian cooking! Everything is soaked in pig fat. He's well again, you know. My father, your grandfather. I'm sorry that you've never known him. We got on famously. I cured him, you know. But what a place! Our relatives are really more Thracian than Greek by now. I've actually seen cousins of mine wearing fox-skin caps!"

I was given not only a full description of my grandfather's household possessions at Abdera but a series of spirited portraits of a family I had yet to meet.

Characteristically, despite a separation of three years, Lais did not ask me once about myself. In fact, she has never shown the slightest interest in my affairs when we are alone together; yet when strangers are present—or when I am not present—she boasts constantly of my mystical powers and religious fervor. But were it not for me, Lais would have had no place at court. I must say that the fact that I have never interested Lais has never caused me pain. I understood her character too well. I also realized early on that whenever she put herself forward, I benefited as well. We were like a pair of accidental travelers made allies by a series of common dangers.

On my side, I always found Lais beguiling. She is easily the most plausible liar that I have ever known; and my life has been spent at courts and with Greeks.

I told Lais that I had requested an audience with Queen Atossa, but so far it had not been granted. She made a series of signs—no doubt to hasten the hour of my reception by the queen.

Lais then confirmed Xerxes' suspicions. Ever since Artobazanes proved to be an effective commander in the field, Darius had begun to speak of a possible change in the succession. The fact that Mardonius had conquered Cyprus also added to the glory of the family of Gobryas.

Meanwhile Queen Atossa had withdrawn into the inner chambers of the third house of the harem. Although no one knew what she was planning, Lais was optimistic. "Atossa will find a way to advance her son. She is simply cleverer than anyone else at court, including"—Lais dropped her voice dramatically as if we were being spied on, which we were not: we were not important enough— "Darius."

"But why doesn't he let Xerxes have the same chance as the others?"

"Because Darius is afraid of the combination of Atossa and Xerxes. Darius may rule in Persia, but Atossa governs. If Xerxes were to be at the head of a victorious army in the plains of . . . of Caria or some such place, and Atossa were at Susa, and the stars were in a certain conjunction . . ."

"Treason?"

"Why not? Such things have happened before. And Darius knows it. That's why he keeps Xerxes home. That's why he allows his other sons and nephews to win all sorts of victories. But Atossa will make the difference."

"You are sure?"

"I am sure. But it won't be easy. We must all help. You can do your part by taking your lawful place as chief Zoroastrian. Your uncle is a fool. You could replace him in a day."

Lais then outlined a strategy whereby I would become the leader of our order. I did not tell her that I would rather be bitten by one of Cybele's snakes. I was not meant to be a priest; yet at the same time I was not at all sure just where my future would lie. I had shown no real aptitude for war. I could always become a councilor of state or a court chamberlain; unfortunately, the eunuchs do that sort of thing better than we. At heart, I wanted only to serve my friend Xerxes—and see far-off places.

A week after the gloomy Xerxes had left for Babylon, I was granted an audience with Queen Atossa. As usual, the door to her apartments was guarded by imposing eunuchs, dressed like kings. I never saw her in those apartments that I did not remember myself as a terrified child, slithering across the red-and-black carpet. The rug was

now quite threadbare but Atossa never replaced anything
—or anyone—that she liked.

I found Atossa unchanged. But then, how can a white
enamel mask change? She was attended by a deaf-mute,
always a good sign. We would be able to talk freely.

I was allowed the privilege of the footstool.

Atossa came straight to the point. "I suspect Gobryas
of magic. I think Darius has been bewitched. I do what I
can, of course. But I cannot undo spells that I have no
knowledge of. So I appeal now to the Wise Lord."

"To me?"

"Yes, you. You're supposed to be in communication
with the one and only god—other than all the other gods
of earth and sky. Well, I want you to invoke the Wise
Lord. Xerxes must be Great King."

"I shall do what I can."

"That won't be good enough. I want you in authority. I
want you to become the chief Zoroastrian. That's why
you're here. Yes. *I'm* the one who ordered you home to
Susa. In the name of the Great King, of course."

"I didn't know."

"You weren't supposed to know. I have told no one.
Not even Lais—who did give me the idea, I'll admit.
She's talked of nothing else since I've known her. Anyway, I've instructed the Magians—yours as well as mine.
I mean ours. If you say the word, your uncle will step
aside. They're all afraid of you and it is even possible
that they might be just a bit afraid of me." Atossa's lips
had been painted a somewhat gaudy coral pink. Briefly, a
smile cracked the white enamel.

"And I'm afraid of the Great King."

"Darius likes you. He would have no objection if you
became chief Zoroastrian. We've already discussed it. Besides, it is not as if he were losing a great general." Atossa's cruelty was never entirely leashed.

"I do my duty . . ."

"And your duty is here at the court. As chief Zoroastrian you will have the Great King's ear. Since he pretends to follow Zoroaster, he will have to listen to you.
That means you'll be in a position to influence him against
the enemy."

"Gobryas."

"And Gobryas' grandson Artobazanes and Gobryas'
son Mardonius, the whole lot of them. Darius is bewitched and we must exorcise whatever demon controls

136

him." Atossa clenched and unclenched her hands. I noted that the statue of Anahita was heavily burdened with chains and odd devices. Plainly, the queen was laying vigorous siege to heaven. Now the Wise Lord himself was to be importuned.

I did not dare say no. If Atossa was a dangerous friend, she was a lethal enemy. I told her that I would go to my uncle. "I'm not sure what he'll say. He likes being chief . . ."

Atossa clapped her hands. A door opened and there was the chief Zoroastrian. He looked terrified, as well he ought. He bowed low to the queen, who stood, out of respect for the Wise Lord.

My uncle then began to chant one of Zoroaster's most famous hymns: " 'To what land shall I flee? Where bend my steps? I am thrust out from family and tribe . . .' "

Thus Zoroaster addressed the Wise Lord at the beginning of his mission. I allowed my uncle to continue well into the text despite the restlessness of Atossa, who preferred unequivocal statements from gods to questions from prophets.

Then I broke in with the exultant promise, the supreme coda, the words of the prophet himself: " 'Whoever is true to me, to him I promise through good mind, that which I myself do most desire. But oppression to him who seeks to oppress us. O Wise One, I strive to satisfy your wish through righteousness. Thus the decision of my will and of my mind.' "

I cannot think that my uncle took any of this very well. He was the prophet's son. I was the grandson. He came first; I came second. But only two men that ever walked this earth have heard the voice of the Wise Lord. The first was murdered at the altar in Bactra. I am the second. Will there ever be a third?

When I had completed the hymn, Atossa turned to my uncle. "You know what is expected of you?"

The chief Zoroastrian was nervous. "Yes. Yes. I go home to Bactra. I shall take charge of the fire altar there. I'll also be busy at work transcribing the true words of my father. On cowhide. The best cowhide. That's after the cow has been killed during a proper sacrifice, where the haoma is drunk *exactly* as Zoroaster told us it should be drunk, not a drop more, in that sunless place . . ."

"Good!" Atossa's voice arrested my uncle's tendency to babble. She told him that I was to be installed immediately. "Whatever ceremonies are necessary will take place at the fire altar here in Susa." Then the chief Zoroastrian was dismissed.

"We shall . . . surround the Great King," said Atossa.

But since the walls in Atossa's apartment always had listening ears, it was Darius who surrounded *us*. The day before I was to be invested as chief of the order, I was commanded to wait upon the Great King.

I was terrified. One always is. Was I about to be executed, maimed, imprisoned? Or hung about with golden chains of honor? The Achaemenid court has never been a place without surprises, usually unpleasant.

I put on priest's robes. That was Lais' idea. "Darius must respect Zoroaster, and his heir." But Lais was nervous, too.

Silently she cursed Atossa. But I could read her lips. "She is senile, arrogant, dangerous." Although the old queen was by no means senile, she had been careless. Our conversation had been reported to the Great King.

6

THE GREAT KING RECEIVED ME IN THE room where he worked. This chamber is still kept the way it was when he was alive. The room is square, with a high ceiling. The only furniture is a table of solid porphyry and, somewhat incongruously, a high wooden stool where Darius liked to perch when he was not walking about, dictating to the secretaries who squatted cross-legged beside the table. When he was not dictating, the clerks would read him reports from satraps, king's eyes, councilors of state, ambassadors. Those documents that only Darius himself could read were written in a special language with a simplified syntax. All in all, much art went into writing for his eyes. But as I have said, he was more at home with figures. He could add, subtract and even divide in his head without, noticeably, using his fingers.

I was announced by the chief chamberlain, a relic of Cyrus' time. As I did obeisance to the Great King the two secretaries slithered past me, quick as serpents. I was to be given something unique, a private audience. My heart beat so loudly in my ears that I barely heard Darius' command, "On your feet, Cyrus Spitama."

With a sense that I was fainting, I straightened up. Although my eyes were respectfully averted, I did note that Darius had aged considerably in the years that I had spent at Sardis. Since he had not bothered to have the hair of his head properly dressed that day, gray curls escaped from under the blue-and-white fillet that he wore, the only ensign of his rank. The gray beard was a tangle.

Darius stared at me a long moment. Inadvertently my right leg began to jerk. I hoped that my priestly robes disguised the outward sign of a most real inner terror.

"You served us well enough at Sardis." Darius was curt. Was this near-compliment preface to an ominous but?

"I serve in all ways the Great King, whose light—"

"Yes. Yes." Darius stopped my ceremonial response. He shoved to one side a pile of papyrus scrolls from the satrapy of Egypt. I recognized the hieroglyphs. Then Darius rummaged through a second pile of documents until he had found a rectangle of red silk on which a message had been painted in gold leaf, a luxurious if impractical form of letter writing.

I could not tell what the language was. Certainly it was neither Persian nor Greek. Darius enlightened me. "This comes from India. It is from the king of some country I've never heard of. He wants to trade with us. I have always wanted to go back to India. That's where our future is. In the east. I have always said so. Certainly there is nothing in the west worth having." Then, in the same tone of voice, he said, "You are not to be chief Zoroastrian. I have decided."

"Yes, lord of all the lands."

"I suspect that you will be relieved." Darius smiled, and suddenly I was almost at ease.

"It has ever been my wish to serve only the Great King."

"The two are not the same?"

"The two cannot help but coincide, Lord." Apparently this was not to be the day of my execution.

"Hystaspes would have disagreed with you." Then, to my surprise, Darius laughed like a highland warrior. In private, he never resorted to the refined cough of the court. "My father thought well of you. He wanted you to be chief Zoroastrian, as does, of course, the queen."

I grew tense again. Darius knew every word that had passed between Atossa and me. Idly the Great King picked at the gold letters on the red silk square. "But I have decided otherwise. You lack the vocation. That has always been as clear to me as it has been to the Wise Lord, who is the first of all the gods." Darius paused, as if expecting me to denounce him for blasphemy.

"I know, Lord, what has always been clear to you." This was the best I could do.

"You are tactful, which is good—unlike your grandfather. Cyrus would have cut off Zoroaster's head if he had ever spoken to him the way he used to speak to me. But I am . . . indulgent." Darius' warrior fingers played with the illuminated scrap of red silk. "In religious matters," he added. "In other matters . . ." He stopped. I could see that he was trying to make up his mind just how candid he could be with me.

I think that, finally, Darius was as straightforward with me as he could be with anyone. After all, the secret of complete power is complete secrecy. The monarch must be the sole knower of all things. He can share bits and pieces of knowledge with this one or that. But the entire terrain must be visible only to him. He alone is the golden eagle.

"I am not happy with the Greek war. Histiaeus thinks he can put a stop to it but I doubt if he can. I can see now that the war won't end until I've destroyed Athens and that will take a lot of time and a lot of money, and at the end I will have added nothing at all to the empire but some stony bits of the western continent where nothing grows except those filthy olives." Darius had the true Persian's dislike of the olive. Our western world is split between those who are nourished solely by the olive and those who have access to a variety of civilized oils.

"I had hoped that in my last years I would be able to move toward the east, where the sun rises. The symbol of the Wise Lord," he added, smiling at me. If Darius believed in anything other than his own destiny, I should have been surprised. "Well, the Greek wars won't take us more than a year or two and I believe that I am good for a year or two . . ."

"May the Great King live forever!" I gave the traditional cry.

"My sentiment." Darius was not at all ceremonious in private. In fact, I got the sense with him on those occa-

140

sions when only the two of us were together that we were rather like a pair of moneychangers or caravan merchants trying to figure out ways of fleecing the customers in the marketplace.

"You can do mathematics?"

"Yes, Lord."

"Are you able to learn languages quickly?"

"I think so, Lord. I've learned some Lydian and—"

"Forget Lydian. Cyrus Spitama, I need money. I need a great deal of money—"

"—for the Greek wars." I had done the unforgivable. Although I had not asked a direct question, I had interrupted him.

But Darius seemed more pleased than not to have a proper conversation with me. "For the Greek wars. For the work that I am doing at Persepolis. For the defense of the northern frontier. Of course, I could increase the tributes paid me by my loyal slaves, but with the Ionian cities in revolt and Caria confused and a new pretender in Babylon, this is not a good time to increase taxes. Yet I must have money." Darius stopped.

In a sense, I must have guessed all along why I had been summoned. "You want me to go to India, Lord."

"Yes."

"You want me to make trade alliances."

"Yes."

"You want me to analyze the nature of the Indian states."

"Yes."

"You would like to add all India to the Persian empire."

"Yes."

"Lord, I can think of no greater mission."

"Good." Darius picked up the red message. "These people want to trade with Persia."

"What have they to offer, Lord?"

"Iron." Darius gave me a great, mischievous smile. "I am told that this particular country is *made* of iron. But then, all India is full of iron, from what I hear, and whoever gets control of those mines can make his fortune!" Darius was like a young merchant contemplating a commercial coup.

"You want me to negotiate a treaty?"

"A thousand treaties! I shall want a full report on the finances of each of the countries you visit. I shall want to

141

know the state of the roads, the methods of taxation, and whether or not they use coinage or barter. Study how they supply and transport their armies. Find out what their crops are and how many harvests a year they get. Give particular attention to their gods. It has been my policy always to support those religions that are truly popular. Once you pretend to honor the local deity, the priesthood is immediately on your side. Once you have the priests, you don't need much of a garrison to keep order. This is vital to us. We Persians are few, and the world is vast. Like Cyrus and Cambyses, I govern the non-Persians through their priests. Now this is where *you* can be most useful to me." Darius became conspiratorial; he even lowered his voice. "I have heard reports that Zoroaster is highly regarded by certain Indians. So you will be not only my ambassador but a priest."

"As a priest, I shall be obliged to proclaim the uniqueness of the Wise Lord. I shall be obliged to attack the devils that the Indians worship."

"You will do no such thing." Darius was very hard. "You will be agreeable to *all* the priests. You will find points of similarity between their gods and ours. You are not to challenge them. One day I shall have to govern India. I shall need the priests. Therefore, you must . . . enchant them." That was an Atossa word.

I bowed low. "I shall obey you in all things, Lord."

With a loud noise Darius dropped his heavily ringed hand on the tabletop. The palace chamberlain promptly appeared in the doorway. He was accompanied by two men. One was an Indian eunuch; the other was the mariner Scylax, whom I had met at Halicarnassus. The Great King treated Scylax almost as an equal, and ignored the eunuch, who was shaking with fright.

Darius indicated the large leather purse that Scylax was carrying in one hand. "You've brought it. Good. I'll get mine."

Darius pushed aside a tapestry depicting Cambyses hunting deer. Curiously enough, I recall no tapestries of Darius in any of the palaces. But Cambyses was everywhere. As far as I know, there is only one tapestry of Cyrus at Susa; it is in the queen's hall—a crude piece of work which moths have not improved.

Behind the tapestry was a deep niche in which was set an ordinary wooden chest of the sort that merchants keep their money in. Darius lifted the lid and rummaged for a moment. Then he produced a small copper shield. Meanwhile, Scylax had removed a similar shield from the leather purse.

I had never before seen a proper traveler's map. In fact, the only map of any kind that I had seen was the somewhat fantastic one that covers an entire wall of the new palace at Babylon. In rare stones, the cities and ports of Babylonia, Asia Minor and Egypt are depicted as they were at the time of Nebuchadnezzar. Since the Babylonians are good mathematicians, the distances are supposed to be accurate.

Darius himself placed the two copper maps of India side by side on the table. Then he began to point out significant differences between his map and that of Scylax. "We are only agreed on the Indus River, which you mapped for me." Darius indicated the long line of the river that runs from the high mountains east of Bactria down to a complex delta that empties into what is called the Sea of India.

Scylax said that his map was the most recent. But he agreed that neither map could be trusted.

Suddenly Darius threw the red silk square onto the floor so that the Indian eunuch could read it. "Who is this message from?" he asked. "And where is it from?" He turned to Scylax. "How much of India did you actually see?"

"The river, Lord. Parts of the delta. The city of Taxila in the north."

"That's mine, isn't it?"

"Yes, Lord. The whole valley to the east of the Indus is now your twentieth satrapy. The border is about here." Scylax touched a spot on the map. "To the east is the land of the five rivers which the Indians call . . . what?" Scylax looked at the floor where the eunuch was busy reading the message.

"The Punjab, Lord Admiral."

"The Punjab. Then, in the north, there is the kingdom of Gandhara . . ."

"My kingdom."

"The king pays tribute to you, Lord," said Scylax tactfully. Then he traced the wriggling length of the Indus River from north to south. "Thirteen months it took me, Lord, from the high mountains to the delta. But at the end, all this was yours."

"Not to mention an annual tribute of three hundred

143

and fifty gold talents in the form of gold dust." Darius positively smacked his lips, a vulgarity denied the rest of us. "That is the largest annual tribute of any of my satrapies, including Egypt. So just think what the yield would be from all this!" The square hand brushed from left to right, from west to east, across the copper disk. Then Darius frowned. "But *what* is all this? My map shows two rivers and three cities whose names I can't read. And then . . . well, look at the shape! My India is like a round disk. Yours is a sort of peninsula. And what happens over here at the farthest edge? Is there a sea? Or do we fall off the end of the world?"

"There is another sea, Lord. There are also high mountains, jungles, and then a great empire, or so they claim."

"Cathay. Yes, I have heard the name. But *where* is it?"

"In the reign of Cyrus, Lord, there was once an embassy from Cathay. They came to us with silk and jade."

"I know. I know. I've seen the inventory. I want to trade with them. But it is hard to deal with a country whose whereabouts is unknown. Oh, Scylax, I dream of cows! I lust for cows!" Darius laughed.

Scylax smiled, though he did not dare laugh.

I was mystified. I had no idea what the reference to cows meant. Later, in India, I was to hear the phrase a thousand thousand times. Cows were the measure of wealth for those Aryan tribesmen who conquered Persia as they conquered Assyria and Greece and India. Although we no longer measure wealth in cows, the highly civilized Indian heirs of those long-dead cattle thieves still say "I dream of cows" when they mean that they want wealth. As a true Aryan chieftain, Darius never ceased to dream of cows—an expression as common to the Achaemenids and to the Indian Aryans as it is obscure to the rest of us.

"Well, Scylax, the time has come for us to acquire more cows. Apparently, we've been asked to pay a visit to the cattle pen. From . . . Where is that place?" Darius stared down at the eunuch.

"Magadha, Great King. The message is from its king, Bimbisara. He sends you greetings from his capital city at Rajagriha."

"What extraordinary names they have! Worse than the Greeks. Well, Scylax—Greek that you are—where is Magadha? It's not on my map."

Scylax pointed to a long river that ran from the northwest edge to the southeastern edge of the map. "That is the river Ganges, Lord. Here, to the south of the river, is the kingdom of Magadha. Rajagriha must be about here. None of it is properly marked."

"I shall want a perfect map of all India, Cyrus Spitama."

"Yes, Lord." I was excited at the thought of the adventure, and appalled at the vastness of India: thirteen months simply to go *down* a river!

"What else does this . . . Indian have to say?"

"He says that his grandfather exchanged ambassadors with the Great King Cyrus. He says that he himself is in close communication with the kingdom of Gandhara . . ."

"*My* kingdom."

"Yes, Great King."

"But this Bimb—whatever—does not acknowledge my sovereignty?"

"All the world does!" The eunuch was trembling uncontrollably.

"But *he* does not. That means we have work to do. He wants to trade with us?"

"Yes, Great King. He mentions iron. Teak. Cotton. Rubies. Monkeys."

"Everything that the heart desires!" Darius struck the map with his forefinger. The sound was like that of a miniature gong. Then he took the red silk from the eunuch and held it close to his face. In old age, Darius was extremely short-sighted. Carefully he detached one of the gold letters from the red silk. Then he put the fragment in his mouth and, like a jeweler, he bit the metal. "Gold," he said happily. "The best quality, too."

Darius spat the gold onto the floor, and gave the eunuch a playful kick. "You will prepare a message to this Sarabimba. Tell him the Great King, the lord of *all* the lands, the Achaemenid, and so on, looks with affection upon his slave and condescends to send him, as ambassador, one close to his bosom, Cyrus Spitama, grandson of Zoroaster, the Aryan prophet—emphasize Aryan, and the fact that we are all one race, separated only by geography. A separation that I personally find intolerable. No, don't put *that* in the message. We don't want to alarm him. Tell him that we will pay for iron in gold coins—if they use coinage—or in kind if they don't. Make the usual list of what our warehouses have to offer. You're an Indian, you know what they'll like. Where are you from?"

"Koshala, Great King. It is the most ancient and glorious of the Aryan kingdoms. It is north of the Ganges."

"Who is your ruler? I can't really call him king. There is only one king on this earth."

"If he still lives, Lord, it is Pasenadi, a holy and good man whose sister is the chief queen of Bimbisara of Magadha and the mother—"

"Spare me the details. But give them all to my ambassador." Darius smiled at me. Dreams of cows made him appear youthful. The straggling gray hair looked almost blond, and the blue eyes were bright. "You must prepare yourself, Cyrus Spitama. And you, down there, must teach him to speak whatever it is they speak in that part of the world. You will travel with my ambassador." Darius gave the eunuch a farewell kick. "Prepare a similar message to this ruler of yours. Introduce my ambassador, and so on."

When the eunuch was gone, Scylax and Darius began to plan the journey—*my* journey.

"You will take the post road to Bactra. That should be nice for you," said Darius to me. "You'll see your old home. I was there last year. It's been entirely rebuilt." He traced a line on the map. "Then you can go along here, by way of the Oxus River to the high mountains. Cross through this pass, which probably doesn't exist. They never do when you need them. Then you're in Gandhara, where you can travel luxuriously down the Indus River as far as . . . where?" Darius turned to Scylax.

"Taxila. From the Indus River it's three days' journey to the city where all the caravan trails converge."

"Trails? Are there no roads?"

"Properly speaking, no, Lord. But the country is flat and the trails are well defined. On the other hand, the jungles are dense. There are many wild beasts, bandits. We'll need a company of soldiers. There are also five rivers to cross before you get to the Yamuna River. Then boats or rafts will take us down into the Gangetic plain to where the sixteen kingdoms are."

"How do you know all this?" Darius was staring at Scylax with some wonder. "You've never been east of the Indus delta."

"I, too, dream of cows, Lord," said Scylax. "In your name, of course!"

Darius gave Scylax an affectionate hug of the sort that any of his sons or brothers would have offered at least an arm for. "You shall have your cows, Scylax. Look after the boy." I was treated offhandedly. "You can have a hundred troops, enough to protect the ambassador but not enough to alarm the cow herders. Also, the usual attendants, map makers, architects, and so on. The eunuch—what's his name?—will prepare suitable gifts for the two rulers. But nothing too rich. After all, as lord of all the lands, I own their lands by right of—of the Wise Lord," he added for my delectation.

Then Darius turned to me. I was startled to find that he was my height. I had always thought of him as a physical giant. The Great King looked me straight in the eyes, and I was totally unnerved. It is not allowed, I remember thinking, as those dark-blue eyes, with their slightly red lids, stared into my eyes. "You must not fail me, Cyrus Spitama. I give you a year—two years at most. In that time, I shall want to know all that I need to know in order to mount an invasion of India. I shall want to go as far as the edge of the world—or to Cathay, whichever comes first."

"To hear is to obey, Lord."

"I look upon India as my last gift to the clansmen. So you must be watchful, clever, inquisitive. You will preach the way of the Truth but you will not threaten those who follow the Lie."

Quite rightly, Darius feared the zeal of the true Zoroastrian. He was not about to alienate sixteen Indian kingdoms because of the religious zealotry of his ambassador.

"I shall do as the Achaemenid commands." To call the Great King by his true name is very nearly the equivalent of swearing an oath to the Wise Lord.

"Good." Darius gave me his hand, which I kissed.

Thus was I ennobled. I could dine at his table, if invited. As it turned out, I was never invited to do so, but my rank was now secure. I was a Persian noble, and if I survived my embassy, my fortune was made.

BOOK FOUR

India

1

FROM SUSA, THE EMBASSY TO THE SIX-
teen kingdoms of India—as we were referred to, rather
sneeringly, by the second room of the chancellery—made
its way to the Tigris River. Then, on flat-bottomed boats,
we descended the river to the delta. Here we found
Scylax, and two triremes that had survived the disastrous
siege of Naxos. I suppose I should have taken that as an
omen. But I was in much too good a humor.

Due to the constant siltage from the rivers, there has
never been a proper port at the delta where the Tigris and
Euphrates come together in a sort of shallow sour lake.
Persians, Babylonians, Assyrians have all tried to establish a port at this most strategic juncture, but the mud that
never ceases to flow from the top of the world to the bottom eventually buries each attempt. In the reign of Darius
there was a makeshift port at the edge of a salt marsh
which could be crossed only if one kept to a series of rafts
that extended for nearly a mile over the mud and quick-
sand. I once saw a camel and its driver vanish beneath
the wet sands in less time than it took for the driver to cry
out.

Scylax had intended to use the ships for a circumnavi-
gation of Africa. But India now took precedence and I
don't think that he was too displeased, although it was
the dream of his life to go all around Africa, something
no man has ever done or is likely to do despite the claims
of the Phoenicians. To hear them tell it, they have charted
every foot of the ocean that girdles the world.

Each trireme needed a hundred and twenty rowers as
well as some thirty other sailors, carpenters, cooks. Since
these ships are made for war and not trade, there is not
much space for travelers as opposed to soldiers. In addition to one hundred troops, I was accompanied by a staff
of twelve men reputed to be experts on India, as well as
by a valuable gift from Queen Atossa—an Indian slave
named Caraka: "He will suit our purposes," she said; and

no more. We were also laden with gifts for the two kings, food for ourselves, and eight horses with grooms. The ships were seriously overcrowded.

To my annoyance, it took Scylax the better part of a week to get us all aboard. But he was right: on long voyages, the initial post assigned each man is all-important. If there is any doubt as to who does what work and where, fights break out and discipline deteriorates. Fortunately, since we were to hug the Persian coastline as far as the Indus River, each night the sailors would pull the ships up on shore and everyone was able to sleep comfortably beneath the stars. Although I did my best to play the part of wise commander, in the most graceful and to me agreeable way, Scylax took command in my name.

I shall never forget the excitement of our departure. At sunrise when the west wind started, Scylax ordered each ship to raise its mast. Then the rowers set to work and for the first time I heard the rhythmic sound of rowers as they chant to the steady beat of the flute player. When this chant coincides with that of a man's inner pulsing, it is possible to become a part of the ship, sea, sky, as in the act of love.

Free of the land, the square sails were hoisted, and as they collected wind the ships tacked this way and that, and the rowers rested. To our left, the desert sparkled in the sun while the hot west wind smelled of sea, of salt and decayed fish. All along this part of the coast the natives have built crude salt pans. Once the sun has burned away the water, the natives collect the residue of pure salt for sale to caravans. They also preserve fish on the spot. These odd people live in curious tents, whose frames are made from the skeletons of whales.

We had not been under sail for an hour when Caraka came to me, ostensibly for my daily lesson in the Indian language; actually, he had other matters on his mind. "Lord Ambassador," he said, and I found it most satisfying to be so addressed even though my new dignity was nothing more than Darius' premonitory shadow in India.

"I've been investigating the ship." Caraka lowered his voice, as if fearful that Scylax might overhear him. But the admiral was in the forward part of the ship, talking to the chief mate.

"A fine ship," I said, rather as if I had built it. From the beginning, I loved the sea; and if I regret anything now, it is the fact that I shall never again hear the chant of the rowers, feel the salt spray in my face, watch the sun rise or set over the ever-changing unchanging curve of the sea.

"Yes, Lord. But the hull is full of *nails!*"

I was startled. "How else do you hold together a ship?" I asked, not quite sure just how a ship is made. Except for a brief visit to Halicarnassus, I had never really observed the workings of a seaport.

"But the nails are *metal,* Lord." Caraka was shaking with fright.

"But wood spikes are not seaworthy." I sounded knowledgeable. Actually, for all I knew, wood spikes were indeed superior to metal nails. As I spoke, I was careful to stand with legs wide apart, in imitation of experienced seamen.

"Lord, I have made this journey before. But I've only traveled in Indian ships, and we use no nails. We don't dare. It's fatal."

"Why?"

"*Magnetic* rocks." The round black face looked up at me with true terror. Caraka had the snubbed nose and broad lips of the original Indian stock, sometimes known as Nagas, sometimes known as Dravidians. These dark people still dominate the south of India, and their language and customs are quite unlike those of the tall, fair-skinned Aryan tribesmen who overthrew their northern kingdoms and republics so long ago.

"What on earth is a magnetic rock?" I asked, genuinely curious if not alarmed.

"There!" Caraka gestured toward the barren, wind-smoothed hills of the coast. "Those hills are made of rocks that contain the power to attract metal. If a ship gets too close, nails fly from ship to rocks and the timbers will fall apart and we shall drown."

Since I saw no reason to disbelieve him, I sent for Scylax and asked if there was any danger. Scylax was soothing. "There *are* certain rocks that do attract metal, but if the metal has first been covered with pitch, then the magnetic powers are nullified. Since all our nails have been carefully shielded, we've nothing to fear. After all, this is my third trip along the coast and I promise you that we'll arrive in India with every single nail in place."

Later I asked Scylax if what Caraka had said was true. Scylax shrugged. "Who knows? Perhaps it's true of certain rocks on certain shores, but it's not true on this coast. I know."

"Then why have you covered the nails with pitch?"

"I haven't. But I always tell the Indians that I have. Otherwise, they'll abandon ship. I've noticed one odd thing, though. No one has ever looked to see if the nails are really covered or not."

To this day, I am curious to know if such magnetic rocks exist. Certainly I never met a single Indian mariner who was not convinced that if so much as a single bit of metal was used in the construction of a ship, it would be extracted by a demonic force and the ship would sink. Indians hold their ships together with rope.

"Not the worst method of shipbuilding," Scylax conceded. "No matter how high the sea or strong the wind, you can't sink because the water just goes through and around the planks."

It is some nine hundred miles from the delta of the Tigris and Euphrates rivers to the delta of the Indus. The strip of desert between the sea and the highlands of Persia must be the bleakest on earth. Since there is little fresh water, the coast barely supports a handful of fishermen, salt makers, pearl divers, pirates.

The third day out, at sundown, just back of a group of coral islands, I saw the fire altar at Bactra, saw my grandfather, saw the Turanians attack, saw the slaughter. Although this magical apparition or mirage lasted only a minute or two, I was transfixed by what I took to be a message from Zoroaster. He himself was reminding me that all men must follow the Truth, and I felt guilty because I had set out on my journey to follow not in the way of Truth, but in the way of the golden eagle of the Achaemenid. Later, in India, I was to feel even more disloyal to my grandfather. Although I never lost my faith in Zoroaster's teaching, the wise men of India did make me uncomfortably aware that there are as many theories of creation as there are gods in Babylon, and of these theories there are a number that I find altogether fascinating —if not true or True.

Democritus wants to know which theory was the oddest. I can answer that one. That there never was a creation, that we do not exist, that this is a dream. Who is the dreamer? The one who wakes up—and remembers.

During the weeks that it took us to reach the Indus River we were either becalmed, and obliged to resort to our rowers, who grew weaker and weaker in the blazing sun, or we were hurled to the northeast by the winds. Under full sail our lives were always at risk, since we were never so far from the spiky coral shore that a sudden gust of wind might have wrecked us. But Scylax was a master mariner who had never lost a ship. Or so he said, to my great unease. Those who have not undergone minor disasters are usually being held in reserve for something major.

Nevertheless, I was able to use those weeks at sea to good advantage. In my youth I was quick to learn new things, and Caraka was an excellent teacher. By the time the blue-black mud of the Indus delta came into view, I had mastered the fundamentals of the Indian language, or so I thought. As it turned out, Caraka had taught me a Dravidian dialect that is almost as unintelligible as Persian to the Aryans of the sixteen kingdoms.

Fortunately, Caraka knew enough Aryan words to help me begin to comprehend not only a new language but a new world, for it is the language of a people that tells us most about what gods they worship and what sort of men they are or would like to be. Although the language of the Indo-Aryan is not at all like what the Dravidians speak, it does resemble Persian, which proves the ancient theory that once upon a time we were all members of the same northern tribe and shared—until Zoroaster—the same gods. Now the Aryan gods have become our devils.

Scylax told me a good deal about his first voyage down the Indus. "In the beginning, Darius wanted all of India. He still does, of course—though, between us, he's much too old for a long campaign. He should've gone east right after I secured the Indus valley for him."

"But he couldn't. There was a rebellion in Babylon. There was—"

"There is always something else to be done. But if you want the world, you must forget insignificant places—like Babylon."

I laughed. It is always a relief not to be at court. Like Scylax, I wore nothing more than a breechclout and an Indian cotton shawl to shield my body from the sun. We looked no different from the rowers. Although Scylax must have been over fifty years old at the time, he had the hard wiry body of a young man. Salt preserves men as well as fish. Sailors always seem younger than they are.

"Babylon is the greatest city in the world," I said.

154

Scylax disagreed. "Once upon a time, maybe. But the cities of India are far richer, grander."

"Have you actually seen any of them?"

"Only Taxila. And Taxila is as large as Sardis, and much richer. But the Indians will tell you that Taxila is nothing more than a frontier town."

"Then why has Darius waited so long?"

Scylax shrugged. "Like the pharaohs and their tombs, I suppose. He thinks that once India is his, he'll die because then there'd be nothing left in the world to conquer."

"Cathay?"

"Is that really a part of the world?" For a professional mariner, Scylax was sometimes unadventurous. Yet to his credit, he was the first to map out, in a systematic way, the ocean of the Indians as far as the island of Ceylon. I say first but that is not quite true. Some years later, when I presented the Great King with a tolerably accurate map of India, he showed me a similar map that had recently been found in the archives of the temple of Bel-Marduk at Babylon. Apparently the Babylonians and the Indians had been in regular correspondence long before Darius and Scylax. In this old world, there is nothing new but ourselves.

Through the wide delta of the Indus, all sorts of streams and tributaries crisscross a considerable area of land. Some of the rich black earth is planted with rice, and some of it is brackish swampland suitable only for waterfowl like the Indian duck, a superb dish if cooked long enough. Here and there, groves of willow trees make beautiful shapes against the leaden sky: the annual rains were a month late that year and the Indians talked of nothing else. Without the rains, half the country dies. That year they need not have worried. The very day that we disembarked upriver at the port of Patalene, the rains arrived in torrents and we were not to be entirely dry again for the next three months. My first impression of India was water. The Greek Thales' theory of creation has its attractions for those who have endured the Indian monsoons.

During the journey upriver to Patalene, Scylax showed me the sights. "Both sides of the river are Persian," he said, with some satisfaction.

"Thanks to you." I was polite.

"Yes," he said, not at all vaingloriously. "Thirteen

months it took me. Fortunately, the people hereabouts prefer an overlord a thousand miles away to one close at hand. They would rather be ruled by the Achaemenid at Susa than by a local king."

"But there is a satrap."

Scylax nodded, and frowned. "I picked the first one myself. He was an Aryan, from the Punjab. Then he died and now we've got his son on our hands."

"Is he loyal?"

"I doubt it. But at least he is always on time with the annual tribute. You've never seen so much gold dust as there is in this part of the world."

From nowhere, a school of dolphins made gleaming arcs all about us. One even leapt across the ship's bow. As the dolphin hung for an instant in the torpid air, he gave us a most humorous look.

"That's good luck," said Scylax.

"*Fresh*-water dolphins?" I had never known that such creatures existed.

"Yes. But only in Indian rivers, as far as I know," he added. Scylax was a dedicated explorer who took nothing on faith. He was always skeptical of hearsay. If he had not seen something himself, he did not report as a fact its existence—unlike those Dorian Greeks who write what they call histories.

We disembarked at Patalene, a large but undistinguished port city. The air was stifling with all the rain that had yet to be released from the oppressively low sky.

I should note here that there are three seasons in India. From early spring to the beginning of summer the sun shines relentlessly, and were it not for the great rivers and the elaborate systems of irrigation, the earth would soon turn to dust and the people die. Then, as summer starts, the monsoon winds blow and there is rain for a third of the year, causing the rivers to flood. This season is followed by the altogether too short winter. One perfect cool day follows another. The skies are a vivid blue, and flowers grow in such profusion that the rose gardens at Ecbatana seem barren by comparison.

Just as I set foot on the dock at Patalene, a huge gust of wind caused our trireme to smash hard against the wharf, and we lost two horses to the river. Then the sky broke in half and rain fell in hot sheets. Completely drenched, we were welcomed by the king's eye who told us, "The satrap is at Taxila. He sends his apologies."

156

We were then escorted to government house, a ramshackle wooden affair with a most imperfect roof. Never before in my life had I been both wet and hot, a disagreeable condition characteristic of the rainy season in that part of the world.

The next day Scylax and I parted. He continued upriver to Taxila, while I began my journey overland to the kingdoms of Koshala and Magadha. I was eager to be on my way; happy to be on my own. I was fearless. I was stupid. I was young. Democritus thinks that I should reverse stupid and young. The first being the cause of the second. But I would not be so impolite as to make such a link. In any event, the king's eye arranged for camels, provisions, guides; and Caraka knew, more or less, the route.

We started out in a northeasterly direction toward Mathura, a city located on the Yamuna River. A hundred miles east of the Yamuna is the Ganges. From north to south, the two rivers run side by side until they arrive at the center of what is known as the Gangetic plain. Then the Ganges makes an abrupt bend to the east, and it is along that west-to-east branch of the river that the central kingdoms and republics and important cities of modern India are located.

Feeling not unlike the Great King, I set forth in a driving rain with Caraka beside me. My entire retinue numbered three hundred men, five concubines and no eunuchs. At Susa, Caraka had warned me that the Indians have such a strong dislike of castration that even animals are not tampered with. Because of this eccentricity, Indian harems are guarded by very old men and women. Although this sounds a bad arrangement, vigorous old people of either sex tend to be not only vigilant but uncorruptible. After all, they have no future to plan for, unlike our ambitious young eunuchs.

I rode horseback, as did Caraka and my personal guards. Everyone else was either mounted on camels or walked along the dirt trail that had been turned by the rains into a sort of trough of thick yellow mud. We traveled slowly, weapons at the ready. But although India is plagued with bands of thieves, they tend to stay home during the monsoon season. In fact, only an ignorant and zealous ambassador would have attempted a thousand-mile journey overland in such weather.

We were stopped by armed troops whenever we came

157

to a frontier, which was at least once a day. Not only are there numerous principalities in that part of India but each principality is subdivided into a number of semi-autonomous states whose chief revenues come from the taxing of caravans. As the Great King's ambassador, I was exempt from such taxes. But, in practice, I made it a point always to pay something. As a result, we were often granted an honor guard, which would accompany us to the next frontier. Presumably the thieves were intimidated by these escorts.

Only a strong king can make the countryside safe for travelers and at that time there was only one strong king in all of India. This was Bimbisara, to whose court at Magadha I had been accredited. Although Pasenadi of Koshala governed a larger, older and richer kingdom than Magadha, he himself was a weak ruler, and Koshala was a dangerous place for travelers.

We rode through jungles where bright parrots screamed, and maneless lions fled at our approach. Once I looked up and saw a tiger crouched on the branch of a tree. As I stared into the bright sun-yellow eyes, he stared into mine. I was terrified. He was, too, and vanished into the green wet darkness like a mirage or waking-dream.

The most dangerous of all Indian animals are the wild dogs. They travel in packs. They are mute. They are irresistible. Even those animals that are swifter than the dogs fall victim to them in the end for the pack is willing, day after day, to trail a deer or a tiger or even a lion until it grows weary and falters, and then, in absolute silence, the dogs attack.

Outside the deserted city of Gandhai, I noticed a series of small burrows arranged in a neat semicircle to one side of the muddy trail. When I asked Caraka what they were, he said, "Each dog digs himself a hole. Then he backs into it and sleeps. Or keeps watch. See? The shining eyes." Through the driving rain, I could make out the bright eyes of the wild dogs. They watched our every move.

That evening, somewhat abruptly, our escort left us at the gates of Gandhai. "They think," said Caraka, "that the city's haunted."

"Is it?" I asked.

"If it is," he said with a smile, "the ghosts are of my people. So we're safe."

We rode down a wide central avenue to the main square of a city that had been built by the original Indians thousands of years before the arrival of the Aryans. The city is very like Babylon, with houses of burnt brick and straight main avenues. To the west of the city are the ruins of a citadel, which the Aryans tore down. Then, for some reason, they drove away the native population and the city has been empty ever since.

"The people who built this city were called Harappas. I suppose that those who were not killed went south." Caraka sounded bitter.

"But that was so long ago."

"Thirty-five generations is not long for us," he said.

"You sound like a Babylonian," I said, which he took as a compliment.

Shortly before the sun set, we moved into a large building that had once been a granary. Although the ancient tile roof was in better condition than the new roof of government house at Patalene, the beams of the ceiling sagged ominously. After we had driven away a colony of angry monkeys, I ordered my tent to be set up at one end of the hall. Then fires were lit, and the evening meal was prepared.

At that time Caraka was introducing me to Indian food —a slow process, since I am a cautious eater. Although my first experience with a mango was disagreeable, the pineapple was an immediate delight. I also liked the Indian fowl, a white-fleshed bird so tame that Indians keep them not only for their eggs and flesh but for the feathers, which are used in cushions. These birds are closely related to what the Greeks call the Persian fowl, a current novelty here at Athens.

As a rule, I dined alone with Caraka. For one thing, the Persian officers preferred their own mess; for another, I was occupying the place, as it were, of the Great King. So I was hedged around with some of his dignity.

"You see what a high culture we had." Caraka indicated the enormous hall. All that I could think of were those weakened beams. "Most impressive," I agreed.

"We built this city a thousand years before the Aryans came." Caraka sounded as if he himself had been the architect. "We were builders, traders, makers of things. They were tent dwellers, cattle herders, nomads—destroyers."

Whenever I asked Caraka—or anyone else—to tell me just who and what the Harappas were, I got no coherent answer. Although their princes and merchants used to roll

159

cylindrical seals on wet clay in order to make what are often quite beautiful picture-writings, no one has ever been able to read their texts.

"They worshipped the mother of all the gods," said Caraka somewhat vaguely. "And the horned god."

But I never learned much more than that from him. Over the years I heard a bit more about such Harappa gods as Naga the dragon, Nandi the bull, Honuman the monkey, as well as various animal and tree gods. Apparently the snake god is the most powerful, while their most ominous manlike deity has a snake coming out of each shoulder like Ahriman.

Without much help from Caraka, I soon learned to speak the proper Indo-Aryan of the rulers. I was startled to discover that both Persians and Indo-Aryans use the same term for that common Aryan homeland, from which also came the Dorian and Achaean Greeks. This homeland is somewhere at the north of the world, which is why the north star is sacred to all Aryans. I must say that I've always found it hard to believe that we are so closely related to those blond, fierce, cattle-keeping tribes who, to this day, descend upon the small dark peoples of the south in order to sack and burn their cities—as the Turanians did Bactra.

A thousand years ago, for reasons long since forgotten, certain Aryan tribesmen chose not to destroy but to settle the southern cities. When this happened in Media and Attica and Magadha, the Aryan tribesmen became civilized by their slaves. Also, despite every sort of taboo, they intermarried. When this happens, the wildest savage becomes like the civilized people that he has conquered. One can see this happening even now when Persia's borders are constantly harassed by those wild folk from the steppes who are today what we once were and would like to be what we are now—civilized.

Incidentally, Cyrus was very much aware of the danger of his Persian highlanders becoming like the luxurious black-haired people that they had conquered. To guard against this, Cyrus insisted upon a strenuous military education for all young Persians. We were never to forget our Aryan heritage. But when Xerxes came to the melancholy conclusion that the Persians are now no different from the people they govern, he abandoned much of Cyrus' educational system. I told him that I thought he was wrong. But he was the Achaemenid.

160

Although the Aryans were established in northern India long before Cyrus, it is my belief that the ancestors of both the Medes and the Persians arrived at what is now Persia at about the same time. But while the Aryan Persians settled the highlands, the Aryan Medes appropriated the Assyrian and Elamite civilizations. Eventually the Medes were so entirely absorbed by the dark ancient races whom they had conquered that by the time of Cyrus, the Aryan king of Media might just as well have been an Assyrian or Elamite king. Due to an accident of geography, the Persian clans were able to maintain their fierce Aryan spirit until Cyrus made himself universal monarch, as they say in India.

On the other hand, unlike the Medes, the Indo-Aryans have managed for close to forty generations to keep themselves unabsorbed by the Nagas or Dravidians or Harappas. They pride themselves on their fair skin, straight noses, pale eyes. Also, most shrewdly, they have divided themselves into four classes. First, the priests, whom they call Brahmans—creatures very like our own Magians; second, the warriors; third, the merchants; fourth, the farmers or artisans. Then there are the original peoples of this land. They are dark, sullen, overwhelmed —like Caraka. Millions of them still live in the north, reluctantly serving their foreign masters.

In theory, the four Indo-Aryan classes may not intermarry with one another, while intermarriage with the original folk is absolutely forbidden. Nevertheless, in the millennium that has passed since the Aryans arrived in India, they have become considerably darker of skin and eyes than their Persian cousins. Yet Indo-Aryans will tell you, quite seriously, that this darkness is due to the fierce sun of the dry season. I always agree.

Just as I was about to withdraw to my tent for the night, a tall naked man appeared in the doorway of the granary. For a moment he stood, blinking in the light. The hair on his head hung almost to his ankles. His fingernails and toenails were as long and as curving as parrots' beaks; presumably, at a certain length, they broke off. He carried a broom. Once the man's eyes were accustomed to the light he moved slowly toward me, sweeping the floor in front of him.

Those of my attendants who were still awake stared at him as dumbly as I. Finally one of the guards drew his sword, but I motioned for him to let the man pass.

"What on earth is it?" I asked Caraka.

"Some sort of holy man. He could be a Jain. Or he could be mad. Or both."

The man stopped in front of me and raised his broom, as if in salute. Then he said something that I did not understand, but Caraka did. "He's mad," said Caraka. "*And* he's a Jain. That's one of our most ancient sects."

"Are all Jains mad?"

"Quite the contrary. But this one says that *he* is the maker of the river crossing, and he's not. He can't be. There have only been twenty-three crossing-makers since the beginning of time."

None of this made the slightest sense to me. "What is a crossing-maker?" I asked. "And why is this man naked? And what is that broom for?"

Without permission, the man carefully swept a place for himself on the ground at my feet. Then he sat crossed-legged; and murmured prayers.

Caraka was so embarrassed by his countryman that at first he refused to tell me anything until I told him that the Great King was particularly interested in all the religions of India, which was true. If Darius was obliged to walk about naked with a broom in order to gain India, he would.

"A crossing-maker is a most holy man. The last one occurred about two hundred years ago. I have heard that a new one has appeared on earth, but I'm quite sure that this naked man isn't the crossing-maker. For one thing, only extremists go about naked—or sky-clad, as the Jains say."

"The broom?"

"To sweep away insects. A Jain must kill no living creature. So they often wear masks in order to keep from inhaling insects. They refuse to be farmers because insects are killed when the land is turned. They can't eat honey, for that would starve the bees. They can't—"

"What *can* they do?"

"They are excellent businessmen." Caraka smiled. "My father was a Jain. But I'm not. The cult is very old . . . pre-Aryan, in fact. The Jains have never accepted the Aryan gods. They do not believe in Varuna, Mithra, Brahma . . ."

"Because they are devils." I then quoted Zoroaster, briefly.

"They may be devils to Zoroaster, but they are true

162

gods to the Aryans. To us, they are nothing at all. We are very different. Aryans believe in a life after death. A heaven for the good. A hell for the bad. We don't. We believe in the passage of souls from one person to another or to a plant or to a rock or to a tree or to an animal. We think that the highest state is nirvana. That is, to be blown out, like a candle. To stop the long chain of being. To exist, finally, at the ceiling of the universe—perfect and still and complete. But to achieve this state one must, as the Jains would say, cross the river. Cease to want the things of this earth. Obey the eternal laws."

For years now I have tried to discover if Pythagoras had ever had any contact with the Jains. I have found no evidence that he did. If he was never told about reincarnation, and if the idea of the transmigration of souls occurred to him all by itself, then there is a possibility that this pre-Aryan notion may be true.

Personally, I find the thought appalling. It is quite enough to be born once and to die once. After death, Zoroaster tells us, each of us will be judged. The good will exist in paradise; the wicked in hell. Eventually, when the Truth has eliminated the Lie, all will be transmuted into Truth. This seems to me to be not only a rational but a highly useful religion. That is why I cannot imagine anything more horrifying than hopping about from body to body, or from snake to wasp to tree. Of course, one is not supposed to remember—as Pythagoras could—earlier incarnations. But that is not really the point. Personally, I am all for nirvana—a word hard to translate. Nirvana is something like the blowing out of a flame, but there are other aspects to the word that are not only impossible to translate but difficult for a nonbeliever like myself to understand.

"How was the earth created?" I asked the usual first question.

"We do not know, and we do not care." Caraka spoke for the holy man, who was still muttering prayers. "Of course, the Aryans say that once upon a time, at the beginning, there were twins—a man and a woman."

"Yama and Yima?" I was startled: these twins were also acknowledged by Zoroaster and they are still worshiped by the country people.

Caraka nodded. "They are the same. Yama wanted a child. But Yima feared incest. Finally she convinced the man that they must mate, and that is how the human race began. But then, who made the twins? The Aryans speak of an egg that hatched the god Brahma. Good. But who laid the egg? We don't know and we don't care. We are like the six blind men who tried to define an elephant. One touched an ear and said, this is not a beast but a leathery leaf. Another felt the trunk and said, this is a snake. And so on. What matters is what is and how what is ultimately transcends itself when one no longer wants those things that make life not only miserable but unholy."

Needless to say, Caraka did not make a speech at all like the one that I have just given. I am trying to distill in a short space a quantity of information that I was to acquire over a number of years.

But I do have a vivid memory of that evening in the granary of the old Harappan city. For one thing, the naked Jain suddenly began to speak, and thanks to Caraka for having taught me the wrong language, I was able to understand a speech that not only astonished me at the time but still reverberates in my memory. "When the ninth before the last of the river-crossers was born, he had a brother who was as evil as he was good. Serpents sprang from the shoulders of the dark brother, and he committed every crime. Just as one brother was entirely good, the other was entirely evil. And so they continued until, at last, the light absorbed the dark and the light prevailed. Thus it will be when the last river-crosser has brought us from the dark bank of the river to the sunlit side."

I did my best to question the holy man. But he could not or would not reason with me. He simply repeated stories, sang songs, prayed. Caraka was not much help either. But I was now eager to find the answer to a question whose solution must exist somewhere on earth.

Was Zoroaster simply revealing the religion that was ours *before* the Aryans conquered Media and Persia? Certainly Zoroaster was not Aryan. As I have said before, I believe that the Spitama family is Chaldean. But that race is now so intermingled with other races that our original religion is quite forgotten or confused. Nevertheless, *if* Zoroaster's so-called reforms were nothing more than a reassertion of the original true religion of the human race, then that would explain the ferocity with which Zoroaster attacked the gods that the Aryans had brought with them from the north.

"They are not gods, they are devils," he used to say.

And the fact that so many of the common people accepted his message means that, secretly, the original divine vision had never been extinguished in their souls. This would also explain why the Achaemenids have never taken seriously Zoroaster's teachings. Except for Hystaspes, they only pretend to honor my grandfather because, as Aryan chieftains, they are still loyal to those tribal gods who gave them all the world to the south of the steppes.

I must say that my real religious education began in Gandhai. As the rain clattered on the tile roof, the naked holy man told us, with all sorts of rhetorical flourishes, that mind is in all things, even rocks.

Incidentally, the word that he used for mind is almost identical with the Greek word that Anaxagoras is given credit for coining. He also told us that nothing is true except from a single point of view. From another point of view, the same thing will appear to be quite different; hence, the story of the blind men and the elephant. Yet there is an absolute truth which can be known only to a river-crosser or redeemer. Unfortunately, our holy man was a bit vague as to just how one gets to be a redeemer. He was one, he told us, because he had fulfilled the five vows, which are: don't kill, lie, steal, be unchaste, seek out pleasure.

This last presented some difficulty, as I remarked to Caraka the next day when we were again on the road. "Suppose that one's pleasure is to walk around naked lecturing Persian ambassadors? That would be breaking the fifth vow, wouldn't it?"

"But suppose he hates lecturing Persian ambassadors?"

"No. He enjoyed himself enormously. I feel that he's not a true river-crosser."

"Or even a Jain." Caraka had been disconcerted by the whole adventure. In some way he seemed to feel that I had been exposed to an aspect of the Dravidian culture that he was not entirely easy with. Although he plainly detested the Aryan conquerors, he had lived all his life amongst them both in India and in Persia. As a result, he was neither one thing nor another. A state in which I have often found myself. After all, I am half-Persian or Chaldean and half-Ionian Greek. I serve the Aryan Great King, yet I am Zoroaster's grandson. I reject the Aryan gods but not their kings. I believe in the way of the Truth but do not know, truly, where it is to be found.

2

SOME FOUR HUNDRED MILES EAST OF the Indus River is the Yamuna River, and the rich city of Mathura. Here we were received by the governor, a small fat man with a violet-and-yellow chin beard. Whereas our barbers try to re-create youthful tints for aging men, the Indian barber is noted for his fantasy. A beard in four colors is considered highly desirable. As a result, there is no sight quite so strange as a gathering of Indian courtiers, each with his rainbow beard, his perilously thick-soled white leather shoes, his bright parasol.

Although the governor had been appointed by King Pasenadi of Koshala, Caraka assured me that Mathura was practically independent, like most of the cities of Koshala. "No one fears Pasenadi. His kingdom is breaking up. And he does not care."

"What does he care about?"

"Eel-wrigglers and hair splitters."

"What are they?"

"Wanderers. Wise men, or so they say." As you can see, the India of fifty years ago was very like the Athens of today where such eel-wrigglers and hair-splitters as Protagoras and Socrates hold forth, and nothing is true or false.

In my old age, I am at last beginning to understand what our world has been passing through. For some time, the original populations of Greece and Persia and India have been trying to overthrow the gods—or devils—of the Aryans. In every country Zeus-Varuna-Brahma is being denied. Since the Athenian mob is still Aryan in its superstitions, few dare question openly the gods of the state. But, privately, they are either turning to pre-Aryan mystery cults or to such radical prophets as Pythagoras—or to atheism. Things are more open in India. On every side, the Aryan gods are being challenged. Such ancient beliefs as the transmigration of souls are once again popular, and the countryside is filled with holy men

166

and ascetics who have exchanged the Aryan gods for the old beliefs. Even Aryan kings have been known to give up their thrones in order to live in jungles, where they meditate and mortify the flesh.

I give full credit to Zoroaster for showing mankind not only the oneness of deity but that simultaneous duality which is a necessary condition of true deity. Truth cannot be true without the Lie, and the Lie cannot be refuted without the True. In consequence, each human life is a battleground between the two.

Democritus sees a contradiction where I see perfect light. But he spends his days with sophists.

At Mathura we were housed in a small, comfortable wooden house, rather like a miniature version of the Median palace at Ecbatana. Unfortunately, in the monsoon season the odor of wet wood is curiously oppressive, and no matter how much incense is burned, the smell of rot persists in every room.

We stayed two weeks at Mathura. During this time, messengers arrived from the kings of Koshala and Magadha. Each wanted me to visit his kingdom first. As we were already in Koshala, Caraka thought that I should present myself to Pasenadi. But since it was Bimbisara who had written Darius, I felt that I was obliged to do him the honor of waiting upon him at Rajagriha. Besides, Bimbisara owned the iron mines that so intrigued Darius.

I sent a messenger up to Susa, reporting on my embassy thus far. I then made arrangements for the next stage of the journey: the crossing of the Yamuna River and the descent of the Ganges River to Varanasi. I had been worried that if the Ganges were in flood we would have to go overland, or even wait in Mathura until the end of the rainy season. As it turned out, both the Yamuna and Ganges rivers were in flood, and we were obliged to wait. Relentlessly, the rains continued to fall, and I grew more and more depressed. On the other hand, Caraka positively bloomed in the rain. Rain is life for these people.

It was at Mathura that I met the most hated—yet often venerated—religious figure in all India.

I had asked the governor to show me about the various temples and religious establishments of the city. He had been most obliging. He had even pretended to know who Zoroaster was. Thanks to his efforts, I spent several days

167

hurrying from one temple to another. I don't know why I bothered. The Aryan gods are always the same, no matter what their names. There is Agni the fire god and Indra the storm god. There are the highly popular mother-goddesses, whose idolatrous sanctuaries would have seemed most congenial to Atossa. And so on.

Early one morning, armed with parasols against the rain, Caraka and I took a stroll through the bazaars. In front of a booth containing snakes in wicker baskets, an old man suddenly stopped me. He carried not a parasol but a wooden staff. Although he was soaked from the rain, he did not notice the water that filled his dark eyes, dripped from his long nose. For a moment we stared at each other. I noticed that his beard was white, unpainted. Finally I asked, "Do you want alms?"

The old man shook his head. "Come with me," he said. The accent was that of an Aryan of the highest caste. As he crossed the marketplace, he did not look back. Obviously he assumed that we would obey him. We did. And, for once, people stared not at us but at him. Some made the sign to ward off the evil eye while others kissed the hem of his wet shawl. He ignored everyone.

"A holy man," said Caraka with his usual sagacity.

We followed the old man through narrow crowded streets to a large square house built around a courtyard whose wooden verandah sheltered a series of large holes. These holes were the entrances to the cells of the monks. Incidentally, this was the first of the many monasteries that I was to see in India.

The old man led us into a long empty room. As he squatted on the packed-earth floor, he motioned for us to do the same. The ground was unpleasantly damp—as is all India in that terrible season.

"I am Gosala," said the old man. "You are from Persia. I am told that your Great King wishes to learn wisdom from us. That is good. But I must warn you that in this land there are many eel-wrigglers who pretend to be conquerors, enlightened ones, river-crossers. You must be on your guard, and you must report to the Great King only what is true."

"And what is true, Gosala?" Tactfully, I refrained from telling *him*.

"I can tell you what is not true." I realized then that I was in the presence of an accomplished teacher. Needless to say, I had no idea who Gosala was. If I had, I might have learned more than I did from our one and only meeting.

"It is believed by the Jains that one can become holy or closer to holiness by not killing any creature, by not telling a lie, by not pursuing pleasure." We were given the usual list of what not to do. This list is common to all religions that wish to purify the soul—or, simply, man. The two are *not* the same, by the way, thanks to the essential duality of creation. The soul comes straight from the Wise Lord. The flesh is matter. Although the first pervades the second, they are not the same. The first is eternal; the second transitory.

"But you, Gosala, are a Jain." Caraka knew exactly who Gosala was.

"I am a Jain. But I have parted company with the one who calls himself Mahavira. He is thought to be the twenty-fourth crossing-maker. He is not."

"Are you?" Caraka was genuinely interested.

"I don't know. I don't care. I loved Mahavira. We were like brothers. We were as one. We observed all the vows together. We reaffirmed the old wisdom. But then I began to study those things that men have forgotten, and we were obliged to part. Because I now know exactly what is true, and I am obliged to tell the truth to anyone who will listen."

"But you just said that you would only tell us what is *not* true." I was quick to remind him of his opening gambit.

"Affirmation evolves from the negative." Gosala was patient. "It is *not* true that any living creature can grow closer to holiness or to nirvana through the conduct of a good life or through the complete observance of all our vows. What *is* true . . ." Gosala gave me a stern look that I found unnerving; he was both serene and relentless. "What is true is that each of us begins as an atom or a life monad. And each life monad is obliged to undergo a series of eighty-four thousand rebirths, starting with the original living atom and proceeding then through each of the elements of air, fire, water, earth and then into such complex cycles as rocks, plants, living creatures of every kind. Once the series of eighty-four thousand rebirths has been completed, the life monad is released, blown out."

I must have looked uncommonly stupid, for, suddenly, as if to please a child, Gosala got to his feet. He pulled from his belt a ball of thread, which he held in his hand.

"Think of this thread as the entire course of a life monad. Now—watch it rise."

Gosala threw the ball of thread toward the rafters. Once the thread had unwound to its full length in the air, it fell to the floor. "Now it is at an end. And that," said Gosala, "is the story of our existence. We change from atom to air to fire to earth to rock to grass to insect to reptile to man to god to—nothing. At the end, all of those masks that we have been obliged to put on and take off are irrelevant, for there is nothing left to mask. That is the truth of our condition. But my former brother Mahavira will tell you that this process can be speeded up by leading a virtuous life, by obeying the five vows. He lies. *Each of us must endure the entire cycle from beginning to end. There is no way out.*"

"But how, Gosala, do you know this to be true?"

"I have spent my life studying our holy wisdom. It has all been revealed to us over the centuries. The process is as plain as that thread on the floor. No one may hasten or alter his destiny."

"But Mahavira teaches righteousness. Is that not a good thing?" Caraka was as mystified as I by Gosala's uncompromising bleakness.

"Mahavira is at that state in his development." Gosala was mild. "He is obviously coming to the end of his own thread. After all, some men are closer to nirvana than others. But whether they do good or ill makes no difference at all. They simply are. They do what they are meant to do, and endure what they must endure, and they come to an end when it is time—and no sooner."

"Why then—" I pulled toward me the near end of the thread, for comfort?—"do you teach? Why do you want to tell me what is not true and what is true?"

"I am near the exit, child. It is my duty. It is also a proof that I am close to the end. So I have no choice in the matter. I am obliged," he smiled, "to play with string."

"You know of Zoroaster?"

Gosala nodded. "From what I have been told, he must have been very young." The old man wrung out his wet shawl. I began to feel wet, watching him. "It is a sign of extreme youth to worry about correct religious procedures, to invent heavens and hells and days of judgment. I do not mean this unkindly," he added. "Thousands of years ago I, too, went through the same state. You see, it is inevitable."

It is inevitable.

That was the chilling message of Gosala, and I have never forgotten it. In a long life I have yet to come across a world view as implacable as his. Although he was much reviled throughout India, there were quite a number of people who saw him as one so close to the exit that they believed every word he said. Naturally, I did not.

For one thing, practically speaking, if Gosala's vision of an inexorable immutable creation were to prevail, the result would lead to a complete breakdown of human society. If good and evil are simply characteristics of a given creature's place along that unfurling string, then there would be no need for right action if one were, say, at the beginning of the string, and without right action there can be no civilization of any kind, much less salvation when the Truth defeats the Lie. Even so, I find it curious that not a day of my life has passed that I do not think of Gosala and his string.

3

SINCE THERE ARE SO MANY RIVERS IN India and no proper bridges, the ferryboat is an absolute necessity. I did not truly comprehend this until it came time for us to cross the swollen Yamuna River. As we put ourselves at the mercy of a pair of villainous ferryboat men, I suddenly realized why the twenty-four so-called saviors of the Jains are called makers of the river-crossing. The Jains see this world as a rushing river. We are born on one bank, which is the life of the world. But then if we submit ourselves to the crossing-maker, we can pass over to the other side, to relief from pain, even to final release. This spiritual ferryboat is the emblem of purification.

The mundane ferryboat at Mathura proved to be nothing but a large raft which was poled across to the other side by a pair of rather weak saviors. I have never studied the Jaina religion sufficiently well to know if they ever enrich their ferryboat metaphor by remarking upon those unfortunates who drown, as we nearly did, in transit to the other side. But we survived the swirling yellow water, just as if we had been duly purified.

We then crossed overland to the Ganges, where several

flat-bottomed boats were waiting to take us some two hundred miles downriver to the old and holy city of Varanasi, which is in the kingdom of Koshala but not far from the border of Magadha.

The journey between the two rivers was uneventful. The land is flat. Much of the original jungle has been cleared, and fields of rice have been planted. During the last century the population of the Gangetic plain has more than doubled, thanks to the ease with which rice can be grown. Not only do the monsoon rains feed that water-hungry crop but when the rains stop, the flatness of the country makes it easy for farmers to irrigate their fields with water from the always deep, swift, surprisingly cold Ganges River.

The roads were as bad as I had been warned. In open country, we followed trails of thick mud. In the jungles, we were at the mercy of guides who were paid by the day. As a result we spent more days than were necessary in that hot green wilderness, where snakes slither in the underbrush and mosquitoes of fantastic size drink the traveler's blood. Although the Persian costume covers every bodily surface except the face and the tips of the fingers, the Indian mosquito's proboscis can penetrate a three-layer turban.

We found the village people to be shy but kindly. According to Caraka, the country folk are of the old pre-Aryan stock, while the cities are the homes of the Aryan invaders. The two groups seldom mingle.

"It is the same here," said Caraka, "as in the Dravidian south."

"But you told me that there are no Aryans in the south."

Caraka shrugged. "That may be," he said. Caraka suffered from the congenital Indian vagueness. "But village people are a different breed from city people. They never want to leave their land and their animals."

"Except," I pointed out, "when they do." Most popular Indian tales concern a village lad who goes to a great city, befriends a magician, marries the king's daughter, and anoints himself with ghee, or clarified butter—a nauseous substance that the wealthy delight in. Periodically, temple priests bathe the images of their gods in this ill-smelling viscous liquid.

Varanasi is a huge city built on the south bank of the Ganges. The inhabitants like to say that it is the oldest

172

inhabited city in the world. Since the world is very large and very old, I don't see how they would know one way or the other. But I understand the sentiment. Babylonians also boast of the antiquity of their city. But whereas in Babylon there are many written records of previous times, there is not much writing to be found in any of the cities of India. Like the Persians, they prefer—at least until recently—the oral tradition.

For over a thousand years the Aryan conquerors have been reciting their songs or hymns of so-called divine knowledge; these are known as the vedas. The language of the vedas is very old and not at all like the modern dialects. Presumably it is the same Aryan speech that the original Persians spoke, and many of the narratives resemble those Persian stories old men still recite in the marketplace. They tell of the same sort of heroes and monsters, of elaborate wars and sudden revelations of divinity. Curiously enough, the Indian deity most often addressed is Agni, the god of fire.

Throughout India, the Brahmans carefully preserve these hymns. But among the Brahmans, there is a good deal of specialization. Some Brahmans are noted for their mastery of those vedas that deal with, let us say, the god Mithra or with a semidivine hero like Rama; others see to it that the sacrifices are performed properly, and so on.

Although the Brahmans comprise the highest Aryan class, the warriors tend to make fun of them and even their inferiors openly mock them in songs and theatrical performances. Brahmans are thought to be lazy, corrupt and impious. How familiar all this sounded to me! Thus do Persians regard the Magians. Yet the gods that the Brahmans serve are taken very seriously by many people. Agni, Mithra, Indra all have their devotees, particularly among the more simple Aryan classes.

I do not believe that anyone on earth understands all the complexities of the overlapping Indian religions. When confronted with a somewhat similar confusion of deities, Zoroaster simply denounced the whole lot as devils and swept them into the holy fire. Unfortunately, as smoke, they keep coming back.

In a heavy rain we docked at a wooden wharf in what looked to be the center of Varanasi. The governor of the city had been warned of our arrival, and we were met by a delegation of very wet officials. We were congratulated on our safe arrival. Most politely, we were told that no

173

one travels in the rainy season. Obviously, the gods were pleased with us.

I was then brought a ladder so that I could climb to the top of an elephant. Since this was my first experience with an elephant, the driver tried to reassure me with the information that these beasts are quite as intelligent as men. Although I suspect that he was not the best judge of men, it is certainly true that elephants respond to a variety of spoken commands; they are also both affectionate and jealous. In fact, each elephant regards his driver as *his* driver, and should the driver show the slightest interest in another elephant, there will be a tantrum. A stable of elephants resembles nothing so much as the harem at Susa.

I sat on a sort of wooden throne beneath an umbrella. The driver then spoke to the creature, and our journey began. Since I had never before traveled so far above the ground, it was a long time before I dared look down at the muddy street, where a large crowd had gathered to see the ambassador from the far west.

Until quite recently, the name of Persia was unknown in the Gangetic plain. But as the growing kingdom of Magadha lacks good universities, the most intelligent of their young men are sent either to Varanasi or to Taxila to be educated. Naturally, Taxila is preferred to Varanasi because it is farther away, and young men always like to put as much distance as possible between themselves and home. As a result, at Taxila, the young Magadhans not only learn of the power of Persia but they are able to meet Persians from the twentieth satrapy.

We were received in the vice-regal palace by the viceroy of Varanasi. Although dark as a Dravidian, he belonged to the Aryan warrior class. At my approach, he bowed low. As I made my usual speech I saw that he was shuddering like a willow tree in a storm. He was plainly terrified, and I was deeply gratified. Let them fear Darius, I thought to myself, *and* his ambassador.

When I had finished my gracious remarks, the viceroy turned and indicated a tall pale man with a fringe of coppery hair just visible beneath a turban of gold cloth. "Lord Ambassador, this is our honored guest, Varshakara, lord chamberlain to the king of Magadha."

Varshakara moved toward me with the ungainliness of a camel. Face to face, we greeted each other in the formal Indian manner. This involves numerous nods of the head and claspings of the hands—one's own hands. There is no physical contact.

"King Bimbisara awaits with eagerness the ambassador of King Darius." Varshakara's voice was surprisingly thin for such a large man. "The king is at Rajagriha, and hopes to receive you there before the rains stop."

"With eagerness the ambassador of the *Great* King looks forward to meeting King Bimbisara." By this time I was able to conduct ceremonial conversations without an interpreter. By the end of my Indian embassy I was teaching the court language to Caraka.

At first I always referred to Darius as the Great King. But when Bimbisara's courtiers started to use that title for Bimbisara, I then referred to Darius as the king of kings. They were never able to match that one.

"It is the happiest of coincidences," said the chamberlain, tugging his green beard, "that we are both in Varanasi at the same time. It is my dearest wish and hope that we will be able to travel together to Rajagriha."

"That would bring us joy." I turned to the viceroy, wanting him to join in the conversation. But he was staring wildly at Varshakara. Obviously it was not I but the Magadhan who had so terrified the viceroy and his entourage.

Intrigued, I set aside protocol and asked, "What brings the Chamberlain to Varanasi?"

Varshakara's smile revealed bright-red teeth; he was a constant chewer of betel leaves. "I am at Varanasi to be near the stallion," he said. "At the moment he is in the deer park outside the city. He doesn't like the rains any more than we do. But presently he will continue his sacred journey, and should he enter Varanasi—" Varshakara did not finish the sentence. Instead, he showed me all his bright-red teeth. Meanwhile, the viceroy's dark face looked like the ashes of a long-dead fire.

"Whose horse," I asked, "is in the deer park? And why is his journey sacred?"

"At least once in the reign of a truly great king, he arranges for the horse sacrifice." I did not like the chamberlain's use of the word great, but I said nothing. There would be time enough to set him straight. In my mind's eye, I saw the eagle of Darius raised high above all India, and dripping with rain.

"A stallion is driven with a broom into the water. Then a four-eyed dog is clubbed to death by the son of a

175

whore. As an Aryan priest, you will grasp the significance of this."

I looked solemn; grasped nothing.

"The body of the dog then floats under the horse's belly to the south where the dead live. After that, the stallion is set free, to roam as he chooses. Should he enter another country, the people of that country must either accept the overlordship of our king or fight for their freedom. Naturally, if they capture the horse, the king's destiny is seriously . . . shadowed. As you can see, the horse sacrifice is not only one of our most ancient rituals but, potentially, the most glorious."

I now understood the nervousness of the viceroy of Varanasi. If the horse were to enter the city, the inhabitants would be obliged either to recognize Bimbisara as their king or to fight. But fight whom?

The chamberlain was happy to tell me. He was enjoying the terror of our hosts. "Naturally, we take no chances with our king's destiny. The horse is always followed by three hundred of our best and noblest warriors. Each is mounted—though not on a mare! The stallion is denied sexual intercourse for a year, and so is the king. At night, he must sleep, chastely, between the legs of his most attractive wife. Meanwhile, here we are. Should the stallion enter Varanasi, then these good people"—Varshakara made an airy gesture that included the viceroy and his suite—"will become subjects of King Bimbisara, which I am sure they would not mind. After all, our king is married to the sister of their present ruler, the king of Koshala."

"We are creatures—all of us—of fate," sighed the viceroy.

"That is why I am here to persuade our friends, neighbors, cousins—you see, we think of the people of Varanasi as being already a part of the Magadhan family—to persuade them not to resist if the stallion should decide to enter the city, and drink deep from the Ganges."

All in all, an inauspicious start to an embassy, I thought, as we were shown our quarters in the vice-regal palace. A war between Magadha and Koshala would certainly disrupt the iron trade; on the other hand, a war between two powerful states can sometimes be resolved by the intervention of a third power. Years before, an Indian king had offered to mediate between Cyrus and the king of the Medes. Naturally, he was turned down by both sides. Although westerners may travel east, easterners must never be encouraged to go west!

For the sake of the iron trade, I hoped that the horse would stay in the deer park. For the future glory of the Persian empire, I hoped that it would get thirsty and drink from the Ganges.

Two days later the stallion turned south, and Varanasi was safe. Although Varshakara was furious, he did his best to appear serene. "You must," he said to me the day after the horse's departure, "come with me to the temple of Agni. He is just like your fire god, and I'm sure you'll want to worship him in an Indian setting."

I did not explain the Wise Lord to the chamberlain. I had already made up my mind that I would talk religion only with Brahmans, holy men and kings. But I was interested to see if my grandfather's influence had spread beyond Persia.

Through what seemed to be miles of narrow, winding, unbelievably crowded streets, we were carried in gilded litters to the temple of Agni, a small ugly building made of wood and brick. We were respectfully received at the door by the high priest, whose head was entirely shaved except for a long topknot. He wore scarlet robes and brandished a torch.

Beside the temple door, a round stone altar was protected from the rain by a canopy. Casually the high priest lit some ghee with his torch. I must say that I was appalled at the sacrilege. *The sacred fire must be lit only in a sunless place.* But I suppose the fact that the sun had not shone once in several months might qualify all India as a sunless place.

Varshakara and I then entered the temple, where a wooden statue of Agni gleams with rancid butter. The god is seated on a ram. In one of his four arms he holds a javelin, representative of fire, while on his head he wears an elaborate wooden crown depicting smoke. Other images in the temple show Agni with seven tongues, and so on. Like most Indo-Aryan deities he has all sorts of personas. In the hearth, he is fire. In the sky, he is lightning. At all time he is the intermediary between man and god because it is the fire that transports the burned sacrifice to heaven; in this last, and only in this, does Agni resemble Zoroaster's fire.

There was a good deal of ritual, most of it quite confusing to a non-Brahman. For one thing, the priests used an archaic language that neither Caraka nor I understood.

"I doubt if they understand it either," he said later. Although Caraka's parents were Jains, he liked to claim that he was a worshiper of Naga, the Dravidian snake god upon whose coils rests the world. Actually, Caraka was irreligious.

After an hour of chanted gibberish, each of us was offered an ill-tasting liquid in a communal cup. Dutifully I took a sip. The effect was swift and infinitely more powerful than that of haoma. But since I do not accept the Vedic gods, my waking dreams were unrelated to the ceremonies at hand. Even so, at one point Agni's four arms appeared to move and by some trick or other the javelin did seem to be afire.

I muttered a prayer to fire, as the messenger of Ahura Mazdah, the Wise Lord. Later I learned that one of the names for the chief Aryan god Varuna is Ashura. This means that he is our own Ahura, or Wise Lord. I then realized that after my grandfather had recognized the central god of the Aryans as the sole creator, he dismissed all the other gods as irrelevant demons. But aside from Ashura-Varuna or Ahura Mazdah, we share nothing with the worshipers of the Vedic gods except the belief that harmony must be maintained between that which creates and that which is created through correct ritual and sacrifice. Yet I cannot help but think that the lunatic jumble that the Indo-Aryans have made of their gods is a sign that they are now moving toward Zoroaster's concept of the unity that contains all things. Is not an infinitude of gods—as at Babylon—very close to being an admission that there is but One?

Ultimately, the sacrifices that are made to this or that devil must be construed by the Wise Lord as offerings to himself. Otherwise he would not let such things be. Meanwhile he sends us holy men to tell us how and when and what to sacrifice. The holiest was Zoroaster.

In India there are all sorts of holy men or teachers of this way or that way, and many of these figures are both fascinating and disturbing. Most reject the Vedic gods and the notion of an afterlife. According to the Vedic religion, evildoers end up in a hell known as the house of clay, while the good ascend to something called the world of the fathers; and that is that. The current crop of holy men believe in the transmigration of souls, a pre-Aryan concept. Certain holy men, or arhats, believe that the process can be stopped; others don't. Quite a few are entirely in-different; they would fit in nicely at one of Aspasia's din-ner parties.

But since the Indo-Aryan devil-worshipers believe that fire is an aspect of the good because fire burns away dark-ness, I did not in the least mind taking part in that cere-mony at Varanasi. The Indians call the image-inducing liquid that I drank soma, obviously a variation of our own haoma. Unfortunately, the Brahmans enjoy their little se-crets quite as much as do our Magians, and so I could not find out how or from what it is made. I do know that at one point I saw—that is, imagined—Agni hurl his fiery lance straight at the ceiling.

I also heard, very clearly, the high priest speak of the origin of all things. To my surprise, there was no talk of a cosmic egg or a colossal man or twins. Instead, he spoke very clearly of a moment when even nothingness did not exist.

I was struck by that image. I have never been able to envisage nothing because it is, I suppose, impossible for *some* thing—a man—to comprehend *no* thing at all.

"There was neither nonexistence nor existence; there was no air, no sky." As the high priest finished each line of the so-called creation hymn, he would strike a small drum that he held in one hand.

"What covered all? and where?" The hymn then tells of a time—which was pre-time—when "there was neither death nor immortality, neither night nor day. But then, because of heat—" Where, I wondered, did the heat come from?—an entity known as the One came into being. "Thereafter rose desire, the primal seed and germ of spirit." From the One came gods and men, this world, heaven and hell. Then the hymn takes a very odd turn.

"Who knows," chanted the high priest, "where it all came from? and how creation happened? The gods, in-cluding Agni, do not know because they came later. So who does know? The highest of all the gods in heaven, does *he* know how it began—or is he ignorant too?"

To me, this sounded like atheism. But then, I have never been able to figure out what, if anything, the Brah-mans actually believe. Although our own Magians are complicated, confused, sly, they are consistent in certain things. The original twins exist for them as the first man and woman. Also, I cannot conceive of any Magian suddenly questioning—at a religious ceremony!—the very existence of the creator-god.

In a highly drugged state I returned to the governor's palace, where Varshakara wanted to talk to me at length of political matters. But I begged off. The soma and the rains and a journey of more than a thousand miles had exhausted me. I slept for three days.

I was awakened, finally, by Caraka.

"Varshakara has offered to escort us to Rajagriha. Shall I tell him yes?"

"Yes." Although still half asleep, I was suddenly aware that something was not right. Then I realized that for the first time in close to four months I could not hear the rain clattering on the roof. "The rains . . ."

". . . have stopped. For a while, anyway. The monsoons withdraw gradually."

"I was dreaming of that horse." This was true. In my dream I was at the tomb of Cyrus near Persepolis. I was mounted on the stallion. In front of me stood Atossa and Lais, each with a sword in her hand.

"This is Persia!" Atossa shouted.

"And *that* is the wrong horse," said Lais firmly; then Caraka awakened me.

I should have had the dream studied at once. Indians are marvelously adept at the interpretation of dreams. But I promptly forgot it and only now, a half-century later, do I recall the dream—vividly, and to no useful purpose.

"The horse is back in Rajagriha," said Caraka. "Everyone's upset, especially Bimbisara. He'd hoped to add Varanasi to his kingdom. Or failing that, one of those little republics north of the Ganges. But, so far, the horse has never left Magadha. I've arranged for you to meet Mahavira."

"Who?" I was still half asleep.

"The crossing-maker. The hero of the Jains. He's in Varanasi, and he's agreed to meet you."

The name Mahavira means great hero. The actual name of the twenty-fourth and last maker-of-crossings was Vardhamana. Although he came from a warrior family, his parents were such devoted Jains that they acted seriously upon the Jaina injunction that the best of all deaths is to blow out one's own life, slowly and deliberately and reverently, through starvation.

When Vardhamana was thirty years old, his parents starved themselves to death. I must say they sound to me like real heroes, if not great heroes. Vardhamana was so impressed by his parents' death that he left his wife and children and became a Jaina monk. After twelve years of isolation and self-abnegation, he achieved a state called by the Indians kevala. This means that he has somehow joined himself in a special way to the cosmos.

Vardhamana was acclaimed Mahavira, and became the head of the Jaina order. When I was in India, the order was made up of some fourteen thousand celibate men and women. The men live in monasteries, the women in convents. A number of the men go without clothes and are known as sky-clad. Women may not be so heavenly adorned.

On a low hill above the Ganges, a group of Jaina monks had converted a dilapidated warehouse into a monastery where Mahavira had spent the rainy season. We had been told to arrive just after the noon meal. Since the monks do nothing more than gobble a bowl of rice that they have begged, the noon meal begins and ends at noon. So, shortly after noon, a pair of monks escorted us into a cavernous damp room where several hundred members of the order were praying loudly. I noticed that most of them do not wash themselves very often, and that many of them seemed to be physically deformed or ill.

Our guides led us to a sort of lean-to which is separated by a curtain from the warehouse proper. Behind the curtain we found the great hero himself. Mahavira was seated cross-legged on a sumptuous Lydian rug. He wore a golden robe. I thought this somewhat unascetic, but Caraka assured me that each of the twenty-four crossing-makers has had, from the beginning of time, his own particular color and emblem. Mahavira's color was gold, and his emblem was the lion.

I suppose Mahavira must have been in his late seventies when I met him. He was a short, thick man with a high, compelling voice. He almost never looked at you when he spoke, which I always find disconcerting. But I was brought up at a court where you must not look at anyone royal. Therefore, if someone does not look at me, I think that I am either with someone royal or with— what? An impostor?

"Welcome, ambassador from the Great King Darius. Welcome, grandson of Zoroaster, who spoke for the Wise Lord, if anyone does."

I was pleased that I was known to Mahavira; displeased at the ambiguity of "if anyone does." Did he mean that Zoroaster was *not* the prophet? I soon found out.

I saluted Mahavira in the elaborate Indian manner while Caraka kissed his feet as a sign of respect. We then sat at the edge of the rug. Behind the curtain, we could hear the monks chanting in unison some endless hymn.

"I have come to teach all men the ways of the Wise Lord," I said.

"If any man can do this, I am sure that it is you." Again the small smile of someone who knew or thought he knew more than one did. I controlled my irritation. For his benefit, I chanted one of Zoroaster's gathas.

When I stopped, Mahavira said, "There are many gods, just as there are many men and many—mosquitoes." This last occurred to him when a large mosquito made a slow circuit of his head. As a Jain, Mahavira could not take its life. As a guest of the Jains, I decided that I would not take its life either. Perversely, the mosquito ended by drinking blood from the back of my hand and not from his.

"We are all the same substance," I was told. Tiny particles, or life monads, assemble and reassemble, in this form and that form. "Some ascend the life cycle," he said. "And some descend."

It is the view of the Jains that the cosmos is filled with atoms. I use the word that Anaxagoras invented for the infinitesimal bits of matter that make up creation. Yet the life monad of the Jains is not exactly the same as an atom.

Anaxagoras would not think of an infinitely small bit of sand, say, as containing life. But for the Jains *every* atom is a life monad. Some monads intermingle and ascend the life cycle from sand and water through the vegetable and animal realms to those higher creatures who possess five senses, a category that includes not only human beings but the gods themselves. Or the life monads disintegrate and descend the cycle. First they lose the so-called five faculties of action as well as the five senses; then they gradually decompose themselves into their constituent elements.

"But when and how did this process of ascending and descending begin?" I asked, fearing the answer that I indeed got.

"There is neither beginning nor end. We are fated to

182

continue from level to level, up or down, as we have always done and will always do until this cycle of the world ends—to begin again. Meanwhile, I am the last crossing-maker in this cycle. We are now descending, all of us."

"You, too?"

"As all things must, I must. But I am the crossing-maker. I at least have been able to make clear as a diamond the life-monad that animates my being."

Apparently a life monad is like a crystal that is dimmed or darkened or colored by one of six karmic, or fated, colors. If you kill someone deliberately, your life monad will turn black. If you kill inadvertently, it will turn dark-blue, and so on. But if you observe faithfully all the rules of the order, you will become pure, but you will not be the crossing-maker. You must be born that.

The certainty with which Mahavira spoke was the result of an ancient religion whose tenets he so entirely accepted that he could conceive of nothing else. When I pointed out to him that the tension between the life monad and those colors that stain it somewhat resembles the struggles between the Wise Lord and Ahriman, he smiled politely and said, "In every religion, no matter how undeveloped, there is often a tension between the idea of what is good and what is evil. But youthful religions fall short of absolute truth. They cannot accept the end of human personality. They insist upon a cave of clay or some sort of ancestral home where the individual may continue as himself for all time. Now, that is childlike. Is it not plain that what did not begin cannot end? Is it not plain that what ascends must also descend? Is it not plain that there is no escape? Except to become complete, as I have done, by integrating myself with the entire universe."

"How was this accomplished?" I was polite; even curious.

"For twelve years I isolated myself. I lived without clothes, ate seldom, was chaste. Naturally, I was beaten and stoned by villagers. But since I knew that the body is unclean, transient, an anchor that holds the ferryboat in mid-passage, I ignored all the body's needs until, finally, gradually, my life monad became clear. Since I am now impervious to all things, I cannot be born again, not even as a king of the gods—always something to be feared, for that sort of grandeur has clouded more than one crystal. In fact, to be one of the high gods is the last temptation, the hardest to resist, the most exquisite. Look at your own Ahura Mazdah. He has chosen to be Wise Lord. But if he had been truly wise, he would have taken the next and final step and integrated himself with that cosmic creature of whom we are all a part, the colossal man within whose body we are all of us simply atoms that will not cease to rearrange themselves over and over again until, with integration, there is a release from the self and like a bubble one floats to the top of that curving starry skull, and it is over and it is done with."

What fascinates me about the Jains is not so much their certainty—a characteristic of altogether too many religions—as the antiquity of their beliefs. It is possible that their atomistic view of man is the oldest known religious theory. For centuries they have studied every aspect of human life and related it to their world view. Although integration is the official goal of every Jaina monk, only a few will ever achieve it. Yet the effort to do so will make for a better rebirth, if there is such a thing.

"Can you remember any of your previous incarnations?"

For the first time Mahavira looked at me. "Why, no. What would be the point? After all, it takes no effort to *imagine* what it must be like to be a lion or the god Indra or a blind woman or a grain of sand."

"A Greek named Pythagoras claims that he can remember all of his previous lives."

"Oh, poor man!" Mahavira looked genuinely unhappy. "To remember eighty-four thousand previous existences! Now, that is indeed hell, if such a thing were to exist."

The number eighty-four thousand reminded me of Gosala. I told him that I had met his former friend.

Mahavira blinked his eyes at me. He looked like a friendly fat monkey. "For six years we were as close as brothers," he said. "Then I ceased to be myself. I no longer cared for him. Or for anyone. I had achieved integration. Poor Gosala has not, cannot. So we parted. Sixteen years later when we met again. I was the crossing-maker. Because he could not bear this, he hated himself. That was when he denied the essential belief of the Jains. If we cannot, some of us, integrate ourselves, then there is no point to what we do. At that instant, Gosala decided that there is absolutely no point to what we do because . . . Did he throw out a ball of string for you?"

"Yes, Mahavira."

Mahavira laughed. "What happens, I wonder, to those

minute particles of the string that detach themselves as it unwinds? I have a suspicion that some will integrate themselves with the whole, don't you?"

"I have no idea. Tell me about this cycle of creation which is ending?"

"What is there to tell? It ends . . ."

"To begin again?"

"Yes."

"But when did these cycles first begin? And why do they go on?"

Mahavira shrugged. "What is endless is without beginning."

"But what about this—this colossal man? Where did he come from? Who created him?"

"He was not created, because he already was, and everything is a part of him, forever."

"Time—"

"Time does not exist." Mahavira smiled. "If you find that too difficult to understand"—he looked at Caraka the Dravidian—"then think of time as a serpent swallowing its tail."

"Time is a circle?"

"Time is a circle. There is no beginning. There is no end." With that Mahavira inclined his head, and the audience was over. As I rose to go I noticed that a mosquito had settled on Mahavira's bare shoulder. He did not stir as it sucked his blood.

One of the monks insisted on showing us through the nearby animal shelter where every sort of wounded or sick animal is lovingly tended in a series of ramshackle huts where I have never before or since smelled such a stench or heard so much howling and baying and lowing.

"Do you also tend human beings?" I asked, cloth held over my nose.

"Others do, Lord. We prefer to help the truly helpless. Let me show you this heartbreaking cow that we found . . ."

But Caraka and I had hurried away.

Later that day I met one of the city's most important merchants. Although the merchant class is looked down upon by the warriors and Brahmans, most of the wealth of the Indian states is controlled by them and they are often courted by their social betters.

I would now give the man's name, but I have forgotten it. He was, curiously enough, in correspondence with the ubiquitous Egibi and sons, the Babylonian bankers. For years he had been trying to exchange caravans with them. "Caravans are the basis of all prosperity." He sounded as if he were quoting some religious text. When I told him of the Great King's desire to import iron from Magadha, he thought that he might be useful. He had, he said, a number of partners in Rajagriha. I would get on with them. Some were bankers, who used money.

By and large, Indians do not strike many coins. Either their trade is conducted through barter or else they use crudely stamped weights of silver or copper. Curiously enough, they mint no gold, even though our Persian darics are highly valued; yet they produce quantities of gold which are mined for them by giant ants. Although I found it odd that these highly civilized and ancient countries are so primitive in regard to money, I was much impressed by their credit system.

Because of thieves, Indians seldom travel with chests of gold or objects of value. Instead, they place their valuables with a reputable merchant of their own city. He then gives them a written statement to the effect that goods of a certain value have been placed with him and he requests his fellow merchants throughout the sixteen kingdoms to provide the holder of the statement with money or goods against the money or goods he is holding. This is done gladly. No wonder! Not only is the money safe, but the lender collects eighteen percent interest on what is borrowed. Fortunately, the merchant who holds your valuables will often pay you quite a good percentage for his own lendings against what is yours.

For safety and convenience, this system is difficult to fault. During my embassy I actually earned a bit more money than I spent. Some years ago I was able to introduce a similar system of credit in Persia. But I don't think that it will ever catch on. Persians are both honest and suspicious, not the best mentality for the conduct of business.

While the merchant and I were talking, an elderly servant woman entered the room with a pitcher of water.

"I must make one of the five sacrifices, if you'll forgive me." The merchant crossed to a niche where a number of crudely-made clay figures were placed side by side on a shelf of elegantly glazed tile. Pouring water onto the floor in front of them, he murmured a series of prayers. Then

186

he gave the pitcher to the servant, who crept from the room.

"That was the prayer to my ancestors. Each day we must perform what we call the five great sacrifices. The first is to Brahma, the world spirit. We recite to him from the vedas. Later we make a libation of water to our ancestors, while to all the gods we pour ghee onto the sacred fire. Next we scatter grain for the animals, birds, spirits. Finally we worship man by offering a stranger hospitality. I have"—he bowed very low to me—"just had the honor of performing two sacrifices simultaneously."

I quoted for him a similar Aryan sentiment that predates Zoroaster. Then my new acquaintance asked me how the Persians educate their young. He was particularly interested in Cyrus' palace school system.

"Our kings should do the same," he said. "But we are very indolent here. I suppose it has to do with the heat, the rains. Our warrior class is taught archery, and some of them actually know how to fight, but not much else. If they can learn by heart a single veda, they are considered educated. All in all, I think that we merchants are the best educated. Of course, the Brahmans learn thousands and thousands of verses of the vedas. But they seldom learn the things that we consider important—like mathematics, astronomy, etymology. The origins of speech fascinate us. Up north, in Taxila, the Persian language was studied long before Darius got control of the Indus River. We have always been fascinated by the words that both separate and bind us. I myself support a school here at Varanasi where we teach the six schools of metaphysics as well as the secrets of the calendar."

Although I was somewhat overwhelmed by the intricacies of Indian education, I agreed to talk to a group of students before I left for Rajagriha. "They will be honored," he assured me, "and attentive."

The school occupied several rooms in an old building just back of a bazaar that specialized in metalwork. The distracting sound of hammers on copper did not exactly improve the quality of my discourse. But the students were indeed attentive. Most were reasonably fair-skinned. A few were of the warrior class; the rest were merchant class. There were no Brahmans.

Democritus wants to know how I could tell who belongs to what class. This is how. When an Indian boy is old enough for what is called his second birth as an Aryan, he is given a cord of three intertwined threads, which he will wear for the rest of his life across his chest, from left shoulder to below the right arm. For the warrior, the cord is of cotton; for the priest, hemp; for the merchant, wool. In Persia we have a somewhat similar rite of initiation but without any visible mark of caste.

I sat in a chair beside the teacher. Although of the merchant class, he was deeply religious. "I am a disciple of Gotama," he told me gravely when we met. "We call him the enlightened one, or the Buddha."

I found the students inquisitive, polite, shy. There was a good deal of curiosity about geography. Just where was Persia? and how many families lived at Susa? They measure population not by the number of individual freemen but by households. At that time there were forty thousand families in Varanasi or, perhaps, two hundred thousand people, not counting foreigners and the non-Aryan natives.

I spoke at some length of the Wise Lord. They seemed interested. I refrained from that fierceness of style which characterized my grandfather's exhortations. Because the Indians accept all the gods, they find it quite easy to accept the idea of only one god. They even accept the possibility that there is no creator at all and that the Aryan gods are simply natural forces of supermen who will one day be extinguished when this cycle of creation ends, as it must, and a new cycle begins, as it will—or so they believe.

I can see how this lack of certainty about deity has led to the sudden recent flourishing of so many new theories of creation. At first I was hopelessly confused. I had been brought up to believe that the Wise Lord was all-encompassing, and I was quite prepared to annihilate in debate anyone who denied the truth of Zoroaster's vision. But no Indian ever denied it. Everyone accepted Ahura Mazdah as the Wise Lord. They even accepted the fact that their own high deities Varuna, Mithra, Rudra were, to us, devils.

"All things evolve, and change," said the young teacher as the class ended. He then insisted that we visit the deer park outside the city. A four-horse chariot had been provided by my merchant friend, so we were able to drive comfortably through Varanasi. Like so many very old cities, the place had simply evolved without plan or straight avenues. Most of the city clings to the riverbank. Many of the houses are four and five stories tall, with a tendency to collapse. Day and night the narrow winding streets are crowded with people, animals, carts, elephants. There are no temples or public buildings of any interest. The vice-regal lodge is simply a house larger than its neighbors. The temples are small, dingy, stinking of ghee.

The deer park contained no deer as far as I could tell. It was simply a charming overgrown park, filled with strange flowers and even stranger trees. Since the common people may use the park as they please, it pleases them to sit about under the trees, eating, playing games, and listening to professional storytellers or even to wise men.

Thanks to four months of rain, the greens of the park were so intense that they made my eyes water. I suspect that even then my eyes were somehow oversensitive, and flawed.

"This is where Gotama sat when he first came to Varanasi." The young teacher pointed at a tree whose only distinction was that no one went near it except to stare, as we were doing.

"Who?" I'm afraid that I had managed to forget already the name that he had told me only an hour before.

"Gotama. We call him the Buddha."

"Oh, yes. Your teacher."

"*Our* teacher." My companion was matter-of-fact. "Under that bo tree, he experienced enlightenment. He became the Buddha."

I listened with less than half an ear. I was not interested in Siddhartha Gotama and his enlightenment. But I was interested to learn that King Bimbisara was a Buddhist; and I remember thinking to myself, Yes, he's a Buddhist in the same way Darius is a Zoroastrian. Kings are always respectful of popular religions.

As we parted I told the young man that I was leaving for Rajagriha.

"Then you are already in the Buddha's footsteps." The young man was entirely serious. "When the rainy season ended, the Buddha left this park and journeyed east to Rajagriha, as you will do. He was then received by King Bimbisara, as you will be."

"But there the likeness must surely end."..

"Or begin. Who knows when or how enlightenment will come?"

There was no answer to that. Like Greeks, Indians are better at questions than at answers.

4

IN GREAT STATE, THE PERSIAN EMBASSY left Varanasi. Normally, the traveler goes by boat down the Ganges to the port of Pataliputra, where he disembarks and proceeds overland to Rajagriha. But since the Ganges was still dangerously swollen, Varshakara insisted that we travel overland by elephant.

After the first day or two of what can only be described as seasickness, one becomes not only used to this sort of travel but also fond of the beast itself. I would not be surprised if elephants *are* more intelligent than human beings. After all, their heads are larger than ours, and the fact that they do not speak might well be an indication of superiority.

What for us is the cool autumn of the year is a hot and stormy time for the people of the Gangetic plain. As the monsoons gradually recede, the moist air is heavy with heat; and one feels rather as if one were floating under water. The strange feathery trees are like sea ferns, among whose fronds bright-colored birds dart like fish.

The road to Rajagriha is unusually bad. When I said as much to Varshakara, he looked surprised. "This is one of our best roads, Lord Ambassador." Then he laughed. A red spray of saliva just missed me. "If the road were any better, we would have armies marching against us every day."

This was cryptic, to say the least. Since Magadha is the most powerful state in India, there is no army that would dare march against it. Unless, of course, the chamberlain was making a subtle reference to Darius. Although I often had difficulty understanding what he said, I had no difficulty at all in understanding him. Varshakara was a merciless man of great ambition. He would do anything to increase the power of Magadha. He would . . . But I shall get to all that in due course.

I was impressed by the richness of the land in the so-called great plain. There are two harvests a year. One is in the winter, the only bearable season; the second is at the time of the summer solstice. Immediately after the summer harvest, rice and millet are planted, and the fields devoted to those crops looked, to my eye, like yellow-green rugs thrown across the flat land. Without much effort, the people are well-fed. In fact, if it were not for the complex task of feeding large urban areas, the Indian villager could live without work. The fruits and nuts from trees, the domestic and water fowl, the thousand and one varieties of river fish provide a bountiful free diet.

But cities require elaborate agriculture. As a result, the enormous cattle herds of the Aryan conquerors are now being deliberately cut back as grazing land is converted to farm land, and there is a good deal of debate about this change in the way the people live. "What is an Aryan without his cow?" the Brahmans ask. They do not, of course, expect an answer.

Just past the forest or jungle to the east of Varanasi, there are many villages. Each settlement is surrounded by a flimsy wooden stockade, designed not to keep out an army but to prevent tigers and other predators from carrying off livestock and children. At the center of each of these somewhat random communities is a rest house where travelers can sleep on the floor for nothing and buy a meal for next-to-nothing.

I was surprised to learn that most Indian farmers are free men and that each village has its own elected council. Although they are obliged to pay taxes to whoever happens to be their overlord, they are pretty much left in peace. No doubt this explains the high crop yield of the Indian countryside. As every landowner on earth knows, a hired farmer or slave will produce exactly half as much food as a freeman who owns the land that he tills. Obviously, the Indian village system is a leftover from an earlier, more pristine age of man.

The journey from Varanasi to Rajagriha took two weeks. We traveled slowly. Except for the heat of the day, the journey was comfortable. Each night elaborate tents were set up for the chamberlain and for me. Caraka shared my tent while the rest of the embassy slept in the rest house of the nearest village or beneath the stars.

Each night I would burn a noxious incense which drives away those insects that feed on sleeping men. But Indian snakes are another problem. Since neither incense nor prayer repels them, Varshakara allowed me the use of a small furry snake-eating creature called a mongoose. Chain a mongoose to a post near your bed, and no snake will disturb your sleep.

Evenings were tranquil. Caraka and I would make notes about what we had seen and heard during the day. We also supervised the making of new maps, since Scylax's map of the interior of India was as inaccurate as the rendering of the coastal area was precise. Then, once the tents were set up, I would usually dine with Varshakara. He was as curious about me as I was about him. Although we told each other numerous necessary lies, I was able to pick up a good deal of useful information about the exotic world that I had only just begun to penetrate. We would recline on divans, which somewhat resemble Greek couches except that they are upholstered and strewn with cushions. Beside each divan was the inevitable spitoon. Indians are always chewing some sort of narcotic leaf.

Indian food is not unlike Lydian. Saffron is much used, as well as a pungent combination of spices called curry. For cooking fat the wealthy use ghee, which keeps for a long time even in hot weather. Eventually, I grew used to ghee. If I had not, I would have starved. What is not fried in ghee is soaked in it. I much preferred the oil that the Indian poor use. Made from a grain called sesamun, it is lighter than ghee and tastes no worse. Sesamun oil is to the masses what olive oil is to the Athenians.

But at royal or rich tables only ghee may be served, and since I ate, doggedly, whatever was served me, I became for the first and only time in my life fat as a eunuch. Incidentally, fatness in both sexes is much admired by Indians. No woman can ever be too fat, while a prince of spheroid proportions is reckoned to be blessed by the gods and perfectly happy.

Yet the chamberlain himself ate sparingly. On the other hand, he enjoyed altogether too much a powerful drink that is made from distilled sugar cane. I also grew to like it. But each of us took care not to drink too much in the other's company. Varshakara regarded me with the same suspicion that I regarded him. As we flattered each other extravagantly in the Indian manner, each waited for the other to make an indiscreet move; neither ever did.

I do remember one conversation in the tent. After an unusually heavy dinner we continued to drink the sugar-cane wine that a servant girl kept pouring into our earthenware cups. I was half asleep; so was he. But I do remember asking, "How much longer is the horse supposed to wander?"

"Until the spring. Another five or six months. Have you a similar ceremony in Persia?"

"No. But the horse is peculiarly sacred to our kings. Once a year our priests sacrifice a horse at the tomb of Cyrus the Great King."

The Indian horse sacrifice made a great impression on me. For one thing, I was struck by the sheer strangeness of fighting a war simply because a horse has chosen to graze in the field of another country. Of course, I had heard those endless verses of blind Homer, who assures us that once upon a time the Greeks attacked Troy—now Sigeum in our part of the world—because the wife of a Greek chieftain had run off with a Trojan youth. For anyone who knows both the Greeks and Sigeum, it is perfectly plain that the Greeks have always wanted to control the entrance to the Black Sea and the rich lands beyond. But to gain that control, they must first conquer Troy or Sigeum. Currently, that is the dream of Pericles. I wish him luck. He will need it. Meanwhile, should Pericles' wife run off with the son of old Hippias of Sigeum, that would make a suitably Greek pretext for war and you, Democritus, can celebrate the result in verse.

We Persians are more candid than other peoples. We admit openly that we created an empire in order to become richer and safer than we were before. Besides, if we had not conquered our neighbors, they would have conquered us. That is the way of the world. It is certainly the way of those Aryan tribes whom Homer sang about in much the same way that the Brahmans of India sing of the heroes of their Aryan past. Incidentally, one Vedic narrative about a young king named Rama may well be the longest hymn ever written. I am told that it takes at least ten years for an intelligent Brahman to learn every line. After having listened to a day or two of this hymn, I think that one can say with some justice that the narrative is even more boring than Homer's story. To me, the only interesting thing about either of these old Aryan stories is the fact that the gods are simply superheroes. There is no sense of true deity anywhere in either story. The Aryan gods are exactly like ordinary men and women except that they seem to live forever; they also have exaggerated appetites which they overindulge, usually at the expense of human beings.

Democritus tells me that the intelligent Greeks have never taken the Homeric gods seriously. That may be. But the huge temple to Athena that is now being built just behind us on the Acropolis is an incredibly expensive memorial to a goddess that is obviously taken very seriously not only by the people but by the rulers of a city that has been named for her. Also, it is still a capital offense in Athens to mock or deny the Homeric gods—in public, at least.

The Indians of my day—and perhaps now, too—were wiser than the Greeks. For them the gods are simply there or not there, depending on your perception of them. The notion of impiety is quite alien to the Indian mind. Not only do Aryan kings enjoy talking to atheists who openly mock the high gods of the Aryan tribes but no Aryan ruler would ever dream of outlawing the pre-Aryan local gods of the country folk.

My grandfather's attempt to make devils of the Aryan gods struck the Aryans of India not so much as a sign of impiety as an exercise in pointlessness. Under such names as Brahma and Varuna, the idea of the Wise Lord is everywhere prevalent. Why, then, they would ask me, deny the lesser gods? I repeated Zoroaster's injunctions: one must purify oneself; cast out devils; convert all men to the True. I did not make a single convert. But then, my mission was political.

Varshakara did not know when or how or why the horse sacrifice began. "It is very old. Very sacred. In fact, after the ceremony of coronation, it is the most important ceremony in a king's life."

"Because it adds new territory to the realm?"

Varshakara nodded. "What better indication of heaven's favor? Had the horse entered Varanasi, our king would have been truly glorious. But . . ." Varshakara sighed.

"I don't want to be irreligious, Lord Chamberlain"— the powerful wine had somewhat loosened my tongue— "but those warriors who follow the horse . . . can they determine its direction?"

When Varshakara smiled, his betel-stained teeth seemed to drip blood. "Even to hint that the horse is guided by anything but fate is intolerable and irreligious . . . and partly true. The horse can be subtly guided, but only to a point. Since cities tend to terrify horses, we usually encourage the horse to walk all around a city. That's quite good enough for us. Control the perimeter of a city, and the place is yours. Naturally, our soldiers will then have to defeat their soldiers. But that part is simple—for us. Koshala is disintegrating and we could very easily have . . . But the horse went south. Our only hope now is that it will turn to the northeast, to the Ganges, to the republics on the other side. That's where the real danger is."

"The republics?"

Again Varshakara showed his red teeth, but not in a smile. "There are nine republics. From the Shakya republic in the northern mountains down to the Licchavi republic just across the Ganges from Magadha, the nine are all united by a relentless hatred of Magadha."

"How can nine small republics be a single threat to a great kingdom?"

"Because at this very moment they are making a federation, which will be as powerful as Magadha. Last year they elected a general sangha."

I suppose assembly is the best translation for this word. But whereas the Athenian assembly is supposedly open to commoners as well as to nobles, the sangha of the Indian republics was made up of representatives from each of the nine states. As it turned out, only five republics ever joined the federation, and those were the states closest to Magadha and so most fearful of King Bimbisara and his chamberlain Varshakara. They had every right to be afraid. These republics stood in relation to Magadha rather the way that the Ionian Greek cities stand in relation to Persia. The only difference is that in the days of Darius, the Greek cities of Asia Minor were not republics but tyrannies.

Even so, I thought the analogy apt. I made it. "It has been our experience that no republic can ever withstand a popular monarchy. Consider the Greeks . . ." I might just as well have mentioned the inhabitants of the moon. Varshakara had a fair notion of what and where Persia was, and he knew something of Babylon and Egypt; otherwise, the west did not exist for him.

I tried to tell him how no two Greeks can ever agree for any length of time on a common policy. As a result, they are either defeated by disciplined outside armies or torn apart from within by democratic factions.

Varshakara understood enough of this to define the Indian word for republic. "These countries are not governed by popular assemblies. Those ended long before we arrived. No, those republics are governed by assemblies or councils made up of the heads of the noble families. What we call a republic is really a—" He used the Indian word for oligarchy.

Later I learned that the ancient tribal assemblies that he had referred to were not pre-Aryan; instead, they were very much a part of the original Aryan tribal system. In free assembly, leaders were elected. But the assemblies gradually faded away, as they tend to do everywhere; and hereditary monarchy took their place, as it tends to do everywhere.

"You're right that we have nothing to fear from any one of these republics. But a federation presents a real danger. After all, only the Ganges separates us from their southern border."

"What about Koshala?" Although my grasp of Indian geography was never to be entirely secure, even then I had a mental picture of that part of the world which was not totally inaccurate. I could see in my imagination the high mountains to the north. They are supposed to be the highest in the world, as if anyone has ever measured them —or seen all the other mountains that there are on this vast earth. But the Himalayas are certainly impressive, particularly when seen from the low flat Gangetic plain. These mountains are the home of the Aryan gods and, more important, the source of the Ganges River. At the foot of the Himalayas are the nine small republics. They are set in a fertile valley between the Rapti River on the west and the thickly forested foothills to the Himalayas on the east. The Gandak River runs more or less through the center of this territory, ending when it joins the Ganges, the northern border of Magadha. The most important of Indian trade routes starts at the far-eastern port of Tamralipti and passes through the republics on its way to Taxila and Persia beyond. Magadha has always coveted that trade route.

To the west of the republics was Koshala, an incredibly rich and populous nation. Unfortunately, King Pasenadi was weak. He could not keep order. He could not collect tribute from many of his own cities because the lords were often in rebellion against him. Even so, in my day, both Aryans and Dravidians agreed that there was on earth no city to compare with Shravasti, the capital of Koshala. Thanks to the accumulated wealth of the past and to the highly civilized nature of Pasenadi, Shravasti was an enchanted place, as I was to discover. For a time, it was my home; if my sons are still alive, they are there.

"Koshala is a danger to us." All the world was a dangerous place for the dangerous Varshakara. "Naturally, it is our policy to support the kingdom against the federation. But, ultimately, statesmanship is the mastery of the concentric circle." Even in the relations between sovereign states, the Indians have evolved intricate rules. "One's neighbor is always the enemy. That is the nature of things. Therefore, one must seek alliances with the country just beyond the neighbor, the next concentric ring. So we look to Gandhara . . ."

"And to Persia."

"And to Persia." I was allowed a brief, bright glimpse of red teeth. "We have agents or well-wishers everywhere. But the federation is far craftier than we. There is not a corner of Magadha that they haven't infiltrated."

"Spies?"

"Worse. Worse! But then, you know. You've been dealing with our enemies, Lord Ambassador."

My heart beat somewhat irregularly. "I have yet to deal, knowingly, with an enemy of Magadha, Lord Chamberlain."

"Oh, I'm sure that you weren't aware that they were. But you've been with our enemies all the same. And they are much worse than spies because they mean to weaken us with alien ideas, just as they have weakened Koshala."

I got the point. "You mean the Jains?"

"And the Buddhists. And those who follow Gosala. You must have noticed that the so-called Mahavira and the so-called Buddha are not Aryans. Worst of all, both come from the republics."

"But I thought your king was a patron of the Buddha . . ."

Between thumb and forefinger, Varshakara blew his nose. Generally speaking, Indian manners are almost as delicate as ours; yet they blow their noses and void in public. "Oh, it has been our policy to let these people come and go as they please. But we keep a close watch on them and I suspect that, very soon, our king will see them for what they are—enemies of Magadha."

I thought of Gosala and his string, of Mahavira and his

197

perfect remoteness from the world about him. "I cannot think that these . . . ascetics have the slightest interest in the rise or fall of kingdoms."

"So they pretend. But had it not been for the Jains, Varanasi would be our city tonight."

The chewing of betel quid ultimately deranges the senses in much the same way that haoma does. Taken too frequently, haoma destroys the barrier between dreaming and waking. This is why Zoroaster laid down such precise rules for haoma's use. Betel-chewing has the same long-range effect, and that evening I decided that Varshakara's mind had been disordered in a most dangerous way. I say dangerous because no matter how distorted his vision of actual things, he was always able to express himself in the most plausible way.

"When the horse entered the deer park, it walked—quite deliberately—to the gate that leads into the city. I know. My agents were there. Suddenly two sky-clad Jains darted through the gate. The horse shied. And ran off in the other direction."

"You don't think that their appearance was just coincidence?"

"Coincidence? No! The federation does not want Varanasi in our hands. And Mahavira was born in the capital of the Licchavi republic. Well, there will be other occasions. Particularly now that we have a new and treasured ally in Persia."

We drank to the alliance.

I hoped that Varshakara's agents had not told him how meticulously the geographers in my retinue were mapping the Gangetic plain. I dreamed of nothing but the conquest of India. I dreamed of cows! The Persian army would occupy Taxila. With that northern base, our armies would sweep down the plain. Although Koshala would put up no resistance, Magadha would fight. We would be faced with formidably armored elephants. Would the Persian cavalry panic? No matter. I was certain that, somehow, Darius would prevail. He always did.

As we talked of those spies and enemies that threatened Magadha, I wondered if Varshakara realized that I was the principal spy of the ultimate enemy. I suppose he did. He was by no means a fool.

Since the beginning of history, there has been a settlement at Rajagriha. This is because of the five protecting hills that make for a natural fortress some twenty miles south of the Ganges. But early in the reign of Bimbisara, the city began to expand onto the plain, and the king built a massive wall of crudely cut rocks in order to enclose and protect not only the new city but also farmland, gardens, parks, lakes. As a result, in case of siege, there is always enough food and water within the walls. At first this troubled me. But then Caraka pointed out that a capital city always surrenders if the rest of the country is cut away from it, like a body from a head.

As we approached Rajagriha the sun was setting, and in the half-light the walls seemed like natural cliffs studded at irregular intervals with clumsily made guard towers. Because India is so rich in timber and mud, stone is seldom used for building and there are few accomplished masons in the country. Important structures are made either of wood or of a combination of wood and mud brick.

The sky was still full of light as we rode into the city. Conch shells were blown in our honor, and the common people crowded around, as they always do when personages are to be seen—not to mention elephants.

The city that Bimbisara had built was on much the same grid pattern that I had so much admired in Babylon and in the abandoned Harappa city. Long straight avenues ran parallel to one another. Each begins at one of the city's gates; each ends at the central square, which is dominated by a huge building, where travelers can sleep and eat for a price.

Just back of the new city are the five sentinel hills and the original town, a confusion of narrow lanes and alleys, much like Sardis or Susa.

The embassy architect and I used to argue whether or not man's first cities had straight streets that met at right angles. He thought that the original cities were simply villages that had got too large, like Sardis or Susa or Ecbatana or Varanasi. Later, when a king actually founded or rebuilt a city, he would be inclined to use the grid pattern. I disagreed. I think that the first cities all followed the grid pattern. Eventually, when those cities deteriorated, the great avenues were broken up and new winding lanes evolved between the new buildings which had been set haphazardly amongst the ruins of their predecessors. We shall never know the answer.

The new part of Rajagriha is impressive. Many of the

houses are five stories high, and all are well made. The king had established a number of building standards that were strictly obeyed. But then, the king was strictly obeyed in all things because the secret service of Magadha—thanks to Varshakara—was a superb instrument. There was nothing that the king did not know—or if not the king, the chamberlain.

Enthroned on my elephant, I could look into second-story windows where behind exquisitely carved lattices, the women are able to watch the life of the city without being seen. Many roofs support charming airy pavilions, where the owners sleep on hot nights.

Most upper-story windows have balconies crowded with pots of flowering shrubs. As we passed, men and women threw flowers in our path. All looked to be friendly.

The air was heavy with those odors that I always associate with India: flowering jasmine, rancid ghee, sandalwood and, of course, decay—not only human but that of the city itself. Wooden buildings have short lives in countries where the rain does not fall so much as flood.

The royal palace is set at the center of a large unpaved square, where there are no monuments of any kind. I suppose that this is because the city is—or was then—so new. Curiously enough, there are no arcades at Rajagriha. In a climate where one is either drenched by the rains or scorched by the sun, the arcade should be a necessity. But it is unknown in Magadha. The natives are content to conduct their business either beneath the brightly colored awnings that edge the avenues or in the blazing sun itself. Most of the city's inhabitants are dark-skinned; some have skin that is blue-black.

Except for a brick foundation, the four-story palace of King Bimbisara is fashioned of wood. But unlike the Median palace at Ecbatana, which is made rather oppressively of cedar wood, Bimbisara's elegant structure contains every sort of highly polished wood, including ebony and teak and silkwood, and the walls of many of the rooms are inlaid with mother-of-pearl or plaques of carved ivory. Each section of the palace has its own characteristic smell, the result of carefully selected aromatic woods combined with incense and flowering plants. Barrel-vault ceilings made the interior of the palace tolerably cool on even the hottest days.

The palace is built around four inner courtyards. Two of these are devoted to the ladies of the harem, and one is used by the court. The king's private courtyard is filled with trees and flowers and fountains. Because the windows that look upon the king's courtyard have all been sealed save for those of his own quarters, no one may spy upon him when he walks in his garden. At least that is the theory. I soon learned that the secret service had made all sorts of spy holes through which they could keep a constant watch on the king whose eyes *they* were meant to be. I have never attended a court so ridden with intrigue, and I was at Susa with Xerxes to the end.

I was lodged with Caraka on the second floor of the palace in what is called the princes' quarters. This was a great honor, or so everyone liked to remind us. We had a suite of six rooms, with a view of the nobles' courtyard on one side and the city square on the other. The rest of the embassy was lodged in a house nearby.

I had warned my principal agents that the country was aswarm with spies and that whatever they said to one another was apt to be overheard. They should also never assume that the listener did not know Persian. Meanwhile, they were to discover the true military resources of Magadha. I say true because I have yet to know of a state that does not so misrepresent its military strength and wealth that, in time, the state ends by deceiving itself.

Not a day passes here in Athens but that I am not told how two or three thousand—or was it hundred?—Greeks defeated a Persian army and navy of two or three million men. The Greeks have so misrepresented those wars that they have finally confused themselves. This is always a mistake. If you cannot count properly, you had better not go to market—or to war.

5

I SHOULD SAY THAT NEVER IN MY LIFE have I seen so much bare flesh as I did in India. But unlike the Greeks, the Indians do not reveal their bodies in order to excite one another; they reveal them simply because they live in a hot country. They wear only two garments. Both men and women wear a kind of skirt, which is tied at the waist with an elaborate belt or girdle. They also wear a shawl, which is knotted or pinned at the neck. Once they are indoors, they tend to shed the upper garment. The court costume differs from ordinary clothes only in the richness of the materials.

Court ladies think nothing of revealing to their social equals breasts with painted nipples, depilated armpits, navels set with precious stones. When the ladies are not too fat, they can be extraordinarily beautiful. They have particularly fine skin, aglow with scented pomades.

Both men and women paint their faces. Eyes are carefully outlined with kohl, a Median fashion adopted by Cyrus and since continued by all the Great Kings and most of the court. It was Cyrus' theory that Persians must look as much like gods as possible, particularly when they show themselves to their foreign subjects. Fortunately, Persians tend to be taller and more muscular than other men, and so with painted eyes and rouged cheeks they do indeed look like splendid living effigies of warrior-gods.

Indian men and women not only outline their eyes with kohl but paint their lips a ruby red with something called lac. There is no doubt that cosmetics do improve one's appearance, but they are a nuisance to put on and take off. While I was at the Indian courts, I was obliged to paint myself, or be painted, twice a day. As a Persian of my generation, I found such a fascination with one's appearance both ridiculous and unmanly—and tiring. Nevertheless, there is something most languorous and appealing about being bathed and oiled by pretty girls; then while an old gentleman washes your eyes with collyrium and tints your beard, he tells you the day's gossip. Incidentally, the Indians wear only chin whiskers—I think that this is because they cannot grow hair on their cheeks.

The day after I was established in the palace, I was sent for by King Bimbisara. Several hundred courtiers were assembled in a long high room with clerestory windows so latticed that the sunlight fell in spangles on the pale-green tiles on the floor.

Varshakara met me at the door to the throne room. He wore a scarlet turban and a translucent shawl held in place by a chain of rough rubies. Like so many plump Indian courtiers, he had breasts like a woman. Like so many Indian men, he wore high platform shoes in order to look taller than he was.

Obviously, Varshakara had gone to a good deal of trouble to impress me. But after the court of the Achaemenid, that of Magadha was provincial, to say the least. I was reminded of Sardis. The chamberlain carried an ivory staff; and he made a short speech to me and my suite of seven Persians. I replied briefly. Then Varshakara led us to the high ivory throne, where Bimbisara, king of Magadha sat cross-legged. Above his gold-turbaned head was a canopy of ostrich plumes.

The old queen sat on a stool to the king's left. Unlike Persian or Athenian women, the ladies of India are free, within limits, to come and go as they please. For instance, an Indian lady may go to a shop with only one old woman in attendance. But she must make her visit at either dawn or dusk so that the shopkeeper will be unable to get a good look at her. Yet, paradoxically, she may show herself practically nude to men of her own class.

The old queen wore an elaborate headdress of pearls strung on what looked to be threads of silver artfully intertwined with her own white hair. She wore a mantle of peacock feathers. She looked most distinguished, even intelligent. For a time I thought that she might be the Indian equivalent of Atossa. After all, she was Bimbisara's chief consort as well as the sister of Pasenadi. But in a court where women are not totally sequestered and where, perhaps more to the point, there are no eunuchs, power is exercised entirely by the king and his councilors. The harem has practically no influence.

To the king's right was Prince Ajatashatru. The heir to the throne was definitely and admirably—by Indian standards—fat. He had the face of a huge baby, whose three soft chins produced as a crop one fine tuft of pale-green beard. The prince smiled frequently, and sweetly. The lobes of his ears were weighted down with diamond earrings, and the thick waist was cinched in by a wide belt of gold links. He had surprisingly muscular forearms.

King Bimbisara was an old man with a long violet beard. I never saw the hair on his head—if he had any—because I never saw him without the elaborate turban of gold thread that is the equivalent of the Persian cidaris. Bimbisara was tall and sinewy, and one could see that in his day he had been a physically strong, even formidable man.

Since I was the shadow, no matter how dim, of the Great King, I did not prostrate myself. But I dropped to one knee. Meanwhile, my escort was opening the chests that contained Darius' gifts to Bimbisara. There were a number of mediocre jewels and several exquisite rugs from Lydia and Media.

When I finished my opening speech, I gave Varshakara the letter that the Indian eunuch had written in Darius' name. With a flourish the chamberlain gave the letter to the king, who did not even look at it. Later I was told that Bimbisara could not read. But he spoke very well indeed, and he used not the old Aryan of the court and the temples, but the modern dialect.

"We welcome you as if you were our brother Darius, whose deeds are known to us, even at this great distance." Bimbisara's voice was as harsh as that of any cavalry commander. He spoke to the point. He never hesitated for a word.

"We are happy that he has received our letter. We are happy that he has sent us you, a holy man as well as a warrior." Actually, if I were Indian, I would not have been of the warrior class. I would have been a Brahman. But I was quite happy to accept Bimbisara's ennoblement because, almost without exception, Indian rulers are of the warrior class and constantly challenge their nominal superiors, the Brahmans.

"We will show you what you want to see. We will exchange our iron for your gold. We will deal with you as if we were indeed brothers and as if only a river separated us instead of all the world." There was more in this strain.

Finally the long day ended with a series of religious sacrifices to those Aryan gods who are as well endowed with extra arms and heads as they are with magical powers and arcane duties.

We were then invited to the king's apartments for a feast, whose first course coincided with the appearance above the palace roof of a full moon, which rested, for one lovely moment, like a golden shield on the steep tile roof.

We dined on a broad verandah that overlooked the king's private gardens. This was a great honor, Varshakara was quick to point out. "Only the royal family and the hereditary ministers are invited here. The king has indeed accepted your Darius as a younger brother."

I was a diplomat. I did not mention the fact that many of Darius' twenty satrapies are richer and larger than Magadha. On the other hand, none has as much iron or as many elephants. I confess that I saw myself as satrap of the sixteen Indian kingdoms—and the nine republics, too! Why not? I wondered what to call my satrapy. Greater India? The Gangetic States? I dreamed of empire, as everyone does in youth. I also realized that the man who makes a single empire of all those states will be a rival to the Great King. As a result of my embassy, it is now Persia's permanent policy to make certain that no Indian state becomes so large that it will absorb the others. After all, as Darius and Xerxes dreamed of conquests in the east, there is no reason why India might not one day produce an emperor who will look enviously to the west.

At the time of my embassy, not only was Bimbisara the most powerful king in all India but he had come very close to being the local lord of all the lands. Through his wife he had obtained a considerable portion of the Koshalan state of Kasi. Since Varanasi is the capital of Kasi, he had hoped that the horse sacrifice would give him an excuse to annex that ancient city. Now he would need a new pretext.

I lay on a divan opposite that of the king. Once again, Bimbisara was flanked by queen and heir. A number of court ladies dined alongside the men. Worse, they let fall their upper garments in what seemed the most casual way. Later I learned that the art of public undress is even more elaborate in India than that of dress itself. Many ladies had rouged their nipples. Some even had complex designs on their bellies. At first I thought that these were tattoos. But they proved to be made of colored sandalwood paste. I have never been so shocked.

Another oddity: we were served our dinner by women. Naturally, it is strange for a Persian not to see any eunuchs, but I had not realized how much I had always taken them for granted until I got to India.

I was given a dozen different kinds of wine and of fruit juices. Fish and game and vegetables appeared at regular intervals for what seemed eternity. In the garden, a half-dozen musicians sat in the light of the full moon and played or improvised a number of odd droning melodies, marked by the irregular beating of a drum. Like Greek music, Indian music takes getting used to. The principal instrument is something like the Lydian harp but with ten strings. Flutes are also popular, and cymbals.

The royal figures hardly spoke during dinner. Occasionally father and son would exchange a few words.

205

The queen was entirely silent. Since she ate a very great deal but was not fat, I assumed that she had a wasting disease, which proved to be the case. Caraka had noticed the same thing when he first saw her. "She'll be dead before the next monsoon," he said with all the confidence of a physician who is not going to be held responsible for the sick person's health. Actually, the queen lasted two more years.

A very pretty woman had been placed beside me. She wore a headdress that must have been four feet high, a fantastic arrangement of jewels and hair. Some of the hair was hers, some not. She removed her shawl, and I saw that each breast was circled by a sandalwood-paste wreath of vermilion flowers—exquisitely drawn, I could not help noting. She was the wife of the minister of war and peace. She was discreetly flirtatious, no doubt acting under orders.

"I am told that in your country the ladies are kept locked up and never seen."

"Except by their husbands—and their eunuchs."

"Their what?"

I explained to her what a eunuch was. It is disconcerting to watch a strange woman who is naked from forehead to navel blush.

The lady was equally disconcerted. "I am not sure that *that* is a subject," she said, and primly changed it. "We may dine with men of our own class. Naturally, the women of any household have their own quarters and there is a certain degree of seclusion, which is normal. In the old days, of course, young men and women were allowed to see as much of one another as they pleased. The girls even fought in battles. As recently as my grandmother's time, ladies were taught poetry and dancing and music. But now only low-class women who cater for the tastes of men are allowed to practice the sixty-four arts, which is terribly unfair, but you know the Brahmans . . ."

"They prescribe?"

"Prescribe and proscribe. They won't be happy until every last one of us is locked up like a Jaina nun."

It is odd—and charming—to talk to an intelligent woman who is not a prostitute. Although the Indian courts are filled with such ladies, I have known only three ladies—outside India—who were truly intelligent: Elpinice, Queen Atossa and Lais. The fact that I knew the last two at all was entirely an accident. Had I been a

206

properly brought up Persian nobleman, I would never have seen either one of them after the age of seven.

"Is there no problem with . . ." I wanted to speak of illegitimacy, the main reason for the sequestration of women. A man's son *must* be his. If there is any doubt, properties, not to mention kingdoms, are at hazard. I searched through my rather small store of Indian words and came up with ". . . jealousy? I mean, ladies of the court dining like this?"

She laughed. She was a jolly young woman. "Oh, we know each other too well. Besides, we are well guarded. If a strange man were to be found in the women's quarters of any great house, much less the palace, he would promptly be impaled on a stake, as well he should be. Naturally, the common people *never* see us, and that includes the Brahmans," she added firmly. "We absolutely despise them."

"They are most learned," I said neutrally. I realized that I was not making much of an impression on her despite my exotic Persian costume. I was also sweating heavily. Before the hot season ended, the Persian ambassador wore Indian clothes.

"Are you married?" she asked.

"No."

"Is it true that you westerners have many wives?"

I nodded. "Just as you do."

"But we don't. Not really. The king is obliged to marry often, for political reasons. But our class seldom marries more than once."

"Then who are the women in your harems?"

"Servants, slaves, concubines. For us the ideal relationship between a man and a woman is that of Rama and Sita." She named the hero and heroine of their holy book. Rama is a hero somewhat on the order of Homer's Odysseus, except that Rama is always honest in his dealings with others. But like Odysseus and Penelope, Rama and Sita are essentially monogamous, and that is why, by and large, a man of the Indian ruling class seldom has more than one wife at a time.

After a splendid course of young peacock, adorned with its own tail feathers, King Bimbisara motioned for me to walk with him in the garden.

As we stepped off the verandah, servants removed the tables, and the dinner guests mingled with one another. There was a good deal of breaking of dishes, a sound I was to grow accustomed to in India, where the servants are as clumsy and incompetent as they are agreeable and intelligent.

The palace garden was full of color, even by moonlight. The scent of jasmine filled the warm air. Night birds sang in the tall trees. The palace resembled a silver mountain that had been carefully squared off. The sealed windows added to the impression.

Bimbisara took me by the arm and led me down a path that the moon had turned to purest silver.

"It is good that you are here."

"I am honored . . ."

The old man heard but did not listen: a habit of royalty. "I am most eager to learn more of Darius. How many soldiers does he have?"

I was not prepared for the swiftness of the obvious question. "In thirty days, Lord, he can assemble an army of one million men." This was more or less true. I did not add that most of the million would be useless village louts. In those days, the Great King's army was less than one hundred thousand highly trained men.

Obviously Bimbisara divided my figure in his head by the customary ten. "How many elephants does he have?"

"None, Lord. But his Lydian cavalry—"

"No elephants? I must send him a few. I have one thousand."

I divided by ten in my head.

"Atop each elephant," said the king, "I place six archers in a metal tower. They are so protected that no one can kill them. They are able to destroy any army."

"But surely the elephants themselves can be killed?"

"They, too, wear armor. They are invincible." Bimbisara was warning Darius through me.

At the center of the garden was a small pavilion, containing a large divan on which Bimbisara reclined while I perched on the divan's edge. Through latticed windows, the moonlight was bright—warm, too, I noticed. India is the only country where the full moon gives off heat. Fortunately, there is always a breeze at night in the hills of Rajagriha.

"I come here often." Bimbisara combed out his scented violet beard with the fingers of both hands. "We cannot be overheard. See?" He indicated the four arched win-

208

dows that were the pavilion's walls. "No one can approach without my seeing him."

"Surely no one spies on the king."

"*Everyone* spies on the king!" Bimbisara smiled. In the moonlight he looked to be made of silver. "While the king spies on everyone. There is nothing in Magadha or Koshala that I do not know."

"And Persia?"

"*You* will be my eyes and ears." He gestured politely. "I am curious about a king who can put one hundred thousand men into the field at such short notice." Thus he proved that he had indeed divided by ten. I did not correct him. I started to tell him about all the lands that Darius governed, but Bimbisara stopped me with "My grandfather sent a message to Cyrus, very like the one that I sent Darius. But there was no answer."

"Perhaps the embassy did not arrive."

"Perhaps. But a generation later Darius' army was on the Indus River. Could that have been a . . . belated answer, Lord Ambassador?"

"Oh, no!" I spoke of Darius' love of peace. Admiration for Bimbisara. Troubles with the Greeks. That much was true. As I babbled, the old man sat motionless in the moonlight, a half-smile on the half-face that he turned to me.

The musicians continued to play nearby. Through one window I could see the verandah where we had dined. A company of nude girls was dancing. Eventually, I became a devotee of Indian dancing, which is like no other on earth. For one thing, the dancer's head moves back and forth upon the neck in a fashion that one would swear was not possible. Meanwhile, the body appears to be quite separate from the head, and the undulations of the hips and belly are marvelously enticing. Many dancers become rich, famous, powerful. In fact, one Magadhan dancer was able to make and keep and administer a considerable fortune without the inconvenience of being anyone's wife or concubine. Receptions to her house were as much sought after as an invitation to the house of Democritus' friend, the prostitute Aspasia.

"Is Darius so serious in his desire to be our friend that he might send us troops to help us break the federation of republics?"

"I am sure that he would." I was thrilled. Bimbisara had given us an opening. I had already figured a way of routing the elephants. They are frightened of mice. At the crucial moment, our troops would set free a thousand rodents. The elephants would stampede, and I would be satrap of Greater India. So I dreamed.

"Perhaps I shall call upon him." Bimbisara played with his beard. "You are also supposed to visit our dear brother Pasenadi of Koshala."

"Yes, Lord. The Great King has a message for the king of Koshala."

"Pasenadi is a good man, but weak. My wife is his sister. She has always said that he will lose his kingdom one day because he has no interest in governing. It is sad, really. When I was a boy, Koshala was the greatest nation in the world. Now it is just a name. Between the arrogance of its nobles and the temerity of its thieves, the kingdom has dissolved. I find this tragic." The half-smile was now a full smile. The tragedy of others has that effect on princes.

"Does King Pasenadi want your help?"

"No. He is unaware of the danger. Unaware or, perhaps, indifferent. You see, he is a Buddhist. In fact, the Buddha usually spends the rainy season at Shravasti. Then he comes to us for a month or two. As you must know, there are many Buddhist monasteries in Rajagriha. We think him most holy."

I could not help but contrast Bimbisara with Darius. The Indian sovereign was truly fascinated by the Buddha, while Darius had no interest at all in Zoroaster.

"Who impressed you more, Lord Ambassador, Gosala or Mahavira?"

I did not ask the king how he knew that I had met the two holy men. I take essential points rather quickly. I had been spied on ever since my arrival in India.

"Each was impressive," I said truthfully. "I found Gosala's view somewhat bleak. If there is no way of altering one's destiny by good actions, then why not behave as badly as possible?"

"I made the same point to him. But he seemed to think that to observe all the vows was a good thing in itself, and if you could observe them successfully, that was a sign that *you* were near the exit. He also believes that a man's life is rather like a pond: if you add no new water, the pond will evaporate. But he rejects the notion that fate—or karma—can be altered by good or bad actions. All is predetermined. You get to the exit when it is your turn, not before. According to him, the gods and the kings of this world are nowhere near the exit." Bimbisara looked sad. I think that he actually believed what he was saying. "I'm afraid that in my next life I shall retrogress. There are signs that I will become Mara, the god of all evil—and of this world. I pray that I shall be spared. I try to observe all the vows. I follow the four noble truths of the Buddha. But fate is fate. Worse than to be a king like me is to be a god."

I could not, of course, disagree. But I did find the thought of being a god most tempting, and confusing. Since the gods cannot die or end until this cycle of creation ends, how is it possible for anyone to become a god that is already in existence? When I asked a Brahman this question, his answer took half a day. I have long since forgotten both halves of that day.

"I am astonished, Lord, by the sense of time your holy men have. They measure existences by the thousands."

"More than that," said Bimbisara. "Certain Brahmans tell us that a really bad karma can only be eliminated by thirty million million million rebirths multiplied by all the grains of sand in the bed of the Ganges River."

"That is a long time."

"That is a long time." Bimbisara was grave. I could not tell whether or not he believed all this. He had a tendency to repeat one's last statement; then change the subject. "Who is king of Babylon now?"

"Darius, Lord."

"I did not know that. A long time ago we used to trade with Babylon. But then too many ships were lost at sea. It was not worthwhile."

"There is the overland route, Lord."

"Yes, and it is my heart's desire that we will soon wear to dust the road between us. Would you like a wife?"

I was too startled to answer. The king repeated himself; then he added, "Since we hope that you will consider Rajagriha as your native place, we would be pleased if you married one of our ladies, just as I shall marry one of your king's daughters, and he will marry one of mine."

"I think that this is an undeserved honor," I said. "But I would be most pleased, Lord."

"Good. We will arrange everything. You have other wives?"

"None, Lord."

"Good. Certain Brahmans take a foolish line about the number of wives one can have, even though our religion is lenient in this matter." Bimbisara got to his feet. The audience was over.

As we walked through the scented silver air to the verandah, I did feel for an instant that Rajagriha was my native city.

6

I WAS MARRIED AT THE END OF THE week of the horse sacrifice. Both ceremonies took place late in winter, a lovely brief season that corresponds to early summer in Ecbatana.

Unlike my marriage, the horse sacrifice was less than a success. After a year of roaming, the stallion had managed to avoid the republican federation as well as Koshala. It was rumored that at one point the desperate Varshakara had tried to chase the horse onto a ferryboat which would have taken it across the Ganges into the Licchavian republic. But at the last moment the horse had shied, and never crossed the Ganges.

With an almost human perversity, the stallion kept entirely to the kingdom of Magadha during its year of wandering. This was a bad omen for Bimbisara. On the other hand, the horse was not captured by an enemy, and that was a good omen. At year's end the horse was brought back to Rajagriha to be sacrificed after a festival of three days.

The horse sacrifice is as strange a business as I have ever come across. The origin of the rite is obscure. All the Brahmans agree that it is Aryan in origin for the simple reason that the horse was unknown in this part of the world until the pale-skinned clansmen arrived from the north. But the Brahmans agree on nothing else. Much of the ceremony is conducted in a language so old that even the priests who recite the sacred hymns have no idea what the words they are chanting mean. In this they resemble the Magians who follow the Lie. But the leading

Brahmans at court did question me closely about those Persian sacrifices that resemble theirs; and I was able to tell them that in Persia the horse is still sacrificed to the sun god by those who follow the Lie. Beyond that, I know as little of the origins of our sacrifices as they do of theirs.

For an Indian ruler the horse sacrifice is all-important. For one thing, it represents a renewal of his kingship. For another, if he is able to enlarge the kingdom that he inherited, he will be known as a high king, or maha-rajah, a rank that certain ambitious Indians would like to pretend is equal to that of the Great King. Tactfully, I would tell them that a maharajah more resembles the pharaoh in Egypt or the king of Babel, titles that Darius bore.

The horse sacrifice took place in a fairground just inside the city wall. A four-story golden tower had been built at the center of a field. Three hundred flagpoles had been so placed as to form a square in front of the tower. As the day was windless, bright banners hung limply from the poles.

While the drugged and docile stallion was being tied to one of the poles, Brahmans attached an animal or fowl to each of the other poles. Horses, cows, geese, monkeys, even gasping porpoises were all to be sacrificed that day. Meanwhile, musicians played. Jugglers and acrobats performed. What seemed to be all of Rajagriha was in the fairground.

I stood at the door to the tower, surrounded by the court. The royal family were inside the tower, preparing themselves for the ritual.

At exactly noon, the king and his five wives came out of the tower. They all wore white. There was not a sound in the fairground, except for the noises of the tethered beasts and fowl, except for the almost human choking of the dolphins.

The high priest himself led the stallion from the flagpole to the king. Then Bimbisara and the wives walked around the animal. One wife oiled the animal's flanks while another put a garland about its neck. Nearby a group of Brahmans acted out some sort of play, a kind of mock marriage, with numerous obscene gestures. I could not understand the language.

The mood in the fairground was curiously solemn. Usually, Indian crowds are noisy and cheerful. But today they felt the magic, I suppose, of an event that seldom happens more than once in the reign of a king despite the ancient tradition that the first earthly king who celebrates one hundred horse sacrifices will overthrow the god Indra and take his place in the sky.

I do not suppose that there is anything quite so boring as an immensely long ceremony conducted in a foreign language, and dedicated to a god or gods that one does not acknowledge.

But toward the end of the mock play, the ceremony became most intriguing. The horse was led back to the point where it had been tethered. The high priest then covered its face with a cloth. Slowly, he smothered the beast. With a crash the stallion fell to the dust and for some minutes the legs twitched in the death agony. Then the old queen walked over to the body. The crowd was now very still. Carefully she lay down beside the corpse. The high priest then covered the old queen and the horse with a silken sheet.

When they were hidden from view he said, in a loud, clear voice, "In heaven you are covered, both. And may the fertile stallion, the seed-deliverer, place the seed within."

It took me a moment to grasp what was happening. After the rites of Ishtar at Babylon, I thought that nothing could startle or shock me. But this did. Under the silken covering, the old queen was expected to place within her the member of the dead stallion.

The ritual dialogue was obscure and obscene. It began with a blood-chilling cry from the old queen. "Oh, Mother Mother Mother! Nobody will take me! The poor nag sleeps. Me, this wonderful little creature, all dressed in the leaves and bark of the pampila tree."

The high priest shouted, "I shall incite the procreator. You must incite him too."

The old queen spoke to the dead stallion: "Come, lay the seed deep into the womb of one who has opened her thighs to you. Oh, symbol of virility, set in motion the organ that is to women the maker of life, which darts in and out of them, swiftly, in darkness, the secret lover."

There was much writhing beneath the coverlet. Then the old queen howled, "Oh Mother Mother Mother, no one is taking me!"

This was followed by obscene byplay between the high priest and a lady. He pointed to her sex. "That poor little hen is so agitated, and hungry. Look how it wants to be fed."

The lady pointed to the priest's sex. "There it wriggles, almost as large as your tongue. Be silent, priest."

All the while, the old queen never stopped her howling of "Mother Mother Mother, no one is taking me!"

The high priest exchanged cryptic obscenities with each of the king's wives. The king himself said not a word. Finally, whatever was done was done. Presumably the old queen had somehow stuffed the stallion's member into her vagina. The coverlet was taken away. The wives of the king sang in unison a hymn to a flying celestial horse. When basins were brought to them, they bathed their faces and hands in a ritual way and chanted a hymn to water. Then all the animals, fowl and fish were slaughtered, and fires were lit.

The old queen sat in a chair beside the dead stallion and watched as four Brahmans efficiently quartered the beast. The high priest then cooked the bones himself. As the marrow sizzled, King Bimbisara inhaled the steam. Thus was he purged of sin. Then sixteen priests each cooked a portion of the horse, and when this was done, there was a great shout from the people. Bimbisara was now universal monarch.

I have heard of all sorts of fertility cults in the wild places of Lydia and Thrace, but the horse sacrifice is the oddest by far and, according to the Brahmans, the oldest. It is thought that the ceremony began as a means of ensuring fertility for the king and his wives. But no one will ever know for certain because no one alive understands all of the hymns that the Brahmans have been memorizing and singing for the past two thousand years. I do know that the ceremony is terrifying to behold. It is as if we had all of us suddenly reverted to a time before time.

Dancing and feasting went on all night. At dawn the royal family retired to their golden tower. Like most of those who had attended the sacrifice, I slept in an open field.

The next day I was told that I was to marry the daughter of Prince Ajatashatru. This was a great honor, as I was constantly reminded. For one thing, as a surrogate for the Great King, I was accepted as being of the warrior class. But since I was not the Great King, I could not marry a daughter of King Bimbisara. Nevertheless, I was

215

sufficiently worthy to take for a wife one of Ajatashatru's twenty-three daughters.

At first I feared that some ancient Vedic law would be produced, obliging me to purchase my wife from her family. But the ancient Vedic law proved to be quite the reverse. I was paid, very handsomely, for accepting as wife the twelve-year-old Ambalika, who had not yet, I was lied to by her loving father, menstruated. Indians consider this a most important detail on the excellent ground that since their women are allowed such freedom, any nubile girl is not apt to remain a virgin for very long in that climate and at that court.

Although the first negotiations were carried out most formally between Varshakara, representing the royal family, and Caraka, representing me, the final agreement was arrived at, most amiably, even charmingly, by Ajatashatru and me in the Five Hills Gambling Hall, the largest of the capital's numerous gambling establishments.

Indians are passionate game-players. They are also reckless gamblers. Fortunes are lost on a throw of the dice or at the guessing-the-numbers game. Under King Bimbisara all gambling halls were strictly supervised by the state. Five percent of the stakes went for the maintenance of the hall. Since no gambler is allowed to use his own dice, the state also makes a nice profit from the rental of dice. Because the hall itself never loses heavily—are the dice loaded? games secretly rigged? or does the law of averages favor the hall?—the revenue to the king is so enormous that the actual amount he receives is one of the best kept secrets in Magadha. Certainly, my embassy never penetrated it.

Although King Bimbisara personally detested gambling and tried to discourage it at court, his heir was a constant habitué of the Five Hills Gambling Hall, the most elegant of the capital's gambling establishments. It was rumored that Ajatashatru himself owned the hall and that he blithely cheated the government of its share of the profits.

My future father-in-law was only a few years older than I. From the beginning, we got on well; but then, when he wanted to be charming, there was no one to compare with him. That evening at the Five Hills Gambling Hall, Ajatashatru was ablaze with charm; had even rouged his nipples, something that court dandies only do on festive occasions.

Arm in arm we entered the main hall, a long narrow

216

room with gaming tables on either side. At the far end, a curtained alcove contained divans covered in Cathay cloth. Here the prince could relax, unobserved, but observing through one of several holes that had been cut in the dusty curtains.

I noticed that as the manager led us to the alcove, none of the gamblers looked at the prince. "You see," Ajatashatru whispered to me, breath heavy with perfume, "I am invisible."

I assumed that it was considered bad form to notice the prince when he took his ease among the common people. Later I learned that it was worse than bad form: it was fatal for the person who dared look at the prince when he was enjoying himself.

As the two of us took our places on divans, the curtains of the alcove were drawn. Then a series of powerful wines was brought us in silver flagons by very young girls. One was not even pubescent, which excited the prince. While he spoke to me he fondled her rather the way a Magian will caress a dog as he discourses solemnly on the proper making of haoma or the creation of the world.

"You will bring us joy and good fortune." The prince smiled. Unlike the chamberlain, he kept his teeth clean with some sort of cosmetic gum that pulls away all particles of food. I sat so close to him that I could see that his entire body had been shaved or depilated. Were it not for those muscular forearms and brutal hands, I would have thought that I was seated beside my future mother-in-law.

"You have done me the sort of honor that cannot be measured in gold and silver. My master the Great King will be pleased."

"We must invite him to Magadha. Not, of course, for the wedding," Ajatashatru added, rather quickly. I always assumed that the secret service in Rajagriha was more or less aware of Persia's intentions. Yet I believe that we had been remarkably subtle in our own spying. Nothing was ever written down by the five men that I had assigned to gauge Magadha's military strength. Each man was obliged to memorize the same facts, on the theory that at least one was bound to return alive to Susa.

When it came to trade routes and manufactories and raw materials, our dealings were perfectly open, and we soon had a good idea of the remarkable wealth of the country. Much of the kingdom's revenue came from taxes levied on the caravans that passed through Magadha; par-

217

ticularly lucrative was the famous southeast-to-northwest trail—the word road is simply not applicable to anything Indian.

The state exercised a monopoly over the making of textiles and weapons. It took the superintendent of weaving three days to show me the various workshops where women work from dawn until night, spinning and weaving. The export of finished cotton is a principal source of revenue for the kings of Magadha. Although I was not shown the arsenals, several members of the embassy were able to discover a few secrets. Although they were surprised by the inefficient way that the iron is worked, they were impressed by the efficient way that weapons and farm implements are assembled.

One set of workmen is responsible for making, let us say, the wooden shaft of a hoe. Another set will then pour molten metal into the mold for the iron head. A third set will assemble shaft and head, while a fourth is responsible for loading the finished articles onto wagons. The speed with which a great many hoes can be made and shipped is marvelous.

Unfortunately, I was never able to interest anyone at Susa in these things. For one thing, Persian nobles disdain trade. For another, as a member of the court I was never able to get to know the sort of people who might have wanted to try to produce objects in quantity.

"You will find my child a perfect treasure. She will be as devoted to you as Sita was to Rama." This was a conventional phrase.

"That she is your daughter is more than enough for me."

"She is closest to me of all my children." Tears came to the bright collyrium-washed eyes. Actually, as Ambalika was later to tell me, her father had never bothered to learn the names of any of his daughters. He was interested only in his sons. "I was terrified of him," said Ambalika later. "We all were. He never actually spoke to me until the day he told me that I was to marry a Persian lord. When I asked him where and what Persia was, he told me that that was none of my business."

"You will also want to meet my precious child's grandfather, Prince Jeta. He is also related to my beloved uncle the king of Koshala. Ours is a beautiful and happy family whose only division, I always say, is the Ganges River. And," he added, the soft face suddenly concentrated by a

218

scowl, "the federation. Oh, my dear, you must give us your wisest counsel." The powerful hand rested for a moment on the back of my hand. The heat from his fingers was intense. The palm wine that we had been drinking notoriously heats the flesh while deranging the senses.

"We are stronger. But they are wilier. They stir up trouble on the frontier. They infiltrate the religious orders. The Jaina and Buddhist monasteries are filled with republican agents. But since my father—may he live forever —is personally devoted to the Buddha, we can do nothing. Worse, in the last year, republican agents have worked their way into the guilds. At this very moment, they control the council of the guild of pottery makers right here in Rajagriha. They also have two members on the council of the weavers' guild. Worst of all, the elder of the shoemakers' guild is an open republican. We are being slowly eaten away from within and— Oh, my dear friend, what are we to do?"

"Purge the guilds, Lord Prince. Eliminate the republicans."

"But, dearest, you don't know our little world. Our guilds are almost as old and almost as sacred as the monarchy. As for purging them . . . Well, *I* would like to smash them to pieces. So would my father, secretly, of course. But they are too powerful. They are too rich. They lend money at exorbitant interest. They maintain their own militias . . ."

"But that is dangerous, Lord Prince. Only the ruler should have the power to raise troops." I had been shocked to discover that not only do the guilds of Magadha dominate the country's commercial life but because the workers in any given trade all live together in the same quarter of the city, they resemble tiny nations: each guild has its own law courts, treasuries, troops.

"Mind you, we control the guilds, up to a point. In wartime the guild militias automatically become part of the king's army. Yet when there is no war . . ."

"They are practically independent?"

"Practically. Of course, the guilds are useful to us. No king, no secret service could ever keep control over a population as large as ours. So the guilds keep order for us. Also, when it comes to setting prices, they usually know better than we what the market's demands are."

"But how can you control them? If I were the . . . elder of the shoemakers' guild, say, I would want to get as much as I possibly could for a pair of shoes. I'd double the price, and people would have to buy because only my guild is allowed to make and sell shoes."

The prince smiled, rather sweetly. He was beginning to react to all the wine that he had drunk. "For one thing, we alone have the power of life and death. We seldom use this power against the guilds, but it is always there, and they know it. Practically speaking, our power is based on the fact that we control all raw materials. We buy cheap and we sell only to make a small profit. For instance, cows are slaughtered at a certain time of year. When this happens, we buy up all the hides and put them in warehouses. When cowhides are in short supply, we sell them at a reasonable price to the guilds. If a guild was tempted to market its shoes at an unreasonable price, we would withhold the leather until they become more reasonable."

Nowhere in the world have I found a monarchial system so delicately and intelligently balanced as to be able to gain the most revenue from the population with the least coercion.

"Will you go to war with the federation?" I was sufficiently drunk to ask the prince the question whose answer all India nervously awaited.

Ajatashatru spread his arms, palms upwards. The fingertips had been painted red. "War is always the very last thing one wants. But had the horse sacrifice turned out differently, we would at least have had a sign from heaven that it was time for us to fight for our survival. As it is . . . I don't know, my dear."

The prince fondled a naked girl of nine or ten who lay across his lap. She had enormous, watchful eyes. I assumed that she was a secret-service agent. In Magadha, agents are recruited young, usually from among homeless orphans.

If the child was an agent, she learned nothing that night. The prince was discreet, as always. Although I had watched him on more than one occasion drink himself into unconsciousness, I never heard him say anything that he did not want the world to know. Wine made him maudlin, affectionate, confused. The "my dear's" would come in Greek phalanxes. The hot hand would press my hand and the arm about my shoulders would bestow a loving hug. That night I was patted, hugged, my-deared and accepted as a member—more or less—of the royal

220

family of Magadha which was separated from its cousins of Koshala by the Ganges River . . . and by the wicked federation of republics. That night at the Five Hills Gambling Hall it was my impression that the decision to go to war had already been made.

"There has never been a soldier to equal my father, you know. Not even your Cyrus the Great. Believe me, Bimbisara was a high king long before the horse sacrifice. After all, it was he who conquered the people of Anga, which gave us the port of Champa, which controls all the traffic down the Ganges to the sea that leads to Cathay."

Ajatashatru now wept, from wine. "Yes, it was Bimbisara who created what is now the most powerful nation in all the world. It was he who built a thousand thousand roads and a thousand thousand causeways over the marshes. It was he . . ."

I stopped listening. When Indians use numbers, they never know when to stop. It is true that Bimbisara did create a lot of dirty lanes, which turn to mud in monsoon weather, but he never managed to maintain even the great caravan route from Champa to Taxila. Also, curiously enough, there are no bridges of any kind anywhere in India. They will tell you that bridges are impractical because of the seasonal floods, but it is my view that they do not have the ability to span rivers even with rafts tied together. Of course, one of the most powerful guilds in Magadha is that of the ferrymen and, as the Indians like to say, no guild has ever dissolved itself.

Later that evening, after the prince had fallen asleep, I gambled for a time with Caraka. But as soon as I began to lose at dice, I stopped. On the other hand, Caraka could not stop. Finally I ordered him to leave the hall. I had not realized until then to what an extent the desire to gamble can make men mad. It is like haoma or sexual passion. But haoma and sexual passion wear off in time, while the need to gamble does not.

I must say that I admired the way that Bimbisara was able to raise, so painlessly, so much revenue from the addictions of the people. For a time, we experimented at Susa with a gambling hall. But Persians are not gamblers —because they are not traders? And only Greeks came to the hall. Since the Greeks invariably lost more money than they could ever pay, the place was shut down.

7

AS SOON AS I HAVE DECIDED HOW ALIKE all human beings are, I am confronted with some great differences between races. Indians gamble. Persians don't. The Vedic gods of India are the Zoroastrian devils of Persia. Why do some men believe that the cosmos is a single entity, while others believe it is many things? Or many things in one thing? Or no thing at all. Who or what created the cosmos? Does it exist or not exist? Did I exist before I addressed this question to Democritus? Do I exist now? Did I exist in another form before I was born? Will I be reborn as something else again? If there were no people on earth to watch the sun cast lengthening shadows, would there be such a thing as time?

Prince Jeta took even greater pleasure than I in pondering what he called first things. He came from Koshala to Magadha to attend his granddaughter's wedding. At our first meeting he invited me to his country house just north of Rajagriha. I was told to come at midday. I was not, he said, to worry about the heat. Ordinarily, at that season, social visits take place in the late afternoon. But as he told me, "You will be as cool at noon as if you were in the country of snow." This was an old-fashioned expression, dating back to the first Aryans. After all, I doubt if a dozen people at the court of Magadha had ever experienced snow.

Caraka and I traveled by canopied wagon. Caraka had just returned from a visit to the iron mines in the south; he had been impressed by their extent. Since our bullock-driver was a spy who understood Persian, we spoke cryptically. How could we tell which ones knew Persian and which did not? The Persian-speakers were all from the northwest—from Gandhara or the Indus Valley. To a man, these northwesterners are taller and fairer than the Magadhans. They also have as much difficulty with the local dialect as we did. In my honor, Varshakara had imported several dozen of them to spy on us.

Prince Jeta's estate was enclosed by a wall of mud brick, pierced by a single wooden gate just off the main road. Since neither wall nor gate was at all impressive, we might have been paying a call on the headquarters of the millers' guild. But once inside the gate, even the anti-Aryan Caraka was impressed.

At the end of a long alley of flowering trees was an elaborate pavilion whose tall arched windows were shaded by awnings of a pale-blue cloth that felt to the touch like silk but proved to be a new variety of cotton cloth.

The scent of flowers and herbs varied from section to section of the gardens. Because the countryside between the Ganges and Rajagriha is entirely flat, Prince Jeta had broken the monotony of the view by building a number of small hills and miniature mountains. The artificial hills were covered with banks of flowers and low trees, while the miniature mountains were made to look like the gray Himalayas. The effect was singularly beautiful.

The interior of the pavilion was dim and, as promised, cool because sprays of water periodically cooled the air by dampening the green shrubbery outside the windows. Eventually a member of my embassy was able to work out the hydraulic principle on which this system was based and, for a time, it was used in the new palace gardens at Babylon. But like all innovations in that city, the system was soon abandoned. Anything later than the modernist Nebuchadnezzar is considered slightly impious. The Babylonians are easily the most conservative people on earth.

Prince Jeta was neither young nor old; his skin was paler than that of the average Magadhan, and there was that curious fold over each eye which is a characteristic of the Himalayan mountain people as well as the Cathayans. For an Indian noble in summertime, the movements of his slender body were surprisingly brisk—no doubt the result of being kept cool by running water, shade trees, magical revolving fans.

Prince Jeta greeted us formally. He then told me how delighted he was that I was marrying his granddaughter, who was, everyone agreed, as light-footed as a gazelle, as fertile as fresh lettuce, and so on. I was pleased that he did not pretend to know the child.

Ceremonies out of the way, we were given a light but delicious meal. "I do not eat meat," he said. "But of course you may, if you choose."

"No." I was relieved. On a hot summer day, the com-

223

bination of meat with ghee made me as dull as any over-fed Brahman. I asked my host if he refrained from eating meat on religious grounds.

Prince Jeta made a delicate, self-deprecating gesture. "I would like to be truly enlightened. But I am not. I do observe the vows as much as possible, but what is possible for me is never much. I am a long way from nirvana."

"Perhaps," I said, "the Wise Lord will find your present intentions the equal to deeds, and he will allow you to cross the bridge of redemption to paradise." I cannot think why I should have been so tactless as to have got onto the subject of religion in the house of a man close to the Buddha. Although I had been taught that ours is the only true religion in the world and that it must be brought to all men whether they—or their demons—like it or not, I was also a courtier and, most important, an ambassador. Darius had said, very firmly, that I was not to denounce other gods or inflict the Wise Lord upon foreigners.

But Prince Jeta chose to deal most amiably with my crudeness. "Indeed it would be gracious of your Wise Lord to assist one so unworthy to pass across his bridge to—uh, paradise." In general, the conception of paradise as the world of the fathers is vague to Indo-Aryans, while it is entirely ignored by those, in particular, who have replaced their Vedic gods with the concept of a long chain of deaths and rebirths that will end either through personal enlightenment or because one of the world's cycles of creation has stopped—in order to start again.

I let drop the subject of the Wise Lord. So, I was sorry to note, did Prince Jeta. He spoke of the Buddha. "You will meet him when you visit us in Koshala, and I shall be heartbroken if we are denied the enormous—how shall I say?—radiance of your presence in Shravasti, not only as emissary of the Great King but, best of all, as grandson of Zoroaster." Like all Indians, Prince Jeta could weave flower garlands with words. Like all Persian courtiers, so can I. But after our meal we let the flowers wither and got to actual subjects.

"We shall walk," said Prince Jeta, taking my arm. Then he led me to an artificial lake, which had been so artfully planted around with reeds and lotuses that one could easily mistake the whole invention for an unusually successful work of nature. Due to some trick of perspective, the lake seemed enormously broad and deep, and bounded at the far end by a mountain range.

At the edge of the water Prince Jeta removed his upper garment. "Do you swim?" he asked.

"That is one of the first things taught us," I said.

Actually, I have never learned to swim properly. But I was able to keep up with Prince Jeta as he paddled decorously across the shallow lake to the miniature mountain range. Bright-colored fish darted between our legs while fiery flamingoes watched us from the water's edge. There was a feeling of paradise in that place that day.

When we were within a few feet of the artificial cliff, Prince Jeta said, "Now hold your nose and dive under the mountain." In an instant, like a sea gull after a fish, he was gone.

Since I did not know how to dive, I carefully ducked my head underwater and kicked my feet. I assumed that I would, presently, drown. But then, for the first time ever, I opened my eyes underwater and I was entranced by the bright fish, the swaying green ferns, the chains of lotuses on their way to the surface. Just as I was almost entirely out of breath, I saw the entrance to a cave. With a great kick I propelled myself into the cave and shot to the surface.

Prince Jeta helped me out of the water. Divans, tables, chairs were placed here and there on the fine white sand. Except that the sand was not white but blue. Everything in the cave glowed with an intense blue light as if beneath the water a fire were burning. This natural effect was the result of several small openings at the level of the lake. Although light and air were able to circulate in the cavern, no one could look in. "Or overhear us," said my host, settling onto a divan. "This is the only place in Magadha where Varshakara cannot listen to us."

"You built this cavern?"

"The mountain, too. And the lake. And the park. I was young then, of course. I had taken no vows. I was still attached to every pleasurable thing in this world, and that sort of attachment is the cause of pain, isn't it?"

"But, surely, there is often more joy than pain. Look at your own marvelous creation—"

"—which I shall have to pay for when I make my next appearance, as a pariah dog." Prince Jeta's manner was so serene that I could not tell if he was serious or not, always a sign of the highest breeding.

But Prince Jeta could be direct. "I understand that you have made a treaty with my cousin Bimbisara."

"We are making a treaty, yes. Iron for Persia. Gold for Magadha. The price has not been decided. I may have to go back to Susa before I can give the Great King's final word."

"I see. When do you come to Koshala?"

"I have no idea."

"I am here not only to help preside at your marriage to my granddaughter but to invite you, on behalf of King Pasenadi, to attend his court as soon as possible."

After a diplomatic interval, I responded to the urgency of my host. "You believe that there will be war?"

"Yes. Soon. Troops are being moved up to the river."

"To invade the federation?"

"Yes . . ." Prince Jeta's eyes looked as blue as the under-mountain pool. Actually, in a normal light, the prince's eyes were what I came to think of as Himalayan-gray, a color or shade that one sees only in natives of that high part of the world.

"What will Koshala do?"

"What will Persia do?"

I was not prepared for a bluntness that more than equaled my own. "It is a thousand miles from Taxila to Magadha."

"We have heard that the Great King's armies travel fast."

"Then you must know that the Great King's army is occupied in the west by the Greeks who—" But I did not think it necessary to explain the Greeks to a man as civilized as Prince Jeta. If he had needed to know about them, he would have known; as it turned out, he knew nothing of Europe.

"Another contingent is on the northern frontier," I said, "fighting the tribes."

"Our cousins." Prince Jeta smiled.

"Thirty or forty generations ago. But whatever our ancient connection, they are now the common enemy."

"Yes, of course. But surely the Great King keeps an army in his satrapy along the Indus River."

"Only for defense. He would never send it to Magadha."

"You are certain?"

"The Great King has controlled the Indus valley for less than a generation. Without a Persian garrison . . ."

"I understand." The prince sighed. "I had hoped . . ." He made a gesture with one hand that was both delicate and intricate. But I had not yet learned the language of hands, as the Indians call it. Their subtlest points are often made not with words but gestures, a form of communication that derives from prehistoric dances.

"You find my son-in-law sympathetic?"

"Oh, yes. He seems most elegant and . . . sentimental."

"He is certainly sentimental. He once wept for a week when his pet bird died."

"But the chamberlain does not weep!" Now, I thought, I shall test whether or not the Magadhan secret service had penetrated Prince Jeta's grotto.

"No. He is a hard man. He dreams of annexing Varanasi. He dreams of the breakup of Koshala."

"Is that only a dream?"

"Pasenadi is a holy man. He does not care for this world. He himself is an arhat. That means he is close to enlightenment, to the ultimate dissolution of the self."

"Is that the reason his kingdom is also close to dissolution, if not enlightenment?"

Prince Jeta shrugged. "Why should kingdoms differ from human beings? They are born. They grow. They die."

"Then why do you care if Koshala now imitates the body of a man three months dead?"

"Oh, I care. I care. Because of the sangha."

Sangha is the word for the order or community of Buddhists. But the word and the concept predate the Buddha by centuries or millennia. In the republics, the sangha is the council of all the heads of family. In some republics, each member of the council or assembly is called raja or king, a nice avoidance of the monarchial principle: if everyone is a king, no one is. In those days no one man ruled in any of the republics.

Since the Buddha himself was the son of a council member in the republic of the Shakyas, he is often referred to as the son of a king. But his father was simply one of a thousand kings who met to administer the republic. But whereas a republican sangha is ruled by half its membership plus one, the sangha of the Buddhists can make no decision without a unanimous vote. Once the Buddha himself was snuffed out, this rule was to cause a good deal of trouble for the order.

"You fear King Bimbisara?"

"No. He is our friend."

"Varahakara?"

Absently or deliberately, Prince Jeta drew a star in the soft white—no, blue—sand. "He is a typical royal chamberlain. For him, the order—any order—is dangerous."

"Republican?"

"Exactly. And since Bimbisara is old and Varshakara is young, it is wise to anticipate the worst." Prince Jeta laughed. "You see why I am a flawed Buddhist? I must concern myself with politics when I ought to be observing the vows."

"Which vows do you *not* observe?" I was most literal in those days. Also, the thousand and one religions of India had me in a state of perfect confusion. Indians appear to accept everything, which is the same as accepting nothing. Whenever I lit the sacred fire in a sunless place, a few curious Brahmans would attend me. They were always polite, and they would ask interested questions. But they never came back a second time. I cannot think how my grandfather would have gone about converting them.

"I am too much of the world," said Prince Jeta. He tossed a pebble into the blue shining pool at our feet. A moment later, what looked to be a school of porpoises swam toward us. But when the porpoises surfaced, they proved to be young girls. Each carried a musical instrument wrapped in water-resistant skins.

"I thought you might enjoy some music. I designed both the mountain and the grotto so that I could hear music at its best. I'm afraid that I don't practice all of the sixty-four arts, but I do know music, the only art that I find closest to—" Wisely, he did not choose to compare to anything what he himself believed to be incomparable.

I cannot say that I enjoyed the concert as much as I did the blue-water light which made all things as incorporeal as a haoma-dream.

I wonder now if all this had been deliberately planned. I do know that many of the things that Prince Jeta proceeded to tell me about the Buddha have remained in my memory. Could the light and the music in some way have combined to induce the sort of vision that we obtain from a sacred haoma or even devils' soma? Only Prince Jeta could know the answer, and he has long since exchanged the body that sat beside me for—what? A minor Indian deity, at the very least, with, one hopes, a mere two arms, and a near-eternity of bliss before the final nothing.

As the music played, Prince Jeta described the Buddha's four noble truths. "The first truth is that all life is suffering. If you don't get what you want, you suffer. If you get what you want, you suffer. Between getting and not getting, human life is like a sputtering fire. Don't you agree?"

"Yes, Prince Jeta." I always say yes, in order to learn more. A proper eel-wriggler like Protagoras or Socrates would want to know just what is meant by suffering. By getting. By not getting. If the splitter of hairs has a sharp enough knife, the fact of life itself can be chopped into nothing. I find this a waste of time. In a blue cavern beneath an artificial mountain, I am willing to accept, if only for the moment, the idea that existence is a sputtering fire.

"We like to delight in the five senses. Certainly, we try to avoid pain or suffering. How is this done? Through the senses, which add fuel to the fire, and make it blaze. So the second truth is that a desire for pleasure or, worse, a desire for permanence in a creation where all is flux, can only make the fire more intense, which means that when the fire drops, as it must, the pain and the sorrow are all the greater. Don't you agree?"

"Yes, Prince Jeta."

"Then it is plain that suffering will never cease as long as the fire is fed. So do you agree that to avoid suffering, one must cease to add fuel to the fire?"

"Yes, Prince Jeta."

"Good. That is the third truth. The fourth truth demonstrates how the fire can be put out. This is accomplished by not wanting."

Prince Jeta stopped. For a moment I listened to the music, which I found oddly attractive. I say oddly because I had not yet become accustomed to Indian music. But since the occasion itself was so enchanting, all things pleased me, and I was more than ever removed from the four truths of the Buddha! I was not in the least detached or released. Certainly, I did not want to be extinguished.

Suddenly I realized that Prince Jeta's fourth truth was nothing at all, which in itself is a truth as some Athenians —and even Abderans—might say. I turned to my host. He was smiling. Before I could put my question, he answered it. "To blow out the flame of this painful existence you must follow the eightfold way. That is the fourth noble truth."

Sooner or later, Indians produce numbers. Since they are the vaguest of mathematicians, I always discount any number an Indian gives me, even though it be thirty million million million times the number of grains of sand in the bed of the Ganges River.

"Eight?" I tried to appear interested. "But I thought there were only four truths."

"The fourth truth requires that one follows the eightfold way."

"And what, Prince Jeta, is *that?*" I was distracted by one of the flautists. She was either off-key or in a key that I had never heard before.

I note for you, Democritus, what the eightfold way involves: One, right views. Two, right intention or purposes. Three, right speech. Four, right action. Five, right living. Six, right effort. Seven, right mindfulness. Eight, right concentration.

At the end, Prince Jeta realized that I was bored. "These things may seem obvious to you . . ."

"No, no." I was polite. "But they are so general. There is nothing specific—like the Wise Lord's very precise instructions to my grandfather on how to sacrifice a bull."

"The Buddha's sacrifices are not of animals but of the animal in the self."

"I understand. But what, specifically, is . . . well, right living?"

"There are five moral rules."

"Four noble truths, one eightfold way and five moral rules . . . At least the Buddha's numbers are not as enormous as those of Mahavira." This was very rude of me.

But Prince Jeta was not upset. "We find Mahavira's views somewhat similar." he said mildly. "But he is only a maker of river-crossings. The Buddha has crossed the river. He is enlightened. He is perfect. He does not exist."

"Except that he is now in residence at Shravasti."

"A body is there. But he is not there."

Since you, Democritus, want to know the five moral rules, I shall give them. The off-key flautist fixed in my memory every word that the prince said. Here are the five moral rules: Don't kill. Don't steal. Don't lie. Don't get drunk. Don't indulge in sex.

I questioned the last rule. "What would happen to the

human race if everyone actually obeyed the five moral rules?"

"The human race would cease to be and that, in the Buddha's eyes, is a perfect thing."

"Even though the Buddhist order would end."

"The aim of the order is to extinguish itself. Unfortunately, no more than a tiny fraction of the human race will ever be drawn to the order, and of those only an infinitesimal number in the course of the millennia will become enlightened. You have nothing to fear, Cyrus Spitama." Prince Jeta was amused. "The human race will continue until the present cycle ends."

"But what is the point to a religion that can only appeal to a few? And of those few, as you've just said, almost none will achieve the ultimate state of nirvana?"

"The Buddha has no interest in religion. He is simply helpful to those who are on the riverbank. He will show them the ferryboat. Should they reach the far side, they will then discover that there is neither river nor ferryboat nor even the two banks . . ."

"Nor the Buddha?"

"Nor the Buddha. The fire will have gone out and the dream of this existence will have been forgotten and the one who has been enlightened will be awake."

"Where?"

"I am not enlightened. I am still too close to the wrong shore."

That is what I was meant to remember of that enchanted if perplexing afternoon in the grotto of Prince Jeta. Later, when I saw and heard the Buddha, I got a somewhat clearer idea of his teaching, which is not really teaching at all.

Democritus says that he sees a resemblance between the Buddha's truths and those of Pythagoras. I don't. Pythagoras and Gosala and Mahavira all believed in the transmigration of souls from fish to tree to man to whatever. But the Buddha was indifferent to transmigration because, ultimately, he did not believe in existence. We are not here, he said. We are not there either. We only imagine that the fire sputters.

Yet one does exist . . . There is absolutely no doubt that I am an old blind man, sitting in a cold and drafty house at Athens, nearly deafened by the sounds of all the building going on just back of us. There is no doubt, in my mind at least, that I am discussing old times with a young relative from Abdera. Therefore, I exist, if barely; more ashes than flames.

To the Buddha the idea of existence was something entirely painful. How right he was! and to be got rid of by eliminating all desire, including the desire to rid oneself of all desire. Obviously, few succeed—at least in eternity. But I am reasonably convinced that those who follow in his way are better off in regard to this world than those who do not.

Odd. I never thought that I would come around to this point of view. Neither did Prince Jeta. "Nothing that I have told you truly matters," he said as we prepared to leave the luminous cave.

"Because the goal of matter is sunyata," I said, rather to his surprise, and to my own earthly delight in my cleverness, "and sunyata is nothingness, which is also your word for the circle that stands for nothing, yet still exists."

For an instant Prince Jeta paused at the edge of the pool. Reflections of blue-water light flickered across his face like so many iridescent spiders' webs.

"You must meet Tathagata," he said in a low voice, as if he did not want even the water to hear him.

"Who is that?"

"Another name for the Buddha. Our private name. Tathagata means the one who has come and gone." With that Prince Jeta himself went. He dived into the water. Gracelessly, I followed.

Years later I discovered that every word that was spoken in the grotto beneath the mountain was carefully taken down by an agent of the Magadhan secret service. Somehow, Varshakara had managed to cut a narrow channel straight through the soft stone of the mountain to the grotto. Fortunately, Prince Jeta was too important to be arrested while the person of an ambassador from the Great King was sacred.

The journey back to Rajagriha was interminable. The dusty road was jammed with people, carts, contingents of soldiers, camels, elephants. Everyone was eager to get back to the city before the sun set and the gates were shut.

I must say I could never get used to the way that Indians relieve themselves in public. You cannot go any distance on any Indian trail without observing dozens of men and women squatting cheerfully at the side of the road. Jaina and Buddhist monks are the worst offenders. Since a monk may eat only what he has managed to beg, tainted food is often put into his bowl, sometimes deliberately. Once the food is in the bowl, he is obliged to eat it. As a result of a truly atrocious diet, most monks suffer from every sort of stomach disorder—in public view.

I saw, perhaps, a dozen Buddhist monks. Each wore castoff rags, and carried a begging bowl. None wore the yellow robes that are today characteristic of the order because, in those days, most dedicated Buddhists still lived in the wilderness, remote from temptation. But eventually the solitary life proved to be at variance with the order's need to record and transmit all the sutras, or words, that the Buddha ever spoke. Gradually those men and women who were truly devoted to the Buddha formed communities. Even during my first visit to India, the order was already a good deal less peripatetic than it had been at first.

The original disciples had traveled with the Buddha and, except during the rainy season, he was always on the move. During his last years, he tended to move in a circle that started and ended at Shravasti, where he spent the rainy season in a park that had been given to the order by Prince Jeta and *not* by a Shravasti merchant named Anathapindika, who used to claim that he had paid Prince Jeta an enormous amount of money for the park. Since Prince Jeta was always careful to avoid credit or praise for anything that he did, Anathapindika is now credited with being the Buddha's most generous patron. I have never known a man quite so noble as Prince Jeta.

When the rains stopped, the Buddha would sometimes revisit his Shakya home in the foothills of the Himalayas. Then he would walk south through the republics, visiting such cities as Kushinara and Vaishali. He would then cross the Ganges at the port of Pataliputra and go south to Rajagriha, where he would spend at least a month in a bamboo grove just inside the city wall. He always slept beneath the trees. He preferred to beg for his food in country lanes rather than in the crowded streets of Rajagriha. During the heat of the day he would meditate beneath a tree, and all sorts of people would come to see him, including King Bimbisara.

I should note here that the sight of holy men squatting beneath trees is a common one in India. Many have been known to sit in the same position for years. Rain-drenched, sun-scorched, wind-flayed, they live on what-

233

ever food is brought them. Some never speak; some never stop talking.

From Rajagriha, the Buddha would move on to Varanasi. Here he was always received like a conquering hero. Thousands of curious people would accompany him to the deer park where he had first set in motion the wheel of the doctrine. Because of the crowds, he seldom stayed long at the deer park. In the dead of night he would leave Varanasi for the northwestern cities of Kaushambi and Mathura, and then, just before the rains began, he would return to Shravasti.

The Buddha was revered by everyone, including those Brahmans who might have regarded him as a threat to their prestige. After all, he belonged to the warrior class. But he was more than a warrior, more than a Brahman. He was the golden one. So the Brahmans feared him because he was like no one else. But then, strictly speaking, he *was* no one. He had come; and he had gone.

8

AFTER AJATASHATRU PAID ME THE dowry, he said, "You must now buy yourself a house. It must not be too large, nor too small. It must be midway between my house and the king's palace. There must be a central courtyard with a well of purest water. There must also be ten different kinds of flowering bushes. Suspended between two trees, there must be a swing that will allow two people to swing together, side by side, for many happy years. The sleeping room must have a wide bed with a canopy of Cathay cloth. There should also be a divan next to a window that looks onto a flowering tree." After itemizing all the things that my house must have, he made two great high arches of his brows and asked, "But *where* is this perfect place to be found? My dear, we must search. There is not a moment to lose!"

Needless to say, Ajatashatru had already found us our ideal house. In fact, he owned it. So I ended by giving back to my father-in-law half the dowry money in order to buy a pleasant if somewhat dilapidated house in a noisy street.

To my surprise, no attempt was made to convert me to

devil-worship before the wedding. I was not expected to do anything more than act out the groom's part in an ancient Aryan ceremony that is not unlike our own. As in Persia, the religious part of the ceremony is performed by the priestly caste. This means that one is not obliged to pay the slightest attention to what they say and do.

In the late afternoon I arrived at the long low wooden house of Ajatashatru. At the entrance I was cheered by a large crowd of common people, who commented favorably on my appearance. I was resplendent, if very hot, in a cloth-of-gold shawl and a turban which a servant had taken one hour to wind and adjust. The king's own barber had outlined my eyes with black and administered lac to my lips. He had then decorated my body with tinted sandalwood paste, transforming my chest into the leaves and branches of a tree whose delicately drawn trunk made its way down my belly to the genitals, which were painted to resemble roots. A glittering serpent circled the calf of each leg. Yes, the barber was a Dravidian and could not resist this pre-Aryan touch. In hot weather, fashionable Indians often cover themselves with sandalwood paste on the ground that it makes them cool. It does no such thing. One sweats like a horse, but at least the sweat smells like the most exotic perfume.

I was attended by Caraka and the entire embassy. By now, we all dressed as Indians. Weather had triumphed over patriotism.

We were greeted at the palace door by Ajatashatru and Varshakara. They were even more gorgeously dressed than I. Varshakara wore Burmese rubies the color of his teeth, while the heir to the throne wore a thousand thousand diamonds, as the Indians would say. Diamonds hung in chains about his neck, covered his fingers, fell in cascades from the lobes of his ears, girdled the huge belly.

According to ancient custom, Ajatashatru offered me a silver cup filled with honey and curds. After I had drunk this cloying mixture, I was led into the central courtyard, where a brightly colored tent had been set up. On the far side of the tent was my as yet unseen bride-to-be, with her mother, grandmother, sister, aunts, female attendants. On our side were the men of the royal family, led by King Bimbisara, who greeted me gravely and kindly. "This day will see joined as one the Aryans of far-off Persia and the Aryans of Magadha."

"You reflect, Lord, as does the Great King Darius, the

true light of the Aryans, and I am happy to be the humble bridge between the twin shining Lords of all the world." I had prepared this nonsense in advance, and a great deal more that can be safely forgotten. All that mattered was the striking of the proper note, which was to pretend that Persia and Magadha were now united against the federation of republics and, if necessary, Koshala.

Flanked by Bimbisara and Ajatashatru, I entered the tent. Silver lamps blazed. Flowers had been made into a thousand thousand—Note, Democritus, that I am now actually thinking in that flowery Indian dialect and then translating my thoughts, such as they are, into stony Greek. The styles of the two languages are entirely unlike, even though many words are similar. Anyway, there were a lot of floral wreaths, and the close air smelled of jasmine and sandalwood.

The ground was covered with Cathayan rugs. One was remarkably beautiful—a blue dragon against a white sky. Later, when Ajatashatru asked his daughter what she most desired, she said the rug. He wept with joy. Nothing, he declared, would make him happier than to see the Cathay dragon rug in the house of his favorite daughter. But we never got the rug. This was the sort of happiness that he tended to deny himself.

The tent was divided in two by a rose-colored curtain. On our side of the curtain, Brahmans chanted passages from the Vedic texts. At enormous length, the perfect love that existed between Rama and Sita was recalled. I was amused to note that the nobles did not even pretend to listen. They were too busy examining one another's costumes and painted skin.

Finally the high priest of Magadha lit a fire in a brazier. Then he was joined by three Brahmans. One held a basin of rice; one held a basin of ghee; one held a basin of water.

The tent was now so hot that I could feel the tree on my chest losing its leaves. I was sweating the way that Cyrus insisted that each Persian soldier must sweat before he is allowed to eat his one and only meal of the day.

From the other side of the rose-colored curtain, we could hear the voices of the ladies as they chanted mantras. Then King Bimbisara whispered something to the high priest. A moment later the curtain was raised, and the ladies of the royal family now faced the men.

My first impression was that the headdresses were almost as tall as the ladies themselves. My wife later told me that since some of the headdresses take a day and a night to arrange, the lady who has been so adorned is obliged to sleep on an inclined board in order not to disturb the marvel that has been created for her.

Between the old queen and the chief wife of Ajatashatru stood a small pretty girl. She might have been six years old—or twenty-six. The red circle that Indian ladies so delight in had been painted between her brows. She was dressed simply, as a virgin.

For a moment the men stared at the women, and the women pretended not to look at the men. I was pleased to see that the breasts of both sexes were covered, a tribute to that original Aryan modesty which has been so effectively undone by the languorous climate of the Gangetic plain.

Finally, the high priest bestirred himself. He took a basket of uncooked rice from a servant woman and made seven small piles on a rug. While this was being done, Ajatashatru crossed the dividing line between the men and the women. As he took his daughter by the hand, Varshakara nudged me. "Go to them," he whispered.

I joined father and daughter at the sacred fire. I had already learned my responses; fortunately, these were few.

"Cyrus Spitama," said Ajatashatru, "Aryan warrior, lord ambassador of the Persian king, take my daughter, Ambalika, and promise that you will observe the Aryan vows, that you will bring her wealth, that you will give her pleasure."

I said that I would do these things as best I could. Then Ajatashatru tied the end of my upper garment to the end of hers. Together Ambalika and I fed the fire with rice and ghee. I found this part of the ceremony comfortable, since we were with the son of the Wise Lord in a sunless place. Then I took the girl by the hand and led her around and around the fire until someone placed a small millstone in front of Ambalika. She stood on the stone for a moment. I still have no idea what the millstone signified.

Uncomfortably knotted together, we took seven steps, making sure that both her foot and mine would rest for an instant on each of the seven heaps of rice. I know what *they* represented: the seven mother-goddesses of pre-Aryan India. Those ladies are eternal, and everywhere. When we had finished hopping across the dragon rug,

237

the high priest sprinkled us with water which was sufficiently cooling to remind me how hot I was; and that was
that. We were married.

But the consummation of our marriage could not take
place until we had slept side by side for three nights. The
origin of this strict abstinence was explained to me at
the time but I have forgotten it. We were also obliged, on
the first night in our house, to watch together the north
star, a reminder to the newlywed Aryan couple that it is
from the north that the tribes originally came . . . and to
which one day they will return?

I liked Ambalika. I was prepared not to. After all, I
have made it a point to expect the worst in life, and the
fact that I am occasionally disappointed in my expecta-
tions is a source of dark solace.

It was about midnight when the last of the wedding
party left the house. My father-in-law was quite drunk.
"My dear," he sobbed, "these tears are the tears of that
unique sorrow which comes from knowing that never,
never again in this life will I know such perfect joy!" As he
blinked his eyes at me the paint from the eyelashes stung
him, producing real tears of pain. Frowning, he rubbed his
eyes with the back of a diamond-sparkling hand. "Oh, my
dearest dear, treat well the lotus of my heart, the favorite
of my children!" In a swirl of perfumed robes and bright
jewels, the royal family departed, and I was left alone
with my first wife.

I looked at her, wondering what to say. But I need
not have worried. Ambalika had been exquisitely trained
in the women's quarters. She was like a worldly lady who
had spent a half-century at court.

"I think," she said, "that after you light the sacred
fire, we had better go up to the roof and look at the
north star."

"Of course. Fire is sacred to us, too," I added.

"Naturally." Ambalika was never to show the slightest
interest in the Wise Lord or Zoroaster. But tales of life at
the Persian court intrigued her enormously.

I lit the fire in a brazier. Everything had been prepared for us by the half-dozen servants who had reported
for duty earlier that day. Ostensibly, they were a gift from
the old queen. Actually, they were all members of the
secret service. How can one tell? If a Magadhan servant
is efficient and obedient, he is a secret agent. Ordinary
servants are lazy, dishonest and cheerful.

238

Together we climbed the rickety stairs to the roof. "Termites," said Ambalika softly. "My lord and master, we'll have to try to smoke them out."

"How can you tell that there are termites?"

"It's just one of the things that we are obliged to know," she said, rather proudly. "Like the sixty-four arts, which I was taught by the old queen, who really does know them. She's from Koshala, where they still believe that ladies should learn such things. Magadha's different. Only the whores are taught the arts here, which is such a pity because, sooner or later, the husbands of ladies find their wives boring and so they lock them up and spend all their days and nights at the halls or in the houses of the whores who are supposed to be perfectly lovely. One of my maids worked for a whore and she told me, 'You think your palace quarters are beautiful—well, wait until you've seen So-and-so's house.' Of course, I'd have to wait forever because I could never visit such a person. But men can. Anyway, I hope that you'll wait until I'm quite old before you start visiting such places."

A tent had been pitched on the roof of the house. By the light of a half-moon, we could see the five smooth hills of the old town.

"There's the north star." Ambalika took my hand and together we stared at what Anaxagoras thinks is a rock, and I wondered, as I often do, just where it was that we all came from. Where had the Aryans first assembled? From the forests north of the Volga? Or from the great plains of Scythia? And why did we come south to Greece, to Persia, to India? And who were the dark-haired people whom we found in the Sumerian and Harappan cities and where did *they* come from? Or did they simply spring from the earth, like so many flowers on a lotus whose time it is to bloom?

Democritus wants to know why the lotus is sacred to eastern peoples. This is why. As the lotus makes its way from the mud to the surface of the water, it forms a chain of buds. Once the lotus bud leaves the water for the air, it opens, flowers, dies; it is then replaced by the next bud of an endless chain. I suspect that if one were to meditate long enough on the lotus, the idea of simultaneous death and rebirth would occur to one. Of course, it may well have been the other way around: a believer in reincarnation decided that the image of the lotus reflected the chain of being.

The north star duly observed, we went inside our roof top tent. I removed my shawl. The tree on my chest had barely survived the rain of my sweat.

But Ambalika was fascinated. "That must've been a lovely tree."

"So it was. Have you a tree?"

"No." She removed her shawl. Since I did not share her father's passion for children, I was relieved to find that she was a fully developed woman. Around each small breast, leaves and flowers had been drawn. At her navel, a white-faced bird stretched its red wings beneath the flowering breasts. "This is Garuda," she said, patting herself. "The sun bird. Vishnu rides him. He brings very good luck, except to serpents. He is the enemy of all serpents."

"Look," I said, and showed her my serpent-ed legs.

Ambalika had a pretty, most natural laugh. "That means you will have to obey our laws or my Garuda will destroy your snakes."

I was restive. "The days we must lie together without making love?"

Ambalika nodded. "Three days, yes. But it won't seem long. You see, I know all the sixty-four arts. Well, most of them, anyway. I'll keep you amused. Mind you, I'm not an expert at any of them. I mean, I'm not a whore. I play and improvise on the lute. I dance quite well. I sing—not so well. I can act in the old plays *very* well, particularly when I play one of the gods like Indra. I prefer acting the part of a man-god. I can also write down poetry that I make up in my head but I can't make it up on the spur of the moment, the way the old queen does, and I don't really fence with a sword or staff, though I'm a good archer. I can make artificial flowers so that you'll think they're real. I can make ceremonial wreaths, arrange flowers . . ."

Ambalika described the varying degrees of proficiency with which she practiced each of the sixty-four arts. I've long since forgotten the full list. But I do recall wondering how any man, much less woman, could have been equally adept at all those things that she named, as well as being a sorcerer, a carpenter, a thinker-up of tongue twisters, and a teacher of birds—particularly the last. Every Indian lady has at least one screeching, brightly plumaged bird that she has taught to say "Rama" or "Sita." When I think of India, I think of talking birds—of rivers and rain, of a sun like god.

Ambalika was as good as her word. She kept me amused and preoccupied for three days and three nights, and though we slept side by side in the roof pavilion, I was able to observe the Vedic law.

When I told her that Ajatashatru had called her his favorite daughter, she laughed. "I never met him until he decided that I was to marry you. Actually, it was the old queen who picked me. I'm *her* favorite granddaughter. Wasn't the horse sacrifice wonderful? The old queen was so excited. 'Now I can die fulfilled,' she told us afterwards. You know, she's going to die very soon. The last horoscope was not good. Look! There's a shooting star. The gods are having a party. They're throwing things at one another. Let's make a wish."

Since I had not yet met Anaxagoras, I could not tell her that what she took to be a handful of pure light was nothing but a chunk of fiery metal on its way to earth.

"Does your father have a favorite wife?" I asked.

"No. He likes new ones. Not wives, of course. They cost you far too much money in the long run, and he's already got three. He might marry another one—or even two. But only after he's king. He couldn't afford a new wife now. Anyway, he sleeps with the elegant whores. Have you ever gone with him to one of their houses?"

"No. When you say he has no money . . ."

"My sisters and I often talk about dressing up as young men and sneaking into a whore's house when she's having a party so that we can see her practice all the arts properly. Or, perhaps, we could go as veiled dancers but, of course, if we were ever caught . . ."

"I'll go. Then I'll tell you what it's like."

"I don't think that's the sort of thing you should say to your very first wife *before* you've experienced her."

"But wouldn't it be much worse to tell her after?"

"True. About my father not having money . . ." The child was quick. She had heard me. She had hoped to distract me. When she failed, she was candid but cautious. She touched one ear, to indicate that we were being spied on. Then she frowned and touched her compressed lips with a reddened forefinger. She was an excellent mime. I was being warned not to discuss the subject in our house, even on the roof at midnight. "He is too generous with everyone," she said in a loud voice. "He wants people to be happy. So he gives them too many presents. That's why he can't afford new wives, which makes us all very

241

happy. Because we want him for ourselves. We don't want to share him." This little speech was a masterpiece of the twenty-eighth art, which is acting.

The next day while we were swinging side by side in the center of the courtyard, she whispered in my ear, "All my father's money is being used to raise an army to fight the republics. That's supposed to be a secret but all the women know it."

"Why doesn't the king raise the army?"

"The old queen says that he really wants peace. After all, since the horse sacrifice he's the universal monarch. So why should he go to war now?"

I did not tell her that Darius, not Bimbisara, was universal monarch because, from the beginning, I assumed that Ambalika's first loyalty would be to her family and not to me. Consequently, I took for granted that whatever I told her of a political nature would be reported to her father or Varshakara. "What does the king think of your father's plans?"

"He doesn't know. How could he? The old queen won't tell him, because she's afraid of my father. I can't think why. After all, she's his mother."

"But the chamberlain would tell him."

"No one knows what the chamberlain tells anyone in secret." Ambalika suddenly looked twice her age. "But he does hate the republics."

"So he has told me."

"Yes, everyone knows what he *says*." She was ambiguous. At the time, I wondered that if there should be a sixty-fifth art, would it be diplomacy or conspiracy?

We were interrupted by the arrival of Ambalika's grandfather Prince Jeta. As this was the third day, he brought us gifts and we entertained him in the main room of the house. Despite the elegance of the furniture and the hangings, it was impossible to disguise the fact that the house would soon collapse from termites and rot. As always, my father-in-law had done well on the transaction.

When Ambalika made as if to withdraw, Prince Jeta motioned for her to stay. "After all, how often does a man get to meet one of his granddaughters?"

Ambalika remained.

Prince Jeta turned to me. "You have been invited, officially, to the court of King Pasenadi." Prince Jeta spoke with none of the urgency that I knew he felt. "The king himself would like to receive you before the rains begin."

"He does me honor." I made the usual speech, adding, "Unfortunately, I must wait until the first consignment of iron leaves for Persia."

"That will be at the beginning of next month, Lord Ambassador." Prince Jeta smiled and I was careful not to acknowledge the slightest distress that he should know of the highly secret arrangements made between Varshakara and me. We had set a price for the iron and we had agreed that the iron be exchanged for gold at Taxila. All in all, I was well pleased with my first commercial treaty. I was not pleased that Prince Jeta knew about it.

"Since your caravan will go through Shravasti, I had hoped that you might accompany it."

"We'll be well guarded, too," said Ambalika, suddenly interested. "You know, there are bands of thieves from one end of Koshala to the other—river pirates, too. Even so, I long to see Shravasti. The old queen tells me that there is no more beautiful city in the world."

"I agree with her," said Prince Jeta. "Of course," he turned to me, "I've only seen the land between the two rivers, as we call our little world."

"Naturally, I shall try to make the trip," I began.

"Oh, say yes!" Ambalika had a child's sense of urgency. Everything must be now. Lais has much the same quality.

Prince Jeta smiled at his granddaughter. "Your husband will also want to meet the Buddha, about whom you've heard such terrible things in the women's quarters."

"That's not true, Prince Jeta. Many of our ladies admire the Lord Buddha." Ambalika was suddenly a tactful royal princess.

"Do you?"

"I don't really know. I can't say that I like the idea of being blown out like a candle. I think that Mahavira is much more interesting."

"Have you seen and heard Mahavira?" Prince Jeta was curious.

Ambalika nodded. "When I was about six, the lady-in-waiting took me to the Jaina convent, which is not far from your house on the river road. Mahavira was sitting in the dirt in front of the convent. I've never seen such a crowd!"

"What did he say that you remember?" Prince Jeta

seemed genuinely interested in his granddaughter. Because she was my wife?

"Well, I liked his description of the creation of the world. You know, how everything is really a part of this giant man, and that we're somewhere around his waist. Of course, Mahavira's geography is not what we've been taught at school, but I did like all those different circles of oceans. There is one of milk and one of clarified butter and one of sugar cane. Oh . . ." She had a habit of interrupting herself. "I particularly liked his description of the first cycle of creation, when everyone was six miles high and we were all twins and each twin brother would marry his sister twin, as they do in Persia today, and there was no work for anyone to do because there were ten trees on which grew everything you would ever want. One tree had leaves that became pots and pans. Another tree grew every kind of food, already cooked. I liked that tree the best. I was a greedy child, I'm afraid. Then there was a tree that grew clothes and another that grew palaces, though I don't see how you could pluck a palace like a banana. But perhaps when the palace was ripe, it would come to rest on the ground, which was made of sugar, while the water was wine . . ." Ambalika interrupted herself again. "But I'm not being serious. I'm only telling you what I remember. He was very old, I thought. I also remember how pleased I was that he was properly dressed, and not sky-clad."

That night our marriage was agreeably consummated. I was pleased. She was pleased. Presumably the Vedic gods were pleased, for nine months later my first son was born.

Not long after the wedding, at the height of the dry season, I was granted a private audience with King Bimbisara. He received me in a small room that looked out upon dry, dusty gardens, loud with swarming locusts.

Bimbisara was to the point. He was always very much the warrior king if not quite the universal monarch. Incidentally, until I went to Cathay I thought that the idea of a universal monarch was peculiarly Aryan, witness our own Great King. But in Cathay I was told that, once upon a time, a single monarch had ruled all the Middle Kingdom—their name for Cathay—in perfect harmony with heaven and that one day he will come again and he will be known as the son of heaven. As there is only one deity, there must be only one universal monarch.

In actual fact, of course, there are as many false gods in the sky and on earth as there are kings and princes in the world. Yet it is clear to me that all mankind hungers for oneness. The Cathayans are in no way related to the Aryans, but they think as we do. Plainly, the Wise Lord has inspired them.

I asked Bimbisara for permission to go with the caravan to Shravasti.

"You are free to go, my son." Bimbisara treated me as a member of his own family, which indeed I was according to Vedic law.

"I am curious to meet the Buddha." Obviously, I made no reference to King Pasenadi's urgent invitation.

"I would give up my kingdom to follow the Buddha," said Bimbisara. "But I am not allowed."

"The universal monarch may do as he pleases." At a king's court, one is never entirely sincere.

Bimbisara tugged at his violet beard. "There is no universal monarch," he smiled. "As you know. And if there was one, he would probably be Darius. I say this only in private, of course. Your Darius is lord of a great many lands. But he is not lord, as he claims, of *all* the lands. As you can see . . ."

"As I can see, Lord King."

"As you can see." He repeated vaguely. "If the Buddha should ask you about the horse-sacrifice, say that I was obliged to pay homage to the Aryan gods."

"Will he disapprove?"

"He never disapproves. He never approves. But, in principle, he holds all life sacred. Therefore, animal sacrifice is always wrong, just as war is always wrong."

"But you are a warrior and a king and an Aryan. You must sacrifice animals to your gods and kill your enemies in war and wrongdoers in peace."

"And to the extent that I am all these things, I may not know enlightenment in this incarnation." There were real tears in the king's eyes, as opposed to those free-flowing fluids that were forever gushing from his son's eyes. "I have often hoped that one day I might be able to put away all this." He touched the jeweled turban that he wore. "Then, once I am nothing, I can follow the Buddha's eightfold way."

"Why don't you?" I was genuinely curious.

"I am weak." With everyone else, Bimbisara was guarded, cautious, cryptic. With me, he was often startlingly candid. I suppose that because I was so entirely outside his world, he felt that he could speak freely to me —of nonpolitical matters. Although I was married to his granddaughter, I was still the Great King's ambassador: one day my embassy would end.

Out of delicacy, no one at court ever referred to my eventual departure. Nevertheless, the return to Persia was always on my mind and, at our last meeting, it was also on Bimbisara's mind. For all he knew, I might decide to continue with the caravan back to Persia. For all I knew, I might very well do just that. My mission had been accomplished. Trade between Persia and Magadha had been established; and there was no reason for it not to continue successfully as long as the one had gold and the other iron.

But at the time of my audience with Bimbisara, I was undecided. I certainly did not intend to abandon Ambalika. On the other hand, I did not know how she might feel at the thought of leaving India. I also dreaded what Ajatashatru might say and do if I told him that I was going home. I would be drowned in tears, if not the Ganges.

"I am weak," Bimbisara repeated, drying his eyes with his shawl. "I still have work to do here. I am trying to set up a sangha of all the village chiefs. I meet them individually, of course. Now I want them to come together at least once a year and tell me their problems."

"You will make Magadha a republic." I smiled, to show that I was joking. I confess that I was somewhat disturbed that he should want to discuss internal politics with a foreigner.

But Bimbisara was simply thinking aloud. "The village chiefs are the secret of our prosperity. Control them, and you flourish. Oppress them, and you perish. I am the first king of Magadha who has known, personally, every chief. That is why I am universal monarch. No, I am not making a republic." He had heard me, after all. "I despise those states where every man with property thinks himself a king. It is unnatural. There can be only one king in any country, as there can be only one sun in the sky or one general at the head of an army. Tell Pasenadi that our affection for him is constant."

"Yes, Lord King." Bimbisara seemed now ready to get to a point, which I was having some difficulty in anticipating.

"Tell him that his sister flourishes. Tell him that she
246

has performed the horse sacrifice. Tell him to disregard those who wish to . . . make trouble between us. They will not succeed, as long as I live."

I looked up at him expectantly. One may stare back at an Indian king. In fact, he would be offended and alarmed if you did not gaze at him directly—but humbly.

"Go to the Buddha. Prostrate yourself before the golden one. Tell him that in the thirty-seven years that have passed since we first met, I have practiced six times a month the eightfold morality. Tell him that only recently have I begun to comprehend the truth of what he once said to me: 'That the only absolute attainment is absolute abandonment.' Tell him that I have made a private vow that in one year's time I shall abandon earthly things and follow him."

No one will ever know whether or not King Bimbisara was serious about giving up the world. I believe that he *thought* he was, which in religious matters counts for slightly more than nothing.

Ajatashatru said farewell to me in the chancellery of his father's palace. For a lover of pleasure, he spent a good deal of his time dealing with the king's privy council and the chief councilor.

At Magadha, the chief councilor does the actual work of administering the country, aided by some thirty councilors, many of them hereditary and most of them incompetent. As palace chamberlain, Varshakara was in charge not only of the court but of the secret police. Needless to say, he was more powerful than the chancellor, and he would have been more powerful than the king had Bimbisara not chosen to rule in close alliance with the village headmen who not only looked upon the sovereign as a friend at a very corrupt and intricate court, but, in his name, they collected taxes, deducted their share and sent on the rest to the treasury. The king was seldom cheated.

As at Susa, various councilors administer different functions of the state. Traditionally, in every reign, the high priest is close to the king. But the Buddhist Bimbisara seldom consulted the official custodian of the Vedic gods whose single moment of glory had been the recent celebration of the horse sacrifice. From amongst the privy council, the king appoints a minister for war and peace and a high judge, who presides over the country's magistrates and hears in his court those cases that do not directly go to the king; he also appoints a treasurer and a chief tax collector. These last two officials are of great importance and, traditionally, they die rich. But under Bimbisara, they were kept on a short leash. He had got around them by his alliance with the village chiefs.

There are a host of sub-ministers who are known as superintendents. Since all raw metals belong to the king, the iron mines are administered by a superintendent who demanded from me no more than a patriotic five percent of the export value of his master's iron, which I paid. Since all forests belong to the king, the elephants, tigers, exotic birds, wood for building and firewood come under a single superintendent. In fact, almost every profitable aspect of Indian life is regulated by the state. There are even superintendents in charge of gambling, of the sale of distilled liquors, of the houses of prostitution. All in all, the system does not work too badly. If a monarch is vigilant, he can, if he chooses, make things happen rapidly. Otherwise, the day-to-day administration of the state is a slow business, which I regard as a good thing. What you do not do can never be entirely wrong. This, Democritus, is a political and not a religious observation.

The thirty members of the privy council sat on low divans in a high-vaulted room on the ground floor of the palace. In a sense, this room corresponds to the second room of our chancellery. As I entered, Ajatashatru rose. As I bowed low—to a father-in-law as well as to a prince—he came toward me, took me in his arms. "You will not abandon us, my dear! Oh, please say you won't!" For once the eyes were not full of tears. They were as bright and shiny as a tiger's when he stares straight at you from a tree's low branch.

I made a graceful, prepared speech. Then Ajatashatru drew me to the far end of the long room. He lowered his voice, as people do in palaces all over the world. "Dearest one, tell King Pasenadi that his nephew cares for him as if he were his own son."

"I shall, Lord Prince."

"Tell him"—Ajatashatru was now whispering in my ear; his breath smelled of curry—"tell him, as delicately as possible, that our police have learned that there will be an attempt on his life. Very, very soon. You understand—and he will understand—that we cannot openly warn him. It would be embarrassing for us to admit that we have agents in Koshala. But you are neutral. You are from outside. You can tell him to be on his guard."

248

"But who are the conspirators?" Then I allowed myself a courtier's inspiration. "The federation of republics?"

Ajatashatru was obviously grateful for a suggestion that had not, for the moment, occurred to him. "Yes! They want Koshala in ruins, which it almost is, anyway. That is why they are working closely, secretly and, oh, so treacherously with the chief conspirator who is"—soundlessly, Ajatashatru mouthed the words—"Virudhaka, the son of the king."

I don't know why I was shocked. After all, the man for whom I was named killed his father-in-law. But a father-in-law is not a father and the Aryan belief in the father's sacredness is an essential part of their code. Did I believe Ajatashatru? I have long since forgotten. But I suspect that I did not. He had a tendency to speak the way a bird sings; he trilled, chattered, made the air vibrate with meaningless sound.

At noon the next day Varshakara accompanied me as far as the north gate of Rajagriha. The first part of the caravan had left before dawn and nearly two miles now separated the head of the caravan from its tail. I was to travel at the center, accompanied by all but a handful of the embassy. I was still not certain whether or not I would return with the caravan to Persia. I had been cut off from the real world for more than two years, during which no message had ever got through to me from Susa. I was feeling isolated, to say the least.

"We regard Pasenadi as a good ally." Varshakara spat a wad of crimson betel juice at a pariah dog, staining the creature's ear.

To the north, as far as the eye could see, a thousand iron-filled bullock-drawn carts moved slowly through a cloud of yellow dust. The smelted iron was of unusually good quality, thanks to a member of my embassy who was able to teach the Magadhans how to smelt iron in the Persian way.

"Because a weak ally is a good ally?" To joke with Varshakara was rather like poking a stick at a tiger in a flimsy cage.

"Sometimes. Sometimes not. But we certainly prefer the old man to his son."

Since the Indian mob at whose center we stood was so loud, there was not much danger of our being overheard.

"Is it true?" I asked.

Varshakara nodded. "Before the end of the rainy season, there will be a new king."

"I hope that I'm not there."

"I hope that you can prevent it."

"How?"

"You must warn the old man. I'm sure that Persia doesn't want a strong king in Koshala any more than we do."

"How can there be a strong king if the Buddhists control the country?"

Varshakara looked surprised. "But they don't. And if they did, what difference would it make?"

Obviously, Varshakara had forgotten his speech to me on the danger Buddhists and Jains present to the established order. Since I thought him mad, I spoke very carefully. "It was my understanding that the monasteries are full of republicans and that they have set out deliberately to weaken Koshala—and Magadha, too."

"Quite the contrary." Varshakara briskly contradicted everything that he had told me on the road from Varanasi. "The Jains and the Buddhists are an enormous help to any king. No, it's Pasenadi himself who is at fault. He is a holy man who thinks only of the next world . . . or of no world, or whatever it is those people believe in. This may be admirable in a man but not in a king. The old fool should have abdicated long ago. Then we could have . . . tamed the son."

Although Varshakara's analysis of Pasenadi's character did not interest me—on principle I never believed a word that he said about political matters—I was intrigued to learn that he now appeared to approve of Buddhism. I asked him why.

Varshakara's answer seemed candid. "Any religion that believes that this world is a kind of illness to be got rid of by prayer and by respecting all life and by not wanting earthly possessions is enormously helpful to a ruler. After all, if people don't want material things, they won't want what we've got. If they respect all life, they will never try to kill us or overthrow our government. Frankly, we do our best, through the secret police, to encourage the Jains and the Buddhists. Naturally, if we ever saw them as a threat . . ."

"But their virtues are entirely negative. They won't work. They are beggars. How can you make soldiers out of them?"

"We don't try. Besides, those are just the monks. The majority of the Jains and the Buddhists simply honor Mahavira and the Buddha, and then they go on about their business like everyone else—with one difference. They cause us less trouble than everyone else."

"Because they are republicans at heart?"

Varshakara laughed. "Even if they were, what could they do? Anyway, the world does not interest them, which is very nice for those of us who absolutely dote on the world as it is."

My bullock cart was now at hand. Varshakara and I said farewell. Then Caraka and I shoved our way through the crowd to where my guards were waiting. Although they were dressed as Indians, they were armed as Persians.

I insisted that the cart be equipped with an awning and cushioned seats. To my surprise, I had been obeyed. Once Caraka and I were seated, the driver's whip touched the flanks of the bullocks and, with a jolt, we began the two-hundred-and-twenty-mile journey to Shravasti.

Ambalika did not go with me because she was sick with the fever. Since there was a good possibility that she was also pregnant, we both agreed that it was dangerous for her to travel. "But you *will* come back, won't you?" Ambalika looked her age, and most forlorn.

"Yes," I said. "As soon as the rainy season is over."

"Then you'll be able to watch me give birth to your son."

"I shall pray to the Wise Lord that I shall be home by then." I embraced her.

"Next winter," said Ambalika firmly, "the three of us will go up to Susa."

9

THE CARAVAN CROSSED THE GANGES AT the river port of Pataligama where the ferrymen are celebrated not only for their clumsiness but for the delight that they take in any sort of disaster. On our account, they had two occasions for high merriment, each involving the loss of a wagonload of iron on a day when the river was as flat and as smooth as a polished-metal mirror.

Because of the sun's heat, we traveled by night and slept by day. We saw no thieves until we entered the forest just south of Vaishali. Here we were attacked by several hundred well-armed bandits who made a great deal of noise but did us no damage. This particular band is esteemed throughout India because no one may join who is not a legitimate son of a third-generation member of the thieves' guild. Thieving is so profitable that this particular guild does not want an age-old business ruined by amateurs.

The Licchavi capital of Vaishali is also the capital of the union of republics, sometimes known as the Vajjian federation.

We were greeted by the governor of the city, who showed us the congress hall where delegates from the other republics meet. But since congress was not in session, the huge wooden hall was empty. We were also taken to the birthplace of Mahavira, an undistinguished suburban house which already has the unmistakable look of a shrine.

It took me a long time to realize that both the Buddha and Mahavira were something far greater than teachers or prophets in the minds of their adherents. They were thought to be *greater than any or all of the gods.* I found this concept as dizzying as it is appalling. Although ordinary Buddhists and Jains continue to pray to Varuna and Mithra and the other Vedic gods, they regard all these gods as *inferior* to the twenty-fourth enlightened one and the twenty-fourth maker of river-crossings on the ground that no god can achieve nirvana or kevala without being reborn as a man. I shall repeat that, Democritus. No god can become enlightened and achieve extinction without first being reborn as a man.

It is astonishing to think that millions of people in my time—now, too, I suppose—actually thought that at a given moment in history two human beings had evolved to a higher state than that of all the gods that ever were or ever will be. This is titanism, as the Greeks would say. This is madness.

While I was in Vaishali, I got the sense that although the republics expected an attack from Magadha, they were having some difficulty in raising troops. This always happens in countries where every man of property thinks himself a king. You cannot fight a war with ten thousand generals. Despite those unrelenting tributes to

252

the wisdom of the people one must endure hereabouts, any fool knows that the people are not only easily manipulated by demagogues but susceptible to bribery. Worse, the people are seldom eager to submit to the sort of discipline without which no war can be prosecuted, much less won. I predict a return of the tyrants to Athens. Democritus disagrees.

It was dawn when we arrived at the north bank of the Ravati River. Shravasti is on the south bank. Since the slow, thick, heat-narrowed river makes a wide curve at that particular point, Shravasti is crescent-shaped. On the land side, it is surrounded by high brick walls and formidable watchtowers. On the river side, there are all sorts of wharves and docks and warehouses—the usual jumble of an Indian river port. A flimsy wooden palisade separates the port from the city proper; obviously the inhabitants do not fear an attack from the river. In a country without bridges and warships, water is the perfect defense. I was pleased to note that the Great King could seize Shravasti in a day. I was equally pleased to note that in the early morning light, the high towers of Shravasti appeared to be made of roses.

Since the caravan was continuing north to Taxila, there was no reason for it to cross the river. So I said farewell to all the embassy except my personal guards and the invaluable Caraka.

As we were ferried across the river I began to comprehend, somewhat, all those Buddhist and Jaina references to rivers and ferryboats, to crossings and the farther shore. In fact, halfway across the river, when I saw how rapidly the caravan on the north shore had begun to shrink while, simultaneously, the walls and towers and temples of the city were expanding, I was reminded vividly of Prince Jeta's image. In fact, approaching the residence of the golden one himself, I found myself *experiencing,* as it were, the image. The shore that I had left was familiar, ordinary life. The river was the torrent of existence in which one might easily drown. Before me was not so much the city of Shravasti as what the Buddhists refer to as "the farther shore from birth and death."

My arrival at Shravasti had been anticipated, and I was met at the dock by a glittering delegation. Prince Jeta himself introduced me to the governor of the city and his suite. These worthies tend to be somewhat fairer of skin and hair than their Magadhan equivalents. They also have about them an air of self-confidence that one seldom encounters at the Magadhan court. But then, King Pasenadi had no pretensions to universal monarchhood; also, he had no chamberlain like Varshakara, whose secret police and sudden arrests made for a constant tension. Whatever Koshala's misfortunes as a state, life was obviously quite pleasant for those able to live in comfort at Shravasti, that most opulent and luxurious of this world's cities.

"Honored guests usually come from the south and then we meet them at the gates, with a most attractive ceremony. But here at the river . . ." The governor apologized for the large mob of dock workers, fishermen, boatmen. They shoved and jostled us, despite a contingent of city policemen who would push back the crowd, which would then push back the police. Although everyone was quite good-natured, it is always an alarming experience to find oneself drowning in the dark odorous flesh of an Indian crowd.

Suddenly the cordon of police broke and the pressure of the mob hurled us against the wooden stockade. Fortunately, my Persian guards saved us from being crushed to death. The Persians drew their swords. The crowd backed off. Then, in a loud voice, the governor gave orders for the gates to be opened. But the gates remained shut. We were now marooned between the suddenly predatory crowd and the wooden stockade.

"This is the way things are in Kashala," said Prince Jeta, striking down a thief's arm that had managed to insinuate itself between two Persian guards.

"Well, the people seem . . . cheerful," I said.

"Oh, they are remarkably cheerful."

"And there are so many of them," I added inanely.

"Oh, yes, fifty-seven thousand families live in Shravasti."

Meanwhile the governor of the city was shouting orders at the top of his voice while pounding on the gates with his fists. After what seemed an entire cycle of Vedic creation, the wooden gates swung creakily open and just inside the stockade, I was relieved to see a line of troops, spears at the ready. The crowd fell back, and we entered Shravasti with more haste than dignity.

Horse-drawn chariots were waiting for us but I said that I preferred to walk, for "after three weeks in a bullock cart my legs are stiff." And so at the head of a somewhat irritable procession. I walked the length of what luckily proved to be the shortest of the four straight avenues that converge on caravan square. Each of the three long avenues begins, respectively, at the southwest, southeast and south gates, and each represents the terminus or point of departure of a caravan route.

The vast wealth of Shravasti is due to geography—the city is at the crossroads not only for the caravans that go between east and west but for those that go from north to south. As a result, the city is dominated by wealthy magnates, which means that, practically speaking, the Brahmans and warriors take second and third place to the merchant class, an anomaly in the Vedic world that is much resented by the displaced or, rather, ignored ruling classes. In peacetime the king and the nobles and the Brahmans are entirely dependent upon the merchants, who are like merchants everywhere—interested in trade, money, peace. It is only in wartime that the ruling classes come into their own, obliging the merchants to take cover until the danger is past.

Prince Jeta believed that the reason why the merchant class supports the Buddhists and the Jains is that the two orders respect all life and disapprove of war. The two orders also appeal to those villagers who worship the pre-Aryan gods. For one thing, villagers prefer peace to war; for another, they detest those huge and wasteful slaughters of horses and bulls and rams that the Brahmans are forever offering up to the Vedic gods. No villager wants to give up his bullock to anyone, Aryan or non-Aryan, man or god. I think it altogether possible that one day the Buddhist and Jaina orders will displace the Aryan gods, thanks to the effort of the wealthy merchants in combination with the non-Aryan population of the countryside.

Until I came to India I had thought of cities as being nothing more than irregular blank walls of different heights arranged haphazardly along winding lanes. Even at Babylon, the houses that look upon the long straight streets are as blank and as windowless as those of any Persian or Greek city. Were it not for the occasional Greek arcade, the monotony would be depressing, particularly in those climates where the common people tend to live out-of-doors all year around.

But Shravasti is unlike the western cities. Every house displays windows and balconies, and the roofs are fantastically turreted. Walls are often decorated with scenes from Rama's endless life. Many of these paintings are beautifully done—or redone—since each year the rains wash them away. Some householders now cover their walls with bas-reliefs, and the effect is delightful.

As the governor and I moved slowly down the center of the crowded avenue, horse-drawn chariots made way for us while rich merchants peered down at us from the tops of elephants. Unlike the crowd at the port, the city people were decorous. But then, they are used to foreigners. They had been Persians before, not to mention Babylonians, Egyptians, Greeks and even visitors from behind the Himalayas, the yellow folk of Cathay.

"To the left," said Prince Jeta, ever the compassionate guide, "are the bazaars and the manufactories." He need not have told me. I could hear or smell the specialty of each of the streets or lanes that led from the avenue. One smelled of flowers; another stank of curing hides. Some quarters were loud with the noise of metal being pounded while others were filled with the sounds of singing birds, to be sold as pets or food.

"To the right are the government buildings, the great houses, the king's palace. While here"—we were now in the enormous central square—"caravans from all over the world meet."

Shravasti's caravan square is an astonishing sight. Thousands of camels, elephants, bullocks and horses fill the largest city square that I have ever seen. Day and night, caravans arrive and depart, load and unload. Three large fountains water both beasts and men while, entirely at random, tents are pitched and booths set up. Everything is bought and sold by imperturbable merchants. Solemnly they hop from wagonload to wagonload, eyes as sharp and glittering as the eyes of those carrion birds which appear once a battle's done.

From caravan square the royal way proceeds to a green park, at whose center is an elaborate wood-and-brick palace. If somewhat less impressive than Bimbisara's recent creation, it is far more beautiful.

By then I was exhausted. So was my escort. They were, also, less than pleased by the long, hot walk that I had subjected them to. Once inside the palace, they got their revenge. "The king has said that you are to attend him the moment you arrive." The sweating chamberlain was very happy.

I was not. "But I am dusty . . ."

"Today the king is indifferent to protocol."

"In that case, the king will not mind if I were to change these clothes and—"

"He may be indifferent to protocol, Lord Ambassador, but he expects to be obeyed in all things."

"But I have gifts from the Great King . . ."

"Another time."

"I'm sorry," whispered Prince Jeta.

As the chamberlain led me through a series of high-ceilinged rooms, inset with plaques of silver, with mother-of-pearl and ivory, I was very much aware that the splendor of the surroundings was in vivid contrast to the grubbiness of my person.

Finally, without ceremony, I was shown into a small room where ogival windows looked onto trees, flowering vines, a marble fountain with no water in it. Silhouetted against the window were two elderly Buddhist monks with shaved heads.

For a moment I thought that I had been brought to the wrong room. I stared dumbly at the two old men. They smiled at me. They looked like brothers. Then the smaller of the two said, "Welcome, Cyrus Spitama, to our court."

As I started to go down on one knee, King Pasenadi stopped me. "No, no. You are a holy man. You must kneel only for those who worship . . . fire, isn't it?"

"We only worship the Wise Lord. The fire is simply his messenger to us." Although I was much too tired to preach more of a sermon than that, I found the king's sweetness relentless.

"Of course. Of course. You worship a sky god. So do we, don't we, Sariputra?"

"Yes, indeed. We have every sort of god imaginable," said the tall, fragile-looking Sariputra.

"Including those that are unimaginable," added Pasenadi.

"The Wise Lord is the only god," I said.

"We also have only gods, too. Don't we, Sariputra?"

"Quantities, my dear."

I was by now used to the way Indian holy men address their disciples . . . as if speaking to small children whom they love. The "my dear's" are gently bestowed, quite unlike the somewhat menacing "my dear's" of Ajatashatru, whose use of endearments was always calculated to keep others off-guard.

"I think that is a contradiction," I said stiffly.

"We have those, too," said King Pasenadi mildly.

257

"In fact, life itself is a contradiction if only because"—Sariputra giggled—"birth is the direct cause, in every single case, of death."

The two old men laughed happily.

Since I was by now in a thoroughly bad temper, I became formal. "I come to you from the Achaemenid, from Darius the Great King, the lord of all the lands, the king of kings."

"My dear, we know, we know! And you will be able to tell us all about Darius when we receive you at our court, in state. Then, and only then, will we receive the messenger—no, the ambassador of that Persian king whose presence in the valley of the Indus River has been a matter of such concern to us all. But, for now, we are simply two old men who would follow the eightfold path. As a king, I cannot go as far as I would like. But, fortunately, I am now an arhat, while Sariputra here is unusually close to enlightenment."

"My dear, I am no such thing! I serve the Buddha and the order, in little ways . . ."

"Listen to him, Cyrus Spitama! It was Sariputra who created the order. It is he who makes all the rules. It is he who sees to it that whatever the Buddha says or has said will be remembered. Why, Sariputra himself remembers every single word that the Buddha has spoken since that day in the deer park at Varanasi."

"My dear, you exaggerate. It is Ananda, not I, who remembers *every* word. All that I do is put those words into verses that even little children can learn." He turned to me. "Do you sing, my dear?"

"No. I mean, not well." I had the sense that I was going mad. I could not believe that one of these two old men ruled a country as large as Egypt, and that the other was the head of the Buddhist order. They struck me as perfect simpletons.

"I can see that you don't see. But you are tired. Even so, you will want to know what happened. In due course, a young lady arrived in Shravasti. She said that she was from the Gotama clan, just like the golden one himself! Oh, I was thrilled! After we were married, the golden one told me what a lovely joke had been played on me. Apparently the Shakyas did not want to mix their noble blood with the royal house of Koshala. On the other hand, they did not dare to offend me. So they sent me a common prostitute. And I married her. But when I found out, was I angry, dear Sariputra?"

"You were in a rage, dearest."

"Oh, no, I was not." Pasenadi looked hurt.

"Oh, yes, you were. You were in such a temper that we feared for you."

"I *seemed* to be, perhaps."

"My dear, you *were*."

"My dear, I was *not*."

Mercifully, some great hand has eliminated the rest of that scene from my memory. It is possible that I fainted dead away.

The Persian embassy was housed in a small building at one end of the palace gardens. Between us and the palace, there were fountains, flowers, trees—and silence. Even the peacocks made no sound—were their tongues slit?—while the band of sacred monkeys would watch us, in perfect silence, from the treetops. At the center of a great city, the king had created a forest retreat.

During the week that I was allowed to prepare myself for the formal presentation to the king, Prince Jeta took me in hand. He invited me to his house, a tall building that overlooked the river. In the prince's civilized company, my encounter with the two silly old men seemed like a fever-dream. But when I told Prince Jeta the story of my reception by King Pasenadi, he was both amused and perturbed. "The old man is like that," he said.

We were seated on the roof of Prince Jeta's house. As the sun set over dull-blue hills, the clouds made strange streak patterns, a characteristic of the start of the monsoon season.

The sky-dome that covers the Indian earth is mysteriously heightened—a trick of light? I don't know the reason but the effect is awesome, and for man diminishing.

"Does Pasenadi's behavior explain why the state dissolves?"

"Things are not that bad." Prince Jeta spoke precisely. "Koshala is still a great power. Pasenadi is still a great king."

I mouthed the word "Spies?"

Prince Jeta nodded. But up to a point, he had meant what he said. "The problem is that Pasenadi is now both an arhat and a king, and it is very hard to be both. I know, in my own small way."

"What is an arhat?"

"The word means 'one who has killed the enemy.' In this case, human desire."

"Like the Buddha."

"Except that an arhat still exists—unlike the Buddha, who has come and gone. There are those who think that since Sariputra is every bit as holy as Gotama, he, too, has achieved nirvana. But this is not possible. Buddha is always singular—in the present tense. In the past, there have been twenty-three Buddhas. In the future, there will be one more Buddha and that will be the end of that, for this cycle of time."

"Sariputra is actually considered . . . holy?"

"Oh, yes! There may be some doubt about Pasenadi, but there is none about Sariputra. After the Buddha, he is the most-nearly-released of all men. Then, of course, he is the sole creator of the order. It was he who gave the monks their rules. Now he and Ananda are assembling every word that the Buddha has said."

"Do they write down these words?"

"Of course not. Why should they?"

"They shouldn't." In those days I believed that whenever holy words were written down, they lost their religious potency. I believed that the Wise Lord's words must live not in writing on a cowhide but in the mind of the true believer. Unfortunately, I could not explain this to my Zoroastrian cousins at Bactra, who had picked up from the Greeks the mania for writing.

Democritus thinks that the first religious texts were Egyptian. Who knows? Who cares? I still believe that the writing down of hymns and sacred stories is bound to diminish religious feeling. Certainly, there is nothing more magical than a religious narrative or injunction or prayer at work in the mind, just as there is nothing more effective than the human voice when it summons from the recesses of memory the words of Truth. Nevertheless, over the years, I have changed. I now want a complete written record of my grandfather's words on the simple ground that if we survivors do not make it, others will, and the true Zoroaster will vanish beneath a stack of illuminated oxhides.

Without ceremony of any kind, we were joined on the roof by a handsome man of forty. He wore full armor, and carried a helmet that looked to be made of gold.

Prince Jeta dropped to his knees. I went to one knee,

assuming, correctly, that this was Virudhaka, the heir to the throne.

Virudhaka was quick to put us at our ease. With a graceful gesture he motioned for us to sit on the divan. "We shall see each other officially tomorrow, Lord Ambassador. But I thought it might be more pleasurable for us to meet like this, with our noble friend."

In the name of the Great King, I agreed. Out of the corner of my eye, I studied the prince. Three questions were very much on my mind. Was he contemplating parricide? If he was, would he succeed? If he succeeded, what would that mean for Persia?

Unaware of my dark thoughts, Virudhaka asked a number of intelligent questions about Persia. Other than Bimbisara, he was the first Indian of high rank to acknowledge the extent of the Great King's power. "In some ways," he said, "Darius seems very close to being the long-predicted universal monarch."

"We think, Lord Prince, that he is the universal monarch." All the color had now gone out of the sky. Night birds soared and dived. The air smelled of rain.

"But shouldn't this universe include Koshala? and the republics? and Magadha? and the south of India? And back of those mountains"—he pointed to the high dark Himalayas—"there is Cathay, a world far larger than Persia and all the western lands put together. Ought not Cathay be subject to the universal monarch?"

"It is said that they claim to have their own universal monarch." I was tactful.

Virudhaka shook his head. "There are many kingdoms in Cathay. But they lack the monarch who will unite them."

"Monarch? Or god?" asked Prince Jeta. "I should think that a true universal monarch would have to be very like a god."

"I thought you Buddhists were atheists." Virudhaka laughed to show that he was serious.

"No, we accept all the gods. They are a necessary part of the cosmic landscape." Prince Jeta was serene. "Naturally, the Buddha ignores them. Naturally, the gods venerate him."

"I steer clear of these matters," said Virudhaka. "I have only one interest. That is Koshala." He turned to me. "We have our problems."

"What kingdom has not, Lord Prince."

261

"Some less than others. Bimbisara now claims to be the universal monarch. You were at the horse sacrifice. So you saw. You heard."

"But I can't say that I understand it. After all, Bimbisara's entire country is not as large or as rich as the Great King's satrapy of Lydia." From the beginning, it was my policy to awe but not to alarm the Indians. I doubt if I was particularly successful. "And Lydia is only one of twenty satrapies."

"That may be," said Virudhaka. "But in this part of the world, only the Indus valley is subject to Persia, and that . . . satrapy is a long way from Koshala. Also, your king must know that we have never been defeated in war. What concerns us is this: Bimbisara claims to be universal monarch. Yet the horse sacrifice went badly. He had hoped to acquire Varanasi. He failed. Now my cousin Ajatashatru is raising an army. This means that when the rainy season ends, he will cross the Ganges and we shall be at war."

"It is my understanding"—I proceeded rather like a swimmer beneath the water—"that Prince Ajatashatru fears only the republics."

"He fears them as much as we do, which is not at all." Virudhaka was sharp. "No, the war will be directed not against the republics but against us. We will win, of course."

"Of course, Lord Prince." I waited for the inevitable request.

"Persia controls the Indus valley."

"But, as you've just said, the satrapy of India is a long way from Koshala."

I let Virudhaka's own words mock him. But he was unabashed. "In the dry season," he said, "five hundred miles need not be a world away."

As we talked we vanished into the moonless night, our disembodied voices mingling with the voices from the riverbank far below. At one point there was a lull in the conversation, and suddenly I felt that we had become extinct. Is this nirvana? I wondered.

But then Virudhaka recalled us to the real world. He was direct, for an Indian prince. He told me that he wanted an alliance with Persia against Magadha. When I asked him what Persia would gain by such an arrangement, the prince proceeded to overwhelm me with good things. "We control the overland route to Cathay. We

262

have a monopoly on the silk trade. We are the center for every important route to and from the farthest east. From Burma we import rubies and jade. Through us you can reach the south of India not only by land but also by water, once the port of Champa reverts to us." There was a good deal more in this vein. Then he told me exactly how many troops would be needed and when they would be needed, and where. Virudhaka's speech to me had been carefully prepared.

As the prince spoke, I could imagine the expression on Darius' face when I told him of all the wealth that I had seen assembled in Shravasti's caravan square. I could also imagine what would be going on in his head when he learned that the prince wanted to make an alliance with Persia. Here, at last, was the perfect pretext for the conquest of all India. The Persian army would be welcomed by Koshala. Magadha would then be crushed and Koshala would be absorbed, painlessly.

Darius was a master of the delicate art of attaching to himself someone else's kingdom. But then, every Persian schoolboy knows by heart Cyrus' famous speech to the Medes: "Through your present submission you have preserved your lives. As for the future, if you behave in the same manner, no ill will befall you, unless it be that the same person will not govern you that governed you before. But you shall live in the same houses and you shall cultivate the same land . . ."

This speech defines the perennial policy of the Achaemenid. Nothing changes for a conquered people but the sovereign; and since the Achaemenid is always a just sovereign, he is usually received with joy, as Cyrus was by the Medes. Also, whenever possible, the Achaemenid tries to leave at least the semblance of power to the old ruling houses. There was no reason why Ajatashatru and Virudhaka could not remain as satraps . . . no reason except that any Achaemenid who trusted either of those subtle princes would be a fool.

"I will do what I can, Lord Prince." I was both enigmatic and encouraging—in the best Susan style.

"There is not much time. The rains are about to begin. When they do, the sea route will be impossible, while the overland trail will be— Where does your caravan stop during the monsoon?"

"At Taxila. I've allowed three months to complete the final negotiations."

"But you could return to Persia when the rains stop?"

"Yes. But since you feel . . . pressed for time, I could send a draft of a treaty between us to the satrap of India. He would then send it up to Susa and we could have an answer before the start of the dry season." Needless to say, I meant none of this. I was playing for time. First the caravan must get through. Then I must report to Darius. Then . . . Who knows?

Virudhaka was now on his feet. We rose too. The three of us were somewhat darker than the night sky. Virudhaka gave me a ritual embrace. "The privy council will prepare a treaty," he said. "I hope that you will work with them. I also hope that you will personally translate the treaty into Persian. That's all-important."

"The king . . ." Prince Jeta said the phrase, and no more.

"The king will agree," said Virudhaka. "He is not yet entirely detached from his kingdom." Then he was gone.

Prince Jeta and I strolled to the parapet and looked down. A thousand small fires burned in the blackness like so many earth-trapped stars. The river people were preparing their evening meal. As we looked down, I whispered into Prince Jeta's ear what I had been told in Magadha.

Prince Jeta made an odd downward gesture with both hands. "They wanted you to tell me this."

"No doubt. But is it true?"

Prince Jeta shook his head. "The son is loyal to the father. Why shouldn't he be? The son has a free hand. Pasenadi seldom interferes. He—" Prince Jeta paused. Then he said, "We are being sent a message. But what is it? What do they really want?"

"They want a war with the republics."

"With Koshala too. But they cannot face both the federation *and* Koshala. So if they could divide Koshala by making trouble between father and son . . ." Prince Jeta did not need to finish.

"It is clever," I said.

"Except that, if we were to tell no one"—Prince Jeta looked at me as if he could actually make out my expression in the dark—"there would be no division, would there?"

We agreed to tell no one of Ajatashatru's warning to Pasenadi. But, of course, each of us intended to use this information to further his own ends because that is the way of courts and the world. Yet I was puzzled because Prince Jeta had seemed puzzled. Had Ajatashatru lied to me? And if he had, why?

10

THE NEXT MORNING, WHILE I WAS BE-
ing dressed in Persian costume for my presentation to the king, the first of the monsoon rains crashed over the rooftops of Shravasti. A few moments later I was joined by the wet and disheveled Caraka.

"There's something wrong," he announced, ignoring the all-attentive barber. "The king has been in council all morning. The prince is on the walls, with the archers—" Caraka stopped, at last aware of the barber.

"Can it be . . ." I began but did not finish a sentence whose meaning Caraka understood.

"I don't know," he said. "I don't think so."

As the barber brushed my lips with lac he smiled. Being a high-ranking member of the Koshalan secret service, he knew what we did not know.

At noon I was escorted to the crowded reception hall. Although the gifts from the Great King had been placed at the foot of the silver throne, the throne itself was empty. The usually serene and rather cold-blooded Koshalan nobles seemed anxious as their voices blended in with the sound of the rain falling on the tile roof. I stood in the doorway, my embroidered splendor unremarked.

Finally the chamberlain saw me. Hurrying forward, he dropped his wand of office. Then he picked it up the wrong way around, saluted me incorrectly and stammered, "I am sorry, Lord Ambassador. You must think us savages. But there's been— Please. Come with me. Your suite, too."

We were shown into a small chamber just off the anteroom. Then the door was not shut, but slammed behind us. Caraka and I exchanged a look. The rain on the roof was now so loud that we could barely hear what must have been a thousand voices cry in unison: "Long life to the king!"

Caraka whispered, "Which king?"

I spread my hands. I was as prepared to deal with Virudhaka as I was with Pasenadi. My only fear was that war might break out between Magadha and Koshala before Darius could take advantage of the situation.

Suddenly a conch shell sounded three blasts. Since this is the traditional call to battle, I was, for the first time, alarmed. Had the royal house been overthrown? Were enemy soldiers in the palace? The chamberlain appeared; he was out of breath, as if he had been running. "The king is on the throne," he said. "This way, Lord Ambassador."

We were hurried into the audience chamber, where a glittering figure sat upon the silver chair. In one hand, a sword; in the other, an ivory sceptre.

The chamberlain announced the arrival of the embassy from the Great King of Persia. Then, escorted by ushers, I walked toward the throne, whose absolutely gleaming occupant bore no resemblance to the wispy monk that I had met my first day in Shravasti. Not until I had saluted the sovereign did I realize that this stern, bejeweled monarch was indeed Pasenadi. The face was as carefully painted and as empty of expression as any Vedic god. There was no trace at all of the giggling monk whom I'd met with Sariputra.

With cold formality the king said, "We hope for good relations with our brother in Persia." The voice was loud, distinct, emotionless. "We shall work to that end. We send him our fraternal blessing. We—"

Pasenadi stopped. He seemed to have lost track of what he was saying. There was a long, slightly embarrassed moment as we stared at the king, who was looking past us at the door. Although I heard footsteps behind me, I did not dare turn my back on the king. Then Virudhaka passed me; he was dripping with rainwater. At the foot of the throne he made a filial salute, and in a voice that only his father and I could hear, he said, "It is true."

Pasenadi put down the sceptre. He got to his feet. He held the hilt of the sword in both hands, as if it were a torch to light some bloody way. "We have just learned that our beloved brother King Bimbisara has been deposed by his son Prince Ajatashatru, who asks for our blessing. We do not give it. Cursed is the son who raises his hand against the one who begat him. Cursed is the land whose sovereign usurps his father's place. Cursed is Ajatashatru."

With remarkable agility the old man skipped down the steps to the floor, and king, prince, councilors of state swept from the room. Then the chamberlain hurried us out of the room. The formal ceremonies of the court at Shravasti were plainly in abeyance, and the Great King's gifts remained unaccepted. Caraka was particularly glum; after all, we had carried those chests of rugs and jewels halfway across the world.

"It's most annoying," he said, "not to have the Great King's gifts acknowledged."

"War takes precedence," I said with statesmanlike sagacity. "But since there can be no fighting until the dry season, we're bound to see the king quite soon."

But we saw neither king nor prince for two months. Daily, despite the rains, delegations from every corner of the kingdom arrived at court. The privy council was in constant session. Meanwhile the street of the metalworkers was shut off to everyone except spies, and it was as a spy that Caraka penetrated the quarter. "Swords, spearheads, armor," he reported. "They work nights as well as days." War had indeed taken precedence over all other activities.

It was Prince Jeta who told me what had happened at Rajagriha. In a council meeting Ajatashatru had asked for permission to cross the Ganges River and attack the federation of republics. Although Bimbisara had agreed that the federation could not withstand the Magadhan armies, he made the point that the subsequent task of governing those quarrelsome states was not worth the effort of a war. Besides, was he not already universal monarch? He took very seriously the horse sacrifice. Too seriously, as it turned out. A few days later, without consulting his father, Ajatashatru claimed Varanasi in his mother's name. Bimbisara was furious; he said that Varanasi was an integral part of Koshala. With that, he dismissed the council.

The next evening, shortly after sunset, Ajatashatru's personal guards entered the royal palace and arrested the king. Since the move had been as swift as it was unexpected, there was no resistance.

"Bimbisara is now being held prisoner at Vulture's Peak. That's a tower in the old town." Prince Jeta betrayed neither surprise nor grief. He knew the world. "It is said that no one has ever escaped from Vulture's Peak."

"What happens now?"

"My son-in-law and your father-in-law is a fierce and determined man who appears to want war. If that is what he wants, that is what he will get."

We were seated on the inner verandah of Prince Jeta's house. Just opposite us a row of banana trees trembled in the rain-scented wind.

"I would not have thought it," I said. "Ajatashatru always . . . wept so easily."

"He was playing a part. Now he will be himself."

"No. He will simply play a new part, without—or perhaps with—all those tears. Most lives at a court," I added, with Brahmanical certainty, "are spent putting on and taking off masks."

Prince Jeta was amused. "You sound like one of us. Only instead of changing masks, we change existences."

"But unlike the courtier, you have no memory of your earlier selves."

"Except for the Buddha. He is able to remember each of his previous incarnations."

"Like Pythagoras."

Prince Jeta ignored this obscure reference. "But the Buddha once said that if he were actually to go to the trouble of recalling every single previous existence, he would have no time left to live out this one, which is the most important of all, since it is the last."

There was a sudden gust of wind. Clusters of unripe bananas were torn from the branches opposite us. The rains fell.

"Bimbisara told me that he hoped to become a monk in a year's time."

"Let us pray that he will be allowed to."

For a time we watched the rain. "How curious," I said finally, "that Ajatashatru should have wanted me to warn Pasenadi against *his* son."

"But how shrewd! While we look for a plot in Shravasti, he executes one in Rajagriha."

"But why go to the trouble of misleading me?"

"To put you off the scent. After all, sooner or later, he must deal with Persia." Prince Jeta gave me an odd look. "One day all of us will have to deal with Persia. We've known that ever since your king seized one of our richest countries."

"Not seized, Prince Jeta. The rulers of the Indus Valley asked the Great King to include them in his empire."

I sounded rather like an eighty-year-old court eunuch from the time of Cyrus.

"Forgive me. I was tactless." Prince Jeta smiled. "Anyway, Ajatashatru wants to make as much trouble for Koshala as he can. What cannot be seized from without must be acquired through division from within. So he tries to turn son against father."

"Has he?"

"He doesn't need to. Pasenadi wants to be both a king and an arhat. That's not possible. So Virudhaka is not . . . happy. And who can blame him?"

Several days later, Caraka presented me with a personal message from Ajatashatru; it was written on cowhide with red ink, a suitable color. Together we deciphered the difficult lettering. The gist was: "You are as close to our heart as always. You are as beloved in our eyes as if you were our own son. You will then mourn, as do I, the death of my father, the universal monarch Bimbisara. He was in the seventy-eighth year of his life and in the fifty-first year of his glorious reign. The court will be in mourning until the end of the rainy season, when we shall expect our beloved son, Cyrus Spitama, to attend us at our coronation."

Needless to say, there was no reference to how Bimbisara died. Some days later we learned that Ajatashatru had personally strangled his father with that silken cord which Indian protocol requires in the case of a deposed sovereign.

I passed a number of uneasy weeks in the steaming, rank gardens of Pasenadi's palace. Neither king nor prince sent for me. There was no message of any kind from Susa. There was even silence from the caravan at Taxila. My isolation was broken, finally, by the arrival of Prince Jeta and the monk Sariputra. They appeared, unannounced, on the verandah. I helped them wring out their clothes.

"I happened to see Sariputra in the garden," said Prince Jeta, "and I told him how much you would like to talk to him." I excused the lie. I was desperate for company, even that of a Buddhist arhat with black gums.

While Caraka sent for wine, Sariputra sat on the floor and Prince Jeta sat on a cushion. I perched on a stool.

The old man bestowed on me what I took to be a smile. "My dear—" he began. Then stopped.

"Perhaps you would like to question him." Prince Jeta looked at me expectantly.

"Or, perhaps," I said perversely, recalling my own spiritual mission, "he would like to question *me*."

"The Buddha has been known to ask questions." Prince Jeta was tactful. "As has Sariputra."

"Yes." There was something in the old man's unremitting benignity that reminded me of a well-fed baby; on the other hand, the sharp eyes were as cold and as unblinking as a serpent's. "Do you like games, my child?"

"No," I said. "Do you?"

"Eternal games, yes!" Sariputra laughed, alone.

"Why," I asked, "have you no interest at all in the Wise Lord and in his prophet Zoroaster?"

"*All* things are interesting, my child. And since it is plainly interesting for you to tell me about your Wise Lord, you must. This very minute! Truth cannot wait, they say. I can't think why. Everything else does. But tell me."

I told him.

When I had finished, Sariputra said to Prince Jeta, "This Wise Lord sounds exactly like Brahma trying to pass himself off as a Persian. Oh, those gods! They change their names from country to country and think that we won't notice. But we always do! They can't fool us, can they? Or escape us. But that Brahma! He is by far the most ambitious. He thinks *he's* the creator. Imagine! Oh, you should have heard him when he came to the Buddha that first time. No, not the first time, the second time. The first time was when he begged the Buddha to set the wheel of the doctrine in motion. Oh, Brahma was very insistent, very persuasive. Because he knows that he'll have to be reborn as a human being before he can obtain nirvana, and when he's reborn the only way that he'll be able to achieve nirvana is through the Buddha. He's not really a fool, you know. He just sounds like one. Anyway, the Buddha allowed himself to be persuaded since Brahma is the best of the gods, which is not saying very much, is it? So the Buddha agreed—that was after their first visit—to set the wheel in motion, which was a great sacrifice for the Buddha, since he himself had already achieved nirvana and is no longer here or there or anywhere, unlike poor Brahma.

"Then Brahma came to him a second time. At Rajagriha it was. We must ask Ananda exactly when and where, he remembers everything, no matter how trivial.

This was all before my time. So Brahma told the Buddha, 'I am Brahma. I am the great Brahma, the king of the gods. I am uncreated. I have created the world. I am the sovereign of the world. I can create, alter and give birth. I am the father of all things.' Now, we all know that this is perfect nonsense. But the Buddha is always polite. He is also sublime. 'If you exist, Brahma,' he said most gently, 'you were created. If you were created, you will evolve. If you evolve, your aim must be release from the fire and the flux of creation. Therefore, you must become what I already am. You must take the last step on the eightfold path. You must cease to evolve and to be.' "

"What did Brahma say to that?" Never before or since have I heard such blasphemy.

"Oh, he was upset. Wouldn't you be? I mean, there he is, just like your Wise Lord—ever so full of himself and ever so powerful, or so he thinks. Yet if he is all-powerful, then he is quite capable of *not* being, a state that he craves but cannot obtain, which is why he begged the Buddha to set the wheel of the doctrine in motion."

"You are absolutely certain that this was indeed the Wise—I mean Brahma who spoke to the Buddha?"

"Of course I'm not certain! This is all a dream, my dear, and in dreams some things make less sense than others. I mean, it all depends on where you are standing when you sleep, doesn't it?"

I confess that I had the sense that I, too, was either dreaming or going mad. "Zoroaster actually heard the voice of the Wise Lord—" I began.

"—just as Brahma heard the answers of the Buddha." Sariputra nodded encouragingly, as if a dull student had succeeded in adding one to one.

"Out of reverence, I am obliged to say that Zoroaster heard the answers of the Wise Lord, and not the other way around."

"I say it the other way around, out of reverence for the Buddha. There is only one Buddha at any given moment."

"There is only one Wise Lord."

"Except when he sneaks off to India and tries to pass himself off as Brahma. Anyway, he's not the only god. He's just the most conceited."

As best I could, I maintained my rigid courtier's mask. "You deny that the Wise Lord is the sole creator of all things?"

"Of course, my dear. And so do you." Then the wicked

old man repeated back to me what I had chanted for him from the holiest of our texts: " 'Ahura Mazdah, before the act of creation, was not the Wise Lord. After the act of creation, he became the Wise Lord, eager for increase, wise, free from adversity, manifest—' I've forgotten the rest of his attributes that you so kindly recited for us just now. My memory is not what it was."

I continued grimly, " '—ever ordering aright, bounteous, all-perceiving.' "

"Yes, yes. 'And by his clear vision Ahura Mazdah saw that the destructive spirit would never cease from aggression . . .' And so he goes and makes a trap for the destructive spirit when he invents, out of infinite time, time of the long dominion. Oh, my dear, this is all so elaborate! If he is the all-powerful creator, why did he invent the destructive spirit to begin with? What is the point? But once it was invented, why must he go to the trouble of battling his own invention? This was really not very wise of him, was it? And then to insist that the human race, another of his inventions, must constantly do battle with his very first creation . . . Well, that is definitely not kind."

"The fact of evil is not kind, Sariputra. But as good exists, so does evil, and the battle between the two must continue until good triumphs at the end of time of the long dominion."

"Since the good will win, anyway, why bother with the battle?"

"Because it is the will of the Wise Lord. Out of himself, he created all human souls at once. And these eternal spirits exist with him until they are obliged to take human form. Then they make a choice. They follow either the Truth or the Lie. If they follow the Truth, they will earn merit. If the Lie . . ."

"Yes, dear child. Slow as my brain is, I have grasped the concept. But why make everyone suffer so?"

"How else is evil to be overthrown?"

"By removing first world, then self. Or if you like—and can—first self, then world."

"The world is. The self is. Evil is. Good is. Contest is—inevitable, and ordained."

"Then it is better *not* to be at all, isn't it? And that can be achieved by following the eightfold way."

The old man was even more maddening than the worst of our local sophists. "All things struggle—" I began.

"—except those that don't," he ended. "But your Wise Lord, just like our own proud, if rather tricky Brahma, is as in the dark as the rest of his creations. He has no idea where he is going any more than he knows where he came from."

"The Wise Lord knows that he will trap and destroy the evil Ahriman in time of the long dominion. When he does, all souls will be saved."

"So he *says*. But he, too, evolves. There was a time when he was not. Then was. Now is. But *will* he be?"

"Before the Wise Lord was the Wise Lord."

"And before that? He says, if you quote him correctly, 'before the act of creation, I was not lord.' If he was not, who was? And where did this creator come from?"

"Time—"

"Ah, time! But where does time come from?"

"Time was. Is. Will be."

"Perhaps. Perhaps not. I talk, dear child, of first things because they interest you. They do not interest us. We have no curiosity about the origin of things, about creation. We have no way of knowing what was first, or if there is such a thing as a first thing in time or space, or outside time or space. It is all the same. Gods, men, ghosts, animals, fish, trees . . . these are all manifestations of a creation in which pain is a constant because all is in flux and nothing remains the same. Is that not true?"

"There is a single source—" I began.

But Sariputra was no longer listening to me. "The first thing I do with our novitiates is to take them to cemeteries where I show them decomposing bodies. We study the new life that springs from the dead. We watch the maggots lay their eggs in the putrefying flesh. Then the eggs hatch and a new generation of maggots eats its fill until in time—of a very very short dominion, my dear—there is nothing but bone left and the poor maggots starve and die. But out of their dust come plants, insects, invisible kernels of life, and the chain goes on and on and on—and who would not want to break that painful chain if he could?"

"The chain breaks when the Wise Lord prevails and all is light."

"I must say that sounds very like Brahma. But as he himself admits—that is, when he's not telling lies—he has no more idea just how things will end than he knows how he himself started. He is in mid-river, like the rest of us. Naturally, his river is greater than ours, but the principle of any river is the same. As you yourself sang so beautifully . . . no, no, *really* beautifully, 'Time is mightier than both creations—the creation of the Wise Lord and that of the destructive spirit.' With *us,* child, time is only a part of the dream from which you must awaken if you are to be enlightened."

"And extinguished?"

"You have learned the lesson, Cyrus Spitama!" The wicked creature applauded me.

Although not one of Sariputra's arguments could be intelligently defended, I remembered Darius' command. I was to learn as well as to teach or, to put it another way, one cannot teach without first knowing just what it is that others believe to be true. In those days I never doubted my mission, which was to bring all men to the Truth. But at the same time I was deeply curious about the origin—if any—of creation; and, somewhat embarrassingly, Sariputra had drawn attention to a curious gap in Zoroaster's perception of divinity. Yes, Democritus, you, too, have noticed the same omission. But that is because you are interested only in what is material. We are interested in what is holy.

I agree that it has never been clear how or when or why the Wise Lord was born out of infinite time, which itself can never be truly understood, since what is infinite is, by definition, not only not yet but *never* yet. But until I met the Buddhists, I did not think it possible for a religion or philosophy or world view of any complexity to exist without a theory of creation, no matter how imprecise. But here was a sect or order or religion which had captured the imagination of two powerful kings and many wise men, and the order had done so without ever taking seriously the only great question: How did the cosmos begin?

Worse, Buddhists regard all gods with the same sort of amiable contempt that educated Athenians do. But the Athenians are fearful of prosecution by public opinion, while the Buddhists are indifferent to the superstitions of the Brahmans. They do not even care enough about the gods to turn them into devils the way Zoroaster did. The Buddhists accept the world as it is, and try to eliminate it.

Meanwhile, in the here and now, they suggest that it is probably better than not for the ordinary Buddhist layman to be joyful, friendly, equable and compassionate; members of the order, however, must relinquish not only the sorrows of this world but the joys as well.

"After we've studied the rotting corpses, I remind the novitiates how truly disgusting the living body is. Since many novitiates are young, they are still attracted to women, which of course links them to the chain of being. So I show them how the body of the most beautiful woman is like a wound, with nine openings that ooze revoltingly, while the whole body is covered with a clammy skin that—"

"Slow as *my* brain is, I have grasped the concept," I said, evening somewhat the score.

"My dear, if you really have, you are now spinning for yourself the wheel of doctrine! Such a clever child." Sariputra looked at Prince Jeta. Although the monk's face was smiling, the eyes were as bright and unblinking as a parrot's. He was a disconcerting figure.

"I think," said Prince Jeta, "that the time has come for our friend to attend the Buddha."

"Why not?"

Democritus wants to know exactly who the Buddha was and where he came from. The first question is probably not answerable. I know that I asked it often enough when I was in India, and I received a marvelous variety of responses. Indians do not have our interest in facts; their sense of time is different from ours, while their apprehension of reality is based on a profound sense that the world does not matter because the world is only shifting matter. They think that they are dreaming.

11

THIS IS WHAT I THINK I KNOW ABOUT the Buddha. At the time that I met him—more than a half-century ago—he was about seventy-two or -three years old. He was born in the Shakya republic, which is located in the foothills of the Himalayas. He came from a warrior family called Gotama. At birth, he was named Siddhartha. He was brought up in the capital city of Kapilavastru. At one time Gotama's father held high office in the republic, but he was hardly a king, as certain snobs at Shravasti and Rajagriha still like to pretend.

Siddhartha married. He had one son, Rahula—which means link or bond. I suspect that the child must have begun life with another name, but I never found out what it was. He certainly proved to be a bond with that world which the Buddha was to eliminate—for himself.

At the age of twenty-nine Siddhartha embarked upon what he called the noble quest. Because he was acutely conscious that he was "liable to birth because of self, and knowing the peril in whatever is liable to birth, he sought the uttermost security from this world's bonds—nirvana."

Siddhartha's quest took seven years. He lived in the forest. He mortified the flesh. He meditated. In due course, through his own efforts—or simply because he had evolved in the course of all his previous incarnations? —he understood not only the cause of pain but its cure. He saw all that was and all that will ever be. In a magical contest he defeated the evil god Mara, who is lord of this world.

Siddhartha became the enlightened one or the Buddha. Since he had eliminated not only himself but the tangible world as well, he is higher than all the gods: they are still evolving and he is not. They continue to exist within a world that he has entirely dissolved. Since enlightenment is an end in itself—*the* great end, the now-eliminated world ought not to have concerned the Buddha. But the world that he had awakened from returned to him, as it were, when the high god Brahma came down from heaven and begged him to show others the way. But the Buddha was not interested. Why speak, he said, of what cannot be described? But Brahma was so insistent that the Buddha agreed to go to Varanasi and set in motion the wheel of the doctrine. He expounded the four truths; and he revealed the eightfold path. Yet at the same time, paradoxically, the entire exercise was—is—pointless because he had abolished this world and all other worlds, too.

"Everything subject to causation," the Buddha said, "is like a mirage." For him, human personality is something like a bad dream—to be got rid of, preferably, by waking up to . . . nothing? There is a point beyond which I cannot follow the Buddha. But then, he is enlightened and I am not.

In every way, the Buddha's teaching is opposed to that of the Wise Lord. For Buddhists and Jains, the world deteriorates; therefore, extinction is the goal of the wise. For Zoroaster, each man must make his way either toward the Truth or the Lie, and in eternity he will be judged for what he did or did not do in the course of only one life. Finally, after a time in heaven or hell, all human souls will share in the Wise Lord's victory over Ahriman, and we shall achieve a perfect state of being that is not so different from the Buddha's sunyata, or shining void—if that is the right translation of a word which explains so precisely the inexplicable.

For the Indians, all creatures are subject to constant reincarnation. Punishment and rewards in any given life are the result of previous deeds, in previous lives. One is totally subject to one's karma, or destiny. For us, there is suffering or joy in time of the long dominion and, finally, union with Ahura Mazdah in eternal time. For them, there is endless death and rebirth, only broken for a very few by nirvana, which is nothing, and sunyata, which is what it is if it is.

Democritus thinks that the two attitudes are not so far apart. I *know* that they are entirely unlike. Admittedly, there is something luminous if slippery about the Buddha's conception of sunyata; in fact, the more I think of his truths, the more I feel that I am trying to catch with two clumsy hands one of those swift eels that writhe at night in hot southern seas, ablaze with cold light. At the core of the Buddhist system there is an empty space which is not just the sought-after nirvana. It is perfect atheism.

To my knowledge, the Buddha never discussed any of the gods except in the most offhand way. He never denied them; he simply ignored them. But despite his formidable conceit, he did not set himself in place of the gods because, by the time he had set in motion the wheel of his doctrine, he himself had ceased to be, which is the ultimate stage of evolution. But while he still inhabited Gotama's flesh, he allowed others to create the sangha in order to alleviate for the chosen few some of life's pain.

At first only men could be admitted to the order. But then Ananda persuaded the Buddha that women should be admitted too. They would live in their own communities, and follow the eightfold path. Although the Buddha was complaisant, he did make a joke, much quoted by misogynists. "Had the order been made up only of men, Ananda, it would have lasted a thousand years. Now that women have been included, it will last only five hundred years." In either case, I suspect he was unduly optimistic.

Toward the end of the rainy season I accompanied

277

Prince Jeta to the park which he may or may not have sold to the merchant Anathapindika for the Buddha's use. Here live a thousand monks, disciples, admirers. Many ascetics sleep out of doors, while pilgrims live in guest-houses and members of the order are quartered in a large building with a thatched roof.

Not far from this monastery, a wooden hut had been erected on a low platform. Here on a mat sat the Buddha. Since the hut was built without walls, he lived in full view of the world.

Sariputra welcomed us to the monastery. He moved like a boy, with a skipping step. He did not carry a parasol. The warm rain seemed never to bother him. "You're in luck. Tathagata is in a mood to talk. We're so glad for you. Since the full moon, he's been silent. But not today." Sariputra patted my arm. "I told him who you were."

If he expected me to ask him what the Buddha had had to say about the Persian ambassador, he was disappointed. I was ceremonious. "I look forward to our meeting." I used the word upanishad, which means not just a meeting but a serious discussion about spiritual matters.

Sariputra escorted Prince Jeta and me to the pavilion that had been built on a platform approached by eight shallow steps—one for each part of the eightfold way? At the first step, a tall heavyset yellow man greeted Sariputra, who then introduced him to us. "This is Fan Ch'ih," said Sariputra. "He has come from Cathay to learn from the Buddha."

"It is not possible *not* to learn from the Buddha." Fan Ch'ih spoke the Koshalan dialect even better than I, despite an accent that was rather worse.

Since Fan Ch'ih and I were to become close friends, I will only note here that he had not come to India to learn from the Buddha; he was on a trade mission from a small nation in southeast Cathay. Later he told me that he had come to the park that day in order to meet the Persian ambassador. He was as fascinated by Persia as I was by Cathay.

We followed Sariputra up the steps and into the hut, where all of those who had been seated rose to greet us except for the Buddha, who remained seated on his mat. I could see why he was called the golden one. He was as yellow as any native of Cathay. Not only was he not Aryan, he was not Dravidian either. Obviously, some tribe from Cathay had crossed the Himalayas to sire the Gotama clan.

The Buddha was small, slender, supple. He sat very straight, legs crossed beneath him. The slanted eyes were so narrow that one could not tell if they were open or shut. Someone described the Buddha's eyes as being as luminous as the night sky in summer. I would not know. I never actually saw them. Pale arched eyebrows grew together in such a way that there was a tuft of hair at the juncture. In India this is considered a mark of divinity.

The old man's flesh was wrinkled but glowing with good health, and the bare skull shone like yellow alabaster. There was a scent of sandalwood about him that struck me as less than ascetic. During the time I was with him, he seldom moved either his head or his body. Occasionally he would gesture with the right hand. The Buddha's voice was low and agreeable, and seemed to cost him no breath. In fact, in some mysterious way, he seemed not to breathe at all.

I bowed low. He motioned for me to sit. I made a set speech. When I was finished, the Buddha smiled. That was all. He did not bother to answer me. There was an awkward moment.

Then a young man suddenly asked, "O Tathagata, is it your view that the world is eternal and all other views false?"

"No, child, I do not hold the view that the world is eternal and all other views false."

"Then, is it your view that the world is *not* eternal and all other views are false?"

"No, child, I do not hold the view that the world is not eternal, and all other views are false."

The young man then asked the Buddha if the cosmos was finite or infinite, if the body was similar or not similar to the soul, if a holy man exists or does not exist after death, and so on. To each question the Buddha gave the youth the same answer or non-answer that he had given to the question whether or not the world was eternal. Finally the young man asked, "What objection, then, does Tathagata perceive to each of these theories that he has not adopted any one of them?"

"Because, child, the theory that the world is eternal, is a jungle, a wilderness, a puppet show, a writhing, and a chain forever attached to misery, pain, despair and agony —this view does not contribute to aversion, absence of desire, cessation, quiescence, knowledge, supreme wisdom and nirvana."

"Is this Tathagata's answer to each question?"

The Buddha nodded. "This is the objection I perceive to these apparently conflicting theories, and that is why I have not adopted any one of them."

"But has Tathagata any theory of his own?"

There was a pause. I must confess that the blood was suddenly high in my cheeks, and I felt as if I had the fever. I wanted, desperately, to know the answer or non-answer.

"The Buddha is free from all theories." The voice was mild. The eyes seemed to be looking not at us but upon some world or non-world that we could not comprehend. "There are things, of course, that I know. I know the nature of matter. I know how things come into being and I know how they perish. I know the nature of sensation. I know how it is that sensation comes, and how it goes. I know how perception begins and ends. How consciousness starts, only to stop. Since I *know* these things, I have been able to free myself from all attachment. The self is gone, given up, relinquished."

"But Tathagata, are you . . . is the priest who is in such a state as yours, is he reborn?"

"To say that he is reborn does not fit the case."

"Does that mean he is not reborn?"

"That does not fit the case either."

"Then is he both reborn and not reborn?"

"No. Simultaneity does not fit the case."

"I am confused, Tathagata. Either he is the one thing or the other or even both things at the same time, yet—"

"Enough, child. You are confused because very often it is not possible to see what is right in front of you because you happen to be looking in the wrong direction. Let me ask you a question. If a fire was burning in front of you, would you notice it?"

"Yes, Tathagata."

"If the fire went out, would you notice that?"

"Yes, Tathagata."

"Now, then, when the fire goes out, where does it go? to the east? the west? the north? the south?"

"But the question is to no point, Tathagata. When a fire goes out for lack of fuel to burn, it is . . . well, it is gone, extinct."

"You have now answered your own question as to

whether or not a holy man is reborn or not reborn. The question is to no point. Like the fire that goes out for lack of fuel to burn, he is gone, extinct."

"I see," said the young man. "I understand."

"Perhaps you *begin* to understand."

The Buddha looked in my direction. I cannot say that he ever looked *at* me. "We often hold this discussion," he said. "And I always use the image of the fire because it seems easy to understand."

There was a long silence.

Suddenly Sariputra announced, "Everything subject to causation is a mirage." There was another silence. By then I had forgotten every question that I had meant to ask. Like the proverbial fire, my mind had gone out.

Prince Jeta spoke for me. "Tathagata, the ambassador from the Great King of Persia is curious to know how the world was created."

The Buddha turned those strange blind eyes toward me. Then he smiled. "Perhaps," he said, "you would like to tell me." The Buddha's bared teeth were mottled and yellow, disconcertingly suggestive of fangs.

I don't know what I said. I suppose I described for him the simultaneous creation of good and evil. Repeated my grandfather's doctrines. Observed those narrow eyes which were aimed—there is no other verb—in my direction.

When I had finished, the Buddha made a polite response. "Since no one can ever know for certain whether or not his own view of creation is the correct one, it is absolutely impossible for him to know if someone else's is the wrong one." Then he dropped the only important subject that there is.

The next silence was the longest of all. I listened to the sound of the rain upon the thatched roof, of the wind in the trees, of the monks chanting in the nearby monastery.

Finally I remembered one of the many questions that I had intended to ask him: "Tell me, Buddha, if the life of this world is an evil, why then *is* the world?"

The Buddha stared at me. I think that this time he might actually have seen me, even though the light inside the hut was now as dim and as green as pond water when one opens one's eyes below the surface.

"The world is full of pain, suffering and evil. That is the first truth," he said. "Comprehend that first truth, and the other truths will be evident. Follow the eightfold way and—"

"—and nirvana may or may not extinguish the self." There was a slight gasp from those present. I had interrupted the Buddha. Nevertheless, I persisted in my rudeness. "But my question is: Who or what made a world whose only point, according to you, is that it causes pain to no purpose?"

The Buddha was benign. "My child, let us say that you have been fighting in a battle. You have been struck by a poisoned arrow. You are in pain. You are feverish. You fear death—and the next incarnation. I am nearby. I am a skilled surgeon. You come to me. What will you ask me to do?"

"Take out the arrow."

"Right away?"

"Right away."

"You would not want to know whose bow fired the arrow?"

"I would be curious, of course." I saw the direction that he was taking.

"But would you want to know *before* I took out the arrow whether or not the archer was tall or short, a warrior or a slave, handsome or ill-favored?"

"No, but—"

"Then, that is all that the eightfold way can offer you. A freedom from the arrow's pain and an antidote to the poison, which is this world."

"But once the arrow has been removed and I am cured, I might still want to know whose arrow struck me."

"If you have truly followed the way, the question will be immaterial. You will have seen that this life is a dream, a mirage, something produced by the self. And when the self goes, it goes."

"You are Tathagata—the one who has come and gone and come again. When you are here, you are here. But when you go, where do you go?"

"Where the fire goes when it's gone out. My child, no words can define nirvana. Make no attempt to catch in a net of familiar phrases that which is and is not. Finally, even to contemplate the idea of nirvana is a proof that one is still on the near-side of the river. Those who have achieved that state do not try to name what is nameless. Meanwhile, let us take out the arrow. Let us heal the flesh. Let us take a ride, if we can, on the ferryboat that goes to the far side. Thus we follow the middle way. Is this the right way?" The Buddha's smile was barely visible in the twilight. Then he said, "As the space of the universe is filled with countless wheels of fiery stars, the wisdom that transcends this life is abysmally profound."

"And difficult to comprehend, Tathagata," said Sariputra, "even for those who are awake."

"Which is why, Sariputra, no one can ever comprehend it *through* awakening."

The two old men burst out laughing at what was obviously a familiar joke.

I remember nothing more of that meeting with the Buddha. I think that before we left the park, we visited the monastery. I believe that I first met Ananda then. He was a small man whose life work was to learn by heart everything that the Buddha was reported to have said and done.

I do remember asking Prince Jeta if the Buddha had said anything to me that he had not said a thousand times before.

"No. He uses the same images over and over again. The only new thing—to me—was the paradox about awakening."

"But it was not new to Sariputra."

"Well, Sariputra sees him more than anyone else, and they tell each other complicated jokes. They laugh a good deal together. I don't know at what. Although I am sufficiently advanced that I can smile at this world, I cannot laugh at it just yet."

"But why is he so indifferent to the idea of creation?"

"Because he thinks it, literally, immaterial. The ultimate human task is to dematerialize the self. In his own case, he has succeeded. Now he has set up the wheel of the doctrine for others to turn as best they can. He himself is come—and he is gone."

Democritus finds these ideas easier to comprehend than I do. I can accept the notion that all creation is in flux and that what we take to be the real world is a kind of shifting dream, perceived by each of us in a way that differs from that of everyone else, as well as from the thing itself. But the absence of deity, of origin and of terminus, of good in conflict with evil . . . The absence of purpose, finally, makes the Buddha's truths too strange for me to accept.

12

IN THE LAST WEEK OF THE RAINY SEA-
son, the river flooded. The yellow waters rose, covered the
quays, burst through the wooden stockade, half drowned
the city.

Those who had tall houses like Prince Jeta simply
moved to the upper stories. But those whose houses were
on a single level were forced to move onto their roofs.
Fortunately, the palace enclave was on a slightly higher
higher ground than the rest of the city, and my own quarters
were flooded only to the depth of an ankle.

On the second day of the flood I was dining with
Caraka and Fan Ch'ih. Suddenly our meal was interrupted by a series of blasts on a conch shell. Then we
heard the ominous sounds of metal striking metal. Since
floods and civil disobedience go together in India, we
were all agreed that those who had been dispossessed by
the river had suddenly attacked the palace.

Attended by Persian guards, we hurried to the palace.
I remember how the hot wind blew the rain in our eyes. I
remember the slipperiness of the mud beneath our feet.
I remember our surprise when we found that the garden
entrance to the palace was unguarded.

Swords drawn, we entered the vestibule, which was
waist-deep in water. Although there was no one in sight,
we could hear shouts in other parts of the building. At the
entrance to the reception hall, we saw an amazing sight.
The king's guards were fighting one another—but very
slowly, because the water hampered their movements. As
we watched this curious dreamlike battle, the doors to
the hall were flung open and a line of spear carriers appeared in the doorway, weapons lowered for attack. At
the sight of the spear carriers, the guardsmen sheathed
their swords. In silence, the fighting stopped. In silence,
King Pasenadi appeared in the doorway; he had a long
chain about his neck, which an officer of his own guard
held in one hand. In the watery silence, the rhythmic

clatter of the king's chain made the sort of harsh music that Vedic gods delight in.

As the king passed us, I bowed. But he did not see me. In fact, no one paid the slightest attention to the Persian embassy. Once the king was out of sight, I waded to the door of the reception hall and saw a dozen dead soldiers floating in the red-streaked yellow water. At the far end of the room, the throne had been overturned and several men were trying to put it back onto the dais. One of the men was Virudhaka.

When Virudhaka saw me, he left to the others the task of righting the silver chair. Slowly he waded toward me, mopping his face with one end of his wet cloak. I remember thinking how odd it was for a man drenched in blood and river water to want to dry his sweaty face with a wet cloth.

"As you see, Lord Ambassador, we are quite unprepared for ceremony."

I dropped to one knee. I had seen quite enough to know what was expected of me. "May the gods grant long life to King Virudhaka."

Caraka and Fan Ch'ih also recited this pious hope.

Virudhaka's response was grave. "What the gods have given me this day, I shall do my best to prove worthy of."

There was a crash as the throne again slipped off the dais. All in all, not the best beginning to a reign.

"It has been my father's wish to abdicate for some years." Virudhaka spoke smoothly. "This morning he sent for me, and he begged me to let him surrender the burden of this world. And so, today, at his insistence, I have, as a good son, granted his wish and taken his place."

Obviously, the Buddha's insistence that this world is a dream had had an effect not only on Virudhaka but on the entire court. No one ever referred, in my presence at least, to the bloody overthrow of Pasenadi. On the few occasions when his name was mentioned, it was said that he had gone into a much longed for retirement in the forest. He was said to be absolutely content; there were even rumors that he had achieved nirvana.

In actuality, later that same day Pasenadi was hacked into a number of small pieces, which were then offered as a sacrifice to the river god. Since the river promptly returned to its banks, the sacrifice was plainly acceptable.

Not long after, Prince Jeta and I met in a crowded street where the air was so filled with dust from the dried

285

river mud that we were obliged to hold dampened cloths to our faces; and took shallow breaths.

As we strolled toward caravan square, Prince Jeta said, "Pasenadi kept promising to go, but at the last moment he always changed his mind. 'Another month,' he would say. Obviously he stayed one month too long."

"Obviously. But he was so old. Why didn't . . . *he* wait?" In India, it is always a good idea to substitute pronouns for great names.

"Fear. *He* is a devout man, and even though it was plain to him that his father was destroying Koshala, he was willing to wait. But when Ajatashatru seized power in Magadha, he knew that there would be war. So he did what he felt he had to do, to save what is left of the kingdom."

We stopped at a booth filled with odd-looking glazed pottery from Cathay, recently introduced by Fan Ch'ih. "Do you approve of what he did?"

Prince Jeta sighed. "How can I? I am a Buddhist. I do not believe in hurting any living thing. Also, the . . . dead man was my old friend. But"—idly, Prince Jeta pointed at a dragon-headed pot—"I am told that there are many creatures like that in Cathay."

"'So Fan Ch'ih tells me. The best medicine is made from dragon's bone." I waited for an answer to my question.

Prince Jeta bought the pot. "If anyone can save this country from Ajatashatru, it is the new king," he said.

"What was the Buddha's reaction?"

"The Buddha laughed—like a lion."

"He is not compassionate."

"How can he be? He has come and gone. Kings are simply a part of that distracting puppet show that the perfect one no longer attends."

During the hot season, Ambalika arrived from Rajagriha with our son. Prince Jeta offered his granddaughter and great-grandson a wing of the river mansion, and I moved in with them. Meanwhile, a message had come to me from Susa by way of Taxila. The Great King denounced me for having paid too much for the shipment of iron, but since I had reopened the old trade route between Persia and Magadha, he was more pleased than not with his slave and I was a hero at court, or so the letter from the chancellor for the east implied. I was to come home immediately.

Carefully, I made my plans. I ordered Caraka back to Rajagriha, where he would act as business agent for the Great King. He would also prepare a second caravan of iron from Magadha, at a more reasonable price than the one that I had agreed to. Ambalika and our son would remain in Shravasti until I sent for them, or until I returned myself.

To everyone's pleased surprise, the war between Magadha and Koshala did not take place. Although Ajatashatru sent troops to Varanasi, he did not try to seize the city. Meanwhile, Virudhaka led the Koshalan army not south to his own beleaguered city of Varanasi, but east to the Shakya republic. In a matter of days, the republic collapsed and its territory was absorbed by Koshala. The federation of republics was now on a war footing.

All in all, I was happy to be going back to Persia, where battles take place at a considerable distance from Susa, and the high crime of parricide is virtually unknown amongst *our* Aryans. Although I found it curiously abominable that India's two most powerful Aryan kings should be murdered by their sons, Prince Jeta seemed not at all perturbed. "We have an old saying, 'Princes, like crabs, eat their own parents.'" Ultimately my embassy to the Indian kingdoms was conducted most bloodily in the astrological sign of the crab.

Practically speaking, I found Virudhaka much easier to deal with than his father. For one thing, he was a superb administrator and, briefly, Koshala was again what it must have been in those great days that everyone so enjoyed telling me about. But then, I have never visited any city in the world where I was not told that I had just missed the golden age. I seem never to be on time.

I was a guest of honor at Virudhaka's coronation, an ancient ritual that took place in a fairground just outside the city. I don't remember much about the elaborate ceremonies except that they seemed a bit hurried.

I do recall the magical moment when the new king took three steps on a tiger skin, in imitation of the three steps that the god Vishnu took when he crossed creation and filled the universe with light. Ananda says that the Buddha did the same thing shortly after his enlightenment. But as far as I can tell, the Buddha himself never seems to have mentioned this remarkable tour of the universe to anyone except Ananda. It was my, perhaps mistaken, impression that the Buddha was not given to such exaggerated gestures.

Although Virudhaka had begged the Buddha to attend his investiture, the perfect one had seen fit to leave Shravasti the night before. He was last seen on the road to the land of the Shakyas. It was later said that the Buddha knew that the king intended to attack his native country and that he wanted to be with his own people when war began. But years later, when I asked Prince Jeta if this theory was true, he shook his head. "The Buddha would not have cared one way or the other. All attempts to involve him in politics failed. To the end, he laughed at the puppet show. It's true that the Shakyas thought that he might help save them because he seemed to approve of their sangha. Perhaps he did. But it was not the Shakyan but the Buddhist sangha that interested him—if anything did."

This conversation took place during my last visit to India. With sufficient luck, Democritus, you will live long enough to be able to say of something that it is the last, and know for certain that what you have said is simple truth. I shall never again look upon scarlet parrots, yellow-eyed tigers, sky-clad madmen. I shall never again travel in that hot flat land where swift pale rivers rise and fall, and there is always a crossing to be made.

"Why did Virudhaka attack the Shakyas?"

At first Prince Jeta gave the official reason. "He wished to avenge the insult to his father. As an arhat, Pasenadi was obliged to forgive the Shakyans for sending him a prostitute for a wife. As a warrior, Virudhaka could never forgive this insult."

"But there must be some other reason." I never accept the official reason for anything. In the second room of the chancellery at Susa, I have myself invented altogether too many noble pretexts for necessary if ugly actions.

"Virudhaka feared the republics as much as Ajatashatru. I suppose he thought that if he were to break them first, he would be more powerful than his cousin. Who knows? Virudhaka had no luck."

But on coronation day Virudhaka seemed blessed by heaven. For one thing, just after he took the last of his three steps on the tiger skin, all the gods came down from heaven and up from hell to greet him, and the crowds cheered this charming spectacle.

"Here comes Vishnu," said Prince Jeta. "He's always first."

Twice the size of a normal man, the god Vishnu loomed over the heads of the excited mob. The god's handsome face was blue-black, and he wore a tall elaborate headdress. In one hand he held a lotus, like the Great King. In the other he carried a conch shell. I was relieved that he had not chosen to wear his other two arms that day. While Vishnu slowly walked toward the tiger skin where Virudhaka stood, the people fell prostrate. Many of them wriggled toward him in order to touch the hem of his robe. Suddenly the fairground seemed to be full of human-headed snakes.

Just behind Vishnu was his wife Lakshmi. The goddess' nipples had been painted vermilion, and the golden skin shone with ghee, as do her statues at the city's gates. As the two high gods adorned Virudhaka with wreaths, the ecstatic crowd began to howl and dance like haoma-drunk Magians.

"What on earth are they?" I asked Prince Jeta.

"On earth, as in heaven, they are the gods of the Aryans!" He was amused at my bewilderment.

Caraka laughed too. "Your Vishnu has been in India too long," he said to Prince Jeta. "He's the same color as one of our old gods."

"I'm sure that they are all related." Prince Jeta's politeness required a change of subject. "Naturally, this is a very rare occasion. Only once or twice in a generation will a king summon all the gods to his side." As Prince Jeta spoke, the baleful red-faced Indra materialized at the far end of the field. In one hand he held a thunderbolt; in the other he clutched a huge flask of soma, from which he swigged. Nearby, all in black, eyes ablaze, stood Agni in a chariot drawn by fire-red horses.

Brilliantly, eerily, from every direction, the Vedic gods solemnly converged upon King Virudhaka.

Prince Jeta was not entirely sure of my reaction. Nor was I, even to this day. Had I, for an instant, believed that the gods were really present? It is possible. Certainly, the performance was awesome. But it was only a performance, as Prince Jeta assured me. "The gods," he said, "are being impersonated by actors."

"But these actors are giants!"

289

"Each god is actually two actors. One sits on the shoulders of the other and the robes cover both of them. The effect is convincing, isn't it?"

"And alarming." I had the sense that I was in a haoma-dream. "Do the people really believe that these are their gods?"

Prince Jeta shrugged. "Some do. Some don't."

"Most do," said Caraka. He turned to Prince Jeta. "You Aryans got the idea from us. At the New Year, when our people come to the temples to make sacrifice, all the gods appear. They threaten the people with plague and famine. So to avoid disaster, the temple priests beg the people to make a contribution to the temple. If our actor-gods put on a really good performance, a temple's revenue can double."

"In that case, was it Brahma or a couple of actors who came to see the Buddha in the deer park?" I teased Prince Jeta.

"I wouldn't know. I was not there." The answer was serene. "But then, neither was the Buddha, since he was already extinguished. So Brahma—or his impersonator—was wasting his time."

I must confess that those huge deities moving about the crowded fairground had a most unnerving effect on me. In a sense, all my grandfather's chief devils were being impersonated, and I saw what a Zoroastrian hell might be like.

But Ambalika enjoyed herself hugely. "They seem so real! Which is just as good as being real, isn't it?" She had attended the coronation in the entourage of the old queen. Ambalika was somewhat plumper than she had been before my son was born. "I'm not too heavy for your taste, am I?" That was her greeting to me when I met her at the city's gate. In a tactless moment I had once complained to her that everyone at the court of Magadha was too fat, including myself. In three years, I had nearly doubled my weight.

"No. You are exactly right."

"If I'm not, tell me." We were in the main garden of Prince Jeta's house.

"I'll tell you." I was entirely delighted by Ambalika. I told her so.

"Then you'll let me come to Susa?"

"If I can."

"Because I'm certain you'll never come back here." Ambalika looked sad but sounded cheerful.

I told her that I was certain to come back for the prosaic reason that "there is bound to be more trade between Persia and Magadha. Koshala, too."

This proved to be true. In fact, before I left Shravasti, I was approached by every important merchant in the city. Each wanted special trade concessions. Although I turned down several fortunes in bribes, I did accept a retainer's fee from the potter's guild in the form of a loan without interest. The loan itself would be paid off by the guild if I saw to it that Persian imports of Indian pottery were not taxed. I made this arrangement so that Ambalika and my children—she was again pregnant—would be taken care of in case Prince Jeta should die or be disgraced. Naturally, I assumed that when I next saw my wife and children, I would be with the lord of all India, Darius the Great King.

In the autumn of that year, I attached myself to a westbound caravan. In addition to my personal guards, I was accompanied by Fan Ch'ih. All the other members of his original expedition had been killed or died of the fever or gone home.

"The people of Cathay don't like to travel." Fan Ch'ih smiled his constant but never annoying smile. "Since Cathay is the world, why go anywhere else?"

"Persians feel the same."

Because the days were dry and cool, we rode horseback. In fact, the weather was so splendid that one was absolutely happy to be young and alive—all in all, a rare sensation.

During our journey to the west I learned a great deal about Cathay, which I shall come to in the proper place. I had expected to impress Fan Ch'ih with the splendors of the Persian empire. Instead, he impressed me with the magnificence—alleged, of course—of the Cathayan world, where once upon a time there had been a single empire known as the Middle Kingdom. But as empires will, this one broke up, and today Cathay is comprised of a number of contending states like India. Also, again like India, these states are not only constantly at war with one another but there is not a duke or marquis or earl in his fortress who does not dream of one day making himself the single master of a recreated Middle Kingdom.

"But this can only happen if the ruler—whoever he is —receives the mandate of heaven."

I remember hearing that phrase for the first time at the same moment that I saw the dreamlike towers of Taxila in the hazy violet distance. Usually the traveler smells a city before he sees it. This time one saw the towers first, then smelled the cook-fires' smoke.

"We call the mandate of heaven, the awesome royal glory," I said. "One of our old devil-gods was its sole bestower and he, and he alone, could give the glory to a ruler, just as he alone could take it away. Now we know that it is not a devil-god but the Wise Lord who bestows or withholds the awesome royal glory."

"Master K'ung would say that the bestower was heaven, which is the same thing, isn't it?"

A few years later I was to meet Master K'ung, and of all men that I have known, he was the wisest. Take my word for it, Democritus. Not that you have much choice. After all, I am probably the only man in the western world who ever knew this remarkable teacher.

No, Master K'ung—or Confucius, as he is also called— was not like Protagoras. Confucius was not clever. He was wise. Eventually I shall try to explain the difference between the two. But my best may not be enough. After all, Greek is the language of the hair-splitter and the debate-winner; it is not the language of the God, as opposed to gods.

BOOK FIVE

The Passing of the Awesome Royal Glory

1

I ARRIVED AT SUSA, FOUR YEARS LESS three days after I had set out on my embassy to the sixteen kingdoms of India, a perfect misnomer even at the time of my departure. In the Gangetic plain there were fewer than sixteen kingdoms, and no one has ever bothered to count how many nations there are to the south. The chancellery agreed with me that future ambassadors would be posted only to the kings of Magadha and Koshala.

Although the court was still at Susa, Darius himself had moved on to winter quarters at Babylon. The chancellery was now preparing to depart while the harem had already begun its slow progress by wagon to the west. Of the royal family, only Xerxes was in residence.

During my absence the harem war had ended with an outright victory for Atossa, as if there had ever been any real doubt. Except for making me chief Zoroastrian, she almost never failed in anything that she undertook. She had obliged Darius to recognize Xerxes as his heir, and that was that.

I was received by the crown prince in the private quarters. As I was about to fall prostrate Xerxes caught me with his left arm and we embraced like brothers.

Looking back, I now realize how fortunate we were. Each was in his prime. Unfortunately, each was unaware of the fact. I was weary of travel. Xerxes was weary of Mardonius. No man ever knows when he is happy; he can only know when he was happy.

We drank Helbon wine while I told Xerxes of my adventures in India. He was enthralled. "I must lead the army!" The pale-grey eyes glowed like a cat's. "The Great King's too old. He'll have to send me. Except"—the brows that normally met in a straight line now formed a cleft—"he won't. He'll send Mardonius."

"You could both go. And Mardonius would serve under you."

"If I'm allowed to go." The light in the gray eyes went out. "He gets everything. I get nothing. He has had a hundred victories. I've had none."

"You conquered Babylon," I said. "Or you were about to just before I left."

"I put down a rebellion, nothing more. But when I asked to be made king of Babel like Cambyses, the Great King said no. He said it was quite enough for me to administer Babylonia, which I do. I've also built a new palace, which I'm allowed to stay in only when he's not there."

I have never been able to decide whether or not Xerxes liked his father. I suspect that he did not. Certainly, he resented the confusion over the succession, and he took as a deliberate insult the fact that he was never given a military command of any importance. Yet he was entirely loyal to Darius; and feared him just as Darius feared Atossa.

"Why are you here so late in the season?" I asked. In private we always spoke directly to each other, and looked each other in the eye.

"Cold, isn't it?" The room was freezing. There's no city in the world with such abrupt shifts in weather as Susa. The previous day had been positively sultry. Yet that very morning when I crossed from my quarters in the north section of the palace to Xerxes' apartments, the ornamental pools had been covered with thin layers of iridescent night-ice and my breath hovered like smoke in the bright air. I could understand how the aging Darius came to abhor cold weather; at the first hint of frost, he would retreat to warm Babylon.

"I'm the Great King's chief mason." Xerxes held up his hands. The short nails were impacted with cement. "He was so pleased with the palace that I built in Babylon—for me, not for him—that he's put me in charge of finishing this one. He's also given me a free hand at Persepolis. So I build and build. Spend and spend. I've replaced most of the Egyptian builders with Ionian Greeks. They're the best at stonework. I've even got some of your Indians as wood-carvers. I've accumulated just about everything, except money. Darius doles it out, a sheep's worth at a time. I don't think I've seen an archer since the Greek wars."

That was the first time I heard the slang word archer, the name the Greeks give to the gold coin that shows the

295

crowned Darius holding a bow in one hand. Current Persian joke: No Greek is impervious to a Persian archer.

Xerxes gave me his version of what had been happening while I was in India. I say his version because there is no such thing as a true account of anything. Each sees the world from his own vantage point. Needless to say, a throne is not the best place from which to see anything except the backs of prostrate men.

"After a long siege, Miletus fell. We killed the men. We shipped the women and children here to Susa. The Great King plans to settle them somewhere nearby so, till then, we've got several thousand very attractive young Milesians living in the old barracks. Take your pick. They've pretty much stopped their weeping and wailing. In fact, I've established one young widow in my harem. She's teaching me Greek, or trying to. She's clever, like all Milesians." This clever lady was the aunt of Aspasia.

We must keep that a secret, Democritus. The Athenians would ostracize Pericles if they knew that the mother of his illegitimate son was the niece of the Great King's concubine. Democritus doubts if the assembly would have the wit to figure out the connection. They wouldn't. But Thucydides would.

A cold wind rattled the awning that had not yet been taken down for the winter. Through the open portico I could see brown leaves whirling. I thought of my school days in that same palace, and I shivered; it seemed always to be winter when I was a child at Susa.

"After we took Miletus, a group of Medes—who else? —set fire to the temple of Apollo at Didyma and burned the whole thing to the ground, oracle and all. Then that idiot Artaphrenes sent a message to all the Greek cities saying that the burning of the temple was in revenge for the burning of the temple of Cybele at Sardis."

"But wasn't it?"

"Brother of my youth, the priesthood of Apollo at Didyma, the priesthood of Apollo at Delos, the priesthood of Apollo at Delphi are all supported by the Great King. Each year he sends them divisions of archers."

Democritus wants to know if we still pay for the Greek oracle at Delphi. No, we do not. The wars are over now. Besides, the priests learned their lesson. Nowadays, oracles seldom comment on political matters.

"Anyway, the Great King has been making apologies ever since. He'll also have to pay to rebuild the temple.

296

And that means less money for Persepolis." In those days, Xerxes could drink half a dozen flagons of unmixed Helbon wine at a sitting without ill effect. On the other hand, even in my youth I always mixed wine with water—like a Greek.

Xerxes ordered the cupbearer to bring us more wine. He then described the collapse of the Carian revolt. "After Miletus fell, that was the end for those yokels. What else? Histiaeus was captured and put to death by the idiot at Sardis, which made the Great King angry because he liked Histiaeus and never blamed him for any of the Milesian business. But of course the charge against the old conniver was piracy, not treason, and he was certainly a pirate during the last years of his life. Your mother was very upset when he was executed." Xerxes always found my mother's intrigues amusing.

"They weren't friends after Miletus rebelled. Or so I gathered. I wouldn't really know." I was always careful to distance myself from the Greek faction.

"Only in the sense that they never saw each other again. But they were still devoted to each other." Xerxes grinned. "I *know*," he said and, of course, he did. Xerxes had a dozen spies in the harem—unlike Darius, who tended to ignore harem intrigues unless they involved Atossa. Needless to say, Darius spied on her constantly and she spied on him. They were like neighboring sovereigns.

"After Miletus, we sent the fleet up the Ionian coast. The Greek cities surrendered. Then our fleet—mostly Phoenicians now—passed through the straits, and the local tyrant was so alarmed that he went home to Athens. I can't think why. As one of the Great King's most loyal vassals, he was perfectly safe. Now he's a traitor."

Thus, casually, Democritus, did Xerxes refer to Miltiades, a minor Persian vassal who less than three years later was elected supreme commander by the Greek allies. He is given credit for the so-called Greek victory at Plataea. Democritus tells me that Miltiades was not at Plataea, but at Marathon. Small details like this are no doubt important to a Greek history. This is a Persian history.

"Then, last spring, Mardonius was given command of both the fleet and the army." Since Xerxes loved Mardonius like a brother, Mardonius' success was all the more unbearable to him.

297

"In less than six months Mardonius conquered Thrace and Macedonia. Not since Cambyses gave us Egypt has anyone added so much territory to the empire. It's lucky for me that he is the Great King's nephew and not his son."

"Why aren't you given the same opportunities?"

Xerxes raised high his right arm, palm open—the traditional gesture of homage to the Great King on state occasions. "My life is too valuable, they say. But how am I to be Great King myself if I've never taken the field? Oh, I need victories! I need to be like Mardonius. Only . . ." Xerxes' arm fell to the table. The open palm became a fist.

"Queen Atossa?"

"Yes. Thanks to her, I am the heir. And thanks to her, I am less than my cousin, less than my brothers, less than you."

"You are certainly more than I."

"Well, yes, of course. But I haven't seen India, and you have. And because of you, we're now in a position to annex a whole world. Well, let's pray that that will be my work. Let's also pray that Darius allows Mardonius to go on fighting the Greeks, which Mardonius wants to do. I can't think why. There's nothing in the west that anyone would want."

"Doesn't the Great King want to avenge the burning of Sardis?"

"Any one of a hundred generals could manage that. All you have to do is burn down Athens. That's easy. And pointless. But India!" Xerxes was happier for all the wine he had drunk. He gripped my forearm; his fingers were roughened from military practice. "When you report to the Great King, tell him that I must—well, no, you can't tell him that he *must* do anything but . . ."

"I can hint. I can also speak to Queen Atossa."

"Don't. She'll want me safe in Babylon."

"If she thought that the conquest of the Indian kingdoms would be easy, she would let you go. She's not a fool, to say the least."

Xerxes used a dagger's tip to clean the mortar from under a thumbnail. "She might be helpful. It's hard to say. We'll see." He smiled. "If I go, you'll come with me."

Happily, we plotted glory, as the young do; an exquisite pleasure denied the old when all plots are at an end, like the spider's web when the spider's dead.

"If we're lucky, we'll have set things in motion *before* Mardonius is up and around." Xerxes suddenly nicked his thumb. Bright blood made two tiny red pearls. He licked the blood away.

"Is Mardonius ill?"

"Wounded." Xerxes tried not to look pleased. "He was ambushed on his way back from Macedonia. By Thracians. A leg tendon was severed. So now he limps about, full of complaints even though he sits every day at the Great King's table. Sits at his right hand when I'm not there, and Darius feeds him from his own plate."

"But if he's wounded, that's the end of the Greek business." I always did my best to divert Xerxes' attention whenever he started to brood on his father's indifference to him. But, no, indifference is not the right word. Darius saw Xerxes as an extension of Atossa, daughter of Cyrus; and Darius was not only in awe of his wife and her son but fearful of them. I shall soon come to the reason for this.

"It should be the end. Certainly, there's nothing else for us in the west except Mardonius' ambition to be satrap of all the Greeks. Luckily, he's not fit for a spring campaign. And I am. So with a bit of . . . good fortune"— Xerxes used the Greek phrase—"I shall lead the Persian army this spring. And we'll go east, not west." Xerxes then spoke of women. He found the subject endlessly interesting. He wanted to know all about Ambalika. I told him. We agreed that my son should be brought up at the Persian court. Xerxes then told me about his principal wife, Amestris. "You know she was chosen for me by Atossa. At first, I didn't know why."

"Because of Otanes' money, I should've thought."

"That was a consideration. But Atossa is deeper than that. Atossa chose Amestris because Amestris is like Atossa." Xerxes smiled without much pleasure. "Amestris studies all the accounts. She administers my household. She spends hours with the eunuchs, and you know what that means."

"She is political?"

"She is political. Atossa wants to make sure that after she dies, I'll be looked after by yet another Atossa. Naturally, I revere my mother. Because of her, I am the heir."

"The eldest living grandson of Cyrus was bound to be the heir."

"I have two younger brothers." Xerxes did not need to

299

say more. It had always been his fear that he would be superseded not by Artobazanes but by one of his own royal brothers. After all, when Darius became Great King, *he* had three older brothers, a father and a grandfather living. Admittedly, this anomalous situation is not apt to recur in Persian history; even so, there are still many precedents for the passing over of the eldest son in favor of a younger one: witness my current master, Artaxerxes.

"We must get you a Persian wife." Xerxes changed the dangerous subject. "You must marry one of my sisters."

"I can't. I'm not one of The Six."

"I don't think that the rule applies to the royal girls. We'll ask the law-bearers." Xerxes finished the last flagon of wine. He yawned contentedly. "The law-bearers will also have to pick a wife for that Indian . . . ?"

"Ajatashatru."

Xerxes grinned. "I shall personally go to his wedding."

"That would be a great honor for Magadha."

"I'll also attend his funeral, an even greater honor."

The next day we left Susa in a hailstorm. After India, I was so used to bad weather that I was not in the least distressed, but Xerxes always regarded bad weather as a sign of heaven's spite and he was forever trying to find some way of punishing the rain or the wind. "What is the point to being lord of the universe," he used to say, "if you can't go hunting because of a storm?"

I tried to teach him serenity, without much luck. Once I even went so far as to describe the Buddha to him. Xerxes laughed at the four noble truths.

I was irritated. I can't think why. I had found the Buddha himself a chilling, even dangerous figure. But one could hardly fault those noble truths which are obvious. "Are they so amusing?"

"Your Buddha is. Doesn't he know that wanting *not* to want is still wanting? His truths aren't noble. They aren't even true. He has no answer to anything. There is no way not to be human except through death." Xerxes was of this world, entirely.

Southwest of the crumbling row of red sandstone hills that marks the natural end of Susa's countryside, the weather became warm and mild; and Xerxes' temper promptly improved. By the time we got to Babylon even he could not fault heaven's arrangements.

Shortly before midnight we were at the city's gates. Tactfully but inaccurately the guards hailed Xerxes as king of Babel. Then, with a roaring sound, the great cedarwood gates swung open and we entered the sleeping city. On either side of the broad avenue that leads to the new palace, the tiny thornfires of the poor shone like earthbound stars. Wherever one is on earth, they are there.

2

SINCE I HAD EXPLORED A WORLD THAT no one at court had ever heard of, much less seen, I felt that my return would cause a good deal of excitement and I was rather looking forward to being a center of attention. I should have known better. The court is all that matters to the court. My absence had not been noted, while my return was ignored.

On the other hand, Fan Ch'ih's appearance made people laugh. Fortunately, he was not distressed. "They look very odd to me, too," he said serenely. "They also smell very bad—like old ghee. I suppose that's because they have so much hair on their bodies. They look like monkeys." Since the bodies of the yellow men of Cathay are almost entirely hairless, their sweat has a most curious odor, like boiled oranges.

I reported to the first room of the chancellery. Nothing had changed there. I was sent to the second room, where the same eunuchs sat at the same long tables, keeping accounts, writing letters in the Great King's name, conducting the tedious business of the empire. The fact that I had been to India interested them not at all. An under-chamberlain told me that I might be received in private audience by the Great King quite soon. But then again . . . The Persian court is eternal in its sameness.

Lais was also unchanged. "You look much older," she said. Then we embraced. As usual, she asked me no questions about myself. She was not interested in India either. "You must go see your old friend Mardonius. Right away. He's absolutely the most powerful man at court." Lais responded to power in rather the same way that a water-diviner's rod will bend if it detects the slightest moisture beneath the earth. "Darius dotes on him. Atossa is furious. But what can she do?"

"Poison him?" I suggested.

"She would if she thought she could get away with it. But as I keep telling her, Mardonius is no real threat. How can he be? He's not the Great King's son. 'Nephews have inherited before,' she says. She's lost four teeth this year. They just fell out. But if you can't understand what she's saying, *don't* let on. Pretend you've understood every word. She's very self-conscious, and she hates to repeat herself. Do you like Xerxes' palace?"

We were on the roof of Lais' apartment in the new palace. To the north, just past the ziggurat, Xerxes' building loomed in all its gold-glazed splendor.

"Yes, what I've seen of it. I've only been to the chancellery."

"The interior is beautiful. And comfortable. Darius likes it so much that poor Xerxes has been obliged to move back here when the court's at Babylon, which it is more and more." Lais lowered her voice. "He's aged." Lais gave me her secret witch-look. In her world *nothing* is natural. If Darius had aged, it was not time's usual work but a magical spell or potion.

With a rustling sound, Lais' ancient eunuch appeared in the doorway. He looked at her. He looked at me. He looked at her again. He withdrew. They knew each other so well that they could communicate without words or signs.

"I have made a new friend." Lais was nervous. "I hope you'll like him as much as I do."

"I've always liked your Greeks. Where is this one from? Sparta?"

Lais has never liked the fact that I can see through her in much the same way that she claims that she can see through others. After all, I am the grandson of the holiest man that ever lived, as well as the son of a sorceress. I have powers denied the ordinary.

Democritus has asked for a demonstration of these powers. I am giving you one. My memory.

The Greek was not much older than I. But then, my mother is not much older than I. He was tall. He had a pale face and Dorian-blue eyes. Except for sandals instead of shoes, he wore Persian dress, and looked most uncomfortable. I had guessed right. He was Spartan. How could I tell? The dark-red hair that fell to his shoulders had never been washed except by the rain.

302

"Demaratus, son of Ariston." Lais' voice was reverent. "King of Sparta."

"King no longer. Son of Ariston no longer. Thanks to Delphi."

"The prophetess has been removed." Lais sounded as if she herself had been responsible for the change.

"Too late for me."

At the time I had not the slightest notion what they were talking about. Later I came to know altogether too much about the so-called Spartan Scandal—a somewhat inapposite title when one considers how many scandals there are in Sparta every year, usually involving bribed officials. Of all the Greeks, the Spartans are the most archer-mad.

The Spartan constitution requires not one but two kings, a stupid arrangement. Demaratus fell out with the other king, Cleomenes, who bribed the prophetess at Delphi to say that Demaratus was not the son of Ariston. Once Demaratus had been *proved* illegitimate, he was king no longer. Hippias had told us that day at Darius' hunting lodge that this would happen; but Hippias had not been believed. The Great King did not think even the Delphi oracle could prove who had sired whom so many years after the act. But the oracle prevailed, and like every other discredited Greek king or tyrant or general, Demaratus promptly came up to Susa, where Darius took him in. Demaratus was given lands in The Troad, and made a general.

We exchanged the usual civilities. Then with a sense of having lived through all of this before with Histiacus, I said, "You are now trying to persuade the Great King to attack Athens in the spring. When Athens falls, will you want the Great King to conquer Sparta, too?"

"Only Athens," said Demaratus. I noticed that the cold blue eyes were the same color as the glazed blue tiles of the Ishtar Gate just opposite us. "The Spartan army is stronger than the Persian army."

"No army is stronger than the Great King's!" Lais said nervously.

"Except Sparta's," said Demaratus. "That is a fact." I admired the ex-king's coolness. I did not admire his feet. He wore open sandals that revealed toes as black as a Babylonian peasant's. Trying to look at neither feet nor hair, I ended by staring at Demaratus' beard. It was so

303

thick with old dust that it looked to be made of baked clay.

"Without allies, Sparta is vulnerable," I said. "Sparta depends on the Athenian fleet. But if Athens falls . . ." I did not state the obvious.

Demaratus gave me a murderous look. Then, irritably, he pushed back the long Persian sleeves. "Eretria, Euboea and Athens. Those are the Great King's targets for the coming year. The matter of Sparta is something else, and will be settled by Spartans. Meanwhile, Mardonius will lead the army again."

Lais looked at me as if I should be pleased. I looked at her in order to remind her that our faction was *not* that of Mardonius and the Greeks but of Xerxes and Atossa.

"Are you certain?" But the question that I put to Demaratus was answered by Lais.

"No," she said. "The physicians say that he'll never walk again."

"Mardonius is the Great King's best general." Demaratus was flat. "If he has to, he can lead the expedition in a litter. But he won't have to. I've seen the leg. It will heal."

"If it doesn't"—and Lais looked suddenly grave and sibylline—"there is no reason why a Spartan king could not lead the army."

Demaratus' black toes clenched like two fists. I looked away. "There is a very good reason why I could not lead the army." The voice was oddly mild. "I am not Persian —yet."

Later that day Lais and I had a furious quarrel. I told her that the last thing in the world "you and I should want is another Greek expedition."

"*Our* future is in the west," Lais proclaimed. "Let Mardonius outshine Xerxes for a year or two. What difference will it make? Xerxes is still going to be Great King one day, and when he is, thanks to Mardonius or Demaratus, he will be the lord of all the Greeks from Sigeum to Sicily, and sea lord, too."

Lais and I were now on different sides. In fact, after that day we did not speak to each other again for several years. Since I supported Xerxes, I did my best to bend Persian policy to the east, while Lais continued to receive all the Greeks at court in order to support their numerous causes. Yet she kept warm her friendship with Atossa. Years later, when Lais and I were on better terms, she told me how she had managed to stay in with both factions.

"I convinced Atossa that I was poisoning Mardonius. Very slowly, of course, so that when he died everyone would blame his death on the leg that wouldn't heal."

"But what did Atossa think when Mardonius didn't die?"

"After he was replaced as general, I said to her, 'What's the point to killing him?' and she agreed that there was none. So I stopped the so-called poisoning."

Shortly after my meeting with Demaratus I was received by Atossa, who deplored the fact that I had turned on Lais. "After all, your mother saved your life."

"*You* saved my life, Great Queen."

"True. But I did it for Lais. How I hate this city." Although the third house of the harem of Xerxes' palace was more sumptuous than its equivalent at Susa, Atossa complained constantly of the heat, the noise, the Babylonians—not that she ever saw any Babylonians other than those who had always been at court.

"Naturally, I am pleased with you." Atossa's speech had indeed been impaired by the recent loss of several crucial teeth. She compensated for this disability by pursing and smacking her enameled lips in a most distracting way.

"I know that you do what you do for Xerxes. I know that you quarreled with your mother about the Greeks and Mardonius. Mardonius—" She checked herself. I suspect now that she was tempted to tell me that her brilliant nephew Mardonius would soon be dead, thanks to Lais. But if that was the moment's temptation, she did not yield to it. Instead, Atossa kicked at the old tattered rug with one bright silver shoe. Wherever she went, the old rug traveled with her. I think that she was superstitious about it. I know that I was.

Atossa addressed the rug. "They say that Mardonius will not be able to take the field this spring." Then she looked straight at me. "Tell me about India."

I told her about India.

The old eyes shone with greed. "Rich, rich!" she kept repeating.

"And easily gained," I said. "By Xerxes."

"He cannot be risked." Atossa was firm.

"He must prove that he can lead the armies before the Great King dies."

305

"Too dangerous. Especially now. In these times. We are all so old. Oh, the tomb!" Because of the impairment to her speech, the queen was particularly hard to follow when she shifted too quickly the subject.

I looked at her dully.

"The tomb. The tomb of Darius." She arranged her lips carefully about each syllable. "It's enraging."

"The moon symbol?" The devil symbol decorates the façade of Darius' tomb, as a balance to the Wise Lord's sun. Hystaspes had died at the tomb—in a rage at the blasphemy. Hystaspes is now *in* the tomb; and the moon symbol is still on the façade.

"That is as it should be." Atossa detached a flower from the garland about her neck and threw it at the image of Anahita in the corner. "The moon is *her* symbol, and I would not lie under any other. No, something else has happened. There is room for only twelve of us in the tomb. Old Hystaspes and two of Darius' brothers are already there on one shelf. Then Darius and I and my sister Artystone will occupy another shelf, while six of the nephews are to fill the remaining two shelves. It was all worked out by Darius and me. Now, only this morning, Darius has assigned the place that was to have gone to young Artaphrenes to Parmys. To Parmys, of all people! She died last week, by the way. Most painfully, I'm told!"

Atossa pressed a thin yellow hand against the spot where her breast had been. "Yes, the same sickness. But I had Democedes. And survived. She had only Egyptians. And died, most painfully. They say that at the end she weighed less than a year-old child." This pleasurable reverie was swiftly dispelled by the thought of Parmys "with us in that rock chamber for all eternity. Oh, I tell you it is intolerable! And mysterious. Of course, there is gossip that— But the point is, *why* has he done the unthinkable? Except to annoy me, which he has succeeded in doing. I cannot bear to think that for all eternity I must lie beside the daughter of a murderer and a traitor and an impostor."

I must say that I had forgotten all about Parmys, the daughter of the Magian usurper Gaumata. Lais had told me how astonished the court had been when Darius announced that he intended to marry her. They were even more mystified by his explanation: "Impostor or not, the Magian was Great King for a year. Therefore, his daugh-

306

ter Parmys is the daughter of a Great King of Persia. Therefore, it is suitable that she be my wife."

"You must promise me in the name of Anahita—well, of the Wise Lord—that when Darius is dead and I am dead you will persuade Xerxes to remove that dreadful woman from the tomb. Swear!"

As I swore, Atossa regarded me with a suspicious eye. "If you break your oath, there is nothing that I will be able to do about it *in the flesh*. But the goddess is strong. The goddess is everywhere." Atossa's red eyes glared at me.

"I shall do what I can. But surely a word from you to Xerxes—"

"He has received that word. But he is forgetful. He is also apt to be influenced by other considerations." She did not elaborate. "So I count on you. On you alone."

Atossa had other complaints. She seldom saw Xerxes. When the court was at Susa or Ecbatana, he was either at Babylon or Persepolis. "He has a mania for building." Atossa frowned. "So did my father, of course. But it is a very expensive hobby, as he discovered. And endless."

Over the years, I was to watch Xerxes create at Persepolis the most beautiful complex of unfinished buildings in the world. When Callias came to Persia for the peace negotiations, I took him to Persepolis. Elpinice tells me that he was so awed by what Xerxes had built that he ordered one of his slaves to make drawings of the principal buildings. At this very moment, the Athenians are busily imitating Xerxes' work. Fortunately, I have seen the originals. Fortunately, I shall never see Phidias' crude copies.

Atossa admitted to a certain loneliness, and isolation. "I have Lais, of course. But she is deranged by Greek politics. Ordinarily I'm perfectly content with the eunuchs. After all, they've been my eyes, my ears, my hands ever since I was a child. But this new crop isn't at all like the old. They are either too much like women or too much like men. I don't know what's gone wrong. In my father's time, they were perfectly balanced and absolutely devoted. They knew what you wanted without being told. Now they are arrogant and dull and careless, and both rooms of the chancellery are a shambles. Nothing gets done properly. I think it's all those Greeks from Samos. They're very good-looking, of course. Even intelligent. But they don't make good eunuchs. They don't make

307

good anything at all, except troublemakers. You know that Lais is conniving again."

"Yes. I've met the king of Sparta."

"In the harem, Lais is known as the queen of Greece. No, I don't mind. If it weren't for her, I'd never know what those troublesome people are up to."

"What *are* they up to?" On serious matters I asked Atossa direct questions, to which she sometimes gave direct answers.

"They want a spring offensive. Athens is to be destroyed, and so on. The whole thing is absolutely useless, but Hippias—"

"Always Hippias."

"Don't interrupt."

"I was echoing, Great Queen."

"Don't echo. Hippias has convinced Darius—again—that the Athenians want him back as tyrant. Darius is getting old." Unlike Lais, Atossa did not whisper treason. She shouted it, knowing that the secret service would repeat every word to Darius. Thus they communicated with each other. Not until after Darius' death did I learn why she did not fear him; why he feared her.

"Darius is muddled. He actually thinks that Athens wants to restore the tyrants now that all the other Greek cities have become democracies."

I was startled. "But surely the Ionian cities are—"

"—are all democracies now. The tyrants are gone, every last one of them. Thanks to Mardonius. At first, Darius was furious. But then he realized how clever Mardonius was." Atossa's eyes were like dusty enamel by torchlight. "Mardonius *is* clever. Too clever, I sometimes think. Anyway, as he went from city to city, he realized that the tyrants were unpopular because they were loyal to Persia."

"An excellent reason for retaining them."

"So I would have thought. But Mardonius is subtler than we. He made it a point to meet the leading Greek merchants. You know, the sort of people who control the rabble when it gets together and starts voting. Then, suddenly, in the Great King's name, Mardonius dismissed the tyrants. Just like that. Now he's the hero of the Ionian democracies. Breath-taking, really."

"Although the tyrants are gone, I'm sure that Mardonius left a queen in Halicarnassus." This was the sort of thing that amused Atossa.

"Oh, yes. Artemisia is still queen. She is also a beautiful widow."

"Actually, she's a rather plain widow."

"All queens are to be regarded as beautiful," said Atossa firmly. "Except by their husbands. Anyway, now, thanks to Mardonius, Persia is in the ridiculous position of being the sponsor of democracy in the Ionian cities while trying to overthrow the Athenian democracy in order to restore the tyranny."

"Mardonius is very bold."

"In my father's time, he would have been flayed alive at the palace gate for having taken upon himself the Great King's prerogative. But this is another time, as I often remind myself." Atossa gave one of her remaining teeth an experimental tap and winced with pain. "It's lucky for Mardonius that he conquered Thrace and Macedonia. Otherwise Darius might have been very angry with him. As it is, Darius listens to Mardonius, and only to him. This season, anyway. And that means that there will be another Greek campaign, with or without Mardonius. Unless . . . Tell me more about India."

Atossa was a highly practical and realistic politician. She knew that, sooner or later, Xerxes must prove himself in war, and in the light of Mardonius' victories, sooner was better. Although Atossa had no fear of Xerxes' failing to win battles—was he not Cyrus' grandson?—she feared that he might be murdered by the Gobryas faction. She also knew that it is far easier to kill a commander in the field than to kill a well-guarded prince at a court.

When I had finished, Atossa said the awesome words "I will speak to Darius." In all the years that I knew her, I don't suppose that I heard her use this phrase more than three times. It was like a declaration of war. Gratefully I kissed her hand. Once again we were fellow conspirators.

I tried several times to see Mardonius, but he was too ill to receive me. The leg had turned gangrenous and there was talk of amputation. Everyone said what a shame it was that Democedes was no longer alive.

Fan Ch'ih was delighted with Babylon. "There are at least six men from Cathay living here, and one is a partner of the Egibis." All the world knows—except Democritus—that Egibi and sons are the richest bankers in the world. For three generations they have financed caravans, fleets, wars. I never knew any of them well, but Xerxes was altogether too familiar with them. Because of his passion for building, Xerxes was constantly short of money and the Egibis were invariably helpful and sometimes reasonable. Ordinarily they lend money at twenty percent. For Xerxes, they would reduce the rate to ten percent, which made it possible for him to start if not complete a dozen palaces during his lifetime, as well as conduct the Greek wars. Xerxes' wife Roxanna was a granddaughter of an Egibi. She was very much ashamed of a connection that very much amused him. "They cannot refuse money to a relative," he would say.

Darius despised bankers, which was curious, since he himself was essentially a man of the marketplace. I suppose that he wanted to eliminate the middle-man. In any case, he financed the realm through tribute and plunder. According to Xerxes, Darius almost never took a loan. "But then, I don't think my father ever understood the system."

I never told the Great King Xerxes that there was very little about finance that his predecessor had not understood. Darius' discounts on money turned in at the treasury were notorious. Although he is supposed to have learned the trick of short-changing the citizens from Hippias, I think that it was the other way around. On the other hand, the gold coinage was always honest in Darius' day. "I am the archer," he would say, ringing one of his coins on the table. "That is my face, my crown, my bow. Men must appreciate my true weight." They did. They do. Only recently has the gold coinage been debased.

I was able to arrange several meetings between Fan Ch'ih and Xerxes. As interpreter, I saw to it that they got on well. Not only was I able to interest Xerxes in India but Fan Ch'ih's stories of the cities of Cathay excited both of us.

"How large the world is!" Xerxes exclaimed at one point. We had just run out of maps and Fan Ch'ih was not very explicit when it came to describing the approaches to Cathay. He did tell us that there were two overland routes. One passed through the high mountains to the east of the old Shakya republic; the other crossed the wide northern desert beyond the Oxus River. Fan Ch'ih himself had come by sea to the Magadhan port of Champa. "But it took me more than a year," he said. "And I don't want to go back that way. I want to find a good overland route—a silk road, connecting us with you."

Later, in Cathay, Fan Ch'ih told me that he had been deliberately vague about the approaches to what they call the Middle Kingdom because he had been overwhelmed by the immensity of Darius' empire. "I had thought Persia would be like Magadha. Instead, I found a universal monarch who, luckily for us, had no idea just how much of a universe there is. So I decided that it would not be a good idea for him to visit Cathay. A Persian army on the Yellow River would be highly disturbing."

Note the contrast between a man of Cathay and a Greek. Out of injured self-esteem, the Greek is always ready to betray his native land. Although the Middle Kingdom is split into dozens of warring states, no man of Cathay—except, perhaps the so-called son of heaven— would dream of asking help from the army of an alien race. The yellow people are not only exceptionally intelligent, they are perfectly convinced that of all the world's people they are unique. In their eyes, *we* are barbarians! That's why only a few adventurous souls like Fan Ch'ih ever leave Cathay. The rest are indifferent to what lies beyond their Middle Kingdom.

Fan Ch'ih had been quick to make a number of business arrangements with Egibi and sons. Skillfully he exploited their passion for silk or Cathay cloth. He sold what he had; bought what he could afford; borrowed against future profits.

While I was still waiting for a private audience with the Great King, Fan Ch'ih had managed to finance a convoy of cargo ships to take him to India, where he would transfer his goods to a caravan. Then he would cross India and enter Cathay through the high mountains, a long and hazardous journey of the sort that young men embark upon without a second thought.

After a brief period of mourning for Parmys, Darius held a levee and I took this opportunity to present Fan Ch'ih at court. At first there were all sorts of objections from the second room of the chancellery. Was the yellow man really an ambassador? If so, from what king? If he was simply a merchant, he could not be received. That was definite. Finally Xerxes intervened and Ambassador Fan Ch'ih was commanded to attend the Great King and present him with the duke of Lu's acknowledgment of the Great King's lordship over him.

At noon we arrived in the hall of columns. Xerxes had only just finished this handsome building, situated to the northwest of the palace. I was received courteously by the court chamberlain. I was treated gravely by the Persian nobles, who have never quite known what to make of me. On principle, they do not like priests. Yet I am no more a priest than I am a noble. Nevertheless, though not one thing or the other, I am close to the royal family, and so all the nobles offer me polite smiles, proffered cheeks, whispered compliments—all except for Gobryas. He never gave me more than a nod. As part of the Atossa-Xerxes faction, I was the enemy. I noted that the old man's whiskers had undergone yet another transformation. From a harsh red, they had changed like autumn leaves to a dull gold.

Although Mardonius was nowhere in sight, more than a hundred of the Great King's sons and nephews were present. For the first time I saw Artaphrenes, the son of the satrap of Lydia. He looked like his father except for the expression of the face, which was positively stone-like with ambition. At his side was the Median admiral Datis, whom I had met years before at the hunting lodge on the road to Pasargada.

The Greek contingent was grouped to the left of the throne. Hippias looked very old; but resolute. He clung to the arm of Milo, now a handsome man. I bowed to Hippias. I embraced Milo, who said with wonder, "You've turned black."

"Too much fire eating," I said, backing off. I did not want to speak to the king of Sparta.

Fan Ch'ih stayed close to me. The nobles stared at him as if he were some sort of strange animal. He stared right back. Although Persian architecture was not to his taste, he did admire the splendor of the costumes. "Only," he asked suddenly, "where are the Egibis?"

"This is the court." I thought that was answer enough.

"I know. I also know that they lend money to the crown prince. So why aren't they here?"

"This is the court," I repeated. "The Egibis are bankers, merchants. The Great King cannot receive them."

"But his family does business with them."

"Yes, but only in private. At court, only the nobles may wait upon the Great King. Isn't it the same in Cathay?"

"It has been said that, perhaps, it was so in the old days." Fan Ch'ih was a master of the uninformative reference, usually attributed to his teacher, Master K'ung.

In each of the Great King's capitals, court ceremonial

conforms to whatever protocol obtained before the creation of the Persian empire. At Memphis, he is pharaoh, and a god. At holy Pasargada, he is clan leader. At Babylon, he is a Chaldean king whose power is granted him by a priesthood who takes the line that although the city might currently belong to a mortal Persian king, the court's ceremonial must never cease to be anything less than an earthly reflection of Bel-Marduk's immortal glory. As a result, musicians play music rather more suitable for an evening with prostitutes than for a levee of the Great King while temple dancers make distractingly obscene movements as they render homage to Ishtar who is Cybele who is Anahita who is Diana who is—everywhere!

At Babylon the high priest of Bel-Marduk acts as master of ceremonies. That day the high priest was in excellent voice. He stood at the entrance to the hall of columns and howled at us in old Chaldean. Then the guards commander roared, "The Great King Darius, lord of all the lands, king of Babel, king of kings!"

Darius appeared in the doorway, the sun behind him. As he put his foot on the long Sardis rug that leads to the throne, we prostrated ourselves.

The Great King was dressed in the purple Median robe that only the sovereign may wear. On his head was the high felt cidaris circled by Cyrus' blue-and-white fillet. In his right hand, he held the golden sceptre; in his left hand, he held the golden lotus. The court chamberlain carried the ceremonial fly whisk and folded napkin. The guards commander carried the footstool. A member of the Babylonian royal family held the traditional golden parasol over the Great King's head. This particular parasol had belonged to the ancient Assyrian kings. A few paces behind the Great King walked the crown prince.

As Darius made his slow stately progress down the center of the hall, the priests of Bel-Marduk began solemnly to chant. Although we were supposed to be looking at the redwash floor, we were all watching the Great King.

Darius was now blond as a Scythian. I looked for signs of age, and found them—always an easy thing to do, except in one's own mirror. Several months earlier, Darius had suffered some kind of paralysis. As a result, he dragged, very slightly, his left leg, and the left hand, which held the lotus, looked stiff. Later I was told that

Darius had no strength at all in the entire left side of his body and that the lotus had been tied to his fingers.

Nevertheless, Darius' face was still handsome and he did not seem to be more than usually painted. The blue eyes were clear. Even so, the contrast between him and Xerxes was altogether too vivid. Xerxes was half a head taller than his father; and he was young. In Xerxes' left hand was a golden lotus. The right hand was still empty.

I suspect that Darius was perfectly aware that there was no one in that hall who was not wondering how long it would be before there was a new occupant of the lion throne—except that the lion throne was not used in Babylon. At the insistence of the priests, the Great King was obliged to sit in a somewhat unimpressive gilded chair that had been used by the Akkadian kings for a thousand years, or so the high priest maintained. When Babylon rebelled for the last time, Xerxes had the chair chopped up and burned. As Xerxes watched the smoky flames, he said, "You see, I was right! It's new wood. They fake everything here."

The cult of antiquity has always been a kind of madness at Babylon. Credit for this must be given to Nabonidus, the last Babylonian king. He spent his life digging up forgotten cities. When Cyrus invaded Babylonia, Nabonidus was so busy trying to decipher the contents of the foundation stone of a thirty-two-century-old temple that he never noticed that he was no longer king until he returned to the city one evening and found Cyrus in residence at the new palace. At least that's the story the black-haired people like to tell. Actually, Nabonidus was captured, imprisoned, freed. He then went back to his digging.

Between Nabonidus and his friend Amasis, the pharaoh of Egypt, the past was—and is—constantly being not only disinterred but imitated. Nothing can ever be old enough or ugly enough for the true lover of antiquity. Worse, all sorts of long-forgotten religious rites have been revived, particularly in Egypt. To Cyrus' ever-lasting shame, he encouraged the antiquarian passion of his Babylonian and Egyptian subjects; worse, it was his policy to identify the Achaemenids with every extinct dynasty of any note. Except for Xerxes, all of his successors have continued the madness. For more than twenty years a dozen Magians labored in a back room of the palace at Susa inventing plausible genealogies for Darius. Eventually he was related to everyone from Zeus to Amon Ra, and always in the direct line!

Darius took his seat. Xerxes stood behind him. We got to our feet and stood, hands in our sleeves, heads respectfully bowed. The Babylonian high priest intoned the Great King's titles; then followed an erotic dance by women from Ishtar's temple. The whole ceremony was very un-Persian.

Armed with lists, the court chamberlain began to whisper into Darius' ear things that he needed to know. Since Darius was now rather deaf, there was a good deal of confusion. Quite often the wrong person was awarded the command of a nonexistent frontier post. Nevertheless, Darius insisted that he alone make every appointment, unlike Xerxes, who turned over to the chancellery all routine assignments. As a result, Darius never lost control of the machinery of a government which Xerxes never mastered.

Darius then spoke of general matters. From time to time he would mispronounce simple words, a characteristic of those who have suffered a partial or whole paralysis of the left side. Democedes once told me that there is absolutely nothing to be done when this has happened. But if the patient is a powerful and willful man, certain herb poultices can be prescribed on the ground that "they will cause the patient practically no harm." He was a rare physician.

All was well on the northern borders, said Darius. The tribes were quiet. There had been civil disobedience in Armenia. The Great King had put a stop to it. There were the usual alarms out of Egypt. But Egypt was like Babylon, filled with religious fanatics, madmen, adventurers. The Great King had restored tranquillity.

As Darius spoke, I watched the Greeks. Demaratus and Hippias jointly headed a group of perhaps twenty exiles. Except for Hippias, there were no longer any tyrants at the court. That era was finished. The current Greeks were disgruntled generals, admirals, magistrates, who felt, often rightly, that they had been ill treated by the various democracies. The Athenians were particularly bitter. But then, the Athenian assembly is uncommonly perverse. Any citizen can be sent packing if a majority of the city's occasionally corrupt but always frivolous assembly votes for ostracism. Sooner or later just about every distinguished man of state is exiled. Democritus thinks that I exaggerate. I don't. One day they will rid themselves of General Pericles simply because he bores them.

"In the matter of the west." Darius crossed his arms. Sceptre and lotus changed sides just as crook and flail do when Egypt's pharaoh chooses to symbolize his dominion over the double realm.

"We are well pleased with our nephew Mardonius. He has broken the power, such as it was, of the western Greeks. The Thracians have sent us earth and water in acknowledgment of our sovereignty. King Alexander of Macedonia has sent us earth and water. He is our slave, forever more. The matter of the western Greeks is settled. There will be no spring campaign."

Although Xerxes was obliged to remain as expressionless as a statue behind his father, I could see his lips begin to part in a half-smile.

There were no smiles from the Greeks. The Great King had spoken from the throne. Only in private audiences could the Greeks argue for war and, of course, they would. Darius would not have a peaceful winter.

The Great King looked about the room. When he saw me, he nodded. "We now receive our ambassador to the sixteen kingdoms beyond the Indus River. We commend Cyrus Spitama for having opened a trade route between our satrapy of India and the countries of . . . of . . ."

There was a good deal of muttering between Darius and the court chamberlain. The chamberlain had difficulty pronouncing the words Koshala and Magadha, which, in any case, Darius could not hear. Irritably, Darius silenced the chamberlain with a prod from the sceptre.

". . . and the sixteen countries," said Darius firmly. "The first caravan arrived at Bactra just before the full moon, with a large consignment of smelted iron. In the coming year we shall receive other metals and textiles and jewels from . . . from these far-off places. Approach, Cyrus Spitama."

Two ushers came forward. They escorted me to the throne.

I prostrated myself at the golden footstool.

"You are now my eyes," said Darius.

The chancellor had already told me that I was to be made king's eye. This meant that as a high officer of state I would be able to draw a comfortable salary from the treasury. I would also be able to stay at any of the royal palaces and travel wherever I chose, at government

316

expense, accompanied by a ceremonial guard and a herald whose cry "Way for the king's eye!" was enough to make half the population of the empire fall to the ground with terror. At regular intervals, each satrapy is investigated by a king's eye. Whatever complaints the citizens have against the satrap and his administration are brought to the attention of the king's eye, who has the power to redress them on the spot. For the time that he is in office, the king's eye is the monarch's surrogate. Since many of the satrapies are enormously rich and complex—I think particularly of Egypt and Lydia and India—a corrupt king's eye dies rich. I was not corrupt. Of course, I was never sent to a rich province. I did one tour of duty in the Ionian cities, where there is no great wealth, and another in Bactria, which is poor.

I expressed my gratitude to the Great King, and to the Wise Lord who had inspired him. Finally, Darius gave me an amiable kick on the shoulder. He had heard enough of my gratitude. As I got to my feet I could see how haggard the painted face was. But the eyes were still bright, even mischievous.

"There is," the Great King announced, "to the east of the east, a land which is known as Cathay." Darius was plainly enjoying himself at the expense of the Greeks, who had not the slightest interest in my embassy. Curiously enough, most of the Persian nobles were equally indifferent to the lure of new worlds to conquer. It was their view that Persia was large enough as it was. They have always lacked curiosity.

"This far-off land is full of cities and rivers, full of gold and cows." Darius was now speaking for his own amusement, and perhaps mine. "The people are descended from a yellow god and they live on either side of a yellow river that never goes dry. Once upon a time they had a heaven-sent ruler. But since he died the nobles do nothing but quarrel with one another, just as we used to do. What was once a single rich kingdom is now an unhappy land of small and turbulent states in need of a great king who will protect them and give them a sound currency and perfect justice. The lord of one of these countries to the east of the east is now ready to offer us earth and water. He has sent us an ambassador."

All of this was somewhat disingenuous, to say the least. Fan Ch'ih was on a trade mission, not an embassy. But Darius knew exactly what he was doing. He wanted to whet the interest of the clans. He wanted to convince them of a fact which he had always known: Persia's future lies to the east, and to the east of the east.

Fortunately, Fan Ch'ih did not understand a word of Persian, and I told him only what I wanted him to hear. Then I told the Great King what *he* wanted to hear. As no one present understood the Indian dialect that Fan Ch'ih and I used, I was able to mistranslate and misinterpret freely.

Fan Ch'ih prostrated himself before the Great King. If nothing else, our inward-looking court was distracted by his appearance. Everyone stared at him. Although there are yellow men in every important Persian city, no noble would have seen one up close unless he was in trade, a not very likely prospect since a Persian noble may not trade or borrow money—in theory, anyway. The yellow people of Cathay are simply a rumor to the court, like those two-headed Africans that Scylax says he saw.

From head to toe, Fan Ch'ih was dressed in crimson Cathay cloth. He was a good-looking man, about my age. Of the warrior class, he had served in the army of one of the leading families of the duchy of Lu. Unlike most young men of his race and class, he wanted to see the outside world. In order to do so, he had made trade with the west the pretext for his journey to India and to Persia.

Fan Ch'ih said, "I do reverence to the Great King." In translation, I changed Great King to universal monarch.

Fan Ch'ih said, "I am here to reopen the overland trade route between Cathay and Persia."

I translated this exactly. I also added, "I come as ambassador from the duke of Lu, a land as large and as rich as Lydia. My master says that should you come to him with your armies, he will offer you earth and water and submit to you as your slave."

This caused some stir in the hall of columns, except amongst the Greeks. For the Greek, what is not Greek is not.

Darius looked very happy. "Tell your master that I shall come to him with all my hosts. Tell him that I shall take with my own hands the earth and water that he offers me. Tell him that I will then make him my satrap of . . . of all Cathay." Darius was superb. He had no more idea what Cathay was like than I did. We might just as well have been talking about the moon. But to the court, Darius sounded knowledgeable, serene, all-powerful.

Fan Ch'ih was plainly puzzled by our exchange, which was considerably longer than his own mild request for the reopening of a trade route.

I said to Fan Ch'ih, "The Great King will protect any caravan that goes from Persia to Cathay. He commands you to make a list for him of those things that your country has to exchange for Persian gold or kind."

"Tell the Great King that I shall obey his command. Tell him that he has answered my heart's desire."

I said to the Great King, "If you come to Lu, you will answer the heart's desire of its ruler, who promises to serve you loyally as satrap of all Cathay."

The performance that Darius and I gave was the talk of the court for the rest of the winter. Even the dullest of the Persian nobles was now intrigued by a possible campaign to the east, and to the east of the east.

Overnight it became the fashion to wear something of Cathay cloth. As a result, every scrap of silk in the market was sold out, to the delight of the Egibi banking interests, who then—as now—control the silk trade. Persian gold would be spent for Cathay cloth, and Egibi and sons would not only make twenty percent on their loan to Fan Ch'ih, they would also make an additional profit on the sale of silk in the markets.

The Great King sent for me the day after the levee. Darius always preferred small rooms to large. In this, he resembled the mountain lion who makes its lair in a cleft in the rock; also, like most of the lords of this world that I have known, he invariably sat with his back to the wall.

I found him peering at a stack of accounts. With age, he could read only if the writing was held very close to his face. I did obeisance. For some minutes he paid no attention to me. As I listened to his heavy breathing, I could hear a somewhat ominous lionlike rumbling in his chest. Finally he said, "Get up, King's Eye. Let's hope you're not as flawed as the King's real eyes."

I studied him intently from beneath respectfully lowered lids. The unevenly dyed hair and beard were in their usual disorder. The unpainted face was sallow. In his stained and rumpled tunic, he could have been a Greek horse trainer. The weakened left arm and hand were arranged in the most natural way on the table's top, and one was not aware of any physical disability.

"You paid too much for the iron."

"Yes, Great King." One did not argue with Darius.

"But I shall want a second consignment. This time we will pay not in gold but in kind. Do you know what these people want?"

"I do, Lord. I've prepared a list and given it to the second room of the chancellery."

"Where it will vanish forever. Tell the councilor for the east that I want the list today." Darius put down the documents that he had been holding in his good right hand. He sat back in his chair. He smiled broadly. The teeth were strong, yellow—yes, lionlike. That is my persistent image for the Great King. "I dream of cows," said the lion, in character.

"They exist, Lord. Millions of them, waiting to be herded."

"How long will it take me to pen them?"

"If the army were to leave for the Indus valley next spring they could spend the summer—which is the Indian rainy season, at Taxila. Then when the good weather starts, in our autumn, you would have four months in which to conquer Koshala and Magadha."

"So from beginning to end, I shall need one year." Darius shoved the documents to one side, revealing the copper map that I had prepared for him. He tapped the metal with the gold ring on his forefinger; there was a ringing sound. "Explain to me the distances. The kind of terrain. And what about all these rivers? I've never seen so many rivers in one country. How swift are they? Will we need a fleet? Or is there enough wood to build one there? If not, will we have to bring the wood? And what sort of boats?"

In the course of one hour, I have never been asked so many questions. Fortunately, I knew most of the answers. Fortunately, the Great King's memory was perfect and he never asked the same question twice.

Darius was particularly curious about Ajatashatru. He laughed when I told him that I was the son-in-law of his vassal-to-be. "It's perfect!" he said. "We'll make you satrap of Magadha. After all, you're a member of their royal family, and it is our policy to change things as little as possible. I suppose we'll have to darken you up a bit. They're all black, aren't they?"

"The common people, yes. But the ruling class is almost as light as we are. They're Aryans, too."

"Whatever that may be. Anyway, we'll dip you in

320

henna. Although, come to think of it, you're pretty black as it is. Now, what about all those people in Cathay? Are they as yellow as that one you brought to court?"

"So I have heard, Lord."

"I've never seen one that close before. The eyes look very odd, don't they? How do I get to Cathay?" Darius was already dreaming of Cathayan cows.

I pointed to the northeast corner of the map. "There is a pass through these mountains. But it is only open in the hot season. It's a six-month journey, they say."

"What about by sea?"

"It would take at least three years—from Persia."

"That means one year from India. We would pass many islands, I should think. Rich islands."

"Islands, peninsulas, the mainland. Fan Ch'ih says that south of Cathay there is nothing but jungle. But he also says that there are a number of good ports—and many pearls." If one wanted to hold Darius' attention, one was always well advised to mention things like pearls.

"Well, we shall collect the Cathayan pearls once we have herded those Indian cows." With a frown, Darius took his left arm in his right hand and pushed it off the table. I felt odd. I had seen his father make the same gesture a hundred times. Darius was suddenly aware of what he had done in front of me. "I can still ride a horse," he said. He was matter-of-fact.

"And lead an army, Lord." I bowed low.

"And lead an army. Xerxes would like to go to India." Darius' smile was sometimes boyish, despite the square straggling beard that almost hid the full, chafed lips. "He complains to you, I know."

I felt the blood rise in my cheeks. Thus, charges of treason began. "Lord, never does he complain . . ."

But Darius was in a good mood. "Nonsense. As I have loyal eyes"—he indicated me—"so I have loyal ears. I don't blame the boy. In fact, I would blame him if he did not complain. He's the same age as Mardonius, and look what Mardonius has accomplished. The queen is responsible for the life my son leads. She wants him safe. So I am guided by her." Darius had a brief fit of coughing. Then he said, "I am not too old to lead the army."

The fact that Darius felt the need to repeat such a declaration was, for me, the first sign that he knew that he had begun to fail. "I've stayed out of those Greek wars because they are not worth my time and effort. I also

321

can't abide the Greeks. At the last levee in Susa, I counted more Greeks than Persians in the hall of columns."

Darius may have had difficulty reading, but he could count with the greatest of ease. "I am surrounded by Greeks, hungry for archers." I was always faintly shocked when Darius used this slang expression. "Of both kinds," he added. "But now I've done with the whole lot of them. There'll be no spring campaign. Mardonius is upset. But I told him, you wouldn't be able to lead the army even if there was a campaign. So he made me a speech about all the battles that have been won by generals in litters, which is nonsense. *I* can still ride from sunrise to sundown." With that non sequitur, Darius convinced me that he would never take the field again. I was delighted. Soon Xerxes would have his chance.

"You've done well." Darius pushed the map to one side. "Tell the chancellery what you think we should send to Cathay. Write those two kings—you know, the Indian ones—that the Great King smiles upon his slaves. The usual sort of thing. And tell them that we shall dispatch a caravan before the end of the coming year." Darius smiled. "Do not mention that I myself will be the caravan master. And that all our merchandise will be metal—swords, shields, lances! Before I die, I shall be . . . What did you say that little man called himself?"

"Universal monarch."

"I shall be the *first* universal monarch. I dream of pearls and silk—of islands and Cathay!"

If Darius had been ten years younger, and I had been ten years older, I am convinced that all the known world that mattered would now be Persian. But, as I had guessed, Darius never again led the clans into battle. In less than five years, he would be lying next to his father in the rock tomb outside Persepolis.

3

MARDONIUS RECEIVED ME ABOARD A houseboat moored to the new palace quay. The commander in chief of the armies and the navies of the Great King looked pale and fragile, and even younger than he actually was. He lay in a hammock that was suspended between two beams. As the boat responded to the river's currents, the hammock swayed of its own accord.

"When the boat rocks, the pain is less," Mardonius said as I crawled down the ladder to his quarters. The festering leg was bare, swollen, black. Two slaves fanned away the flies. A brazier of burning sandalwood could not disguise the smell of rotting flesh that filled the cabin. "Ugly, isn't it?"

"Yes." I was to the point. "Cut it off."

"No. I must have two legs."

"You can die of this sort of rot."

"The worst is over. Or so they say. If it isn't . . ." Mardonius shrugged; then grimaced with pain from the effort.

All about us, we could hear the usual sounds of a busy port. Men shouted and hawsers creaked and the circular Babylonian boats made a slapping sound as they moved against the river's current.

"Doesn't the noise bother you?"

Mardonius shook his head. "I like it. When I shut my eyes, I think I'm still with the fleet. Do you want to sail with me next spring?"

"To Thrace?" I don't know why I was so tactless as to mention the place where not only was he wounded but a part of his fleet was lost in a storm.

Mardonius frowned. "Yes. Thrace, too. Where your relatives are now in rebellion."

"Abdera may be in rebellion, but not Lais' family. They are all pro-Persian."

"I met your grandfather. I had no idea he was so rich."

"I've never met him, I'm sorry to say. I do know that he was always loyal to the Great King."

"He's Greek." Mardonius tugged at the cords of his hammock to make it swing along a wider arc. "Why have you been exciting Xerxes with those tales of India?" Mardonius was accusing.

"He asked me. And I told him. If you like, I'll tell you the same stories. Our future is in the east."

"That's because you were brought up on the eastern frontier." Mardonius was irritable. "You have no idea what Europe is like. How rich it is—in silver, grain, people."

"Darius tried to conquer Europe, remember? He was badly beaten."

323

"That's treason," said Mardonius, with no attempt at lightness. "The Great King has never been defeated."

"Just as his commanders are never wounded?" I always spoke as an equal to Mardonius. I don't suppose that he liked it, but since he and I and Xerxes had been as one for so many years, he could hardly complain. Finally, Mardonius was more fond of me than I was of him. This always gives one an advantage. Since I could never command an army, I was no threat to him. He also thought that he could influence the advice that I gave to Xerxes.

"That was a stupid mistake." Mardonius shifted his weight in the hammock. I tried not to look at the leg and, of course, looked at nothing else.

"There's no reason why *you* couldn't lead the armies into India." I was absolutely committed to the so-called eastern policy and have never wavered from it to this day. But Mardonius was the sole executor of the western policy. He did not have an easy task. The Great King had lost interest in Europe after his defeat on the Danube; his days were spent fretting about the northern tribes, and thinking up new ways of making money. By and large, Darius had had no real desire for further conquests until I fired his imagination with my tales of India and Cathay.

For several hours Mardonius and I argued in that stinking cabin, whose constant rocking made me somewhat ill. Although Mardonius knew of my private audience with Darius, he was too shrewd to ask me what had been said. Perhaps he already knew. There are not many secrets at the Persian court. It was already common knowledge that I had come down to Babylon with Xerxes.

"I want Xerxes to lead the next Greek expedition. I'll be second in command." I could see that Mardonius thought that he was being subtle. "Atossa won't let him go." I was not at all subtle.

"But Amestris will make him go." Mardonius smiled. "She is a great influence on our friend."

"So I've heard. Does she want him to go?"

"Of course she does. She hates seeing me get all the glory. I don't blame her. That's why I'm willing to share the credit for the conquest of Europe."

"Exactly how much of Europe do you expect to acquire?" This was a real question. In those days we knew even less than we know now about the extent and variety of the western lands. Phoenician traders had given us a good idea of the ports or potential ports along the northern coast of the Mediterranean. But the interior of that densely forested and largely empty continent was then, as it is now, a mystery, not worth unraveling—in my view, of course.

"On principle, we should destroy Athens and Sparta and bring the inhabitants here, as we did the Milesians. Next, I would occupy Sicily. It is an enormous island where we can grow enough grain to feed all Persia, which will make us less reliant on this damned barley." Mardonius made a face. "If you want to understand the Babylonians, just think of barley—and palm wine. They live on nothing else, and look at them!"

"They're quite handsome, as black-headed people go."

"I'm not speaking of beauty. I don't want prostitutes. I want soldiers, and there are none here."

But soon there were. Almost the entire Greek faction at court joined us in the cabin.

The aged Hippias and I embraced. "This will be my last campaign," he whispered in my ear. Although he was old and the teeth in his mouth were loose, he could still ride a horse as if he and the horse were one. "I dreamt last night that my mother held me in her arms. That is always a good sign. I am now certain that I shall soon be in Athens, offering a sacrifice to Athena."

"Let us hope so, Tyrant." I was polite.

Demaratus was not. "Let us hope that there is a campaign." The Spartan looked at me without pleasure, and the others took their lead from him. Even Milo's rosy face was sad at the thought that I might be, truly, an enemy.

As I excused myself, Mardonius insisted that I come see him again. "Next time I'll have a map of Europe for you, of the sort that should gladden any king's eyes." He laughed. The Greek conspirators did not.

The sun was hot as I climbed the steps from the wharf to the low gate that marks the end of the avenue of Bel-Marduk. Here my guards and herald were waiting. I had almost forgotten them. I was still not used to the pleasures and annoyances of high rank. It is one thing to be honored in a strange country like Magadha where one knows little of the people and cares less, and quite another to walk or ride down the main avenue of Babylon, attended by guards whose swords are drawn, and by a herald whose clear voice proclaims, "Way for the king's eye!" And way is made. People shrink as if from a fire that might burn them, which the king's eye is.

When the court is at Babylon, the city is overcrowded. The temples are busy not only with religious services and ritual prostitution but, most important of all, with money-changing and moneylending. It is said that banking was invented by the Babylonians. This may be true. But it is also true that, elsewhere, and quite independently, the Indians and Cathayans have worked out their own systems. I was always struck by the fact that the interest rates in each part of the world are usually the same. Yet there has been little or no regular contact between the three lands. I find this truly mysterious.

I made my way on foot through the narrow, winding side streets. Thanks to the herald and the guards, I was able to reach the main offices of Egibi and sons without too much jostling—and spitting. The black heads take revenge on their Persian masters by spitting on them whenever a sufficiently large crowd provides adequate cover.

The façade of the world's most important banking establishment is a featureless mud wall in which is set a plain cedar door with a small window. At my approach, the door opened. Black slaves with ritually scarred faces bowed me into a small courtyard where I was met by the head of the family, a smiling little man named Shirik. When my herald proclaimed the presence of the king's eye, he dropped to his knees. Respectfully, I helped him up.

Shirik was amiable, watchful, and entirely unimpressed by me. He showed me into a long high room whose walls were lined with shelves on which were stacked thousands of clay tablets. "Some of those records go back more than a century," he said. "To the days when our family first came to Babylon." He smiled. "No, we were *not* slaves. There is a legend that we were Jewish captives, brought here after Jerusalem fell. But we were never slaves. We had established ourselves in Babel long before their arrival."

We were joined by Fan Ch'ih and the Cathay man who served Shirik. We sat at a round table, surrounded by clay tablets that represented millions of sheep, tonnes of barley, stacks of iron and nearly all the archers ever minted.

I think that I might have done well at banking had I not been so carefully trained to be neither a priest nor a warrior. Although I have the Persian noble's contempt of trade, I lack his passion for war and hunting and drinking wine to excess. Although I have a priest's deep knowledge of religion, I am not certain *what* is true. Although I once heard the voice of the Wise Lord, I confess now in my old age that to hear and to listen are two different things. I am puzzled by creation.

Shirik came to the point. "I am willing to finance a caravan to Cathay. I am impressed by Fan Ch'ih. So is my colleague, from the neighboring duchy of Wei." Shirik indicated his yellow assistant, an unprepossessing creature with a blind eye, pale as moonstone. Shirik was precise in all his references. He knew that Wei was not a kingdom but a duchy. To the extent that he was able to obtain the information that he needed—no, craved—he got everything right. Except for Darius, I have never met a man with such a passionate interest in the details of this world.

"Naturally, there are difficulties," said Shirik, beginning to place the borrower on the defensive.

"Numerous but surmountable, Lord Shirik." Fan Ch'ih was now beginning to learn to speak a sort of Persian that nicely complemented Shirik's own oddly accented but entirely fluent Persian. Shirik was Babylonian, and to this day the people of Babel avoid learning Persian on the never admitted ground that, sooner or later, the Persians will either go away or be absorbed by Babylon's older and superior culture.

For a time we discussed the approaches to Cathay. The safest seemed to be overland from Shravasti to the mountain passes. We were all agreed that the sea route is endless, and that the trail from Bactria to the east is not passable because of the Scythian tribes. While we talked, Shirik moved the ivory disks of an abacus so swiftly that they made a blur like a hummingbird's wings.

"Naturally, a single caravan is worthless." Shirik offered us wine in solid-gold cups whose bright grandeur was in startling contrast to all those dusty tablets that lined the walls, so like the tumbled mud bricks of some dead city. But then, those unprepossessing but entirely alive tablets had made possible the golden cups.

"Let us say that the caravan reaches Lu or Wei. Let us say that a second caravan returns safely to Babylon with goods whose value are in excess of what was sent out. Let us say that all this happens, even though the odds are seven to one that the first caravan will not arrive and eleven to one that if it does, the return caravan will never reach Babylon." I assumed that he had, somehow, worked out these odds on the abacus.

"But I am willing to gamble. For five generations it has been the dream of our family to open a route between Babylon—that is, Persia—and Cathay. We have always had our connections with the Indian kingdoms." Shirik turned to me. "The merchant-banker that you did business with at Varanasi is a valued colleague of ours. Of course, he and I shall never meet in this world, but we manage to correspond once or twice a year, and do what business we can."

It took less than an hour for Shirik to make his offer to me. "We believe that this enterprise would be a great success if you were to accompany the caravan as the Great King's ambassador to the Middle Kingdom. As you know, the Cathayans still pretend that their empire exists."

"It does," said Fan Ch'ih, "and it does not."

"An observation," said Shirik, "worthy of the Buddha."

I was amazed to hear the name of the Buddha on the lips of a Babylonian banker two thousand miles from the banks of the Ganges River. There was little that Shirik did not know about the world he was obliged to deal with.

"I would also suggest, most humbly, that you take your leave before the start of the spring campaign."

"There will be no spring campaign," I said.

Shirik smiled his gentle, secret smile. "I cannot contradict the king's eye! I am too humble, Lord. So let me say that should there be, by some miracle, a combined land-and-sea attack on Eretria and Athens, the expense of mounting that invasion will be enormous. Should such a campaign take place, Egibi and sons will be obliged to make their contribution, ever so gladly, gladly! Let me say. But in light of these military expenditures, I would suggest to the king's eye who honors us with his presence today, that he whisper in the ear of that glorious sovereign whose eye he is, that an embassy should be sent to Cathay before the Persian fleet leaves Samos."

"There will be no Greek war this year." I was firm in my ignorance. "I have spoken—" I almost made the error that the courtier must never make: repeat in public a private conversation with the Great King.

"—to the Lord Admiral Mardonius, yes." Swiftly, Shirik saved me from indiscretion. "Your dearest friend, after your truly dearest friend, the Lord Xerxes the crown prince, the viceroy of Babel . . . Yes, yes, yes." He treated me rather the way that a Greek philosopher who happens to be a slave will treat his master's son. He was both subservient and imposing, courteous and contemptuous.

"Yes," I said. "I have just come from Mardonius. There will be no war. He's not physically able to lead the expedition."

"The last part is all too true. Lord Mardonius will not lead the Great King's forces. But there *will* be a war. The decision has been made. The command will be divided. I tell you no state secrets for if these were indeed high secrets, how would poor Shirik of the house of Egibi know them? One commander will be Artaphrenes, the son of the satrap of Lydia. The other will be Datis the Mede. Six hundred triremes will rendezvous at Samos. They then will sail for Rhodes, Naxos, Eretria, Athens. But you know all this, Lord. You take pleasure in allowing a humble old man to make a fool of himself by telling you what is known to all who attend the Great King's councils."

I did my best to pretend that I was indeed a repository of state secrets. Actually, I was entirely taken aback. Although I was not surprised that the banker might know things that I did not, I was fairly certain that Mardonius knew nothing of the spring campaign, and I was entirely certain that Xerxes was ignorant of his father's plans. If Shirik was correct, then, for reasons unknown, the Greek faction had once again persuaded the Great King to commit himself to a war in the west.

I agreed with Shirik that embassy and caravan should travel as one, and I said that I would propose myself to the Great King as ambassador. But as we made our plans I could think of nothing but Darius' duplicity. He had promised me an invasion of India. Naturally, Great Kings are not obliged to honor promises made to their slaves. Yet by Darius' own admission, Persia's interest was to the east. Why had he changed his mind?

In those days Xerxes liked to wander about Babylon in disguise. He would wear a Chaldean cloak in such a way that the hood covered the telltale square-cut beard. With face covered, he looked like a moderately unsuccessful young merchant from some upriver village. When Atossa remonstrated with him about these adventures, he would say, "If they are going to kill me, they will kill me. If it happens, it happens." Eventually, it happened.

In our youth, thanks to Atossa, Xerxes was never entirely on his own. Wherever he went, guards were always close at hand. Even so, I must say that those expeditions always made me uneasy. "Why expose yourself like this?"

"I enjoy it. Anyway, since no one ever knows in advance just when I plan to vanish—including me—that rules out ambush, doesn't it?"

Xerxes and I vanished the day after my conference with Shirik. My heralds and guards were dismissed, while Xerxes' personal guards were dressed to resemble farmers come to market. Then, contentedly, Xerxes led me through the quarter of those privately owned brothels which are far superior to the temple establishments. In a good private house, it is possible to dine well, listen to music, enjoy the resident girls who come from every part of the world. The girls are often lovely; and always clean.

Xerxes' favorite house was in an alleyway between the back wall of the temple of Ishtar and the camel market. The owner and mistress of the revels was a bewhiskered woman who had no idea who we were. But she always remembered with simulated fondness the handsome gray-eyed young Persian who paid her well and made no trouble. At the door she greeted us with her usual "Gallant young princes, you are like the sun in a dark place! Enter, enter!"

Somewhat incongruously, she spoke the language of the old Babylonian court, where she had spent her childhood as, she claimed, a concubine of Nabonidus. But the other house owners in the district assured us that she had been not a concubine but a cook. Babylonian malice is always elaborate and amusing if one is not the butt.

"By now," said an aged competitor, "the old thing really believes that she was queen of Babylon. But she was the lowest of the low. I can't think why you nice lads go near her place. She has every sort of disease. And, of course, she's a eunuch. Didn't you know? Haven't you noticed the little beard?"

As always, we paid in advance, which delighted Xerxes. He enjoyed pretending that he was an ordinary mortal. As always, I paid for both of us. The crown prince may not carry a purse. We were then shown into a large room at the top of the house, where we lay side by side on a low divan.

Remembering Xerxes' preference for Helbon wine, our hostess sent us a dozen flagons. Each was delivered by a

330

different girl—an amiable way of showing us the house's wares. In another room, Phrygian music was played. When the last girl had set down the last flagon of wine and departed, I told Xerxes about my visit to Shirik.

Xerxes lay back on a cushion, cup in hand; he shut his eyes and murmured, "No."

"Didn't the Great King tell you?" I asked. The room was warm and the smell of frankincense permeated everything, including the wine. I cannot think why people are so attached to that cloying scent. I suppose because it is so rare. The satrap of Arabia provides the Great King with more than sixty thousand pounds a year, as tribute.

"My father tells me nothing. We talk about building. We talk about"—Xerxes made a large gesture to indicate the satrapy of Babylon—"all this, and how it *should* be governed, as opposed to the way I govern it. He finds fault." Xerxes sighed. "Datis is no threat. But my cousin Artaphrenes . . ." The voice trailed off.

"Let's hope he's inherited his father's military prowess. I was there when Sardis burned, thanks to the old man's negligence."

"Gobryas was never good at war, and look at *his* sons." Suddenly Xerxes smiled for the first time since I told him the news. "Well, at least Mardonius will not be in command." Xerxes clapped his hands, and a girl appeared in the low doorway. "I want Lydian music," he said. "And Lydian food."

In no time at all, we were provided with both. While course after course was brought us, melody after melody was played us on twelve-string harps. Between courses, we were able to talk.

"I did my best," he said. "I told Darius we should go east next spring." Xerxes plunged his hand into an earthenware pot filled with honeyed kid and pine nuts.

"What did he say?"

"He agreed. He said, 'Yes, we should go east.' That's his way, of course. He said should and made me think that he had said would. But . . . something's odd. He really was excited by what you told him."

"Then why—"

"I don't know why. I never know why. Obviously, the Greeks at court have been to work on him. Particularly Hippias. He has some hold over my father. I can't think what. Yet every time the old man says, 'By Athena and Poseidon, I swear that I shall once again make sacrifice

331

on the Acropolis' "—Xerxes mimicked to perfection Hippias' sonorous voice, in which an old man's quaver had only recently begun to sound—"Darius gets tears in his eyes and swears to help him."

"What about the king of Sparta?"

"Ask your mother." Xerxes was sour. "I've had no dealings with him. I suppose he wants us to restore him to power. What else? He's supposed to be a good soldier. Let's hope Lais teaches him to bathe occasionally."

"Lais and I have quarreled."

"Over the Greeks?"

I nodded. "And you. And Mardonius."

Xerxes raised himself up on one elbow. He pulled me so close to him that the side of my face was pressed against the soft curling beard, and I could smell the sandalwood scent of his clothes and feel the warmth of his lips as he whispered into my ear, "Is she poisoning Mardonius?"

I drew back. "No," I said in an ordinary voice. "I don't think that the girl loves him at all."

"But I was told that she does, that she pines for him, day after day, a drop at a time, in the cup." Xerxes was amused at our game.

"I think that the girl wants certain people to *think* that she is in love when she is not."

Xerxes nodded. "I understand. Even so . . ."

To my delight, a pair of Indian dancers performed for us. Twins from Taxila, they were astonished when I addressed them in their own language. I asked them to perform the famous nautch dance, and they obliged. Xerxes was fascinated at the way their bellies moved first in one direction and then in the other. During the intervals between the dances, he told me that he was still not entirely certain of the succession.

"There is no way that you cannot succeed." I confess that I was somewhat bored with what I took to be groundless fears. Xerxes had been crown prince for several years. He had no rival.

"Gobryas still wants his grandson to succeed," Xerxes was obsessed. "And Artobazanes has never forgotten that once upon a time, he was crown prince."

"I must say I'd almost forgotten."

The court had been at Ecbatana when Darius suddenly announced that he was leaving for the northeast frontier and since Persian—actually, Median—custom requires that whenever the ruler leaves the country, an heir must be designated, he chose his eldest son, Artobazanes. At the time, Xerxes and I were perhaps thirteen or fourteen years old. I thought nothing of the announcement until Lais asked me how Xerxes had reacted. When I said not at all, she shook her head. Years later Xerxes told me what an effort it had been for him to disguise his terror. "After all, if Darius had not come back from the frontier, Artobazanes would have been Great King and all of Atossa's sons would have been put to death."

As we finished flagon after flagon of wine, Xerxes spoke of his brother Ariamenes as a potential threat. Ariamenes was also satrap of Bactria, a territory prone to rebellion. "Spies tell me that he plans to take my place."

"How?"

"Poison. Rebellion. I don't know."

"What does Atossa think of this . . . son of hers?"

"It was Atossa who warned me." Xerxes shook his head, in a puzzled way. "You know, of all my brothers and half-brothers the only one that I ever liked was Ariamenes, who means to kill me."

"Unless you kill him first."

Xerxes nodded. "Unfortunately, Bactria is far away. That is why I had hoped"—he let his hand rest on my shoulder—"that you would take the northern route to Cathay—through Bactria." Xerxes gave me a slow blink of his cat's eyes.

I turned to ice. "That is a most . . . awesome commission." How, I wondered desperately, was I going to kill the satrap of Bactria in his own capital?

"Well, you've not been given it yet. But bear in mind that you may one day be obliged to demonstrate your love for your brother-in-law."

Dumbly, I looked at him through the same haze of wine that he looked at me. Then Xerxes embraced me. He was jubilant. "I've had it out with the law-bearers. And I've won. On new year's day, you will marry my sister."

"I am not worthy." That is the usual response. But, for once, I thought it apt. Who was I to marry a daughter of the Great King? I said as much, and more. But Xerxes ignored my demurs. "We must have you in the family. At least. I must have you in the family. Atossa is delighted."

"What does the Great King say?"

"At first he was not pleased. But then he started to talk

about Zoroaster and about what a disappointment he's been to your grandfather's followers, whom he values above all the Magians. You know the sort of harangue he gives when he wants to get something for nothing. Anyway, by the time he'd finished, he had convinced himself that it was his idea that you marry one of his daughters in order to mingle the blood of Cyrus the Great with that of holy Zoroaster. Mingle *my* blood, that is, since he's no more related to Cyrus than you are."

The rest of the day that we spent in the brothel is something of a blur. I remember sharing the Indian twins with Xerxes. I remember vomiting. I remember that our hostess gave me some powerful potion that immediately cleared my head, which then began to ache.

At sundown Xerxes and I made our unsteady way through the jostling crowds to the new palace. At the foot of the ziggurat I asked, "Which of your sisters am I to marry?"

"You're going to marry . . . uh . . ." Xerxes stopped. He thought hard; then shook his head. "I don't remember. I've only met two of the five. Anyway, Atossa says that the one you're getting is the best of the lot. Why don't you ask Lais? She knows the harem."

"I no longer talk to her."

"Well, ask Atossa. Or just wait and see." Xerxes grinned in the brazen light. "After all, what difference does it make? You're marrying an Achaemenid, and that's all that matters in this world."

4

FOR REASONS UNKNOWN, THE GREAT King had turned his face once again to the west. There would be no expedition to the east in his reign. I said farewell, sadly, to Fan Ch'ih. I married, gladly, the Great King's daughter; and for the next five years I enjoyed various high offices at Darius' court, including the much-sought-after rank of king's friend, a title that I still hold but would not dare use at the present court. It has always been my view that one's title and one's actual status ought, reasonably, to coincide.

As king's eye, I was sent to inspect the Ionian cities. I

enjoyed that tour of duty. For one thing, I was made much of, not only because of my rank but because I was half-Greek. For another, I was able to visit Abdera, where I met my grandfather, who received me like an only son. He was rich. He was witty. He was a sophist before the tribe was invented. Of course, Protagoras was a young woodcutter on his property and it is possible that he influenced my grandfather. It is equally possible that my grandfather influenced him. I also met my uncle— *your* grandfather Democritus. He was a young man of eighteen. He was interested only in money. I shall not pursue a subject you know better than I.

From Abdera, I set sail for home. This uneventful sea journey ended at Halicarnassus, where we made landfall one bright dawn when the stars were still to be seen in the west. As I went ashore, I half expected to find my younger self gaping not only at his first view of the sea but at the mature specter of the impressive king's eye that he was to become. But instead of my youthful self, I saw the grown-up Mardonius in the flesh. He was sitting on the end of the mole, surrounded by fishermen unloading their nets.

"Way for the king's eye!" my herald bawled.

"Way is made." Mardonius got to his feet and bowed low. "Welcome to Halicarnassus."

"Lord Admiral!" As we embraced I could feel the fleshless body through his heavy cloak. It had been two years since he was wounded, and he was still not recovered. But though the face was pale, the lively blue eyes reflected with the clearness of a child the morning's bright sea light.

"I am entirely out of the world," he said as we crossed the waterfront to the street that leads up the hill to Artemisia's palace. "Invisible. Forgotten."

"Invisible to the court. But not forgotten. What are you doing here?"

Mardonius paused at the foot of the hill. He was breathing hard and sweat shone on his brow. "When I lost my command, I told the Great King that I would like to retire from court."

"Forever?"

"Who knows? I mean, the only true forever is death. Isn't that so, dear cousin?" He gave me an odd look. "Who would have thought that you'd ever marry into our family!"

"Their family." And I mimicked his tone: "Dear cousin."

"Mine, too, by blood. Yours through marriage. And Xerxes' unswerving love." As we began the ascent to the sea palace, Mardonius took my arm. He did not limp so much as swagger, the body swinging from side to side as he tried not to put too great a weight on the shattered leg. Halfway up the hill he let go my arm. "Climbing is the worst," he gasped; and sank onto a limestone ledge.

I sat beside him. Below us the houses of the town looked like so many game dice strewn at the rough edge of the purple channel that separates the mainland from the dark-green mountains of the island of Cos. Home of the god Pan, I thought—then checked myself. I thought of the pirates who live in those lovely mountains, of the island's lax civil administration, of the taxes in arrears. I was very much the stern inspector, the entirely incorruptible king's eye.

Mardonius then told me that "As soon as the young Artaphrenes and Datis left for Greece, I came to Halicarnassus. And I've been here ever since."

"Regaining your strength?"

"Yes." Mardonius gave me a somewhat challenging look. "I expect to be in command next year."

"But will there be a campaign next year? Once Athens is destroyed, what's the point?" I picked at a small stone fish that had been imbedded in the limestone, a relic from the time of the Babylonian flood.

"The point is Greater Greece. Sicily. Italy." Mardonius grinned. "I never showed you my map, did I?"

"No. But then, I never showed you *my* map of the Indian kingdoms."

"We shall never agree."

"No. But why should you care?" I was somewhat bitter. "You always win. You have some sort of magic over the Great King. When you say attack the Greeks, he attacks."

"Hippias has the magic. He is the sorcerer." Mardonius was serious. "I only pray his spells are still effective. Old as he is, he's with the fleet. All our Greeks are, except Demaratus, who stays at Susa, where he has the Great King to himself."

"What do you think Demaratus wants?"

"The world! What else is worth having?" Mardonius positively shouted in my ear; and the pale face turned, briefly, coral-pink. That was when I realized that not only was he going to recover but he would once again obtain if not the world, the command of the Great King's forces.

A goatherd with his flock approached us. He bowed low; said something in dialect and moved on. Plainly, he had no notion who we were. We were simply foreigners on the way to the sea palace.

Mardonius's reaction was the same as mine. "We govern millions of people," he said, with a certain wonder, "and they never even know our names."

"Not ours, perhaps. But they know that Darius is the Great King."

Mardonius shook his head. "That goatherd doesn't know who Darius is."

I disagreed; and so we made a bet. While Mardonius rested on his rock perch, I made my way through the flock of goats to the herder, who looked alarmed. I said something to him; he said something to me. I found his primitive Dorian dialect as baffling as he found my Ionian Greek. Eventually we worked out a language suitable for my purpose, which was, simply, to ask, "Who is your sovereign?"

"Demetrius, young lord. He owns the whole of the back of that mountain over there. He owns this flock."

"But who is Demetrius' lord?"

The man frowned, and thought. As he wrestled with this new concept, a louse took advantage of the stillness to make a swift journey from the hair that was pulled back from the herder's left ear to the tangled beard that started halfway up his cheeks. The louse found a safe refuge in the beard forest, and I was pleased; those who are not by nature hunters side with the hunted.

"I don't know," he said at last.

I pointed to the gray palace above us. "What about the queen?"

"Queen?" He said the word as though he had not heard it before.

"The lady who lives up there?"

"Oh, *the lady!* Yes, I've seen her. She rides a horse like a man. She's very rich."

"She is the queen of Halicarnassus."

The man nodded. The phrase was plainly unfamiliar to him, "Yes, yes," he said. "The goats are straying, young Lord."

"But who is *her* lord?"

"Her husband, I suppose."

"She is a widow. Yet there is one person above her, and he is her sovereign."

Once again I had produced an unfamiliar word. "Sovereign?" he repeated. "Well, I don't come over to this side of the mountain all that much. There are a lot of people here I don't know."

"But surely you know the name of the Great King. He is your sovereign and he is my sovereign, and everyone in the world knows his name."

"And what would that be, young Lord?"

Mardonius was delighted to win the bet. I was not. "There must be some way of reaching those people," I said.

"Why bother? He looks after his goats and pays some sort of rent to a landowner who pays tax to the queen who pays tribute to the Great King. So what more can we want of a yokel like that? Why should he bother his head with who we are, or who Darius is?"

As we made our way to the top of the cliff, sweat covered Mardonius' face like a warm Indian rain. "The court is not the world," he said somewhat unexpectedly.

"No." I was very much king's eye. "But it is our world —and theirs, too. Whether they know it or not."

"You have never been to sea." Mardonius' response was cryptic. When I reminded him that I had crossed the southern sea, he shook his head. "That's not what I meant. You've never commanded your own ship. There is nothing like it."

"Yes, sea lord." I mocked him amiably. But he could not respond; he was again out of breath. We sat on a broken column just opposite the palace and watched the suppliants come and go.

"What news of Xerxes?" Mardonius mopped his face with a sleeve. The sun had lost its dawn-chill, and the heat now seemed to rise from the earth itself.

"He's at Persepolis," I said. "Building."

"Building?" Mardonius picked up a pine cone. "That's no life." He pulled back the cone's hard leaves in search of nuts. Finding none, he threw the cone at the tree that bore it. "I told the Great King that Xerxes should lead the armies against Athens." This was a lie, but I made no comment. "Darius agreed."

"Yet Xerxes was not allowed to go."

Mardonius rubbed his hand over the rough granite surface of the column. "Xerxes must have victories," he said, caressing the stone as if it were a horse. "Last year when I realized that I wasn't going to be strong enough to take the field, I advised Darius to call off the spring offensive in the west and send the army to that monkeyland of yours."

"Is this true?" The question was rude. Because I did not know the answer.

"A Persian noble may not lie," said Mardonius, not smiling. "Even," he added, "when he does." He looked in pain. "Yes, it's true. I want only one thing—to be the conqueror of the Greeks, and I don't want to share that distinction with Artaphrenes and Datis. So I had hoped that this year Xerxes would take the army across the Indus River."

"Then next year you would take the army west?"

"Yes, that's what I wanted. But that's not what I got."

I believed Mardonius. After all, it was no secret that he wanted to be satrap of the Greeks in Europe. Since it now looked as if young Artaphrenes would enjoy that high office, I changed the subject. "Is Queen Artemisia contented with her position?"

Mardonius laughed. "Which one? She has several."

"I speak as king's eye. She ignores the satrap. She deals directly with the Great King. The satrap is not happy."

"But Artemisia is happy, and so are the people. This is a Dorian city, and the Dorians tend to worship their royal families. And then, of course, she's popular in her own right, as I discovered. When I dismissed the Ionian tyrants, I dismissed her, too. So she sent me a message, saying that if I wanted to replace a dynasty as old as the gods of the Aryans, I would have to fight her in the field."

"Hand to hand?"

"There was that implication." Mardonius grinned. "Anyway, I sent her a soothing message, followed by my handsome person, with leg intact."

"Did she greet you on the floor?"

"On the throne. Then on the bed. Floors are for the very young. She is a formidable woman and I'd give a . . . I'd give my *bad* leg to marry her. But that is not possible. So I live quite openly with her, as if I were consort. It's amazing. These Dorians are not like other Greeks, or anyone else. The women do as they please. They inherit property. They even have their own games, just like the men."

Except for Halicarnassus, I have never visited a Dorian city. I suspect that Halicarnassus must be the best of the lot, just as Sparta is the worst. The independence of the Dorian women always annoyed Xerxes. Eventually he divorced or sent away his Dorian wives and concubines on the ground that he could not bear their melancholy. They actually resent being sequestered in the harem! I have found that there is no attitude so bizarre that one will not encounter it sooner or later if one travels far enough.

Artemisia received us in a long low room with small windows that looked toward the sea and dark-green Cos. She was somewhat stouter than I remembered, but the golden hair was still golden and the face was agreeable despite the recent birth of a second chin.

My herald announced me, as is the custom. The queen bowed not to me but to my office, as is the custom. After she had welcomed me to Halicarnassus, I told her of the Great King's affection for his vassal. In a loud voice she swore obedience to the Persian crown; then our attendants withdrew.

"Cyrus Spitama is a ruthless inspector." Mardonius was now in a good mood. "He has sworn to increase the tribute you pay by half." He stretched himself out on a narrow bed that had been so placed that he could see the harbor from the window. He told me that most of his days were spent watching ships come and go. That morning, at first light, when he had recognized the sails of my ship, he had hobbled down to the port to greet me.

"My treasury is the Great King's." Artemisia was formal. She sat erect in a high wooden chair. I sat almost as erect in a chair that was not quite as high as hers. "So is my army, and so am I."

"I shall tell that to the lord of all the lands."

"You can also tell him that when Artemisia says that she is his, she really is. But not for the harem. For the battlefield."

I must have looked as surprised as I was. But Artemisia was perfectly placid in her belligerence. "Yes, I am willing, at any time, to lead my army into any battle that the Great King sees fit to fight. I had hoped to join the spring offensive against Athens, but I was rejected by Artaphrenes."

"So now we console each other," said Mardonius. "Two generals without a war to fight."

Artemisia was somewhat too masculine for my taste. Physically, she was a well-fleshed woman, but the fair hard face that she turned toward me was that of a Scythian warrior. All she lacked was the mustache. Yes Mardonius told me that of the many hundreds of women that he had known, she was the most satisfying to make love to. One never knows what others are really like.

We spoke of the war in Greece. We had heard no news since Artaphrenes burned the city of Eretria and enslaved its inhabitants. Presumably, he had occupied Athens by now. Thanks to Mardonius' removal of the Ionian tyrants, the democratic element at Athens was pro-Persian, and the city was not expected to put up much resistance. After all, most of the leading men at Athens were either pro-Persian or in Persia's pay or both.

As I spoke of our victory at Eretria, Mardonius fell silent and Artemisia looked concerned. This was not a subject calculated to delight our wounded lion. She cut short my profound analysis of the military situation in Greece: "We have heard that you were recently married to the daughter of the Great King."

Mardonius brightened. "Yes, he's my cousin now. One day he's a sort of Magian, guzzling haoma, and the next day he's a member of the imperial family."

"I am *not* a Magian." I never cease to be annoyed when people say this, as Mardonius knew. Boyhood friends are like that, when they are not open enemies.

"So he says. But let him near a fire altar and he'll grab the sacred twigs and chant the—"

"Which of the noble ladies is mother to your wife?" Firmly, Artemisia silenced Mardonius.

"The Queen Atossa," I responded formally, "daughter of Cyrus the Great, for whom I was named." I was somewhat surprised that Artemisia did not already know my wife's name. But perhaps she did; and chose to pretend that she did not.

"We are so far away, here by the sea," she said. "Do you know that I have never been up to Susa?"

"You'll come with me when I go back to court." Mardonius slowly raised and lowered his bad leg, exercising the muscles.

"I don't think that would be tactful." Artemisia gave

341

us one of her rare smiles; she looked womanly, even handsome. "What is this great lady your wife's name?"

"Parmys," I answered.

Democritus wants to know more about my marriage. He is intrigued by my wife's name. So was I. After listening to Atossa castigate Darius' wife Parmys, I could not believe my ears when the court chamberlain told me that I was to marry Atossa's daughter Parmys. I remember asking the eunuch to repeat the name, which he did, adding, "She is the most beautiful of Queen Atossa's daughters." That is a conventional court expression, which means if not the opposite, nothing at all. When I asked if she was called Parmys after the daughter of the usurper, the chamberlain could not or would not answer.

Atossa was less than enlightening. "Parmys is a significant name for an Achaemenid, that's all. You'll find her very bad-tempered but intelligent. Two qualities *I* wouldn't want in a wife, if I were a man, which I'm not, worse luck. Anyway, it is who not what she is that matters. Take her. If she becomes too disagreeable, beat her."

I took her. I beat her once. It did no good. Parmys was a woman of furious temper and strong will, an Atossa gone entirely wrong. Physically, she resembled Darius. But features that looked handsome when arranged on the Great King's face managed to look all wrong on hers. When we were married she was eighteen, and horrified to get me for a husband. At the least, she had expected one of The Six; at the most, the crown of some neighboring kingdom. Instead, she was wife to a mere king's eye. To make matters worse, she was a dedicated devil-worshiper and would stop her ears at any mention of Zoroaster. She so offended me on one occasion that I struck her as hard as I could with the back of my hand. She fell across a low table and broke her left wrist. It is said that a woman will love a man who treats her violently. This proved not to be true in the case of Parmys. From that moment on, she hated me more than ever.

For several years I had my own establishment at Susa, and Parmys shared the women's quarters with Lais, who, needless to say, liked her very much. There is no end to Lais' perversity. I kept no concubines in the house, as it was not large enough; and I took no more wives. So the two ladies were much together. I have never had any desire to know what they talked about. I can imagine their conversations all too well.

342

After a daughter was born dead, I stopped seeing Parmys. When Xerxes became Great King, I asked him to take her back, which he did. She died while I was in Cathay. This is a very unhappy story, Democritus, and I see no point in dwelling on it.

I questioned Artemisia about her relations with the satrap. As king's eye, I was intent on righting wrongs and making a certain amount of necessary trouble. Artemisia answered my questions with serene good humor. "We have an excellent relationship. He never comes to see me and I never go to see him. I pay tribute directly to the treasury at Susa, and the treasurer seems content. *He* has visited me several times."

"Who is treasurer?" Mardonius liked to pretend that he did not know the names of any of the officials in the chancellery on the ground that he was too great for mere clerks. But he knew, as we all did, that the empire is governed by the clerks in the chancellery and by the eunuchs in the harem.

"Baradkama," I said. "He is thought to be honest. I know that he demands complete accounts of what is spent at Persepolis, and if a single consignment of cedarwood is not accounted for, heads roll."

"I wish I were as well served," said Artemisia. "In my small way."

Suddenly a lyre was struck in the next room. Mardonius groaned; and Artemisia sat very straight in her chair.

In the doorway stood a tall fair-haired man, dressed as a beggar. He held a lyre in one hand and a walking stick in the other. Rather clumsily, he played the lyre with the hand that held the stick. As he approached us he tapped the floor with his stick, the way so many blind men like to walk but not I. Few people seem to know that the blind are able to sense the presence of an obstacle before they come to it. I don't know the explanation for this, but it is a fact. As a result, I seldom stumble, much less walk into a wall. Nevertheless, certain blind men—usually beggars—like to advertise their infirmity by tapping a stick in front of them as they walk.

"Hail, O Queen!" The blind man's voice was loud and not at all pleasing. "And hail to thee, O noble Lords! Let a humble bard delight you with the songs of his ancestor, blind Homer, who sprang from yonder mountain-crossed fast-river-blessed Cos. Yea, I am of the blood of him who sang of those Argives who sailed 'gainst high-gated Troy.

343

Yea, I, too, sing the songs that Homer sang, tales of beauteous Helen and false Paris, of doomed Patroclus and his testy catamite Achilles, of lordly Priam and his calamitous fall! Attend me!"

With that, the bard sang at hideous length, to the accompaniment of an imperfectly strung lyre. Not only was the singer's voice unpleasant, it was deafening. Oddest of all was the song that he sang. Like all Greek-speakers, I know by heart quantities of Homer and I recognized many of the verses that fell—no, were ejected—from the blind man's lips like stones launched by a sling. First he would sing us a verse from Homer's *Iliad,* crudely emphasizing the six stresses to the line. Then he would sing an entirely new verse whose seven stresses to the line often contradicted entirely the meaning of what had gone before. I had the sensation that I was dreaming the sort of dream that one sometimes has after too large a Lydian dinner.

When, finally, the bard stopped, Mardonius lay as still as a dead man while Artemisia sat rigid in her chair and the king's eye gaped—or, perhaps, stared is the better word.

"Lord Cyrus Spitama," said Artemisia, "let me present to you my brother Prince Pigres."

Pigres gave me a low bow. "A humble bard takes pleasure in singing for an Argive lord."

"Actually, I'm Persian," I said, rather stupidly. "I mean, I'm half-Greek of course . . ."

"I could tell! The eyes! The brow! The commanding presence, so like Achilles!"

"Then you're not blind?"

"No. But I am a true bard, descended from Homer, who lived across those straits." He pointed at the window. Although Homer was born not on Cos, but on Chios, I said nothing. "His music flows through me."

"So I heard." I was polite. Then I remembered his characterization of Achilles. "Surely Achilles was older than Patroclus, and surely, neither one was a catamite. Weren't they lovers in the Greek fashion?"

"You must allow a certain license to my inspiration, noble lord. Also, it is no secret that my ancestor believed that Achilles was the younger man but dared not say so."

"Pigres is Homer born again," said Artemisia. I could not tell if she was serious. Mardonius now lay with his back to us; he snored.

"The Persian Odysseus sleeps," Pigres whispered. "And so we must speak softly," he said, raising his voice. "But, oh, it is a long way from here to his home in Ithaca, where his wife Penelope plans to put him to death because she likes being queen of Ithaca, her harem filled with men."

"But surely Penelope was happy to receive Odysseus and—" I stopped. Rather late, I had got the point. Pigres was raving mad. It has been said that Pigres only pretended madness because he feared Artemisia, who had seized the crown that was lawfully his at the time of their father's death. If this story is true, then what had begun as a performance had ended as reality. Wear a mask too long and you will come to resemble it.

During the years of Artemisia's rule, Pigres had reworked the entire *Iliad*. After each of Homer's lines, Pigres wrote one of his own. The result was maddening, particularly when sung by him. He also wrote an unusually clever narrative about a battle between some frogs and mice which he modestly attributed to Homer. One summer afternoon he sang me this work in a perfectly pleasant voice and I was very much amused by the sharp way that he mocked all the pretensions of the Aryan warrior class—a class to which I do and do not belong. I applauded him sincerely. "This is marvelous work!"

"It should be," he said, tilting back his head and pretending to be blind. "Homer composed it. I merely sing it. I am his voice only."

"You are Homer born again?"

Pigres smiled; put his fingers to his lips; tiptoed away. I have often wondered what became of him in Artemisia's damp sea palace.

It was at Halicarnassus that we received the bad news from Greece. I forget who brought us the message. Some merchant ship, I suppose. I've also forgotten exactly what we were told. But I do know that Mardonius and I were both so alarmed that we left Halicarnassus the next morning and together went up to Susa.

5

To THIS DAY ATHENIANS REGARD THE battle of Marathon as the greatest military victory in the history of warfare. They exaggerate, as usual. What happened was this. Until Datis sacked Eretria and burned the city's temples, Athens was ready to surrender. The Athenian democratic party was headed by the Alcmaeonids, the clan of our noble Pericles; and they had let it be known that if Persia would help them drive out the aristocratic party, they were more than willing to acknowledge the Great King as overlord. Precisely what they planned to do with Hippias is not clear. Although the democratic party had often been allied with the Pisistratids, the age of the tyrants was at an end and even the word itself was now accursed, a word that had once been a reflection of divinity on earth.

I have never understood why the tyrants fell into such disrepute. But then, the Greeks are the most volatile and fickle of all races because they are so easily bored. They cannot bear for things to go on as they are. In their eyes, nothing old can be good, while nothing new can be bad —until it is old. They like radical change in everything except their notion of themselves as a deeply religious people, which they are not. Persians are the opposite. Great Kings may come and go, often bloodily, but the institution of kingship is as immutable with us as it is in India and Cathay.

When Datis destroyed the city of Eretria, he lost the war. Had he made an alliance with the democrats of Eretria, they would have offered Darius earth and water, and then, with Eretrian backing, he could have moved on to Athens, where he would have been made welcome.

Democritus thinks that even if Eretria had not been destroyed, the Athenians would have resisted Persia. I doubt it. Years later, when Athens' greatest commander, Themistocles, was expelled by the people that he had saved, he came up to Susa. I often talked to him about the Greeks in general and the Athenians in particular. Themistocles was confident that had Eretria been spared, the battle of Marathon would never have been fought. But when Eretria was destroyed, the panicky Athenians called upon their allies to come to their defense. As usual, the Spartans sent their regrets. This belligerent race is remarkably ingenious at finding excuses for not honoring military alliances. Apparently the moon was full—or not full—or whatever. Although I have never investigated the matter, I would not be surprised if the Persian treasury had paid the Spartan kings to stay home. Baradkama, the treasurer, used to complain that of all those who received secret funds from the treasury, the Spartans were the greediest and the least reliable.

Only the Plateans answered the desperate call of the Athenians. And so, just opposite the narrow channel that separates Eretria from Attica, the Athenian and Plataean troops took their stand in the plain of Marathon under the leadership of the former tyrant Miltiades. With consummate political skill, this one-time vassal of the Great King had managed to get himself elected general of Athens, in the conservative interest. Naturally, he was hated by the democrats. But thanks to Datis' mistake at Eretria, both factions rallied around him and our forces were stopped. No, I will not fight again a battle which, at this very moment, in every tavern of the city, old men relive at joyous length. I will say that Athenian losses were as great as Persian losses. But who in Athens believes that such a thing could be true?

In good order, our troops boarded the ships. Then Datis ordered the fleet to sail straight to the Piraeus. He hoped to be able to seize Athens before the Greek army returned from Marathon. As Datis' fleet rounded Cape Sunium, the Alcmaeonids signaled him that the city was empty and that he should attack.

But just off Phaleron, Datis was delayed by winds and by the time the winds fell, the Athenian army was within the city and the Persian expedition was at an end. Datis sailed for home. In Halicarnassus we knew nothing more than the fact that Datis and Artaphrenes had been turned back.

I have never seen Mardonius in such good spirits. He started to put on weight, and from time to time he even forgot to limp. "Next year I'll be in command," he said as we rode out of Halicarnassus. The smell of fermenting

347

grapes was heavy in the air, and dark seething olives were thick upon the ground. "They've had their chance," he crowed. "*And* failed! I should've known. Years ago the sybil at Delos said I would die master of all Greece." He turned to me, face glowing. "You can come with me. I'll make you governor of Athens . . . No, that won't do. You don't want to be governor of a lot of ruins. I'll let you have Sicily."

"I prefer India," I said.

As it turned out, neither dream was fulfilled.

Darius was furious at Datis' failure. Out of loyalty to the elder Artaphrenes, Darius never blamed the younger. He simply put him on the inactive list—to Xerxes' delight. But when the crown prince asked if he might lead the next expedition against Athens, the Great King said that there was not enough money. He would need time to fill the treasury, build a new fleet, train more armies.

The last years of Darius' life were unexpectedly peaceful. He had now accepted the fact that he would never again lead an army. He had also come to believe, wrongly, that there were no generals whose competence he could trust. Although Mardonius was still Darius' favorite, the Great King liked to treat his ambitious nephew as a man of his own age, with the same sort of infirmities.

"What a pair we are," Darius would say in the gardens of Ecbatana as he walked slowly up and down, clinging to Mardonius' arm. "Two old soldiers who've seen their day. Look at that leg of yours! I'd cut it off if it were mine. Nothing wrong with a wooden leg, once your fighting days are over. And they're over for us. Oh, it's sad!"

Darius enjoyed torturing Mardonius. I can't think why. After all, he liked his nephew better than any man of my generation. I suppose that when Darius realized that he himself would never fight again, he wanted Mardonius to join him in his redundancy—and grief. Yes, it was grief that one saw in the old Darius' eyes when he watched the young officers at their exercises.

Mardonius was less than pleased to be removed from the roster of the active. Once, in the gardens at Ecbatana, I saw him do a ghastly jig to show Darius how well his leg had healed. Actually, Mardonius was never able to walk properly again. On the other hand, he could ride well enough; and he had no trouble at all in his war chariot, where he was strapped into place so that the bad leg bore no weight at all.

The court during Darius' last years was lively—and dangerous—with plots and counterplots. I can't say I remember that aspect of those days with much pleasure. For one thing, I had nothing to do. After being complimented on my work as king's eye, I was relieved of my duties and given no new post. Yet I was never out of favor. I was still Darius' son-in-law. I still bore the title king's friend. What had happened was what so often happens at a court. I was no longer of any use to the sovereign. Also, I think that whenever Darius saw me in attendance, he was reminded of those cows that he had once dreamed of—and now would never herd. No one enjoys being reminded of all that he has *not* accomplished in his life.

It was apparent to the court that the age of Darius was drawing to an end. That is, in theory we realized that he would not live much longer, but in fact none of us could conceive of a world without him. Darius had been Great King all our lives. We had known no other. Even Xerxes could not really imagine himself in Darius' place, and it could never be said that Xerxes lacked confidence in his own majesty.

Atossa continued to dominate the harem. She had done her best to forward the eastern policy; and she had failed. But then, no adventurous scheme was apt to appeal to Darius in those last years. He spent most of his time with his inner council. Daily he saw the guards commander Aspathines and the treasurer Baradkama. Darius was putting his house in order.

The sudden death of Gobryas cleared the air. In fact, some weeks after Gobryas' death, the former crown prince Artobazanes retired from court and moved to Sidon. He never came up to Susa again. Atossa had now lived long enough to witness the total defeat of the Gobryas faction.

Although the Greeks were less in evidence than usual, Demaratus had become an intimate of Darius. No doubt Lais' witchcraft had been more than usually effective. Certainly, it was to her credit that he was now much cleaner than before, and no longer smelled like a caged fox. The other Greeks were either dead or out of favor.

Xerxes continued to build palaces. There was nothing else for him to do except, secretly, to assemble the men and eunuchs that he would need to serve him once Darius was dead. It was at about this time that Xerxes took up with Artabanus, a young Persian officer distantly related to the Otanes clan. Artabanus was poor; and he was ambitious. In due course Xerxes would give him the command of his personal guard, while from the second room of the chancellery Xerxes took as personal chamberlain Aspamitres, a eunuch of unusual charm.

Xerxes and Mardonius were once again as close as—I was going to say brothers, but in a royal family, kinship is apt to beget not loyalty but blood. In any case, they were friends once more and it was understood that Mardonius would be Xerxes' chief general. So, with great subtlety and much care, Xerxes selected the men who would contrive his ruin. Even with hindsight, I cannot say that any of his appointments was wrong in itself. Ultimately, there is good luck and bad luck. My friend's luck was bad—something he knew at the time, but I did not.

During the last year of Darius' life, I met several times with the Egibis in order to send out a private caravan to India. But something always went wrong. At about this time, I received a message from Caraka. He had sent a second convoy of iron from Magadha to Persia. Unfortunately, somewhere between Taxila and Bactra, the caravan vanished. I assume that the Scythians seized it. Before I left India, Caraka and I had worked out a private code. As a result, I was able to learn from what looked to be a sober commercial report that Koshala no longer existed, that Virudhaka was dead, that Ajatashatru was the master of the Gangetic plain. Since Prince Jeta was in good favor with Ajatashatru, my wife and two sons —the second child was a boy, too—were safe. Beyond that, I knew nothing. I missed Ambalika, particularly on those rare occasions when I was with Parmys.

Five years after Fan Ch'ih's departure, he sent me a message. He was still not in Cathay. But he said that the caravan was making progress. He had found a new approach to Cathay, and he had high hopes of opening up a silk road between Cathay and Persia. I read the letter to Xerxes, who was sufficiently interested to send on a copy to the Great King. A month later I received a formal acknowledgment from the councilor for the east, then— silence.

In a sense, Mardonius was responsible for the death of Darius. As Mardonius regained his health, he became once more the center of what was left of the Greek faction at court. He was particularly wooed by Demaratus. Incidentally, I forbade Lais to receive any Greek in my house. While I was home, she obeyed me. But whenever I was away from Susa, every Greek hanger-on at court converged upon my house and there was nothing that I could do about it, short of expelling Lais—not the sort of thing one does to a Thracian witch.

Mardonius wanted a final Greek war, while Xerxes wanted a victory in the field, any field. Mardonius tempted Xerxes with glory. Together, they would conquer Greece. Xerxes would be overall commander; Mardonius his second in command. Since there was no longer any talk of India, I was excluded from their councils. I was not unhappy. I had always disapproved of the Greek wars because I knew the Greeks. Xerxes did not.

It is my impression that Darius wanted peace. Although, at the time, he had been angry with Datis for failing to destroy Athens, he certainly did not brood over the matter. After all, Darius never took Athens or any other Greek city seriously. How could he, when their leading men were forever coming up to Susa to beg him to help them betray their native cities? Although Darius admired the Greeks as soldiers, he was deeply bored by their quarrels with one another. Finally he said, "Two campaigns are enough." The first had been an unqualified success, while the second had been not only inconclusive but expensive. There was no need for a third campaign.

But that did not stop Mardonius. He brought pressure to bear on everyone, including Queen Atossa, who agreed, finally, that the time had come for Xerxes to take the field. The retirement of Artobazanes had done much to allay her fears, and Xerxes seemed to have no rival. These combined pressures on Darius proved to be disastrously successful.

The Great King summoned us to the hall of seventy-two columns at Susa. Although I had no presentiment that this would be Darius' last public appearance, I do remember thinking how changed he was from the vigorous young conqueror that I had first seen in that same hall. Where once a lion had moved amongst us, a fragile old man now crept toward the throne. The Great King was in his sixty-fourth year.

Democritus wants to know how old Xerxes was at the time. Xerxes, Mardonius and I were all thirty-four. Herodotus thinks that Xerxes was only eighteen. So much for what is called history. Although our youth had left us, old age was as far away as childhood.

As Xerxes helped his father into the high gold throne, every eye was on the failing sovereign and his successor. Darius wore the spiked war crown. In his right hand he clutched the gold sceptre. As discreetly as possible, Xerxes picked up his father's useless left arm and placed it on the arm of the throne.

Xerxes stepped down from the throne. "The king of kings," he said in a voice that carried throughout the hall. "The Achaemenid!"

We stood erect, hands in our sleeves. Looking at the row of young princes and nobles, I thought of Xerxes and Mardonius and myself and Milo so many years ago. Now a new set of youths had replaced us, just as Xerxes would soon replace the diminished figure on the throne. There is nothing like the unchanging court of Persia to remind one of time's impartial passage.

When Darius spoke, the voice was weak but carefully pitched. "The Wise Lord requires us to punish the Athenians who burned our holy temples at Sardis."

This was the formula that the chancellery always used to justify any expedition against the western Greeks. More than once, I remonstrated with the chamberlain. I also spoke to Xerxes. I did everything possible to get them to change the formula, but the chancellery is like the proverbial mountain which cannot be budged. When I told them that the Wise Lord would have wanted those temples destroyed by the Greeks or by anyone else, no one at the chancellery paid the slightest attention to me. I also got no help from the Zoroastrian community. In order to be the most honored priests at court, they were—and are—quite happy to be the most ignored. They have long since disregarded my grandfather's command to convert all those who follow the Lie. To be honest, so have I. Only the community at Bactra is still relatively pure, and militant.

"We have ordered six hundred triremes to be built. We are levying troops from every part of the empire. We are increasing the tribute that each of the satrapies must pay."

Darius pointed the sceptre at Baradkama, who then read the tax roll. There was a soft sighing sound in the hall as each of the nobles noted those tax increases that affected him or his estates. Although the Persian clans are exempt from taxes of any kind, they are expected to provide those troops that form the core of the Persian army. In a sense, it is the Persians who pay most dearly when the Great King goes to war.

Once the treasurer was finished, Darius resumed. "Our son and heir Xerxes will lead the expedition." Xerxes had been waiting all his life for such a command; yet his face did not change expression.

"Our nephew Mardonius will command the fleet."

This was a surprise. Everyone had expected Mardonius to be appointed second in command. Perhaps the post of admiral implied as much; perhaps it did not. The Great King chose not to elaborate. I looked at Mardonius, who stood to the right of the throne. Mardonius' lips curved beneath his sculptured beard. He was happy. I was not. I would go to Greece with Xerxes. If I survived the campaign, I might one day return to India and visit Ambalika and our sons. I confess that I was deeply depressed. I saw no future for Persia in the west. More to the point, I saw no future for me except in the east. The collapse of my marriage to Parmys had made Ambalika seem all the more desirable to me. Democritus wants to know why I never took other wives. The answer is simple: I lacked the money. Also, in the back of my mind, I had always thought that one day I would either settle in Shravasti with Ambalika or bring her and—most important—my sons back to Persia.

At the end of the audience, Darius used his right arm to push himself to his feet. For a moment he stood, swaying slightly; the weight of the Great King's body rested entirely on the right leg. When Xerxes made a move to help him, Darius gestured for him to stand back. Then Darius began the slow, hesitant, painful descent from the throne.

On the last step of the dais, Darius swung the weakened left leg forward onto what he took to be the floor. But he had miscalculated. There was still one more step. Rather like a tall gilded door slamming shut, the Great King swung toward us on his right leg and slowly—very slowly, so it seemed to the stunned court—he fell face down upon the floor. Although he still clasped in one hand the sceptre, the crown fell off and I saw, with horror, that the hoop of lethal gold was rolling straight toward me.

I threw myself on my belly. Since there was no precedent for what had happened, we all played dead, did not dare stir as Xerxes and the court chamberlain helped Darius to his feet.

As the Great King was half carried, half dragged past me, I could hear his heavy breathing and I could see upon

353

the dull redwash floor a trail of bright fresh blood. He had cut his lip; he had broken his good arm. The Great King had begun to die.

There was no Greek war that year or the next. The war was postponed not because of Darius' disability but because Egypt chose to go into rebellion rather than pay the new tax levies. And so the army that the Great King had raised for the conquest of Greece was now to be used for the pacification and punishment of Egypt. From one end of the earth to the other, heralds proclaimed that Darius would lead the army in the spring, and Egypt would be destroyed.

But three months later, when the court was at sultry Babylon and Susa was buried beneath the worst blizzard in anyone's memory, the Great King died at the age of sixty-four. He had reigned for thirty-six years.

Death took Darius in—of all places—Queen Atossa's bedchamber. They had quarreled. That is, he had wanted to quarrel with Atossa, or so she said. "I tried to keep the peace, as always."

I was in her private apartment at Babylon. This was the day before we were all to go to Pasargada for Darius' funeral and Xerxes' coronation. "I knew how ill he was. He did, too. Even so, he was in a terrible rage, supposedly at me but really at himself. He could not bear his own weakness, and I couldn't blame him for that. I can't bear mine, either. Anyway, he came to me, secretly, in a lady's litter with curtains drawn. He could no longer walk. He was incontinent. He was in pain. He lay *there*." Atossa pointed to a place between her chair and me. "I knew he was dying. But I don't think he knew. One doesn't, you know. At a certain point when one is ill, all notion of time stops and you think you'll never die because you're still here, not dead. You *are*, and that is all. Nothing will change.

"I tried to divert him. We used to play at riddles when we were young. Oddly enough, he liked word games, the more elaborate the better. So I tried to distract him, proposed several games. But he was not—to be distracted. He criticized Xerxes. I said nothing. He criticized me. I said nothing. I know my place." Atossa was given to exaggeration for effect.

"Then Darius praised our son Ariamenes. 'He is the best of all my satraps. Thanks to him the northern tribes were driven out of Bactra.' You know how Darius liked to carry on about those savages. 'I want Ariamenes to lead the army into Egypt. I've sent for him.' I'm afraid I couldn't keep still at that point. 'Xerxes was promised the spring command,' I said. 'And Xerxes is your heir.' Then Darius started to cough. I can still hear that awful sound."

To my surprise, tears were streaming down Atossa's face; yet the voice was perfectly steady. "I should like to say that our last meeting was peaceful. But it was not. Darius could never forget that the only legitimacy he had on this earth was through me, and he hated his dependency. I can't think why. He may have got the crown through cunning, but with the crown he got me, too, and because of me he was the father of Cyrus' grandson. What more could the man want? I don't know. I always found him hard to fathom. But then, I saw very little of him these last years. Of course, his mind was unsettled by illness. I could see that. Even so, I never thought that he would send for Ariamenes. 'You'll start a civil war,' I said. 'Ariamenes will want to succeed you. But we won't let him. That is a promise,' I said. Oh, I was hard. And Darius was furious. He tried to threaten me, but could not. The coughing had left him without any breath. But he glared at me, and made the sign of a knife cutting a throat. That gesture so infuriated me that I threatened *him*. 'If you encourage Ariamenes, I swear to you that I shall go myself to Pasargada. I shall raise with my own hands the standard of the Achaemenid. I shall summon the clans and *we* will make the eldest grandson of Cyrus our Great King.' Then . . ."

Atossa sat back in her chair. "Darius raised his right arm and made a fist. Then the arm fell on the side of the litter. He opened his eyes very wide. Looked at me the way he used to look at strangers. Remember? Polite, but ever so distant. Then he stopped breathing, all the while staring at me, ever so politely."

Atossa blinked eyes that were now sand-dry. Then she was all business. "Ariamenes is on the march to Susa. There will be civil war."

But thanks to Xerxes, there was no civil war. The day after Darius' death, Xerxes left Babylon at the head of the ten thousand immortals. He took possession of the palace at Susa, and the treasury. From Susa he sent his father-in-law Otanes to confer with Ariamenes. I have never known the full details of that meeting. I do know

355

that Ariamenes was won over without bloodshed. I assume
that he was heavily bribed. In any case, as a proof of
good will, he agreed to attend the coronation of Xerxes at
Pasargada. I must say that it is very much to Xerxes'
credit that he did not put to death his presumptuous
brother. In these matters, leniency is usually a mistake,
since the man who can forgive the man who forgives him
is rare indeed. But Ariamenes proved to be an exception.
He was loyal to his brother. Later he died a hero's death
in the Greek wars.

At the beginning Xerxes understood men; and their
vanity.

6

ON A BRIGHT COLD DAY THE BODY OF
Darius was placed in the rock tomb next to old Hystaspes
and the unfortunate Parmys—whose remains were soon
to be removed at Atossa's urgent request.

Dressed as a simple warrior, Xerxes entered the small
fire temple that stands just opposite the tomb of Cyrus.
The rest of us waited outside. I have never been so cold.
It was the sort of icy day that makes the hairs in one's
nostrils freeze, while the sun blazes with the sort of intense light that gives no heat. I remember that the sky
was perfectly clear except for the white plumes of smoke
that rose from the fires where a thousand bulls would
soon be offered up to the Wise Lord.

Inside the temple, Magians presented Xerxes with a
simple dish of sour milk, herbs, dates. After he had tasted
the traditional food, he put on the gold-embroidered Median cloak of Cyrus. Then Ariamenes presented Xerxes
with Cyrus' war crown, which he held in his hands until
the Arch-Magian indicated the exact moment of the winter solstice. At that propitious instant Xerxes placed the
crown upon his head and became Great King. Actually,
the winter solstice had occurred earlier that day, but Magians are seldom precise in such matters, worse luck.

When Xerxes appeared at the door of the temple, we
cheered him until our voices broke. I have never been so
moved as I was that winter day when my lifelong friend
stood before us, wearing the cloak of Cyrus and holding

high the lotus and the scepter. I remember thinking that the gold-turreted crown on Xerxes' head looked like an earthly—no, *un*earthly—fragment of the sun itself. So the reign began.

The court stayed at Persepolis for a month. During this time I drafted his first proclamation. It is carved on a cliff not far from the tomb of Darius. Xerxes had wanted to begin with praise of himself, in imitation of those ancient Elamite kings who are forever threatening the reader or listener with their awesome might. But I persuaded Xerxes to imitate his father, who had begun *his* first proclamation by praising the Wise Lord. Needless to say, I was under great pressure from the entire Zoroastrian community.

When Xerxes finally agreed to acknowledge the primacy of the Wise Lord, I found myself for the first and only time in my life popular with every one of my numerous uncles, cousins, nephews. Several years later they were even more pleased when I persuaded Xerxes to drop all pretense that he ruled in Babylon and in Egypt at the pleasure of the local gods.

"A great god is the Wise Lord, who created this earth, who created man, who created peace for man—" That last phrase was Xerxes' own contribution, not mine. Unlike most rulers, he never enjoyed war for its own bloody sake. "—who made Xerxes king, one king of many, one lord of many . . ." And so on. Then we listed all the lands that he governed. Although the recent disturbance in Bactria was mentioned in a somewhat minatory way, no mention was made of the revolt in Egypt. That was too delicate a matter. I was also able to persuade Xerxes to denounce the devas and their worshipers in far stronger terms than Darius had ever used. But Xerxes somewhat spoiled the effect by celebrating a characteristic of the Wise Lord called Arta—or righteousness. Now, if one regards Arta as simply an aspect of the *single* deity, no blasphemy has been committed. But in recent years the common people—encouraged by certain Magians—have tended to regard mere aspects of the Wise Lord as separate deities. I'm afraid that Xerxes himself inclined to this heresy. He prayed quite as much to Arta as he ever did to the Wise Lord. He even named his son, our present Great King, Arta-Xerxes.

When Xerxes announced that the court would remain at Persepolis for a month, I was surprised that he was willing to be parted for such a long time from the harem. When I alluded to this, he smiled. "You don't know what a relief it is not to be advised by Atossa and Amestris." He also thought it auspicious that his reign should begin in the heart of the Persian homeland, surrounded by clan leaders.

At the coronation feast, fifteen thousand of the empire's most important men dined in the main courtyard of Darius' winter palace. I once saw the list of the animals slaughtered for that particular feast. I don't think a single sheep or goose or bull was left alive in all the highlands. But despite the vast expense, the affair was highly auspicious, or so we thought. The grandees ate and drank for nine hours. Many were ill. All were ecstatic. The awesome royal glory had passed, in the most suitable way, to the true Achaemenid. This does not often happen.

Xerxes himself dined with his brothers in a curtained alcove just off a hall where sat one hundred king's friends. A thick green-and-white curtain separated Xerxes' alcove from the room where we feasted. Later the curtain was drawn back and he drank with us. Later still, he went out into the courtyard and the cheering of the clans sounded like ocean waves when they strike the shore, rhythmically, in accordance with the moon. Yes, Democritus, beneath the surface of the outer seas, there are powerful tides of a sort that do not exist in the Mediterranean, where waves are caused by capricious winds. No, I do not know the reason for this. Somehow, ocean tides follow the waxing and the waning of the moon, in much the same way that the periods of women do.

I sat between Mardonius and Artabanus. We were as drunk as everyone else. Only Xerxes remained sober. He mixed water with his wine, something that he rarely did. He was on his guard. After all, at the foot of his golden couch sat Ariamenes. The would-be usurper was a sturdy youthful man, with the arms of an ironworker. I was still deeply suspicious of him. We all were, except Xerxes.

I found Artabanus highly agreeable. I cannot say that I took him very seriously, even though I knew that Xerxes was about to make him commander of the palace guard—a position of enormous power, since the guards commander not only protects the Great King but supervises the day-to-day maintenance of the court. Because Darius had always kept his guards commanders on a short leash, I assumed that Xerxes would do the same.

Artabanus was a blond blue-eyed Hyrcanian a year or two younger than Xerxes. It was rumored that he liked to drink distilled barley from a human skull. Whatever his private habits, his public manners were most civilized. Certainly, he was deferential with me. I'm afraid that I found him dull, which was just the impression that he wanted to make on us all. As it turned out, we were the dullards, not he.

The guards commander at the Persian court is usually kept in check by the court chamberlain. The wise sovereign does his best to keep those two officials permanently at odds, which is not hard to do. Since the chamberlain must have access to the harem, he is always a eunuch. Since virile soldiers are contemptuous of all eunuchs, a satisfactory hostility is bound to exist between guards commander and court chamberlain. On the recommendation of Amestris, Xerxes had already appointed Aspamitres court chamberlain. All in all, the court was pleased. Everyone knew that when Aspamitres took a bribe, he gave good value in return. He was also an excellent administrator, as I discovered on the day of Xerxes' coronation.

At about the third course, Mardonius and I were moderately drunk. I remember that the dish before us was venison, cooked exactly the way I like—basted with vinegar and served with cock's combs. I had eaten one piece. Then, mouth full, I turned to Mardonius, who was drunker than I. He spoke of war, as usual. "Egypt is better than nothing," he said. "I don't mind. Not really. I want to serve the Great King." We were still not used to the fact that that awesome title was now attached forever to our boyhood friend. "Even so, it's a year wasted from . . ." Mardonius belched, and lost his train of thought.

"From Greece. I know. But Egypt's more important than Greece. Egypt is rich. And it's ours—or was." At that moment I reached for another piece of venison, only to find that the plate was still there but the venison was gone. I cursed aloud.

Mardonius stared at me dully. Then he laughed. "Mustn't grudge the slaves what's on the plate."

"But I do!" And I did.

Suddenly Aspamitres was at my side. He was young, pale, sharp-eyed; he had no beard, which meant that he had been castrated before puberty, as the best eunuchs are. He had observed everything from his place just below Xerxes' golden couch.

"You were not finished, Lord?"

"No, I was not. Nor was the Lord Admiral."

"We shall punish the offenders."

Aspamitres was nothing if not a serious figure. In an instant, the venison reappeared. Later that night six servants were executed. As a result, the lively trade in food from the royal table was considerably diminished, if never entirely discontinued. Old customs are hard to break. But at least during the early years of the reign of Xerxes, one was able to eat most of one's dinner in relative security. For this improvement, we had Aspamitres to thank.

At the time, it was rumored that since Aspamitres' seventeenth year, he had been the lover of Queen Amestris. I would not know. I only repeat what people used to whisper. Although harem ladies—even queens—tend to have complex relationships with their eunuchs, I doubt that our revered Queen Mother Amestris would have so used Aspamitres, despite the fact that his genital member was reputed to be unusually large for someone castrated as early as the tenth or eleventh year.

Democritus now reports the very latest gossip from the Agora. Apparently the Greeks want to believe that the queen mother is currently having an affair with the present court chamberlain, a eunuch of twenty-three who wears an artificial beard and mustache. Let me assure the scandal-loving Athenians that the queen mother is in her seventieth year, and indifferent to the joys of the flesh. More to the point, she has always preferred power to pleasure, like her predecessor Queen Atossa. I think it possible that the *young* Amestris might have dallied with eunuchs. But that was another world, now lost.

The lost world was a most beautiful one for us. Particularly that winter in Persepolis when all things seemed possible—except that one would never be comfortable again. The palaces were incomplete. There was no city to speak of, only the huts of the workmen and a brand-new complex of buildings that had been built around Darius' treasury. These storerooms, exhibition rooms, porticoes and offices were used, temporarily, to house the clerks of the chancellery.

Mardonius and I shared a small, airless, icy room in the harem of the winter palace. Since the women's quarters had been designed to accommodate Darius' relatively modest collection of wives and concubines, they were inadequate for Xerxes' so-called city of women. Consequently, the first order that Xerxes gave as Great King was to his architects. They were to extend the women's quarters in the direction of the treasury. Ultimately, part of the original treasury had to be pulled down in order to accommodate the new harem.

One afternoon Xerxes sent for me. "Come see the tomb of your namesake," he said. So together we rode a considerable distance to the tomb of Cyrus the Great. Set on a high platform, the small white limestone chapel has a portico of slender columns. The stone door has been carved to look like wood. Back of that door, Cyrus lies on a golden bed.

Although the Magian in charge of the tomb was plainly a devil-worshiper, he promptly intoned a hymn to the Wise Lord for our benefit. Incidentally, the custodian lives in a house close to the tomb, and once a month he sacrifices a horse to the spirit of Cyrus—an ancient Aryan custom, much deplored by Zoroaster.

Xerxes ordered the Magian to open the tomb. Together we entered the musty chamber where the wax-preserved body of Cyrus lies on its golden bed. Next to the bed there is a golden table piled high with marvelous jewels, weapons, robes. They glowed in the flickering light of the torch that Xerxes held.

I must say it is an odd feeling to look at a famous man who has been dead for more than half a century. Cyrus wore scarlet trousers and a cloak of overlapping golden plates. The cloak had been pulled tight at the neck in order to hide the gash made by the barbarian's ax. Casually Xerxes pulled open the cloak, revealing the dark cavity where Cyrus' neck had been.

"The spine was cut through," said Xerxes. "I don't think he was so handsome, do you?" Xerxes stared critically at the face under its layer of clear wax.

"He was old," I whispered. Except for a slight grayness of the skin, Cyrus might indeed have been sleeping and I, for one, did not want to wake him. I was awed.

Xerxes was not. "I shall want an Egyptian to preserve me." He was most critical of Cyrus' embalmers. "The color's bad. So's the smell." Xerxes sniffed the musty air and made a face. But I smelled only the various unguents that had been used by the embalmers.

"Sleep well, Cyrus Achaemenid," Jauntily Xerxes saluted the founder of the empire. "You deserve your rest. I envy you." I was not always certain when Xerxes was serious and when he was not.

Xerxes had made an office for himself in what is known as Darius' annex, even though it was built entirely by Xerxes when he was crown prince. Callias tells me that this graceful building is currently being copied by Phidias. I wish him luck. The annex was the first building in the world to have a portico on each of its four sides. Democritus doubts that this is true. I would have doubts, too, if I spent my days with philosophers.

Shortly after the visit to Cyrus' tomb, Xerxes sent for me officially. Aspamitres met me in the vestibule of the annex. As always, he was eager to please. In fact, thanks to Aspamitres, the indolence and bad manners of Darius' chancellery clerks had been transformed overnight. The clerks were now helpful and eager and they remained helpful and eager for almost a year, when they became— yes, indolent and bad-mannered. But that is the nature of chancellery clerks, not to mention eunuchs.

I was led past worktables that had been arranged in rows between bright-colored columns made of plaster-covered wood, much the cheapest way to build columns; also, plaster is more easily decorated than stone. I am told that Phidias intends to make all his columns from pure marble. If he is indulged in this folly, I predict an empty treasury for the Athenians. Even today, the granite columns in the main buildings at Persepolis have not been entirely paid for.

Charcoal-burning braziers made Xerxes' room comfortably warm; incense from a pair of bronze tripods made it uncomfortably smoky. But then, incense always gives me a headache, doubtless because I associate it with devil-worship. Zoroaster inveighed against the use of sandalwood and frankincense on the ground that these perfumes are sacred to devils. Although our Great Kings profess to believe in the unique Wise Lord, they allow others to treat them like gods on earth. I find this paradox unpleasant. But it is easier to change the sun's course than to alter the protocol of the Persian court.

Xerxes sat at a small table in the windowless chamber. For an instant, in the lamplight, he looked to my somewhat awed eye like Darius. I fell forward. In a high voice

Aspamitres recited my names and titles. Then, quickly, he slithered from the presence.

"Get up, Cyrus Spitama!" The voice was that of the old Xerxes. I stood and stared at the floor, as is the custom.

"The king's friend may look at his friend. At least when we're alone." So I looked at him and he looked at me. He smiled and I smiled. But nothing was the way it was, nor would it be, ever again. He was king of kings.

Xerxes came straight to the point. "I must compose my autobiography before I go to Egypt, which means I haven't got much time. I want you to help me write the text."

"What does the king of kings want the world to know?"

Xerxes pushed toward me a tattered sheaf of papyrus, covered with Elamite writing. "This was the only copy of Cyrus' autobiography that we could find in the house of books. You can see it's almost worn out. Apparently he never got around to rewriting it. The text hasn't been changed since the year I was born. I'm mentioned, by the way. Anyway, we'll have to work from this as best we can."

I looked at the Elamite text. "The language is very old-fashioned," I said.

"So much the better," said Xerxes. "I want to sound exactly like Darius who sounded like Cambyses who sounded like Cyrus who imitated the Median kings and so on back to the beginning, whenever and wherever that was." I remember thinking that although Darius had invariably talked about the pseudo-Mardos as a predecessor, Xerxes never mentioned him.

The Great King and I worked for three days and three nights to compose his official autobiography. When we were finished, copies were sent to every city of the empire as a tangible expression of the sovereign's will and character. In the first person, Xerxes described his ancestry, his accomplishments and his intentions. This last part is particularly important because the Great King's personal testament can be used in any court of law as a supplement to the official law code.

We worked like this. Xerxes would tell me what he wanted to say. I would then make notes for myself. When I was ready to dictate, the secretaries were summoned. While I declaimed in Persian, my words were translated simultaneously into Elamite, Akkadian and Aramaic, the three written languages of the chancellery. In those days,

Persian was seldom written down. I must say that I always marveled at the speed with which the chancellery secretaries are able to render Persian sentences into other languages. Later, translations would be made for the Greeks, Egyptians, Indians, and so on.

When the entire work had been recorded, it was then read back to Xerxes in each of the three chancellery languages. He listened carefully. Then he would make changes and clarifications. Ultimately, the most important task of a Great King is to listen to each word of a chancellery text. At the beginning of Xerxes' reign, not a word went out in his name that he had not carefully examined to make sure that it was indeed true shadow to his meaning. At the end, he no longer listened to anything but music and harem gossip.

On the night of the third day the final texts were read to Xerxes, who personally affixed his seal to each version. All in all, I think that our work was superior to Darius' vainglorious and inaccurate account of his usurpation.

After Aspamitres and the secretaries withdrew, Xerxes clapped his hands. The cupbearer materialized like a swift ghost or mirage. He poured the wine; drank from Xerxes' cup; left as swiftly as he had appeared. Xerxes was always amused by the cupbearer's ritual. "Everyone thinks that if the wine's poisoned, the taster will drop dead immediately. But suppose the poison's effect is slow? It could take the two of us months to die."

"Isn't the ritual supposed to discourage the cupbearer from poisoning the sovereign?"

"Yes, assuming he has no antidote. But a clever assassin could kill us both so slowly that no one would know." Xerxes smiled. "Look at the way Lais kills people with those Thracian mixtures of hers."

I am always embarrassed by any reference to Lais' reputation as a witch and murderer. Actually, I cannot think of anyone that she herself ever killed. But I do know that she used to make up all sorts of potions for Atossa, and it is hardly a secret that any harem lady who displeased the old queen was bound, sooner or later, to suffer from some mysterious and satisfyingly terminal illness.

"It is strange to be here." Xerxes was unexpectedly melancholy. "I never believed that it would happen."

"But it was quite clear that Darius was dying."

"Of course. But I never believed he . . ." Xerxes twirled

364

the red-and-black cup back and forth in his hands like a Samian potter. "I am too old."

I stared at him, amazed and speechless.

Xerxes removed the heavy golden collar from around his neck and let it fall onto the cedar tabletop. Idly he scratched himself. "Yes, I'm too old to . . ." Again he paused. He seemed to be speaking not to me but to himself. "I have had no victories. No real ones, that is." He tapped his copy of our handiwork. "I have put down rebellions. But I've not added so much as a handful of earth or a cupful of water to my father's realm. All I have done is build."

"You are the greatest builder that ever lived!" I did not exaggerate. I believe that Xerxes is—was—no, *is* the most splendid creator of cities and buildings that ever lived, and I include those provincial savages who assembled Egypt's profoundly dull pyramids and pylons so many ages ago.

"Is that of any real account?" Xerxes was wistful. I had never seen him in so defeated a mood. It was as if the gift of all the lands had given him not joy but pain, and apprehension. "I think that my life was entirely wasted. All I've ever done is wait and wait, and now I am thirty-five . . ."

"Hardly old! Look at Mardonius."

"I have looked." Xerxes smiled. "He staggers about like an old man. No, this"—with a swift gesture Xerxes drew in the air the crown—"should have come ten years ago, when I was the same age as Darius when he killed the Great King."

"Great King?" I stared at Xerxes. "You mean the usurper Gaumata?"

"I mean the Great King." Xerxes finished the cup of wine and dried his lips with the back of an embroidered sleeve. "You don't know?"

I shook my head.

"I thought you did. I know that Atossa told Lais. Obviously, your mother is more discreet than mine. Anyway, it's time that you knew the high bloody secret of our family."

The prince who confides a secret often passes, simultaneously, a sentence of death upon the hearer. I suddenly felt very cold. I did not want to hear what I heard. But I could not stop him. He was eager that I should know what only a handful of people at that time knew,

"Darius was never the Achaemenid. He was distantly related to the family. But so is every Persian clan leader. When Cambyses left for Egypt, he made his brother Mardos regent. It was agreed that should anything happen to Cambyses, Mardos would become Great King. In Egypt, Cambyses was poisoned. I don't know by whom. Cambyses himself thought that the local priests were responsible. Anyway, the poison worked slowly. He suffered terribly. Much of the time he was deranged. But whenever he was himself, he was perfectly lucid." Xerxes paused; idly he rubbed the edge of the gold collar with his thumb. "Despite what we have all been taught, Cambyses was quite as great a sovereign as his father, Cyrus."

I listened, hardly able to breathe.

"When word came up to Susa that Cambyses was ill, Mardos made himself Great King. When Cambyses heard the news, he promptly denounced his brother Mardos and started for home. En route, Cambyses was again poisoned, this time by someone close to him. If you remember, he is supposed to have cut himself with his own sword. I think that part of the official story is true. But the sword had been rubbed with a fatal poison, and Cambyses died. Mardos was now the legitimate Great King. He had no rival. He was popular.

"But then rumors began to circulate. It was said that Mardos was not really Mardos. It was said that Mardos had been murdered by a pair of Magian brothers and that one of them, Gaumata, was impersonating the dead man. As all the world knows, Darius and The Six killed the pseudo-Mardos, and Darius made himself Great King. Then Darius married Atossa, daughter of Cyrus, sister and wife of Cambyses, sister and wife of the so-called pseudo-Mardos. As a result, Darius made his son, me, the legitimate Achaemenid."

Xerxes clapped hands. The cupbearer appeared. If he had overheard, he made no sign. But then, he would not have dared.

When the cupbearer was gone, I asked the obvious question. "Who did Darius kill?"

"My father killed the Great King Mardos, the brother of Cambyses, the son of Cyrus."

"But, surely, Darius *thought* that he was killing the Magian Gaumata, the pseudo-Mardos . . ."

Xerxes shook his head. "There was no Magian. There was only the Great King, and Darius killed him."

In silence, we drank our wine.

"Who," I asked, knowing the answer, "was the man who poisoned the sword of Cambyses?"

"The Great King's spearbearer." Xerxes spoke with no particular emotion. "Darius, son of Hystaspes." Xerxes sat back from the table. "Now you know."

"I did not want to know, Lord."

"But now you do." Again, I was struck by Xerxes' sadness. "Now you know that I am who I am because my father killed both my uncles."

"How else are thrones gained, Lord?" I gabbled. "After all, Cyrus killed *his* father-in-law and . . ."

"That was war. This was—unholy. Treacherously and with no motive other than to rise, a Persian clansman struck down the chieftains of his own clan." Xerxes smiled, lips shut. "I thought of my father when you told me about those two Indian kings who were killed by their sons. I thought, Well, we are no different. We are Aryans too. But we know, as those Indians must know, that whoever breaks our most sacred law is cursed, and so are his descendants."

Xerxes firmly believed that he would be punished by fate for what his father had done. I disagreed with him. I told him that if he were to follow the Truth, it would make no difference to the Wise Lord that his father had followed the Lie. But Xerxes was haunted by all those devils and dark powers that my grandfather had tried to banish from this world. Xerxes believed that whatever the father had not been obliged to pay for in blood, the son would be forced to pay. Sooner or later, Xerxes believed, the old gods would avenge the murder of two Great Kings; and only holy blood can wash out the stains left by holy blood.

"Did Hystaspes know?" I asked.

"Oh, yes. He knew. He was horrified. He hoped that by devoting himself to Zoroaster he could expiate the crime of Darius. But that's not possible, is it?"

"No," I said. "Only Darius could have done that, with the Wise Lord's help." I was too stunned to be reassuring.

"I thought not." Xerxes turned his cup upside down on the table. He was finished with the wine, and he was sober.

"Well, there is blood upon my throne. Atossa thinks

that that is normal. But she is half-Mede, and they are not like us in these matters."

"When did you learn all this?"

"As a child. In the harem. The old eunuchs used to whisper. I would listen. Finally I asked Atossa. At first, she lied. But I was persistent. 'If I don't know the truth,' I said, 'how will I know when to seize the awesome royal glory for myself?' Then she told me. She is a ferocious woman. But I don't need to tell you that. She saved your life. She saved my life, too, and she put me here."

"How did she manage to save *her* life?" I asked.

"With cunning," said Xerxes. "When Darius killed Mardos, he sent for Atossa. He intended to put her to death because she alone knew for absolute certain that the man he had murdered was indeed her husband and brother, the true Mardos."

"Didn't the rest of the harem know?"

"How could they? While Cambyses was alive, his brother Mardos was regent and the regent is not expected to make himself at home in his brother's harem. But when it was known that Cambyses was finally dead, Mardos quickly married Atossa, to her delight. He was her favorite brother. A year later, when Darius came up to Susa, he spread the rumor that Mardos was not Mardos but a Magian impersonator. Then Darius killed the so-called impersonator. Now there was only one person left on earth who knew the truth. Atossa."

I have heard three versions of what happened next: from Atossa herself, from Lais and from Xerxes. Each story varies a bit from the other but the general sense is as follows.

When Darius came to Atossa in the harem, he found her seated in front of a life-size statue of Cyrus the Great. She wore the queen's diadem. She was entirely at her ease, or gave that impression. Gracefully she motioned for her attendants to withdraw.

Then, like an Indian cobra, Atossa struck first. "You have killed my husband and brother, the Great King Cambyses."

Darius was taken entirely by surprise. He had expected Atossa to fling herself at his feet and beg for her life. "Cambyses died of a wound," said Darius, allowing himself to be put on the defensive, a mistake that he would never have made in war. "Of an accident, self-inflicted."

"You were king's friend. You were his spearbearer. You rubbed the poison onto the sword's tip."

"Because you say so does not make it true." Darius had begun to rally. "Cambyses is dead. That is a fact. How he died is no business of yours."

"What concerns the Achaemenid is my business, and mine alone. For I am the last. I have proof that you killed my husband and brother, the Great King Cambyses . . ."

"What is this proof?"

"Do not interrupt," hissed Atossa. When she wanted, she could sound like a proper pythoness. "I am the Achaemenid queen. I also know—as you know—that you killed my husband and brother, the Great King Mardos."

Darius had started to back away from this alarming woman. Now he stopped. "He was your husband, but he was not your brother. He was Gaumata, a Magian."

"He was no more a Magian than you are. He was the Achaemenid, which you are not, and can never be."

"I am Great King. I am the Achaemenid." Darius had now placed an ivory chair between himself and Atossa. I am quoting from Atossa's version. "I killed the Magian, the impostor, the usurper . . ."

"You are the usurper, Darius, son of Hystaspes; and one word from me to the clans, and all of Persia will go into rebellion."

This brought Darius to his senses. He swept the chair to one side and moved toward the seated queen. "There will be no word from you," he said, face close to hers. "Understand? No word. Because all those who choose to believe that the Magian was really Mardos will be put to death."

"Go ahead, little adventurer. Kill me. Then see what happens." Atossa gave him what must have been, in those days, a lovely smile: white pearls instead of black. It was, incidentally, at this point that Atossa found herself uncommonly attracted to the blue-eyed auburn-haired usurper, or so she told Lais. The fact that she and Darius were the same age increased rather than diminished her unexpected lust.

Atossa made her life's boldest move. "I have already dispatched agents to Babylon, to Sardis, to Ecbatana. Should I be killed, they are to reveal to the military commanders of our loyal cities that Darius is twice a regicide. Remember that Cambyses was admired. Remember that

Mardos was loved. Remember that they were the last sons of Cyrus the Great. The cities will revolt. That is a promise. You are a bold young man and nothing more— as yet."

The as yet was the beginning of an elaborate peace treaty, whose principal condition was laid down by Atossa. If Darius married her and made their first son the heir, she would tell the world that he had indeed killed a Magian whom she had been forced to marry. Although each made various concessions to the other, the main article of the treaty was honored by both sides.

Democritus wants to know if Atossa had really dispatched those agents to Babylon, and so on. Of course not. She was never more splendid than when she was improvising toward some great end. Did Darius believe her? No one will ever know. What we do know is that as a result of her bluff, Darius never ceased to fear as well as admire Atossa. For the next thirty-six years, he did his best to exclude her from the business of government, and it must be said that, occasionally, he succeeded. On her side, Atossa was delighted with the youthful regicide; and saw in him a superb administrator of her father's empire. The result of that blood-stained treaty was Xerxes. Unhappily, he was the sort of man who anticipates balance in all things. If one end of the board that rests on the log goes down, the other must go up. Since Darius had not suffered for his crimes, the son would.

I have revealed these matters, Democritus, not just to confound the man from Halicarnassus. Quite the contrary: his version is a fine tale for children and Darius is its shining hero. The actual story is darker and reflects no credit on our royal house. But I think it necessary to know the truth in order to explain the nature of my beloved Xerxes. From the first moment that he knew the true story of his father's rise, he saw with perfect clarity his own bloody end. This foreknowledge explains why he was who he was, and did what he did.

Happily, before the month was over, Xerxes had put aside his melancholy. He kept both rooms of the chancellery working day and night. He personally counted the gold and silver in the treasury. Together we inspected the contents of the house of books. I read to him all sorts of ancient records, particularly those that dealt with India and Cathay.

"You want to go back, don't you?" We were covered

with dust from old brick tablets, moldering papyrus, bamboo strips.

"Yes, Lord, I want to go back."

"The year after next." Xerxes brushed the dust from his beard. "I promise we'll go, once Egypt is back in the fold. I haven't forgotten what you told me. I also haven't forgotten that sooner or later, old though I am, I must add to my patrimony."

We both smiled. I was no longer expected to take seriously Xerxes' references to his advanced age. Yet, looking back, I think that he had convinced himself that his time as a soldier had come and gone. War is a very young man's work.

Before the court left Persepolis, Xerxes reinstated me as king's eye. I was then commanded to accompany Ariamenes to Bactria. I was expected to use my ears as well as my eyes. Although Xerxes had treated his brother leniently, he did not trust him. Now that I understood the family better, I was in no position to say that his doubts were frivolous.

Ariamenes accepted my company with reasonable grace. Despite the considerable retinue that we traveled with, we were obliged to pay the always humiliating tax to the brigands who control the trail through the Persian highlands.

I did not recognize Bactra. After the great fire the entire city had been so rebuilt that it now resembles Shravasti or Taxila more than Susa. What had once been a crude frontier settlement is now an eastern city, with nothing Persian about it.

At first Ariamenes was highly suspicious of me. But in the end, we got on well enough. We got on even better when I found practically no irregularities in his conduct of the government. I found him altogether mysterious as a man. To this day I have no idea why he went, if only briefly, into rebellion. I suppose the strangeness and the remoteness of Bactria might have had something to do with it. Beyond the mountains to the south is India; across the deserts to the east is Cathay; at the north are the cold forests and barren plains of the tribes. Civilization does not begin until one has traveled three hundred miles to the west. At the edge of everywhere, Bactria is nowhere.

Bactria is also quite as much a mood as a place, and the mood is wild, violent, ecstatic. The Bactrian Magians who follow the Lie are amongst the strangest people on earth. They are constantly besotted with haoma. They are cruel beyond belief. Despite the teaching of Zoroaster and the stern injunctions of three Great Kings, they continue to tie down the sick and the dying alongside the dead. Scorched by the sun and chilled by the snows, the dying cry out for help that no one dares provide. Vultures and dogs feed not only on corpses but on the living.

When I complained to Ariamenes, he said, "I can do nothing. The Bactrians fear the Magians more than they do me. Why don't *you* stop them? You're the prophet's heir. They'll listen to you."

Ariamenes was amusing himself at my expense. He knew that where Zoroaster himself had failed, his grandson was not apt to succeed. Yet I did take up the matter with the leaders of the Zoroastrian community. Most of them were related to me, and several were sympathetic. Nearly all were . . . worldly, I suppose the word is. Pretending to follow the Truth, they pursued money and honors. They assured me that the practice of exposing the not-dead would be stopped. Yet it goes on to this day.

A large shrine had been built over the spot where Zoroaster was murdered. I felt very odd indeed, standing in front of the fire-scorched altar, whose shallow steps had once been drenched with golden haoma and blood. I said a prayer. My cousin, the head of the order, chanted a response. Then, standing before the fire-altar, I described to a dozen of my relatives—small, dark Chaldean-looking men—the death of the prophet and the words that the Wise Lord saw fit to speak to me through those dying—dead?—lips.

They were deeply moved. So, in fact, was I. Yet as I spoke the familiar words, I did not actually recall them the way that they had sounded when I first heard them. Repetition has long since robbed me of true memory. Nevertheless, standing before the haunted altar, I did catch a sudden glimpse of myself as a child, eyes bedazzled by death and deity.

I was then shown the room of the oxhides. Here a dozen scribes sit listening to old members of the community recite Zoroastrian texts. As the old men chant, the verses, or gathas, are written down. Since I had heard some of these gathas from my grandfather's lips, I noticed that slight alterations were being made—deliberately? In some cases I think that my grandfather's words are being altered for a new generation. But, more often, the reciter has simply forgotten the original, which is why I have finally come around, reluctantly, to the view that it is important that these things be recorded now while errors are relatively few.

With the current and universal penchant for writing everything down—when, where, why did it begin? The actual words of Zoroaster, the Buddha, Mahavira, Gosala, Master K'ung will be preserved for future generations even though, paradoxically, a written text is far easier to corrupt than the memory of a priest who has learned a million words by rote and dares not change one of those words for fear he will lose all the rest. On the other hand, it is quite easy to make up a brand-new text on a cowhide and then claim that it is very old, and authentic.

Already, in my lifetime, Zoroaster's injunctions against the improper use of haoma have been altered to conform to the Magian tradition. Recently the quality of Arta, or righteousness, has been turned into a god, while the deva Mithra has never been entirely expunged from the Zoroastrian faith because, as my last living contemporary cousin says most piously, "Is Mithra not the sun? And is not the sun the sign of the Wise Lord?" So, slyly, one by one, the devils return. What man wants to worship, he will worship. My grandfather shifted certain emphases. That was all.

When I told the community that Xerxes had promised to acknowledge no god but the Wise Lord, they were most pleased. "Even though," as the chief Zoroastrian observed, "the Magians who follow the Lie are not apt to follow the Great King."

In some detail, I was told of the daily battles that took place between our Magians and theirs. I was also told of the endless disagreements between the Zoroastrians at court and those who had stayed in Bactra.

Although I did my best to appear entirely at their service, I got the impression that I was something of a disappointment to these small dark men of the frontier. They had expected me to be one of them. Instead, they were confronted with a blue-eyed man who spoke the Persian of the court. As king's eye, I was altogether too much a part of the secular world, and I am sure that it seemed every bit as strange to them as it still seems to me that of all the people on this earth I should have been the one to hear the voice of the Wise Lord. Because of that one moment in my childhood, I am, to this day, regarded as

373

Persia's holiest man. It is ludicrous. But then, what we are is seldom what we want to be while what we want to be is either denied us—or changes with the seasons.

Am I not wise, Democritus? Now that winter's come for me and the ice is black, I know exactly who and what I am—a corpse-in-waiting.

BOOK SIX

Cathay

1

TWO YEARS AFTER XERXES' ACCESSION
to the throne, I was accredited ambassador to all the kingdoms, duchies, states which comprise that far-off land we
call Cathay, a world that no Persian had ever seen. The
journey that I had hoped to make with Fan Ch'ih I now
would make with a caravan sponsored by Egibi and sons.
Two Cathayans were assigned me as translators while
Bactrian cavalry and foot soldiers acted as military escort.

Needless to say, the second room of the chancellery
opposed my embassy but the Great King had spoken and
so, to justify what the treasurer considered wasted money,
I was commanded to inaugurate, formally, a trade route
between Persia and Cathay, a task rather like building a
ladder to the moon. But I was more than willing to try.
Although I would have preferred to take the long, relatively safe journey through India—and see Ambalika and
my sons—Fan Ch'ih's letter had made it clear that the
northern route beyond the Oxus River was the shortest,
if most dangerous approach to Cathay. So I went north.
This proved to be stupid. But then, stupidity is a quality
common to youth. Democritus tells me that he, too, would
have gone to Cathay by the shortest way. Thus, my point
is proven.

Fan Ch'ih had told me that since smelted iron is virtually unknown in Cathay, there would be an excellent
market for the best Persian metal—and metalworkers.
Egibi and sons agreed. They would finance the caravan
—despite those depressing odds against our ever returning, which Shirik had worked out on his abacus. Nevertheless, he would take the chance, he said: "If you can
open the northern route, then we shall have—for the first
time—a proper silk road." Traditionally, all land approaches to Cathay are called silk roads. In exchange
for the smelted iron, Egibi and sons would want a thousand and one things, ranging from silk to dragon's bone

for medicinal purposes. Luckily for me, old Shirik's stomach disorders could only be soothed by an infusion of powdered dragon's bone from Cathay. As a result, he had a personal as well as a business interest in the success of my mission.

At the beginning of spring I left Bactra for the rising sun. My description of the long journey east is kept locked in an iron chest in the house of books at Persepolis and only the Great King has the key to the chest, provided he has not lost it. In less than a year I found a way to Cathay that was not previously known to anyone in the west. But since I am a Persian and king's friend, I have no intention of revealing to the Greeks *any* details of my journey to Cathay. Also, without the maps and the star sightings that we made, I could not give more than a vague description of a journey which took place—how long ago?—thirty-eight years by my reckoning.

After we crossed the Oxus River, we traveled through miles of grazing land. Here live the northern tribes. They attacked us more than once, but since I had a thousand Bactrian troops for escort, the tribes did us no damage. After all, the Bactrians are themselves closely related to those fierce nomads who inhabit the steppes. And the desert.

The desert! I should think that that eastern desert is the largest on earth. Certainly, it is the most deadly. All of our horses died. Fortunately, most of the camels survived. Many of the men did not. Of the two thousand camel drivers, soldiers, attendants who had left Bactra one bright spring morning, only two hundred survived the crossing of a desert that seemed never to end except, briefly and cruelly, in the most astonishing mirages. Suddenly, up ahead, we would all see a swift mountain stream or a waterfall or a cool snow falling in deep woods. Invariably, some of the men would throw themselves into what looked to be a refreshing lake or stream. Men died, mouths choked with scorching sand.

Although the eastern desert is filled with oases, one needs a reliable guide to find them. No such guide was available to us; the desert tribes saw to that. In fact, had we not known that Cathay was in the direction of the rising sun, we would have been hopelessly lost. As it was, our journey lasted a month longer than it needed to, and cost us many lives. Toward the end, in order to avoid the mirages as much as the heat, we traveled only at night.

377

The moment the sun appeared over the flat gray horizon, we would make burrows in the sand like Indian dogs; and, heads covered with cloth, we slept like corpses.

Despite my long conversations with Fan Ch'ih, I knew very little about the geography of Cathay. I did know that most of the Cathayan states are located between the Yangtze and Yellow rivers, but I had no idea how far apart the rivers are or what sea they empty into. Fan Ch'ih had told me that his native country of Lu was located in a basin formed by the Yellow River. Beyond that, I knew nothing of Cathay, or its extent.

The desert ended in grazing land where yellow-faced herdsmen studied us at a safe distance. They made no attempt to molest us. Since there were numerous springs and much game, we lived well off the country. Finally, just as the weather turned cold, we came to the westernmost end of what proved to be the Yellow River, a deep, dark, crooked stream flowing through low coniferous green hills which looked to us like the Aryan home of the fathers.

We made camp in a grove of bamboo trees at the river's edge. While the men bathed and caught fish, I made inventory. We had lost many men and horses, but thanks to the indestructibility of the camels, we still had most of the consignment of iron as well as sufficient arms to protect ourselves from all but an army. During the week that we remained encamped beside the river, I sent out a dozen messengers. Only one returned—as the prisoner of an army, which proceeded to surround us.

A thousand cavalrymen astride ponies stared at us with the same wonder that we stared at them. Although I was used to Fan Ch'ih's yellowness, these men were the color of dark honey. Their faces were round, noses flat, slit eyes aslant. They wore thick quilted tunics and curious riding caps. Each appeared to be a part of his short-legged pony. Thus, on a gray day, with the season's first snow falling, I was introduced to the newly organized cavalry of the duchy of Ch'in, the westernmost of the Cathayan states.

For nearly six months my two Cathayan attendants had been teaching me the rudiments of their complex language; as a result, I was able to communicate with the cavalry commander. Not that there was much for us to talk about. As his prisoners, we were escorted, under guard, to Yang, the capital of Ch'in.

I don't remember much about the journey, except that I was surprised that the cavalry commander had never heard of Persia. I also remember that when I told him that the shipment of iron was destined for Lu, he laughed and spat upon the ground, thus demonstrating Ch'in's disdain for Lu.

I had imagined that the cities of the yellow people would be rather like those of the Gangetic plain. Instead, I was startled to find that the people of Yang were silent, even grim; and dressed alike in long gray tunics. The streets of the city reminded me of an army camp. All behavior is carefully regulated. Men are obliged to walk down one side of the street, while lower-class women must walk down the other. Upper-class women are properly sequestered. Even the central market-place is eerily quiet, thanks to a horde of inspectors who constantly check the weights of the sellers, the coinage of the buyers. Those who break any of the numerous laws are either killed or mutilated. What looked like half the population lacked an ear or a nose or a hand. I saw no one smile in public, including the troops who are everywhere.

During my first days in Ch'in I wondered whether or not Fan Ch'ih had deliberately misled me: this was not the Cathay he had described. Later I was to discover that Ch'in is not only unlike the rest of the Middle Kingdom, it resembles no other place in the world with the possible exception of Sparta.

My caravan attendants were confined to an empty warehouse just inside the wall of the city. I myself was escorted, more or less respectfully, to a low wooden building at the center of the city where I was—rather less than more—respectfully locked in a small cell.

I have never felt so entirely desolate. Although I could make myself understood in the language, no one would speak to me. Silent men brought me food. They tried not to look at me because when they did, they were plainly alarmed by what they saw. Blue eyes disturb Cathayans. Fair skin disgusts them. Fortunately, my hair was not red or I would have been immediately sacrificed to one of the so-called star gods.

I was not ill-treated. I was simply not treated at all. Once a day I was fed, either rice or a sort of meat soup. But when I tried to talk to the servants they seemed not to hear me. For a time I thought they were deaf-mutes.

Eventually, I was sent for not by the duke of Ch'in, to whom I was accredited, but by the chief of the council of ministers, a polite old creature who looked somewhat

379

like the Cathay man that I had met in Shirik's office at Babylon. The prime minister was called Huan something. I have forgotten his second name. But then, I was never able to sort out Cathayan names. Each man of quality has a public name, a private name, a secret name, an attribute name, all in addition to his various titles. Also, each dresses according to rank. Some wear fox fur; others wear lamb's wool; others red silk. Each man of rank wears a girdle or belt from which hangs various jeweled ornaments denoting rank, family, country. It is quite a good system. Since one can always tell at a glance a stranger's rank, one knows just how to treat him.

Huan's audience chamber was like the inside of a beautifully polished wooden box. Most of the state buildings in Cathay are of wood while the houses of the poor are of mud brick with reed roofs. Only fortresses are made of stone; and very crude they are. All buildings are constructed according to the four cardinal points, north, south, east, west. Each of those points has its own characteristics: sleep with your head to the north and you will die, and so on.

Although I had not known it at the time, I had been confined in the prime minister's house. As the principal officer of state under Duke P'ing, Huan presided over a council of six ministers, each from one of the six noble families who control Ch'in. Apparently Duke P'ing was addicted to a powerful drink made from fermented millet. As a result, he had spent most of his reign in seclusion at his palace, surrounded by concubines and drinking cronies. Once a year he would appear at his family's ancestral temple and make sacrifice to heaven; otherwise, he might just as well have been one of those ancestors for all the influence that he exerted on the administration of the state.

Needless to say, I knew none of this at my first meeting with the prime minister, who greeted me with what I took to be the most exquisite Cathayan courtesy. Actually, he was treating me like an expensive slave.

Huan gestured for me to squat opposite him. Although I was to become fluent in the Cathayan language, I never ceased to be confused by it. For one thing, the verbs have no tenses. You never know if something has already happened, is happening, will happen; for another, since nouns are neither singular nor plural, you can never be certain just how many wagons of silk you will receive for your smelted iron. Yet, to be precise—unlike the language—the people of Cathay are not only excellent businessmen but often honest.

As I proceeded to set forth all the titles of the Great King and described briefly but vividly his power, Huan listened politely. Then he said, "You have come to trade with us, I would assume." Each time he made a statement he would nod his head as if to make certain that we were in agreement.

"To trade with all the countries of Cathay, yes."

The head nodded again, but this time the nod meant disagreement; the effect was unnerving. "Yes. Yes. But, again, no. There is only one Cathay. There is only one Middle Kingdom. Whatever divisions there might be within the Middle Kingdom are temporary and unhappy and"—he looked triumphant—"nonexistent."

"Yes, yes." I imitated him, even to the nod. "But I know that there is a duke here in Ch'in and a duke in Lu and one in Wei . . ."

"True. True. But each duke reigns only at the pleasure of the son of heaven, who alone has the mandate because he alone descends from the Yellow Emperor."

None of this made the slightest sense to me, but I persevered. "Yes, Lord Huan. We know of this puissant monarch. And the Great King sends him greetings through my unworthy self. But where, may I ask, is he to be found?"

"Where he is. Where else?" Huan's head bobbed up and down. He seemed unnaturally happy.

"Then I shall go to him. I shall go to where he is."

"Yes. Yes." Huan sighed. We stared at each other. In the next few years I was to hear all sorts of variations on the theme of the emperor who is and is not where he is and is not. In actual fact, there has been no true emperor of heaven for three hundred years; although the duke of Chou styles himself emperor, he is scorned by all.

The Cathayans are nearly as vague as the Indians when it comes to the past. But they all agree that a long time ago there was a dynasty of emperors known as Shang. For a number of generations these emperors possessed the mandate of heaven or, as we would call it, the awesome royal glory. But seven or eight hundred years ago the mandate was withdrawn, as sooner or later it always is, and a western tribe of barbarians occupied the

381

Middle Kingdom and established a new dynasty known as Chou.

The first Chou emperor was called Wen. He was succeeded by his son Wu. Two years after Wu received the mandate—that is, after he butchered the last of his Shang opponents—he became seriously ill and not even broth of dragon's bone could reverse his illness. Finally his younger brother Tan, the duke of Chou, offered himself to heaven in place of his brother. The Cathayan heaven, by the way, differs from the Aryan heaven or any other sort of heaven that I have ever heard of in that it is a shadowy place presided over not by a god or gods but by the dead ancestors, starting with the first man, the so-called Yellow Ancestor or Emperor. Consequently, virtuous Tan did not cry out to a Cathayan equivalent of the Wise Lord; instead he addressed three earlier royal ancestors. It should be noted here that the religion of these people is a very peculiar religion if only because it is practically no religion at all. Although their so-called star gods are not unlike our devils, the worship of these minor deities is peripheral to the welfare of the state which depends upon maintaining harmony between heaven and earth. This is achieved by carefully observing those ceremonies that honor the ancestors.

The three dead kings were so charmed by Tan's offer to take his brother's place that they allowed Wu to recover from his illness; best of all, they did not demand Tan's life in exchange for their benevolence. Tan is a hero to many Cathayans, as is his father, Wen. Since Wu is the epitome of military ruthlessness, he is not always admired. Needless to say, the dukes of Ch'in claim direct descent from Wu, and they deny the legitimacy of the Chou pretender who descends from Wen. The Ch'inese speak constantly of the hegemony, which they regard as rightfully theirs. In this case the hegemony means the overlordship of all the warring states that now make up the Middle Kingdom. Thus far, heaven has so loved the Cathayans that it has denied the dukes of Ch'in the mandate. As I later discovered, the rulers of Ch'in are hated by all Cathayans, including the Ch'inese, whom they oppress. When I say the rulers I don't mean the dukes. I mean the council of six who govern Ch'in; and of the six I mean Huan, who was certainly one of the most remarkable men that I have ever met, as well as one of the very worst.

I was held captive for six months. My attendants were

sold into slavery and the iron ore was confiscated. I managed to save my life by persuading Huan that I alone knew the process whereby iron ore can be smelted. Actually, I had learned a good deal about the making of iron from watching the smelters that I had brought to Magadha. In those days Persia was the most advanced of all nations when it came to smelting iron. The Cathayans were the least advanced. Now, thanks to me, the Ch'inese are competent ironworkers.

I was treated well enough. I often dined with Huan alone. Occasionally I attended him when he paid calls on the other nobles. But I was never presented to the duke.

Once I had decided that I was in no immediate danger, I began to ask Huan almost as many questions as he asked me. He enjoyed what he took to be my barbarous candor. But he did not always enjoy my questions. "Why hasn't the duke been replaced? After all, he does not rule."

"How terrible!" Huan looked shocked. Quickly he traced some magical design—to ward off evil?—on the edge of the mat where he was sitting. We were in a low-ceilinged room that faced upon a garden in which a row of plum trees were in pale, fragrant bloom.

"Oh, too barbarous! Really, too barbarous! Even for a person from beyond the desert."

"I apologize, Lord Huan." I looked humbly at the polished wood floor between us.

"It is so terrible to hear the thought *expressed* that I shudder and, oh, how my mind aches!" He clasped his stomach where Cathayans believe that the mind dwells. "Our duke is sacred because he descends from the Emperor Wu. He and he alone possesses the mandate of heaven. Even a barbarian must know that."

"I do, Lord Huan. But as you have said yourself, the Middle Kingdom is not yet his. The balance between earth and heaven—that great bellows, as your wise men call it—is not yet in proper balance."

"True. True. But it is, of course." Yes, that is exactly what he said. I was never able to get entirely used to the way the Cathayans confuse future, past and present in their tense-less language.

Huan appeared to be saying that the mandate of heaven was already Duke P'ing's. Actually, he meant that one day it would be his because it was already his and had been his because he was who he was. There is a good deal of subtlety in the Cathayan language; and endless confusion.

"But meanwhile there is the emperor at Loyang."

"He is *not* the emperor. He is duke of Chou."

"But he is descended from Wu's father, Wen. And Loyang is the holy capital of the Middle Kingdom."

"Even so, he is simply one of the fifteen dukes of the Middle Kingdom. And of those fifteen dukes, only eleven are descended from one or another of the twenty-five sons of the Yellow Emperor, who invented fire, whose descendant saved the world from the flood of water and then received from heaven the great plan with its nine divisions, the plan which eventually came into the possession of his descendant the Emperor Wu, from whom it passed down the generations to *him*, the one who looks south." Huan bowed reverently in the direction of the ducal residence. The expression the one who looks south is used to describe the heaven-mandated emperor. I don't know why. Doubtless, an astrologer might have an explanation. I have often thought that it might have had something to do with the Aryan or north star. In any case, on public occasions the emperor always stands to the north of his people.

Once mandated, the emperor is a living reflection of heaven, that ghostly residence of a line of emperors which extends back to the Yellow Ancestor, who created all things when he pushed apart a sort of cosmic egg, whose upper half became heaven while the lower became earth. Only through man's propitiation of heaven can harmony be kept between the two halves of a divided whole. Needless to say, religious rites are of enormous importance to the Cathayans. Like many primitive people, they believe that there will be no autumn harvest if, say, the spring terrace play is incorrectly performed—and a most intricate ceremony it is, involving numerous actors, dancers, singers and musicians, as well as the ruler, who alone may speak to the royal ancestors as they look down upon him and all his works, and smile—or frown.

"Then Duke P'ing has already received the appointment of heaven." I bowed my head very low when I said the duke's name, and lower still at the mention of heaven.

"Yes, yes." Huan smiled. But of course Duke P'ing lacked the appointment, as did the actual pretender at Loyang. That is the continuing crisis of Cathay. As a result, there is not a Cathayan ruler who does not dream of obtaining the hegemony, and heaven's appointment—in that order. But it seems most unlikely that any one ruler will ever be able to subjugate his neighbors the way Cyrus or even Ajatashatru did.

As far as I can tell, the Middle Kingdom is larger than the Gangetic plain but smaller than the Persian empire. A hundred years ago the northern state of Tsin almost obtained the hegemony; then the southern state of Ch'iu became as powerful as Tsin and so heaven's mandate continued to be withheld. That is the way things were when I was in Cathay, and I doubt if there has been any change. Despite protests to the contrary, no ruler wants the Middle Kingdom united—except by himself. Such is the balance or nonbalance there.

Early in my captivity I managed to dispatch a message to Fan Ch'ih at Lu. Although he was my only hope of ever getting home to Persia, I had no idea whether or not he had the power to free me because I was never told just what my status was. If I was a slave, he could buy me. But whenever I suggested to Huan that a ransom might be paid for my release he would say, "But you are an honored guest." Then he would clap his hands and I would be escorted back to my cell, whose door was never locked because I could never escape. I was as conspicuous in Ch'in as a black man at Susa. More so. There are hundreds of black people at Susa while, as far as I could tell, I was the only white person in Ch'in.

When I came to speak the language with some ease, Huan questioned me in some detail about the administration of Persia. Although he showed no interest in the Great King, when it came to such things as the fixing of prices in the market, establishing interest rates on money lent, keeping control of the population through the police and secret service, he was more than eager to listen to my stories of Persia and the Indian kingdoms.

I recall one dinner party where I was treated as an honored guest by Huan, who always enjoyed showing me off to his fellow nobles. On that occasion, most of the council of state was present. As we knelt on mats, servants shuffled into the room with stools, which were set beside each diner. I always wanted to sit on the stool, but that is the one thing you cannot do at a formal Cathayan dinner party. The stool is there only to lean against. Since even the Cathayans find kneeling for several hours uncomfortable, the stool is useful for shifting one's weight about.

In front of each diner was an array of dishes and cups. A minister is allowed eight dishes; I was allowed six. To one's left is a dish of meat that has been cooked on the bone, as well as a bowl of rice; to one's right, a dish of sliced meat and a bowl of soup. This order must never be varied. In a circle outside these dishes, other dishes are arranged; they contain minced and roasted meat, steamed onions, pickles, and so on. Boiled fish is served in winter with belly to the host's right; in summer the belly is to the left. Dried meat is folded to the left. Spouts of jars face the host. And so on, and on.

The ritual of a Cathayan dinner party is almost as elaborate as a religious ceremony. For instance, if one is of a lower rank than the host—which I was thought to be—one is required to pick up the dish containing rice or millet or whatever is made of grain; then one bows to the host and declines the dish while pretending to depart. The host then gets to his feet and implores the guest to remain, which he does. I have never heard of a case when the guest actually left. But since everything that can happen in the world has happened, that must have happened too. I should not like to have been the guest who left the dining room.

There were other niceties which one had to observe, but I have forgotten them. On the other hand, I am not apt to forget the splendid cooking that one finds in all the noble houses of Cathay. Even the cooked food that one buys in the market is of high quality, and there is no pleasure on earth to equal that of dining aboard a boat tied to a willow tree in the Wei River at the time of the summer moon.

Once the various ceremonies are attended to, a Cathayan dinner party can be almost as sophist-like as one here at Athens. Of course, Cathayan manners are more formal than Athenian manners. What manners are not? Nevertheless, the conversation in Huan's dining room was occasionally sharp and to the point. There were even arguments toward the end of a meal when too much millet wine had been drunk.

I remember enjoying my first plate of the famed baked suckling pig, a somewhat inadequate description of a dish that begins with a suckling pig which has been stuffed with dates and baked in straw and mud; once the pig is baked, the mud is broken off and the meat is sliced and fried in melted fat; then the slices are boiled with herbs for three days and nights and served with pickled beef and vinegar. There is nothing so delicious in all Lydia. I fear that I gorged myself at Huan's table—something that one is not supposed to do at a Cathayan dinner, but everyone does.

After Huan had explained to me how the pig had been prepared and I had extolled, sincerely, the result, he said, "But you must dine like this in your country." He nodded encouragingly.

I nodded too; and said, "No, never. You have achieved that perfection which we merely seek."

"Oh, no, no!" Then Huan turned to the other guests, saying, "Cyrus Spitama, despite his curious name and characteristic paleness, is a very sharp weapon." A sharp weapon is the Cathayan phrase for a clever person.

The others looked at me with more than polite interest. But then, I don't believe that any of them had ever seen a white person before. Certainly, they were always surprised when I spoke their language. As a barbarian, I was expected to grunt like a pig.

Politely, a noble asked me about Persia. Where was it? How far away? When I explained that it was a thousand miles to the west of Champa—a port that they had all heard of—a dozen heads nodded with disbelief.

"He tells me," said Huan with his almost toothless smile, "that in his country all men are subordinate to the state and that the state alone is the measure of what is good and bad."

The nobles nodded and smiled, and I did the same. Needless to say, I had *never* told Huan any such thing.

"But surely," said one old man, "even in a barbarous land, heaven's decrees take precedence over those of the state."

Huan looked at the roof beam as if it were heaven. "As long as the mandate has been given the ruler, the ruler's will is absolute. Isn't that the way you told me it was in your happy country?" Huan smiled at me.

"Yes, Lord Huan." I was not about to contradict my captor.

"But surely"—and the old man turned now in my direction, glad to use me as surrogate for the first minister —"there are certain laws of heaven that your ruler must obey?"

Huan answered for me. "No. There are none, as long as the mandate is his. These western barbarians believe, as do we, that the state is a chain that starts with the individual who is linked to the family which is linked to the village which is linked to the state. Each link in the chain must be strong. Each link contributes to the whole, which is the state. In the happy country of our honored guest" —a bob of the head in my direction—"men are no longer the way they were at the beginning when each man lived only for himself, which meant that if you brought two men together, you had two different ideas of what was good and bad, which is a very bad thing since no one can deny that all the suffering in the world begins with a disagreement between men as to what is good or bad. Well, the barbarians of Persia are wiser than we. Yes, yes! They believe that if each man is allowed to act and think as he pleases, there can be no order, no harmony, no state. And so, finally, the wise ruler, when he receives the mandate of heaven, must tell his people that what he thinks is right is right for all men and what he thinks is wrong is wrong for all men. But, of course, there are always some who will disobey their ruler and so the Persian king has said, 'Should any voice be raised against the official good, whoever hears that voice must report it to his superior.' How wise that rule is! How truly wise! Everyone is obliged to report to the ruler or to his officials any wrongdoing or even the hint or suggestion that wrong might be done. The result? Perfect happiness! Because the western barbarians have eliminated all disorder and disharmony. Everyone serves a state which is based upon . . . what was that marvelous phrase, Cyrus Spitama? Oh, yes! The principle of agreement with the superior."

Huan bowed to me as if I were the imaginary Persian monarch who had invented this unholy system of government. A few years later I learned that Huan's dinner party had proved to be historic. For more than a generation there had been much argument amongst the Ch'inese nobles on how the state should be governed. Huan believed that the only way to govern Ch'in was to enslave the people to a degree never before attempted in Cathay or anywhere else, including Sparta. Everyone was encouraged to spy on everyone else. Families were broken up so that able-bodied men could be moved from army to agriculture to road-making or whatever. Since merchants and artisans tend to come and go as they please, Huan proposed that these activities be outlawed. Finally, in order to establish the state's absolute primacy, he worked, secretly, to destroy his own class, the aristocracy.

Needless to say, Huan's fellow nobles were not altogether happy with his theories—not to mention practices. There was a good deal of polite dissent at the dinner party. Some years later the dissent grew less polite and Huan was murdered by a rival faction. But he had done his work well. Although merchants and artisans continue to prosper and the aristocracy has kept its power, ordinary men and women are obliged to live in barracks, their lives entirely ordered by the state. Should anyone object to Huan's rule of heaven, he is hacked in two and his remains are displayed on either side of the city gate.

As we ate baked suckling pig, the old man addressed Huan through me. "In the time of our ancestors, each man lived according to the dictates of his inner nature and there was much kindness in the world and little struggle. Surely your Persian king would like his subjects to live as their ancestors did, in harmony with heaven and themselves."

Huan clapped his hands gleefully. "But when I asked this wise barbarian the very same question, he said, and I hope I quote you exactly . . ."

"Oh, you will! You will, Lord Huan!" I sounded like one of those Indian birds that have been taught to speak.

"You told me that men were good to one another in early times because people were few and things were many. Now people are many, and things few. Even in the far-off time of the Emperor Yu, life was so hard that Yu himself worked in the fields until he wore all the hair off his shins. But now there are ten thousand times as many people as there were in the age of Yu. So, for the common good, we must control them in order that they not hamper one another. How can this be done? I confess that I myself was not clever enough to think of a solution. But your wise Persian king provided me with an answer." Huan bowed in my direction, obliging me to bow so low that my stomach gurgled. The Cathayans take very seriously the stomach's noises. I prayed that the sounds from my stuffed belly were in no way seditious.

" 'Utilize human nature,' said the Persian king. 'Since men have their likes and dislikes, you can control them by rewards and punishments, which are the handles by which the ruler maintains his supremacy.' "

389

"But should these . . . handles fail the ruler, what then would this wise Persian prescribe?" The old man looked at me; the eyes were bloodshot; the veins at his temples throbbed. He hated Huan. There was no doubt of that.

"The word that the wise Persian used was 'force.'" Huan was benign.

"'Force,' he said, 'is the stuff that keeps the masses in subjection.'"

Despite the marvelous food, I cannot recall a more alarming dinner party. Through me, Huan was challenging his fellow nobles. Luckily for the Ch'inese, the nobles did not embrace all of Huan's harsh precepts, and he himself never ceased to be more than what he had been for so many years, first amongst equals. But through his efforts, the lives of the common people have been so changed that nothing short of a collapse of the state can ever save them from that slavery he had consigned them to. At least the Spartans are trained to love their state, and take for granted their brutish lives. The people of Ch'in do not love their masters, to say the least.

The dinner party ended when everyone invoked heaven to grant the duke a long life. I was somewhat startled by the vehemence with which the dinner guests addressed heaven. After all, the duke was powerless; yet the nobles wept real tears at the thought that he might die. I attributed their emotion to millet wine. But three months later, when Duke P'ing did indeed die, I realized that those tears had been genuine.

On that fateful day, I was awakened at dawn by a clanging of bells. This was followed by an irregular beating of drums. From one end of the city to the other, there was a sound of wailing.

I dressed quickly and hurried into the courtyard just as Huan climbed into his chariot. He was dressed in old clothes and looked like a beggar. With a cry the charioteer lashed at the four horses, and they were gone.

According to one of the stewards of the household, "the duke died just before the sun rose. They say that when he had taken too much wine, he called for the eunuch to help him vomit, which he did. But instead of vomiting wine, he vomited blood. Oh, this is a terrible day for Ch'in! A black day, truly, truly!"

"Was he so loved?"

"By heaven, yes. Otherwise he would not have been the one who looks south, would he? Now he is gone." The steward burst into tears. It seemed that everyone in Ch'in was weeping. I was mystified. I knew that Duke P'ing had not been popular. More to the point, he had existed only as a ceremonial puppet, manipulated by the six families. What, then, was the reason for so much grief?

I found out during the funeral ceremonies. I stood with Huan's household in the square at whose center is the ducal residence. Except for a row of flagpoles just opposite the entrance, the building is inferior to the prime minister's palace. The display of banners signifies that the one who lives within possesses heaven's mandate. On this day the banners were black and red, and highly ominous. Since no breeze stirred the thick cloth, they drooped in the hot sun. The day seemed to be without air. Although I yawned constantly behind my sleeve, I could never get quite enough breath. I put this down not only to the heat but to the heavy breathing of the ten thousand solemn men and women who stood in perfect silence, staring at the palace gate. Although the people of Ch'in must be the quietest and most obedient on earth, I used to find their stillness somewhat alarming—like a presage to earthquake.

The doors to the palace opened. Huan and the council of state appeared, followed by a highly lacquered palanquin resting on the shoulders of a dozen soldiers. Atop the palanquin lay the duke. The corpse was dressed in scarlet silk and a thousand jewels. On its breast lay a splendid disk of dark-green jade, the symbol of heaven's favor.

A long procession of slaves emerged from the palace carrying chests of silk, golden tripods, leather drums, ivory statues, gilded weapons, featherwork screens, a silver bed. All these rich objects were to furnish the ducal tomb at a breath-taking cost. I know. Huan asked me to make a complete accounting of what had gone into the tomb so that the sum might be allowed for in the budget that was to be presented at the council of state when it waited upon the new duke.

At the far end of the square, Huan and his fellow ministers took their places at the head of what proved to be a mile-long funeral cortege. Just behind the chariots of the nobles was a wagon drawn by eight white horses. The body of Duke P'ing was so strapped to a board that he seemed to be driving the wagon's horses. The effect was distinctly unpleasant. The objects for the tomb were

391

placed in other wagons, along with several hundred ladies of the harem. Behind their veils, they wept and moaned.

It took more than an hour for the chariots and wagons to cross the city to the south gate. Here Huan made a sacrifice to some local devil. Then he led the cortege along a winding road to the valley where the kings are interred beneath artificial mounds not unlike the ones at Sardis.

Quite unexpectedly, I was given a ride in a red-lacquered wagon by a tall, lean man who said, "I have a passion for white people. I used to own three. But two are dead and the third is sickly. You may kiss my hand. I am the duke of Sheh, a cousin of the late duke of Ch'in as well as of the dukes of Lu and Wei. But then, we dukes are all related to one another through our common ancestor the Emperor Wen. Where do you come from?"

I did my best to tell him. Although the duke knew nothing of Persia, he had traveled more in the west than any of the Ch'inese that I had met. "I spent a year at Champa," he said. "I can't say I liked it. The weather was either too hot or too rainy. And the people are much too dark for my taste. I'd hoped that they would be white like you. But I was told that if I wanted to find white people, I'd have to keep on traveling for at least half a year and I couldn't bear the thought of being so long out of the world." He pinched my cheek; stared intently at the fold of flesh between his fingers. "You turn red!" He was delighted. "Just the way my other slaves did. I never tire of watching the red come and go. You don't think Huan would sell you to me?"

"I'm not at all certain," I spoke most carefully, "that I am a slave."

"Oh, I'm sure you are. You're a barbarian, even though you don't fold your robe to the left. You really ought to, you know. It's more amusing for us. And your hair should be loose. You mustn't try to look too civilized or you will lack novelty. Anyway, you are definitely a slave. You live in the minister's house. And you do what he tells you. I should say that you are very much a slave. I can't imagine why Huan hasn't told you. Very wicked of him, really. But he is so timid. He probably thinks it bad manners to tell you outright that you're a slave."

"Prisoner of war, I would have said."

"War? What war?" The duke of Sheh stood up in the wagon and looked about him. "I see no armies," he said.

The gray-green countryside was certainly peaceful as the funeral cortege twisted like a silent, interminable snake between those jagged limestone hills that mark the ducal burial grounds.

"I came as an ambassador from the Great King."

The duke was moderately interested in my story. Although Persia meant nothing to him, he was very much aware of Magadha. When I told him that I was married to a daughter of Ajatashatru, he was most impressed. "I've met several members of that family, including Ajatashatru's uncle who was viceroy when I was at Champa." The duke became very animated, even gleeful. "I'm sure whoever owns you will be able to get a splendid ransom from the king, which is why I must get you away from Huan. Then I'll sell you to your father-in-law. You see, I'm always short of money."

"But I would have thought that the ruler of Sheh would be supported most richly by . . . by heaven!" I was slowly learning the elaborate style of the Cathayans. Nothing spoken ever quite means what it appears to mean, while the arm, hand and body gestures are intricate beyond belief. I never began to master them.

"The Sheh of which I am duke is no longer the Sheh that it was, so I've never set foot there. I prefer to travel with my court and visit my numerous cousins and collect dragon's bone. You have probably heard that I have the largest collection of dragon's bone in the world. Well, what you have heard is true. I have. But since the bones always travel with me, I need to maintain ten thousand wagons, and that is very expensive. But if I can sell you to the king of Magadha, I shall be rich indeed."

The duke of Sheh was a fantastic figure who greatly amused the Cathayans. He was born Sheh Chu-liang, the illegitimate son of a duke of Lu. Not content with this ambivalent status, he styled himself duke of Sheh. But Sheh is not a country. The word means holy ground—the earth mound that stands at the edge of every Cathayan state. The duke liked to pretend that once upon a time there had been, somewhere, a state called Sheh whose hereditary duke he was. Absorbed by predatory neighbors, Sheh had ceased to exist and all that was left of this lost world was its vagabond duke. Whether or not he was truly ducal—through Lu—is a fine point that Cathayan nobles delight in discussing. On the other hand, since his descent from the Emperor Wen was a fact, all of Cathay's sovereigns were obliged to receive their honored cousin. As the duke was constantly on the move from court to court, he was able to keep his living expenses to a minimum. He maintained a score of elderly retainers, fourteen equally aged horses, six wagons—ten thousand is a form of Cathayan hyperbole which means countless—and one chariot with a broken axle.

There were those who thought the duke enormously rich but very mean. Others thought that he was a poor man who lived on trafficking in dragon's bone. He used to collect these huge rocklike fragments in the west country where they are fairly common; then he would sell them to physicians in the east, where dragons are scarce. I had the good fortune never to see one of these alarming creatures, but I was told that the duke had slain more than thirty. "In my youth, of course. I am not what I was, I fear." He constantly painted likenesses of these beasts, which he sold whenever he could.

As the funeral cortege approached the high mound that marked the resting place of what the Ch'inese claim is the Emperor Wu, the duke suggested that we find some way to get me away from Huan. "You must have some influence with him. I mean, if you didn't, he'd have killed you by now. He's easily bored, like so many timid men."

"I don't think that I have the slightest influence on the minister. He uses me in small ways. At the moment, I keep his accounts."

"Are you a skilled mathematician?" The duke turned and squinted at me. The falling sun was now on a level with our eyes; it seemed to have burned away the air. Never before or since have I had such difficulty breathing as I did in the hot season of Ch'in.

"Yes, Lord Duke." I was so eager for him to buy me that I was ready to tell any lie. "My people built the pyramids as an exercise in celestial mathematics."

"I've heard about them." The duke was impressed. "Well, I shall think of something. You think, too. It's a pity you're not a criminal because there's always an amnesty for criminals when a new duke takes the throne. Even so, we might be able to persuade the new duke to free you if Huan will let him, which I doubt. On the other hand, if you're free, how can he sell you? That's a bit of a riddle, isn't it?"

I agreed. But then, I agreed with everything that this delightful madman had to say. He was my only hope of leaving Ch'in, a place that I was eager to escape from—an eagerness that was increased, if such was possible, by the funeral ceremonies that took place at the mound of the Emperor Wu.

The carriage and wagons formed a semicircle in front of the conical hill which contained if not the legendary Wu, then at the very least a monarch of demonstrable antiquity, since the mound was covered with that symbol of majesty the dwarf pine, which takes a thousand years to mature into those graceful hieratic shapes that Cathayans admire.

Since the wagons and chariots were arranged according to rank, the duke of Sheh and I were quite close to the prime minister, and so we had an excellent view of the proceedings. Behind us, in quiet ranks, several thousand of the common people fanned out over the low silver-gray hills.

I don't know what sort of ceremony I expected to see. I assumed that there would be sacrifices, and there were. Fires were lit southwest of the mound, and a great number of horses, sheep, swine and doves were butchered.

In the division of the sacrifice, as in everything else, the government is ingenious. Each person is given a tally stick, which entitles him to so much and no more of the cooked meat of the sacrificed beasts and fowl. As a result, not only is there always enough for everyone but there are no unseemly riots of the sort that mar Babylonian and even Persian ceremonies. I am told that Huan was responsible for this innovation, which was eventually adopted by all the Cathayan states. When I tried to introduce the principle of the tally stick to the Magians, they rejected it. They prefer the unseemly chaos that attends all their haoma-drenched rites.

The new duke stood to the north of us. As ritual requires, he was alone. He looked as old as, if not older than, his predecessor. But then, according to the duke of Sheh, he was not one of the dead man's sons but a cousin. The ministry had rejected all of Duke P'ing's sons in favor of an obscure first cousin who was "noted for his stupidity. He'll do very well from the ministry's point of view."

"Do the ministers always choose the sovereign?"

"He who has received heaven's appointment chooses as ministers only his loyal slaves." The duke's voice was suddenly shrill. As I came to know him, I realized that if

395

he was not indeed two separate people inside one body, he certainly possessed two entirely different manners. One was confiding and sly, marked by a low-pitched voice; the other was highly cryptic and distinguished by a voice that was monotonous, thin, high. He made it clear that this was neither the place nor the time to discuss the anomalous position of his ducal cousins. As I soon learned, they are, with few exceptions, powerless; and their realms are governed by hereditary ministers, either alone or in combination with other hereditary office-holders. The mandate of heaven is no more than a golden dream of what might be but never is and, perhaps, never was.

In a loud voice the new duke of Ch'in addressed his ancestors. I did not understand a word that he said. While he spoke to the sky, slaves bore the chests, tripods, furniture into what looked to be a natural cave at the foot of a steep limestone cliff. All the while, music played. Since there were some three hundred musicians playing simultaneously, the effect was peculiarly distressing to a foreign ear. Later I came to like a good deal of Cathayan music. I was particularly charmed by those stones of different size which make such lovely sounds when struck with hammers.

As the duke finished the address to the ancestors, the palanquin that bore the body of his predecessor was hoisted high on the shoulders of a dozen men. The music stopped. In silence, the palanquin was carried past the new duke into the cave. Once the body was out of sight, everyone exhaled. The effect was eerie—like the first breath of a summer storm.

I turned to the duke of Sheh. He was hunched like a molting bird at the edge of the wagon, bright eyes on the cave. The men who had carried the body into the cave did not come out. Instead, a hundred veiled women moved in slow procession toward the cave. Some were wives of the late duke; others were concubines, dancers, slaves. The women were followed by a separate procession of men and eunuchs headed by the old nobleman who had attended the baked suckling pig dinner. A number of the men were guards' officers; others were high-ranking courtiers. They were followed by musicians, carrying their instruments; by cooks and waiters who carried bamboo tables on which had been arranged an elaborate feast. One by one, the women and the men entered what was obviously not just a cave but an enormous room carved in the limestone.

Once the last of what proved to be five hundred men and women had vanished inside the cave, the new duke spoke again to his ancestors in heaven. This time I understood, more or less, what he said. He praised the ancestors by name. This took some time. Then he asked the ancestors to accept his predecessor in heaven. He referred to Duke P'ing as the all-compassionate one. In Cathay a dead man is never referred to by his proper name on the sensible ground that if he is called by name, his spirit is apt to come back to earth and haunt one. If the all-compassionate one was accepted by heaven, the duke swore that he would never omit any of the rituals that keep in harmony heaven and earth. He asked the blessings of all the ancestors for the orphan. I had no idea whom he was talking about. Later I learned that the ruler often refers to himself as either the orphan or the lonely one, since, of necessity, his father, or predecessor, is dead. He refers to his principal wife as that person, while the people call her that person of the duke's. *She* refers to herself as the little boy. I don't know why. They are unusual, the Cathayans.

From inside the cave, music began to play. Apparently a feast was in progress. For an hour we stood facing north while the new duke faced south. For an hour we listened to the music from inside the cave. Then, one by one, each of the instruments fell silent. The last sound was that of a bronze bell tolling. Every eye was now on the entrance to the cave. Beside me, the duke of Sheh was trembling. At first I thought that he was ill; but he was simply excited.

When the bronze bell ceased its ringing, the duke of Sheh gave a long sigh. But then everyone sighed, as if by prearrangement. Suddenly the men who had carried the palanquin emerged from the cave. Each man held in his right hand a sword; each sword dripped blood.

Gravely the men saluted their new master, who raised his face to heaven and gave a howl like that of a wolf. From all of his subjects to the south came an answering howl. I have never been so terrified. What I had taken to be men were wolves in masquerade. And now, before my eyes, they had begun to revert to their true nature. Even the duke of Sheh joined in the howling. Snout toward heaven, he bared preternaturally long teeth.

397

I still hear that terrible howling in those dreams where I relive that awful moment when the twelve blood-streaked men emerged from the cave, their duty done. Five hundred men and women had been killed so that their corpses might attend for all eternity their lord.

Although human sacrifice is hardly unknown in our part of the world, I have never seen it practiced on such a scale as it is in Cathay. I was told that when a true son of heaven dies, as many as a thousand members of the court will be put to death, which explained the sudden odd intensity of those prayers for the duke's health at the end of the baked suckling pig dinner. Alive, the duke was merely contemptible; dead, he could take many of them with him. Actually, according to Ch'inese custom, only one of the council of ministers is sacrificed and he is chosen by lot. As luck and the highly tricky Huan would have it, the old minister who had defied him at dinner drew the unfortunate yarrow stick.

The cave was sealed. There was music, dancing, a feast. Later a mound would be built to cover the entrance to the tomb. Needless to say, a ducal tomb is such a great temptation to thieves that the beautiful and costly objects placed beside a duke's bier are usually in circulation not too long after the funeral.

Huan refused to sell me to the duke of Sheh. "How," said Huan, "can I sell an ambassador who is free to come and go?"

"In that case, Lord Huan, perhaps the time has come for me to go, in the company of the duke of Sheh."

This impertinence caused my master to smile. "Surely you would not want to risk your life in the company of a man who looks for dragons in wild country, who fights with brigands, who consorts with witches. Oh, the duke of Sheh is a dangerous man to know! I could not let one that I have come to love confront such dangers in a strange land. No, no, no!"

That was that. But I had made up my mind to leave. When I told the duke of my resolve, he proved to be unexpectedly resourceful. "We shall disguise you," he whispered. We were at the prime minister's weekly audience. Petitioners from all over Ch'in were allowed to approach Huan, who stood at one end of a low-ceilinged room. Gold tripods to Huan's left and right symbolized authority.

The prime minister received each petitioner with a

quiet courtesy that was entirely unlike his fierce political views. He was shrewd enough to know that you can never enslave a reluctant people without first charming them. Certainly, you must convince them that your way is their way and that the chains which you have forged for them are necessary ornaments. In a sense, the Great Kings have always realized this. From Cyrus to our current enlightened lord, Artaxerxes, the diverse peoples of the empire are allowed to live pretty much as they have always lived, owing the Great King no more than annual taxes, in exchange for which he gives them safety and law. Huan had managed to convince the admittedly barbarous and remote Ch'inese that although there had once been a golden age when men were free to live as they pleased, that age ended when—and how he loved to use the phrase!—"there were too many people and too few things."

Actually, Cathay is relatively underpopulated and many parts of that rich land are empty. Except for a half-dozen cities with populations of a hundred thousand, Cathay is a land of stone-walled villages set in rolling countryside between the two rivers. Much of the country is densely forested, particularly to the west, while to the south there are Indian-like jungles. Consequently, except for the well-disciplined and entirely controlled Ch'inese, Cathayans tend to move about a good deal. If a farm is washed out by a flood, the farmer and his family will simply shoulder their plows and the ancestral hearthstone, and move on to another country where they will begin again, paying tribute to a new overlord.

The most important travelers are the shih. There is no equivalent word—or class—in Greek or Persian. To understand the shih, one must understand the Cathayan class system.

At the top is the emperor, or son of heaven. Currently, he was and perhaps will be but certainly, he *is* not. As I say this, I suddenly realize how clever the Cathayans are to have a language without a past, future or present tense. Below the emperor, there are five orders of nobility. The highest is that of duke. With odd exceptions, like the mad duke of Sheh, the dukes are the titular and sometimes actual rulers of states, which makes them equivalent to our kings and tyrants; and like our kings and tyrants, who recognize the Great King as overlord and source of legitimacy, each of these dukes has received, in theory, his authority from the son of heaven, who does not exist. If he were to exist—that is, exercise hegemony over the Middle Kingdom—he would probably be the duke of Chou, the direct descendant of the Emperor Wen, who established the Chou hegemony over the Middle Kingdom. Certainly he would *not* be the duke of Ch'in, who descends from Wen's brutal son Wu.

The eldest son of a duke is a marquis, and when the duke dies he becomes a duke, barring an all-too-common untoward accident. The other sons of the duke are also marquises, and while the eldest son of the second son will retain that title, the other sons will drop to the next order of nobility, and their sons to the next, and theirs to baron. The sons of a baron—the lowest aristocratic order—are shih. During the six or seven centuries since the establishment of the Chou hegemony, the Chou descendants now number in the tens of thousands, and those without rank are shih or, let us say, knights, who retain only one hereditary privilege: a knight can go to war in a chariot, assuming that he can afford to maintain one.

In recent years there has been a considerable increase in the ranks of the knights. These not-quite noblemen are everywhere. Many specialize in administration, rather the way our eunuchs do. Many are army officers. Many teach. A few devote themselves, rather like Zoroastrians, to keeping uncorrupt those religious observances that maintain a proper harmony between heaven and earth. Finally, the knights administer most of the Cathayan nations, serving those hereditary officers of state who have managed to usurp the powers if not the divinity of the dukes.

The highways of Cathay are crowded with ambitious knights. If one of them fails to find a position in, say, the ministry of police at Lu, he will move on to Wei, where his services may be valued more by the local administration than they were at home. Human perversity being what it is, a knight's chance of employment is usually best the farther he is from his native land.

Consequently, at any given moment, thousands are on the move. As they tend to maintain close communication with one another, they form a sort of middle kingdom of their own. In place of a son of heaven, there are now ten thousand knights who govern Cathay, and though the states are constantly at war with one another, the knights are often able to mitigate the savagery of their masters—

except at Ch'in, where they have little or no influence over Huan and his fellow despots.

Finally, a new element has been introduced in the class system. There is now a category—one cannot say class—known as gentlemen. Anyone can become a gentleman if he observes the way of heaven, a complicated business that I shall get to when I describe Master K'ung, or Confucius, as he is also known. He is given credit for having invented the idea of the gentleman, a notion of great appeal to the knights, and to hardly anyone else.

As Huan accepted petitions and listened to the complaints of the people, the duke of Sheh and I plotted my escape. "You must shave off your beard." The duke pretended to admire a feather screen. "We shall get you women's clothes. You will travel as one of my concubines."

"A *white* concubine?"

"Precisely the sort of concubine who would appeal to the duke of Sheh, as all the world knows." The duke looked amused. "But we'll take no chances. You'd better darken your face. I'll send you a coloring I use myself. And of course you'll also be veiled."

"Will your retinue be searched?" I knew the strict guard that was kept not only at the gates of the city of Yung but at checkpoints throughout Ch'in. People were forever trying to escape Huan's entirely rational rule.

"They would not dare! I am a fellow sovereign. But if they do . . ." The duke made the universal gesture of bribery.

Suddenly Huan was at our side. He had the gift of noiseless ubiquity. I often thought of him as resembling the earth shadow of a fast-moving cloud.

"Lord Duke . . . honored Ambassador! I can see that you admire my screen of feathers."

"Yes," said the duke of Sheh very smoothly, "and I was about to explain to your guest its meaning." I looked at the screen and for the first time actually saw it. Eight black birds against a stormy sky.

"You would know its meaning, Lord Duke." Huan turned to me. "There is nothing that our lord of Sheh does not know about our ducal family, which is also his family."

"Quite true. The great-grandfather of the late all-compassionate one was my great-uncle. He was called P'ing. One day he received from the north a group of musicians. They told him that they knew all the music that had been played at the court of the Emperor Wu.

Duke P'ing was skeptical. Who wouldn't be? Everyone knows that most of the sacred music of the original Chou court is either hopelessly corrupt or entirely forgotten. He told them as much. But the music master—who was not blind, a suspicious detail, since every proper music master must be blind—the music master said, 'We shall prove that we can bring heaven close to earth.'

"So they began to play. The music was strange and other worldly. Other-worldly but *not* heavenly. Out of the south, eight black birds appeared, and danced on the terrace of the palace. Then a huge wind swept through the city. The tiles flew off the palace roof. The ritual vessels were smashed. Duke P'ing fell ill, and for three years nothing grew in Ch'in, not even a blade of grass."

Huan smiled at me. "The Lord Duke knows well this sad, this cautionary tale. I take it most seriously, you know. In fact, that's why I always keep this screen near me so that I shall never be tempted to play the wrong music. We do not want, ever again, to see eight black birds swoop down upon us from the south."

That very night, the duke's steward bribed one of Huan's servants to come to me at midnight in my cell. I was given a razor, face paint, women's clothes. Quickly I transformed myself into an unusually tall Cathayan lady. I then followed the servant through the dimly lit palace, fearfully aware of the creaking of the floorboards as we crept past a pair of sleeping—that is, drugged—guards to a side door that opened into a walled garden. Here the steward of the duke of Sheh was waiting. Fortunately the night was moonless—starless, too, because of heavy clouds, full of rain.

Like spirits of the dead, we hurried through twisting, narrow streets; we hid in doorways whenever a contingent of the night guard approached, their bronze lanterns casting shafts of light before them like fiery lances. Since no citizen was allowed to leave his house from sundown to sunrise, Yang resembled a city of the dead. The steward had permission to be abroad, but I had none. I don't know what excuse he had ready should we be stopped. Fortunately, with a sound like ten thousand drums, a storm broke over the city.

Through a flood of rain we made our way to the city gate where the wagons of the duke of Sheh were ready to depart. The steward lifted up the floorboards of one of the wagons and motioned me to hide in a space slightly smaller than I was. Once I was wedged into place, the boards were nailed down. Although the storm was so loud that I did not hear the order for the duke's entourage to leave, I felt the wagon jolt beneath me as the driver started the mules and we rattled through the gate.

As I had expected, the Ch'inese police caught up with us two days later when we were in the Hanku Pass. The wagons were thoroughly searched, and my hiding place was discovered. But I was not in it. The duke had taken the precaution to station scouts along the road from the city. He knew that when I was found to be missing, Huan would suspect him of having engineered my escape. The scouts signaled one another by holding up highly polished bronze shields that reflected the sun's light from station to station.

As soon as we knew that the police were almost at hand, I took refuge in a tree while the wagons continued past. When the police arrived, the duke was superb. He reminded them that he was a cousin to their new duke as well as a direct descendant of the Yellow Emperor, of the Emperor Wen, and of all the rest. Nevertheless, he would allow them to search the wagons; and he hoped that their sacrilegious behavior would not be unduly punished by his ancestors in heaven.

The police searched the wagons; scrutinized every single one of the duke's attendants, male and female; were plainly astonished not to find me. In a totally regulated state like Ch'in, no one vanishes without official connivance. Finally they gave the convoy permission to continue on its way but, to my horror, the police accompanied the wagons for the next five days, and they did not leave the duke until the convoy had arrived at the stone monument that marks the border between Ch'in and Chou.

I was obliged to keep not only out of sight of the police but out of range of the wolf packs that stalked me curiously, eyes like green-yellow fires in the night. I slept in trees, always carried a heavy stick and cursed the fact that my woman's costume included no weapons. I saw a black bear; I saw a brown bear. If either saw me, he showed no interest. Although brigands are supposed to live in that dim forest, I encountered no human being. Had I not been able, from time to time, to hear the sounds of the duke's convoy, I would have been entirely out of the world of men.

Whenever I found a pond or stream, I drank water the way animals drink, on all fours. I ate strange berries, roots, fruits. I was often ill. Once I thought I saw a dragon, gleaming in the half-light of the forest. But the dragon proved to be an odd pinnacle of shining green and white jade, the most beautiful of all stones.

I stood in a copse of feathery trees at the juncture of the Wei and Tai rivers, and watched as the police saluted the duke of Sheh, and turned back into the forest. On the far side of the Tai River, I could see the cultivated fields of Chou. Going from Ch'in to Chou was like passing from night to day.

On the Chou side of the river the duke was received with deference by the frontier commander, who examined his passport perfunctorily and graciously waved him toward Loyang, the capital of the Middle Kingdom. My own entrance into Chou was less formal. I floated across the Tai River beneath a rude raft of willow branches.

The duke was astonished to see me. "What a joy!" He clapped his hands. "Now I shall get the ransom money from Magadha. Oh, I am delighted! Surprised, too. I was positive that if the wolves didn't get you, the wolf-men would." That was the first time—on Chou soil, needless to say—that I heard what the civilized Cathayans call the barbarous Ch'inese.

The duke gave me food from his own store of provisions, and presented me with one of his own wide-skirted gowns of loosely woven fine threads, as well as an almost new outer robe of black lambskin. Once all ducal emblems had been removed, I looked like a knight—no more, no less. Yet I felt most uncomfortable. For the first time since I was a boy, I did not have a beard. I looked exactly like a eunuch. Fortunately, many Cathayan men do not wear beards, so at least I was not conspicuous.

2

FOR THE FIRST TIME SINCE I ARRIVED in Cathay, I began to enjoy myself. Although I was still a captive, if not a slave, the duke was a delightful companion, eager to show me the true Cathay. "You must not base your view of the Middle Kingdom on Ch'in, which is barely a part of the realm, despite the somewhat irregular descent of their dukes from the Emperor Wu. Even so, these crude provincials lust for the hegemony! But heaven is kind, and the mandate has not been bestowed on anyone. When it is granted, I am certain that it will be awarded to my beloved cousin the duke of Chou. You'll find him inspiring. But flawed. He acts as if he were already the son of heaven, which is the height of presumption. Of course, all the dukes of Chou have suffered from the same delusion on the ground that heaven's last decree was indeed bestowed upon their ancestor. But that was three hundred years ago, and the mandate was lost when an unholy league of barbarians and nobles killed him. The emperor's son fled here to Chou and proclaimed himself emperor. But, of course, he lacked the hegemony. So he was really only duke of Chou, which is why, to this day, we have nothing more than a shadow son of heaven at Loyang, the shadow capital of a very real Middle Kingdom. The duke of Chou is *nearly* emperor. But that is not good enough, is it? Particularly when Chou is one of the weakest of the duchies and sooner or later some neighbor—probably the wolfmen—will take it over. Meanwhile, we all look to Loyang with tears in our eyes, hope in our stomachs."

The duke then told me about his great-grandmother, who had also been the great-grandmother of the present duke of Chou. A woman of infinite pride, she always referred to herself as the little boy. One day the wing of the palace where she lived caught fire and all the ladies fled except the little boy, who remained seated in her receiving hall, serenely telling fortunes with yarrow sticks. When a maid servant begged the duchess to leave the burning palace, the old lady said, "The little boy cannot leave the palace unless escorted by the son of heaven or by a male relative whose rank is no lower than that of marquis and, of course, the little boy must never be seen outside the palace without a lady-in-waiting who is older than the little boy." Then she went on with her fortune-telling, a popular Cathayan pastime.

The maid servant hurried off to find someone of sufficiently high rank to escort the duchess to safety. But there was no one at the palace higher in rank than earl; and there was no lady-in-waiting older than the duchess. So, faces shielded with damp cloths, the earl and the maid servant entered the blazing palace, where they found the old lady still seated on her silken mat, arranging yarrow sticks.

"Please, that person of the son of heaven," said the earl, who was also her nephew, "come with me."

The duchess was very angry. "This is unheard of. I may not leave my quarters unless chaperoned by an older woman and by a man of my family whose rank may not be lower than that of marquis. To do otherwise would be unseemly." And so the duchess burned to death, in the name of seemliness, a quality that is all-important to the Cathayans.

This lady's death was a source of endless discussion in Cathay. Some regard her as a figure to be admired and emulated. Others think her ridiculous. "After all," said Fan Ch'ih, "she was neither a maiden nor a young married woman. She was a very old lady who need not have worried about who chaperoned her. She was not modest. In fact, she was vain like all the other members of the house of Chou. And vanity is never seemly in the eyes of heaven."

As we approached the outskirts of Loyang, human traffic increased. All sorts of men and women were making their way to the capital. The rich rode in chariots or were borne in litters. Poor farmers carried their produce on their backs. Rich farmers and merchants presided over bullock-drawn wagons. The common people were well-dressed and smiling, unlike the dour Ch'inese, whose features, incidentally, are quite unlike those of the eastern Cathayans. The people of Ch'in tend to be bronze-colored with flat noses. The people of Chou and the inner states are paler in color than the Ch'inese and their features are more delicate. But all of the indigenous Cathayans are black-haired, black-eyed, round-headed, with almost hairless bodies. Curiously enough, like the Babylonians, they are known as the black-haired people to the Chou warrior class, which conquered the Middle Kingdom at about the same time that the Aryans came into Persia, India, Greece. Where were the Chous from? The Cathayans point to the north. It would be interesting if we shared a common ancestor.

We entered Loyang through a tall stone gate, set in a crude brick wall. I felt immediately at home. The crowds are like those one sees at Susa or Shravasti. The people laugh, shout, sing, hawk and spit; they buy, sell, gamble and eat at a variety of booths in every street.

Near the central market, the duke bought a boiled carp from a man at a stall. "The best carp in Cathay," said the duke, tearing off a piece and giving it to me.

"I have never tasted a better fish," I said with a fair degree of honesty.

The duke smiled at the fish seller. "I always come to you first when I'm in Loyang. Don't I?" The duke was gracious despite a mouth full of fish.

The man bowed low, wished the duke long life; received a coin. Next the duke bought a large leaf which had been made into a funnel containing bees that had been fried in their own honey. He commended the dish highly, but I found it odd. Since my days in Lydia, I have never cared for honey.

The duke of Sheh always took rooms in a large building opposite the ducal palace. "This house belonged to a connection of my family," he said, somewhat vaguely. After all, he was related to everyone. "But then it was sold to a merchant who rents out rooms at a very high rate, except to me. He makes me a special price because I'm a member of the imperial family."

Although the duke did not treat me as a captive, I knew that that was exactly what I was. When we traveled he kept me either in his own room or in a room with his steward. I was never out of his sight or that of some member of his retinue.

After Ch'in, I found Loyang such a charming place that I did not realize for quite some time that both city and nation were close to economic collapse. Neighboring states had seized most of Chou. Only the ambiguously divine figure of the duke kept the rulers of Cheng or Wei from occupying Loyang itself. As it was, everyone more or less maintained the fiction that the duke was the son of heaven—all the while stealing his land and mocking, behind his back, his pretensions.

Loyang had the somewhat startled look of a great capital that has only recently lost the empire that sustained it. Babylon has the same slightly dilapidated and disappointed air. Yet Loyang was full of music, games, jugglers; and, of course, ceremony.

We attended the rites of the new year which are celebrated in the ancestral temple of the dukes of Chou. The building must have been unusually beautiful when it was first built shortly after the arrival of the last emperor's son, three centuries earlier.

The temple has a high, steep roof whose tiles are beautifully glazed in a wavy pattern of alternating green and gold. The wooden columns are decorated with the intricate duck-weed pattern that only the son of heaven may use. The temple's foundation is of stone, while the walls are made of dark wood and covered with weapons both ancient and modern. In theory, the entire armory of the nation is kept in the ancestral temple of the ruler. In practice, only token weapons are kept in these temples. When the ruler was simply a clan leader, he ensured his primacy by the direct ownership of all weapons. But that was long ago, when the community was nothing more than a family that obeyed its father, who was himself a son not only of his own chieftain-father but of heaven, too.

At one end of the vast interior is a most curious terracotta statue of a man, somewhat larger than life. He is dressed like a warrior of the dynasty before Chou; his mouth is covered with a triple seal. At the base of the statue is the inscription "Least said, soonest mended." Why there should be a statue to caution in the ancestral hall of the Chous is totally obscure; unless, of course, the message is perfectly plain and means what it says.

The current son of heaven proved to be a brisk little man of forty, with a long pointed beard. He wore an elaborate ceremonial robe on whose back a dragon had been picked out in gold thread. In one hand he carried a large disk of green jade attached to an ivory stick, the outward symbol of heaven's fickle mandate.

The duke of Chou stood alone at the north end of the room, the altar at his back. Between him and the court stood the marshals of the left and the right; they are the great officers of the realm. Next came the hereditary priests; then the various masters of music and ceremony, the courtiers and the guests of Chou. Because of the high rank of the duke of Sheh—a rank quite as specious as that of the so-called son of heaven—we were able to watch close-to-an-interminable ceremony in which, according to the muttered comments of my master, "The whole thing's a botch. Too scandalous!"

The duke was particularly outraged when the succession music was played. "This may be played *only* in the presence of one who has both the mandate and the hegemony. Oh, it is perfect sacrilege!"

The succession music was composed more than a thousand years ago. While it is played, extraordinarily costumed dancers act out the peaceful succession to the throne of a legendary emperor called Shun. Properly played and mimed, this music is supposed to bind together in perfect harmony earth and heaven.

Democritus wants to know how music can be remembered for a thousand years. So do many Cathayans who maintain that the original music has been either corrupted or totally forgotten over the centuries and that what one hears today at Loyang is a travesty of the original, and because it is a travesty, the mandate of heaven has been withdrawn. I wouldn't know. I can only say that the effect is bizarre to western ears—and eyes.

When the music and mime ended, the duke of Chou asked the Yellow Emperor for heaven's blessing upon the Middle Kingdom. Then the son of heaven reinstated all the lords of Cathay. This part of the ceremony was as impressive as it was meaningless.

Solemnly the duke of Chou motioned for the lords of the Middle Kingdom to approach him. Fifteen splendidly dressed men scuttled toward the duke. I should mention here that whenever a person of inferior rank presents himself to a person of superior rank, he lowers his head, raises his shoulders, inclines his body, bends his legs so that he will seem as small as possible in the presence of the great one.

Just short of the duke, the fifteen resplendent figures stopped. Then the marshals of the right and left presented the duke with fifteen bronze tablets covered with the beautiful and for me never-to-be-comprehended Cathayan script.

The duke took up the first tablet; then he turned to an elderly man in a silver robe. "Come near to me, beloved cousin."

The old man moved crablike toward the duke. "It is heaven's will that you continue to serve us as our loyal slave. Take this"—the duke thrust the tablet into the old man's hands—"as a token of heaven's will that you will continue to serve both us and heaven as the duke of Wei."

I was most impressed. Within the dusty hall, whose dark beams were half eaten away by termites, all the dukes of Cathay had gathered in order that their authority might be renewed by the son of heaven. There are eleven dukes of the inner states, and four dukes of the so-called outer realms. As each duke received the emblem of authority and renewal, music played, priests chanted; and the duke of Sheh laughed softly. I did not dare ask him why. At first I thought he was simply angry that what Sheh there was, was his no longer. But when the duke of Ch'in received with cringing gratitude the mark of sovereignty, I was startled to see that he was not the same man whom I had last seen howling like a wolf at the mound of the Emperor Wu.

"That's not the duke," I whispered.

"Of course it isn't." My eccentric master giggled.

"But who is he?"

"An actor. Each year the fifteen dukes are impersonated by actors. Each year the son of heaven pretends to renew the authority of the real dukes. Oh, it is perfectly scandalous. But what is my poor friend to do? The real dukes won't come to Loyang."

"I thought you said they all accept him as son of heaven."

"They do."

"Then why don't they do him honor?"

"Because he is not the son of heaven."

"I don't understand."

"Neither does he. Not really. Yet it is simple. As long as they *pretend* that he is son of heaven, none of them can claim the mandate. That's why this performance is so necessary. Since each duke dreams of one day seizing the mandate, all the dukes are agreed that it is best, for now, to act as if the duke of Chou is really what he says he is. But sooner or later some duke will obtain the hegemony, and when that happens, Loyang will vanish like a dream and the Yellow River will be red with blood."

As the actor-dukes withdrew, the son of heaven proclaimed, "Here at the north stands the lonely one. The mandate of heaven is *here!*"

There was then a fearful noise from the musicians, and a hundred men with fantastic feather headdresses and animal tails began a series of dances that was as extraordinary as anything that I ever saw at Babylon, where *all* things are to be seen. In the midst of a whirl of harsh colors and strange sounds, the son of heaven withdrew.

"They are playing the music of the four cardinal points," said the duke. "Purists dislike it. But purists dislike any innovation. Personally, I prefer the new music to the old. That's heresy in some quarters, but these are heretical times. Proof? There is no duke in Sheh."

I cannot remember how long we stayed at Loyang. I do remember that for the first time since I had been made captive, I felt almost free. I attended numerous dinner parties with the duke, who enjoyed showing me off. Not that I was much of a success. Cathayans in general and the courtiers at Loyang in particular have little interest in the world beyond what they call the four seas. Worse, I looked odd and spoke their language with a disagreeable accent, two plain deficiencies not apt to ensure popularity. To my surprise and the duke's disappointment, hardly anyone was interested in the western world. What is not the Middle Kingdom does not exist. In Cathayan eyes we are the barbarians, and they are the civilized. I have found that if one travels far enough, left becomes right, up down, north south.

Yet I found the general seediness of the court at Loyang remarkably appealing. The courtiers wanted only to be amused. They played word games that I could not follow. They gossiped wickedly about one another. They dined well on chipped plates, drank from dented cups, wore frayed robes with elegance.

Wandering about Loyang, one got the sense that once upon a time it must have been an impressive if somewhat primitive capital. One also got the sense that its day was forever past. Like ghosts, the attendants of the son of heaven went about their ceremonies, ineptly performed according to the duke of Sheh; and like ghosts made lustful flesh, they enjoyed themselves as if they suspected that their day was done and that the court they served was but a fading shadow of a world forever lost.

We visited the Hall of Light, an ancient building dedicated to the Wise Lord—I mean heaven. It is curious that I find the two concepts interchangeable; yet whenever I mentioned the Wise Lord to Cathayan priests, they looked ill at ease; changed the subject; spoke of the Yellow Emperor, of royal descendants, of the mandate . . . that eternal mandate! They cannot or will not deal with the notion that there is a first and guiding principle to the universe. They have no conception of the war between the Truth and the Lie. Rather, they are concerned with maintaining a harmonious balance between heaven's cloudy will and earth's tempestuous follies. They believe that this is best done by carefully observing those elaborate ceremonies that propitiate the ancestors.

The duke was shocked to find the Hall of Light filled

with musicians, jugglers, vendors of food. The effect was most cheerful, but hardly religious.

"I can't think why he allows this!"

"What should be happening here?" I watched with fascination as a group of dwarfs did complicated acrobatics, to the delight of a crowd that threw small coins at the small performers.

"Nothing. This is supposed to be a refuge where one may contemplate the idea of light. And, of course, religious ceremonies are held here. I suppose the duke collects rent from the vendors. Even so, it is shocking, don't you think?"

The duke was answered not by me but by a melodious voice behind us. "Most shocking, Lord Duke! Most distressing! But that is the condition of man, is it not?"

The owner of this beguiling voice proved to be a gray-bearded man with unusually *open* eyes for a Cathayan; eyes bright with good humor—or sadness. The two are often the same, as this remarkable man liked to demonstrate.

"Li Tzu!" The duke greeted the sage with an exquisite balance of respect and condescension. If I have not said so before, tzu is the Cathayan word for master or sage. I shall now refer to Li Tzu as Master Li.

"This," said the duke to Master Li, "is the son-in-law of the king of wealthy Magadha." The duke seldom forgot my royal connection, which he hoped would one day make him rich. "He's come to us to be civilized. And now"—the duke turned to me—"you've met the wisest man in all the Middle Kingdom, the keeper of the archives of the house of Chou, the master of all the three thousand arts . . ." The duke was lavish in his praise of Master Li. Like so many impoverished nobles, he felt obliged to make up with effusive compliments and elaborate manners for all the outward panoply and state that he could not afford.

Master Li showed more than polite interest in my foreign-ness; he was also the first Cathayan to realize at a glance that I could not be a native of Magadha. Although he had not heard of Persia, he was aware that there was a land filled with blue-eyed people beyond the Indus River; and since he wanted to know what we knew, he invited the duke and me to dine with him at the edge of the grounds for the sacrifice to earth. "The lonely one has been pleased to allow me the use of the old pavilion. We shall eat frugally, and talk of Tao." The word tao means the way. It also has many other subtle meanings, as I was to discover.

We made our own mundane way through a group of half-nude dancing girls. As far as I could tell, they never actually danced; rather, they lounged about the Hall of Light, waiting for someone to buy their favors. The duke was horrified by the blasphemy. "I never thought that any son of heaven, no matter how—" Wisely, he did not finish the sentence.

Master Li serenely filled the gap. "—how compassionate! Yes, the orphan is deeply compassionate. He wants only to make the people happy. He does not strain after what is impossible. He is an adept of wu-wei." In the Cathayan language, wu-wei means do nothing; and to Master Li the art of doing nothing is the secret not only of ruling but also of human happiness. Does Master Li really mean doing nothing at all? No, Democritus. Master Li means something even odder than that. Presently I shall try to interpret him.

We walked through the busy alleyways of Loyang. I don't know why I felt entirely at home. I suppose because I had been so long in the desert, the forest, savage Ch'in. The people of Chou must be the most cheerful on earth, and if they find sad their comedown in the world, they disguise the fact beautifully. Also, like so many busy people, they practice wu-wei without knowing it. Yes, Democritus, that is a paradox, soon to be examined.

The ground for the sacrifice to earth is in a park to the north of the city, not far from that conical mound of earth which is to be found at the edge of every Cathayan city. This mound is known as sheh, or holy ground, and symbolizes the state; it is always close to a grove of trees that are not only characteristic of the region but sacred. At Chou, the chestnut tree is holy.

In the third month of each year, the so-called spring terrace play is performed in these grounds. Actually, this is not one play but a number of alternating plays, dances, ceremonies. If the spring terrace play is not a success—that is, precise in its ritual—there will be a poor harvest or no harvest at all. The terrace is a ridge of earth where the worshipers can sit and observe the ceremonies. On this one occasion of the year, men and women may mingle freely. Since the spring terrace play is the high point of the year for all Cathayans, various magnates curry favor with heaven—and the people—by financing the festivities, rather the way they do nowadays in certain Greek cities. Originally these fertility rites were somewhat like those that are still celebrated in Babylon, where both women and men are prostituted in order to ensure a good harvest. But over the years the Cathayan spring terrace play has become quite decorous—inaccurate, too, according to both the duke and Master Li. I wouldn't know. For some reason I never attended this ceremony during my years in the Middle Kingdom, but if I had, I would not have known whether or not the play was ill or well done.

As we passed the earth mound, the duke of Sheh was relieved to find that not so much as a blade of grass grew on its surface. "If the holy ground is not kept perfectly clean . . ." The duke made a sign to ward off evil. Then he bowed to the earth altar, which is square because the Cathayans believe that the earth is square, just as they think that heaven is round; at the south of every city there is a round altar to heaven.

Master Li led us across a narrow stone bridge to a charming pavilion on a limestone crag whose base was circled by a narrow, swift, white-foaming stream. I must say that I have never seen anything quite as strange or lovely as the Cathayan countryside, at least that region between the two great rivers. The hills are of every fantastic shape imaginable, while the trees are quite unlike anything to be found in the west. Also, whenever one travels, there are unexpected waterfalls, gorges, vistas whose cool blue-green depths are as magically inviting as they are perilous, for Cathay is a haunted land of dragons and ghosts and outlaws. Although I saw neither ghost nor dragon, I did see many brigands. Cathay's beautiful, seemingly empty landscape is a hazardous place for the traveler. But then, wherever one goes on this earth, all things are spoiled by men.

The pavilion was made of yellow brick with a steep tile roof. Moss grew in every fissure, and bats hung from beams wreathed in cobwebs. The old servant who prepared our meal treated Master Li as an equal; and ignored us. We did not care. Hungrily we devoured fresh fish to the soothing sound of fast water striking rocks.

As we knelt on rustic mats, Master Li discussed the meaning—or a meaning—of Tao. "Literally," he said, "Tao means a road or a way. Like a highway. Or a *low* way." I noticed that Master Li's hands looked as if they were made of fragile alabaster, and I realized then how much older he was than I had first thought. Later I learned that he was more than a century old.

"Where," I asked, "does the way—*your* way, that is —begin?"

"*My* way would begin with me. But I don't have a way. I am part of the Way."

"Which is what?"

The duke of Sheh began to hum contentedly, and pick his teeth. He enjoyed this sort of discourse.

"Which is what is. The primal unity of all creation. The first step that a man can take along the Way is to be in harmony with the laws of the universe, with what we call the always-so."

"How is this done?"

"Think of the Way as water. Water always takes the low ground, and permeates all things." I had the uneasy sense that I was again in the Gangetic plain, where complex things are expressed so simply that they become utterly mysterious.

To my astonishment, Master Li saw into my mind. "My dear barbarian, you think me deliberately obscure. But I can't help myself. After all, the doctrine of the Way is known as the *wordless* doctrine. Therefore, whatever I say is pointless. You can no more know what I know to be the Way than I can feel the pain in your left knee, which you keep shifting on the mat because you are not yet used to our way of sitting."

"But you perceive my discomfort without actually feeling it. So perhaps I can perceive the Way without following it, as you do."

"Very good," said the duke, and belched to show his satisfaction not only with the meal but with us. The Cathayans regard the belch as the mind-stomach's sincerest utterance.

"Then think of the Way as a condition in which there are no opposites or differences. Nothing is hot. Nothing is cold. Nothing is long. Nothing is short. Such concepts are meaningless except in regard to other things. To the Way, they are all one."

"But to us they are many."

"So they seem. Yes, there are no *real* differences between things. In essence, there is only the dust that makes us up, a dust which takes temporary forms, yet never

415

ceases to be dust. It is important to know this. Just as it is important to know that it is not possible to rebel against the fact of nature. Life and death are the same. Without the one, there cannot be the other. And without the other, there cannot be the one. But, finally, neither exists except in relationship to the other. There is nothing but the always-so."

Although I found this conception of a primal unity acceptable, I could not overlook those differences which Master Li so blithely drowned in his sea of the always-so. "But surely," I said, "a man must be judged for his actions. There are good actions and bad. The Truth and the Lie . . ." I spoke as the grandson of Zoroaster. When I had finished, Master Li answered me with a curious parable.

"You speak wisely." The old man bowed his head courteously. "Naturally, in the relative conduct of a given life there are seemly actions and unseemly ones, and I am sure that we would agree as to what is proper and what is not. But the Way transcends such things. Let me give you an example. Suppose you were a maker of bronze—"

"Actually, he is a smelter of iron, Master Li, a useful art which the barbarians have mastered." The duke looked at me as if he himself had invented me, out of primal unified dust.

Master Li ignored the duke's aside. "You are a maker of bronze. You want to cast a bell, and you have prepared a crucible for the molten metal. But when you pour out the fiery metal, the bronze refuses to flow. It says, 'No, I don't want to be a bell. I want to be a sword, like the flawless sword of Wu.' As a bronzemaker, you would be most distressed with this naughty metal, wouldn't you?"

"Yes. But metal may not choose its mold. The smelter has that choice."

"No." The softly spoken no was as chilling in its effect as Gosala's thrown string. "You may not rebel against the Way, any more than your hand can rebel against your arm or the metal against the mold. All things are a part of the universe, which is the always-so."

"What are the fundamental laws? And who was their creator?"

"The universe is the unity of all things, and to accept the Way is to accept the fact of this unity. Alive or dead, you are forever a part of the always-so, whose laws are simply the laws of becoming. When life comes, it is time.

When life goes, this is natural, too. To accept with tranquillity whatever happens is to put oneself beyond sorrow or joy. That is how you follow the Way, by achieving wu-wei."

I was again puzzled by that phrase, which means, literally, do nothing.

"But how is our world to function if one is entirely passive? Someone must cast bronze so that we may have bells, swords."

"When we say do nothing, we mean do nothing that is not natural or spontaneous. You are an archer?"

"Yes. I was trained as a warrior."

"So was I." Master Li looked as unlike a warrior as it is possible to look. "Have you noticed how easy it is to hit the mark when you are idly practicing on your own?"

"Yes."

"But when you are in a contest with others, when there is a golden prize, don't you find it more difficult to hit the mark than when you are alone or not in competition?"

"Yes."

"When you try too hard, you become tense. When you are tense, you are not at your best. Well, to avoid that sort of tension is what we mean by wu-wei. Or to put it another way, cease to be self-conscious in what you do. Be natural. Have you ever cut up an animal for food?"

"Yes."

"Do you find it difficult to separate the parts of the body?"

"Yes. But I'm not a butcher or a Magian—I mean a priest."

"Neither am I. But I've observed butchers at work. They are always swift, always accurate. What is hard for us to do is simple for them. Why? Well, I once asked the lonely one's chief butcher how it was that he could dismember an ox in the time it would take me to clean a small fish. 'I don't really know,' he said. 'My senses seem to stand still, and my spirit—or whatever—takes over.' That's what we mean by wu wei. Do nothing that is not natural, that is not in harmony with the principles of nature. The four seasons come and go without anxiety because they follow the Way. The wise man contemplates this order, and begins to understand the harmony implicit in the universe."

"I agree that it is wise to accept the natural world. But even the wisest man must do all he can to support what is good and to defy what is evil . . ."

"Oh, my dear barbarian, this idea of doing is what makes all the trouble. Don't *do!* That's the best doing. Rest in the position of doing nothing. Cast yourself into the ocean of existence. Forget what you take to be good, evil. Since neither exists except in relation to the other, forget the relationship. Let things take care of themselves. Free your own spirit. Make yourself as serene as a flower, as a tree. Because all true things return to their root, without knowing that they do so. Those things—that butterfly, that tree—which lack knowledge never leave the state of primal simplicity. But should they become conscious, like us, they would lose their naturalness. They would lose the Way. For a man, perfection is possible only in the womb. Then he is like the uncarved block before the sculptor shapes him, and in so doing spoils the block. In this life, he who needs others is forever shackled. He who is needed by others is forever sad."

But I could not accept the passivity of Master Li's doctrine of the Way any more than I could comprehend the desirability of the Buddha's nirvana.

I asked Master Li about the real world—or the world of things since the word real is apt to inspire the Taoist sage to pose a series of self-satisfied questions as to the nature of the real. "What you say, I understand. Or *begin* to understand," I added hastily. "I may not follow the Way, but you have given me a glimpse of it. I am in your debt. Now let us speak practically. States must be governed. How is this to be done if the ruler practices wu-wei?"

"Is there such a perfect ruler?" Master Li sighed. "The busy-ness of the world of things tends to preclude absorption with the Way."

"We dukes may only glimpse the road that you wise men take." The duke of Sheh looked very pleased with himself, and somewhat drowsy. "Yet we honor your journey. Deplore our own high busy place. Wait for you to tell us how to govern our people."

"Ideally, Lord Duke, the prince-sage who governs ought to empty the minds of the people while filling their bellies. He must weaken their will while strengthening their bones. If the people lack knowledge, they will lack desire. If they lack desire, they will do nothing but what is natural for men to do. Then good will be universal."

As statecraft, this did not differ too much from the precepts of the brutal Huan. "But"—I was most respectful—"if a man should acquire knowledge and if he should then desire to change his lot—or even change the state itself—how would the prince-sage respond to such a man?"

"Oh, the prince should kill him." Master Li smiled. Between two long incisors, there was only dark gum. He suddenly resembled one of the sleeping bats overhead.

"Then those who follow the Way have no feeling against taking human life?"

"Why should they? Death is as natural as life. Besides, the one who dies is not lost. No. Quite the contrary. Once gone, he is beyond all harm."

"Will his spirit be born again?"

"The dust will reassemble, certainly. But that is not, perhaps, what you mean by rebirth."

"When the spirits of the dead go to the Yellow Springs," I asked, "what happens?" In Cathay, when someone dies, the common people say that he has gone to the Yellow Springs. But should you ask them where and what that place is, answers tend to be confusing. From what I could gather, the notion of the Yellow Springs is very old; it seems to be a kind of eternal limbo, like the Greek Hades. There is no day of judgment. The good and the bad share the same fate.

"It would seem to me that the Yellow Springs are everywhere." Master Li stroked his right hand with his left. A magical gesture? "If they are everywhere, then no one can go there, since he is already there. But, of course, man is born, lives, dies. Although he is a part of the whole, the fact of his brief existence inclines him to resist wholeness. Well, we follow the Way in order not to resist the whole. Now, it is plain to all, or nearly all"—he bowed to me—"that when the body decomposes, the mind"—he patted his stomach—"vanishes with the body. Those who have not experienced the Way find this deplorable, even frightening. We are not frightened. Since we identify with the cosmic process, we do not resist the always-so. In the face of both life and death, the perfect man does nothing, just as the true sage originates nothing. He merely comtemplates the universe until he becomes

419

the universe. This is what we call the mysterious absorption."

"To do nothing—" I began.

"—is an immense spiritual labor," ended Master Li. "The wise man has no ambitions. Therefore, he has no failures. He who never fails always succeeds. And he who always succeeds is all-powerful."

"There is," I said, "no answer to that, Master Li." I was already used to the circular argument which is to the Athenians what the wheel of the doctrine is to Buddhists.

To my surprise, the duke challenged Master Li on the subject of how best to govern. "Surely," he said, "those who follow the Way have always opposed the death penalty on the ground that no man has the right to pronounce such an awful judgment upon another. To do so is the very opposite of wu-wei."

"Many followers of the Way agree with you, Lord Duke. Personally, I find the matter of no consequence. After all, nature is ruthless. Floods drown us. Famine starves us. Pestilence kills us. Nature is indifferent. Should man be unlike nature? Of course not. Nevertheless, I find sympathetic the notion that it might be better to let our world go its own way and not try to govern it at all, since truly good government is not possible. Everyone knows that the more good laws the ruler makes, the more thieves and bandits will be created in order to break those laws. And everyone knows that when the ruler takes too much for himself in taxes, the people will starve. Yet he always does; and they always do. So let us live in perfect harmony with the universe. Let us make no laws of any kind, and be happy."

"Without law, there can be no happiness." I was firm.

"Probably not." Master Li was blithe.

"I am sure that there must be a right way to govern," I said. "Certainly, we are well acquainted with all the wrong ways."

"No doubt. But, finally, who knows?" He bent like a reed to every argument.

I was growing impatient. "What," I asked, "*can* a man know?"

The answer was swift. "He can know that to be at one with the Way is to be like heaven, and so impenetrable. He can know that if he possesses the Way, though his body ceases to exist, he is not destroyed. The Way is like a cup which is never empty, which never needs to be filled. All complexities are reduced to simplicity. All opposites are blended, all contrasts harmonized. The Way is as calm as eternity itself. *Only cling to the unity.*" Master Li stopped. That was that.

The duke sat very straight, head held high; he was sound asleep and snoring softly. Below us the water sounded like a seashell held close to the ear.

"Tell me, Master Li," I asked, "who created the Way?"

The old man looked down at his now folded hands. "I do not know whose child it is."

3

I WAS NEVER PRESENTED TO THE SON of heaven. Apparently there was no protocol for the reception of a barbarian ambassador who was also a slave. I did watch several ceremonies at which the duke of Chou presided. Since he always gave the appearance of divinity, he looked perfectly suited to his symbolic role. A good thing, according to my master, "because he is less intelligent than most people."

We often took walks with Master Li and his disciples. Plainly, the duties of the archivist of Chou were not onerous; he was always free to talk to us at length about his wordless doctrine. He gracefully dismissed my grandfather's dogma of good and evil on the ground that the primal unity precluded such small divisions. I chose not to argue with him. I did describe for him Gosala, Mahavira, the Buddha, Pythagoras. He found only the Buddha interesting. He admired the four noble truths, and thought the Buddha's triumph over the senses consistent with wuwei. "But how," asked Master Li, "can he be so certain that when he dies he will be snuffed out?"

"Because he has achieved perfect enlightenment."

We were standing near the altar of earth. A high wind knocked leaves from the trees: winter was near. A dozen young men of the knightly class stood at a respectful distance. "If he thinks he has, he has not. Because he is still thinking." This easy play on words delighted the young men; they giggled appreciatively.

The duke said, "Wisdom! Wisdom!"

I made no defense of the Buddha. After all, neither

421

the Cathayan way nor the Buddhist noble truths has ever appealed to me. Each requires the banishment of the world as we know it. I can see how this might be a very desirable thing, but I cannot see how it is to be accomplished. Yet I am grateful to Master Li because, inadvertently, his performance that afternoon at the altar of earth set in train those events that made it possible for me to return to Persia.

Master Li sat on a rock. The young men made a circle about us. One asked, "Master, when the Cloud-spirit met Chaos, he asked him what was the best way to bring into harmony heaven and earth, and Chaos said that he didn't know."

"Wise is Chaos." Master Li nodded approvingly.

"Most wise," said the young man. "But the Cloud-spirit said, 'The people look to me as a model. I must do something to restore a balance in their affairs.'"

"Presumptuous," said Master Li.

"Most presumptuous," the young man echoed. But he persevered. "The Cloud-spirit asked, 'What shall I do? Things are very bad on earth.' And Chaos agreed that the world's basic principles are constantly violated and the true nature of things constantly subverted. But Chaos said that the reason for this is—"

"—the mistake of governing men." Master Li completed what was obviously an ancient dialogue. "Yes. That was —and is—a wise observation."

"But," said the young man, "the Cloud-spirit was not satisfied . . ."

". . . never is." Master Li's cloak was billowing about him in the sharp wind, and the strands of white hair on his head stood straight up. "But he should have been convinced when Chaos told him that the idea of *doing* in the world is what makes all the trouble. *Desist!*" Master Li's voice was suddenly as loud as that of a bronze bell struck with a hammer in a high wind.

"But, Master Li, are we to follow Chaos and not the Cloud-spirit?" The young man looked as if he might be asking an actual question instead of taking part in a litany.

"In this matter, yes. Particularly when Chaos said, 'Nourish your mind. Rest in the position of doing nothing, and things will take care of themselves. Never ask the names of things, do not try to figure out the secret workings of nature. All things flourish of themselves.'"

"Beautiful," said the duke of Sheh.

"Your word for Chaos—" I began.

"—is also one of our words for heaven," said Master Li.

"I see," I said, not seeing at all. Since things cannot flourish without order, heaven must be the antithesis of Chaos. But I was not about to engage the old master in a debate. He had the advantage of knowing what all the words of his language meant—and that is the secret of power, Democritus. No, I will not explain myself just yet.

One of the young men was not as delighted as the others with Master Li's celebration of inactivity. He came forward, head bowed; a slight youth, his whole body was atremble—whether from the cold wind or from awe, I could not tell. "But surely, Master, the Cloud-spirit's desire for harmony between heaven and earth should not be disregarded. After all, why else do we pray to earth in this place?" The young man bowed to the nearby altar.

"Oh, we must observe what is proper." Master Li tightened his cloak about him; sniffed the sharp smell of snow upon the air.

"Would Chaos disapprove of such observances?"

"No, no. Chaos would accept them as natural as the . . . the fall of the year. Or the winter sleep of the root in the ground. Do nothing that is not natural—and ritual is natural—and all will be for the best."

"Then, Master, do you agree that if a ruler could for just one day submit himself to ritual everyone under heaven would respond to his goodness?"

Master Li looked up at the young man and frowned. The other disciples were wide-eyed. Even the duke was suddenly attentive. Some sort of heresy had been spoken. The young man shuddered convulsively, as if with fever.

"What is this goodness that you refer to?" The normally seductive voice of Master Li was shrill.

"I do not know. All I know is that through correct ritual, goodness can be attained. And for the state to flourish, goodness must have its source in the ruler himself. It cannot be got from others."

"The son of heaven reflects heaven, which is all things, as we know. But this goodness, what is it if it is not wu-wei?"

"It is the thing done as well as not done. It is not doing to others what you would not like done to yourself. And if you are able to behave in this way, there will be no feelings of opposition to you, or—"

Master Li gave a somewhat unceremonious hoot of laughter. "You are quoting Master K'ung! Even though you must know that he and I are as unlike as the bright side of the hill is to the dark."

"But surely, light or dark, it is all the same hill," said the duke mildly.

"No thanks to Master K'ung. Or Confucius, as the vulgar name him. You must go to Wei, my boy." Master Li was helped to his feet by two disciples. The shivering youth was silent, eyes to the ground. "Or wherever Confucius happens to be for the moment. He stays no place for very long. He is always greeted with deference. But then he starts to harangue and annoy officials, even rulers. Why, he once tried to instruct the son of heaven himself! Oh, it was mortifying. But then he is a vain and foolish man, who thinks of nothing but holding public office. He lusts for worldly distinction and power. Years ago he held some little office in the ministry of police at Lu. But since he's only a knight, he could never be what he wanted to be, which was the minister. So he moved on to Key. But the prime minister found him—I quote the minister's very words: 'Impractical, conceited, with many peculiarities, including an obsession with the details of old ceremonies.'" Master Li turned to the duke of Sheh. "Later I believe that your cousin"—Master Li smiled into the freezing wind—"the late duke of Wei, gave him a minor post."

The duke nodded. "My cousin, the incomparable one, did appoint him to some post or other. But then the incomparable one died. Rather," he said to me, "the same sort of death that recently visited the all-compassionate one at Ch'in. Neither could stop drinking millet wine. But the incomparable one was as charming as the all-compassionate one was boorish." The duke turned to Master Li. "Actually, Confucius left Wei before the incomparable one died . . ."

"We heard that there had been a quarrel between Confucius and the ministry of the incomparable one." Master Li pulled his cloak over his head. We were all growing cold.

"If there was, it's been patched up. Only yesterday, the son of heaven told me that Confucius is once more in Wei, where our young cousin Duke Chu regards him most highly."

"Mysterious are the ways of heaven," said Master Li.

I was freezing; and bored with so much talk of a man I knew nothing about. Although Fan Ch'ih had liked to quote Confucius, I remembered little of what Fan Ch'ih had said. It is hard to take seriously another world's wise man, particularly at second hand.

"Confucius has been invited to return to Lu by Duke Ai," said the shivering young man; his face was as gray as the clouds in the winter sky. The light was failing.

"Are you certain?" The duke condescended to look at the youth.

"Yes, Lord Duke. I've just come from Lu. I wanted to stay and meet Confucius. But I was obliged to come home."

"I *am* sorry," whispered Master Li. Malice made his ancient face look almost young.

"So am I, Master." The young man was straightforward. "I admire Confucius for all those things that he does not do."

"Yes, he is noted for what he does not do." The duke was quite serious, and I was careful not to laugh.

Master Li caught my eye, and smiled collusively. He turned to the young man. "Tell us which of those things he does *not* do that you most revere."

"There are four things he does not do that I revere. He takes nothing for granted. He is never overpositive. Or obstinate. Or egotistical."

Master Li responded to the young man's challenge. "Although it is true that Confucius takes little for granted, he is certainly the most positive, the most obstinate, the most egotistical man within the four seas. I met him only once. I found him respectful until he began to lecture us on the proper observances of this-and-that ceremony. As I listened to him I thought to myself, With such self-importance, such consequential airs, who could live under the same roof with this man? In his presence, what is purest white looks blurred, while the power that is most sufficing becomes inadequate." These last lines were in verse, beautifully rendered, with the north wind for accompaniment. The disciples applauded. The trembling youth did not. Then all light left the sky and it was night, and winter.

On the way back to our quarters the duke spoke affectionately of Confucius. "I was never a disciple, of course. My rank made that impossible. But I used to listen to him whenever I was in Lu. Also, I used to see him in Wei,

And come to think of it, didn't I see him in . . ." While the duke rambled inconsequentially, I had but one thought: We must go to Lu, where I will find Fan Ch'ih; if he is still alive, he will set me free.

The next few days I affected such interest in Confucius that the duke caught fire. "He is truly the wisest man within the four seas. In fact, he is probably a divine sage, as well as an intimate friend of mine. Master Li is superb, of course. But as you may have noticed, he's not really of *this* world because he's already a part of the Way, while Confucius is a guide for the rest of us *to* the Way." The duke was so pleased with this last statement that he repeated it.

I responded rapturously, "Oh, what I would give to sit at the feet of a divine sage!" I sighed. "But Lu is so far away."

"It's not at all far away. One goes east, along the river for about ten days. Quite an easy trip, actually. But you and I are going south across the great plain to the Yangtze River and from there to the seaport of Kweichi and then . . . on to the land of gold!"

But I had planted a seed which I nurtured daily. The duke was tempted. "After all," he mused, "Lu has a number of seaports, inferior to Kweichi but still serviceable." Apparently one could find a ship for Champa there. Although leaving from Lu would lengthen the sea voyage the land journey would be shortened. The duke confessed that he did not fancy crossing the great plain with a convoy of dragon's bone. The great plain is aswarm with thieves. Also, he was obliged to admit, there was a large market for dragon's bone in Lu.

Each day the duke became more tempted by the thought of Lu. "I am an uncle *by blood* of Duke Ai, a charming youth, who's now been on the throne for eleven years. My half-brother, his father, was extremely musical. My half-brother his uncle was not. The uncle was duke until he was driven out by the barons, as you know. But, of course, you don't know. How could you?"

We were walking in a grove of mulberry trees not far from the knoll where the unwanted newborn babies are left to die. As we strolled, the catlike sounds of dying babies mingled with the chatter of southbound birds. Cathayans put to death at birth any deformed male and most of the females. Thus do they keep in balance a population that shows no sign at all of getting to be too large. I was never able to understand why the custom of infant exposure should be so resolutely practiced in such a large, rich, empty country.

Naturally, the practice is universal and necessary: no society wants too many breeding females, particularly the Greek states where the soil is too poor to sustain a large population. Nevertheless, sooner or later, every Greek city becomes overcrowded. When this happens, numbers of people are sent away to start a new colony, in Sicily or Italy or Africa—wherever their ships will take them. As a result, Greek colonies now extend from the Black Sea to the pillars of Heracles—and all because of the harsh terrain of Attica and most of the Aegean islands. The Greeks like to boast that their prowess in war and sport comes from the selective way in which they kill off not only unwanted females but imperfect males. Only the strong—not to mention the beautiful—are allowed to survive, or so they say. But Democritus thinks that the Athenians must have grown lax in recent years. He tells me that most of the male population of this city are highly ill-favored, as well as susceptible to all sorts of disfiguring diseases, particularly those of the skin. I wouldn't know. I am blind.

When I asked Fan Ch'ih why the Cathayans always pretend that there are too many people in their lovely empty world, he used the same phrase that the dictator Huan had used: "When we were few and things were many, there was universal happiness. Now that things are few, men many . . ." I suppose that there is some religious reason for all this. But I was never able to find out what it was. When the Cathayans choose not to tell you something, they are exquisitely and tediously uninformative.

The duke reminisced about his half-brother Duke Chao, who had been driven out of Lu some thirty years earlier. "He was a bad-tempered man. Much older than I. Although he was not our father's favorite, he was the heir. Everyone acknowledged this, even the hereditary ministers. Chao was *always* respectful of me. In fact—and this is very important to remember—he privately acknowledged that I took precedence over him because my title, which came to me through my mother, the duchess of Sheh, is the oldest title in the Middle Kingdom." Even at that time I knew that my master had invented for himself not only a dynasty but a country. Actually, he was the son of either the third wife or the first concubine of the old duke of Lu. No one seems certain which. But all agreed that he might well have been styled marquis had he not preferred to be the self-invented duke of the non-existent holy ground.

My fantastic master peered at the hill where lay, amongst ten thousand tiny white bones, a half-dozen blue-gray babies. Lazy vultures hovered in the bright wintry air. I thought of the dead and dying at Bactra. Said to myself a prayer for the dying.

"Trivial things can set in motion great catastrophes." The duke paused. I looked attentive. In the Middle Kingdom, one never knows what is a proverb and what is nonsense. To a foreign ear, the two can sound perilously alike.

"Yes," the duke continued, arranging the jade, gold and ivory ornaments on his belt, "a cockfight changed the history of Lu. A cockfight! Heaven never ceases to laugh at us. A baron of the Chi family owned a formida-ble fighting bird. A connection of the ducal family owned another. So they decided to pit their birds against each other. The contest was held outside the High South Gate of the capital city. Oh, what a tragic day. I know. I was there. I was very young, of course. A boy."

I later learned that the duke had not attended the celebrated cockfight. But since he had so often said that he was present on that famous occasion, I am certain that he had come to believe his own story. It took me many years to get used to people who tell lies for no purpose. Since Persians must not lie, they do not lie—generally speaking. We have a racial horror of not telling the truth which goes back to the Wise Lord. Greeks have no such feeling, and they lie imaginatively. Cathayans lie conve-niently. Most eunuchs and the duke of Sheh lie for plea-sure. But I do the duke an injustice. With him, truth and fantasy were so mingled that I am certain that he never knew which was which. He lived in a made-up world at a sharp or right angle, as Pythagoras would say, to the always-so.

"The Chi baron put a subtle but swift-acting poison on the spurs of his fighting bird. After a brief skirmish, the ducal bird fell dead. I don't need to tell you that there was a good deal of ill feeling that sunny day at the High South Gate. Half the city was there, including Duke Chao himself. The Chi family were delighted. The ducal family were not. There were all sorts of fights as the baron collected his money purses. The wicked baron then retired to the Chi palace for the night. The next morning there was a crowd outside the palace. During the night, the poison had been detected. Furious, the duke himself arrived with his personal guard. He ordered the arrest of the baron. But, disguised as a servant, the culprit had already slipped out of the house and fled north to Key. Duke Chao gave chase. Then—"

Abruptly, my master sat down on a stump; he looked grave, portentous. "These are bad times for the Middle Kingdom." He lowered his voice as if someone might overhear us; yet it was plain that we were entirely alone. "The Chi family came to the aid of their relative. So did the Meng family. So did the Shu family. These are the three baronial families that rule illegally in Lu. At the Yellow River, their troops attacked my brother's army. Yes, the heaven-appointed duke of Lu, the descendant of the Yellow Emperor, the descendant of Duke Tan of Chou, was attacked by his own slaves and forced to swim across the Yellow River and take refuge in the duchy of Key. And though Duke Chao was kind to him he would not help him regain his rightful place. The Chi family is too powerful, their private army is the largest in the Middle Kingdom, and they lord it over Lu. In fact—oh, I shudder even to say this!—the head of the family *on more than one occasion has worn the ducal insignia*. The impiety! The impiety! Right then and there, heaven should have made plain its decree. But heaven was silent. And my poor brother died in exile." Just as the sleeve was about to cover once again the duke's eyes, a swarm of black birds diverted his attention. He studied their formation, in search of omens. If he found any, he said nothing. But he did smile and I took that to be a good omen—for me.

"Who succeeded your brother, Lord Duke?"

"Our younger brother, the open-hearted one. Then he died, and his son succeeded him, my lovely nephew Duke Ai."

"And the Chi family?"

"They now obey their duke in all things. How can they not? To do otherwise would be to oppose heaven's will. You will see them cringe in the presence of the heir of the glorious Tan."

I was elated. We were going to Lu.

It was spring when we left Loyang. The first almond blossoms had opened, and the fields were turning from muddy red-brown to yellow-green. On every side, flowering dogwood looked like pink clouds fallen to earth. I must say that all things seem possible when new leaves unfold. For me, the spring is the best time of the year.

We traveled by land. Once or twice the duke tried to go by river barge, but the current was too swift. Incidentally, these barges can go upriver as well as down. To travel against the current, lines from the barge are attached to a team of oxen that then pulls the barge upstream. The oxen travel along special roads cut out of the soft stone that edges the river. In this way, even narrow gorges can be navigated in every season of the year except early spring, when unexpected floods make river travel dangerous.

I was charmed by the countryside. The soil is rich. The forests are magical. Best of all, we were never far from the silvery river. At night, its soft, rushing sound became a part of pleasant, soothing dreams.

Occasionally our road brought us to the riverbank itself. Oddly shaped islands looked as if they had been dropped into the silver water by some god or devil. Many resembled miniature limestone mountains, covered with cypress and pines. On each island there is at least one shrine to the deity of the place. Some of these island shrines are beautifully made with glazed tile roofs; others are rough work, dating from the time of the Yellow Emperor—or so the people say.

In the midst of a pale-green and yellow bamboo grove, the duke's steward gave a terrible cry. "Lord Duke! A dragon!"

Sword in hand, the duke leaped to the ground and took up his position behind the rear wheel of his personal wagon. Everyone else vanished into the grove, except for a dozen knights who had elected to travel with us from Loyang. They drew their swords. I was alarmed; and curious.

The duke sniffed the air. "Yes," he whispered. "He is nearby. He is very ancient. Very fierce. Follow me."

As the duke made his way into the bamboo grove, the new shoots bent before him as if he were some sort of celestial wind. Then we lost sight of him. But we could hear his shrill cry: "Death!" This was followed by the

430

noise of some large beast crashing through the grove in the opposite direction.

A moment later the duke returned, pale face bright with sweat. "He escaped, worse luck! If only I'd been on horseback, I would have had his head by now." With one sleeve, the duke dried his face. "Of course, they all know me, which makes it even more difficult for me to bring one to earth."

"But they are only beasts," I said. "How can beasts know people by reputation?"

"How does your dog know you? He's a beast, isn't he? Anyway, dragons are in a class by themselves. They are neither human nor beast but something else. Also, they live practically forever. It is said that some are as old as the Yellow Emperor. And they know their enemy, as you saw just now. One glimpse of me, and he fled in terror."

Later one of the knights told me that he had actually seen the so-called dragon, which proved to be a water buffalo. "I was standing beside the steward on the first wagon. Either the steward is blind or he deliberately pretended to see a dragon." Then the young knight told me an amusing story about the duke. In fact, the story is so amusing that before I left Cathay I had heard at least a dozen versions of it.

"As you know, the duke of Sheh has a passion not only for dragon's bone but for dragons."

"Oh, yes," I said. "He has killed many."

The young knight smiled. "So he says. But in the Middle Kingdom there are few if any dragons left, except in the mind of the duke of Sheh."

I was startled. After all, there are dragons in almost every country and many reliable witnesses have described encounters with them. When I was a child there was a famous one in Bactria. He used to eat children and goats. Eventually he died or went away.

"But if there are so few," I asked, "how do you explain the quantities of dragon's bone that the duke collects, particularly in the west?"

"Old, old bones. Once upon a time there must have been millions of dragons within the four seas, but that was in the time of the Yellow Emperor. What bones you find nowadays are so old that they've turned to stone. But your duke is a madman on the subject of living dragons, as you know."

"He's hardly mad. He makes quite a good living selling dragon's bones."

"Of course. But the duke's passion for living dragons is something else. Some years ago he visited Ch'u, a wild southern country on the Yangtze River, where dragons can still be found. Naturally, word spread that the famous devotee of dragons was staying in the capital, in a bedroom on the second floor of a small guesthouse.

"One morning, at dawn, the duke awakened with a start; sensing that he was being spied on, he got up and went to the window and pulled back the shutters and there, staring at him, teeth bared in a friendly smile, was a dragon. Terrified, the duke hurried downstairs. In the main hall he stumbled over what looked to be a rolled-up carpet. But it was not a carpet. It was the tail of the dragon, which saluted him by banging up and down on the floor. The duke fainted dead away. And that, as far as we know, is the closest that the duke of Sheh has ever got to a living dragon." Although I never dared ask the duke if this story was true, he himself alluded to it our first day at Ch'u-fu.

The capital of Lu is much like Loyang, but considerably older. It is built on that grid pattern which is a characteristic of those cities founded by the Chou dynasty. But between the four broad, straight avenues, there are countless side streets so narrow that two people cannot pass unless each flattens himself against a wall, all the while running the risk of being drenched by the contents of a chamber pot. Yet the smells of a Cathayan city are more agreeable than not because pungent foods are cooked on braziers at every crossing and sweet-smelling wood is burned in private as well as in public houses.

The people themselves have a curious but not disagreeable odor, as I have noted before. A Cathayan crowd smells more of oranges than of sweat. I don't know why. Perhaps their yellow skin has something to do with their odor. Certainly, they eat few oranges; and bathe far less often than Persians, whose sweat has a much stronger smell. Nothing, of course, can compare with the fragrance of those woollen drawers that Athenian youths put on in the fall of the year and do not change until the fall of the next year. Democritus tells me that the upper-class young men wash themselves daily at the gymnasium. He says that they use not only oil to make their skins glossy but water as well. But why, once clean, do they put on those filthy woollen drawers? In matters like these, Democritus, do not dispute the remaining senses of a blind man.

The ducal palace is not unlike that of the son of heaven —which is to say, the palace is old and dilapidated and the banners in front of the main door are torn and dusty.

"The duke is away." My master could read the message of the banners as easily as I can—could—read Akkadian script. "Well, we must make ourselves known to the chamberlain."

I was surprised to find that the entrance hall to the palace was empty except for a pair of drowsy guards at the door to the inner court. Despite my master's assurance to the contrary, the duke of Lu is as powerless as the so-called son of heaven. But at least the duke of Chao has a symbolic role to enact, and his palace at Loyang is always crowded with pilgrims from every part of the Middle Kingdom. The fact that the duke's possessions of heaven's mandate is a fiction does not deter the simple folk. They still come to gaze upon the lonely one, to receive his blessing, to make him an offering in either money or kind. It is said that the duke of Chao lives entirely on the proceeds of the faithful. Although the duke of Lu is wealthier than his cousin at Loyang, he is nowhere near as wealthy as any of the three lordly families of Lu.

While we waited for the chamberlain, the duke told me his version of the dragon story. It was much the same as the one that I had heard from the young knight except that the protagonist was not the duke himself but a pretentious courtier, and the moral was: "Avoid false enthusiasm. By affecting to like what he did not know, a very silly man was frightened to death. In all things, one must be faithful to what is true." The duke could be remarkably sententious; but then, I have yet to come across a really inspired liar who was not positively lyric on the virtue of truth-telling.

The chamberlain saluted the duke with every mark of respect, looked at me with polite wonder; then told us that Duke Ai was in the south. "But we expect him any moment. The messengers found him yesterday. You can imagine how distraught we are, Lord Duke."

"Because my illustrious nephew has gone hunting?" The duke raised one eyebrow, a signal that more information was needed.

"I thought you knew. For three days now we have been at war. And if the duke does not report this state of affairs

433

to the ancestors, we shall lose. Oh, it is a terrible crisis, my lord. As you see, all Lu is in a state of chaos." I thought of the placid everyday crowds that I had just seen in the streets of the capital. Obviously, chaos is a relative matter in the Middle Kingdom, and as I have already noted, the Cathayan word for chaos is also a word for heaven—for creation, too.

"We've heard nothing, Chamberlain. War with whom?"

"Key." Whenever the hegemony is spoken of—and when is it not?—this nation to the north of the Yellow River is always considered the one most likely to receive heaven's mandate. Originally, Key's wealth came from salt. Today Key is easily the richest and most advanced of all the Cathayan states. Incidentally, the first Cathayan coins were struck there, which makes Key a sort of eastern Lydia.

"The army of Key is at the Stone Gates." This is the border between Key and Lu. "Our troops are ready, of course. But there can be no victory until the duke goes to the temple of the ancestors and reports first to the Yellow Emperor and then to our founder, Duke Tan. Not until he has made his report will we receive their blessings."

"Have you consulted the shell of the prescient tortoise?"

"The shell has been prepared. But only the duke can interpret heaven's message."

At moments of crisis in any Cathayan realm, the outer side of a tortoise shell is coated with blood. The chief augur then holds a rod of heated bronze to the inner shell until fissures or designs appear on the blood-coated surface. Theoretically, only the ruler may interpret these signs from heaven. Actually, only the chief augur knows how to interpret the pattern, a process even more complex than the Middle Kingdom's usual form of divination, which involves the throwing of yarrow sticks. Once the sticks are thrown at random, their hexagonal relationship to one another is duly looked up in an ancient text called *The Book of Changes*. The resulting commentary is not unlike the sort of thing the pythoness at Delphi produces. The only difference is that the book does not demand gold for its prophecies.

The chamberlain assured us that as soon as Duke Ai had fulfilled his ceremonial duties, he would receive his ducal uncle. Although the ducal uncle hinted broadly that an invitation to stay in the palace would not be rejected out of hand, the chamberlain chose not to understand him. In a bad mood, the duke withdrew.

We then went to the central market, where the duke's steward was already negotiating with the dragon's-bone sellers. I cannot think why I so much enjoy Cathayan markets. Obviously, the sheer foreign-ness must have something to do with it. After all, a market is a market anywhere on earth. But the Cathayans are more imaginative than other people. Their displays of food resemble exquisite paintings or sculpture, and the variety of things on sale is infinite: baskets from Ch'in, banners from Cheng, silk cords from Key—ten thousand things.

The duke was too important to speak to the retailers of his commodity but he did acknowledge their deep bows with a series of hieratic gestures. Meanwhile, under his breath, he was saying to me, "I knew we should've gone south. If there's a real war, we'll be caught in it. Worse, my nephew will be too busy to look after me properly. There will be no official reception, no acknowledgment of esteem, no place to stay." This last concerned him most. He hated to pay for lodgings—or anything else, for that matter.

I noticed that the war interested the market people not at all. "Why aren't they more excited?" I asked as the duke and I made our way through the crowded market, all things marvelously vivid beneath the low sky. For some reason, the Cathayan sky seems closer to earth than it does elsewhere; no doubt heaven is constantly peering at the dukes, trying to decide to whom to give the mandate.

"Why should they be? There's always some sort of war between Key and Lu. Terrible nuisance, of course, for the duke and the court but of no real concern to the common people."

"But they could be killed. The city could be burned . . ."

"Oh, we don't have that sort of war here. This isn't Ch'in, where war is a bloody business because the Ch'inese are wolfmen. No. We are civilized. The two armies will meet at the Stone Gates—as usual. There'll be a skirmish or two. A few hundred men will be killed or wounded. Prisoners will be taken and held for exchange or ransom. Then there will be a treaty. Our people love making treaties. At the moment there are ten thousand treaties between the states of the Middle Kingdom, and since each of those treaties is sure to be broken, that means yet another treaty to replace the old one."

Actually, affairs of the Middle Kingdom are not as bad or as good as the duke led me to believe. Sixty years earlier the prime minister of the weak state of Sung had arranged for a peace conference. As a result, an armistice was declared. For ten years there was peace in the Middle Kingdom. Ten years is quite a long time, as human history goes. Although there have been many minor wars in recent years, the principles of the armistice of Sung are still given lip service by everyone, which explains why no single ruler has yet thought the time auspicious to seize the hegemony.

The duke proposed that we go to the great temple. "I'm sure we'll find the Chi family there, committing their usual blasphemies. Only the legitimate heir of Duke Tan can speak to heaven. But the Chi family do as they please, and the head of their family, Baron K'ang, likes to pretend that he's the duke."

The great temple of Duke Tan is as impressive as the temple at Loyang, and much older. Duke Tan founded Lu six centuries ago. Shortly after his death, this temple was built to his memory. Of course, the actual age of any structure anywhere is always moot. Since most Cathayan temples are made of wood, I am fairly certain that even the most ancient temple is simply a phoenixlike recreation of a long-vanished original. But Cathayans maintain—as do the Babylonians—that since they are always careful to duplicate, exactly, the original buildings, nothing really changes.

In front of the temple a thousand foot soldiers were drawn up in battle array. They wore leather tunics. Elmwood bows were slung over their shoulders. Long swords were attached to their belts. The troops were entirely surrounded by children, streetwomen, food vendors. At the far end of the square, sacrificed animals were roasting over altar fires. The mood was more festive than warlike.

The duke asked one of the guards at the temple's door what was happening. The guard said that Baron K'ang was inside, addressing heaven. The duke's mood was definitely sour when he rejoined me in the crowd. "It's really frightful. Sacrilegious, too. He's not the duke."

I was curious to know just what was going on inside the temple. My master did his best to explain. "The pseudo-duke is telling the ancestors, who are not *his* ancestors, that the realm has been attacked. He is saying that if heaven and all the ancestors smile upon him, he will stop the enemy at the Stone Gates. Meanwhile, he is offering the ancestors all the usual sacrifices, prayers, music. Then the commanding general will cut his nails and—"

"He will what?"

The duke looked somewhat surprised. "Don't your generals cut their nails before battle?"

"No. Why should they?"

"Because whenever someone we know dies, we cut our nails before the funeral, as a sign of respect. Since men die in war, our commanding general prepares in advance, as it were, for the funeral by putting on a robe of mourning and cutting his nails. He then leads his army through an ill-omened gate—that's the Low North Gate here—and takes to the field."

"I'd have thought that a general would want to associate himself only with good omens."

"He does," said the duke, somewhat irritably. Like most people who enjoy explaining things, he hated to answer questions. "We go by opposites, as does heaven. Leave by the unlucky gate, return by the lucky gate."

I have learned in my travels that most religious observances make no sense unless one has been accepted into the inner mysteries of the cult.

"He will also address thirteen prayers to the number thirteen."

"Why thirteen?"

The duke bought a small fried lizard from a vendor. He offered me no part of it, which I took to be a bad sign; doubtless he would have thought it a good one. "Thirteen," he said, mouth filled with lizard, "is significant because the body has nine apertures"—I thought of Sariputra's gruesome description of those orifices—"and four limbs. Nine and four make thirteen, or a man. After a celebration of the number thirteen, which is man himself, the general will pray that his men be free from death spots. A death spot," he said quickly, before I could ask another question, "is that part of the body *least* guarded by heaven, and so, most susceptible to death. Years ago I was told where my death spot was and I've been most careful never to expose it. In fact—"

But I was to hear no more of the duke's death spot. At that moment the bronze temple doors swung open. Drums

437

were pounded with jade sticks. Bells were jangled. Soldiers waved bright silken banners. All eyes were now upon the doorway, in which stood the hereditary dictator of Lu.

Baron K'ang was a small fat man with a face as smooth as that of the shell of an egg; he was draped in a robe of mourning. Solemnly he turned his back to us and bowed three times to the ancestors within. Then a tall handsome man came out of the temple; he, too, wore a robe of mourning.

"That is Jan Ch'iu," said the duke. "The steward of the Chi family. He'll lead the Chi army to the Stone Gates."

"Is there no Lu army?"

"Yes. The Chi army." Like most Cathayans, the duke had no conception of national armies. In almost every country, each clan has its own troops. Since the most powerful clan will have the most troops, it exerts the most power in the realm. The only exception to this rule is Ch'in, where Baron Huan had managed to bring together in a single army not only all the troops of his fellow nobles but every able-bodied man in the land. The result is a Spartan military state, an anomaly in the Middle Kingdom.

In order to ensure victory, the dictator and his general performed a number of arcane rites in full view of the people.

"Who," I asked, "will win the war?"

"Key is a richer and more powerful state than Lu. But Lu is peculiarly holy and ancient. Everything the people of the Middle Kingdom regard as wise and good is associated with the founder of this city, Duke Tan."

"But to win a war, it's hardly enough to be wise and good and ancient."

"Of course it is. Heaven decides these things, not men. If it were left to men, the wolves of Ch'in would enslave us all. But heaven keeps the wolves at bay. I suspect that this will be a brief war. Key would not dare upset the balance of the world by conquering Lu, even if it could, which is doubtful. Jan Ch'iu is a fine general. He is also devoted to Confucius. He even went into exile with him. But seven years ago Confucius told him that his duty was here, and he has been the Chi steward ever since. In my view, he has many good qualities, even if he is a commoner. That is why I have *always* been polite to him." The duke bestowed his highest accolade.

The dictator embraces his general. Sacrificial flesh was then offered to each soldier. When the roasted meat had been bolted down, Jan Ch'iu shouted a command, which I did not understand. From the opposite side of the square, a chariot containing two men clattered toward us.

Needless to say, the duke recognized the officer in the chariot. He always said that more people had been presented to him than to any other personage in the Middle Kingdom. "He's the second in command. He's also a disciple of Confucius. In fact, the Chi family is administered by Confucius' protégés, which is why Baron K'ang has sent for him after all these years." The duke stared at the second in command, who was now saluting the dictator. "I can't remember the man's name. But he's a dangerous sort. I once heard him say that none of us ought to live by the work of others. I was stunned. So was Confucius, I am happy to say. I remember his answer, which I've often quoted. 'You must do what you were meant to do in your station of life, just as the common people must do what they are meant to do. If you are wise and just, they will look to you, their babies strapped on their backs. So don't waste your time trying to grow your own food. Leave that to the farmer.' Confucius also made the very good point . . ."

I had ceased to listen. I had recognized the second in command. It was Fan Ch'ih. I thought rapidly. Should I go to him now? Or should I wait for him to return from the war? But suppose he was killed? If he was, I knew that I would spend the rest of my life as the slave of the mad duke of the holy ground. During our stay at Loyang I had come to realize that the duke was far too scatter-brained to undertake the long and hazardous journey to Magadha. I would remain his slave for the rest of my life, following him from place to place like a pet monkey to be shown off, having my cheek pinched so that the Cathay men could see the red come and go. Between such a life and death, I chose death—or escape. I made my decision in that crowded square before the great temple of Lu.

I shoved my way through the crowd; ducked between a line of soldiers; ran toward Fan Ch'ih. As I was about to speak to him, two members of the Chi guard seized my arms. I was only a few yards from Baron K'ang, whose face was expressionless. Jan Ch'iu frowned. Fan Ch'ih blinked his eyes.

"Fan Ch'ih!" I shouted. My old friend turned his back to me. I was terrified. According to Cathayan law, I was now a runaway slave. I could be put to death.

As the guards began to drag me away, I shouted in Persian, "Is this the way you treat the Great King's ambassador?"

Fan Ch'ih swung around. He stared at me for an instant. Then he turned to Jan Ch'iu and said something that I could not hear. Jan Ch'iu motioned to the guards, who let me go. Cringing in the Cathayan manner, I approached Fan Ch'ih. I had not been so frightened since I was a child squirming on Queen Atossa's rug.

Fan Ch'ih got down from the chariot, and my heart, which had stopped its beating, started again. As Fan Ch'ih embraced me he whispered in my ear in Persian, "How? What? Be quick."

"Captured by the Ch'inese. Now a slave of the duke of Sheh. Did you get my messages?"

"No." Fan Ch'ih broke the embrace. He walked over to Baron K'ang. He bowed low. They exchanged words. Although the egglike face of the dictator betrayed no emotion of any kind, the egg itself ever so slightly nodded. Then Fan Ch'ih got into the chariot. Jan Ch'iu mounted a black stallion. Commands were shouted. Half walking, half running, the Chi family troops crossed the square in the direction of the ill-omened Low North Gate.

Baron K'ang's eyes were upon his army. I did not know what to do. I was afraid I had been forgotten. As the last soldier left the square, the duke of Sheh was at my side. "What a display!" he said. "I am humiliated! You have behaved barbarously. Come away! This instant." He pulled at my arm. But I stood as if my feet had been nailed to the packed red earth.

Suddenly the dictator looked at us. The duke of Sheh assumed his courtly manner. "Dear Baron K'ang, what a pleasure to behold you on this day of days! When victory is in the air for my beloved nephew the duke of Lu."

Cathayan manners are nothing if not rigid. Although my master was little more than an impoverished scrounger, every Cathayan court received him as a duke; and although there is hardly a real duke in the Middle Kingdom who is not regarded with contempt by his hereditary ministers, there is not a duke who isn't treated, both in private and in public, as a celestial figure, true descendant of the Yellow Emperor.

Baron K'ang made the absolute minimum of those physical gestures that are required when a lowly baron, even if he be master of the state, finds himself in the presence of a duke. When Baron K'ang finally spoke, the voice was as expressionless as the face. "Your nephew whose slave I am should be here before nightfall. I assume that you will stay with him."

"Actually, I'm not certain. I spoke to the chamberlain just now. He seemed most flustered, which is understandable. After all, this is a tortoise day, hardly an everyday experience. But then, a visit from the duke's uncle is not an everyday experience either, is it, Baron?"

"Heaven does seem to want to spoil us, Duke. You are welcome to stay in my cheerless hovel."

"That's very good of you, Baron, I must say. I'll find your steward myself. Don't give me a second thought. I'll manage." The duke turned to me. "Come along," he said.

This was the moment that I looked at Baron K'ang. He looked past me at the duke. "Your slave will remain with me."

"You are gracious! Naturally, I had hoped that you'd let him sleep inside the palace, but I was not going to make a point of it."

"He will stay in the palace, Duke. As my guest."

Thus was I liberated. The duke of Sheh was furious, but there was nothing he could do. Baron K'ang was dictator, and that was that.

I was assigned a room in the Chi palace by a respectful under-steward, who told me, "The master will receive you tonight after the tortoise auguries."

"Am I a slave?" I was to the point.

"No. You are an honored guest of Baron K'ang. You may come and go as you please, but since the duke of Sheh may try to get you back . . ."

"I will neither come nor go. I'll stay right here, if I may."

It was after midnight when I was sent for by the dictator. He received me cordially, as far as I could tell: neither his face nor body betrayed any sort of emotion. When I had finished the prescribed series of bows, twitches and hand gestures, he motioned for me to sit on a mat to his right. Behind a feather screen two women played mournful music. I assumed that they were concubines. The room was lit by a single bronze lamp filled with what the Cathayans call orchid-perfume fat oil. Although not made from odorless orchids, this oil is delicately per-fumed from some sort of flower; it is highly expensive.

"As you see, I have put you in the place of honor to my right," said the baron.

I bowed my head. But I was somewhat puzzled. In the Middle Kingdom, the place of honor is to the left of the host.

The baron anticipated my bewilderment. "In peace-time the place of honor is to the left. In wartime, it is to the right. We are at war, Cyrus Spitama." He said the strange name with no difficulty; reputedly, he had the best memory in all Cathay. "You are a slave no longer."

"I am grateful, Lord Baron—" I began.

With a graceful wave of the hand, I was interrupted. "Fan Ch'ih says that you are related to the Great King beyond the western desert. He also tells me that you be-friended him. So we can do no less for you than what you did for our friend and kinsman."

Tears came to my eyes. I was overwrought, to say the least. "I am eternally grateful—"

"Yes, yes. In this matter, as a host, I do no more than follow the wisdom of Confucius."

"I hear the praises of this divine sage wherever I go," I said. "He is almost as admired as you . . ." The baron then allowed me to flatter him at such length that I real-ized to what extent the expressionless face was indeed a work of art, not to mention hard work. Like most men of power, Baron K'ang could not get enough praise, and in me he had a panegyrist quite beyond anything he had ever encountered within the Cathayan four seas. In fact, I pleased him so much that he promptly sent for a wine made from fermented plums. While we drank he asked me innumerable questions about Persia, Magadha, Baby-lon. He was fascinated by my descriptions of court life at Susa. He wanted to know in detail how the satrapies are governed. He was delighted that I understood the art of smelting iron. He hoped that I would instruct his metal-workers. He asked me to describe Persian war chariots, armor, weapons.

Then, suddenly, he stopped; became apologetic. "It is unseemly that two cultured men should talk so much of war, an activity best left to the louts that excel at it."

"But under the circumstances, our conversation is un-derstandable, Lord Baron. Your country is at war."

"All the more reason that I should let my thoughts

dwell on those things which truly matter. Such as how to bring to the realm one single day of perfect peace. Should this ever occur, sweet dew, tasting of honey, will fall upon the land."

"Has such a thing ever happened, Lord Baron?"

"All things have happened. All things will happen." I *believe* that this is what he said. In a language without tenses, one is never certain. "How long will you honor us with your presence?"

"I should like to return as soon as possible to Persia. Naturally . . ." I did not finish a sentence that only he could finish.

"Naturally," he echoed. But he did not pursue the subject. "I saw the duke of Sheh at court tonight." Something close to a smile began to alter the lower part of the egg. "He was most distressed. You are his friend, he said, as well as slave. He saved you from the wolfmen. He had hoped to travel with you to Magadha, where your father-in-law is the king. He had hoped that, together, as partners, you would be able to open a permanent trade route to Champa and Rajagriha."

"He intended to hold me for ransom. There was no question of a trade route."

Baron K'ang nodded amiably. "Yes," he said informally. There are, by the way, two kinds of yes in the Cathayan language. One is formal; the other informal. I took it as a good sign that he chose to be informal with me. "I am most interested in King Ajatashatru. Early in his reign he wrote the son of heaven at Loyang. Copies of the letters were sent to each of the dukes. Your awesome father-in-law said that he was interested in trade with us. I assume that he still is."

"Oh, yes. In fact, he had hopes that I might prove to be the link." I could not believe what I was saying. Obviously, too long and close an association with the duke of Sheh had made me quite as fantastic as he; also, the plum wine was unexpectedly strong and deranging. I spoke at length of my mission to bring together in a single world Persia, India and Cathay. I described in detail a circular caravan route from Susa to Bactra to Ch'in to Lu to Champa to Shravasti to Taxila to Susa. I made no sense. But the baron was polite. Unlike most rulers, he listened attentively. In his own unemphatic way, he made swift judgments during slow speeches. He was always quick to detect the significant word not spoken, as well as the false note sounded. I came to admire, even to like him. But I never ceased to fear him.

When I finally gave out a breath, much to my own relief, he said that the trade route that I had envisaged was also a dream of his. This was polite. After all, it has been the dream of many travelers for several centuries. He knew little of Persia and the west, he said, but he did have some slight knowledge of the kingdoms of the Gangetic plain. He then described them in considerable detail, ending with "Ajatashatru is now universal monarch. He has destroyed Koshala. Except for a few mountain republics, he has the hegemony—" There was a pause; then he added, "—of India."

"Ajatashatru is truly a marvelous warrior, a just ruler." The plum wine produced a number of epithets more suitable for carving on a cliff to edify peasants than to decorate, as it were, a conversation with the man who appeared to be, thus far at least, my liberator.

"I find it curious," said the baron, when I had at last stopped babbling, "that Persia and now India each has a monarch who has received heaven's decree."

"I thought that the decree could come only to the son of heaven, to the master of the Middle Kingdom."

"That is what we have always thought. But now we are beginning to realize just how much world there is beyond the four seas. And I am beginning to suspect that we are but a single grain in the great barn. Anyway, I take it as a good omen that the mandate is once more being given, even if it be to barbarians in far-off lands."

"Perhaps," I said, too boldly, "it will come to the duke of Lu."

"Perhaps," he said. "Or to another," he added. A servant brought us eggs that had been kept underground for several years. We ate them with tiny spoons. The eggs tasted delicately musty. Although I was later to bury many eggs at Susa and Halicarnassus, they simply putrefied. Either Cathayan soil is different from ours or they prepare the eggs in some secret way.

The baron saw to it that I answered more questions than I asked. He was insatiably curious about the west. But then, he was curious about everything. He was like a Greek.

When I ventured to ask him about that evening's tortoise-shell auguries, he shook his head. "I may not discuss this. You must forgive me." But I could tell by the

444

tone of his voice that the auguries had been excellent. "Usually our relations with Key are good. But when they gave asylum to Duke Chao—not a good man, I fear—a certain tension developed between the realms. We thought it most unkind of them to harbor our enemy so near to the Stone Gates, where he could act as a rallying point for every sort of malcontent. We protested. But the old duke of Key was a stubborn man. He was also fond of making trouble. So he encouraged the pretensions of our former duke." The baron sighed softly, and belched loudly. "Fortunately, in the natural course, Duke Chao died. After that, all was well between our two countries. Or so we thought. But then . . . Oh, we are living in a most *interesting* period!" Cathayans use the word interesting rather the way that Greeks use the word catastrophic. "Duke Ting succeeded his brother Chao, and my unworthy grandfather was commanded to take office as prime minister, a task he was as little suited for—or wanted, as I." Thus do great Cathayan lords express themselves, rather like eunuchs getting ready to raid the harem larder. "When my grandfather died, one of his secretaries, a creature called Yang Huo, made himself prime minister. Since he was only a knight, this was not at all proper. Oh, we were deeply discouraged." The baron put down his spoon. Together we listened to the workings of his devious mind. Then preserved apricots were brought us. Of all fruits in Cathay, this is the most esteemed. I have never liked apricots. But I consumed with apparent relish whatever the dictator offered me.

As usual I learned not from Baron K'ang but from others, the true nature of that deep discouragement. Yang Huo had seized the government. For three years he was absolute dictator. Like so many illegitimate rulers, he was enormously popular with the common people. He even tried to make an alliance with the duke against the three baronial families. "I serve Duke Ting as his first minister," he used to say, "in order that the Chou dynasty may regain its rightful supremacy in Lu. When this happens, the mandate of heaven will descend upon our duke, heir of the godlike Tan."

Duke Ting had sense enough to keep as much distance as he could between himself and the usurper. Literal distance: the duke was forever hunting. He only came to the capital when he was obliged to address the ancestors. I must say, if I'd been in his place I would have made an alliance with Yang Huo. Together they could have destroyed the baronial families. But the duke was timid. Also, he had not the imagination or knowledge to think of himself as an actual ruler. For five generations his family had been dominated by the three families. So he went hunting.

Eventually Yang Huo overstepped himself. He tried to kill the father of Baron K'ang. But the Chi forces rallied around their chieftain, and Yang Huo fled to Key with most of the national treasury. The government of Lu asked that the rebel be sent back, with the stolen treasury. When this request was ignored, relations between Key and Lu worsened.

The baron assured me that even as we spoke, Yang Huo was plotting his return, in order, as he said, to create "a Chou in the east"—that is, a restoration of the original celestial emperor. Yang Huo must have been a highly persuasive man. Certainly, he had many secret admirers in Lu, particularly among those who favor what they call the old ways. As far as I know, he never returned. The Chi family is much too powerful and Baron K'ang is—or was—too clever and formidable. When I met the baron, he had been prime minister for eight years. But though he was absolute dictator, he still feared Yang Huo. He had also been shaken by the recent revolt of one of his ablest commanders, the warden of Castle Pi.

Ever since the breakup of the Chou empire, the nobles have been building themselves fortresses. At first these castles were intended to provide protection against thieves and hostile armies. But gradually, over the years, the fortresses have become the visible and outward sign of a given family's strength. Through marriage, treachery, all-out revolt, each family tries to gain as many fortified places as possible. Since the Chi family currently controls the largest number of fortified places in Lu, they govern one million people in an uneasy alliance with their rivals the Meng and Shu families. Needless to say, the duke has no castles. In fact, he owns nothing but his palace, for whose maintenance there is never enough money. Yang Huo had promised to change all that; he had even spoken of razing the Chi castles. I suspect that it was not the attempted murder of the old baron, but this threat to the fortresses, that caused Yang Huo's downfall.

A dozen years before my arrival in Lu, the warden of Castle Pi went into rebellion against his Chi masters. For five years he held the stronghold. Finally he was obliged to give it up and take refuge in Key. It was no secret that Baron K'ang believed him to be the principal instigator of the war between Key and Lu, even though others felt that that honor should go to Yang Huo. In any case, the warden had shrewdly set himself up as yet another supporter of the ducal family. He, too, wanted to create "Chou in the east."

The baron alluded to this rebellion. As usual, he was less than direct. "It is plainly heaven's will that we are to be denied absolutely serene lives. Yet we propitiate heaven and we perform every traditional rite. Unfortunately, we have ill-wishers to the north . . ." Baron K'ang paused to see if I had caught the double meaning. I had. Key is to the north of Lu, while the phrase "to the north" also means the celestial emperor. "You know our ways, I see. I meant, of course, Key, which harbors our enemies. I cannot think why. We have never taken in a single opponent of their government. Men are unfathomable, aren't they?"

I agreed. Actually, I have always found men quite fathomable. They look entirely to their own interest. On the other hand, how men choose to interpret or explain the fact of, let us say, creation is often mysterious to me.

As I sat with Baron K'ang in that dimly lit room, the delicate music filling the air about us like the reverberation of a sound rather than the sound itself, I knew that he meant to use me. In his elliptical way, he was testing me. He was applying, as it were, heat to the interior of the tortoise shell so that he might be able to read the mysterious script that was bound to appear upon the blood-coated outer surface. I remained as still as—as a tortoise shell.

"The restoration of the house of Chou is our dream," he said somewhat unexpectedly.

"Is this imminent?"

"Who can say? In any case, first the hegemony, then the mandate." Suddenly two tiny parallel lines marred the upper sector of the egg shell. The baron was frowning. "There are those who believe that the process can be reversed. Although I do not believe this, many wise and not-so-wise men think that such is the case. They believe that if a rightful duke is given his ancient *worldly* primacy, heaven's decree will follow. Recent . . . adventurers have encouraged this false idea. That is why our army is at the

Stone Gates. It is easy to handle adventurers." The upper part of the egg was smooth once again. "We do not fear traitors. But we fear—and respect—our divine sages. You know the teachings of Confucius?"

"Yes, Lord Baron. Fan Ch'ih told me a great deal about him when we were together in the west. And, of course, all educated men discuss him. Even Master Li," I added with a smile. I was beginning to sense the wind's direction.

"Even Master Li," he repeated. The lower part of the egg now displayed, briefly, two small indentations. The dictator had smiled. "They do not love each other, these wise men." He spoke in a soft voice. "Confucius is returning to Lu, at my request. He has been gone fourteen years. During this time he has traveled in nearly every land within the four seas. He likes to think that he was exiled by my revered father, the prime minister. But I assure you that this was not the case. Confucius exiled us. He is very strict. When the duke of Key made a gift to my father of a number of religious dancers"—the phrase the baron used for religious dancers was not unlike the Babylonian phrase for temple prostitutes—"Confucius thought that my father ought not to accept this gift on the ground that it was unseemly. He gave the traditional reason: such dancers are meant to weaken the resolve of the men who own them. Most courteously, my father said that he regarded the gift as a sign that the government of Key wished to make amends for the fact that they were harboring the traitor Yang Huo. Confucius then resigned all his offices. He was chief magistrate of the town of Chung-fu, a charming place that you must visit while you're here. He was also assistant to the superintendent of works . . . no, no, I'm mistaken—he had been promoted from that office. He was under-minister of police, an important office which he filled most competently."

I watched the baron as he spoke to the wall behind my head. The wind's direction was now unmistakable. He knew that I was a friend of Fan Ch'ih's. Fan Ch'ih was a disciple of Confucius; so was the Chi steward Jan Ch'iu. I began to make connections.

I made the necessary connection. "Did Confucius go to Key?"

"Yes."

We drank plum wine; listened to music; passed between us a smooth fragment of jade to cool our hands.

448

I have never known anyone in any country at any time to occupy the sort of place that Confucius did in the Middle Kingdom. Through birth, he was the premier knight of Lu. This meant that he took precedence immediately after the lord-ministers of state. Nevertheless, he came from a poor family. It was said that his father had been a minor officer in the army of the Meng family. Like the other baronial families, the Mengs conducted a school for the sons of its retainers. Confucius was the most brilliant student ever to attend that school. He studied the *Odes*, the *Histories, The Book of Changes;* he made himself an expert on the past so that he might be useful in the present. As son of the premier knight, he was also trained to be a soldier. He proved to be an excellent archer until middle age clouded his eyes.

Confucius supported himself and his family—he had married at nineteen—by working for the state. I believe that his first job was as a clerk attached to the state granaries. Presumably, he was accurate in his accounts because, in due course, he made his way up the ladder of government service whose terminus, for a knight, is a post such as the one that he had held in the ministry of police.

It is an understatement to say that Confucius was not generally popular. In fact, he was hated and resented not only by his fellow clerks but by the high officers of state as well. The reason for this was simple. He was a nag. He knew exactly how and precisely why things should be done, and he was never shy in expressing his opinions to his superiors. Nevertheless, irritating as he was, he was too valuable a man to ignore; and so he rose as far as he could. By the time he was fifty-six he was under-minister of police, and that should have been that. He had had a successful career in government. He was generally honored if not liked. He was the acknowledged authority on the celestial empire of the Chous. Although he himself wrote nothing, he was the principal interpreter of the Chou texts. It was said that he had read *The Book of Changes* so many times that the thong which holds together the bamboo-strip pages had to be replaced a half-dozen times. He'd worn out the leather in rather the same way that he had worn out the patience of his colleagues in the administration of Lu.

At some point, Confucius became a teacher. I could never find out when or how this began. It must have happened gradually. As he got older and wiser and more learned, young men would come to him with questions about this or that. By the time he was fifty, he must have had thirty or forty full-time disciples, young knights like Fan Ch'ih who would listen to him by the hour.

Although he was not unlike one of those philosophers that we see—or rather, that I *hear* at Athens—he took practically no money from the young, and unlike your lively friend Socrates, he did not ask questions in order to lead the young to wisdom, Confucius *answered* questions; and many of his answers came from a positively archival memory. He knew the entire recorded as well as remembered history of the Chou dynasty. He also knew the history of their predecessors the Shang. Although many Cathayans believe that Confucius is a divine sage—one of those rare heaven-sent teachers who do such a lot of harm—Confucius himself steadfastly denied not only divinity but sagacity. Nevertheless, he became so celebrated outside Lu that men from every part of the Middle Kingdom came to visit him. He received everyone courteously; spoke of what was and of what *should* be. It was his description of what should be that got him into trouble.

Confucius started life as a client of the Meng family. Then he received office from the Chi family. But despite the patronage of the baronial families, he never let them forget that they had usurped the dukes' prerogatives. He wanted this situation rectified by, first, the restoration of the Chou rituals to their original form and, second, by the ceding of the barons' illegal powers to the rightful duke. When these two things were done, heaven would be pleased and the mandate would be bestowed.

This sort of talk did not exactly delight the barons. But the Chi family continued to indulge the sage. They also gave preferment to his disciples. Not that they had much choice: all the Confucians were superbly trained by their mentor in administration and war. Finally, since Confucius tried to keep the peace between the states, the barons could not fault him for that—at least not openly.

Confucius was often sent to peace conferences, where he invariably overwhelmed the other participants with celestial learning. He was even, sometimes, useful. But despite his years of work as an administrator and a diplomat, he never learned tact. Baron K'ang gave me a celebrated example of the sage's bluntness. "Not long before Confucius left Lu the first time, he attended a celebration at our family's ancestral temple. When he saw that my father had engaged sixty-four dancers, he was furious. He said that since the duke had only been able to afford eight dancers when he addressed his ancestors, my father should not have used more than six dancers. Oh, how Confucius scolded my father, who was very amused!"

The actual story was not at all amusing. Confucius had made it very clear to the old prime minister that since he was flagrantly usurping the sovereign's prerogative, he was sure to suffer heaven's anger. When the baron told Confucius to mind his own business, the sage withdrew. As he left the room he was heard to say, "If this man can be endured, who can *not* be endured?" I must say my grandfather never dared go as far as that.

Confucius tried to persuade Duke Ting to dismantle the fortresses of the three baronial families. No doubt, the duke would have done so if he could. But he was powerless. In any case, if only briefly, the two men conspired against the three families; and it is fairly certain that they were responsible for the revolt of the Chi fortress at Pi. Evidence? Shortly after the warden of Castle Pi fled to Key, Confucius resigned all of his offices and left Lu.

Stories differ about what happened in Key. But everyone agrees that both Yang Huo and the warden of Pi tried to enlist the services of Confucius. Each promised to overthrow the baronial families and restore the duke to his rightful place; each asked Confucius to serve him as prime minister. Confucius was said to have been tempted by the warden's offer. But nothing came of any of this because Yang Huo and the warden never joined forces. If they had, Fan Ch'ih is certain that they could have driven out the barons and restored the duke. But the adventurers were as suspicious of each other as they were of the barons.

Confucius did not stay long in Key. Although his discussions with the two rebels were not satisfactory, the duke of Key was delighted with Confucius and invited him to join the government. The sage was tempted. But the prime minister of Key was not about to have such a paragon in his administration, and the offer was withdrawn.

For the next few years Confucius wandered from state to state, looking for employment. At no point did Confucius ever want to be a professional teacher. But since we always get what we do not want in life, he was besieged by would-be students wherever he went. Young knights and even nobles were eager to learn from him. Although Confucius appeared to be speaking of the restoration of the old ways in order to please heaven, he was actually the leader of a highly radical movement whose intention was, very simply, to sweep away the corrupt all-powerful and ever-proliferating nobility so that there might once more be a son of heaven, who would gaze southward at his loyal slaves, amongst whom a clear majority would be highly trained knights in the new Confucian order.

This was the background to the return of Confucius to Lu in his seventieth year. Although he was seen as no personal threat to the regime, his ideas so troubled the nobles that Baron K'ang decided to put a stop to the wise man's wanderings. He sent him an embassy in the duke's name. This wise man was implored to come home; high office was hinted at. Confucius took the bait. He was now en route to Lu from Wei.

"Let us hope," said my host, "that our little war with Key will be finished before he comes."

"May it be heaven's will." I was pious.

"You will hear a good deal about heaven's will from Confucius." There was a long pause. I held my breath. "You will be lodged here, close to me."

"The honor—" I was not allowed to finish.

"And we shall see to it that you return, somehow, to your native land. Meanwhile . . ." The baron looked down at his smooth little hands.

"I shall serve you in every way, Lord Baron."

"Yes."

Thus, with no further word spoken, it was arranged that during my stay at Lu I would spy on Confucius and report secretly to the baron, who feared Yang Huo and the warden, who regarded with deep suspicion his own guards commander Jan Ch'iu, who found unnerving the moral force of Confucius and his teachings. Sometimes it is wise to confront rather than evade what you fear. That is why the baron had sent for Confucius. He wanted to learn the worst.

4

THE CAPITAL CITY OF LU REMINDED ME
of Loyang. Of course, all Cathayan cities are more or less
alike. There are the astonishingly narrow, twisting streets,
the noisy market places, the quiet parks where altars to
heaven, rain and earth are set. The city of Ch'u-fu was
more ancient than Loyang, and smelled of charred wood,
the result of a half millennium of fires. Although I did not
know it at the time, Lu was considered somewhat back-
ward by such up-and-coming states as Key, whose capital
city was regarded with rather the same awe that Sardis
used to be by us. Nevertheless, the duke of Lu was the
heir of the legendary Tan, whose name is on everyone's
lips in much the same way that Odysseus is constantly
referred to by the Greeks. But whereas Odysseus is noted
for trickiness, Tan was overwhelmingly noble and self-
sacrificing, the model not only for the perfect Cathayan
ruler but, more to the point, of the perfect gentleman—a
category invented or appropriated by Confucius. Although
most gentlemen are knights, not all knights are gentlemen.
Gentle or seemly behavior is the Confucian ideal. I shall
try to describe what that is in the proper place.

Whenever Confucius had anything important to say, he
would invariably ascribe it to Tan. But then, he used always to say, "I do nothing but transmit what was taught
to me. I never make up anything of my own." I suppose
he believed this and I suppose that, in a sense, it could be
true. Everything *has* been said before, and if one knows
the recorded past, one can always find a venerable pretext for action—or aphorism.

Two weeks after I moved into the Chi palace, the war
between Lu and Key ended. Jan Ch'iu and Fan Ch'ih
had won a remarkable—that is to say, an unexpected—
victory. They had even managed to seize the town of
Lang on the Key side of the border. It was reported that
both Yang Huo and the warden of Pi were to be seen
fighting in the Key army against their own countrymen.

453

In this respect, Cathayans are like Greeks. Loyalty to oneself takes precedence over patriotism.

Democritus twits me. He has just asked me about those Persian adventurers who have overthrown Great Kings to whom they had sworn allegiance. This is not exactly comparable. True, we have had our share of usurpers. But I can think of no case where a disgruntled Persian of rank ever joined a foreign army in order to invade his native land.

I was treated as a guest of the Chi family; and given the title honored guest. I was also received at the ducal court. Even though Duke Ai exercised no power, Baron K'ang not only deferred to him ceremonially but consulted him when it came to matters of state. Although there is no recorded instance of the baron ever having taken the advice of the duke, their relations were superficially smooth.

When the victorious Chi family army returned to the capital, I attended a reception for the heroes in the Long Treasury, a building just opposite the ducal palace. As part of the prime minister's entourage, I wore for the first time the court apron—a curious garment of silk that sweeps in a semicircle below a wide leather belt to which are affixed one's various badges of rank in gold, silver, ivory and jade. Needless to say, my belt was plain except for a small knob of silver, which identified me as honored guest.

About fifty of us followed Baron K'ang into the main hall of the Long Treasury. Previously this building had been the stronghold not only of the treasury but of the dukes. When Duke Chao tried to regain his rightful powers, he took refuge in the Long Treasury. But the troops of the three families overwhelmed his guards and set fire to the building. Chao escaped the fire; the building did not. There was a good deal of debate whether or not to rebuild this symbol of ducal power. Baron K'ang finally gave permission, and the year before my arrival in Lu, the Long Treasury had once again risen from the ashes.

To the north of the room stood Duke Ai. He was a lean, well-favored man, with the legs of the dedicated huntsman; that is, the sort of legs which obligingly bend themselves in order to fit snugly the sides of a horse. He wore a startling robe of blue and gold, a garment that had once belonged to the legendary Tan.

The Meng and Shu families were already in attendance, as well as the ducal family and retainers. Amongst them I saw the glowering duke of Sheh. At least he glowered when he saw me.

Baron K'ang bowed to the duke; wished him long life; complimented him on *his* victory against Key. Then the baron presented Jan Ch'iu to the duke, who responded with an address that was so celestial and archaic that I understood very little of it.

As Duke Ai spoke I examined the long high room, an exact replica of the one that had been burned. A tall, rather crude statue of Duke Tan stood opposite Ai; otherwise, there were no furnishings except for the courtiers. In their brilliant robes they made a charming spectacle, and the room looked more like a garden in spring than a gathering of grimly ambitious men.

After the address from the north, there was music. And a ritual dance. And a good deal of millet wine, which everyone drank too much of. At a certain point the duke slipped away—a sad sign of power lost: universal protocol requires that no one may leave a room before the ruler. But Baron K'ang, not Duke Ai ruled at Lu.

Once the duke was gone, people began to move about. There was much bowing, cringing, trotting. I always found Cathayan protocol both ludicrous and nerve-wracking. On the other hand, Fan Ch'ih was not impressed by the way we order such things at Babylon.

Finally, as I knew he would, the duke of Sheh found me. He had drunk too much. "If I live to be ten thousand years . . ."

"I pray that such is the case," I said quickly, bowing and cringing as if he were a real duke.

"I hope never again to encounter such ingratitude."

"I was helpless, Lord Duke. I was taken captive."

"Captive." He pointed at the silver knob on my belt. "Honored guest! You . . . whom I saved from certain death . . . are a slave. *My* slave. Paid for by me. Fed by me. Treated as something human by me. Now you have betrayed your benefactor, your savior!"

"Never! My gratitude to you is eternal. But Baron K'ang—"

"—has been put under some sort of spell. I can recognize the signs. Well, I've warned my nephew the duke. He's keeping an eye on you. One false step and . . ."

Where that false step might have taken me I shall never know because Fan Ch'ih came between us. "Dear friend,"

455

he said to me. "Lord Duke," he said to my former master.

"All honor for this day," the duke muttered to Fan Ch'ih and walked away. I never saw him again. Yet I had been sincere when I said that I would always be grateful to him for having saved me from the wolfmen of Ch'in.

Fan Ch'ih wanted to know in detail everything that had happened to me. I did my best to tell him. He kept shaking his head and murmuring, "It is not seemly, not seemly," as I recounted my numerous vicissitudes in the Middle Kingdom. When I had run out of breath, he said, "You saw to it that I got back here. I shall see to it that you go to Persia. That is a promise."

"Baron K'ang has also promised to help me, thanks to you."

Fan Ch'ih looked grave, an expression one seldom saw on that merry face. "It won't be easy, of course. Not right now."

"I thought I might find a ship that was going to Champa and—"

"There aren't many ships that set out for Champa. And the few that do seldom arrive. Those that do arrive . . . well, they arrive without passengers."

"Pirate ships?"

Fan Ch'ih nodded. "You'd be robbed and thrown overboard the first night out. No. You'll have to go on your own ship or a government ship with a cargo. Unfortunately, the state is without money." Fan Ch'ih spread the fingers of both hands palm upward; then he turned his hands over, the Cathayan gesture for emptiness, nothingness, poverty. "First, Yang Huo stole most of the treasury. Then, there was the cost of rebuilding this." He indicated the long room in which the flowerlike courtiers had begun to go, as it were, to seed. "Then there were the various troubles, and now, finally, this war with Key, which we did manage *not* to lose." Cathayans delight in understatement; revel in the cryptic aside.

"You won a marvelous victory. You've added new territory to Lu."

"But what we've gained is not equal to what we've spent. Baron K'ang will have to impose new taxes. That means you'll have to wait until we have the money to send you back. Next year, perhaps."

I did my best to look pleased. Actually, I was desolate. I had already been gone from Persia for nearly five years.

"For selfish reasons, I'm delighted you're here." Fan

Ch'ih smiled; his face resembled the autumn moon. "Now I can pay you back for all that you did for me at Babylon."

I said that I had done nothing, and so on. Then I asked, "Is there a banking firm like Egibi and sons in Lu?"

"No. But we have all sorts of merchants, shippers, sea captains, greedy men."

Somehow or other, during this conversation, the name of Confucius was mentioned. I cannot remember in what context. But I do recall how Fan Ch'ih's eyes suddenly gleamed with pleasure. "You remember all the stories that I told you about Master K'ung?"

"Oh, yes. Yes! How could I forget?" My enthusiasm was not feigned. I had a task to perform.

Fan Ch'ih took my arm and led me through the crowd of courtiers. Although their manners were as precise and exquisite as ever, their voices were now a bit too loud. It was all reminiscent of the Persian court, with one exception: the Cathayan ruler—or, in this case, rulers—leaves at the first sign of drunkenness, while the Great King stays to the end. Because of this ancient Persian custom, Herodotus now tells us that it is only while drunk that the Great King devises policy. Actually, the reverse is true. Every word that is said at a royal drinking party is recorded by a scribe, and any order that the sovereign gives while drunk is carefully scrutinized in the neutral light of the next day. Should the decision be less than coherent, it is quietly forgotten.

I followed Fan Ch'ih through the crowded hall. I noticed Baron K'ang slipping out a side door. He had taken the victory of his troops with the same equanimity that he took everything else. In many ways he was a model ruler. I shall always admire him, strange though I found him— and his world.

Beneath the somewhat ominous statue of Duke Tan stood Jan Ch'iu, surrounded by a dozen well-wishers. A quick glance told me that all were of the knightly class, including the general himself. Fan Ch'ih presented me to his commander. We exchanged the usual formalities. Then, most decorously, Fan Ch'ih turned me in the direction of a tall, thin old man with a pale face, large ears, bulbous forehead, scanty beard, and a mouth more suited for the dietary requirements of a grass-eating hare than a meat-eating man. The two front teeth were so long that even when the mouth was shut, the yellow tips could be seen shyly resting on the lower lip.

"Master K'ung, allow me to present my friend from Persia, the son-in-law of two kings, the—"

"—the honored guest," said Confucius precisely: he had looked at my belt; seen the meager symbol of my entirely ambiguous rank.

"Premier Knight," I replied. I was now a competent belt-reader. We exchanged the usual formalities. Although Confucius was meticulously correct in the way he spoke, he gave an impression of absolute straightforwardness. One has to know the Cathayan language to realize just how difficult this is.

I was then presented to a half-dozen of the master's disciples. They had shared his exile. Now they were home again. They all looked very pleased with themselves, particularly a bent little old man who proved to be Confucius' son, yet looked his father's age. I cannot remember anything else of consequence that was said. The conversation was entirely about Jan Ch'iu's victory, which he modestly ascribed to Confucius' teachings. I think he was actually serious.

Some days later Fan Ch'ih took me to the master's house, a nondescript building close to the rain altars. Since Confucius' wife was long since dead, he was looked after by a widowed daughter.

In the mornings, Confucius would talk to anyone who came to see him. As a result, in no time at all, the inner court of the house became so full of young and not-so-young men that the master was often obliged to take the whole lot of them into the mulberry grove near the rain altars.

In the afternoons, Confucius received his friends or disciples. The two were the same because he was never not the teacher and the friends were never not disciples. Questions were constantly put to him about politics and religion, good and evil, life and death, music and ritual. He usually answered a question with a quotation, often from Duke Tan. Then, if pressed sufficiently, he would adapt the quotation to the question at hand.

I remember vividly my first visit to his house. I stood at the back of the inner courtyard. Between the sage and me a hundred students squatted on the ground. As I have already said, Confucius took little or no money from these young men. But presents were acceptable if they were modest. He liked to say, "No one who wants instruction from me has ever been denied it, no matter how poor he is—even if all he can bring is some dried meat." But there was a corollary to this. He did not waste his time on the stupid. "I only teach someone who's bubbling with eagerness, with excitement, who wants to know what I know." He called both students and disciples "little ones," as if they were children.

Since I had only the vaguest knowledge of the texts that Confucius quoted, I was not exactly an ideal, bubbling, excited student. Yet when the master spoke in his slow, rather high voice, I found myself listening carefully, even though I only half understood what he was quoting. But when he chose to interpret an ancient text, he was as clear as the waters of the Choaspes River.

I remember one question that he was asked by a definitely bubbling and overexcited youth: "If our Lord Duke should ask Master K'ung to serve in his government, what would Master K'ung do?"

Fan Ch'ih whispered in my ear, "This may be a clue."

Confucius looked at the youth for a moment. Then he quoted some old maxim. " 'When wanted, then go; when set aside, then hide.' "

Fan Ch'ih was delighted at this elegant evasion. I was not much impressed. Everyone knew that Confucius had spent his life trying to find a ruler who would, at best, let him govern the state; at worst, listen carefully to his advice. Even at seventy, the old man's ambition to rule was as strong as ever.

"Would you interpret that quotation, Master?" The young man was nervous. I wondered if Baron K'ang had told him to ask the question. "It is believed by many that you have been sent for in order to guide the state."

Confucius smiled; he had most of his teeth. "Little one, I know you think that there is something that I'm keeping from you, some secret or other. Believe me, I have no secrets. If I did, I would not be me."

"Excellent," whispered Fan Ch'ih in my ear.

I remember only one more exchange from that morning. An earnest, dull youth said, "In my village they say that you are known to be very learned, but they wonder why you've never actually done anything in the world or made a real name for yourself."

The other students gasped. Fan Ch'ih stiffened. Confucius laughed. He was genuinely amused. "Your friends are absolutely right. I've never really excelled at anything. But it's never too late, is it? So I shall start practicing. Today. But what? Archery? Chariot-racing? Chariot-racing! Yes, I shall enter the races as soon as I am ready." Everyone laughed with relief.

That afternoon I again joined Confucius. This time only a dozen of his closest friends were present. He seemed not to mind my presence. I remember thinking that perhaps it was true what he had said about having no secrets. But if there were secrets, it was my task to discover them and report to Baron K'ang.

Confucius sat on a mat in the guest hall. He was flanked by his oldest disciple, Tzu-lu, and by his most beloved disciple, the youthful but sickly Yen Hui. In the background lurked the prematurely aged son; in the foreground was *his* son Tze-ssu. Confucius treated the grandson as if he were the son, and the son as if he were an acquaintance, because the son was a fool. That seems to be a law of families. Whatsoever the father is, the son is not.

The disciples speculated, openly, about Baron K'ang's plans for Confucius. So did the master: "I came home because I was assured that I was needed, and to be needed is to serve the state, in any capacity."

Yen Hui shook his head. "Why should the master waste his valuable time on the business of office?" When Yen Hui spoke, his voice was so low that we all had to lean forward, ears cupped. "Isn't it best that you talk to us, to the young knights who come to see you, to the officers of state who consult you? Why should you burden yourself with the ministry of police when you alone can explain to men the way of the ancestors and so lead them to goodness?"

Tzu-lu answered Yen Hui. "You've heard the master say ten thousand times, 'He who holds no rank in a state does not discuss its policies.' Well, Baron K'ang has sent for Confucius. That means he needs him. That means that that harmonious state of affairs which we have dreamed of since the time of the Chou is close at hand."

There was then a lengthy argument between the two points of view. Confucius listened to each speaker as if he expected to hear words of shattering wisdom. That he was plainly not shattered by what he heard seemed in no way to surprise him. Tzu-lu was a fierce old man, not at all the sort of person, one would have thought, to attach himself to a wise man—unlike Yen Hui, who was gentle, contemplative, withdrawn.

Fan Ch'ih spoke of the high esteem that Baron K'ang had for Confucius; in fact, just recently, the prime minister had mentioned the possibility of appointing Confucius chief justice. Most of the others thought that this would be a suitable honor. All chose to ignore the fact that since Confucius was only a knight, he could not hold *any* of the great offices.

Finally, when Confucius spoke, he did not address himself directly to the issue. "You know, when I was fifteen I set my heart upon learning. At thirty, I had my feet planted firmly in the ground. At forty, I no longer suffered from . . . perplexities. At fifty, I knew what were the biddings of heaven. At sixty, I submitted to them. Now I am in my seventieth year." The master looked at the edge of the mat on which he was seated. Carefully, he smoothed out a wrinkle that was imperceptible to us. Then he looked up. "I am in my seventieth year," he repeated. "I can follow the dictates of my own heart because what I desire no longer oversteps the boundaries of what is right."

No one quite knew how to interpret this. As it turned out, no one was obliged to because at that moment Jan Ch'iu entered the room with the news that "Our lord would like for the master to attend him at the palace."

The Tzu-lu faction were delighted. They were positive that Confucius was to be given office. Yen Hui looked sad. But then everyone looked sad when Jan Ch'iu added, "I mean our lord, Duke Ai."

Confucius smiled at his disciples, aware of their disappointment. "Little ones," he said softly, "if out of the entire *Book of Songs* I had to take one phrase to cover all my teaching, I would say 'Let there be no evil in your thoughts.' "

I seldom saw Baron K'ang in private. Since the victory against Kcy had exhausted the national treasury, the prime minister's days were spent devising new and ingenious taxes which the equally ingenious citizens of Lu usually managed to avoid paying. I was reminded of the ruinous cost of the Greek wars that had forced Darius to levy such high taxes that Egypt had gone into rebellion.

Finally, after several meetings with Confucius, I reported directly to Baron K'ang at the Long Treasury. I found him seated at the head of a large table covered with bamboo strips, on which were listed the state's accounts.

At a second table, clerks arranged and rearranged other strips; made notations; added and subtracted. Behind the baron, the statue of Duke Tan stared at the ceiling.

"Forgive me," said the baron, not rising. "This is the day that we check the state's inventories. A time of discouragement, I fear."

In Cathay, as in India, each state maintains reserves of grain. When grain is in short supply, the reserves are sold off at a small profit. In times of plenty, the grain is kept off the market. Weapons, farm implements, cloth, wagons, bullocks and horses are also maintained by the state not only as commodities to be sold when necessary but as reserves to be used in bad or interesting times. It was no secret that everything was now in short supply at Lu, including the coinage which was being not too subtly clipped.

As I advanced on tiptoe, shoulders hunched, head wagging with feigned humility and incredulity—the usual approach to a high official—the baron motioned for me to sit beside him on a low stool.

"Honored guest, your days are not too wretched, I pray, in this unworthy city." Cathayans can talk like this by the hour. Fortunately, Baron K'ang never made these conventional sounds for more than a moment at a time; usually he was all business. He was not unlike Darius—Darius the huckster, that is. Not Darius the Great King.

"You have seen Confucius four times."

I nodded, not at all surprised that I'd been spied on.

"Duke Ai has received him a number of times, which is highly appropriate."

"But *you* have not received him, Lord Baron." I put the question in the form of a statement, a useful Persian art as yet unknown in the Middle Kingdom.

"The war." The baron gestured at the clerks at the other long table. This meant that he had not yet spoken in private to Confucius.

"It is my impression that he thinks you sent for him in order to use him."

"That is my impression, too." Baron K'ang looked very solemn, a sure sign that he was amused. During my three years in Lu, I got so that I could read his face with the greatest of ease. At the end, we seldom exchanged words. We did not need to. We understood each other perfectly. I was also led to understand, from the beginning, that I was going to have to work very hard indeed for my release from his charming cage.

I made my report. I repeated everything of interest that Confucius had said, and almost everything that Fan Ch'ih had said on the subject of the master. When I was done, the baron said, "You must interest him."

"I am not sure that that is possible." I allowed myself a forbidden smile. In the presence of a superior the courtier must always look humble and apprehensive—by no means a difficult task at any of the volatile Cathayan courts.

It was the genius of the Chou dynasty to mitigate man's destructive nature through intricate rituals, observances, manners and music. A man of the court must know and act upon three hundred rules of major ritual. The mat he sits on must be straight, bedclothes must be exactly one and a half times the length of the sleeper, actual names of the recent dead must not be mentioned, and so on. In addition to the three hundred major observances, the true gentleman must also know and be able to practice three thousand minor ones. To spend one's time with a truly punctilious Cathayan gentleman is a most disturbing experience for a foreigner. Your companion is forever making mysterious hand gestures while looking up to heaven or down to earth, not to mention rolling his eyes from side to side, whispering prayers, assisting you when no help is needed while allowing you to flounder entirely when a degree of help might be useful. Even Baron K'ang's silences, cryptic utterances, uses or nonuses of the facial muscles were all a part of the nobleman's code, somewhat modified for a foreigner's benefit. Yet when men of power are together—anywhere on earth—they tend to disregard many of the niceties which they show to the public. Darius always spat in private; and laughed like a soldier.

"You must interest him." Thus, the baron ordered me to spy directly on Confucius.

"What subjects should I bring up in order to . . . interest him?" Thus, I accepted the commission.

"You are the grandson of a divine sage. That will interest him." After a long and boring list of so-called interesting subjects, the baron came to the point. "The subject of Key is deeply interesting to him, and to me. I believe that very soon we shall have unusual news from Key. When it comes, I have no idea what his response will be. After all, he is close to Duke Chien. He was often in the company of the warden of Pi . . ."

"The traitor!" I was properly outraged.

"To give him his proper name, yes. I am also aware that the warden offered to make Confucius prime minister of Lu if Confucius would help him betray his native land."

I was, for the first time, intrigued. "Did Confucius agree?"

"That is for you to discover. Certainly, the warden made a strong case for the return, as he would put it, of all power to the duke of Lu, who has never—as we know —lost one scintilla of that true power given to him by the celestial ancestors." The conviction that the hereditary ruler is all-powerful is central to the gentleman's thirty-three hundred ritual observances. Everything that the dictator did he did in the name of Duke Ai.

"Was that the reason for the war? The restoration, as they falsely call it, of the duke."

"Yes. The warden persuaded Duke Chien that now was the time to attack. Naturally, Key would like to diminish us, even absorb us. But then, over a year ago, Confucius crossed the Yellow River and settled in Wei. I don't know why. I would like to know why. Had he fallen out with the warden, as he tends to fall out with everyone? Or was it a ruse to make us think that he had no connection with our enemies in Key or with the recent war?"

I had never heard the baron speak quite so directly. I was equally direct. "You think that Confucius is a secret agent of the warden?"

"Or of Duke Chien. Now, even if he were, it would be of no importance except for the fact"—the baron looked me straight in the eye, something a Cathayan gentleman ought never to do—"that his disciples occupy positions in every ministry of our government. My own best general is a devoted Confucian. Your good friend and my second steward, Fan Ch'ih, would give his life for the master. Well, I would prefer that no lives be given. Do you understand me?"

"Yes, Lord Baron."

It was Baron K'ang's fear that the Confucians in his own government combined with the forces of Duke Chien might bring him down, particularly now that he lacked the resources to fight a second war. The baron had brought Confucius home not only to keep an eye on him but to neutralize him should there be a new war. In a sense, I was an ideal agent for the baron. I was a barbarian: I had no allegiance to anyone but the baron, who alone had the power to send me home. Although he did not trust me any more than I trusted him, neither of us had much choice in the matter. I accepted the commission in good faith. I would make myself interesting to Confucius—not the easiest of endeavors, since the world outside the four seas is of no concern to Cathayans. Fortunately, Confucius proved to be unique. He was fascinated by the world of the four barbarians: that is, those who live north, south, east and west of the Middle Kingdom. In fact, whenever he grew discouraged, he would say, "I think I shall just get aboard a raft and float out to sea." This is the Cathayan formula for going native in some wild and uncivilized part of the world.

"How," I asked Baron K'ang, "am I to get him all to myself?"

"Take him fishing," said the baron, going back to the gloomy task of trying to salvage a state close to financial collapse.

As usual, the baron was right. Confucius had a passion for fishing. I cannot remember exactly how I got him to join me at the stream that runs through the willow grove just north of the rain altars, but one bright morning in early summer there we were, just the two of us, each equipped with bamboo pole, silken line, bronze hook, wicker basket. Confucius never fished with a net. "What pleasure can there be in that?" he would ask. "Unless your livelihood depends upon catching as many fish as you can."

Wearing an old quilted robe, Confucius sat cross-legged on the damp green riverbank. I sat next to him on a rock. I still remember how the silver surface of the slow river reflected the sun's light. I still remember that the white spring sky that day contained not only a hazy sun but a half-moon, like a ghost's skull.

We had the river to ourselves. Incidentally, this was the first time that I was able to observe the master without his disciples. I found him most agreeable, and not at all priestly. In fact, he was disagreeable only when someone powerful behaved in an unseemly way.

Confucius proved to be a master angler. Once a fish had taken the hook, he would ever so delicately shift the line this way and that; it was as if the line was moved not by a human hand but by the river's own current. Then, at precisely the right moment, he would strike.

After one long silence he said, "If only one could go on and on just like this, day after day."

"Fishing, Master?"

The old man smiled. "That, too, honored guest. But I was referring to the river, which never stops, which always is."

"Master Li would say that everything is already a part of the always-so." There is no better way of getting a man to let down his guard than to mention his rivals. But Confucius was not to be drawn out on the subject of Master Li. Instead, he asked me about the Wise Lord. I answered at my customary length. He listened non-committally. I did get the impression that he was more interested in the day-to-day life of a good Zoroastrian than in the war between the Truth and the Lie. He was also curious about the various systems of government that I had encountered in my travels. I told him what I could.

I found Confucius to be a most impressive man in spite of the fact that I could not begin to appreciate the vast learning for which he was honored in the Middle Kingdom. Since I knew nothing of the rituals, the odes, the histories that he had committed to memory, I could not delight in the ease with which he quoted from these ancient works. In fact, I could not always tell when he was quoting and when he was extrapolating from an old text. As a rule he spoke quite simply, unlike so many of the Greeks who make simple matters difficult with syntax and then, triumphantly, clarify what they have managed to obscure with even more complex syntax.

I was startled to find how often this traditionalist sage was at odds with received opinion. For instance, when I asked him what the latest tortoise-shell auguries had foretold, he said, "The shell asked to be reunited with the tortoise."

"Is that a proverb, Master?"

"No, honored guest, a joke." And he showed the length of his two front teeth in a smile. Like so many people whose teeth are distorted, he suffered from stomach trouble—for which he was greatly admired. In Cathay, constant loud disturbances in that region of the body signify a superior mind forever at work.

Confucius discussed the poverty of the state. "Only yesterday Duke Ai asked me what he should do. So I asked him if the state had collected all of this year's tithes and he said yes, but the war had cost so much that there was nothing left."

"All the tithes will have to be increased," I said, recalling the glum figure of the baron at work in the Long Treasury.

"But that would be most unwise," said Confucius, "and unfair. After all, if in good times the ruler is willing to share in the plenty, then in bad times he should be willing to accept the fact that he is not going to have as much to spend as he would like to have."

I reported this comment to the baron because I thought that it might mean that Confucius was eager to weaken the state in the event of an attack from Key. The baron thought this possible but unlikely. "He has always taken that view. He thinks the people owe the state a fixed part of their income and no more; and he is angry whenever a government alters what he regards as a sacred contract."

Confucius told me of a wise man whom he had known in his youth. Apparently this statesman—he was the prime minister of one of the least powerful duchies—assembled and conformed all the laws of the Middle Kingdom and had them inscribed on bronze, much the way Darius did when he gave us our law code. The sage—Tzu-Ch'an by name—also worked out a new series of economic arrangements, to the horror of the conservatives. But his reforms proved to be so effective that today he is one of the most admired of modern Cathayans. Certainly, Confucius was generous in his praise of his mentor. "Tzu-Ch'an had the four virtues of the perfect gentleman." A fish tugged at the master's line. Delicately he flicked his pole downstream; then, more sharply, upstream. "He's hooked," he said happily.

"What are the four virtues?" I asked. Everything is numbered east of the Indus River.

As Confucius cautiously pulled in his line he listed these precious qualities: "The perfect gentleman is courteous in private life. He is punctilious in his dealings with the prince. He gives the common people not only their due but more. Finally, he is entirely just in dealing with those who serve him, and the state."

"Tzu-Ch'an sounds like a divine sage." I was polite. Actually, the wise man sounded to me like one of those

467

masters of the commonplace who are always quoted at such length by the dull.

Confucius let the fish weary itself at the river's edge. "I doubt if we shall ever see a divine sage in our time. But we can always hope to find a perfect gentleman."

"You are considered to be that, Master. If not more." I spoke to him as if to a ruler.

But Confucius seemed not to take himself for granted in quite the same way that most eminent men do. "What I am considered to be and what I am are two different things. Like the fish, which is one thing in the water and another on the plate. I am a teacher because no one will allow me to conduct the affairs of a state. I'm like the bitter gourd: they hang me on the wall as a decoration, but I am not used." He said this without any apparent bitterness. Then he landed the fish, a sizable perch. With swift gestures he unhooked the fish, threw it into the wicker basket, prepared the hook once more with bait and cast his line—all this in the time it takes an ordinary person to phrase the response to a question whose answer he knows.

When I complimented Confucius on his expertness as a fisherman, he laughed and said, "I don't hold high office. That's why I have so many skills."

"It is said that the duke of Key offered you high office."

"That was the old duke. And that was many years ago. Lately, I have talked to his son. Duke Chien is a serious man. But I have no influence in Key."

"That is plain, Master." I began to fulfill Baron K'ang's commission. Simultaneously, I hooked a fish.

"Why is that so plain, honored guest?" Confucius was one of the few wise men who actually asked questions in order to find out what he did not know. As a rule, this world's sages prefer to bait the listener with carefully constructed questions in order to elicit answers that will reflect the wise man's immutable views. This is a very easy thing to do, as you observed the other day, Democritus, when I obliged Socrates to answer *my* questions. In this darkness, where I perpetually sit, I can *hear* you smile. Well, you'll see that I'm right one day. Wisdom did not begin in Attica, though it may yet end here.

"Because of the recent war, Master, which you would have opposed."

"I was not in Key when the war began." Confucius

looked at my taut line. "Downstream, but easily," he advised. I moved the pole but not easily; and lost the fish. "Too bad," he said. "It takes the lightest touch. But then, I've fished this river all my life. I know the current. I'm surprised that anyone would think that I might have encouraged the war." Confucius knew exactly what *I* was fishing for. One could not fool him on his own ground, and I did not try.

I was to the point. "It is thought that you wanted the warden of Castle Pi to restore the duke to power."

Confucius nodded; and let out his line. "It's quite true that I've spoken to the warden. It's true that he offered me office. It's true that I said no. He is an adventurer, and not serious." The old man looked at me suddenly. The eyes were paler than those of most Cathayans. "It is also true that there shall never be a proper balance between heaven and earth until we restore the old ceremonies, music, manners and dynasty. We live in evil times because we are not good. Tell that to Baron K'ang." It did not disturb him that I had been assigned to spy on him. In fact, he used me as a means of communicating with the prime minister.

"What is goodness, Master?"

"Whoever submits himself to ritual is good." A cloud of gnats gathered about us. "Don't stir," he said. "They'll move on." We sat very still. They did not move on. I found myself breathing in gnats. But the master was oblivious to them. "A gentleman or a ruler"—Confucius again showed his front teeth in a smile—"the two can be the same, you know—must do nothing in defiance of ritual. He should treat everyone in the same courteous way. He should never do anything to anyone that he would not like them to do to him."

"But surely, when a ruler puts a man to death for a crime he is doing something that he would not like anyone to do to him."

"Presumably, the man who is put to death has defied ritual. He has committed evil in the eyes of heaven."

"But suppose he is serving his country in a war?" By now both Confucius and I were fighting off the gnats. He used his fan; I used my wide-brimmed straw hat. Finally the gnats began to depart in groups, like military units.

"War involves a different set of rituals. It is when a nation is at peace that the good ruler must be on his guard, must avoid the four ugly things."

Again the numbers! Since I was expected to ask what these four ugly things were, I did. Meanwhile, the last of the definitely ugly gnats had moved on.

"First, putting a man to death without having taught him what is right; that is called savagery. Second, to expect a task to be completed at a certain date without having given the worker warning; that is oppression. Third, to be vague in the orders you give while expecting absolute punctiliousness; that is being a tormentor. Finally, to give someone his due in a grudging way; that is contemptible and petty."

Since one could hardly deny the ugliness of these things, I made no comment. He expected none. "What exactly do you mean by ritual, Master?" The word for ritual is constantly used in Cathay and means much more than mere religious observance.

"The ancient rites of Chou purify us while the sacrifice to the ancestors binds earth to heaven in perfect harmony *if* the ruler is good and the rites are accurately performed."

"At Loyang I watched the ancestral ceremonies. I'm afraid that I found them confusing."

Confucius had hooked another fish. The bamboo pole bent in an arc. The fish was heavy but the angler's hand was light. "Anyone who understood all of the ancestral sacrifices could deal with everything under heaven as easily as I . . . catch—" With a powerful jerk, Confucius flipped the pole upward and a fat bream sailed over our heads. We both laughed with pleasure. It is always agreeable to see something done marvelously well. "—this fish." As Confucius completed the sentence the fish fell into a lilac bush. I retrieved it for the master, who said, "All the ancestral ceremonies are a bit like catching fish. Too hard a tug and you break your line or pole. Too soft a tug and you'll lose the fish—the pole, too."

"So to be good is to act in accordance with heaven's will."

"Of course." The old man put away his latest conquest. "What," I asked, "is heaven?"

Confucius took rather longer than usual in baiting his hook. He did not answer until the line was once again cast. I noticed that the daytime moon had vanished. The sun was now aslant in the white sky.

"Heaven is the dispenser of life and death, good fortune and bad." He was aware that he had not answered my question. I said nothing. He continued, "Heaven is where the original ancestor dwells. When we make sacrifice to heaven, we make sacrifice to him."

I caught an eel. I thought that my wriggling eel was an excellent representation of Confucius on the subject of heaven. He was not specific—for the excellent reason that he did not believe in heaven any more than he believed in the so-called supreme ancestor.

Confucius was an atheist. I am certain of that. But he believed in the power of ritual and ceremony as conceived by the long-dead Chou dynasty because he was devoted to order, balance, harmony in human affairs. Since the common people believe in all sorts of star gods and since the ruling class believe in their direct descent from a series of celestial ancestors who watch them closely from heaven, Confucius strove to use these ancient beliefs in order to create a harmonious society. He emphasized the Chou dynasty because—aside from the charm of Duke Tan's admonitions—the last son of heaven was a Chou. Therefore, to create a united Middle Kingdom, it was necessary to find a new son of heaven, preferably from that family. But since Confucius rightly feared the emergence of the wrong sort of ruler, he constantly emphasized what he claimed to be the virtues of the old dynasty. Although I am fairly certain that he made up a good deal of what he said, Fan Ch'ih swore to me that Confucius did nothing but interpret actual texts. To which I answered, "Then he interprets them only to suit present occasions." Fan Ch'ih saw nothing wrong with that.

When I told him Confucius' joke about the tortoise shell, he frowned. "That was unseemly."

"Why?"

"The art of divination originates with the ancestors. They also gave us *The Book of Changes*, which the master venerates."

"Yet he smiled."

Fan Ch'ih looked unhappy. "It is no secret that the master is not as interested in divination as he ought to be. In fact, he is said to have said that a man makes his own future by complying with the laws of heaven."

"Which he does not believe exists."

Fan Ch'ih was shocked. "If you think that, you've not understood him. Of course, you're a barbarian." He grinned. "You serve that very peculiar god who created

471

evil so that he would have an excuse to torture his other creations."

I did not dignify this blasphemy with an answer.

As far as I know, Confucius was the only Cathayan who had no interest at all in ghosts or demons or the spirit world. One might almost think that he did not believe in them. I questioned him several times on the subject, but never got a very satisfactory answer.

I do remember that just as I was trying to get the eel off my hook, I asked Confucius, "What of the dead? Where do they go? Are they judged? Do they rise again? Or are they born again?" The eel's twisting made it impossible for me to get the hook out of its jaw. "Is there not *some* merit in doing good which will be rewarded in heaven? And if not, then why—"

"You'd better let me unhook that eel," said the master. With a skilled gesture, the old man flipped the eel from the line to the basket. Then he dried his hands on the grass. "How well," he asked, "do you know life?"

"I'm not sure I know what you mean. I know my own life. I've traveled in strange lands, met all sorts of people . . ."

"But you've not met all races, all men?"

"Of course not."

"Then, honored guest, since you do not yet understand life, how can you understand death?"

"Do you understand life, Master?"

"Of course not. I know a few things. I love learning. I have tried to understand this world. I listen to everyone. I put to one side what seems doubtful and I'm cautious about the rest."

"You do not believe in divine revelation?"

"Such as?"

I told him of the time that I heard the voice of the Wise Lord. I also described the vision of Pythagoras, the enlightenment of the Buddha, the other-worldly experiences of our own Magians—admittedly haoma-induced, but still true vision. The old man listened, and smiled—or gave that impression: the tips of the two front teeth were always visible. As a result, Confucius' usual expression was one of gentle amusement.

When I finished, Confucius drew in his line and neatly put away his tackle. I did the same, less neatly. For a moment I thought he had forgotten what we had been talking about. But as he got to his feet, with some help from me—he had brittle joints—the master said, most casually, "I've heard many stories like the ones you've told me and I used to be tremendously impressed by them. So much so that I, finally, decided that the time had come for me to try meditation. I spent a whole day without food, a whole night without sleep. I was entirely concentrated. And then what do you think happened?" For the first time he addressed me informally. I had been accepted.

"I don't know, Master."

"Nothing. Absolutely nothing. My mind was a perfect blank. I saw nothing at all. I understood nothing at all. That is why I think it is better to study real things in a real world."

We walked slowly through the trees just back of the altars. Confucius was recognized and saluted by all the passers-by; he responded benignly, courteously, distantly.

In front of the altars a loutish knight suddenly appeared. "Master!" He greeted Confucius rapturously.

"Tzu-Kung." The master's greetings were correct; but no more.

"I have great news!"

"Tell us."

"You remember when I asked you if there was any one precept that I could and should act upon all day and every day?"

Confucius nodded. "I remember, yes. I told you, 'Never do to others what you would not like them to do to you.' "

"That was more than a month ago and now, thanks to you, Master, what I do not want others to do to me I have no desire—believe me!—no desire at all to do to them!"

"My dear," said Confucius, patting Tzu-Kung's arm, "you have not quite got to that point yet."

5

I REPORTED TO BARON K'ANG. I DON'T know what impression my account of that first conversation with Confucius made. He listened gravely; then asked me to remember everything that had been said

473

about the former warden of Pi. He seemed more interested in him than in the duke of Key.

When I ventured to say that I thought it most unlikely that a man like Confucius would ever try to overthrow a state, Baron K'ang shook his head. "You do not know this great man as well as we do. He disapproves of the current order. You heard what he said about my revered father, the hereditary prime minister: 'If this man can be endured, anything can be endured.' That was said openly, before the first exile."

"Why didn't your father put him to death?"

The baron made a rolling gesture with one hand. "Because he is Confucius, we put up with his bad temper. Also, he knows heaven's way. So we must honor him. But we must also keep a watchful eye on him."

"At *seventy,* Lord Baron?"

"Oh, yes. The annals of the Middle Kingdom are crowded with wicked old men who tried to tear the state to pieces." Then the baron told me that I was to teach the state metalworkers how to smelt iron. I was also to see Confucius as often as possible, and make regular reports. The baron granted me daily access to his person, which meant that I could attend his court whenever I chose. For some reason I was never accepted at the levees of either the Meng or Shu family. But I was always welcome at the ducal court.

I was provided with a modest salary, a pleasant if chilly house near the foundry, two servants and two concubines. Cathayan women are easily the most beautiful on earth, and the most subtle when it comes to pleasing men. I became inordinately fond of both girls. When Fan Ch'ih told Confucius about my venery, the master laughed and said, "All my life I have searched for a man whose desire to build up his moral power was as strong as his drive for sex. I thought that perhaps our barbarian was he. Now I must go on looking."

Generally speaking, Confucius did not laugh much in the time that I knew him. Quite soon after his return, things started to go very wrong. I was present at the court when Duke Ai announced, "My dearly beloved cousin the duke of Key has been murdered."

Despite protocol, there was an audible gasp in the room. Although the premier knight did not gasp or move or do anything unseemly, he did turn very pale.

Apparently a baronial family in Key had decided to

474

seize power in much the same way that the Chi family had taken power from the dukes of Lu. The friend and patron of Confucius was murdered in front of his own ancestral temple. When Duke Ai had finished speaking, Confucius asked permission, as premier knight, to address the throne.

When permission was granted, he said, "I beg forgiveness for not first bathing my head and limbs, as becomes a suppliant. But I did not know that I would find myself in such a situation on this dreadful day." Although the old man's voice kept cracking with tension, he made an eloquent speech to the effect that the murder of a lawful monarch is an affront to heaven, and must be punished. "In fact, if the murder is not promptly avenged, all the nations are apt to forfeit heaven's sympathy."

The duke's response was dignified. "I share the premier knight's horror at my cousin's murder. I will do what *I* can to avenge him." The duke looked properly fierce, as befits a man without power. "Now I suggest that you take this matter up in council with the Three."

Confucius went straight to Baron K'ang, who told him bluntly that there was nothing anyone in Lu could do about a murder in Key. Confucius was furious; he was also helpless.

That evening Fan Ch'ih came to my house at the foundry. As the two girls served us fried rice cakes—we lived frugally in those postwar days—Fan Ch'ih told me, "We've expected this ever since the war."

"The murder of the duke?"

Fan Ch'ih nodded. "He wanted to restore all power to Duke Ai. But when he lost the war, he lost the support of his own barons. And so, with a degree of help from outside, they killed him."

"Help from outside?" Suddenly I remembered what Baron K'ang had said about certain events that were in train.

Fan Ch'ih put his finger to his lips. I motioned for the girls to withdraw. When we were alone, Fan Ch'ih told me that Baron K'ang had conspired with the barons in Key to kill the duke. This explained why the baron had been so eager for me to find out not only what Confucius might do or want to do but, more important, to what extent Jan Ch'iu and Fan Ch'ih would be influenced by Confucius' predictable anger at the murder of a prince who was also a personal friend. Not unreasonably, Baron

475

K'ang's constant fear was treason. Certainly, he had every reason to be apprehensive. In his lifetime, a Chi servant had made himself dictator of Lu; the warden of his own castle had gone into rebellion; and the duke of Key had invaded the realm. If the baron was a deeply suspicious man, who could blame him?

"I've tried to put his mind at rest," I said. "But I don't think that the baron takes me very seriously."

"He might. You are from outside."

"When do you think that I'll be able to go—*inside*?" Although my days were pleasant in that charming if somewhat dangerous land, I was often overwhelmed with loneliness. I still recall most vividly the sense of strangeness that engulfed me one morning in autumn. The first girl had wanted me to go early to market and look at a pair of expensive pheasants. I remember how cold the dawn was. I remember that the night mist was still in the air. I remember that the market itself was—is—a constant delight. During the night, wagons and carts roll into the city with produce. Vegetables and edible roots are then exquisitely arranged, according not to price but to color, size and beauty. Round tubs contain live fish, both freshwater and salt-water, as well as octopuses, prawns and crabs. Exotic and costly delicacies are also available: bear's paws, gelatinous bird's nests, the fins of sharks, the livers of peacocks, buried eggs from the time of the Yellow Emperor.

Just as the sun rises over the market and the mist begins to burn away, the buying and selling is at its most intense. The scene is delightful and I was usually a contented part of it. But that particular morning, standing in front of a row of wicker cages filled with bronze-colored pheasants, I was suddenly overwhelmed with loneliness. I have never felt so out of the real world. There I stood, surrounded by people of an alien race whose language I barely understood, whose culture was so remote from anything that I had ever known. Should there actually be an Aryan home of the fathers or a Hades, I am sure that one would feel in that limbo rather the way that I felt, looking at pheasants through eyes blurred with tears. I was reminded of that passage in Homer where the ghost of Achilles mourns for his old life in the world beneath that sun which he will never see again. At that moment I would rather have been a shepherd in the hills back of Susa than the son of heaven. Although such moments of weakness were rare, they were no less excruciating when they did come. I still dream sometimes that I am surrounded by yellow people in a marketplace. When I try to escape, cages filled with pheasants bar my way.

Fan Ch'ih was consoling. "We'll go together. Soon. The baron likes the idea. And he should. After all, I've found what I think must have been the original silk road to India. We could start tomorrow except . . ."

"No money?"

Fan Ch'ih nodded. "It's worse than you think. The Chi treasury's almost empty. The ducal treasury is permanently empty."

"What about the Meng and Shu families?"

"They're suffering, too. Last year's harvest was bad. The war was disastrously expensive, and we gained nothing except Lang, the poorest town in Key."

"You said that there are no bankers here but surely there must be wealthy merchants who are willing to lend money to the state."

"No. Our rich pretend to be poor. As a result, no one lends money because . . . well, life is so fragile here."

No more fragile than anywhere else, I thought. But it is true that the long periods of relative peace and stability at Babylon and even Magadha had made complex banking procedures possible. The Middle Kingdom is too fragmented for any very elaborate system of borrowing and lending.

"Tomorrow"—Fan Ch'ih looked unhappy, despite the presence before him of the dish of the four seasons which the girls had taken four days to prepare, a dish that one would like to contemplate and savor for yet another four days—"Baron K'ang will announce new taxes. They are to be levied on everyone. No one is to be exempt. It's the only way we'll be able to pry the money from the rich."

"And ruin everyone else." I was alarmed. The war tax had been levied a few months before, to the dismay of every citizen. At the time, Confucius had warned the government that the tax was excessive. "Worse," he had said, "by taking so much for the state, you reduce everyone's ability to create more wealth. Even the bandit in the forest never takes more than two thirds of a merchant's caravan. After all, it is to the bandit's interest that the merchant prosper so that there will always be something for him to steal." I asked Fan Ch'ih if Confucius had been consulted.

"No. Baron K'ang does not want another lecture. Jun

Ch'iu is going to post the proclamation on the wall of the Long Treasury. Then he and his soldiers will go from house to house and collect what they can."

"I hope that the baron knows what he is doing."

"He knows what he has to do." Fan Ch'ih was not at all happy. Aside from the public unrest that the new taxes would create, the entire government was concerned with Confucius' reaction. I always marveled at the awe in which this powerless old man was held. Although no ruler would give him the office he wanted or heed his advice either political or religious, every official wanted his benediction. I still do not understand how a single scholar without political power or wealth could have established such a position for himself. Doubtless, heaven had given him a decree when no one was looking.

The day that the new taxes went into effect, I was at the house of Confucius. A dozen of the disciples were arranged in a semicircle about the master, who sat with his back against the wooden column that supported the ceiling to the inner room. The old man's back seemed to bother him for he would press first one shoulder blade, then the other against the hard surface of the wood. No one mentioned the latest tax assessment. Confucius' views on the subject were too well known. Instead we spoke, not unfittingly, of funerals and mourning, of the dead and what was owing to them. Tzu-lu sat on the master's left. Yen Hui sat on the master's right. In another part of the house, Confucius' son was dying. Death was in the air.

"Certainly," said Confucius, "one cannot be too strict when it comes to mourning. We owe that much to our memory of the dead. I would even adhere to the old rule that a man who has wailed in the morning at a funeral should not raise his voice in song that night."

Although everyone agreed that one could not be too punctilious in observing funeral rites—for instance, one must never sacrifice to the dead after eating garlic or drinking wine—there was some disagreement about how long one ought to mourn a parent as opposed to one's child, friend or wife.

A young disciple said, "I am convinced that a year's mourning is quite enough for one's father; yet the master insists on a full three years of mourning."

"I *insist* on nothing, little one. I simply conform to custom." Although Confucius was his usual mild self, I could not help but notice the somewhat anxious looks that he would direct to the sickly Yen Hui.

"But isn't it customary to suspend all ordinary business when you mourn for your father?"

"That is the custom," said Confucius.

"But, Master, if a gentleman does not practice all the rites of religion for three years, the rites will decay. If he makes no music, he will lose the art. If he doesn't plant his fields, there will be no harvest. If he doesn't whirl the drill in the wood, there'll be no new fire when the old fire burns out. Surely, a year without doing these necessary things is more than enough."

Confucius shifted his gaze from Yen Hui to the young disciple. "After only a year of mourning," he asked, "would you feel comfortable eating the best rice and wearing fine brocades?"

"Yes, Master, I would."

"In that case, do so. By all means. Only remember"— and the soft voice rose slightly—"if the true gentleman hears music at a time of mourning, the music will sound harsh to his ears. Good food will have no taste. A comfortable bed will be like a stony field. That's why he finds it easy, and proper, to abstain from such luxuries. But if you really feel at ease indulging yourself, why, go right ahead!"

"I knew that you would understand, Master." Much relieved, the disciple excused himself.

When the youth had gone, Confucius shook his head. "How very inhuman! That young man's father has been dead for only a year and now he wants to stop all mourning. Yet when he was a child he spent his first three years in the arms of his parents. One would think that the least he could do would be to mourn his father for the same length of time."

Although Confucius encouraged me to ask questions, I seldom did when others were present. I preferred to question the sage when we were alone together. I had also discovered that when he had a fishing rod in his hand, he was at his most communicative. He would even ask me questions, and listen carefully to the answers. Therefore, it was to my own surprise that I found myself asking Confucius a question in front of the disciples. I suppose that I was affected by the general tension. Confucius' son was dying; Yen Hui was ill; the master was so outraged by the new taxes that schism within the ranks of the disciples was a distinct possibility. In order to distract, as well as to learn, I heard myself ask, "I have noticed that in parts of the Middle Kingdom, men and women are put to death when a great lord dies. In the eyes of heaven, is this seemly, Master?"

All eyes were suddenly turned upon me. Since there is not a society on earth that does not perpetuate ancient customs which profoundly embarrass thoughtful contemporaries, my question was definitely unseemly.

Confucius shook his head, as if to condemn with a physical gesture a practice that he was obliged to explain if not justify. "Since the time of the Yellow Emperor, it has been the custom for the great people who have died to take with them their loyal slaves. In the west the custom still flourishes, as you witnessed in Ch'in. We are less traditional here in the east. But that is because of the duke of Chou, whose words on the subject place the whole matter in a somewhat different light."

Whenever Confucius mentioned the duke of Chou, one could be fairly certain that he himself was about to subvert custom in the name of the legendary founder of Lu, whose sayings seemed never to contradict Confucius' own views of things. "Since our rulers like to be served in their tombs as they were served in their palaces—a seemly desire and entirely traditional—it has been the custom to put to death all sorts of useful men and women, horses and dogs. This is proper, up to a point—a point that the duke of Chou elucidated so beautifully, as he did everything. He noted the fact that human bodies quickly deteriorate and that their flesh soon turns to earth. In no time at all, the most beautiful concubine that ever lived will lose her form and turn to common clay. Now, the duke of Chou said, 'When these slaughtered men and women turn to clay, they lose their original shape and function. So let us substitute for temporary flesh, true clay images that have been so fired that they will last forever. In either case, the great lord is surrounded by clay. But if the images about him are made of clay that has kept its shape, then his spirit will be able to gaze upon the loyal slaves forever.' "

The disciples were pleased. Whether or not the duke of Chou had ever said such a thing did not matter. Confucius had said that he had said it, and that was enough. Certainly, every intelligent Cathayan agreed that human sacrifice on a large scale is wasteful and pointless—and

480

condemned, according to Confucius, by the Chou dynasty. "Of course," Tzu-lu noted, "the people of Ch'in have little regard for human life."

"True," I said. "In fact, when I asked the dictator of Ch'in why he felt obliged to put so many people to death for unimportant crimes, he said, 'If you wash your head properly, you will always lose a few hairs. If you don't wash your head at all, you will lose all your hair.'"

I sensed, to my surprise, that most of those in the room agreed with Huan. But then, the people of the Middle Kingdom tend to favor the death penalty for crimes that we would punish with a simple mutilation or even a beating.

The subject of funerals, of mourning, of what is owing the dead, fascinates the Cathayans even more than it does us. I never realized quite why until Tzu-lu suddenly asked the master, "Do the dead know that we pray for them?"

I was aware—who was not?—that Confucius always had a deep dislike for the unanswerable question. "Wouldn't you agree," he asked, "that it is quite enough that *we* know what we are doing when we honor them?"

"No." As Confucius' oldest and fiercest disciple, Tzu-lu did not in the least mind contradicting the sage. "If spirits and ghosts do not exist, then I see no reason why we should bother to propitiate or serve them."

"But if they do exist?" Confucius smiled. "What then?"

"We ought to honor them, of course, but—"

"Since we cannot know for certain, is it not best to do as our ancestors did?"

"Perhaps. But the expense of a funeral can ruin a family." Tzu-lu was stubborn. "There must be some other, more reasonable way of serving both spirits and the living."

"My old friend, until you have learned how to serve living men properly, how can you hope to serve them when they are dead?" Confucius looked, inadvertently I should think, at Yen Hui, who looked at him and smiled; suddenly every detail of the young man's skull was visible beneath the loosened skin.

"Besides," Confucius went on, "the world that matters is this world, the living world. But since we love and respect those who came before us, we observe those rites which remind us of our unity with the ancestors. Yet the real significance of these rituals is not easily grasped, even by the sage. For the common people, the whole thing is a mystery. They regard such ceremonies as services rendered to propitiate frightful ghosts, which is not the case. Heaven is far. Man is near. We honor the dead for the sake of the living."

Confucius' evasions on the subject of heaven always fascinated me. I wanted to question him further, but we were interrupted by the arrival of Jan Ch'iu and Fan Ch'ih. They squatted at the back of the room like schoolboys late for their lesson.

Confucius stared at Jan Ch'iu for a long moment. Then he asked, "Why are you late?"

"Affairs of state, Master." Jan Ch'iu's voice was low.

Confucius shook his head. "I may not hold office but if there had been state business this evening, I would have known." There was an embarrassed silence. Then Confucius asked, "Do you approve of the new taxes?"

"This morning I posted the assessments on the wall of the Long Treasury, at the order of Baron K'ang."

"That is well known." For once the tips of the two front teeth were no longer visible; the old man had so set his rabbit's mouth that he looked uncharacteristically stern, like some devil-god of lightning. "I did not ask you whether or not you had posted the new assessments: I asked you if you approved of them."

Jan Ch'iu looked desolate and nervous. "As steward of the Chi family, I am obliged to obey the prime minister."

Confucius was as close to rage as it was possible for him to be. "In all things?" he asked.

"I have duties, Master. And it has always been your rule that one must serve one's lawful lord."

"Even when he requires you to commit sacrilege?"

Jan Ch'iu looked puzzled. "Sacrilege, Master?"

"Yes, sacrilege. Last spring Baron K'ang went to Mount T'ai. He offered jade to the spirit of the mountain. Since only the sovereign may do that, he committed sacrilege. Did you assist him in those ceremonies on Mount T'ai?"

"Yes, Master."

"Then you have committed sacrilege." Confucius snapped shut his official fan. "Have you begun to collect the new taxes?"

Jan Ch'iu nodded, eyes to the floor.

"What you are doing is unjust. The taxes are excessive. The people will suffer. You should have tried to stop Baron K'ang. You should have warned him of the consequences of what he is doing."

482

"I did warn him that the taxes were . . . would be re-sented."

"When the ruler refuses to act justly toward the people, his servant is obliged to resign. Your duty was plain. You should have given up your post as steward of the Chi family."

Throughout the room there was the hissing sound of breath suddenly inhaled. I was witnessing something that had never happened before. Confucius had denounced a disciple—a disciple who happened to be one of the most powerful men in the state. Jan Ch'iu got to his feet. He bowed low to the master and withdrew. Fan Ch'ih remained. Smiling pleasantly, Confucius changed the subject.

For a time, Lu seemed to be on the verge of revolution. I was reminded of Egypt's response to Darius' war levies. There is always a point beyond which you cannot drive people, and when that point is reached, either the ruler must enslave them all or he must find some clever way to retreat from his position.

Confucius now became the center for those anti-Chi knights who served the duke and also the Shu and Meng families. Although the barons objected to the taxes, they dared not confront Baron K'ang. Like Duke Ai, they made cryptic remarks. Like Duke Ai, they did nothing. Not only was the Chi family army powerful, it was loyal to the dictator. Also, the day before the new taxes were posted, Baron K'ang increased the pay of every one of his soldiers. In difficult times, loyalty is expensive.

During this tense period I spent my days at the foundry. Since Baron K'ang did not send for me, I did not attend the Chi court. Needless to say, I did not visit Confucius. I also avoided the ducal court, always a center of dissent. In fact, I saw no one except Fan Ch'ih, who would come to see me. He was my only link with the dangerous world of the court.

Fan Ch'ih liked to come to the foundry and watch the iron smelters. He found the process fascinating. I found the Cathayan metalworkers fascinating. I have never known any people so quick to learn and master new techniques. Although I was officially in charge of the state's iron production, I had very little to do after the first few months. The metal-workers now knew everything that their Persian counterparts knew; and I was redundant.

A week after the tax levy, Fan Ch'ih paid me a call. I turned over the works to my chief assistant and stepped out of the heat and glare that molten metal makes into a hazy violet evening, marked by the slow falling of large flakes of snow. As we strolled toward my house I was told the latest news. Apparently Baron K'ang was in complete control of the situation. The taxes were being collected and the state was reasonably secure from internal dissension. "But the master has refused to see Jan Ch'iu. Or Baron K'ang."

We were in the street of the Shang potters. The Shang are the dark-haired pre-Chou inhabitants who were conquered by the northern tribes. Before the Chous came into the Middle Kingdom, the Shang were priests and administrators, masters of reading and writing. Now they have no power. They make pottery. But, lately, many of Confucius' gentlemen are of the old Shang stock. Thus, slowly, the dark-haired people return to power, as they appear to be doing everywhere in the world. Zoroaster, the Buddha, Mahavira—even Pythagoras—are reviving the old religions of the pre-Aryan world and, slowly, the horse god is dying everywhere.

"Isn't it dangerous," I asked, "for Confucius to challenge Baron K'ang?" We stood in front of a pottery stall. Since each Shang shop contains a single lantern that makes the yellows and reds and blues of the glazed pottery glow like so many coals in a furnace, Fan Ch'ih suddenly looked to be a rainbow made flesh.

Fan Ch'ih smiled. "This is 'Chou in the east.' Or so we claim. Our divine sage is safe, no matter what he says."

"He says that he is not a divine sage."

"He is modest, a sign of divinity if there ever was one. But he is cruel. Jan Ch'iu suffers."

"He could end his suffering by resigning as steward."

"He won't resign."

"Then he prefers to suffer?"

"He prefers power to goodness. This is not uncommon. But he would like to be good as well as powerful, which is uncommon. He thinks that this is possible. The master disagrees."

Fan Ch'ih bought us roasted chestnuts. As we peeled them we burned our fingers; as we ate them we burned our mouths. All the while, soft clinging flakes of snow like icy feathers fell from dull silver sky to dull silver earth.

"You must speak to him," said Fan Ch'ih, mouth full of chestnuts.

"To Jan Ch'iu?"

"To Confucius. You are a neutral figure, an outsider. He'll listen to you."

"I doubt that. Besides, what can I say?"

"You can say the truth. The state suffers because there is no harmony between the ruler and the divine sage. Now, if Confucius will receive Jan Ch'iu . . ."

I said that I would do what I could. Meanwhile, I asked—yet again—about my return.

Fan Ch'ih was not optimistic. "Nothing can be done this year. The treasury's still in deficit. But I do know that Baron K'ang is very interested in the overland route to India."

"Your silk road?"

"My silk road, yes. But such a trip would be a major undertaking."

"I grow old, Fan Ch'ih." To this day, I associate utter loneliness with snow falling, chestnuts burning.

"Bring together Baron K'ang and Confucius. If you do, you'll get what you want." Although I did not believe him, I said that I would do what I could.

The next day was the last day of the old year, and so I went to Confucius' ancestral shrine. I could not have selected a worse moment. For one thing, the expulsion rite was in full swing. This is easily the noisiest ceremony on earth. Everyone races about, blowing horns, beating drums, shaking rattles. It is believed that only by making the most noise possible can the evil spirits of the old year be driven out to make way for the good spirits of the new year. During the expulsion rite, it was Confucius' custom to put on court dress and stand atop the eastern steps of the ancestral shrine. When the noise was at its most deafening, he would speak soothingly to the ancestral spirits. He would tell them not to be frightened or amazed by the awful racket. He would entreat them to remain where they were.

But to my astonishment, Confucius had not taken his usual position on the steps to the shrine. Was he ill? I hurried to his house. Or tried to hurry: every few steps and I was stopped by the antics of the exorcists and their official madmen.

For a sum, an exorcist will go from house to house,

driving out evil spirits. The exorcist is accompanied by four very noisy men who are called the madmen. Whether or not these creatures are really mad is unimportant. Certainly, they behave in the most grotesque manner possible. Each wears a bearskin over his head and shoulders; and carries a pike and shield. Once inside a house, the madmen inspire the servants to ecstasies of ear-shattering shrieks while the exorcist darts about the house, howling epithets at the evil spirits that live in the cellar, the eaves, the back rooms.

The whitewashed façade of Confucius's house had been smeared with saffron-yellow paint. I never did find out the significance of those daubings. As the front door was ajar, I stepped inside. I expected to see some sort of religious ceremony. But there were no priests or even students in the outer room, which was tomb-cold.

As I crossed the outer hall I heard the sound of wailing from within the house. Thinking that it was an exorcist, I stopped in my tracks and tried to recall the proper etiquette. Was it permissible to enter someone's house during the expulsion rite?

I was enlightened by a disciple who had slipped into the hall behind me. "The son is dead," he whispered. "We must pay our respects to the father." He led me into the private quarters.

Dressed in mourning, Confucius sat on a plain mat, back to the wooden column. The room was half filled with disciples. Everyone looked not only sad but shocked.

I saluted the master, who responded with his usual courtesy. We both made the gestures that are required on the saddest of occasions. As I knelt beside Tzu-lu, he murmured, "There is no consoling him."

"How could there be when it is the height of sorrow to lose one's eldest son?" I spoke the traditional line.

"He has lost more than that," said Tzu-lu.

At first I did not understand what he meant. Conventionally speaking, the worst thing that can happen to a man is the loss of the eldest son. I joined in the chants; repeated the prayers; made consoling sounds. But Confucius was now genuinely weeping, as well as wailing ritually.

Finally, respectfully but firmly, Tzu-lu said, "Master, you have abandoned all restraint. Is such weeping seemly?"

Confucius stopped his wailing; tears gleamed on his

cheeks like snail tracks. "Is it seemly?" he repeated. Then, before Tzu-lu could answer, he began to weep fresh tears. Simultaneously, he spoke in a surprisingly steady voice, "If any man's death could justify abandoned weeping, it is *his*."

I realized then that Confucius did not believe in an afterlife. Whatever he might say, ritually, about heaven as the resident of the ancestors, he himself did not believe that there was such a place. Even so, I was still somewhat surprised that he would be demoralized by the death of a son who had meant very little to him. In fact, the son had often been a source of embarrassment to the father. More than once he had been accused of taking money from Confucius' students and keeping it for himself. Worst of all, he had been stupid.

Then an old man whom I had never seen before said, "Master, let me have your carriage so that I can use it to make a proper frame for my son's coffin."

I was more and more mystified. Who was this old man? Who was the dead son? Abruptly, Confucius stopped weeping. He turned to the old man. "No, my friend, you may not have it. You are bereft, which is natural. I am equally bereft. No, doubly bereft, for I have lost my own son, such as he was, and now I have lost your son, too, the best and wisest of all young men."

It was then that I realized that Yen Hui was also dead. Twice, in quick succession, the master had been struck by . . . heaven.

Yen Hui's father began, disagreeably, to whine. "Then, is it not all-important that such a brilliant youth receive every possible honor? Was he not the wisest man's wisest pupil?"

Confucius blinked his eyes, and annoyance replaced grief. Contrary to what people may think, the old are always more swift to change their moods than the young. "Your son was like a tree which I was able to nurse until it had flowered. But the tree did not live long enough to bear fruit." Confucius paused; he took a deep breath; then he spoke without apparent emotion. "I cannot allow my carriage to be used for a coffin frame, because when my own son was buried—not that I mean to compare the two—I did not grant him a coffin frame either. First, because it would not be seemly and, second, because I am the premier knight and, as such, I may not proceed to the tomb on foot. Custom requires me to ride a chariot. Since this is the law, we have no choice in the matter."

Although the father of Yen Hui was plainly displeased, he did not dare press the matter. But Tzu-lu did. "Surely, Master, we must bury Yen Hui with all possible ceremony. We can find wood for a coffin frame without depriving you of your carriage. Certainly, we must do Yen Hui every honor. We owe it to heaven. We owe it to the ancestors. We owe it to you who taught him."

There was a long silence. Then Confucius lowered his head and whispered as if to himself, "Heaven has stolen from me what was mine."

No sooner was this blasphemy spoken than heaven responded. An exorcist burst into the room, followed by four howling madmen. As they danced about, rattling bells, striking drums, shouting insults at all the evil spirits of the old year, Confucius slipped out of the room; and I hurried across the city to the Chi palace.

I found Fan Ch'ih in that part of the palace which corresponds to the chancellor's second room at home. Here the business of the state is daily conducted by fair-skinned Chou knights and black-haired Shang gentlemen. I could never find out how many of these officials were Confucians. I suspect, a majority.

Fan Ch'ih had already heard about the two deaths. "This is very sad, of course. Yen Hui was a remarkable man. We shall all miss him."

"What about the son?"

Fan Ch'ih made a noncommittal gesture. "At least all this sadness gives us time to breathe."

Jan Ch'iu joined us. Although he looked exhausted, he welcomed me with the ceremony that is due an honored guest. He, too, had heard the news. "I wish that I could go to him. I know he must be suffering. What did he say?"

I repeated Confucius' remark about heaven.

Jan Ch'iu shook his head. "That was not seemly, as he will be the first to admit when he no longer suffers."

"In earlier days," said Fan Ch'ih, "he would never have said such a thing, no matter how distressed he might have been by heaven's will." Both Jan Ch'iu and Fan Ch'ih were more upset by Confucius' uncharacteristic lapse than they were by the death of the paragon Yen Hui.

"Will you attend the funeral?" I spoke to Jan Ch'iu.

"Of course. It will be a grand affair. The father's seen to that."

I was surprised. "But the master said that the ceremonies for Yen Hui must be as simple as those for his own son."

"He will be disappointed." Jan Ch'iu was flat. "I've already seen the plans. The father showed them to me this morning. Honored guest"—with one forefinger he touched me lightly on the forearm, a gesture of trust—"as you know, I am not welcome in the master's house. Nevertheless, it's urgent that I see him as soon as possible."

"He'll be in mourning for three months at least," said Fan Ch'ih. "And no one will be able to talk to him about . . . other matters."

"We shall have to find a way." Again the forefinger rested on my arm, light as a butterfly. "You are a barbarian. You are a priest. You interest him. Above all, you have never angered or displeased him. If you wish to do us a kindness—and I mean this country, not simply the family that I serve, try to arrange a meeting between him and Baron K'ang."

"Surely, the baron can simply send for him. As premier knight, he will have to come."

"But as divine sage, he cannot be sent for."

"He denies—" I began.

"In the Middle Kingdom," said Jan Ch'iu, "he is the divine sage. That he denies the fact so vehemently is simply proof that he really is what we know him to be. Baron K'ang needs Confucius." Jan Ch'iu looked me in the eye. This is often a sign that a man is lying. But the steward had no reason to lie to me. "We have many, many troubles."

"The taxes?"

Jan Ch'iu nodded. "They are exorbitant. But without them, we cannot pay the army. Without the army . . ." Jan Ch'iu turned to Fan Ch'ih, who told me of the latest threat to the state.

"Next to Castle Pi there is a sort of holy ground called Chuan-yu. It was made autonomous by Duke Tan himself. Although this place is within the borders of Lu, it has always been independent. The fortress of Chuan-yu is almost as formidable as Castle Pi."

I began to understand. "So the former warden of Pi . . ."

" . . . has been subverting Chuan-yu." Fan Ch'ih's

irresistibly cheerful face was at odds with the tension in his voice. "It is only a matter of time before we have another rebellion on our hands."

"Baron K'ang would like to raze the fortress." Jan Ch'iu played with the ornaments on his sash. " 'If we don't do it now, my son or grandson will have to do it,' he said. 'We cannot permit such a powerful fortress to remain in the hands of our enemies. Naturally, Confucius will object to an attack on this holy place, on any holy place.' " Jan Ch'iu looked at me for the second time. I was quite unnerved. For one thing, like so many Chou knights, he had the yellow eyes of a tiger. "As ministers to the baron, we agree with him. As disciples of Confucius, we disagree with him."

"Do you really think that anyone can convince Confucius to do something so—unseemly?" I understood their dilemma, and saw no way out.

"We must try." Fan Ch'ih smiled. "*You* must try. Tell him that he must receive Baron K'ang. Tell him that he will be offered high office. Otherwise . . ."

"Otherwise the baron will tear down the castle, anyway." I was to the point.

"Yes," said Jan Ch'iu. "But the castle does not concern me so much as the final days of Confucius. For many years we have worked toward one end: to bring to power the divine sage so that he can set things right."

"Now you are trying to tell me that he can only come to power if he allows the baron to set something wrong." I was sharp.

Jan Ch'iu was quick to take the offensive. "Rightly or wrongly, Baron K'ang thinks that Confucius worked to overthrow the Chi family when he was dealing with the treacherous warden of Pi. Rightly or wrongly, the baron thinks that the recent war was instigated by Confucius. Rightly or wrongly, the baron thinks Confucius may one day try to use his prestige throughout the Middle Kingdom to make himself the son of heaven."

"If any of this is true, your divine sage is guilty of treason." I remembered to smile the court-smile.

"Yes," said Jan Ch'iu, and did not smile. "Fortunately, we won the war and our old enemy the duke of Key is dead."

I now saw the full dimension of the plot. "Baron K'ang . . ." I was going to say "murdered the duke." But

490

I chose discretion. " . . . was then able to save the state," I finished lamely.

Fan Ch'ih nodded. "Now all that's left to be done is to root out the rebels in Chuan-yu. Then we can sleep easily. Since the rebels at Chuan-yu are the last hope of the baron's enemies, only their fortress stands between us and perfect peace."

"But first the master must agree to its dismantling."

Jan Ch'iu shook his head. "Whether he agrees or not, the walls of Chuan-yu will be torn down. But should he agree whole-heartedly, the dream of ten thousand wise men will come true. Confucius will be invited to lead the state. He has always said, 'Give me three years, and I can make things right.' Well, before it's too late, I want him to have those three years. We all do."

I was never able to understand Jan Ch'iu. I believe that he was genuinely devoted to the master; after all, he had proved his loyalty when, some years earlier, he had gone into exile with Confucius. Yet Jan Ch'iu was equally loyal to Baron K'ang. He hoped to make a bridge between—well, heaven and earth, and if I were to help him construct such a bridge, I would be sent home. That was the agreement we came to in the Chi palace on the evening of the dark day that Confucius reproached heaven for Yen Hui's death.

As Fan Ch'ih escorted me to the vestibule of the Chi palace, I commented on the cold way that Confucius had dealt with Yen Hui's father. Why shouldn't Yen Hui have a splendid funeral? And why shouldn't Confucius break with custom and walk instead of ride in a carriage?

"I'm afraid you've not got the point to the wisest man that ever lived," said Fan Ch'ih.

"Since I am not at all wise myself, how could I?" I made all the usual Cathayan humble demurs.

"For Confucius, the moral life is all that matters. This means that whenever personal desire or interest conflicts with right action, then those desires and interests must be set to one side. As a man, he wants to honor Yen Hui. But as an upholder of what is right, he cannot break with what he knows to be right behavior."

"So the humble Yen Hui gets a humble burial?"

"Yes. A man has certain duties to sovereign, parents, friends, humanity. But these duties sometimes conflict. Obviously, duty to the sovereign takes precedence over duty to a friend. Of course, there are all sorts of ambiguities. For Confucius, our rightful sovereign is Duke Ai. For us, it is Baron K'ang. In a sense, Confucius is right. In a sense, we are right. But he will not give way, and we may not give way. So there is—unhappiness."

"Who determines, ultimately, what is right?" I was at the great door to the palace.

"Heaven, honored guest."

"What is heaven, Under-steward Fan Ch'ih?"

My friend smiled. "Heaven is what is right." We both laughed.

I think that for all practical purposes, the Confucians are atheists. They do not believe in an afterlife or a day of judgment. They are not interested in how this world was created or for what purpose. Instead, they act as if this life is all there is and to conduct it properly is all that matters. For them, heaven is simply a word to describe correct behavior. Because the common people have all sorts of irrational feelings about heaven—a concept as old as the race—Confucius has cleverly used the idea of heaven in order to give a magical authority to his pronouncements on the way that men ought to treat one another. But then, in order to impress the educated, both Chou and Shang, he took care to make himself the greatest scholar in the Middle Kingdom. As a result, there is no Chou text that he cannot quote to his own advantage. Yet despite my deep dislike of atheism and my irritation with many Confucian strictures, I have never known a man with such a clear idea of how public and private affairs should be conducted. Even Democritus finds intriguing my no doubt faulty memory of his sayings. If one is going to eliminate the creator of all things, then it is a good idea to replace the creator with a very clear idea of what constitutes goodness in the human scale.

6

I DID MY BEST TO BRING TOGETHER disgruntled sage and edgy dictator. At first I made little headway. For one thing, Confucius was still in mourning for both his son and Yen Hui; for another, his own health was deteriorating. Nevertheless, he continued to teach. He had also got interested in writing the history of Lu. "I think it might be useful," he said to me, "to show how and why ten generations of dukes have been powerless."

I asked him what *he* thought was the principal reason for the decline of ducal power and the rise of the hereditary ministers.

"It began when the early dukes farmed out tax collection to the nobility." Confucius was always matter-of-fact in his analyses. "Eventually the nobles kept the taxes for themselves and, as everyone knows, whoever controls the treasury controls the state. It is also a fact that no dynasty lasts much longer than ten generations. It is also a fact that if power has passed to the barons"—the old man smiled his rabbit's smile—"they can seldom maintain their rule for more than five generations. I have the impression that today, after five generations of power, the Chi, Meng and Shu families are no longer quite what they were."

I did not dare deal directly with Confucius. Instead I cultivated Tzu-lu on the ground that he alone always spoke his mind to Confucius. "After all," he said to me, "if I hadn't stopped him, he'd have joined forces with the warden of Pi. He actually believed that scoundrel when he said he would make a Chou in the east. I told Confucius that he would be a fool to have anything to do with the warden. If there is ever a Chou in the east, it will come naturally and because the master has made it clear to everyone that such a thing is not only desirable but possible."

By then Tzu-lu had agreed with me that the time had come for Confucius to make his peace with Baron K'ang. "Don't worry," said Tzu-lu, "I'll handle him."

After much negotiation, Confucius accepted an invitation to visit the baron in his so-called forest shack. On a bright day in summer, escorted by a company of Chi soldiers, we left the city in a light wagon, drawn by four horses.

"I hope," the Baron had said to me when the final arrangements were being made, "that he won't mind if I receive him in my father's old hunting lodge. I can only pray that its rustic simplicity will appeal to his sense of proportion." The baron's egglike face betrayed, as usual, no emotion when he added, "You, Cyrus Spitama, honored guest, have done us a service that we shall not soon forget."

The journey through the forest was pleasant. Birds of

every sort were on the wing, newly arrived from the far south, while the trees were in early leaf and wild flowers filled the air with those delicate perfumes that make me sneeze uncontrollably.

The first night we dined royally on game and fish fresh-caught. We slept in tents. We saw no dragons, trolls or bandits. But we did meet, the next morning, a solitary hermit-sage; and like most solitary hermit-sages, he could not stop talking. There is nothing like a vow of silence to loosen the tongue.

The man's hair and beard had not been cut or washed in years. He lived in a tree not too far from the forest trail. As a result, he was well known to travelers in that part of the world. Rather like an Indian monkey, he would dart about, taunting strangers. He enjoyed contrasting the simple perfection of his life with the worldliness of everyone else. Cathayan hermit-sages are every bit as tiresome as the ones to be found in the Gangetic plain; fortunately, they are not yet as numerous.

"Ah, Master K'ung!" he saluted Confucius, who had got down from the wagon in order, decorously, to relieve himself in a grove of wild mulberry trees.

Confucius greeted the man politely.

"Tell me, Master K'ung, is there a crime greater than having too many desires?"

"To have one *wrong* desire is a crime." Confucius was mild. He was used to the insults of the hermit-sages. They wished, like the Buddha, to eliminate a world that he wanted only to rectify. They had withdrawn; he had not.

"Is there a disaster greater than not being constant?" asked the wild man.

"To be discontented with one's proper role in life might be called a disaster."

The hermit-sage was not at all pleased to have his rhetorical questions answered so literally. "Is there any misfortune greater than being covetous?"

"Doesn't it depend on what is coveted? To covet what is good in heaven's eyes is hardly a misfortune."

"Do you know what heaven is?"

"For you who follow Master Li"—Confucius knew his enemy—"it is the Way, which may not be described in words. So I shall defer to Master Li and not describe it in words."

The hermit-sage was not exactly delighted with this answer, either. "Master K'ung, you believe in the supreme importance of the ancestral sacrifice, as performed by the son of heaven."

"Indeed I do."

"But there is no longer a son of heaven."

"There was. There will be. Meanwhile, the ancestral sacrifice still continues, if less than perfect in the absence of the lonely one."

"What is the meaning of the ancestral sacrifice?"

I was surprised that Confucius was taken aback by what must have been for him that rarest of all things on this old earth, a new question. "What is the meaning of the ancestral sacrifice?" he repeated.

"Yes. How did it begin. What does it signify? Explain it to me, Master K'ung."

"I cannot." Confucius looked at the wild man as if he were a tree that had somehow fallen in his path. "Anyone who truly understood the sacrifice could deal with all things under heaven as easily as this." And Confucius placed the forefinger of his right hand against the flattened palm of the left.

"Since you do not understand the most important of all our sacrifices, how can you begin to know heaven's will?"

"I merely transmit the wisdom of the wise ancestors. Nothing more." Confucius began, as it were, to walk around the tree in his way. But the hermit-sage was not about to let him go; he put his hand on the master's arm.

"This is not seemly," said Fan Ch'ih, striking down the encroaching arm. As Confucius took his place in the wagon, the wild man's expression was rather more close to hate than to the cool do-nothingness prescribed by the celebrators of the always-so.

I could not resist taunting him. "How," I asked, "did all this come into existence? Who created the universe?"

For a moment I thought that the wild man had not heard me. He certainly did not look at me; his eyes were on Confucius' bent back. But then, just as I was about to move on, he said or quoted, "The spirit of the valley never dies. This is called the mysterious female. The gateway of the mysterious female is called the root of heaven and earth. It is there within us all the while. No matter how much you draw upon it, it will never run dry."

"Does that mean that we came from the waters of some primal womb?" My question was not answered. Instead, the hermit suddenly shouted at Confucius. "Master K'ung, is it your belief that evil should be repaid with good?"

495

Although Confucius did not look at the man, he answered him. "If you repay ill with good, how on earth are you going to reward good? With ill?"

By this time I was in the wagon. I heard Confucius mutter under his breath, "The man's an idiot."

"Like Master Li," said Tzu-lu.

"No." Confucius frowned. "Master Li is clever. He is wicked. He has said that since the ancestral rites are wearing thin, loyalty and good faith are vanishing and disorder has begun. To my mind, he preaches a truly *disorderly* doctrine."

I do not think that I have ever in my life seen a private dwelling as beautiful as the forest shack of Baron K'ang's father. Curiously enough, none of my companions had ever laid eyes on the estate that the old dictator had created for himself some fifty miles south of the capital.

In the midst of a large clearing in the forest, a series of terraces had been so constructed that, as one ascends the steps to the highest pavilion, one seems to be floating on what looks to be a vast green sea, bounded to the south by a range of violet island-mountains still covered with winter's snow.

At the foot of the first terrace we were met by a chamberlain, who accompanied us to the highest level. The forest shack is a complex of rooms, halls, galleries and pavilions built on four artificial terraces at the center of a series of marvelous gardens. Wherever one stands, inside or out, one sees sky, flowers, trees. The gardens and the palace had been created by architects from Ch'u, a southern country on the Yangtze River, famed throughout the Middle Kingdom for its splendid buildings, gardens, women—and dragons, as the duke of Sheh discovered to his horror.

Ornamental ponds reflected the watery light of a pale-skied noon. Pale-green duckweed covered the surface of the water like a net in whose delicate meshes were caught lotuses. At water's edge, yellow orchids bloomed like butterflies frozen on the wing. All the garden attendants were dressed in leopard skins. I don't know why. I do know that the effect was not only bizarre but mysteriously beautiful and entirely typical, I was told, of a Ch'u garden.

At the ultimate level, there is a two-story building made of highly polished red stone. Cringing politely, the chamberlain showed us into a hall that was as high and as wide and as long as the building itself. We were all overwhelmed by the beauty and lightness of the interior—all, that is, except Confucius, who looked very grim indeed.

The highly polished gray-green stone of the interior makes a vivid contrast to the red exterior. At the hall's center an enormous black marble column, sculpted to resemble a tree, supports a ceiling whose radial teakwood beams have been carved to resemble branches, heavy with every sort of gilded fruit.

Directly opposite the main door, an arras of kingfisher-blue hides the entrance to the palace proper. As we gaped, invisible hands or ropes drew the arras to one side, revealing Baron K'ang. Our host was dressed simply but correctly. As he saluted the premier knight correctly, if not simply, the head bobs, hand twitches, shoulder wriggles, breath hisses were endless. Plainly, this was to be a supremely formal and high and significant occasion.

After Confucius had given all the correct responses, the baron led us into a long gallery which overlooked a series of terraced gardens. Here we were served a banquet by a dozen astonishingly beautiful girls from Ch'u. They are an integral part of the furnishings if not the architecture, and we were all bedazzled except Confucius. He sat in the place of honor and made all the correct observances. But he kept his eyes averted from the servitors. None of us had realized that such luxury existed anywhere in Lu. Although the Chi family palace in the capital is a large building, it is suitably austere, as befits the administrative center of an impoverished state. For reasons of his own, the dictator had decided to show us an aspect of his life that few were ever privileged to see. We were highly impressed, as he meant us to be. Confucius was appalled— as the baron meant him to be? I am still not sure.

The banquet was delicious and we drank far too much honey-flavored jade-dark wine and ate course after course of dishes that were served us in the southern fashion. That is, bitter food alternates with salty food which alternates with sour which alternates with pepper which is succeeded by sweet. I recall seethed tortoise; goose in sour sauce; casseroled duck; roast kid with yam sauce; dried flesh of crane with pickled radishes—and the famed bitter-sour soup of Wu.

Except for Baron K'ang and Confucius, everyone gorged himself most disgustingly. The sage and the dictator ate sparingly and sipped rather than drank wine.

Between courses, young women performed the highly

seductive dances of Cheng, to the accompaniment of zither, pipes, bells and drums. Then a fascinating beauty from Wu sang a series of love songs that even Confucius felt obliged to praise for their refinement—and antiquity. By and large, he detested all music that has been composed since the time of Chou.

I remember the conversation in bits and pieces, still illuminated and perfumed in my memory by the splendid day, food, music, women. At one point the baron turned to Confucius. "Tell me, Master, which of your disciples most loves learning?"

"The one who is dead, Prime Minister. Unfortunately, Yen Hui had a short life. Now," said Confucius with a hard look at those of his disciples who were present, "there is no one to take his place."

The baron smiled. "Naturally, you are the judge, Master. Even so, I would have thought Tzu-lu wise."

"Would you?" Confucius bared the tips of his front teeth.

"I also think him a proper person to hold office in the state. Would you agree to that, Master?" Thus, not so delicately, was Confucius being bribed.

"Tzu-lu is efficient," said Confucius. "Therefore, he should hold office." Tzu-lu had the grace to look embarrassed.

"What about Jan Ch'iu?"

"He is versatile," said Confucius flatly. "As you know, since he already holds office."

"Fan Ch'ih?"

"He is able to get things done, as you already know."

Jan Ch'iu and Fan Ch'ih had now ceased to enjoy the feast, as the baron amused himself at their expense. He was also communicating, in some secret way, with Confucius. "I am well served by your disciples, Master."

"Would that goodness were equally well served, Prime Minister."

The baron chose not to respond to this sharp response. "Tell me, Master. What is the best way to make the common people respectful and loyal?"

"Other than by example?" I was suddenly aware that not only was Confucius in a towering rage but even the frugal meal that he had made was beginning to disagree with him. The baron looked attentive, as if Confucius had not yet spoken. "Treat men with dignity." Confucius frowned and belched. "Then they will respect you. Promote those servants of the state who are worthy and train those who are incompetent."

"How beautifully true!" The baron affected delight with this banality.

"I am happy that you find it so." Confucius looked more than ever sour. "Certainly the reverse must never be practiced."

"The reverse?"

"Do not try to train those who are already worthy. Do not promote the incompetent."

Fortunately, the conversation was interrupted by a mournful Ts'ai ballad. But when it ended, Baron K'ang began again his respectful if challenging questions. "As you know, Master, crime has increased enormously since you served with such distinction as under-minister of police. I myself—the humble slave of the duke—have had my own house robbed three times. What would you do to stop this epidemic of lawlessness?"

"If people were not acquisitive, Prime Minister, you couldn't hire a burglar to rob anyone. On the simple ground that there would be nothing to take."

The baron ignored this—savagery. There is no other word to describe the master's response. Confucius was plainly outraged by the display of wealth that the baron saw fit to flaunt at a time when the state was impoverished. "Yet it is wrong to steal, Master. And those of us who rule—well, how should we go about making the people obey the law?"

"If *you* follow a straight road, who will follow a crooked one?"

We were all most uncomfortable at this point; and somewhat drunk. But the baron showed no sign of distress. "I believe, Master, that each of us is set upon a road which *appears* to him to be straight. Those who choose to take the crooked road—well, what should the ruler do about them? Should they be put to death?"

"You are supposed to be a ruler, Prime Minister, not a butcher. If you honestly want what is good, the people will want the same. A gentleman is like the wind, and common people are like grass. When the wind passes over a meadow, the grass always bends." Confucius was once more his usual serene self.

The baron nodded. I had the impression that he was actually listening. But for what? Treason? I was most uncomfortable. We all were, except Confucius, whose mind, as opposed to stomach, seemed for the moment to be at peace.

"But do the common people understand the way of the gentleman?"

"No. But they can be induced, by proper example, to follow it."

"I see." The baron had a fit of hiccups, which the Cathayans regard as an audible manifestation of inner wisdom. Even Confucius looked less stern, as he realized that he was being listened to carefully by his antagonist. "Tell me, Master, is it possible for a ruler who does not follow the way to bring peace and prosperity to his people?"

"No, Prime Minister. It is not possible."

"Then what about the recent duke of Wei? He was a thoroughly disreputable man who allowed himself to be manipulated by his concubine, a woman you once visited, I believe."

At this most unpleasant dig, Confucius frowned. "If I have ever done wrong," he said, "I pray that heaven will forgive me."

"I am sure that heaven has. But explain to me why heaven did not punish this disreputable ruler? Ten years ago, he died old and prosperous and content."

"The late duke saw fit to engage the services of the best foreign minister, the most devout high priest, and the finest general in the Middle Kingdom. That was the secret to his success. In his appointments, he followed heaven's way. This is rare," added Confucius, staring pointedly at the dictator.

"I daresay that few rulers have ever had at hand such good and virtuous servants as the late disreputable duke." The dictator was bland.

"I daresay that few rulers have ever been able to recognize what is good and virtuous when they see it." Confucius was sublimely—and devastatingly—at his ease.

We were all quite nervous except for the master and the dictator. They seemed to be enjoying their duel.

"What is good government, Master?"

"When the near approve and the distant approach."

"Then we are honored that you who were far away from us have now approached." This was very smooth indeed. "It is our prayer that your presence among us means approval of our policies."

Confucius stared rather rudely at the prime minister.

500

Then he made his stock—and somewhat disingenuous—answer. "He who holds no office in a state does not discuss its policies."

"Your—little ones hold high rank." The baron indicated Jan Ch'iu and Fan Ch'ih. "They help us to make good laws, sensible decrees—"

Confucius actually interrupted the dictator. "Prime Minister, if you insist on governing the people with rules, regulations, decrees and punishments, they will simply evade you and go about their business. On the other hand, if you were to govern by moral force and personal example, they will come to you of their own accord. They will be good."

"What, Master, is goodness?"

"It is the way of heaven as practiced by the divine sages."

"But since you yourself are a divine sage—"

"No! I am not a divine sage. I am imperfect. At best, I am a gentleman. At best, I have one foot on the path, and no more. My Lord Baron, goodness is a recognition of the likeness of all things, and he whose heart is in the smallest degree set upon goodness will be aware of this likeness and so he will find it impossible to *dis*like any man."

"Even the bad?"

"Especially the bad. To pursue righteousness is a life's work. In fact, the basic disposition of a true gentleman is righteousness, which he puts into practice according to ritual, modestly setting it forth and faithfully bringing it to completion. Certainly, to attain wealth and power by unrighteous means is as far from the ideal of a gentleman as a floating cloud."

The baron was every bit as unrighteous as most rulers; yet he bowed his head, as if in awe. "Nevertheless," he said to the silken mat on which he sat, "for a humble servant of the state, what, practically speaking, is righteousness?"

"If you do not already know, I cannot tell you." Confucius sat up very straight. "But since I am sure that, deep in your belly, you know what is right as well as any gentleman, I will remind you that it involves two things: consideration for others and loyalty to others."

"When I am considerate, Master, what do I do?"

"You do *not* do to others what you would not like them to do to you. That is simple enough. As for loyalty, you

501

owe that to your sovereign if he is righteous. If he is not, you must transfer your loyalty, even though you may suffer by so doing."

"Tell me, Master, have you ever met anyone who cared deeply for goodness, who truly hated wickedness?"

Confucius looked at his hands. I was always struck by his unusually long thumbs. When he answered, his voice was low. "I cannot think of anyone who ever managed to do good with all his might, even for a single day."

"Surely, *you* are entirely good."

Confucius shook his head. "If I were entirely good, I would not be here with you, Prime Minister. We dine in luxury while your people starve. That is not good. That is not righteous. That is not seemly."

Anywhere else on earth, Confucius' head would have been promptly separated from his body. We were all of us terrified. But, curiously enough, Confucius had done the wisest thing possible. By openly attacking the dictator on moral grounds, he made it clear that he was in no way politically dangerous to the Chi family. At worst, he was an annoyance. At best, he was an ornament to their regime. The truculent wise man who finds fault with everyone is often the safest man in the realm—rather like a court jester, and as seldom heeded. It had been Baron K'ang's fear that Confucius and his disciples were in league with Key; that they were working, secretly, for the overthrow of the baronial families and the restoration of the ducal powers. As it turned out, Confucius' performance at the forest shack convinced the dictator that he had nothing to fear from the Confucians.

At length, Baron K'ang explained to Confucius why the state needed new revenues. He also apologized for the lavishness of his establishment on the ground that "it was built by my father, not by me. And much of it was a present from the government of Ch'u."

Confucius was silent. The storm had passed. As the conversation became general, the dancers became more and more erotic in their movements. I have no memory of how I got to bed that night. I only recall awakening the next morning in a red-walled bedroom with vermilion woodwork inlaid with jet. As I sat up in bed a beautiful girl pulled back the long blue silk bed curtains. She offered me a basin whose interior showed a golden phoenix rising from the flames—the best of omens, I thought, as I vomited. I have never been so ill—or in such beautiful surroundings.

The next few days were idyllic. Even Confucius seemed at ease. For one thing, with much pageantry, Baron K'ang had invested him as a minister of state and it now looked as if, finally, the bitter gourd was to be taken down from the wall and used.

Or so everyone thought except Tzu-lu. "It is the end," he said to me. "The long journey is over. The master will never be given an opportunity to govern."

"But he is minister of state."

"Baron K'ang is kind. And clever. Confucius has been publicly honored. But he will never be used. It is the end."

On our last day at the forest shack, I was summoned to Baron K'ang's office. He was entirely genial. "You have served us well," he said. For an instant a smile was actually perceptible on the egg-smooth face. "Thanks, in part, to your good offices, our divine sage is no longer at odds with us. There is also peace in a land whose borders are as quiet as the eternal sleep of Mount T'ai."

As usual, the dictator's elliptical style needed interpreting. Later Fan Ch'ih told me that that very morning, word had come the holy city of Chuan-yu had fallen to Chi family troops and the citadel had been dismantled. Best of all, from the dictator's point of view, there had been no response at all from across the border. The rebellious warden was old. The rebellious Yang Huo was thought to be dead. The new duke of Key was preoccupied with internal matters. For the moment, Lu—and its dictator—were at peace. Although we had not known it at the time, our reception at the forest shack had been for Baron K'ang a celebration of the success of a long and tortuous foreign and domestic policy. The investiture of Confucius as minister of state was a symbolic if empty gesture, calculated to delight Confucius' admirers and bring to an end the dissatisfaction of the knights and gentlemen who administered the state.

"But we are also in your debt for showing us the western way of making metal. Your name—barbarous as it is —has already been recorded with honor in the annals of Lu." He looked at me as if I had just received at his hands a treasure of gold.

Tears in my eyes, I thanked him for this extraordinary show of esteem. He listened for a while as I turned one graceful Cathayan phrase after another, like a potter glazing a plate. When I finally paused for breath, he said, "I wish to establish once again the silk road to India."

"Once *again*, Lord Baron?"

The baron nodded. "Yes. It is not generally known, but in the days of the Chou—when the son of heaven looked to the south from Shensi—there was regular overland commerce between us and the barbarians of the Gangetic plain. Then came this long . . . interlude. Without a true son of heaven, many things are not what they were. Although the silk road has never been entirely abandoned, regular commerce stopped nearly three hundred years ago. Now, I have always maintained—as did my immaculate father—good relations with Ch'u, the beautiful nation to our south. You may have looked with a favorable eye upon the Ch'u gardens that we have created here. Well, they are as nothing when compared to the entire land of Ch'u, which is one enormous garden, watered by the Yangtze River." At some length the baron told me the history of Ch'u. Heart fluttering like a trapped bird, I pretended to listen.

Finally the dictator came to the point. "Now that we have peace within and without the realm, thanks in part to you, dear friend, our duke will conclude a treaty with the duke of Ch'u and together we shall sponsor an overland expedition to India and you will bear gifts from our ruler to the king of Magadha."

Then, as if by magic, the room was filled with merchants. Two were Indians. One was from Rajagriha; the others from Varanasi. They told me that they had come to Cathay by sea. Just south of Kweichi, they had been shipwrecked. They would have drowned had they not been saved by two of the many mermaids who abound in the southern sea. These creatures live both under the sea and on the land—or at least on remote rocks, where they weave beautiful cloth from seaweed. Mermaids are notoriously well-disposed toward men, and when they weep—usually after having been abandoned by a human sailor—their tears form perfect pearls.

At length, we discussed the expedition. Although Baron K'ang had given the impression that the journey was being undertaken solely as a reward to me for services rendered the Chi family, I soon discovered that this was no more than usual Cathayan hyperbole. In fact, at least once a year a caravan would set out from Key and move on to Lu; and then proceed south to Ch'u. At each stop, new merchandise would be added. I soon realized, with some bitterness, that I could have left Lu years earlier than I did. But, to be fair to the dictator, he wanted me to earn my passage. When I had done so, he let me go. All in all, he was an admirable ruler. No doubt of that.

I don't recall much about the rest of the time that we spent in the forest shack. I do remember that unlike the overjoyed Jan Ch'iu and Fan Ch'ih, Confucius seemed not at all elated by his high office. Tzu-lu was equally dour. I did not begin to understand why until we arrived at the city's gate. As our wagon rolled past the inner gate, a sentry asked one of our guards, "Who's the illustrious old man?"

"A minister of state," said the guard officiously. "The premier knight, Confucius."

"Oh, yes." The guard laughed. "He's the one who's always saying that even though it's no use, you have to keep on trying."

Although Confucius' face did not change expression, his entire body shuddered, as if from illness. The deaf Tzu-lu had not heard what the sentry said, but he did notice the shudder. "You must look to your health, Master. This is a bad season."

"What season is not?" As it turned out, Confucius *was* ill. "And what does it matter?"

Confucius had surrendered not so much to the prime minister as to time. At the forest shack he had accepted the fact that he would never lead the state. He still hoped that he would be used in some way. But the dream of putting to rights his native land was at an end.

7

THE REST OF THE SUMMER WAS TAKEN up with preparations for departure. Lu merchants who wanted to trade with India were told to assemble their goods at the central warehouse. I met all the merchants and made myself as useful as possible. I promised to obtain at Magadha what privileges I could for this or that raw material or manufacture. Although trade with India was still not common, the Cathayan merchants had a very shrewd understanding of what Indians value. I have always thought that each race has a memory quite apart from that of its spoken or written annals. From father to son, certain kinds of information are passed on. Despite the fact that three centuries had passed since there was regular trade between east and west, most Cathayan merchants seem to know at birth that silk and pearls and furs, feather screens and jade and dragon's bone are valued in the west, where the gold and rubies and spices that easterners so much desire can be found in abundance.

The master of the expedition was a marquis from Key. In the course of the summer, he paid me a visit. I saw to it that he was deeply impressed by my connection with Ajatashatru, who was now, according to the latest news, master of all the Gangetic plain except for the Licchavi republic. At the marquis's request, I agreed to act as liaison between the expedition and the government of Magadha. Whether or not I was still in favor with my tempestuous father-in-law was a question that I thought unwise to raise. For all I knew, Ambalika and my sons might be dead. Ajatashatru might be insane. Certainly, if he were so minded, he could put me to death for desertion—or for his own amusement. He was always referred to in worried tones by knowledgeable Cathayans.

"There has never been such a bloody king," said Fan Ch'ih. "In the last few years, he's burned to the ground a dozen cities, slaughtered tens of thousands of men, women, children."

Since I knew Ajatashatru to be even worse than the Cathayans suspected, I made him out to be far better than they feared. In any case, we would simply have to take our chances. Besides, I was reasonably certain that he would want the silk road opened to regular traffic. Therefore, he would not want to inhibit trade by robbing and murdering legitimate merchants. Or so I told myself —and the nervous marquis of Key.

Shortly after our return from the forest shack, Confucius took to his bed. A week later, word began to spread throughout the Middle Kingdom that the divine sage was dying.

As soon as we heard the news, Fan Ch'ih and I hurried to the master's house. The street in front of the house was crowded with silent, watchful, sad young men. Tzu-lu had given orders that only the original disciples could attend the deathbed. I was admitted only because I was with Fan Ch'ih.

506

In the outer room, thirty disciples were gathered. They were dressed in mourning. I could smell the smoke from the aromatic leaves that were being burned in the bedroom. Although the smell is not unpleasant to men, it is sickening to evil spirits—or so the Cathayans believe. Inside the bedroom a dirge was being sung.

When Fan Ch'ih heard the singing, he began to weep. "This means he really is dying. That song is sung only when the spirit is leaving the body."

In Cathay, if one does not pray both to heaven and earth to look after a dying man, he will come back and haunt those who were not willing to placate, on his behalf, the two halves of the original egg. Cathayans believe that each man has two spirits inside him. One is a life spirit, which ends when the body dies. The other is a personality spirit, which continues to exist as long as it is remembered and honored with sacrifices. If the remembered spirit is not correctly honored, the ghost's revenge can be horrendous. Even at that sad moment, I could not help but think how confused every religion is. Confucius himself did not believe in spirits or ghosts. Presumably, his disciples did not believe in them either. Yet at the moment of his death, Tzu-lu insisted that all the old outmoded ceremonies be performed. It would be as if my grandfather at the moment of *his* death had asked the devil-goddess Anahita to intercede for him with the keepers of the Aryan home of the fathers.

The disciples in the courtyard joined in the dirge. I felt uncomfortable and out of place. I was also genuinely saddened, for I had come to admire the wise, unyielding old man.

Then the singing stopped. Tzu-lu appeared in the outer room. He looked ghastly, almost as if he were the one who was doing the dying. Jan Ch'iu stood behind him.

"The master is unconscious. It is nearly over." Tzu-lu's voice cracked. "But if he should regain his senses, we must do him honor." Tzu-lu motioned to one of the disciples who held in both arms a large bundle. "Here are the robes that are worn by the retainers of a great minister. We must put them on. Quickly!"

Tzu-lu, Jan Ch'iu, Fan Ch'ih and four other disciples pulled on the ill-fitting robes. Then they filed into the bedroom, singing the praises of the great minister of state. Since no one stopped me, I followed them.

Confucius lay on a simple mat, head to the north —

507

where the dead reside. He was very pale; and his breathing was irregular. In a brazier, aromatic leaves burned.

As Tzu-lu and the other retainers began to sway and moan, Confucius opened his eyes. He looked startled; like a man awakened from normal sleep. "Tzu-lu!" The voice was surprisingly strong.

The disciples stopped their keening, and Tzu-lu said, "Great Minister, we are here to serve you in death as in life. We have performed the rites of expiation. We have called upon the sky-spirits above and the earth-spirits below . . ."

"My expiation began long ago." The pale face began to darken with returning strength. "I need no rites. Either what I have done in my life is good in the eyes of heaven or it is not. All this is . . . superfluous." The old man blinked his eyes; became aware of the costumes that the disciples were wearing. "What on earth are you got up as?"

"Retainers of a great minister," said Tzu-lu tearfully.

"But I am not a great minister."

"You are minister of state . . ."

"That is nothing, as we all know. Only a great minister can have retainers who wear such clothes." Confucius shut his eyes. "This is travesty, Tzu-lu." Then the eyes opened again; they had become bright and alert. The voice was stronger, too. "When you pretend that I'm something that I'm not, whom do you fool? The court? They know better. Heaven? No! I prefer to die"——there was a slight trace of a smile at the corners of his mouth——"according to my humble station."

Tzu-lu said nothing. Jan Ch'iu filled in the awkward silence. "Master, I have brought you a special medicine." Jan Ch'iu offered the old man a small stoppered bottle. "It is a gift from Baron K'ang, who prays for your recovery."

"Thank him for the prayers. And for the medicine." With some effort Confucius raised one hand as if to take the bottle. But when Jan Ch'iu tried to put it in Confucius' hand, he made a fist and said, "Since I don't know what's in the bottle, I don't dare take it. Besides"——and the front teeth were revealed at last in the famed rabbit's smile——"the prime minister must know that a gentleman cannot take medicine from any doctor whose father and grandfather have not previously served his family."

Confucius did not die. By late summer he had applied

to Baron K'ang for a proper ministry. When he was told that none was immediately available, he realized that the bitter gourd was now on the wall for good.

With apparent good grace, Confucius proceeded to divide his time between the study of the Chou texts and his students. It is said that Confucius' private school was the first in all the Middle Kingdom that was not connected with a noble family. Confucius himself had been educated in the private school of the Meng family. Now he was the educator of the entire knightly class, as well as a number of nobles. More important, he was a maker of gentlemen. Before Confucius, no one below the level of knight could aspire to the rank—no, not rank—the quality of a gentleman. Confucius said that anyone who followed the proper way with diligence could become a gentleman. The dispossessed Shang scholars were pleased. The Chou nobility was not.

Confucius also devoted a good deal of time to sorting out the annals of Lu. He thought it important to know exactly what happened during those years when the dukes lost their power. He spent many happy, dusty hours with the annals, made available to him by Duke Ai. In Cathay, only the great families possess books in any quantity. According to Confucius, most of these books are an absolute hodge-podge because the writing—which is up and down rather than from side to side—is done on strips of bamboo that are then bound together by a leather thong which goes through a hole at the top of each strip. In time the thongs wear out. When they do, the order of the strips often gets jumbled. It was Confucius' dream to put in proper order as much of the Chou literature as possible. This meant separating ancestral hymns from court songs, and so on. All in all, a prodigious undertaking. I have no idea if he lived long enough to complete the task. I should doubt it.

I saw him for the last time back of the rain altars. He was walking with a number of young students. When he saw me, he smiled. I joined the group; and I listened for a while. Although he said nothing to them that I had not heard before, it was always interesting to observe the way in which he adapted his wisdom to different men and situations. He particularly disliked those who simply repeated smugly what they had memorized, like so many Indian birds. "To learn and not to think over what you have learned is perfectly useless. To think without having first learned is dangerous." On the other hand, he did not take well to eel-wrigglers. I remember once listening to a young man turn Confucius' own words back on him. The master took this cleverness with apparent serenity. But as we walked away, he groaned, "How I hate glibness!" He would not have liked Athens.

I think, Democritus, that even your teacher Protagoras would agree with Confucius' strictures on how necessary it is to examine what you've learned. Confucius also thought that a teacher must always be able to reinterpret the old in terms of the new. This is obvious. Unfortunately, it is also obvious that few teachers are able to do anything but repeat, without interpretation, old saws. For Confucius, true wisdom is to know the extent of what you don't know quite as well as you know what you do know. Try that on your friend Socrates—or that demon he likes to talk to. Democritus thinks me unfair to Socrates. If I am, it is because I have known great and wise men of a sort not to be found in this place—or epoch.

When Confucius and the disciples reached the river's edge, I said, "Master, I am leaving. I want to say goodby."

Confucius turned to the disciples. "Go home, little ones." Then he put an arm through mine, a gesture of intimacy he seldom made even with Tzu-lu. Together we walked to the exact spot where we had first fished together three years before. "I hope that you will sometimes think of us here when you are—there." He was too polite to refer to there by its proper Cathayan name: land of the barbarians.

"I shall. Often. I have learned many things from you, Master."

"Do you think so? I would be pleased, of course, if you had. But we are so different."

"The same heaven covers both Persia and Cathay." I was sincere in my affection for him.

"But the *decrees* are not the same." The old man showed the rabbit's teeth. "That is why you still believe in the Wise Lord and the day of judgment and all that fiery . . . terminus to things."

"Yes. But even so, the way of righteousness for us—on earth—is your way, too."

"Heaven's way." He corrected me. We were at the river's edge. This time he sat on the rock where I had first

510

sat. I knelt beside him. "I no longer fish," he said. "I've lost the skill."

"Does that ever go?"

"What does not? Except the idea of goodness. And ritual. I know you laugh secretly at our three thousand three hundred observances. No, don't deny it. I understand you. That is why I would like you to understand us. You see, without ritual, courtesy becomes tiresome. Caution becomes timidity. Daring becomes dangerous. Inflexibility becomes hardness."

"I never laugh at you, Master. But I'm sometimes puzzled. Even so, you've taught me what a true gentleman is —or ought to be. And that is what you are."

The old man shook his head. "No." The voice was sad. "The true gentleman is good. Therefore, he is never unhappy. He is wise. Therefore, he is never perplexed. He is brave. Therefore, he is never afraid. Much of my life has been spent in fear, perplexity, unhappiness. I am not what I would want to be. That is why, to tell the truth, I have failed."

"Master, you are a famous teacher . . ."

"A passable charioteer is more famous than I. No. I am not known. But I don't blame heaven, or even men." He pushed a strand of white hair off the bulbous forehead. "I like to think that in heaven men get credit for how they live and what they've aspired to be. If this is true, I am content."

We listened to the cries of birds from nearby orchards; to the cries of women as they drove away the hungry birds. "Master, do you believe in heaven?"

"Earth is a fact." The old man tapped the moss-covered ground.

"Is heaven a fact?"

"So we have been taught by the Chou, and before the Chou by the Shang."

"But aside from their teachings, their rituals, do you believe?"

"Years ago when I was first in Key, I heard and saw the succession dance. I was stunned. I had never before realized what perfect beauty was, what perfect goodness was. For three months afterward, I was in a daze. At last I understood what heaven must be like because on earth I had been so close to perfection, to goodness."

"But where did this music come from? Who created it?"

As Confucius folded his hands, the long thumbs crossed

511

each other. "If I tell you from heaven, you will ask me who created heaven. And I will not answer that question because there is no need to know what we cannot know. There is so much for us to deal with here. In heaven's *name,* we have created certain rituals which make it possible for us to transcend ourselves. In heaven's name, we are obliged to observe certain customs, manners, ways of thought that make for harmony, for righteousness, for goodness. Words which are not ever easily defined." The old man frowned. "The single great obstacle in my own way—in every man's way—is that of the language. Important words are cloudy with too many meanings and non-meanings. If I had the power, I would redefine every word." He paused, then smiled mischievously. "So that it would conform with its original Chou meaning."

"But all these ceremonies, Master! I mean, what did you think of Tzu-lu's performance when you were so ill?"

Confucius scowled. "The robes were positively blasphemous."

"I meant the prayers to heaven and earth for your spirit when you yourself don't believe in spirits."

"That," said the master, "is an exquisite point. I favor the ritual because it comforts the living, shows respect for the dead, reminds us of our continuity with all those who have gone before. After all, they outnumber us by the millions, which is why I cannot believe in ghosts. If these spirits were all about us, there'd be no room for the living. We'd see a ghost at every step."

"But what about all those people who say that they have seen the spirits of the dead?"

Confucius gave me a quick side-long look, as if not quite certain how far he might dare go with me. "Well," he said, "I've talked to many people who think that they've seen the spirits of the dead, and I always ask them one question, which shocks them. Was the ghost naked? Invariably, they tell me, the spirit is wearing the clothes that he was buried in. Now, we know that silk and linen and lamb's wool are inanimate and soulless. We also know that when a man dies, his clothes rot just as he does. So how can his spirit put them on again?"

I was not certain how to take this. "Perhaps the spirit only seems to be dressed," I said feebly.

"Perhaps the spirit only *seems.* Perhaps the spirit does not exist at all except in the mind of a frightened man.

Before you were born, you were a part of the primal force."

"That is close to what Zoroaster tells us."

"Yes, I remember." Confucius was perfunctory. I could never interest him in the Truth. "When you die, you rejoin the primal force. Since you had no memory or consciousness of the primal force before you were born, how can you retain any of this brief human consciousness once you have died and returned to the primal force?"

"In India it is believed that you will be reincarnated on earth, as someone else, or something else."

"Forever?"

"No. You keep on returning until the present cycle of creation comes to an end. The only exception is the one who has attained enlightenment. He snuffs himself out *before* the cycle of creation ends."

"Once he is . . . snuffed out, where does he go?"

"It is hard to describe."

Confucius smiled. "I should think so. It has always seemed to me clear that the spirit which animates the human body is bound to return at death to the primal unity from which it came."

"To be reborn? Or judged?"

Confucius shrugged. "Whatever. But one thing is certain. You cannot rekindle a fire that has burned out. While you burn with life, your seed can make a new human being but when your fire is out, no one can bring you to life again. The dead, dear friend, are cold ashes. They have no consciousness. But that is no reason not to honor their memory, and ourselves, and our descendants."

We spoke of divination. Although he was not a believer, he thought that the forms and rituals were useful to men. In matters that had to do with improving men in their relations with one another, Confucius reminded me of a gardener who is forever shaping and pruning his trees so that they will bear better fruit.

We spoke of the state. "I am resigned," he said. "I am like the vase of Duke Tan in the ancestral temple. Have you seen it?" When I said that I had not, he told me how the vase had been put in the temple by the duke himself at the time of the founding of Lu. "When the vase is empty, it stands upright, and is very beautiful. But when it is filled, the vase rolls to one side and everything that was in it spills onto the ground, which is not beautiful.

513

Well, I am that empty vase. I may not be filled with power and glory, but I am upright."

At the end, in the shadow of the ancient rain altars, Confucius gave me the ritual—what else?—embrace of a father saying farewell to a son that he will never see again. As I left the old man, my eyes were blinded with tears. I cannot think why. I do not believe what he believed. Yet I found him altogether good. Certainly, I have not encountered anyone else in my travels who could compare with him.

BOOK SEVEN

Why the Ganges River Turned Red With Blood

1

THE JOURNEY FROM LU TO MAGADHA over the silk road took nearly one year. Much of the time, I was ill. But so was everyone else—sick with that fever which is so prevalent in those hideous southern jungles. Although a third of the expedition died on the road, the Key marquis regarded our losses as, comparatively, slight.

I no longer remember, in any detail, the exact route that we took. If I did, I would not tell it to any Greek. In due course I wrote an account of the journey, and I assume that my notes are locked away in the house of books at Persepolis.

There were times in the course of that terrible year when I very much doubted if I would ever again see Susa. There were also times when I ceased to care. The fever has that effect. One would rather die than be hounded day and night by fever-demons. Confucius thinks that the spirit world does not exist. If it does not, then who and what are those nightmare creatures that haunt us during the fever? They are real at the time; therefore, demonstrably, they *are* real. Democritus questions my logic. But you have never been ill, much less ghost-haunted.

My role in the expedition was never entirely clear. Although I was an honored guest of Lu and a son-in-law of the king of Magadha, I was also a sort of slave. The Key marquis treated me well enough; even so, I felt that he regarded me as nothing more than a convenience; and, if necessary, a highly disposable convenience.

When we arrived at the Ganges river port of Champa, I asked the marquis to let me go on ahead to the capital. At first he refused. But I was in luck. Since the viceroy at Champa had once met me at court, he did me such honor that the marquis could hardly keep me captive in what was, after all, my own country. I agreed to meet the marquis in Rajagriha. Then I left Champa with a contingent of Magadhan troops. Needless to say, I had no intention of going to Rajagriha. For one thing, I was not eager to

516

meet my father-in-law again. For another, I wanted to see my wife and sons at Shravasti.

Twenty miles east of Champa, I parted company with my military escort. They went on to Rajagriha while I joined a second detachment of Magadhan troops. These men had been posted to the republican border, and their commanding officer was more than pleased to accompany the king's son-in-law; in fact, he was terrified of me. I soon realized why.

Although even in Cathay we had heard stories of Ajatashatru's cruelty, I had tended to discount them. I knew, of course, that he was ruthless. Crablike, he had devoured his own father. But that was more the rule than the exception in the Gangetic plain. Certainly, I had never thought him wantonly cruel. But I was wrong.

For one thing, I was astonished by the extent of the devastation that I saw in what had once been the proud and prosperous republican federation. As we traveled north through those conquered realms, it was as if the earth itself had been put to death. Nothing grew where once there had been fields of millet, orchards, grazing land.

When we came to a field strewn with fire-darkened bricks, the commander said, "This was the city of Vaishali." The destruction had been total. Dogs and cats and birds of prey, snakes and scorpions and lizards now occupied the ruins of what had been, only a decade before, a prosperous city where I had been shown the congress hall and the shrine to Mahavira.

"Naturally, the king plans to rebuild the city." The commander kicked at a pile of bones.

"When he does, I am sure that it will rival Rajagriha itself," I said loyally. Although I was careful not to allow myself to seem anything but a loyal son-in-law of what the Indians took to be the greatest monarch that ever lived, curiosity occasionally got the better of me. "Was there much resistance here? Was it really necessary to raze the entire city?"

"Oh, yes, Lord Prince! I was here. I took part in the battle, which lasted eight days. Most of the fighting was over there." He pointed to the west where a row of palm trees marked the shrunken river. "We drove them back from the river's edge. When they tried to take refuge in the city, we stopped them at the walls. The king himself led the charge through the main gate. The king himself fired the first building. The king himself cut the throat of the republican general. The king himself turned to red the waters of the Ganges River." The captain was now chanting rather than speaking. Already Ajatashatru's victories were being rendered into verse so that future generations would be able to sing of his glory, and bloodiness.

Twelve thousand republican soldiers had been impaled on either side of the road that goes from Vaishali to Shravasti. Because the final battle had taken place in the dry season, the corpses had mummified in the hot sun. As a result, the dead soldiers still looked to be alive, their mouths wide open, as if gasping for air or screaming: death must have come slowly high on those wooden stakes. I was somewhat surprised to see that each man had been carefully emasculated: Indians frown on this practice. Later, in Shravasti, I saw on sale many exquisitely cured scrotal sacs and, for at least a season, they were very much the fashion as money purses. Ladies wore them tied to their belts, as a sign of patriotism.

We skirted the border of what was left of the Licchavi republic. Although the capital city had been destroyed, the rest of the republic still fought on. "They are a very wicked people," said my escort. "The king is very angry with them for not surrendering."

"I don't blame him. Let us pray that he punishes them —and soon!"

On a beautiful cool, cloudless day in autumn, I entered there was no hatred in the young man's voice. He was as much a victim of Ajatashatru's bloodiness as the endless rows of brown, twisted corpses to our left and right.

As we proceeded along the north road, a vulture came to rest on the shoulder of a mummified soldier. With almost human curiosity, even delicacy, the vulture peered into the socket where the eye had been and gave an exploratory peck; finding nothing, the bird flew away. He had arrived too late for the banquet.

On a beautiful cool, cloudless day in autumn, I entered Shravasti. Fortunately, Ajatashatru had spared the capital of Koshala. When I left Shravasti, I was twenty-seven or -eight years of age. I was now forty years old, and my face had been so burned by sun and wind that it looked like a teakwood mask. Worse, the hair that framed the mask was entirely white. Worst of all, the owner of the mask was no longer young.

Prince Jeta's river house appeared unchanged. I

knocked on the main door. A servant peered suspiciously at me through a small window in the door. When I told him who I was, he laughed. When I threatened him, in the name of Ajatashatru, he disappeared. A few moments later the door opened, and a respectful steward received me. Although I was a stranger to him, he told me that he knew all about the man from the west who had fathered the two sons of Ambalika. Thus, I learned that my wife and sons were alive. As for Prince Jeta . . .

My old friend was seated in the inner garden. He was indeed my *old* friend. I would not have recognized this emaciated creature as the vigorous man that I had known and admired.

"Come close," he said. Since he did not move to greet me, I crossed to where he lay on a couch. It was not until I embraced him that I discovered that he was entirely paralyzed from the head down.

"It happened last year." He sounded apologetic. "I would have preferred a swift departure, but it has been decided that I am to die in slow stages. Obviously, my last incarnation was happy. But I must not complain. After all, I've lived long enough to see you again."

Before I could answer, we were joined by a stout middle-aged woman and two solemn blue-eyed boys. I did not recognize Ambalika until she spoke. "Look at you!" She went immediately on the attack. "You're *old!* Oh, my poor husband—and lord." We embraced. I would not say that our reunion much resembled that of Odysseus and Penelope. But then, I had no suitors to kill off—that I knew of.

My older son was already a man; the younger was on the verge of maturity. The hot sun of the Gangetic plain ripens all things quickly, as if fearful that there will be insufficient time for reproduction.

The boys stared at me with wonder. I stared at them. The combination of northern blue eyes with dark southern skin was most striking: they were very handsome.

"I think they're lovely too," said Ambalika after the boys had been sent away. "But, of course, everyone here regards them as demons because of those blue eyes. They have endless problems. But once they're grown. . . ." Ambalika stopped. We stared at each other across the fragile body of Prince Jeta. I was beguiled, as always, by Ambalika's charm. I have never known a woman so delightful to be with. She was like a man to talk to, but not a

*states*man, like Queen Atossa. As for her appearance . . .
well, the Indian sun had done its work. She was definitely
overripe. The body was shapeless and the chins were numerous. Only the eyes were the same; they shone exactly
the way they had that night when we watched together
the north star.

"Begin," said Prince Jeta, "at the beginning."

I did. I told them whatever I thought would interest
them. I was surprised that neither wanted to hear of
Persia. When I was first married, Ambalika had talked of
nothing else. But then she had expected to go with me to
Susa. Now she had lost all interest in the west—and me.

On the other hand, Cathay fascinated both of them.
As it turned out, Prince Jeta was part of a consortium
that was involved in the reopening of the silk road.

"Now," I said, throat dry from so much talk, "you tell
me what has happened here."

Ambalika made the delicate warning gesture which
meant that we were being spied upon. Then, in a raptur-
ous voice, she said, "My father is now the universal monarch. We delight in his victories. In his wisdom. In his
kindness." There was a good deal more in that uninformative vein.

When I asked about the Buddha, Prince Jeta said, "He
achieved nirvana four years ago."

"After eating a very heavy dinner of pork and beans."
Ambalika was now her usual uncautious self.

"That is only hearsay." Prince Jeta was not pleased
with her levity. "All we know for certain is that he left us
peacefully. His last words were: 'All things are transitory.
Work out your salvation with diligence.' "

"Is Sariputra still head of the order?"

Prince Jeta shook his head. "He died before the Buddha. Ananda is now in charge. They're all in residence,
by the way."

"Busy arguing about what the Buddha said or did not
say." Ambalika was as intolerant as ever of the other
world and its devotees.

"Ananda is a good custodian," said Prince Jeta, without much conviction. "He sees to it that the monks continue to memorize everything that the Buddha said, just
as they did when he was alive."

"Except"—and I spoke from sad personal experience
of priests—"the Buddha is now no longer here to correct
them."

"True. And I don't need to tell you that there are already serious disagreements about what he may or may not have said."

"There will be more." Over the years I have never ceased to be astonished and infuriated by the new doctrines that the Zoroastrians conveniently issue in my grandfather's name. Just before I left Susa for the last time, I paid a call on the chief Zoroastrian. When he ascribed to my grandfather some nonsensical verses I told him, very sharply, that Zoroaster had never said any such thing. With a straight face, the charlatan replied, "You are right. The prophet did not say it in *this* life. He spoke those verses to me in a recent dream, and ordered me to write them down the moment I woke up."

Thus Truth is defeated by the Lie—at least in the time of the long dominion. Well, those false priests will feel the molten metal. That is a fact.

The next few weeks were most pleasant. Although the stout Ambalika no longer attracted me in a sexual way, I found her not only companionable but clever. Our first night together, she led me out onto the roof that overlooked the river. I remember that the moon was in decline, that the smoke of the cook-fires on the quay beneath us were as pungent as ever, that nothing ever changes in India.

"No one can hear us now." We sat side by side on a divan, the moon's light directly in our eyes. Far off to the east, one could just make out the Himalayas, a dark mass against the sky.

"Where is your father?" I had no intention of meeting that volatile figure if I could avoid it.

"In the dry season, he's always with the army. So he's probably somewhere on the Licchavi border. They're very stubborn. I can't think why. If they surrendered, he might save a few. Now he'll kill them all."

"He really is the universal monarch, isn't he?" Since I did not know to what extent my wife was her father's partisan, I was guarded.

"Well, there's been no horse sacrifice but . . . Yes, he is the first of all the kings in our history."

We watched shooting stars, and listened to someone play an out-of-tune zither beneath us.

"I suppose you've married again?" She asked the question without any particular emphasis.

"Yes. I am—or was—married to the Great King's sister. She's dead now."

"Were there children?"

"No. My only children have you for a mother."

"I'm honored." Ambalika's tone was grave, but she was plainly mocking me.

I ignored the mockery. "As far as I know, there is no precedent for someone like me to have sons in a far-off land, by a king's daughter."

"*Persia* is the far-off land." Ambalika was sharp. "*We* are home."

"I thought that you wanted to go back with me to Persia."

Ambalika laughed. "Let us say that I should like to go to Persia quite as much as you'd like to have me there!"

"I would like—"

"Don't be silly!" She was suddenly very like the young girl I had married. "You wouldn't know what to do with me and I certainly wouldn't know what to do in a country full of snow and ice and blue-eyed people." She shuddered at the thought.

"But our sons—"

"—must stay here."

"Must?" I was suddenly angry. After all, they were *my* sons, and I very much wanted to take them home to Susa, with or without their mother.

"Yes, must. Anyway, you have no choice in the matter. Neither do I," she added. "It's my father's will. He likes the idea of Persian grandsons. He thinks one day they'll be useful."

"To send on embassies? But if they've never visited their homeland, what use will they be?"

"He'll find one. Don't worry. Anyway, he's sent for old Caraka. To teach them Persian."

I was pleased that Caraka was still alive. According to Ambalika, he had been superintendent of the ironworks at Magadha.

"What about Cathay?" she asked, adjusting her spangled shawl against the warm night wind. "Did you marry anyone there?"

"I had two charming concubines. But no wife."

"No children?"

"No. Cathayan women have mastered the art of not having babies."

522

Ambalika nodded. "I have heard that. Of course we have certain spells that always work, except when they don't."

"Cathayan women drink some sort of potion. But when you ask what it is, they simply giggle. As a people, they're very secretive. Anyway, my two girls were delightful. You would have enjoyed them."

"I would enjoy almost *any* company here. As the single wife of an invisible husband in the house of a grandfather who has no concubine under the age of sixty, I'm rather on my own. What did you do with the girls when you left Cathay?"

"I sent one home to her village with enough money to get herself a husband, and the other was taken into the household of a friend." Fan Ch'ih had been so enamored of my second concubine that I was delighted to be able to make him a present which he genuinely appreciated.

"I shall be denied their company." Ambalika sounded almost sad. "But then, soon, I shall be denied your company, shan't I?"

"I must report to the Great King," I said.

"And once you've done that, you'll be far too old ever to come back here." Ambalika's bluntness had always startled—and charmed—me. In the dark, listening to her clear, mocking voice, I was able to ignore the hoops of flesh that had so entirely smothered the slender girl whom I had married in what seemed, even then, to have been another life.

"Would you like me to stay?"

"I don't think so," she said. "We've been apart too long."

"What about the king?"

Ambalika was silent. I put my arm about her shoulders. This was a mistake. The illusion of youth created by darkness was dispelled by touch. But we remained in each other's arms for some time; and she told me of the bloody times through which the countries of the Gangetic plain had passed. "We were particularly frightened when the army of Koshala was destroyed. In fact, we were all set to leave the city when the king sent us word, secretly, that we were to stay, that Shravasti would be spared because the Buddha was in residence!" She laughed softly into my neck. "My father's interest in the Buddha is not unlike mine. But he knew that the Buddha was popular. He also knew that the Buddhist order hated King

Virudhaka for having destroyed the Shakya republic. Of course, no one suspected then that my father was going to eliminate all the other republics once he was crowned in Shravasti. Anyway, the people here greeted Father as if he were some sort of liberator. And, so far, he has behaved himself."

"Does he see you?"

"Oh, yes. We're very friendly and, of course, he's delighted with his grandsons. He always asks me about you, hopes to see you again, weeps . . ."

"Still?"

"Still. But now there's so much more to weep about than there was." Beyond that single sentence, Ambalika made no criticism of her father. But women are always attracted to power. I do not think there could ever be a conqueror so bloody that most women would not willingly lie with him in the hope of bearing a son who would be every bit as ferocious as the father.

2

SHORTLY BEFORE THE ANNUAL CARNIval that takes Shravasti by storm when all days are given over to pleasure, Prince Jeta and I paid a call on Ananda at the Buddhist monastery. I accompanied Prince Jeta's litter on foot.

"I seldom leave the house," he murmured as we made our way through the cheerful crowds. "But I want to be present when you talk to Ananda. He'll be delighted with your Cathayan stories." Because Prince Jeta had been fascinated by my accounts of Confucius and Master Li, he assumed that the new leader of the Buddhist order would be equally interested. That was the only sign of naïveté that I was ever to detect in my old friend. If there is one thing the professional priest detests, it is being told about a rival religion or system of thought.

The bamboo park was now entirely devoted to the Buddhist order. The hut where the Buddha had lived was surrounded by a low wall while, nearby, a large new building was going up. "A convent," said Prince Jeta. "Ambapali is building it. And she will be the first nun."

"The courtesan from Vaishali?"

"Yes. After the Buddha died, she came here . . . with all her money. A lucky thing, too."

"Yes. I saw the ruins of Vaishali."

"She is devoting the rest of her life to the order. I deeply admire her. She is very holy."

"Also very old," I could not help but add. It is quite common for successful courtesans to turn to religion or philosophy when their beauty goes. It will be interesting to see what becomes of Aspasia.

Ananda somewhat resembled the Buddha, a likeness that he did nothing to minimize. With many bows, the head of the sangha escorted Prince Jeta's litter into the main hall of the monastery. I followed.

Several hundred youthful monks were reciting the Buddha's words. I noticed that many of them were wearing newly made yellow robes. This was an innovation. In the old days they could only wear those scraps of cloth that they had begged.

Ananda showed us into a low-ceilinged room at the back of the monastery's third courtyard. "Here I do my best to remember," he said.

As Prince Jeta's litter bearers withdrew, Ananda turned to me. "I remember you with delight," he said. "Sariputra spoke so highly of you."

When Prince Jeta told Ananda about my Cathayan adventures, the holy man affected interest. But it was Prince Jeta, not Ananda, who asked me to expound the wisdom of the Cathayans. I did so, briefly. Ananda was politely bored. Finally he said, "Master Confucius strikes me as entirely too much of this world to be truly serious."

"He believes that the world of men is the only world there is," I said. "That's why he thinks it such a serious matter, our behavior in the only world there is."

"We would agree on that last part, certainly, and his notion of what constitutes a true gentleman is very close to what we know to be true. That's why I find it so strange that he has not yet noticed what is so obvious—the fact of nirvana. Just as he seems to be well on the way to the four noble truths"—Ananda made a loud vulgar popping sound, as tongue struck the inside of an inflated cheek—"he stops."

"I don't think he cares to go any further than this world."

"That is to be pitied."

"I think it unnecessary to pity Confucius." I spoke

more sharply than I intended, and Prince Jeta's head shifted from Ananda to me.

Ananda smiled. "Our pity is general, my dear. Our pity is for all living things. To be alive is to be trapped in the cycle of birth and rebirth. Only he who was here and went away can be said to have achieved what should be the deliberate aim of all men."

"Master K'ung would not agree." I was surprised to find myself speaking as if I were a disciple of Confucius. Actually, I had been horrified by his total indifference to the Wise Lord. Not only had he been indifferent to the *idea* of creation, he had refused to accept that duality which is implicit in all things. Although Confucius was entirely of this world, I defended him to Ananda. There is no end to human perversity. I suppose that one is always tempted to challenge those who think that they and they alone possess the truth or the way or the key to the mystery.

"What is Confucius' idea of death?" For Prince Jeta's sake, Ananda was affecting interest.

"I don't really know. I suspect that he doesn't think it matters. He is interested in life . . ."

"Trapped in life! The poor man!"

"Who is not—trapped? Confucius is an honest man. He is often sad. He confesses to imperfection, something very rare, I have found, when dealing with this world's holy men." Ananda accepted my insult with a bland smile. I continued, "He wanted to govern a state for the general good. When this was denied him, he suffered, and because he suffered, he told everyone that was proof that he was by no means a perfect sage."

"By no means a perfect sage," repeated Ananda. "Are you certain that he showed no sign at all of wanting to break out of the cycle of birth and death and rebirth?"

"I don't think he accepts the cycle."

"That is ignorance, I fear."

"No, not ignorance. Simply another kind of knowledge. He envisages a primal unity from which we come and to which we go."

"That is perceptive, very perceptive." Ananda turned to Prince Jeta. "It is a proof of the absolute wisdom of the Buddha that even in barbarous Cathay, a teacher is able to glimpse the truth—not *understand* it, mind you, but he does sense it." Ananda smiled at me. "We are very pleased to hear this." The little man's complacency was deeply annoying.

"I'm sure," I said, "Confucius would be pleased to know that in a far-off land his truths are also perceived, if only dimly."

Ananda ignored not only what I said but the challenge offered. He turned to Prince Jeta. "You will be happy to know that we have finally perfected a system of drainage that is unique—at least for Shravasti. We have diverted the waters of an underground creek so that it now runs directly under the privies. We have also . . ." He spoke at great length of hygiene, always a problem for Indian cities.

Finally, politely, Ananda turned back to me. "I seem to recall that when you were here the first time, you had quite different beliefs from what you appear now to have. At that time you believed in a supreme god, a single creator of the universe. Now, thanks to the teachings of this Cathayan, you are concerned only with . . . deportment in the everyday world."

I had not counted on his remembering what I had said about the Wise Lord so many years before. This was foolish of me. When it comes to memory, the professional priest is worse—or better—than the poet.

"I have not changed," I said. "I still believe in the Wise Lord. I only mention the teachings of Confucius to demonstrate—" I stopped, unable to recall just what it was that I *had* meant to reveal by quoting the worldly Confucius.

"To demonstrate the similarities between his way and the way of the Buddha. Of course, I understand." Ananda smiled, infuriatingly. "Certainly," he went on, "your Cathayan, by rejecting the idea of a creator-god like Brahma or the Wise Lord, shows the beginnings of true intelligence."

I took this blasphemy with, I hope, the same imperturbability that he had used to deflect my earlier challenge. "It is true intelligence," I said, "to realize that nothing can start from nothing. Therefore, the world had to start from something. The world had to be created, which it was—by the Wise Lord."

"But who created him?"

"He did."

"Out of what?"

"Out of nothing."

"But you just said that nothing can start from nothing."

Yes, Democritus, I had fallen into the oldest trap of

all. I shifted ground, swiftly. "Nothing is not the word I meant. Let us say that what there was then and is now and will be is the always-so." Without thinking, I had appropriated Master Li's concept. "It was from the always-so that the Wise Lord created the earth, sky, man. Created the Truth and the Lie . . ."

"Oh, dear." Ananda sighed. "This is very primitive. Do forgive me. I don't want to hurt your feelings. I respect your deep faith in what your grandfather thought was true. But even your Cathayan friend has gone beyond the notion of an all-powerful sky god like the Wise Lord or Brahma or heaven or whatever you want to call him or it. You know, there was once a Brahman who used to get very angry with the Buddha. Finally he said, 'How can you reject Brahma the creator? Don't you realize that whatever happiness or sorrow, whatever feeling a man has comes to him from a supreme deity?' "

"What did the Buddha say to that?" Obviously Prince Jeta had not heard this part of the doctrine before—because it was a recent revelation?

"I quote the Buddha's answer," said Ananda. He shut his eyes and started to chant, " 'So, then, owing to the creation of a supreme deity, men will become murderers, thieves, unchaste, liars, slanderers, abusive, babblers, covetous, malicious, and perverse in views. And so, for those who choose to fall back on the creation of a god as the essential reason, there is neither the desire to do, nor the effort to do, nor necessity to do or not to do this or that deed.' "

"Good," whispered Prince Jeta.

"Nonsense!" I was furious. "That is only a part of it. After the Wise Lord created himself, and his shadow evil, he created man and he gave man a choice: serve the Truth or serve the Lie. Those who serve the Lie will suffer at the final judgment, while—"

"How very, very complicated," said Ananda. "And so typical of one of those supreme deities. All that malice. All that silliness. After all, if he is supreme, why does he allow evil to exist?"

"So that each man can make his choice."

"If I were a supreme deity, I wouldn't go to the trouble of creating either evil or man or anything at all that was not entirely pleasing to me. I'm afraid that when it comes to explaining your supreme deity, you're obliged to work backwards. Evil exists. You cannot explain why.

So you turn your creator into a sort of cruel sportsman who plays games with human life. Will they or won't they be obedient? Shall I or shall I not torture them? Dear child, it's all too primitive. That's why we've long since abandoned the very notion of a supreme deity. And so, I gather, has your friend Confucius. He realizes, as do we, that to accept such a monster means an endorsement of evil, since evil is his creation, too. Happily, we look past Brahma, past the Wise Lord. We look to the nature of the universe and we see that it is a circle without beginning or end, and for the one who follows the middle way, it is possible to look straight through the circle and to realize that the entire thing is an illusion—like eternity. Finally, for practical reasons, we think that men behave better in a world where there is no supreme deity endorsing mischief and confusing the simple. As your Confucius so wisely said, 'Heaven is far. Man is near.' "

I did not pursue the subject. Atheists can always get the better of those who believe in the Wise Lord. We know what is true. They do not. I found Confucius sympathetic because he did not attempt to remove heaven from atop the earth. He accepted what he could not understand. But the Buddha defied heaven with indifference. I do not think that there has ever been on this earth a man so arrogant. In effect, he said, "I exist. But when I cease to exist, I shall exist no longer, and there will be no existence at all anywhere. What others take to be existence is illusion." This is breath-taking.

Democritus says that *his* breath is not taken away. He thinks that the Buddha means something else. Creation continues, says Democritus, and the only anomaly is the flawed self which observes creation. Remove the self and matter remains, as always. The always-so? I cannot follow any of this. For me what is, is.

3

DURING THE NEXT WEEKS I DEALT with the various merchants and guilds who wanted to do business with Persia. I was by now something of a merchant myself. I knew what could be sold at Susa; and for how much. I quite enjoyed the hours of haggling in the tents that are set up in the central market. Needless to say, whenever I found myself in the company of an important merchant or guild treasurer, the name of the Egibis would be mentioned. In a sense, that firm was a sort of universal monarch. Wherever one goes in the world, its agents have already been there, and done business.

I did not find it easy talking to my sons. At first they were wary of me. I had the sense that, in some way, they resented their own differentness and blamed me for it. Nevertheless, I did manage to gain the confidence of the elder boy. He was inordinately proud of his grandfather, the king.

"He will be the first lord of all creation." We were crossing the central market, where my son had watched me accept a series of loans from a corporation of merchants. I must say that he had done his very best to conceal his warrior-class scorn of the merchants that I was dealing with.

"What do you mean by lord of all creation?"

"The king looks to the west. The king looks to the east." The boy was obviously quoting from some palace text.

"You think that he has designs on your father's country?" I asked.

The boy nodded. "One day the whole world will be his because there's never been anyone like him. After all, there's never been a master of all India before."

"All India? What about the Licchavis? And the kingdom of Avanti? And *our* province of India? And what about the south?"

The boy shrugged. "These are details. But when Ajatashatru rode into this square—I was a child then but I still remember the way he looked—he was like the sun. And the people welcomed him just as if he were the sun after the long rains."

I did not suggest that they might have been terrified of their new ruler who did resemble that relentless midsummer sun which scorches the fields and makes a perfect desert.

"Does he like you?"

"Oh, yes. I am in favor." The boy was already the size of the warrior that he would soon be. Although he had my eyes—also, the eyes of the Thracian witch Lais—he was entirely strange to me. But I could tell that he was ambitious and energetic. He would make his way at the court of Magadha. There was no doubt of that.

"Would you like to see Persia?" I asked.

The teeth were very white; and the smile was charming. "Oh, yes! My mother has told me so much about Susa and Babylon and the Great King. And whenever old Caraka comes to see us, he tells me stories, too."

"Would you like to go back with me?" I did not dare look at him. In the land of the dark people, there is something strange about two pairs of blue eyes looking one into the other, as if into mirrors . . . only, one of the mirrors was framed by darkness.

"I must finish my studies, Father." The answer was expected. "Then I'm to go to the university at Taxila. I don't want to go, but my grandfather has commanded me to study languages. So I must obey."

"Perhaps he'll use you as an ambassador, like me."

"That would be an honor twice over." The boy was already a courtier.

My younger son was dreamy, and shy. When I finally got him to talk, he wanted to hear stories about dragons and mermaids. I did my best to delight him with tall tales. He was also interested in the Buddha. I suspect he may have inherited from his great-grandfather the sort of mind that looks quite naturally upon the other world. In any case, neither of my sons wanted to leave India. Although I was not surprised, I was deeply disappointed.

The day before my caravan was to start for Taxila, I sat beside Prince Jeta's litter on the roof of the river house.

"I shall die quite soon," he said. He turned his head toward me. "That is why I'm so pleased that I was able to see you again."

"Why? Once you're dead, you'll forget me." Since Prince Jeta enjoyed laughing at death, I made myself as amusing as possible on the subject, not the easiest task. Even now I am still not used to the idea of abandoning this admittedly decrepit body for the long walk to the far end—or so I pray to the Wise Lord—of the bridge of the redeemer.

"Ah, but to have talked to you in my last days may alter my destiny in some important way. Because of you, I may be closer to the exit when I'm reborn."

"I would have thought that you are only a step away from nirvana."

"More than a step, I'm afraid. I am linked to sorrow. My next rebirth may well be worse than even this." He looked down at the paralyzed body.

"We are born only once," I said. "Or so *we* believe," I added politely.

Prince Jeta smiled. "What you believe makes no sense, if you'll forgive me. We can't conceive a god who takes an immortal soul, allows it to be born once, plays a game with it, then passes a judgment on it and condemns it to pain or pleasure forever."

"Not forever. Eventually, in eternity, all will be as one."

"I'm not sure that I quite grasp your idea of eternity."

"Who can?" I changed the subject; spoke of my sons. "I had hoped that they might go back with me. Ambalika, too."

Prince Jeta shook his head. "That's not practical. They would find themselves as out of place there as you have found yourself here. Besides . . ."

Prince Jeta stopped. He had seen something across the river. I looked, too. The plain between the mountains and the river was filled with what looked to be a dust storm. Yet the day was windless.

"What on earth is it?" I asked. "A mirage?"

"No." Prince Jeta frowned. "It is the king."

I shuddered in the warm sunlight. "I thought he was on the Licchavi border."

"He was. Now he is here."

"I think I should leave before he arrives."

"Too late," said Prince Jeta. "He will want to see you."

"But since he doesn't know I'm here, I could—"

"He knows that you're here. He knows everything."

The next morning, at dawn, I was commanded to attend the king across the river. I bade farewell to Ambalika, as if for the last time. She was soothing. "You're his son-in-law. The father of his favorite grandsons. You've nothing to fear." But even as she spoke, I had the sense that she was saying farewell to me for the last time.

There is nothing on earth to compare with an Indian army. For one thing, it is not an army—it is a city. Imagine a tented city of two or three hundred thousand men, women, children, elephants, camels, horses, bullocks, all moving slowly across a dusty landscape, and you have some idea of what it is like when an Indian king goes to war. Greeks are scandalized by the fact that the Great King goes to war with his women and his furniture and his flasks of Choaspes water—by the fact that even the immortals are allowed to travel with their women and personal slaves. But when it comes time to fight, Persian attendants and baggage are kept well to the rear. Not so in India. The king's city simply engulfs the enemy. First, the elephants charge the opposing army. Should the enemy lack elephants, the battle will end at that point. Should there be resistance, spearmen and archers go into action. Meanwhile, markets, taverns, workshops, armories so fill up the enemy's territory that he is undone by the sheer mass of people and things that have been flung at him.

When two armies of equal size attack each other, ultimate victory goes to the army that manages to kill the other side's leader. Should neither leader die, the result is an endless melee—two cities hopelessly mixed up. There are stories of kings' armies that have got themselves so confused that each side was obliged to call a truce in order to sort things out.

It took my charioteer and me an hour to get from the first sentry across the river to the heart of the military encampment where Ajatashatru's golden tent has been pitched. I had more the sense of being in a vast bazaar than in a military camp. Slowly, slowly we rode through markets, past arsenals and slaughterhouses to the inner city, where the tents of the king and his court had been pitched.

At the entrance to the royal tent, the charioteer stopped, and I got down. A chamberlain led me into a nearby tent where a slave presented me with a silver basin full of rosewater. Ritually, I washed my hands and face in the rosewater; then a second slave dried me with a linen cloth. I was treated respectfully, but in silence. Once I was cleaned I was left alone. Although time passed slowly, imagination worked quickly. Since I assumed I would be put to death, there was no form of execution that I did not vividly imagine in every sickening detail. I was contemplating slow suffocation—of which I have a horror—when Varshakara appeared at the tent opening. I reacted rather the way a swimmer does when he realizes that what he took to be a floating tree is actually a crocodile.

But the chamberlain put me at my ease. "You are *almost* unchanged," he said as we embraced.

"You are the same!" Actually, Varshakara was indeed exactly the way he had been when we first met so many years before at Varanasi. Ever a master of treachery, he had made with consummate ease the transition from the service of the murdered father to that of the killer-son. The chin whiskers were now bright-red to make up for the red teeth, which were gone.

We spoke of Cathay. He was eager for every scrap of news and, fortunately, I had more than scraps to feed this predator.

"You must make me a report," he said finally. "We are *very* interested in reopening the silk road. As we told your companion—who is still at Champa, by the way."

I was not surprised to learn that the chamberlain had already opened negotiations with the Key marquis. I wondered, uneasily, what my Cathayan colleague had had to say about me. After all, I had abandoned him. But Varshakara said nothing more on the subject.

Then there was a sound of thunder all about us: drums were heralding the approach of Ajatashatru. We went outside, and I stared with some awe at what must have been the largest elephant on earth . . . a white elephant that ambled toward us like some slow-moving bejeweled mountain. On top of the elephant was a pavilion of silver set with diamonds. Inside this glittering structure was a huge shimmering golden figure.

"Ajatashatru!" Every voice acclaimed the king. Blessings were screamed at him. Musicians made a terrible racket. Petitioners fell prostrate in the dirt.

When the elephant halted, a ladder was placed beside it. Two professional acrobats scurried to the top of the ladder. Then they tugged the king to his feet and helped him, slowly, to descend.

Ajatashatru was now the fattest man I had ever seen. In fact, he was so heavy that his legs could not support the weight of the swollen body. As a result, he either walked, as he did now, with an arm on the shoulders of each acrobat, or he leaned on a pair of thick ivory staffs. As he shuffled slowly forward, head, neck and shoulders all merged into a single thickness, he looked like a gross golden spider.

My eyes were upon the ground as Ajatashatru approached. I had hoped that he might stop and acknowledge me, but without a word he slid past me. Fixedly, I stared at the scarlet rug. Like the Great King, Ajatashatru never put his foot on uncovered earth.

Several hours later Varshakara came to me and smiled ingratiatingly. For some reason, I missed the bloody tusks; wondered whether or not he had been forced to give up chewing those mentally deranging betelnut quids; recently a person knowledgeable in such matters told me that one can hold the quid between the inside of the cheek and the toothless gums—and enjoy mental derangement.

Varshakara led me into the presence. Ajatashatru was sprawled upon an enormous divan, surrounded by a thousand silk-covered pillows. Within close reach were a dozen small tables covered with dishes of food and flagons of wine; also, within close reach, were a dozen very pretty pre-pubescent girls and boys. With age, my father-in-law's sexual tastes had undergone no change. But then, I have found that whatever men are in youth they will be in age, if to no good effect.

A boy of eight or nine was lovingly wiping the king's face with a linen napkin. Ajatashatru's body was agleam with sweat. He could not walk across a room without suffering from exhaustion. Although I assumed his life must be nearly over, the face was unchanged. If anything, because of the fat, my father-in-law looked far younger than I did. I have noticed that in those countries where the heat is intense and bodies mature early and age swiftly, men and women deliberately make themselves fat in order to retain if not the beauty of adolescence, the charm of the infantile.

Ajatashatru beamed. "Dearest!" The huge baby's face stared at me eagerly, as if I were something to put in its mouth. Then he flung wide arms from which the silk-encased fat hung like Sardis bed bolsters. "Come to me!"

I came to him. As I leaned forward to kiss the nearest hand, I stumbled and fell onto the divan. The children giggled. I was terrified. At Susa—at any court—one would be put to death on the spot for such an approach to the sovereign. But I was forgiven.

The king grabbed me under the arms and half lifted, half dragged me across the divan as if I were a doll. Obviously, the fat arms were still powerful. As I fell against the vast bosom that reeked of a hundred conflicting perfumes, carmined lips kissed my face in exactly the same eager way that a child lavishes love on a doll—which a moment later it will break.

"My darling! Without you, life has been a burden, without joy! How many a night have we wept ourselves to sleep, wondering why it was that our dearest, most darling son-in-law deserted us. Oh, naughty! Naughty!"

With that, Ajatashatru picked me up and dropped me down beside him. I fell back into a pile of cushions. Next to him, I felt like a fragile bowl beside an elephant. There was no etiquette that I knew of for such a situation. I looked as respectful and as attentive as I could, sprawled beside what must easily have been the largest king on earth.

"Darling Darius!" I should mention that he persistently called me Darius during our interview. Needless to say, I did not correct him. Like so many absolute monarchs, he was not very good at remembering names. In Persia, the Great King never appears in public without a chamberlain who will whisper into his ear the names of those who approach him.

"How my poor child has hungered for the sight of you! Has been famished for news of you! Has thirsted to know your whereabouts!" The verbs that Ajatashatru employed gave a clue to what was on his mind. Immediately the children began to offer him food and drink. He was the only man I have ever known who could speak clearly with a full mouth. But then, he seldom stopped either eating or talking.

When I was at last allowed to speak, I told him of my many failed attempts to return to Magadha. As I spoke, he gargled wine noisily in his throat. When I told him of my captivity in Cathay, he listened intently. Between puffs of fat, the dark eyes were as brilliant as ever. When I had finished my recital—interrupted at regular intervals by exclamations of delight, amazement, affection—Ajatashatru finished off a tumbler of wine and said, "You will describe the silk road to Varshakara."

"Yes, Lord King."

"In detail."

"Yes, Lord King."

"Make a map."

"I shall, with joy."

"You *are* my darling, aren't you?" He hugged me. "You'll show me the way to Cathay, won't you?"

"*You*, Lord King, will go to Cathay?"

"Why not? Next year is going to be very, very dull. The naughty Licchavis will have been defeated, and Pardyota—remember him? The king of Avanti? He has been wicked. But I don't think it'll take us more than a month or two to conquer Avanti. You'll stay and watch me teach him a lesson. You'll enjoy it. That's a promise. Because I am a very, very good teacher."

"I know, Lord King. I saw the ruins of Vaishali."

"Oh, I am pleased!" The eyes glowed. "Did you see the impalements alongside the road?"

"Yes! They were superb, Lord King. In fact, I've never seen so many captives put to death all at once."

"Neither have I. Naturally, everyone tells me that I have set some sort of record, but you know how insincere people can be. Even so, I honestly believe that no king ever impaled so many naughty men as I did that day. It was thrilling. You've never heard so much howling. Particularly when we castrated them *after* they were impaled. I thought I'd go deaf. My hearing is extremely sensitive. What were we talking about?"

"Cathay, Lord King."

"Yes. Yes. I'll want to go there myself, with the main army. You can act as guide."

When I told him that, with luck, it would take his army no less than three years to get to the border of the Middle Kingdom, he began to lose interest. He shuddered when I described the steaming jungles, the high mountain passes, the discomforts and fevers of that long journey.

"If what you say is true, I shan't go myself. That's obvious. But I shall send out an army. After all, I'm universal monarch, am I not?"

"Yes. Yes, Lord King!"

"And since Cathay is a part of the universe, they'll know immediately that I now possess . . . what do they call it?"

"The mandate of heaven."

"Yes. They'll realize that I've had it for ever so long now. All in all, I'd be wiser to go west, don't you think? The distances aren't so great. And there are no jungles to worry about. And all those charming cities to stay at. And, of course, Persia is very much a part of my universe. Isn't it, dearest?"

"Oh, yes, Lord King." I was growing more and more uneasy. Although Ajatashatru's army was no threat to the satrapy of Bactria, much less to the Persian empire, I could see myself kept like a monkey on a leash as the king slowly made his way into Persia—and certain defeat.

Although I did my best to deflect him from a Persian adventure, Ajatashatru was euphoric at the thought of what he kept calling *"my"* universe." He blamed the republicans for having kept him from "traveling to the rising sun, to the setting sun, to the north star. Oh, I know how much there is to my universe, and how little time there is for me to visit all my peoples, but I must make the effort. I owe it to . . . uh, heaven." He had grasped rather quickly the Cathayan religio-political system. He was certainly enchanted by the notion that hegemony is the true begetter of the mandate. Since he was now confident that he already possessed the first, he was now ready to receive the other "just as soon as I take a few trips to see all my good yellow peoples and blue-eyed peoples, too. Imagine owning millions of people with eyes like my grandsons! Enchanting boys, by the way. If only for them, we are in your debt, Darius."

Then, in the course of an elaborate and seemingly endless meal, we were interrupted by bad news. The army of Avanti had crossed into Magadha. Varshakara looked very grave. Ajatashatru looked very annoyed. "Oh, the wicked, wicked man! Such a bad king! Now we shall have to kill him. Very soon. My darling!" The king kissed my face rather as if it were a plate. Then he gave me a tremendous shove, and I fell off the divan. "Go to your charming wife. Wait for us in Shravasti. We'll be in residence before the rains start. Meanwhile, we shall turn the kingdom of Avanti into a desert. That is a promise. I am god on earth. The equal of Brahma. I am the universal monarch. Do give my love to . . . to . . . uh, my daughter." He had forgotten Ambalika's name. "And kiss your two enchanting blue-eyed boys for me. I am a doting grandfather. Go away."

My last meeting with Ambalika was surprisingly cheerful. We sat side by side in the swing at the center of Prince Jeta's inner courtyard—one of the few places where we could not be overheard. I told her that I had seen the king. "He's going to war against Avanti!"

"He won't have an easy victory," said Ambalika.

"Do you think the war could last for more than a season?"

"It could go on for years, like the nonsense with those tiresome Licchavians."

"Then I don't suppose he'll want to invade Persia this year."

"Did he say he wanted to *invade* Persia?"

I nodded. I was noncommittal.

"Well . . ." Ambalika was thoughtful. We swung up and down, over the flowering shrubs. "If he were younger, I think he might succeed. Don't you?"

"Persia is the most powerful empire on earth." I thought that that was a reasonably neutral remark.

"But my father is the greatest general on earth. Or was. Well, we'll never know now. The war with Avanti will drag on and on, and Father will die from indigestion, and you . . . what will you do?"

"Go back to Susa."

"With your caravan?"

I nodded. I did not tell her that I meant to slip out of the city that evening, without the caravan. Yet I think that she must have suspected that I had something like that in mind because suddenly she said, "I want to marry again."

"Who?"

"My half-brother. He's fond of me. He's very good with my sons. He'll make me his first wife, and we'll live here in Shravasti. He's viceroy, you know. I don't think you've met him. Anyway, I shall have to marry him fairly soon because Prince Jeta's going to die any day now and when he does this house goes to his nephew, a poisonous creature, and we'll be homeless."

"But you're already married," I reminded her.

"I know. But I can be a widow, can't I?"

"Shall I kill myself? Or will the king do that for you?"

"Neither." Ambalika gave me a charming smile. "Come inside. I've something to show you."

We went to her bedroom. She opened an ivory chest and withdrew a papyrus document. Since I have difficulty reading Indian script, she read for me an account of the lamentable death of Cyrus Spitama at Susa in the "something-or-other year of the reign of the Great King Xerxes. Now, you figure out the date—which should be six months from now. Then fill in the top and the bottom with some Persian writing, saying that this letter comes from the chancellery. You know, all very official."

I also knew the Indian religion. "You can't remarry. That's the law."

Ambalika had thought of everything. "I've talked to the high priest. He'll say that you and I were never properly married. The Brahmans can always find an error in the ceremony if they want to. They want to. So I shall then marry my brother, very quietly."

"And we shall never meet again?"

"I should hope not!" Ambalika's cheerful ruthlessness was chillingly reminiscent of her father. "Anyway, you won't want to come back here. You'll be too old, for one thing."

"My sons . . ."

"They are," she said, very evenly, "where they are meant to be."

So it was that I wrote out a description of my own death to which I forged the signature of the first clerk of the chancellery at Susa. Then, an hour before sunset, I left the house. I did not see my sons or Prince Jeta. What coins I had I folded into a cloth belt that I wrapped about my middle. In the general market I bought an old cloak, sandals, a staff. A few minutes before the west gate was shut for the night, I left the city.

I have no idea whatever became of my sons. Caraka would have sent me messages if he had thought I was still alive. But I assume he believed Ambalika when she announced my death.

From the Egibis I used to get news of Ajatashatru. The war with Avanti proved to be quite as long and indecisive as the war with the Licchavi republic had been. Finally, in the ninth year of Xerxes' reign, Ajatashatru died what was said to be a natural death. Since the succession was confused, the makeshift empire that he had created in the Gangetic plain promptly fell apart.

When I think of India, gold flares in the darkness behind the lids of these blind eyes. When I think of Cathay, silver gleams and I see again, as if I were really seeing, silver snow fall against silver willows.

Gold and silver; darkness now.

BOOK EIGHT

The Golden Age
of Xerxes
the Great King

1

IN THE SPRING OF THE EIGHTH YEAR
of the reign of Xerxes, I came up to Susa after six years
at the east and at the east of the east. The eager young
man who had set out from Bactria no longer existed. A
middle-aged specter rode through the gates of Susa. I was
surprised that people could actually see me. I was not at
all surprised that no one recognized me. Since I had been
given up for dead years before, I was a ghost to the court.
Worse, I was a ghost to myself.

But my sense of unreality was soon dispelled or,
rather, replaced by the unreality of the world that I had
come back to. Nothing was the same. No, that is not quite
true. The chancellery was the same, as I discovered when
I was received in the second room by a sub-chamberlain
whom I had known when he was wine bearer in the harem. He was a Syrian who liked to know everything. He
was often teased because he asked so many questions. He
was feared because he never forgot the answers.

"This is most unsettling, King's Friend." The eunuch
used my last remaining title. The clerks of the first room
had been quick to tell me that I was no longer king's eye.
"Naturally, we are pleased to see you. But . . ." He did
not finish.

I answered for him. "I've been legally declared dead,
and my estate has been seized by the treasury."

"Not by the treasury. Or at least only a small portion.
Your distinguished mother has the bulk of your property."

"She is alive?"

"Very much so. She's with the court at Sardis."

"Sardis?" I was surprised. "Since when does the Great
King hold court at Sardis?"

"You've not heard *any* news?" The second room looks
upon a garden. I noticed that spring was late.

"Very little. I know that the Greek wars were continued. I know that the Great King burned Athens to the
ground." I had learned this in Shravasti from an agent of
the Egibis. "Beyond that I know nothing."

542

"Much," said the sub-chamberlain, "has happened."

This proved to be an understatement. Shortly after I left for Cathay, Xerxes had asked the priests of Bel-Marduk to make him a present of certain gold objects in their treasury. "I asked for nothing of a sacred nature," he told me. "Even so, they refused. I was altogether too lenient. I put nobody to death. But I did confiscate a number of gold odds and ends and melted them down to make darics to pay for the Greek wars. Then I went up to Susa."

Several weeks after Xerxes left Babylon, one of the innumerable pretenders to that ancient throne was encouraged by the priests of Bel-Marduk to declare himself king of Babel, which he did. He put to death our hideous old friend Zopyrus. Then he himself was killed by a rival who held off the Persian army for more than a year. Finally, Babylon fell to Xerxes' brother-in-law and best general Megabyzus, son of the murdered satrap Zopyrus.

"The Great King's vengeance was terrible," said the sub-chamberlain, shaking his head with awe. "He melted down the statue of Bel-Marduk so that no one can ever again take the statue's hand. Then he tore down all the temples to Bel-Marduk and dismissed those priests that he did not kill. Next, he tore down the city walls. He razed the ziggurat. He confiscated the lands and property of the leading merchants—"

"Including that of the Egibis?"

"No." The eunuch smiled. "Egibi and sons is now established here at Susa. Then the Great King split Babylonia into two satrapies and abolished the title king of Babel. Now he styles himself, simply, 'Xerxes the Great King.' Today Babylon is a provincial city, and a thousand years of history are at an end."

"Where does the court winter now?"

"Persepolis."

"Which is freezing in the winter."

The eunuch sighed. "We are loyal slaves." He intoned the usual formula, which I repeated.

When I asked what had become of all those tonnes of gold from Babylon, I was told that they had been used for the invasion of Greece. "Used—and used up, I fear," said the eunuch. "Those wars have been ruinous!"

"But successful. Athens has been destroyed."

"Oh, yes! Yes!" But the eunuch's enthusiasm was plainly false. Close questioning revealed a part of the story which is so well known here at Athens that I only

543

repeat it, Democritus, to give you a glimpse of how it looked to the other side.

Xerxes himself commanded the invasion. He proceeded overland from Sardis. With him were three of the six army corps, or sixty thousand men—not six million or whatever number Herodotus came up with in order to flatter the Athenians. The entire fleet accompanied the army.

The Greeks were in a state of panic. Since the oracles at Delphi and Athens all agreed that the Great King was invincible, it was suggested that the Athenians might be well advised to surrender their city and move onto Italy. As an afterthought, the oracle at Delphi said that the city's wooden walls might be of use. That was when the ill-favored and ill-regarded Themistocles chose, somewhat tortuously, to interpret the phrase wooden walls to mean wooden ships.

But the eunuch from the chancellery only knew the court's version of the war, which he told me. "Exactly two years ago this month, the Great King was at Troy, where he sacrificed a thousand cattle to the Trojan goddess."

This was a shock. I had just been delighted to learn that Xerxes by rejecting the titles pharaoh of Egypt and king of Babel had rejected those countries' gods. But then, for reasons of drama rather more than of politics, he had made a crucial sacrifice not to the Wise Lord but to a Trojan goddess whose name not even the eunuch could remember.

"But the point to the sacrifice was well taken, King's Friend. As you know best of all, the Great King has learned by heart a good deal of the Greek Homer. So, after the sacrifice, he stood among the old ruins and said, 'I shall avenge Troy, destroyed by invading Greeks. I shall avenge my ancestor, Priam the king. I shall avenge all Asia for the wanton cruelties of the Greeks. As the Greeks attacked Asia to bring back a Spartan whore, I shall attack them in order to wash out a stain of dishonor that has been upon us for so many generations. Athens will burn, as Troy burned. Athens will burn, as Sardis burned. Athens will burn, and I myself shall set the torch. I am retribution. I am justice. I am Asia.' " Then the armies of Persia crossed the Hellespont into Europe.

Xerxes' rationale for the invasion of Greece was ingenious. Since there is not a Greek anywhere on earth who does not take personal pride in the barbarous attack that his ancestors made on the Asiatic city of Troy, the Great

King now held all the Greeks responsible for the sins of their ancestors. Xerxes was quite sincere in all this. He truly believed that, sooner or later, the gods—which don't, of course, exist—demand a strict accounting for any evil done them.

At first, the war went well. Fleet and army in perfect coordination came down the coast of Thessaly. En route, a king of Sparta was killed with all his men. Four months after Xerxes made his speech at Troy, he was in Attica. The Athenian leader Themistocles ordered the evacuation of the city. Most of the men went on board those ships which were, he said, Athens' wooden walls. Carefully, Themistocles conformed to the letter if not the spirit of the oracle at Delphi, and most Athenians chose to agree with him. They had no choice. Since the Persian forces were invincible, it was either flight by sea or death on land.

In the presence of Xerxes, the city of Athens was burned to the ground and Troy—not to mention Sardis—was avenged. Meanwhile, Themistocles was in secret communication with Xerxes. The Athenian commander made the usual Greek requests for land and money, and Xerxes was more than willing to indulge this wily enemy. As a demonstration of good faith, Themistocles told Xerxes that since the Greek fleet was preparing to set sail for Sicily, Xerxes must attack immediately if he wanted a total victory. Curiously enough, only Queen Artemisia suspected a trap. She had, by the way, got her wish, and personally commanded the forces of Halicarnassus. Although she was incompetent in the field, she was a shrewd analyst of the Greek mind. Incidentally, whenever Artemisia went into battle, she wore an artificial beard, modeled on Mardonius' natural one. Although deeply annoyed by this travesty, he never complained.

Despite Artemisia's warning, Xerxes gave the order to attack. One third of the Persian fleet was lost because of the disloyalty or incompetence of certain Phoenician captains. When Xerxes rightly punished these officers, the remaining Phoenician and Egyptian commanders deserted and Persia was left with half a fleet. Yet on land we were supreme, and Attica was ours. Nevertheless, the double-dealing Themistocles was given credit by all the Greeks for a great naval victory. What began as an act of treachery on his part ended as the so-called salvation of Greece.

Xerxes did not blame Themistocles for the debacle.

How could he? The Greeks did not win. The Persians lost, thanks to those Phoenician captains. Themistocles then warned Xerxes that the advance guard of the Athenian fleet had set sail for the Hellespont, with orders to destroy the bridge between Europe and Asia. In order to protect the bridge, Xerxes hurried overland to Byzantium. On the way, he stayed overnight with my grandfather at Abdera, a great honor as well as a source of endless political trouble for Lais' family. Even to this day, they are known as medizers.

Xerxes left one army corps in Greece, under the command of Mardonius. A second army corps guarded the long overland route from Attica to the Hellespont. A third army corps was used to maintain order in the Ionian cities.

Since Mardonius still controlled the Greek mainland, all those Greek leaders who were opposed to the administration at Athens came to his headquarters at Thebes. The anti-Persian Greeks were totally demoralized. Nevertheless, Mardonius was obliged to burn Athens a second time, as a lesson to the conservative party. Of all the Athenians, they alone refused to accept the Great King as their master. The demoralized conservatives continued to beg Sparta for help, but none was forthcoming. Traditionally, Spartans are faithless allies. Also, and perhaps more to this particular point, Sparta's leaders are usually in the pay of Persia.

For a time it looked as if Mardonius had succeeded in his mission. But then the Spartan regent Pausanias became greedy. Suddenly, finding the moon in an auspicious position, he led the Spartan army into Attica and asked Mardonius to make him a present of a chest of gold, upon whose receipt he would withdraw. But Mardonius wanted a total victory over Sparta and its Greek allies. He did not pay the gold. He, too, was greedy—for honor. By allowing his ruling passion avarice to be overruled by love of glory, he destroyed himself. It is always a mistake to act out of character.

Mardonius attacked the Spartan army. The Spartans were routed. But when they tried to flee, they found that the road back to the Peloponnesus was blocked by our troops and that their supplies of food had all been seized.

Mardonius had got his wish. Greece was his. But he wanted to make one final triumphant gesture. Astride a white charger, Mardonius led the final attack against the remnants of the Spartan army. In the melee, the white charger was killed and Mardonius was thrown to the ground. Before he could get to his feet—a slow matter, for he was very lame—a Greek smashed in his head with a rock. So died my friend Mardonius, who had dreamed of the sea-lordship of all the isles, who had wanted to be master of all the Greeks. If any death can be called good, Mardonius' was. Not only did he die instantly, he died believing that he had got his wish and that Greece was indeed his. Mysteriously, the body was never found. Over the years, Mardonius' son was to spend a fortune in the search for his father's bones.

On the field of Plataea, the false Pausanias was declared the savior of all Greece. Meanwhile, Ionia had gone into rebellion, and Mardonius' army corps—commanded now by Artabazus—was obliged to return to Asia, where a good part of the Persian fleet had been destroyed on the beach of Cape Mycale. Worse, two Persian army corps had been overwhelmed by Greeks. It is ironic that the decisive military victory which the Greek allies could never achieve on their own ground in Europe was unexpectedly theirs less than a hundred miles to the west of the Great King and his court at Sardis.

With amazement, I listened to the sub-chamberlain's account of all the disasters that had befallen Persia. "And that is why," he said, as if in explanation, "the Great King will not come up to Susa until the beginning of summer, when his son Darius is to be married."

"The Greek wars are over," I said. What more could be said? Mardonius is dead, I thought to myself. Youth is over.

The sub-chamberlain shrugged. "They say that Pausanias wants to make himself king of Greece. If he should try, we may be in for a very long war indeed."

"Or for a very long peace."

We were joined by an elderly eunuch whom I had known when I was a child in the harem. Warmly, we greeted each other. Then he said, "You may attend her now."

"Her?" I looked at him stupidly.

"The queen mother, yes."

"Alive?" I could not believe it.

Nor could Atossa. She had shrunk to the size of a child's doll—and like a doll's, the head was now far too large for the fragile, diminished body.

Atossa lay in a silver bed at the foot of the statue of

Anahita. As I prostrated myself she raised one hand for an instant; then let it fall onto the coverlet. Thus was I greeted.

"Get up." The voice was now as husky as a man's.

We stared at each other, like a pair of ghosts who have just met in the vestibule of the Aryan home of the fathers.

"Surprised?"

I nodded, dumbly.

Atossa smiled, revealing one last tooth. Although I had some difficulty understanding the way she spoke, the queen's voice was as strong as ever, and the old eyes still glittered. "You look," she said, "very old."

"You look, Great Queen—"

"—like something that they forgot to place in the tomb. It is ridiculous for anyone to live so long."

"A blessing for us." With surprising ease I assumed the courtier's style. I had been fearful that I might have lost the knack. Cathayan and Indian dialects were now so mixed with Persian and Greek in my head that I was often at a loss for the simplest phrases. Even today I am uneasy with words. As I talk Greek to you I think in a Persian that is hopelessly adulterated with eastern languages, while my current dreams are peculiarly unsatisfactory. Since I no longer see anything in life, I seldom see much of anything in my sleep. But I do hear voices; and often I no longer understand what they are trying to tell me.

Atossa stopped my courtier's flow with a shake of her head. "Stand there," she said, pointing to a spot between the head of the bed and the statue of Anahita. "It is painful for me to move my head. Or anything else, for that matter." She shut her eyes. For a moment I thought that she had drifted off to sleep—or even died. But she was simply gathering her forces. "I don't suppose you expected to find me alive. Or to find Mardonius dead."

"The first is a joy—"

"—beyond description." She mocked us both. "But the second is a serious matter."

"It was my impression"—I was obliged to proceed tactfully—"that Mardonius was responsible for all the . . . happenings in Greece."

"Yes. He conquered Greece. Beneath the heavy enamel paint, something like a delicate flush of color showed in the cracks. "Then he was killed."

548

"By the Greeks?"

Atossa's mouth set in a straight line, not an easy thing to do when only one tooth is left. "Let us hope so," she said. "But it is possible that a certain faction at court might have killed him. The body was never found, which is very unlike the Greeks. For all their faults, they are most reliable when it comes to giving up the bodies of their enemies."

Even on her deathbed, Atossa continued to spin her webs. Like an ancient spider, she was still eager to catch bright things. "You will," she said at last, "find that the court is a very different place from what it was in our day." Thus, casually, she made me her contemporary. "The harem is the center."

"So it was in . . . our day."

Atossa shook her head; and winced from the pain. "No. In those days Darius ruled through the chancellery. In a small way, I was able to accomplish certain things. But not through the harem. I was obliged to use the chancellery, too. Now there are five hundred women in the harem. At Persepolis, the three houses are so full that the harem has been expanded to include all the old administrative buildings of the winter palace. My son—" Atossa stopped.

"He was always susceptible." I put the case as tactfully as I could.

"Amestris is strong. I congratulate myself on having picked her. She understands women, eunuchs and the Great King. But she has no gift for administration. I was well-trained. She was not. Do you realize that I am the last person on earth to remember my father Cyrus?" At the end of her life, Atossa tended to stray from the subject, to say aloud what normally she would only have thought. "And hardly anyone remembers my brother Cambyses. But I do. I also know who killed him." She gave me a secret smile. She had forgotten, if she'd ever known, that Xerxes had told me the true story of his father's bloody rise. Then she regained the present. "I am counting on you to help my son. You and I are all that's left from the old days. And I'll soon be gone. Amestris cares only for her three sons, which is normal. She is also jealous, which is a dangerous fault. I never cared who shared Darius' bed. Not that he was very interested in women. And I was a special case, of course. I was not just a wife: I was the Great King's partner, *the* queen. But Amestris is different.

549

Very different. She has put to death, secretly and sometimes not so secretly, at least twenty of my son's favorites . . ."

"Why does he give her such a free hand?"

"Don't interrupt! You've no manners at all. But then, you never did. You're a Greek Magian. Or a Magian Greek. You'll be happy to know that Lais is now a great power in the harem because she makes herself very useful to Amestris."

"Magic?" I murmured.

"Magic? Nonsense! Poison." Atossa looked more amused than not. "Whenever the Great King takes a particular fancy to someone, the girl loses her color in a week. The second week she suffers from stomach cramps. The third week she loses all taste for food. The fourth week she dies—of seemingly natural causes. Your mother is certainly the best witch that I've ever known, and I was brought up with Chaldeans. There are too many drunken promises." I was mystified by this sudden shift. Atossa grudged the time that it took to make necessary connections; there was not much time left.

"Drunken promises?" I repeated.

"Yes. Yes." The answer was irritable. Atossa had always hated explaining things that seemed obvious to her. "Xerxes is drunk more often than not. When he is, Amestris—or anyone nearby—will ask him for something and, of course, he grants them whatever it is they want. The next day he realizes too late what he's done. But the Great King may not break his word."

This is something, Democritus, that the Greeks have never been able to grasp. Not only is it impossible for a Persian to lie, but once he has made you a promise he cannot go back on it. I attribute most of the disasters that have befallen Persia to this noble trait or custom.

Democritus reminds me that in this answer to Herodotus, I have said that whatever was decided upon in drunken council is reviewed the next day in a sober light —and accepted or dismissed. That is indeed the case. But I was referring to high councils and to gatherings of law-bearers, not to those occasions when the Great King alone is—not himself. Also, and this is really what I am talking about, on certain ceremonial occasions those close to the Great King may ask him for whatever they please, and he is obliged to grant them what they want. Obviously, a shrewd—and sober—sovereign can so maneuver things

550

that he will never give away anything that he does not want to. Also, those close to the Great King are not exactly eager to displease him by an abuse of privilege. But when the Great King is drunk he loses control; and terrible things can happen. When Xerxes gave up the world for the harem, the women and the eunuchs took advantage of his confused state.

"I don't know what influence you will have on him. Very little, I should think. But she'll see you."

I picked up this rapid shift. "Queen Amestris receives men?"

Atossa nodded. "It is now agreed that *I* set the precedent. Naturally, you'll never see her alone, as you see me now, defenseless before you, an easy prey for masculine lust." Atossa laughed suddenly, and I realized that in the lifetime that I had known her I had never heard her laugh before. She sounded just like Darius—or Cyrus? In Atossa's final days she was like a man or, to be precise, she was like a Great King.

"Xerxes encourages Amestris to meet with the councilors of state, with the law-bearers, with the guards commanders, with all the people *he* ought to see but prefers that she see on his behalf. Empires are not governed in this fashion. Not for long, anyway. Do you know that he falls in love? Imagine! My father, brothers, Darius—not one of the lot ever took a woman seriously. Women were for pleasure, and nothing more—except for me. Not that I ever gave much pleasure. But I didn't have to. I am part of the governance of Persia. Xerxes must always be in love. Notice I have spoken Greek," she said, "to describe a state of sexual enthusiasm which is not Persian. Or ought not to be."

Atossa frowned so deeply that the white enamel on her forehead suddenly fissured like a dry river bottom in high summer. She spoke in jagged, almost breathless sentences. "The wife of Masistes. His half-brother. Xerxes saw her with Amestris. In the harem. At Sardis. An accident, of course. The ladies are chattering. Xerxes suddenly appears. Sees his brother's wife. Falls in love with her. Sends her messages. Presents. Everyone knows. It's too shameful."

"Did the lady respond?"

"No. She's a clever woman. And plain. I can't think what Xerxes wants her for. To make confusion, I suppose. Well, he's succeeded. Amestris is furious. Masistes is terrified. The lady is crafty. She has a beautiful daughter aged thirteen. Xerxes has arranged for this girl to marry the crown prince. He thinks that when this happens, the mother's gratitude will be so great that she will surrender herself to him. Cyrus Spitama, my son will lose his throne." Atossa pulled herself up on the bed. The effort was great. But so was the will. "He is destroying us all. Masistes is a son of Darius. He is satrap of Bactria. He is popular. Xerxes will drive him into rebellion."

"What is to be done?"

"I don't know." Atossa shut her eyes. The soft lamplight seemed to hurt her eyes. "He seldom comes to me anymore. He knows I disapprove of the way he lives. He also knows that I'll soon be on that stone shelf at holy Pasargada. So I am not to be noticed."

Atossa opened her eyes, gave me a speculative look. "*You* may still be able to talk to him. I pray to the goddess that he will listen. I will even pray to the Wise Lord," she added. "But be prepared for surprises. Xerxes is not the man you knew. He is not the son I bore."

2

OUTWARDLY, XERXES WAS LITTLE changed. He had grown somewhat stout from drink, and his beard had been dyed the same fox-red color that the barbers had used for Darius. Otherwise, he treated me just as he did when we were boys.

I should note that the court's arrival from Sardis was like that of an invading army. The harem was so vast that the road from the northwest was crowded for a hundred miles with wagons full of furniture and chests of gold and silver and, of course, the women and the eunuchs and the household slaves. Since Lais always traveled with her ever-loyal—to her, if to no one else—Greeks, she was one of the last to arrive.

Shortly after the Great King's arrival, he held his first audience. As the ushers led me toward him, he stared with astonishment. Then he raised the golden sceptre in greeting and announced his delight at the successful conclusion of my embassy. Later that evening he sent for me to join him in his bedroom.

Despite all my years at court, I had never before seen the fabled bedroom furniture of the Great Kings. For once fable and reality coincide. A century ago the Samian goldsmith Theodore had fashioned an elaborate grape vine of solid gold which curves about and around and above the bed, giving the impression of a metallic vineyard whose vines produce not grapes but precious stones. The famous gold plane tree is opposite the bed. Since it is somewhat less high than a man, it is a bit of a disappointment. One had always heard that a man could stand in its shade. Next to the bed, on an ivory stool, there is a huge golden bowl filled with scented water.

Xerxes lay upon the bed. Beside him was a table on which had been arranged several flasks of Helbon wine. There were two golden cups. As I did obeisance he said, "Get up. Come here. Let me see you!"

Affectionately he embraced me with his left arm, while the right hand was busy filling the cups with wine.

"I never thought I'd see you again. Sit down. On the bed. Forget protocol. No one can see us—except for Amestris' spies. They're peeking at us through holes in the wall. Once a month I have the holes sealed. Once a month she has them reopened. She likes to know who joins me in bed. *This* will puzzle her!" Xerxes grinned. Despite thick folds of puffy skin above and below the eyes, he looked younger than he was. Except for a slight tremor of one hand, he seemed healthy; certainly, he looked younger than I did.

"You must," he said, after a long look at me, "use my barber. Dye your hair. Everyone knows we're the same age. So you make a fool of me when you go about with all that white hair."

We drank. We talked of the past. Of Mardonius. "Oh, we had such a victory! All Greece was ours except the Peloponnesus. Wait, I told him before I left. The Spartans will either surrender or they'll come into Attica. Then you'll be able to buy them off. Or smash their army. Which is what he did. *We* were the winners at Plataea. But that wasn't enough for Mardonius. No. He wanted to be world hero. So he was reckless. And they killed him. They always do," he added obscurely. "And we lost our one chance to destroy the entire Spartan army. Then the business at Mycale . . ." The voice trailed off. I wondered —but did not dare ask—who it is that always kills world heroes.

"Anyway, we'll soon be back." Xerxes brightened at the thought, an effect that was assisted, literally, by the wine. In those days Xerxes' cheeks turned scarlet when he drank. Toward the end of his life they ceased to turn scarlet because they were permanently the color of fresh blood. "Thanks to my Spartan regent Pausanias, the victor of Plataea." Xerxes finished off a second cup of wine. "He wants to be king of all Greece. To be me, in other words. So he's asked for my help. Secretly, of course. He's up at Byzantium now. He wants to marry a daughter of mine. Then, with my help, he'll occupy Athens. And so on."

"Can you trust him?"

"Of course not!" Xerxes' mood was improving. "But he'll be useful to us. He's already sent me a number of Persian captives, as a sign of good faith. What's that old saying? Never trust a Greek who gives you a present. Well, I don't trust him but I suspect that he can make a lot of trouble for his fellow Greeks. Now then"—Xerxes was mischievous—"what did you think when Atossa told you that I'm bound to lose my throne because of time ill spent in the harem?"

I was terrified; and showed it. "Is the time ill spent?" I could think of nothing else to say.

"How do I know what she said?" Xerxes smiled. "I always know. I wish I didn't. But I have no choice. Atossa is something like the weather here at Susa—either too hot or too cold." Xerxes poured me a cup of wine from a new bottle. As I gulped it down, I wondered if it was poisoned. "Yes, I'm in love with a certain lady who happens to be my brother's wife, which is why I may not command her to love me. But I think I can win her. I've arranged for my son Darius to marry her daughter. The boy's very handsome, by the way. I haven't seen the wife-to-be. But she's in luck. One day she'll be queen of Persia. More important, in spite of what Atossa says, gratitude will oblige her mother to join me in this bed. Next week, I should think. The day after the wedding."

I spent an hour with my old friend. My first impression was that he had changed hardly at all. But when I left him, I realized that something very odd had happened or, rather, had not happened. Xerxes never once asked me about India or Cathay. In fact, during the fourteen years that were still left him, he almost never alluded to my embassies. He had lost all curiosity about the world. He had turned in upon himself. He cared for nothing but the harem and the completion of those buildings that he had begun in his youth.

When the suspicious Spartans quite rightly put Pausanias to death for being a Persian agent, Xerxes hardly noticed that he had lost his chief ally in the Greek world. But by then he had convinced himself that, as a dutiful son, he had fought the war which his father had intended to fight. Lacking Darius' luck, Xerxes had failed to hold for any length of time the mainland of Greece. But he had the pleasure of twice burning Athens to the ground. He had avenged Troy and Sardis and, all in all, he was well pleased with the outcome of the Greek war.

Democritus reminds me of Aeschylus' play *The Persians*, which someone read to me when I first came to Athens. The play is perfect nonsense. For one thing, I can promise you that I never once heard Xerxes praise the Athenians—or any Greeks. Certainly, he would never have called them bold and daring. And—how does the ridiculous line go?—"These sad eyes saw their violent and splendid deeds." Read me that speech I laughed at. How . . . Yes, due to "wretched fortune, I was born to crush, to ruin my own native land."

Practically speaking, not only did Xerxes not ruin his native land but he thought that he had done quite well by his patrimony. He had wanted to teach the Greeks a lesson, and he had. He had only one complaint: the cost of the war. "Every bit of gold that I got from Babylon was spent in Greece. So the lesson is plain: Never go to war against a poor country, because no matter how it turns out, you lose."

I doubt that this sentiment would have appealed very much to Aeschylus because it is hard for a Greek to realize that Greece is small, and poor; that Persia is large, and rich. That life is short. Short.

I attended the wedding between Crown Prince Darius and Masistes' daughter. Two thirds of those in attendance at court were unknown to me. But since most were descendants of The Six, I recognized the names if not the faces of the new generation. The marriage was also the occasion for me to take once again my place at the court of the Great King—this time as an elder! Although I was treated with the respect that is owed the lifelong friend of a middle-aged sovereign, I myself was of no real interest to anyone. The court was as inward-looking as the Great King. More to the point, I had been away too long. I also lacked money. It took me ten years to get back my various properties from the treasury, not to mention from Lais, who was not as pleased as she ought to have been to see her only son again. But then, I have noticed that many parents are more thrilled than not to outlive grown children.

Since Lais had been living in *my* rooms in my house, it was with numerous and unbecoming complaints that she moved back into the women's quarters. Although Lais was not ill pleased to see me alive, she kept within seemly bounds a mother's natural joy. "We really had no way of knowing." Sadly she watched her chests and divans leave my bedroom for the somewhat cramped women's quarters. "Besides, the law says that after three years' absence, you're supposed to be quite dead."

Lais had changed hardly at all. If anything, a slight increase of weight now made soft and youthful a face that had begun to look, in her early middle age, over-hard and determined.

"I'd planned to receive guests this evening." This was the day after the last of the wedding ceremonies.

"Go right ahead." I was amiable. We were more like old acquaintances than mother and son. "Shall I join them?"

"You won't be disagreeable?" She sounded apprehensive.

"Greeks." No one ever changes, I thought to myself. "You're not still conspiring?"

"More than ever." Lais held her head high, doubtless reminding herself of the goddess Athena. "This is the moment we've all been waiting for. Our fortunes have never looked brighter."

"Brighter? Oh, yes! Glorious, in fact." I could not restrain myself. "We've lost two of our six army corps, half the fleet, and the treasury is empty. So what makes you think that *our* fortunes have never looked brighter?"

I was told. At length. By Lais. Later, by Demaratus. He was still a handsome man, if somewhat gnawed by time. He was now comfortable in his Persian clothes, and though decent Persian shoes covered his feet, I assumed that he'd learned to wash. Among the Greek émigrés at dinner was a beautiful young man from Cos named Apollonides. Xerxes had taken a fancy to him. No,

556

Democritus, not because of his beauty but because of his skill as a physician. Needless to say, on account of his looks, he was allowed nowhere near the harem. Ordinarily, physicians are the only men who can come and go in that part of the palace but, traditionally, they must be very old like Democedes or very ill-favored or both. Although physicians are carefully watched by eunuchs, everyone agreed that with someone like Apollonides, fate must not be tempted.

"My cousin Pausanias has already shown his good faith. He sent back five of the Great King's glorious relatives." Demaratus had learned to speak a flowery, rather disagreeable Persian. In fact, his manners were now more Persian than Spartan, and I was not sure that I didn't prefer his old crude self. Spartans are used neither to luxury nor to relative freedom. When these two things coincide, as they do at the Persian court, the Spartan is demoralized.

"But surely the Spartans won't let Pausanias make an alliance with us." From the first, I was certain that Pausanias was doomed. He was arrogant; he was greedy; he was stupid. These attributes tend to attract the joyous attention of those goddesses whom the Greeks nervously refer to as the kindly ones. Actually, they are the furies.

"You don't know Sparta." Sparta's former king was serenely condescending. "Pausanias is regent. He can do as he likes as long as the ephors are in his pocket. That is, as long as he sees to it that there is gold in *their* pockets. Oh, he'll be master of all Greece, in the Great King's name, of course."

Lais was thrilled—as always. There is nothing like a Greek conspiracy to bring a youthful gleam to her eye. On the subject of Greek politics, she is, very simply, demented.

After dinner the conspirators were joined by a very important man indeed. I had known Megabyzus slightly when we were young. He was a son of Zopyrus, the mutilated satrap of Babel whom Xerxes and I had managed to avoid on our first trip to Babylon. During my years in the east, Megabyzus had so distinguished himself militarily that Xerxes had given him his daughter Amystis for a wife. Incidentally, by an earlier marriage, Megabyzus had a son named for his grandfather Zopyrus. This is the same Zopyrus who was recently in Athens making trouble for his native land. Although it is true that the young man

557

has a legitimate grudge against our royal house, that is no reason for him to act like a Greek.

Physically, Megabyzus was a giant—is a giant, I assume: he has a knack for survival. Not long ago, during a royal hunt, he saved the Great King Artaxerxes from a lion. Unfortunately, no subject may kill an animal before the Great King has made the first kill. Although Artaxerxes was grateful to Megabyzus for saving his life, he was outraged that an ancient custom had been flouted. Megabyzus was sentenced to death. But Amystis joined forces with Queen Mother Amestris, and together they persuaded the Great King to send Megabyzus into exile. It is said that he is now a leper. But all this was in the future when we first met under Lais' watchful eye.

There was the usual—that is, endless—discussion of Greek affairs. I noticed that Megabyzus was noncommittal. I also noticed that he kept looking at me, as if for some sort of signal. I was mystified. Finally, as the Greeks were beginning to grow drunk, I motioned to Megabyzus to join me in my workroom, which is just off the dining hall. As we left the room Lais gave me a furious look—in my own house!

"I am interested in the east," said Megabyzus. Needless to say, not even a Lydian orchestra could have ravished my ear more than that single phrase.

For an hour we talked of India and Cathay. The conversation that I was never to have with Xerxes, I had with his general. There was no doubt at all in Megabyzus' mind where our future lies. "There's no money now, of course." But the giant head nodded yes instead of shaking no. "It will be several years before we can mount an invasion."

"But you want that?"

"As much as you do." We looked at each other. Then we shook hands. We were allies. In the next room the Greeks were singing Milesian love songs.

"What do you think of Pausanias?" I asked.

"What can you think of last year's savior of Greece who is now offering to sell us Greece in exchange for a royal wife and a silken robe? He is a passing cloud."

"But when the cloud passes . . ."

"We shall cross the Indus River."

"Darius dreamt of cows."

"Then," said Megabyzus, "you and I will herd them for his son."

Unfortunately for Persia, Xerxes preferred herding women. Also, as he got older, he was more and more interested in what he could not or ought not to have. Even as we were talking excitedly of the eastern policy, Xerxes had fallen in love with his son's new wife. Unable to seduce the mother, he now set about seducing the daughter.

Since Amestris—the present queen mother—has been for so long a power at the Persian court, I should try to correct the false impression of her that currently obtains in the Greek world. Like her predecessor and model Queen Atossa, Amestris is highly political. As Otanes' daughter, she has her own private revenues, which means that she is not dependent financially on the Great King. In fact, I suspect that there are times when it is the other way around. Although Amestris receives men as if she herself were a man, there has never been the slightest hint of scandal—with a man. Eunuchs are another matter. In any case, she is much too formidable for love affairs. Like Atossa, she has always been dedicated to her sons. Like Atossa, she was able to force an unwilling Great King to grant the title crown prince to her eldest son. It appears to be a royal rule everywhere on earth that the sovereign is always reluctant to name his heir for a number of reasons that are perfectly obvious if not always sensible.

At Susa, Amestris occupies the so-called third house of the harem. When Xerxes enlarged the palace, he added considerably to the queen's apartments. As a result, she now has her own chancellery, as well as numerous apartments for ladies-in-waiting, eunuchs, and so on. Traditionally, at the Persian court, the queen mother takes precedence over the queen consort. In theory, when Xerxes became Great King, the third house should have remained in the control of his mother. But Atossa preferred her old apartments. "It doesn't make much difference *where* I am," she said to me, with a sly smile, "as long as I am. Amestris is welcome to the third house."

Surprisingly, relations between the two ladies were good. Amestris never forgot that it was Atossa who had made her queen, and unlike most people, Amestris does not hate those who have helped her. She was also aware that the old queen still controlled the chancellery. It is said that no satrapal appointment was ever made without Atossa's consent. She also had a good deal to say about which army commander would be posted to what satrapy to keep an eye on the local administration. The matching of satraps, who are relatively independent, with army commanders, who are directly subject to the Great King, is a subtle art. One mistake, and you will have civil war on your hands.

At least once a day Amestris would visit Atossa in her apartments, and they would compare notes on matters of state. The two ladies were often attended by the court chamberlain Aspamitres. He was sufficiently shrewd to serve each woman loyally.

Although I was disappointed that, once again, the eastern policy came to nothing, the actual day-to-day life of the court was very pleasant indeed. With the seasons, we made our rounds from Persepolis to Susa to Ecbatana and back again. Life was serene, and splendid; happy, too. I was still ambitious. I wanted glory for myself. I wanted glory for Xerxes. But the Great King preferred to conduct his campaigns not in the Gangetic plain or on the banks of the Yellow River but in the houses of the harem. As a result, the hegemony of the whole world is still a dream.

A month after the wedding of Darius to Masistes' daughter, I met Queen Amestris on the day that followed upon the unlucky night that Xerxes first seduced his new daughter-in-law. I was alone with Queen Atossa. The aged Atossa no longer made any pretense that a chaperone was needed. On the other hand, the relatively young Amestris comported herself as freely as a man. During those golden years, our palace women were the freest that they have ever been. Naturally, if a harem lady was caught alone with a man, she would be strangled to death, and the man would be buried alive, a fate rather worse than what befalls the Athenian adulterer, who is forced to receive in his anus a large radish, something as apt to give pleasure as discomfort hereabouts.

Amestris is a tall, slender, fragile woman. She has a melodious voice, dark eyes, fair skin; she blushes easily; she is gentle and hesitant in manner. Although she appears to be quite unlike her predecessor, she is every bit as formidable as Atossa was. I suspect that Atossa—whom I knew better—was the more intelligent of the two. On the other hand, Amestris has now governed Persia for a longer time than Atossa ever did. Also, Atossa was obliged to share power with Darius, while Amestris has never shared power with anyone. She governs her son Artaxerxes as she governed his father Xerxes; and she governs well. Certainly, she must be given a good deal of credit for Persia's long peace, whose decrepit symbol I am, shivering with cold in this drafty house.

Amestris entered Atossa's bedroom without ceremony. "It has begun," she whispered. Then she saw me. "Who's that?"

Atossa was bland. "He is your brother-in-law, Cyrus Spitama. At least he used to be. He was married to Parmys."

Amestris ordered me to rise. I found her polite, even shy. "We have followed your adventures in the east with much interest." She spoke formally. "You must attend us in the third house, and tell us more."

Amestris not only has a first-rate set of spies, she has an excellent memory. She knows exactly who is good for what and how best to use him. In Amestris' eyes, I represented the eastern policy—and Zoroaster. Since neither subject has ever interested her, I am not close to her—a good thing, in my view.

Atossa sent me from the room. I waited in the long hall where Atossa's secretaries prepared her correspondence. Then, an hour later, I was summoned to the bedroom. Amestris was gone and Atossa's white enamel mask looked like a shattered bowl. She told me what had happened. Then she said, "My son is mad."

"What can be done?"

Atossa shook her head. "Nothing. He will go on. But *his* son hates him now, which is dangerous. And Amestris hates the girl, which is dangerous—for the girl. For the mother, too. Amestris holds the mother responsible. I don't. I said, 'I know the wife of Masistes and she is not like other women. When she said no to Xerxes, she meant it.' But Xerxes is stubborn. He had hoped to win her over with this marriage and he failed. So now he's in love with the daughter. Amestris says that the moment he welcomed the girl to his son's house, he wanted her. And now he has got her."

Atossa sank back onto the bed's mound of small pillows. The red eyes glared at me, like the Wise Lord's fire. In a low, hard voice, she pronounced an epitaph: "I speak in the presence of Anahita, the true goddess. There will be mourning for the dead in this house." Atossa looked up at the face of the goddess. She murmured a Chaldean prayer. Then she looked at me. "I have just asked the goddess to grant me a wish. The next person to be mourned in this house that my father built will be me."

Anahita answered Atossa's prayer. Two days later the old queen died in her sleep. Since the court was about to leave for Persepolis, everyone commented on her thoughtfulness. Thanks to the timing of her death, there would not have to be a special expedition to Pasargada for the funeral; instead, the body would travel with the court, as if she were still alive.

3

XERXES WAS MORE SHAKEN BY ATOSsa's death than I might have expected. "She was our last link with the beginning." Xerxes was seated in his gilded wagon. As king's friend, I rode beside him. In front of us were the purple gorges that mark the boundary of holy Pasargada. "As long as she lived, we were safe."

"Safe, Lord?"

"She had power." He made some sort of magical gesture. I pretended not to notice. "As long as she lived, she could keep the curse at bay. Now she's gone . . ."

"The Wise Lord will judge each of us in his own good time." But my invocations of the Wise Lord's mercy and wisdom made no impression on Xerxes. As he grew older he reverted more and more to devil-worship. He even moved Atossa's statue of Anahita into his own bedroom, where it did not look at all out of place beside the gold plane tree. Ultimately, I failed Hystaspes. I never did convert Xerxes to the Truth.

I have just figured that Atossa could not have been more than seventy years old at the time of her death. This comes as something of a surprise to me, for she always looked and acted as if she had been present at the creation of the world. As the years passed, Atossa did not age so much as dry out, like a papyrus leaf on a rock in the sun— a leaf on which was written most of the story of the Persian empire.

The death of Queen Atossa cast a shadow over the new year's celebration. Xerxes was gloomy. Queen Amestris was withdrawn. Masistes looked apprehensive. The crown prince glowered at one and all. According to Lais, only the crown princess was contented. Lais often visited the second and first houses of the harem and, with some wonder, she told me that the girl was envied by all the women. The girl was as good-looking as she was stupid. Through stupidity, she made a fatal error. This is what she did. Amestris had woven with her own hands a robe for Xerxes. The girl fancied the robe and begged Xerxes to give it to her. Like a fool, he did. The crown princess wore the robe on a visit to the third house of the harem. Amestris received her graciously, even tenderly. She pretended not to recognize the familiar robe. I should note here that it is never possible to know what Amestris thinks or feels. A compassionate smile can precede summary execution, while a scowl may be the signal that one is about to get one's heart's desire. But it took no special wisdom for everyone to realize that, sooner or later, Amestris would avenge herself for this insult.

That year at Persepolis the new year's day celebration was unusually magnificent. During the long procession I myself led the empty chariot in which sits, if he is so minded, the Wise Lord. Although the great hall of the hundred columns was still unfinished, Xerxes held court there and all the satraps from every part of the empire, as well as the nobles, officials, clan leaders each paid him homage with a flower.

Later, in private, among close friends and family, the Great King anointed his head, according to custom. This is the occasion when those present have the right to ask him for whatever they want, and whatever is asked for, he must grant. Needless to say, the requests are seldom excessive. After all, one is forever the Great King's slave.

This particular ill-omened year, the ceremony of the anointing of the Great King's head proceeded as usual. There is always a bit of comedy when the king's friends gather about. This time the amusement was provided by Demaratus. He was drunk and more than usually flowery —not to mention bold. He asked the Great King for the right to enter Sardis in state, wearing a king's crown, "as I am forever king of Sparta."

For an instant Xerxes was taken aback by the sort of effrontery which, on any other occasion, would have been a capital offense. Luckily, Megabyzus saved the day by remarking, "Demaratus hasn't brains enough for a crown to cover." Everyone laughed, and the crisis passed.

As Xerxes moved among his friends, he gave nothing that he would not ordinarily have given on such an occasion, and everyone was pleased. Then he withdrew to the harem. Incidentally, he was entirely sober when he left us.

Lais was in the harem; and told me what happened next. "Queen Amestris was all smiles. She kissed the Great King's hands. Then she whispered what seemed to be endearments in his ear. He looked terrified. Said 'No!' in a loud voice. She said 'Yes' in that sweet child's voice of hers. The two left the room. No one knows what they said or did. But when they returned Xerxes was white; and Amestris was smiling. She had asked Xerxes for the wife of Masistes, and Xerxes was obliged to grant her wish." Amestris was shrewd enough not to ask for the real offender, the crown princess. The girl was royal; the mother was not. More to the point, Amestris believed that the mother was entirely responsible for the liaison between Xerxes and his daughter-in-law.

Xerxes sent for Masistes and begged him to divorce his wife. He even offered Masistes one of his own daughters to take her place. Since Masistes had no idea what had happened, he told Xerxes that it was ridiculous for him to give up a wife who was also the mother of his grown children.

Xerxes was furious, and the brothers quarreled. When Masistes withdrew, he said, "Lord, you have not killed me yet."

When Masistes got home, he found his wife. She was still alive. But her breasts had been cut off, her tongue torn out, and she was blind. Masistes and his sons fled to Bactria, where they went into rebellion. But they were no match for Megabyzus. In a matter of months Bactria was subdued, and Masistes and all his family were put to death.

It is not generally known that Xerxes never again spoke to Amestris or set foot in the third house. But, curiously enough, this in no way affected the queen's power. She continued to involve herself in politics. She continued—continues—to govern Persia. Odder still, she was soon on excellent terms with the crown princess. But then, Amestris could charm anyone, particularly her three sons. And of the three sons, she made herself most agreeable and useful to the second, our present Great King Artaxerxes. All in all, Atossa chose her own successor well.

4

THE NEXT DOZEN YEARS WERE THE HAP-
piest of my life. Admittedly, I was middle-aged. Admittedly, my friend Xerxes had withdrawn from the world.
Even so, I still think of that time as curiously splendid.
There were no wars of any consequence, and the life of
the court was more than ever delightful. Never before or
since have the harem ladies enjoyed so much freedom.
Those who wanted to take lovers had no very great difficulty. In some curious way, I think that Xerxes was
amused by all the intrigue. Certainly, as long as no lady's
behavior was blatant, he was complaisant.

Only Queen Amestris was above suspicion. That is to
say, she never had an affair with a man. She was far too
shrewd to give Xerxes any cause for invoking the law of
the Aryans. But she did conduct a long and highly discreet
affair with the eunuch Aspamitres.

The queen's daughter Amytis was not so wise as her
mother. Openly, she took a succession of lovers, which infuriated her husband Megabyzus. When he complained to
Xerxes, the Great King is supposed to have said, "Our
daughter may do as she pleases."

Megabyzus is then supposed to have answered, "And
if it pleases her to break our oldest laws, you will let
her?" And Xerxes said, "Since she is an Achaemenid, she
cannot break our laws."

Looking back, I realize that this exchange—or something
very like it—signified the beginning of the end. Crown
Prince Darius hated Xerxes for having seduced his wife.
Megabyzus was angry that Amytis' adulteries were con-
doned by her father. Also, some years earlier, a member
of the royal family had seduced the virginal granddaughter
of Megabyzus. On this occasion, Xerxes had taken prompt
action. He ordered the seducer to be impaled. But the harem rallied around the offender, a man named Sataspes.
To please the royal ladies, Xerxes ordered Sataspes to circumnavigate Africa, something only the Phoenicians

claim to have done. For a year or two, Sataspes skulked about north Africa. Then he went up to Susa, claiming to have gone all around Africa. No one believed him, and he was put to death.

Even so, Megabyzus was less than pleased. He had wanted vengeance at the time, not two years later. Finally the queen herself was disaffected, and it was Amestris who finally made it possible for the awesome royal glory to pass to her son.

In the autumn of the twenty-first year of Xerxes' reign, I was in The Troad with Lais. Xerxes had given Demaratus a considerable estate, and the former Spartan king was now more Persian horse-breeder than Greek conspirator—a change entirely for the better. Although Demaratus and Lais lived together as man and wife, she refused to marry him. She enjoyed her freedom too much. She also did not want to share the considerable fortune that she had amassed over the years, thanks to her friendship with Atossa. "I come and go as I please," she used to say —and no doubt still says to this day, if she is alive on Thasos.

We were at Demaratus' stables inspecting a newly arrived Arabian stallion. It was a cloudy gray morning, and the south wind smelled of sand. A servant came to us from the main house, shouting, "He is dead!" And the lovely time was at an end.

As far as I can tell, this is what happened. With the queen's blessing, Aspamitres and the guards commander Artabanus killed Xerxes while he slept—an easy task, since Xerxes had not gone to bed in years without first drinking a half-dozen flasks of Helbon wine. They also killed his charioteer—and brother-in-law—Patiramphes.

The night of the murder, Crown Prince Darius was at the hunting lodge on the road to Pasargada. When Darius was told the news, he hurried up to Susa—and into a trap. Everyone knew that not only did Darius hate his father but he wanted, quite naturally, to be Great King. So the conspirators let it be known that it was at Darius' order that Patiramphes had killed the Great King, obliging the loyal Artabanus to kill Patiramphes.

The conspirators then went to the eighteen-year-old Artaxerxes and told him that his brother Darius was responsible for the murder of their father. If Artaxerxes agreed to the execution of his brother, they promised to make him Great King. I have reason to believe that Artaxerxes knew even then exactly what had happened. But Artabanus controlled the palace guard, and Artaxerxes was powerless. He did as he was told. The next day, when Darius arrived at Susa, he was arrested by Artabanus. Condemned as a regicide by the law-bearers, he was put to death.

I have no idea what exact part the queen played in the execution of her eldest son. Although she had agreed to the murder of Xerxes, I cannot believe that she had anything to do with the execution of Darius. I suspect that once events were in train, she lost control. I do know that when she learned through her spies that Artabanus planned to murder Artaxerxes and make himself Great King, she summoned Megabyzus and made a secret alliance with him. As army commander, Megabyzus was even more powerful than the guards commander Artabanus. Although Megabyzus had approved the murder of Xerxes, he was loyal to the dynasty.

With half an army corps, Megabyzus overwhelmed the palace guard and Artabanus was killed. Then Aspamitres was arrested. As the queen's lover, the court chamberlain expected to be spared. But he had tried to supplant the Achaemenids, and Amestris was in a towering rage. It was the queen who gave the order to put Aspamitres in what is known as the trough, a sort of wooden coffin that covers the trunk of the body while leaving limbs and head exposed to sun and wind, to insects and reptiles. Of all deaths, the trough is supposed to be the slowest and the most disagreeable—next, that is, to old age.

I, Democritus, son of Athenocritus, wish to insert at this point in the narrative of my great-uncle, Cyrus Spitama, a conversation that I had with him an hour or so after he had dictated to me the story of Xerxes' death. As a good Zoroastrian, he thought that all essential questions had been answered. But he was too intelligent, finally, to ignore contrary evidence. Although I am fairly certain that he would not have wanted me to reproduce his words on that occasion, I think that I owe it not only to his memory but to our joint quest to report what he said.

We took a walk in the Agora. It was midsummer; and very hot. The sky was like metal gone blue with heat, and the bone-white mud city looked to be abandoned. The Athenians were at home, having their dinner—or in the gymnasiums, escaping the heat. This was the time of day my uncle most liked to walk about the city. "No Athenians!" he would say. "No noise. No shouting!" Due to all the clothes that he wore, he was never hot. Years later, when I came to travel in Persia, I dressed as Persians do and found that light clothes that do not touch the skin will keep one cool on the hottest day.

At the porch to the Odeon, Cyrus decided to sit in the shade. He always knew exactly where he was in the Agora or anywhere else that he had been taken to once. We made ourselves comfortable on a step of the Odeon. Opposite us, Mount Lycabettus looked more than ever odd, like a jagged rock dropped by some ancient titan. Irrationally, the rational Athenians dislike the mountain. They say it is because wolves live there, but I think it is because the mountain does not fit the rest of the countryside.

"From the time I came home from Cathay, I knew that there would be a bloody end to the matter. That's why I distanced myself—from the court. I could never distance myself from Xerxes. He was more than a brother to me. He was a twin to me, my other self. With him gone, I am only half what I was."

"While he . . . is what?"

"The Great King is at the bridge of the redeemer." Cyrus said no more—and there was nothing more to say because if Zoroaster is right, Xerxes is currently bubbling away in a sea of molten metal.

"Suppose," I said, "there is no bridge, no Wise Lord . . ."

"How can *I* suppose that?" But since the old man did suppose that a good deal of the time, he was interested in my answer.

"Zoroaster says that there was a time when the Wise Lord did not exist. Well, isn't it possible that when we die, we go to wherever it is that the Wise Lord came from?"

Cyrus whistled a strange little tune that must have had some religious significance, since he always whistled it whenever faced with a contradiction or gap in the Zoroastrian theory. He had, by the way, nearly all his teeth; he could eat anything. "There is no way," he said at last, "to answer that question."

"Then perhaps the easterners are right, and the question of creation is not to be answered." Actually, I now know the answer to the question, but in those days I was ignorant. I was at the start of a lifelong quest—at whose sad end Cyrus had arrived. Sad because the only important question was still unanswered—for him.

The old man whistled for a moment, his eyes shut; one pale hand made a tight whorl of a tuft of his beard, always a sign that he was deep in thought. "They are wrong," he said at last. "Everything that we perceive starts somewhere and stops somewhere. Like a line drawn in the sand. Like a . . . piece of string. Like a human life. What they try to do in the east is to close the line. To make a circle. With no start. With no stop. But ask them who drew the circle. And they have no answer. They shrug. 'It is *there*,' they say. Around and around they think they go. Forever and ever. Endless. Hopeless!" He shouted the last word; and shuddered with horror at the thought of no terminus to things. "We see a definite beginning. A definite end. We see good and evil as necessary, warring principles. The one to be rewarded after death; the other to be punished. The whole to be achieved only at the end of the end."

"Which is the start of . . . what?"

"Perfection. Deity. A state unknown to us."

"But there is a flaw in this conception. Zoroaster does not know for what purpose the Wise Lord was created."

"Nevertheless, he was created. He is. He will be. But . . ." The old man opened wide his blind eyes. "There *is* something missing. Something I could not find anywhere on this earth in the course of a long life." Thus, by his own admission, Cyrus' quest had failed. Yet by relating to me in such detail his failure, he made it possible for me to understand what he could not—the nature of the universe.

I am not sure to what extent the old man believed in his grandfather's primitive theology. Certainly any deity that had created life in order to torture it must be, by definition, entirely evil. Put another way, the Wise Lord did not create Ahriman. The Wise Lord *is* Ahriman, if one is to follow through to the end the logic—if that's the word!—of Zoroaster's message.

To my uncle's credit, he was deeply shaken by what he had heard in the east. Although he continued to go through the motions of being a dualist, he tended—in dark moments—to sound as if he thought that the circle might not be, after all, a better symbol of our estate than the straight line which starts and stops.

Ultimately, there is neither straight line nor circle. But to understand how things are, one must advance beyond the present childlike phase of human existence. Gods and devils must be abandoned along with those notions of good and evil which have relevance to day-to-day life but mean nothing to that material unity which contains all things and makes them one. Matter is all. All is matter.

5

I ATTENDED THE CORONATION OF ARTA-xerxes at holy Pasargada. Although I was graciously reinstated as king's friend, I did not press this advantage. Young sovereigns do not enjoy relics of previous reigns, and so I prepared to retire to my estates south of Halicarnassus. My public life was at an end. Or so I thought.

Shortly before I left Persepolis, I was sent for by the Great King. Naturally, I was terrified. Who had made trouble for me? That is the question one always asks oneself whenever the usher raises the staff of office and intones: "The master has summoned his slave. Come with me."

Artaxerxes was seated in a small office at the winter palace. I don't recall why he was not living in Xerxes' new palace. I suppose that, as usual, construction was going on.

At eighteen, Artaxerxes was a handsome if fragile youth. Since the beard was not yet full-grown, the face had a somewhat girlish look. In childhood he had suffered from an illness that had stunted his left arm and leg. In consequence, the right hand was considerably larger than the left. That is why when we want to speak of the Great King without actually using his name, we call him the long-handed one.

Standing to the right of the Great King's chair was the new guards commander, Roxanes, a formidable figure who had distinguished himself in the Greek wars. To the left of the chair was the beautiful physician Apollonides;

he was much in favor for having recently saved the Great King's life from a wasting fever.

As always, Artaxerxes was amiable with me and, as always in his presence, I was disconcerted to see Xerxes' eyes now set in an entirely different face. It was as if my dearest friend were looking at me out of his son's face.

"We have need of you, King's Friend." The boy's voice was still weak from his bout with the fever.

I announced my readiness to give my life for my new master.

Artaxerxes came straight to the point. "The widow of Artabanus is a Greek woman. Thanks to her, Artabanus was harboring a Greek exile. Since you were close to my father the Great King and since you are also half-Greek, I want you to translate for me what this man has to say, and then I want you to give me your opinion of him."

With that, Artaxerxes clapped his short left hand into the palm of his long right hand. The cedar doors opened, and two ushers escorted a short stocky man into the presence. There was a long moment as the man and the Great King looked at each other, quite against protocol. Then, slowly, the man dropped to his knees and again, slowly, did obeisance.

"Who are you, Greek?" asked Artaxerxes.

From the floor came the answer, "I am Themistocles, son of Neocles. I am that general of Athens who destroyed the fleet of the Great King Xerxes."

Artaxerxes looked at me. Somewhat shakily, I translated this astonishing speech. But to my surprise, Artaxerxes smiled. "Tell him to stand up. It is not every day we receive so famous an enemy."

Themistocles got to his feet. Thick gray hair grew to within three fingers of straight dark brows that shadowed black, luminous, watchful eyes. Plainly, he was in no awe of the Great King—or anyone else. But he was tactful, quick, prescient.

"Why didn't Artabanus present you to my father?"

"He was afraid, Lord."

"But you are not?"

Themistocles shook his head. "Why should I be? On two occasions, I served your father well."

"My father did not regard the loss of a third of his fleet at Salamis as a useful service." Artaxerxes was amusing himself.

"No, Lord. But just before that engagement, I sent the

Great King a message. I told him that the Greek fleet was preparing to escape. I told him that this was his chance to strike..."

"He struck," said Artaxerxes. "To no good purpose."

"He struck, Lord, and would have won the battle had it not been for the treachery of his own Phoenician captains."

This was both true and untrue. Needless to say, I was not about to get above my humble station as translator. Artaxerxes listened carefully to my literal translation; then he nodded. "What," he asked, "was the second service you rendered my father?"

"I sent him a warning that part of the Greek fleet intended to destroy the bridge between Asia and Europe."

"That is true," said Artaxerxes. Again, the story was true and untrue at the same time, and highly typical of this cunning Greek. Since Themistocles wanted the Greeks to stand fast and defeat the Persians, he forced Xerxes to attack them; thus, he obliged the Greeks to fight for their lives—which they did. Then the Phoenicians deserted and the Greeks won the battle or, to be precise, the Persians lost it. This was as much a surprise to the Greeks as it was to the Persians. The warning that the bridge across the Hellespont would be destroyed was Themistocles' master stroke. He wanted Xerxes out of Europe. As he told his cronies here at Athens, "Under no circumstances, destroy the bridge. If we don't let Xerxes go home to Persia, we're going to have a lion loose in Greece. Cut off the Great King's retreat, and he'll come out from under that gold parasol with a sword in his hand and the most powerful army in the world at his back."

Thus, Themistocles managed to serve both Greece and Persia at the same time. But since gratitude is unknown to the Greeks, Themistocles was ostracized. Later, when Pausanias tried to interest him in subverting Greece, he refused to join the conspiracy. This was un-Greek of him, to say the least. Or, perhaps, he did not trust Pausanias. Unfortunately, ambiguous letters from Themistocles to Pausanias were produced at the latter's trial, and the Athenians ordered Themistocles to come home so that they could execute him for treason. He fled to Persia, to the household of Artabanus, whose wife was related to Themistocles' mother—a lady from Halicarnassus, by the way.

In the light of General Pericles' recent and highly peculiar law that no one can be a citizen of Athens unless both parents were native to the city, it should be noted that Athens' two greatest commanders, Themistocles and Cimon, would not have qualified as Athenian citizens. The mother of each was an outlander.

"Tell us," said the Great King, "of this annoying Greek who has taken to piracy in our waters."

"Piracy, Lord?" Themistocles was not yet adept at interpreting the oblique style of our Great Kings; they affect never to know anyone's name or place of origin. To the end of her life, Queen Atossa maintained that Athens was located in Africa and that its inhabitants were pitchblack dwarfs.

"Eurymedon," said Artaxerxes with grim precision. The Great King knew that place. All Persians do. The Greeks who boast of Marathon and Salamis and Plataea as marvelous victories do not realize that none of these engagements was of the slightest significance to Persia. The fact that the Greeks were able to hold their own in the burned-out cities of Attica is hardly the stuff of military glory. But Persia was hugely shaken by Cimon's victory at the mouth of the Eurymedon River. In fact, I have often thought that the completeness of Cimon's victory on Persian soil was the beginning of the end of Xerxes. From that moment on, the politics of the harem and the politics of the army began to converge, and the Great King was thrown down.

"Cimon, son of Miltiades—" Themistocles began.

"Our treacherous satrap." The Persians will never forget that Miltiades was for so many years a loyal slave of the Great King, enjoying vast estates on the Black Sea.

"—the victor of Marathon."

"Where is that?" Artaxerxes blinked his father's eyes.

"A place of no importance." As translator, I was able to observe Themistocles' nimble mind in action. As he got the range of the Great King, he adjusted his own style accordingly. "In any case, Lord, this pirate is my enemy, too."

"Who can approve of piracy?" Artaxerxes glanced at Roxanes, who was rigid with dislike of the man whom he always referred to as the Greek serpent.

"At Athens, Lord, there are two factions. One would very much want peace with the king of kings. I am of that party. On our side, we have the common people. Against us are the landowners, who overthrew the tyrants. Today Cimon is what I was yesterday, the general of Athens, and the cause of the common people was damaged when I was ostracized."

"But surely, if you were ostracized, that means a majority of the common people voted against you." Artaxerxes was torn between continuing to pretend ignorance of this unimportant African city and the usual passion of a very young man to win a point and be thought clever. Xerxes never made that mistake. Perhaps he should have.

"Yes, Lord. But they had been inflamed against me by the anti-Persian conservatives. It was said that I was plotting with Pausanias to overthrow the Greek states. In any event, as you may have heard, Lord, Greeks tire very quickly of their leaders. Because I was leader of the people did not mean that the people liked or appreciated my leadership."

"Now you are an exile and the pirate attacks the mainland of our empire. What shall we do?"

"I have a plan, Lord."

Themistocles was the most subtle Greek I ever met. Whatever he wanted to do, he found a way to do—at least once. He was a true Odysseus. But before he revealed his plan to the Great King, he asked for one year in which to learn Persian because "Your language is like one of your extraordinary carpets, intricate, subtle, beautiful. I cannot express myself through an interpreter, no matter how able."

The Great King gave Themistocles a year. He also gave him a fine estate at Magnesia. Then he gave him the long hand to kiss, and sent him away.

After Themistocles had left the royal presence, Artaxerxes clapped both hands, turned very pink and shouted, "I have him! I have the Greek!"

As it turned out, Themistocles had no specific plan, other than to wait for the inevitable ostracism of Cimon, which came four years later. During those years Themistocles not only learned to speak Persian without accent, he was given the governorship of Magnesia. He was also charged with the building of a new navy and with the training of our sailors in the Greek fashion. In those days Persian ships were floating fortresses, unwieldy in battle and highly susceptible to fire. Themistocles made modern the Persian fleet.

Would Themistocles have led an expedition against his own people? The conservatives here at Athens think that

that was his intention. Certainly, Elpinice is convinced of his treachery. But she is dedicated to the glorious memory of her brother Cimon. It is my view that Themistocles wanted nothing more than to live and die in peace and comfort, which is what he did. Five years after his arrival at court, Themistocles died. Some say that he killed himself. I am sure that he did not. It is a general law that great men do not live long once they are separated from the people whom they ennobled.

During the ten years that Cimon was ostracized, Athenian power deteriorated noticeably. An attempted invasion of Egypt was crushed by Megabyzus. In fact, everything that the so-called party of the people has undertaken has failed, excepting the conquest of the nearby island of Aegina and a victorious skirmish or two in the environs of Athens. Without Themistocles and Cimon, Athens was—and is—of no particular consequence in the world.

When Cimon returned from exile, he was given command of the fleet. But he had lost his best years. Worse, the Athenians had lost those same years, too. When Cimon died at Cyprus, the Athenian empire ended and the Persian empire was secure. Ephialtes and Pericles are poor substitutes for such heroes.

Do not, Democritus, repeat these thoughts to those who might disagree with an old man who has seen more of this world than he ever intended—much less wanted—to see.

6

My last years in Persia were, I thought, simply my last years. I enjoyed retirement. I never went up to Susa. I busied myself with making notes for the second room of the chancellery. I wrote about the silk road, Cathay, Ajatashatru. My notes were politely acknowledged, and promptly consigned to the house of books.

I often met with the Zoroastrian community. Now that I was old, I was treated with reverence. But I could never interest the Zoroastrians in any of the ideas of deity or non-deity that I had come across in the east. I also noted with more resignation than alarm that the simplicity of

575

the Wise Lord is being fragmented. The old devil-gods are returning in the guise of *aspects* of the One who is Two but will be One again at the end of time of the long dominion. Devil-gods do not give up easily. Recently the Great King erected an altar to Arta, or righteousness— as if that *quality* were some sort of god.

The ostracism of Cimon had one good result—for Persia, that is. When Cimon reigned at Athens, there was not a chance of peace between the empire and the Greek allies. But when Cimon was brought down, the democratic leader Ephialtes promptly restored power to the people's assembly. When Ephialtes was assassinated for his pains, the leadership passed to the young Pericles, whose first move was to make peace with Persia. He sent an embassy to Persepolis, headed by Callias.

So it was that, in my sixtieth year, I was commanded to attend the Great King at Persepolis. I was serene. But then, I am no longer distressed or fearful when summoned by anyone in power, and that includes our local potentate General Pericles. Death is near, kings are far, to paraphrase Confucius.

I had not visited Persepolis since the time of Artaxerxes' coronation. When I presented myself at the winter palace, I found that I was unknown to all but a few of the eunuchs in the second room of the chancellery. They wept when they saw me. Eunuchs tend to get sentimental with old age. I don't. Rather the contrary. But it is quite true that we aged creatures are all that remains of the reign of Darius, and of the high noon of Persia. We have a lot to gossip about—if not to weep for.

I was given an extremely cold and uncomfortable room in Xerxes' palace, which was—and no doubt still is —unfinished, while my servants were quartered in the shantytown that has grown up outside the walls of the royal enclosure.

I must say that I half hoped that I might be put to death for some imaginary crime. For one thing, my sight was going, which means one is obliged to listen carefully to others—the ultimate cruelty. For another . . . my day was done. Unfortunately, I was in high favor.

I was sent for not by the Great King but by the queen mother, Amestris. She had furnished most splendidly the third house of the harem. Although the rooms are small, she has managed to make them opulent. In the room where she received me, the walls are entirely covered with plates of gold leaf, fashioned to imitate the leaves of the lotus. She herself seemed to be wrapped in the same material. Once the ushers had withdrawn, we were alone. I took this to be a tribute to my advanced age.

"You are the last," Amestris whispered; and blushed.

After three days at court I was quite used to hearing myself acclaimed, reverently, as the last. I made a number of aged rumbles to demonstrate to the queen that not only was I the last but, very shortly, the last would be gone, too. Who, I wonder, is next to last? Perhaps Amestris. She had not aged well, I thought. She has become very thin, and the once pretty face is heavily lined. Yet she wears almost no paint on her face. I suppose the grotesqueness of Atossa's face during the final years had a cautionary effect on her daughter-in-law.

"Do sit," she said, proving that in her eyes I was plainly near extinction. Since I was—am—rather lame, I sank gratefully onto a stool beside her ivory chair. She smelled of myrrh. This most expensive unguent was kneaded so heavily into her skin that the wrinkled sallow skin had a curious nacreous glow.

"You loved my husband the Great King." Tears came to her eyes. I think that she was quite sincere. After all, it is possible to acquiesce in the death of someone that you love. I could not. But the Achaemenids can—and do. "We are the last—who loved him."

At least I was now able to share my terminal status with someone else. But I chose tact. "Surely, our Great King and his brothers and sisters—"

"Children do not feel what we feel," she said sharply. "You knew Xerxes as a man and a friend. I knew him as a husband. *They* knew only the Great King. Besides, children are heartless. Hasn't that been your experience?"

"I do not know my children."

"You mean those two sons that you left in India?"

"Yes, Great Queen." As with everyone else at court, the house of books contains all sorts of information about me, amassed over the years by secret agents. Suddenly I wondered why Amestris had gone to the trouble of looking me up. I was mildly uneasy. Although I long for death, the actual business of dying can have its unpleasant side.

"They were alive as of last year. The chancellery received a fairly detailed report from our trade mission at

577

Shravasti. But your wife Ambalika is dead. Women don't last long in that climate."

"So it would seem, Lady." I felt nothing. Ambalika had died for me at our last meeting when she had so briskly arranged my official death.

"Ambalika married her brother after you left. I must say I can't fathom their customs. I mean, she was still your wife. Of course, girls are always the worst." With a frown, Amestris reverted to the subject of children. She had her own very much in mind. It was common knowledge that the queen mother hated her daughter Amytis, whose passionate affair with the beautiful Apollonides was well known even then. After much reminiscence of Xerxes, Amestris came to the point. "The Greeks want peace. Or so they say."

"Which Greeks, Great Queen?"

Amestris nodded. "That is always the problem, isn't it? At the moment, there are two separate embassies here. One is from the Greek city of Argos, a place much loved by Xerxes, if one can love anything so . . . shifting as a Greek city. The other comes from Athens."

I must have looked surprised.

Amestris nodded. "We were surprised too. We *think* that they come to us in good faith. But who can tell? The Athenian ambassador is Callias, the brother-in-law of Cimon."

"An aristocrat?"

"Yes. Which means anti-Persian. But whatever he is, he was chosen to negotiate with us by the present government, which is democratic." Amestris could be specific in a way that denied the Great King, who must at all times be rather like the deity, permeating each atom of a discussion without ever making a specific distinction. On the other hand, Amestris is rather like a superior eunuch, the sort that never stops reading chancellery records, and knows a thousand and one details about a thousand and one things, often without grasping the main thing, as Atossa always did.

"Hippias' grandson is talking to the Argive embassy." Amestris gave me her shy smile. "We thought it might be tactless to use the tyrant's grandson as go-between with the Athenian democrats. So it would please us if you were to deal with Callias."

I accepted the commission.

From the beginning, Callias and I got on famously. He

told me his stories about Marathon, and the first few times I enjoyed them very much. Then I was bored by them. Today I enjoy them again. So little remains the same in this life that one can only take pleasure in a man who persists in telling you, year after year, the same stories in precisely the same words. In a world of flux, the boredom of Callias is a constant.

I showed Persepolis to Callias and the rest of the embassy. They were duly awed not only by the wealth of Persia—for which they were prepared—but by the extraordinary architectural marvels that Xerxes had created. Two of the Athenians were builders. One of the two is close to Phidias and I am sure that just back of this house, amidst all the noise and thievery, a replica of the winter palace at Persepolis is being constructed, as a symbol of *Athenian* genius!

I am not allowed to discuss details of the treaty. They were secret fourteen years ago when the talks began, and they are still a secret now that the peace has been in effect since Cimon's very timely death in Cyprus three years ago. I *can* say that each party has agreed to keep to its own sphere. Persia will not interfere in the Aegean. Athens will not interfere in Asia Minor. Contrary to legend, there is no signed or sealed treaty because the Great King may deal only with his equals. Since he is king of kings, he has no equals. Therefore, he can only appear to assent to a treaty. Because Persian feeling was still violently anti-Greek as a result of the business at the mouth of the Eurymedon River, negotiations were kept secret. Only the Great King, the queen mother and I know all the details.

Finally, when Cimon was dead and General Pericles was firmly in control of the state, the treaty was accepted by both sides and I was sent here to Athens as the corporeal symbol of our superb treaty. Let us hope that the peace will last longer than the symbol, who has no intention of enduring another winter in this dreadful city, this drafty house, this deranged polity.

You are to bury my remains, Democritus. I want to be restored as quickly as possible to the primal unity. What a curious slip! I am quoting Master Li. I don't mean primal unity, of course. I mean the Wise Lord, from whom our spirits come, to whom our spirits—cleansed of the Lie—return at the end of time of the long dominion.

For your delectation, Democritus, I should note that during my last audience with the queen mother, I was

579

charmed and delighted by a twenty-year-old eunuch named Artoxares. He was of enormous help to us as we worked out the details of the treaty. If it is true that Amestris enjoys his incomplete favors, I commend her taste. He is not only intelligent but beautiful as well. He is also said to have had an affair with Apollonides, the lover of Amytis. One day, I fear, these two powerful ladies will confront each other. When they do, I shall, for the first and last time, be thankful that I am an exile in Athens.

BOOK NINE

The Peace
of Pericles

1

LAST NIGHT GENERAL PERICLES CELE-
brated the third year of my embassy with an evening of
music at the house of Aspasia. Like everything else to do
with my seldom acknowledged, much less celebrated embassy, the party took place in relative secret, and at the
last minute. Shortly before sundown, as I was getting
ready for bed, Democritus arrived with the news that
the general would like to see me. We hurried across
town, our faces hidden by shawls so that the conservatives might not know that the infamous representative of
the Great King was conspiring with Pericles to enslave
Athens.

Two Scythian policemen stood guard at the head of the
lane—one cannot call it a street—which leads to the
house of Aspasia. They asked Democritus our business.
He gave them some sort of password, and we were allowed to enter the lane.

I was overheated when we arrived. The summers here
are as hot as the winters are cold. In fact, the climate is
almost as bad as Susa's, if that is possible. But then, I am
now uncommonly susceptible to heat, cold. Last night I
was drenched with sweat when I arrived at Aspasia's
house.

Democritus tells me that the interior is very elegant.
But how would you know? Despite your great-
grandfather's wealth, the house at Abdera where you
were brought up is rustic—to say the least. Of all the
houses hereabouts, only that of Callias seems to me to be
both comfortable and splendid. Certainly, I am aware
that there are rugs on the marble floors and the braziers
burn sweet-smelling wood.

One enters Aspasia's house through a long, narrow,
low-ceilinged corridor that leads to a small courtyard. At
the right of the courtyard there is a porticoed reception
hall, a room not much larger than the one we are sitting
in now, trying to escape the sun's heat.

I knew immediately that I was in the house of a Milesian lady. Expensive perfumes adorned the air, and the musicians played so softly that one was not obliged to listen to the music. This is a rarity at Athens, where the citizens are so little musical that when they do attend a concert, they strain to hear every note in an effort to figure out why they should be charmed. The Ionian Greeks of Asia Minor are different. They regard music as a complement to conversation, food, even love-making. Music is a part of the air that they breathe, not a mathematical equation to be solved by Pythagoras.

There were a dozen people in the room when we arrived. Democritus tells me that, actually, there were ten guests, as well as a number of slaves from Sardis who played music, served food. I was greeted by Evangelos, Pericles' steward. Although this celebrated figure is usually in the country looking after the general's farms—and two legitimate sons—for the last week he has been in the city celebrating with the rest of Athens the trophy of victory that the assembly had just voted Pericles. Ostensibly, the trophy is being given for the reconquest of Euboea. Actually, the trophy is for the astute way that Pericles handled the Spartan king last winter when the Spartan army occupied Attica, and the Athenians were huddled behind their long walls.

When the message to surrender arrived from the Spartan headquarters at Eleusis, the assembly was tempted to do just that. After all, the Spartan army is the best in the Greek world. Why resist them? Athens is a sea power, not a land power. But Pericles had no intention of surrendering anything. He arranged a secret meeting with the Spartan king, a wide-eyed adolescent who had never before been out of the Peloponnesus. Aware of the king's youth and inexperience, the suspicious Spartan elders had assigned a special adviser to keep close watch over their boy-king. But, as Pericles later remarked, this sort of Spartan precaution simply doubles the price. The boy-king got three gold talents, to be held for him at Delphi, while the adviser—a shrewd statesman—got seven gold talents on the spot. Once king and adviser had been paid off, the Spartan army went home. The boy-king was fined an enormous sum by the elders, while the special adviser fled to Sicily, where, presumably, he now enjoys his wealth. "My only problem," said Pericles at the party, "is how to explain this payment to the assembly."

Aspasia's advice was direct. "When you submit your accounts, simply say, 'For necessary expenditures—ten talents.'"

I have a hunch that that is exactly what Pericles will do. Certainly, everyone knows that the Spartans were bribed. When I complimented Pericles on how little the peace had cost Athens, his response was somber. "I did not buy peace," he said. "I bought time."

But my narrative is out of order. Although General Pericles was not in the house when we arrived, Aspasia more than made up for his absence. She has a lovely speaking voice, sings Milesian songs with much delicacy, recites poetry better than anyone else I have ever heard. Of course, I think no language on earth is more beautiful than well-spoken Ionian Greek. Yes, Democritus, it is even more beautiful than Persian.

"I've wanted to meet you from the first day you arrived in Athens." She held my hand in both of hers. She gives the impression that she means every word she says to you.

When I praised her courage in having me to her house, she laughed. "I've always been called a medizer. Personally, I don't care. But there are times when . . ." The voice trailed off. I cursed my blindness yet again. What I would have given to be able to study that face! Democritus says that Aspasia is small, and somewhat thinner than last winter. The hair is light-brown, and not dyed—or so he thinks. You are not yet as expert in these matters as I am, or was.

Aspasia presented a number of men to me. One was Phormio, Pericles' right hand in the assembly. Another was a general named Sophocles. Years ago, when he was in his twenties, he wrote a tragedy that won first prize at the festival of Dionysos. Old Aeschylus was so furious at being second to this young upstart that he moved to Sicily, where that sharp-eyed eagle put an end to their rivalry with a well-aimed turtle. I always enjoy thinking about the death of Aeschylus.

Sophocles is something of a scandal here because he lusts, openly, after young men of his own class. For some reason this is taboo at Athens. Although Athenian citizens are encouraged to have affairs with adolescent boys of their own class, once the boy has grown a proper beard, he must give up having sexual relations with other citizens. He is expected to get married and begin a family.

Then, his duty done, he is encouraged to find a boy to love in order to continue the—what?—training, I suppose, of a new citizen and soldier. Such customs are not unknown elsewhere, particularly amongst our Aryan cousins, the northern tribes. Even so, I don't entirely understand the powerful taboo against sexual relations between grown men who are also citizens of Athens. Although slaves and foreigners are fair game for those men who like that sort of sexuality, two grown citizens who wish to have an affair must forfeit all rights to public office.

So far, Sophocles has been able to hold office *and* seduce youthful citizens. But Pericles is deeply annoyed with him. Recently he reprimanded his friend and fellow general. "You must set an example," said the commander in chief. "Never touch one of your own soldiers. Avert your eyes when they are bathing." But Sophocles continues to scandalize the Athenians. It is said that whenever he pays a call on a friend, the young men of the house are told to hide. Incidentally, since General Pericles has never shown the slightest interest in boys, he is considered to be heartless. This is a very unusual society.

Aspasia led me to a low couch. I sat on the edge while she sat at my feet, like a granddaughter. Wine was brought us. I heard the laughter of girls in the background. If Aspasia does not procure women for Pericles, as his enemies maintain, she certainly manages to attract to her house the most talented of the professional ladies in the city. I have not enjoyed myself so much in years as I did last night. Although such pleasures at my age are not only unseemly but dangerous, I was pleased to be reminded—for the first time since I left India—how delightful it is to mix in company intelligent women with men of the first rank. This is something undreamed of in Persia. So, I suppose, one must give the Athenians credit for having invented a new and delightful kind of society.

Democritus thinks that the credit must go, specifically, to Aspasia. He tells me that not only are the other Athenian companions not in her class but their evenings tend to be drunken and dull. Democritus would know. Thanks to a princely allowance from his father, he is able to spend as much time as he likes in the houses of professional ladies. He has also been able to avoid falling into the clutches of a grown man. All in all, you must be grateful to a destiny that has been so benign—thus far. No wonder you laugh so much.

I asked Aspasia about Anaxagoras.

"He is in Corinth."

"Will he come back?"

"I don't know. I hope so."

"I'm sure he will. I heard Pericles' defense." Heavily veiled, I had gone to the assembly. Thucydides attacked Anaxagoras—and his theories. Pericles defended his friend —and ignored the theories. I cannot say that I was much impressed by either orator. Pericles is a fluent and graceful speaker who is able, when he chooses, to strike a positively Phrygian note of passion. I use a musical term because the general uses his voice like a musical instrument. But at the trial of Anaxagoras, the Periclean lyre was muted. Both speakers were distracted by such recent events as the Spartan invasion, the loss of Boetia, the revolt of Euboea. In a sense, Pericles was on trial at a time when he was more than ever needed. Finally, when the assembly decided that Anaxagoras was neither a medizer nor an atheist, they were simply showing their confidence in Pericles. Thucydides took hard his defeat in the assembly. He promises to return to the attack another day. I am sure he will. Tactfully, Anaxagoras left Athens after the trial. I must say I miss him almost as much as Pericles does.

I complimented Aspasia on the wine, the music, the perfumed air.

Aspasia laughed, a pleasant sound. "My house must seem very poor, indeed, compared to the harem of the Great King."

"How do you know that I would know anything about the harem?"

"You were the confidante of the old queen, and you are a favorite of the queen mother. Oh, I know all about you!" Indeed she did. Apparently the Greek women of the Persian harem have managed, somehow, to keep in communication with their equivalents in the Greek cities. I was surprised at how much Aspasia knows about court life. "But then, my father served the Great King—as the conservatives remind us every day."

"Miletus was a city much loved by the Great King," I intoned. Actually, Miletus has given Persia more trouble than all the other Greek cities of Asia Minor combined. Xerxes wanted to raze it to the ground.

Pericles joined us so silently that I was not aware of his

presence until I felt a hand on my shoulder and heard the famous voice murmur, "Welcome, Cyrus Spitama."

"General." As I tried to rise, the hand on my shoulder kept me seated.

"Don't move, Ambassador. I'll sit beside you."

Aspasia went to fetch wine for the general. I noticed that the party continued just as if the ruler were not in the room. The body seated next to me on the couch was indeed, even in darkness, a formidable presence. I had not realized that Pericles is so much taller than I. "We have neglected you," he said. "But not from choice."

"I understand, General."

"You know that it was I who sent Callias up to Susa to make peace."

"Yes, we knew that then."

"I hope that you also know how opposed I was to the Egyptian expedition. For one thing, it was a flagrant violation of our treaty. But since I've never been able to present the treaty to the assembly in a proper way, I wasn't able to invoke it. Anyway, presented or not, the treaty remains in force, as far as the present government is concerned."

"The Great King would say the same."

"We have lived this long!" Pericles clapped his hands—with joy? I could not tell simply from the voice. "You knew Themistocles." This was a statement, not a question.

"Yes. I acted as interpreter when he first came to Susa."

Pericles stood up. He offered me his arm, a thickly muscled soldier's arm. I struggled to my feet. "I would like to talk to you," he said. "In private."

Pericles led me through the room. Although he paused to speak to this man or that, he never addressed any woman except Aspasia. He showed me into a small stuffy room that smelled of old olive oil. "This is where I work." He arranged me on a stool. We were so close to each other that I could smell his sweat—like heated brass.

"I was twenty-eight," he said, "when Themistocles was ostracized. I thought he was the greatest man this city had ever produced."

"But now—" I began a courtier's response, but the general interrupted me; he is not much of one for flattery—in the Persian style, that is. As a Greek, he hungers for the Attican variety. "I've changed my mind since then. He was a greedy man. He took money from everyone, including the tyrant of Rhodes—which was inexcusable.

Worse, after he got his hands on the tyrant's money, he did nothing to help him."

"Perhaps this was Themistocles' way of proving that he was a true democrat." I could not resist a small joke at the expense of Pericles' party.

The joke was ignored. "Themistocles proved that his word meant nothing. But in his day he was our greatest military leader. More to the point—or, perhaps, *to* the point—he understood the world better than any man I have ever known."

"Including Anaxagoras?"

"Anaxagoras understands many of the secrets of creation. Those things are important, of course, and very deep. But I was speaking of politics. Themistocles understood what the people would do long before they themselves knew. He could see into the future. He could tell us what was going to happen next, and I don't think this gift of his came from Apollo. No. I think he could predict the future because he entirely understood the present. That's why I want to know—" Pericles stopped. I had the sense that he was staring at me.

"What would you like to know, General?"

"I want to know what Themistocles said to you about Athens, about Sparta, about Persia. Naturally, if you don't want to tell me, I will understand."

"I'll tell you what I can." I was honest. "That is to say, what I can remember, and my memory of the recent past is not good. I can tell you every word that Darius the Great King said to me thirty years ago, but I've already forgotten most of what Thucydides said to me at the Odeon last winter."

"You're in luck. I wish I could forget him. But he won't let me. He's a wrestler, you know. And a bad one. The sort that clings and clings and then, secretly, bites. Athens is much too small for both of us. Sooner or later, one of us must go. Because—" Again, Pericles stopped himself. He has a tendency to self-pity, which takes the form of affecting never to understand opposition. At the last meeting of the assembly, his behavior was positively childish. Pericles was criticized for spending too much of the empire's money on new buildings. Instead of saying that if he didn't spend the money, half the population would be out of work, Pericles said, "Very well. I'll use my own money to finish the buildings. Then all the buildings will be dedicated not to the city but to me." Since a chorus of "No's" had been carefully rehearsed in advance, he got his appropriation—and saved his own fortune.

Pericles takes these political matters entirely too personally. But then, this is a small city, and since the leading men know each other far too well, their attacks upon one another are always personal and calculated not only to wound but to fester.

In any event, at Pericles' urging, I did my best to recall the only private conversation I ever had with Themistocles. It took place at Magnesia, a year or two before his death. I cannot remember why I was in that part of the world. But I do remember that when word spread along the highway that the king's friend was approaching. Themistocles sent me a messenger. Would I be his guest at the governor's house? Naturally, being Persian, I was pleased that the great man remembered me. Naturally, being Greek, I knew that he wanted something from me.

I remember that it was late afternoon—in the summertime, I think. We sat together in a beautiful loggia overlooking the gardens of his considerable estate. Over the years, Themistocles had amassed an enormous fortune which he had managed, somehow or other, to spirit out of Athens before his fall from power.

"There has been a misunderstanding between me and the satrap at Sardis." Themistocles poured us wine with his own hands. "A small matter but . . ." In the Greek fashion, he threw out some wine onto the pavement. "Years ago," he continued, "I set up a statue at Athens called the water bearer. It was a memorial to the time when I was water surveyor, a very difficult job which I think I handled rather well. The statue is bronze—old style, of course, but everyone always liked it. Anyway, after the fall of Athens, the Persians took the statue and set it up in the temple of Hera at Sardis." Yes, Democritus, he said "the fall of Athens."

"So I asked the satrap if I might buy the statue from the temple and send it back to Athens—you know, as a symbol of the peace between the Persians and the Greeks, and so on. The satrap was furious. He has now accused me of insulting the Great King, of treason, of . . ." Themistocles discussed at considerable length the satrap's threats. He was genuinely shaken by their exchange. I did my best to soothe him. I told him that I would set matters right with both the chancellery and the third house of the harem. Certainly, the peace treaty was of more importance to the Great King than a single statue. Unfortunately, at about this time, the Athenians saw fit to attack our province of Egypt. In a rage, the Great King ordered Themistocles to assemble the fleet. A week later Themistocles died—of a horse's bite, it was said; and the statue of the water bearer remains at Sardis to this day.

Once I had reassured Themistocles that the Great King would not be swayed by a mere satrap of Lydia, we discussed a thousand and one things. He had a quick and curious mind. He asked many questions and he listened to many, if not all, of my answers.

I asked him questions, too. Certainly, I asked him about Egypt. Even then, everyone knew that disaffected elements within Egypt were looking for aid from outside. Would the Athenians help the Egyptians rebel against Persia? Themistocles' response was firm: "Unless the Athenians are entirely mad—not to be ruled out, may I say, from personal experience"—he smiled—"they will never attack the mainland of Asia or Africa. What would be the point? They could never win. There are not enough of them."

I repeated this speech to Pericles, who murmured, "Yes, yes. He's right. About there being too few of us, that is. Go on. Please."

I told Pericles the rest of what I remembered. The dialogue was something like this:

"I am certain that there is no more danger to Athens from the Great King." Themistocles gave me a side-long glance to see just how seriously I took such a statement from a Persian pensioner.

I was neutral. "I am no longer in the Great King's confidence. But I agree with you. The Great King wants only to maintain what he has. If my prayers are granted, we will one day go to the east . . ."

"And if *my* prayers are answered, the Athenians will go to the west."

"Did he say where?" Pericles was now so close to me that I could feel on my cheek the heat of his face.

"Yes. Themistocles spoke of Sicily, of Italy. 'Europe must be Greek,' he said. 'We must look west.' "

"Exactly! Now, what did he say about me?" I was amused to find that Pericles has all the usual public man's vanity. Fortunately—or unfortunately—the public man almost always ends by confusing himself with the people that he leads. When General Pericles thinks of Athens, he thinks of himself. When he helps one, he helps the other. Since Pericles is gifted and wise—not to mention cunning—Athens *ought* now to be in luck.

Although I could not remember whether or not Themistocles had mentioned his political heir, I invented freely. One is never under oath when talking to a ruler. "Themistocles felt that you were the logical successor to *his* successor Ephialtes. He told me that he did not take seriously the fact that you are under a curse because of your descent from the Alcmaeonids . . ." I threw this in because I was curious to learn Pericles' reaction to the fact that many Greeks think that he and his family are still under a divine curse because, two centuries ago, one of his ancestors killed an enemy in a temple.

"As everyone knows, the curse was lifted when our family rebuilt Apollo's temple at Delphi." From this perfunctory answer, I cannot tell whether or not Pericles believes that the curse is still in effect or not. If it is, Athens will suffer because Pericles *is* Athens, or so he thinks. As I grow older, I tend more and more to believe in the longevity of curses. Xerxes expected to be murdered and I am sure that, at the end, he showed no surprise, assuming that he was granted a moment's reflection before the awesome royal glory passed, in a welter of blood.

I played the courtier. "Themistocles spoke of you with respect—unlike Cimon, whom he hated." This last was true.

"Cimon was a dangerous man," said Pericles. "I should never have allowed him to come back. But Elpinice outwitted me. Yes, I was taken in by that evil old creature. I still don't know how she did it. They say she's a witch. Perhaps she is. Anyway, she came to me dressed as a bride. I was shocked. 'You're too old,' I said, 'to wear perfume and dress like that.' But she argued with me like a man, and she got her way. Cimon came home. Now he's dead, while Thucydides . . . Well, the city is too small for him and me. One of us must go. Soon."

Pericles rose. Once again the strong arm helped me to my feet. "Let us re-join the guests and celebrate the peace with Sparta and the peace with Persia."

"Let us celebrate, General, the peace of Pericles." I spoke with perfect sincerity.

Pericles replied, with what I took to be perfect sincerity, "I would like future generations to say of me that no Athenian ever wore mourning on my account."

    *   *   *

I, Democritus of Abdera, son of Athenocritus, have organized these recollections of Cyrus Spitama into nine books. I have paid for their transcription, and they can now be read by any Greek.

A week after the reception at the house of Aspasia, Cyrus Spitama died, swiftly, without pain, while listening to me read from Herodotus. That was nearly forty years ago.

During those years I have traveled in many countries. I have lived in Babylon and Bactra. I have traveled to the source of the Nile and I have gone as far east as the banks of the Indus River. I have written many books. Yet when I came back to Athens this year, no one knew me—not even the garrulous Socrates.

I think that Cyrus Spitama was correct when he said that the curse upon the Alcmaeonids still continues. Pericles was a great man, greatly doomed. At the time of his death, twenty years ago, Athens was being battered from without by the Spartan army and from within by the killing plague.

Now, after twenty-eight years of constant and de-bilitating warfare, Athens has surrendered to Sparta. This spring, the long walls were pulled down and as I write these lines there is a Spartan garrison on the Acropolis.

Thanks, in large part, to the education that I received from Cyrus Spitama, I have been able in the course of a long life to work out the causes not only of all celestial phenomena but of creation itself.

The first principles of the universe are atoms and empty space; everything else is merely human thought. Worlds such as this one are unlimited in number. They come into being, and perish. But nothing can come into being from that which is not, or pass away into what is not. Further, the essential atoms are without limit in size and number and they make of the universe a vortex in which all composite things are generated—fire, water, air, earth.

The cause of the coming into being of all things is the ceaseless whirl, which I call necessity; and everything happens according to necessity. Thus, creation is con-stantly created and re-created.

As Cyrus Spitama was beginning to suspect, if not believe, there is neither a beginning nor an end to a creation which exists in a state of flux in a time that is truly infinite. Although I have nowhere observed the slightest trace of Zoroaster's Wise Lord, he might well be a concept which can be translated into that circle which stands for the cosmos, for the primal unity, for creation.

But I have written on these matters elsewhere and I mention them now only to express my gratitude to the old man whose life story I am pleased to dedicate to the last living survivor of a brilliant time, Aspasia, the wife of Lysicles, the sheep-dealer.

ABOUT THE AUTHOR

GORE VIDAL wrote his first novel, *Williwaw* (1946), at the age of nineteen while overseas in World War II.

During four decades as a writer, Vidal has written novels, plays, short stories and essays. He has also been a political activist. As a Democratic candidate for Congress from upstate New York, he received the most votes of any Democrat in a half century. From 1970 to 1972 he was co-chairman of the People's Party. In California's 1982 Democratic primary for U.S. Senate, he polled a half million votes, and came in second in a field of nine.

In 1948 Vidal wrote the highly praised international best seller *The City and the Pillar*. This was followed by *The Judgment of Paris* and the prophetic *Messiah*. In the fifties Vidal wrote plays for live television and films for Metro-Goldwyn-Mayer. One of the television plays became the successful Broadway play *Visit to a Small Planet* (1957). Directly for the theater he wrote the prize-winning hit *The Best Man* (1960).

In 1964 Vidal returned to the novel. In succession, he created three remarkable works: *Julian, Washington, D.C., Myra Breckinridge*. Each was a number-one best seller in the United States and England. In 1973 Vidal published his most popular novel, *Burr*, as well as a volume of collected essays, *Homage to Daniel Shays*. In 1976 he published yet another number-one best seller, *1876*, a part of his ongoing American chronicle, which now consists of—in chronological order—*Burr, Lincoln, 1876, Empire*, and *Washington, D.C.*

In 1981 Vidal published *Creation*, "his best novel," according to the New York *Times*. In 1982 Vidal won the American Book Critics Circle Award for criticism for his collection of essays, *The Second American Revolution*. A propos *Duluth* (1983), Italo Calvino wrote (*La Repubblica*, Rome): "Vidal's development... along that line from *Myra Breckinridge* to *Duluth* is crowned with great success, not only for the density of comic effects, each one filled with meaning, not only for the craftsmanship in construction, put together like a clock-work which fears no word processor, but because this latest book holds its own built-in theory, that which the author calls his 'après-poststructuralism.' I consider Vidal to be a master of that new form which is taking shape in world literature and which we may call the hyper-novel or the novel elevated to the square or to the cube."